For Lisa
thanks for the lessons.

Reprisal
A Novel

This is a novel, a work of fiction. The characters and events in this book are fabricated, written solely to entertain. Any similarity to anyone living or dead is simply a coincidence.
Exceptions: Mentioning some individuals: Adm Elmo Zumwalt, USN, Adm Lee Baggett jr, USN, Capt. David Work, USN, Cdr, R.D. Rinesmith, USN, COMINDIV 72, Lt. R.A. Phalan USN, some officers and men* of the USS Namakagon, USS Firm, USS Truxtun, USS Henry B. Wilson, USS Kittyhawk and other commands where men whom the author knows of or has served with, is done specifically to salute them and thereby thank them for the memories.
References to senior politicians and senior military figures and policy makers during the Vietnam War are made for realism and express the opinion of the author only. All places and characters in San Diego and Hong Kong are composites of places therein and of characters known there and are not meant to identify a specific place or individual: Exception: Frenchies restaurant (no longer in operation). Though it provides great memories, was dressed up a bit for this novel.
*before women served at sea.

ISBN: 1-4196-3134-9

To order additional copies, please contact us.
BookSurge, LLC
www.Amazon.com
1-866-308-6235
orders@booksurge.com

VINCE
HUNTINGTON

REPRISAL
A NOVEL

2006

Reprisal
A Novel

To My Wife And Mirror, Sally, Who Looked Over My Shoulder For Years And Optimistically Urged Me On: "You Have Stories To Tell, So Get Writing."

And ...

I Also Humbly Offer This Book To Salute Anyone Who Ever Felt Duty-bound To Leave Home And Go Somewhere On Behalf Of Their Country ...to Do Something They Weren't Really Sure About, To Not Come Home The Same As They Were, Or ...for Some, To Not Come Home At All.

CHAPTER ONE
Things Fall Apart

Commander David Selesky finally said something to Master Chief Paul Vincent that made sense. After counseling him for weeks regarding his failing marriage, the mid-forties navy psychiatrist asked: "If you didn't know Rachael, Paul, would you be looking for Rachael?"

Why was the question of *staying* or *leaving* suddenly so clearly answered?

"No. I'd not be looking for Rachael." He replied evenly to the psychiatrist.

"And if you went home tonight and there was a note from her saying something such as: 'all things considered, Paul, I want a divorce.' What is your *first* feeling? Your *first* one, not after thinking it over as you are prone to do, and *then* decide *what* to feel." Selesky emphasized the key words to keep Paul centered.

"Relief." Paul answered easily, more easily than Selesky thought he might. "Some confusion, some skepticism, but overall, *relief*. How'd I do coach?"

"SO?" Selesky asked with a sort of 'duh!' built into the question.

"So? That's it." Paul said and without saying anything else left the counseling center on the Naval Station San Diego and headed to meet with Rachael, at their home, with a new determination.

Within five minutes he drove the less than a mile to his rented duplex in the naval housing area on McCandless Boulevard, a block or so south of the Chief Petty Officer's Club. Inside the house, afraid to wait for fear his new energy and clarity might leave him, he spoke right up.

"I want a divorce, Rachael." Hands in trouser pockets, eyes tracking the red shaded tips of Rachael's now wringing hands, he braced for another of their unsettling conversations. His usually very expressive face was featureless; no visual evidence of the anxiety and determination behind the blunt comment.

"I want a divorce, Rachael." He repeated.

The use of the "D" word grated her insides and for the first time in their eleven-year marriage Rachael truly lost control. As though choreographed, her mouth dropped open, her ever-present drink glass dropped silently to the carpet, her hands folded at her lap, her knees collapsed forward and she sagged from a standing position as though someone had removed the plug from a blow-up doll. On the floor, her mouth formed the word 'divorce', but without sound.

Paul snapped toward her, reaching for her hands, a flash robotic return to the familiar where he would, without thought, fix everything for her, giving himself away. She raised her hand for his but the flat emptiness of her touch awakened him to what he was doing. He dropped her hand quickly.

"Divorce?" Rachael muttered. "You don't love me? You *hate* me?"

He didn't answer, cautious of falling into old patterns.

"You do hate me." She said, now jerking her hand away.

"I do not hate you, Rach." He said, knowing that was true.

"You love me?" She asked in a semi-whine.

"Love you?" He thought. "No." And that was also true.

Pushing unsteadily to her feet, she spoke in standard everyday Rachael anger-based style. "Love or hate. It's one or the other, Sailor Boy."

It was suddenly too clear. The opposite of love is *not* hate. It is, *nothing*, it's not feeling anything, flat, empty. He stepped back, drew in a steadying breath and restated the power-taking sentence, and added his new information.

"I want a divorce, Rachael. I feel nothing for you now." This time the drama of his sentence became surrealistically visible and cream-colored words literally poured from his mouth into the room and hovered in the space between sailor and his wife. Just as Paul thought he could reach out and feel them, the block shapes divided into tiny paper airplanes that circled to the floor. The cream and brown colors clashed with the worn navy-housing blue carpet.

Rachael spoke: "No divorce big shot! You're going to Vietnam. No divorce. *That* will not be." Her words formed their own paper planes, tumbling across the carpet. 'Does she see them too?' he wondered.

Captured by the realness of the floating words, he was sure he had gone insane. He had to hear *and* see his strength again.

His "I want a divorce, Rachael" now detonated into the room, booming from his mouth as ten-inch cut clay letters, clacking to the floor and forming a clearly defined wall: 'D-I-V-O-R-C-E', facing her.

Rachael blurted: "The last time, Vietnam changed you." Her words, one-inch blocks of brittle clay, plinked against his words and fell innocuously to the floor.

"You and Ben sneaking the money while I was gone changed me." Paul said evenly, distracted by the flying letters.

Lips opened and closed in the center of the frozen mask that was Rachael's face. "Ben *made* me steal." Cream-colored alphabet soup behaving like large butterflies came from her lips and flitted about her head and to a place on the growing wall of words. She did not see a wall. 'I've gone crazy.' He was certain.

"Stop talking." He said without thinking. The wall collapsed silently into off-white dust. "No more talking." He repeated as he turned to leave.

"But, you're going to Vietnam." She whined.

He stopped at the front door but was afraid to look at her. She was gazing toward the floor, her empty drink glass again in her hands. She tried humoring him with the even-settled tones of her best parental voice, the voice she used so successfully to control everything so well for the eleven years of the marriage. "We'll talk about it when you return, Paul, for sure."

Did it work? She wondered.

He grasped the doorknob in a strong hand and rotated with a snap to face her. There was no wall of letters. He spoke with a new freedom directly to her eyes. "We have talked about it already, Rachael. I want a divorce.'

"Goddamn you, Paul Vincent, what if you die in Vietnam?" She yelled and dropped to her knees where she'd spilled the drink.

He opened the door.

Suddenly very weak looking, she tossed forward toward him from the floor and dramatically extended one arm. "What if you die?" She repeated.

"Goddammit, Rachael." He barked half expecting to see the words again form between them. But no! Not acknowledging the craziness of the illusion nor of the drama presented by Rachael's outstretched hand, he spoke clearly to her question with a purposeful tinge of drama. "With you? In this life? I'm already dead."

He walked away from her and from their house.

Completely deflated, Rachael surrendered all self-control. She whispered something, but it was muffled as her face pressed into her folded hands against the carpet. She listened to his footsteps fade outside. Sadly, absently, she lifted her head to where her gaze could reach the table where a gaudy eight by ten frame held their arm-in-arm, wedding picture. With her right hand, she pointed a shaking finger at his photo then poked it into her other palm. Suggesting a doll with a pin poking it, she expressed a caustic prayer. "I *hope* you die there, I *hope*, you die."

Master Chief Radioman Paul Vincent had always mistrusted self-pity when he heard someone whining about being victimized, but since walking out on Rachael he truly felt pushed around by outside forces. He tested his complaint on his shipboard friend of many years, Abie Lake, a rather handsome career sailor.

"Destiny is after me, Abie. Has me paying a penance of some sort."

"A penance saved is a penance earned, ol' Chief." Abie kept a distance.

"Fuck you, Abie, not cute." Paul wanted serious attention from his only close black friend. Abie put a more earnest face in place while his friend and boss returned to complaining. "I'm trying to focus on deploying, but I've got ..." He searched for swords.

"Too many wives bearing down?" Abie interrupted. "Too much ship needin' attention?"

"Both true, Ab."

Paul had known for some time the troubles between he and Rachael had kept him from concentrating on his navy job and on the fact his brand-new nuclear-powered guided missile destroyer was only a week from its deployment to Vietnam.

"We've neglected training, Abie. As ship's Command Master Chief, I'm technically responsible for freakin' near everything, or at least, pretending like I am. As I look around, I see we're not up to speed. We've got a long way to go, and, and I'm distracted by the Rach."

"Whose' pushing you on the ship?" Abie wondered, knowing most officers respected Paul and let him make his own schedules.

"The X.O., and Lieutenant Stumpf mostly. The Captain is aware I've been in-country twice. He's got everyone thinking I've got the nuts and bolts on how to lecture everyone on board to become *Vietnam familiar ...*"

"I was hoping for that, too, Chief." Abie said with a smirk.

"Fuck you." Paul said to his black friend. "If Rachael would back off, accept it all, I could get my work done here."

"You really want it to be over with her?" Abie seemed doubtful. He'd known them both for years. Lake had liked Paul since the early sixties when they served together on the U.S.S. Firm, a minesweeper home-ported in Long Beach. He and his wife had partied with Paul and Rachael. Black couple with white couple brought some eyes from some people but neither Paul nor Rachael seemed distracted by racial stares, comments or discriminating behaviors. Abie had been drawn to friendship since he watched the then young chief petty officer Paul Vincent handle a fight between white and black sailor.

"But he's a nigger and he shouldn't sit at the same table as whites." Arlo Butrice, a seaman from South Alabama yelled toward Vincent as he was shoved away by the chief.

"This ain't *Ala-godamned-bama*, Butrice." Vincent advised. "Straighten up. Wise up. You're in a different society. Prejudiced crap won't go here."

"Well, I just hate 'em, niggers. And I aint'a gonna' quit hatin' 'em."

Vincent pulled up close to the red-faced and puffing Butrice and took a hunk of the man's shirt in his right fist. "You can do anything you want down inside of your private places, Butrice." Vincent said, on guard as to whether Butrice or the black seaman named Robert Lillard might go at it again. "On my ship, Butrice, from out here, all such feelings will be kept in social control. Is that clear?"

Butrice seemed afraid of the Chief both physically and because of his rank. Picking his hat from the dark blue-gray deck, he straightened it into place on his chestnut brown crew cut and shook his head back and forth. "Don't want to hurt no one. I'll just stay away from him and them others."

"Do what you gotta' do, Butrice. Remember what I said."

Lake liked the idea a man could be asked to be smart enough to keep his own ideas inside of him, but decide to join with the rules of the society majority he was functioning in. Over the next few months, he and Paul became friends.

"I wouldn't a married ol' Rachael, myself," Abie blurted back in the moment. "But, I thought you two fit okay."

Paul shot Abie a 'fuck you' look.

"Hey, boss. You've given' a divorce and it isn't takin'. It ain't bein' taken by Rachael an' I can't even tell if it's takin' with you."

Abie was right. Paul had assumed Rachael would take her naive looking blond head and fade to wherever it is people go when they've been told they were no longer wanted. Instead of fading, though, she was as present as ever. Her attorney generated antagonism-based demands in letters timed to arrive at every mail call. Three to five times a day there was an aggressive telephone call from Rachael to the ship's quarter-deck, aiming to accomplish exactly what Paul would hate the most. A display to the crew that the ship's Master Chief Radioman wasn't managing his personal life.

His own attorney, a cold-hearted divorce specialist who had demanded his fees in advance resolutely insisted he have no contact with Rachael. That demand pulled Paul two directions. In a recent therapy session, Commander David Selesky, the navy psychiatrist who once counseled Rachael and Paul's troubled marriage was insistent Paul go against his attorney's advice and keep speaking with the angry Rachael.

"Face her." Selesky had urged calmly as he sipped from a cup of coffee. "Find out exactly what she needs to hear to be able to end the marriage." The composed voice changed then, to one like an objective parent. "Just don't let her manipulate you with anger or with those helplessness ploys she uses." Selesky smiled from the counseling center chair across from Paul. Both feet on the floor, cup and saucer balanced in his hands, he spoke with visible concern for his patient.

"You've already learned in here that you're one of those guys who's happy only if he has some woman to make smile.' Selesky made sure Paul was looking at him and stuck out his lower lip. Tormenting him purposely, Selesky brushed an imaginary tear from the corner of his right eye. "Her tears get you, control you, and, my friend, have ruled your life, even to this instant."

"If she didn't cry, it *would* be easier to go on with my life." Paul admitted, following the doctor's train of reason.

"Its clear she baited and switched you"

"Baited and switched?"

"Advertised one thing but delivered another."

"Advertised what …delivered what …which?"

"Advertised she'd have a baby …right?"

"Yes."

"Then delivered what? A baby? No baby." He mocked a Scottish accent complete with rolled R's. "She ended up naught but a barren woman? Yes, a barren and unfruitful gentlewoman. Aye, the sadness of it 'tall." The accent over-spoken and falling flat, Selesky resumed his even-toned advisor voice. 'Well, maybe not such a gentlewoman …say?" Paul seemed untouched by the sarcasm. Selesky impatiently returned to his therapist voice.

"I've asked her openly in therapy, Paul. Did she change her mind about wanting a baby with you? Or, did she *ever intend* to have a baby. She would not meet my eyes. Further," Selesky continued, wanting to keep his patient focused on himself and to not return to the near neurotic habit of fixing Rachael, "she is overall very secreted about herself, Paul. I *believe* the baby-stuff was all voice-work …to keep you in place. And don't forget, she really did forge your name on that loan paperwork monkey business with her brother Ben. That's a crime. Technically, Paul, in the eyes of the law, she's a criminal."

"Ben makes her do the stealing. She gave *him* the money."

"C'mon, Paul. They say if someone steals, they'll lie and also cheat. She's three for three so far."

"But, the pressure from Ben …" Paul stopped talking, caught in his growing hatred for Rachael's younger brother. While Paul admitted Ben to be a nice looking man he also felt Ben carried a sort of wife-beater look about him.

"Quit defending her, for Chris-sake." Selesky snapped. "Did Ben use a gun? No. Did he harm her? No. Wake up and sniff the empty bank account. Those brothers take precedence over you. She really gave the savings to Brother Ben. That was baby-money, crib money, baby-clothes money."

At that point Selesky reached over and offered two fingers on Paul's wrist as an expression of sincere regard. "Can't you see?" He said evenly. "She played the ploy until you wouldn't be manipulated by it any longer. Now she can say to all of her drinking pals, 'poor me, my husband left me and went off to Vietnam'."

Selesky's subjective face changed back to a supportive grin. "If you would have died in Vietnam last year, or next month? She'd look great in black."

Paul winced. Selesky kept talking.

"You face her now. Call her up and go see her. Show yourself you *can* stay away from her." His voice became instructional. "If not," he continued, "you'll re-create this whole thing with some new future woman."

"How true is that?" Paul seemed bothered. "Or is it just psychobabble?" He asked.

"It's true. And, it's also psychobabble," Selesky nodded emphasis, "Even with ..." He snapped his finger to thumb lightly. "What's-her-name, the Hong Kong fling?"

"Cynthia?"

"Yes. Cynthia." Selesky looked directly at Paul. "She's been waiting in the wings for some time for you to escape from Rachael." Ordinarily, he accepted any comment Selesky made as being seeped in valuable therapeutic tea to be examined until all hidden meanings were exposed and understood. However, the openly critical comments about Rachael, and now the challenging remark over Cynthia made Paul uneasy.

"I can't rely on any Cynthia waiting in any wings. Its all I can do now to deal with deploying and with Rachael's anger."

But, Selesky's tee-peed fingers and exploring gaze soon evoked a sense that the room existed for Paul to come clean, go into his mind, sort through the loosely labeled Cynthia files and see if her presence does shape his thoughts and plans.

"My defensive friend? Where *does* Cynthia come in?"

Paul had met Cynthia quite by chance nearly ten years earlier. Instantly infatuated with one another, they had tumbled gladly into a charged three-day affair. He meant to return completely to Rachael when his ship left port on the fourth day. Yet, unlike other deployed flings sailors call 'what's-her-name-affairs', quickly forgotten, the Cynthia memories would only go into a sort of remission.

Talking to Abie one day as he showed a snapshot of Cynthia that had recently arrived in the mail, he tapped his head with one finger. "I know it'll never go anywhere, Abie ...but, God, she keeps floating close to the surface here in my head."

"Well, I've never seen the woman in person like," Abie cracked, "but based on this picture, red sweater an' those big tuu-tuus and all? She'd float about anywhere she pleases."

"Yeah, maybe it's just my draw to that Valentine of a body."

"Those tuu-tuus would draw anyone, Paul." Abie said feeling safe making the cracks because the woman was not anyone of real value to Paul.

'Yeah, well ...maybe that's all it is now."

Certain that his draw to Cynthia was likely some dark side shallowness that had run away with itself, Paul had worked steadily to make a marriage and a life with Rachael even though he would spend time with Cynthia again and again over the years.

"The primal human need to make babies is powerful, isn't it, Paul?" Selesky asked rhetorically. Paul wasn't sure how that applied to him but Selesky wasn't going to drop it. "You were willing to wait it out with Rachael to have a family." She kept stalling. As she stalled, you kept Cynthia in view. Any man would agree they both look like good breeders ..."

Paul interrupted. "I'm *that* basic? A fuckin' blind like breeder? Bullshit, I told you anyway, Cyn can't have a baby."

"That's what she says." Selesky said, looking away.

"You say there might be some gigantic primordial plot against all the players to get sperm to the egg.

"Who knows for sure, Paul. But it sure looks like you can't stay unattached, trying to get *something* to happen between you and the right woman."

Paul faced Selesky from the coffee pot counter in the corner away from the door. He poured and creamed coffee, wiped the stirring spoon with a tissue, picked up the large white cup, leaned back into the counter and drank, using both hands.

Paul responded to all of Selesky's positioning.

"After eleven years of stalling? It sure took a ton of bricks to fall on this stupid shit. Also, the way Rachael hung out more and more at Ben's bar. He was dragging her to his lowlife side of society. I was beginning to worry about having a baby with a woman who drank every night. That September, '67?" Paul said, his eyes returning to their original wattage. "She flatly and finally and clearly said it. He pointed with one finger without unwrapping from the coffee cup. " ...right out in that waiting room to this office. 'No baby with you'."

That afternoon snapped back into his mind. They sat in the crowded waiting room on a sunny San Diego September afternoon. Waiting for their appointment with Selesky and his co-therapist, Sarah Barkley, Paul suspected something was stirring in her. Rachael sat on a plastic and chrome chair, elbow in palm, inhaling her cigarette nervously, exhaling with an exaggerated hiss. With her legs crossed, too much thigh showed from under the mini skirt. One restless foot swung back and forth, the shoe hung precariously from her toes. She confirmed alienation when she eventually leaned over and whispered harshly to Paul, drawing a score of stares.

"That Sarah Barclays' just one more bitch shrink like that ass, Selesky. I don't trust them with our lives." Then, she returned to full voice. "They're out to make me wrong over this baby shit. Well, no baby for me, pal, never and ever. There, it's said"

Looking at him then jerking away, she tossed her cigarette to the floor, jumped to her feet and startled everyone by yelling: "I'm leaving here. I'm not seeing any of them, EVER. And no baby."

She stomped out. He could remember watching her rear-end swinging in the short gray skirt, her blonde hair bouncing just above her shoulders, she refusing to look back as he called her name. She plunged into her car, and the smell of the Sears tires spinning and catching on the dusty asphalt worked its way into the waiting room.

Selesky had stayed quiet during Paul's reverie.

Bringing his coffee with him, Paul dropped back into the present in the familiar chair across from Selesky. He breathed a sigh and agreed with his doctor. "No baby with me. God, my happiness, my life actually, sure was in her hands all those years."

Selesky looked up from his chair. "You've now begun a new life, Paul."

"Yep." He forced a grin. "That fire is out. I'm getting a divorce. Now, I get to go to Vietnam again. Aren't I lucky?" He brimmed with sarcasm.

"And to Cynthia again?"

"Maybe so. Maybe no."

The once dimming images of Cynthia began to smile back into his needy mind. His eyes moved toward the ceiling. Selesky's fingers reformed the oft-present teepee.

Not sure how consciously he had manipulated his transfer orders, within a year of the first liaison with Cynthia he was on a new ship, a mine-sweeper, the USS Firm, returning to Hong Kong. Once in the city, he still remembered her telephone number. Confident, he had dialed 428-9330 and said just one word into the worn black Bakelite mouthpiece with the cloth covered cord.

"Cynthia?"

And she said four words to him. "Oh Yes. Hotel Cathay."

Within an hour, at the Hotel on Tung Lo Wan Road, they carnivorously re-ignited the entanglement. Over years then, each time he visited her city, the unrestrained passion continued and eventually, in time, a safe intimacy developed and surely increased. In 1966, he managed to get a six-month tour of duty with the Hong Kong Shore Patrol and they were together almost every day and many nights. He believed then that he had truly grown to love being *with* the strikingly beautiful Dutch woman, but as a folly only. He remained truest to the idea of Rachael, an American, and having a family in the States, and all.

"Where are you?" Selesky asked quietly.

"Hong Kong. Cynthia. Strange set of choices. If I could have had Rachael *and* children as we'd planned? I would have settled for it all with her. Row house, two cars in the driveway, play Monopoly, Boy Scouts, picket fence, freezer full of dead animal flesh, insurance policies paid up ...be a grandfather some day ...all that. But with her saying no? The whole idea of children and of middle-America goes out the window. Like I'll settle for something completely different now."

"You have work to do there, Paul."

"Fuck work" Paul snapped at the judgmental statement. "Rachael was work. Life and kids with her would have been more work. It's over. It's different. Cynthia can't have kids so she's a complete other side of the picture." He thought of Abie's comment about Cynthia.

"Abie says she's night and day from Rachael. She's educated, in med school. Sophisticated, Dutch and says she couldn't live in the U.S. mostly because of our politics toward Vietnam. She's probably a qualified bleeding heart."

"So, with her it's Hong Kong and an international sort of x-patriot life?"

"Whatever that means." Paul declared. "Maybe not even able to marry her. She stays married to Kurt." He sat the coffee cup on a side table. "I think I'm nuts, David." He told him about the floating words and letters.

"You sound nuts." Selesky said frankly. "Why her and not a new woman somewhere between the two desires, easier to manage geographically, financially, a woman who actually can have kids?"

"Because, when Cynthia first walked into the room I was hit with a message that somehow, if she were in my life, it would be better, all my needs met. And, I 'can't shake that message. That sort of shit."

"That is shit all right, B-U-L-L shit, you know. Those feelings came from within *you* ...not radiated magically from her. That was simply a sign you were very needy."

"She doesn't see my kindness as weakness like Rachael did."

"Stop, stop." Selesky begged and stood up, his signal to end the hour. "I'll write to the Pope ... St Catherine, move over for Saint Cynthia."

"I've told her in a letter about divorcing. Asked if she'd consider ...you know." His face became solemn. So did Selesky's.

"What did she reply, Paul?"

"Should'a had an answer by now."

Back on the ship, Paul continued to be pulled in several directions. The stress of waiting for Cynthia's answer grew to agonize him. The ship's hurried preparation for the war overworked him and Rachael's persistent calls irritated him. Distracted, overworked and irritated showed through. Abie tried to tease him out of it all.

"You act like a puppet with his strings all tangled, Chief."

"Huh?"

"Outside forces jerkin' your strings. Re-actin' rather than actin'? You need relief an' you spell relief—D-i-v-o-r-c-e."

"Hey."

Abie put one hand on his friend's shoulder. "C'mon. Let's go ashore, get drunk, badmouth women overall, Rachael in particular if you want to."

"Reports are overdue. The Captain's after me ...will I train as Officer of the Deck? Do I want to be recommended for a commission?"

"Not sure about becoming an officer?"

"Never thought of it before, but now ...maybe! Cap'n said he's gotta' know now for the next convening board ...tomorrow morning. Am I in or out?"

"Sanity is overdue."

Paul looked up, then pointed aft. "Company."

Lieutenant Harry Stumpf, their division officer was hurrying toward the two men.

"Ah shee'it." Abie mumbled.

Looking flustered, his eyes fused on his Master Chief, the young Lieutenant bumped his way through small groups of men who were carrying boxes of goods aboard ship. Making eye contact with Vincent, a smile cracked over Stumpf's fleshy face.

Lieutenant Stumpf relied heavily on his Chief but they did not have the stereotyped 'old Chief, young officer' relationship. The 32 year old Stumpf kidded Vincent about being promoted so young, then 33, to Master Chief.

"Master Chief's are supposed to be fifty something, or older, like McCullough. Grizzled looking farts with wrinkled necks like they been climbing masts for forty wind blown years, give or take. You can't be a Master Chief and run around the ship lookin' as sleek and trim as we young officers." He would smile, self-pleased. "Your youth doesn't fit your title and I'm tired of wardroom prattle that the operations department has a 'boy Master Chief'. From now on, I'm calling you 'Pappy', Pappy. At least then I'll have the *illusion* you're old enough to give me sound advice." Vincent disliked the nickname but of course, the more he complained, the more it was used.

Calling his Master Chief 'Pappy' was only one small sign that navy tradition wasn't all that important to Stumpf nor to many of the sailors who came into the navy to avoid an Army tour as a drafted rifle soldier. Those close to Stumpf knew he disliked the navy and wanted to resign his commission as soon as Vietnam was over, but everyone also knew this would be a difficult move for the man. Harry Stumpf's father was vice admiral Frederick Stumpf, Commander in Chief, U.S. Pacific Fleet. No one could quite figure out how to take advantage of that fact.

"Here comes the Admiral's not-favored son." Lake warned.

Seeming to have to be in full throttle just to manage life as a navy officer, the lieutenant puffed up to Vincent and Lake and took a deep breath. The opening smile changed to a practiced pained expression. "Pappy? Thanks for waiting." Adjusting his clear-framed glasses upward with one finger, Stumpf began shifting his 240 pudgy pounds from one foot to the other as though waiting for Vincent or Lake to open the conversation. Lake, who often harassed the division officer over the issue with his admiral father, threw in a paraphrased quip that usually prompted a rise from Stumpf.

"You still thinkin' 'bout tellin' Daddy you don't like workin' for the family company?"

Stumpf turned to Abie as if just noticing Lake was present.

"Hi, Lake." He adjusted his glasses again as though giving Lake the 'finger', and looked at Vincent. As was often the case, he began to whine. " If we don't get the maintenance schedules to him by eight AM, the exec's going to kill me, Chief." His eyes moved back and forth from Vincent to Lake. He didn't seem to know what to do with his hands and ended up folding them at his chest. He readjusted the glasses again by wrinkling his nose and face in a set of gross practiced but unconscious movements. "I'm under the gun, Chief. Can you do the reports by morning?" He whined.

That prompted a mocking whine from Lake, double emphasizing most words. "Mister Stumpf. Me an' Pappy was jus' go-in' ashore to swear off wo—-men."

"I need the report."

"He needs time off." Lake's protective position seemed in order.

Paul resented the two direction tug. In the old days, before he carried so much enlisted rank, he'd have been ordered to stay aboard and finish a report, ordered off to a school, ordered to train as O.O.D. The old days of having no authority, no decisions, no questions, thereby no guilt *and* no freedoms actually seemed pretty good to him at that moment.

But, it wasn't the old days. It was January, 1968 and he was the ship's Master Chief, the crew's most senior enlisted man. He pulled his hat from his head, wiped at the sweat band with one finger, tried a smile that didn't develop and soothed the needs of his boss.

"I've already planned working the night on them, Mr. Stumpf."

"Thank you, Pappy."

"Call me, Chief."

"Okay, Chief Pappy." Stumpf grinned openly and looked silly doing so.

Feeling rejected, Lake slipped both Vincent and the Lieutenant a close to the heart but unseen international finger sign, and left the ship.

Realizing most of life's setbacks are self-inflicted made it a little easier for Paul Vincent to eventually shake the victim feeling. He went below decks to his quarters and spread overdue bookwork all over the small metal desk and onto half his adjacent bunk. For comfort he clicked on the fluorescent desk lamp and killed the overhead lights. For company, he clicked on a San Diego radio station and let a talk show drone into the small quiet room. The radio host was a well-known conservative and most of his callers were in agreement to continuing in Vietnam. If they weren't, the host became a hawkish bully.

"You 'fuzzy-headed-liberals'. Afraid of the heat? Leave the kitchen. Afraid of a war? Leave the world. Ha-ha!"

"But, but, but, the M.I.A., the P.O.W and K.I.A. figures go up every day."

"Hey pinko, your cowardice ratio is what goes up. Along with the commie body bag count … AND …the Dow Jones."

After goading the callers into raging anger, he would cut them off the air without a warning and continue preaching to his choir. To Vincent, the caller's frustrations and the host's goading seemed childish when compared to the actuality of the killing war as he had seen it in the Mekong Delta and the Plain of Reeds. But, for company, he let it prattle on over his shoulder. He was adjusting again to soon being part of the war that seemed to divide the country with each daily newscast.

Around ten PM, the radio messenger brought him his mail and messages. In the small stack of papers and envelopes were two new phone demands from Rachael. He impulsively took Selesky's advice and decided to confront her. For privacy, he walked out on the pier to a pay telephone. No answer at home. He looked up *Benny's Bistro*, certain to reach her there.

"The number you have reached is no longer in service … "

Why would she insist he call but not be reachable? Why is the bar's phone disconnected? He clacked the telephone into its rack and jerked the booth door opened.

He returned to his room and to the remaining mail stack, sorting through the envelopes automatically. There were several Rachael credit card bills, a notice on overdue auto registration, a second letter that day from Rachael's attorney, a surprise bill for two hundred dollars from his own attorney, and last, true excitement: The much anticipated letter from Cynthia.

The instant he popped it open with an index finger, her soft toned British-over-Dutch accent slipped into the air.

My Dearest Paul

Your letter reads like my one to you that went unanswered so many years ago. But I had left you a way out in my letter. You've left me no way out in yours. So, I will answer yours.

Your plea for us to become one turns my heart over and over . . and of course, I must consider it. But, there is bad news in the way.

Kurt's father is desperately ill in the south of France. We must go there. You recall, you met him years ago. He is 81 now and we both feel he will die. I cannot tell if Kurt will want to stay in France until father's end—but he may. Thoughts of missing seeing you in Hong Kong because of this pulls my heart and fuels my desire to divorce Kurt—but, I can't tell if I would be divorcing Kurt's kindness honestly, or if I am being propelled by an immediate need to be loved by you. I will do all I can for us to return before your ship reaches H.K. I need objectivity and with you this strongly in my mind, I have none.

Now, what are good things to reveal?

Kurt sends his love. Mini skirts have made their way to H.K. I have one tucked away but I don't do it the way the long-legged lassies do. And that makes me sad because I know you are a leg-man.

I also have a 'virginal white' off the shoulder dress to meet you in. I have new wai-das. One especially for our first evening together. One for playtime, later. Yes, when packing, I ran across our tape measure. Remember it? Of course you do. I would pack it to Europe but Kurt has no appreciation for such games. I have tucked it safely next to my (our) bed for when we are one again. Hearing that you are coming, albeit eventually, it is nice to look forward to shelving my vibrator.

Mia also sends love to her Mr. Paul.

With deepest need and love

Cyn

Made anxious by the mixed news and the confusing reference to an unanswered letter, he could not wait for another exchange by mail.

He awakened the chief who ran the ship's retail store, badgered him for several rolls of quarters and went ashore again, this time to telephone Hong Kong. It was one a.m. If nothing else, he wanted to remind her he might have *once* been a leg man, but no longer, since her.

The call clicked through the trans-Pacific systems in less than three minutes.

"Hong Kong, Wanchai Exchange." A sudden chill went through him. The office he was speaking to was less than a mile from Cynthia's home. Although the woman's voice sounded somewhat like she was standing in a well, the words were clear.

He asked for the familiar number. "428-9330, please ...and I'm in California. Please do not cut me off."

"Connecting number now." She was very impersonal.

Mia answered on the fourth ring. The old housekeeper's greeting jerked him immediately back to the exotic times when he had telephoned in just this way, to set up a few minutes or a few hours with Cynthia.

"Mia? It's Paul Vincent...—Hello...hello?"

"Oh, Mr. Paul, Mr. Paul." She giggled so hard as to make her normally accented phrases even more difficult to understand. "Cyn an' Mr. Kurt in France. Cyn in France. No call now."

"No Cyn? No call?" He felt empty.

"No Cyn, Mr. Paul. Four days now gone, five days." The empty feeling worsened.

"You Hong Kong, Mr. Paul?" Mia sounded very troubled.

"I'm California, still. You okay? When she come back?" Paul caught himself insultingly speaking in short phrases although he long ago learned Mia understood his English very well.

"No know when come back—Mr. Kurt or Cyn to call Mia."

It took several seconds for him to face that the call had ended. It was almost another minute before the telephone beeped loudly in his hand. He returned it mindlessly to the hanger and eased the booth door open. The second time he'd been rejected from that booth that night.

He returned to Truaxe, to his quarters and tried not to brood. Sitting backward in his padded metal chair, he numbly opened Rachael's attorney's letter wondering truly if anything else could go wrong. In bold black on gray, he held page after page of certified copies of forms. Rachael's self-invested thoughtlessness closed in on him. She, or Ben was proving to be the kinds of people who could publish the crooks guide to major cities. One of them really had forged his signature on a very bad loan agreement, and she was going to milk it. The paperwork stipulated that as a limited partner in Ben's bar business, Vincent was obligated to prop it up with an additional five hundred dollars by the end of the following day, or some bargain-basement letter-head-only Thrift and Loan would attach the equity in the small house he and Rachael were buying, now rented to a navy family in Norfolk, Virginia. He crushed the letter and tossed it toward the corner trash basket. It missed. He stepped to retrieve it, picked it up gingerly and dropped it purposefully into the can. He took a deep breath. Nothing improved. Connecting with Cynthia wasn't working. Disconnecting from Rachael wasn't working either. All the new information mixed with the old and spun in familiar but dead-end streets.

"Out of control." He said into the air and flung the ball-point pen to bounce off Rachael's smiling eight by ten that still hung above his pillow. It didn't change her incongruous smile and he protested. "You won't get the last laugh." But even as he said it he wondered how he and an attorney he hardly knew could manage the legal mess from a deployed ship while his primary thoughts were on staying healthy in a war zone and hooking up with Cynthia who was now off to Europe.

He spun the padded chair around and turned to the paperwork, catching himself laughing aloud at the incongruity. "My fucking world's on fire and I sit here testifying on paper that unnecessary equipment tests have been made that haven't been made so a Lieutenant who hates the navy won't be yelled at by an executive officer whose trying to not be yelled at by a Commanding Officer who can't be yelled out for fear of losing his place on the ladder toward becoming an admiral. But!" He thought. "Maybe that's what Master Chief's are here to do."

He spent until five a.m. in creative writing, bringing the maintenance reports into some sort of order.

At six A.M. he was awakened by loud knocking.

"I don't kid no Master Chiefs this early inna' mornin'. Your wife's *really* at the quarterdeck, right now, sittin' inna' chair I took her. "

The Chief's eyes refused to open until he rubbed life into them. He pushed himself up from his bunk and looked with disbelief at the young messenger who stood with one foot in the doorway of the dimly lit quarters.

"Christ." His anxiety awoke, twisted in his gut and knotted like a wringing towel.

The messenger shifted nervously. "You comin' up, Master Chief?"

Vincent stepped into his khaki trousers, fell back on the bunk and reached for yesterday's socks. "Wait." He snapped to the messenger. "Throw that light switch."

Florescence flickered from two overhead fixtures and caused his eyes to feel hammered, then burn, then become watery. With two index fingers he pressed his eyelashes down against his cheekbones until he felt snapping wet clicks in his eyes. The eyes opened slowly then and with only a little burning sensation.

"Wait." He repeated. Regardless of Selesky's encouragement, he plainly didn't want to have the same old arguments again; no baby, too much drinking, brother Ben and the 'other-brother' Nick in charge, bad sex, no money, her working Ben's low life bar. She had recently countered his complaints about Ben and Nick by reminding him he should have realized how important the brothers were to her when they first married. To check for reason in that repeated remark once again, he slipped a tape of their life together into rapid rerun.

Married in 1957, they had each been twenty-two. Almost immediately, 15 year old Ben, who Paul saw as an under socialized juvenile troublemaker with the brain power of a sand dab, and 14 year old Nick, who had the attention span of a flash bulb, entered their lives to stay. Until the marriage, the boys had lived with their alcoholic parents and had no goals for life beyond a job prospect of setting pins at the *Belleview* Bowling Alley in Steubenville. Rachael's marriage to a steady person had given her mother and father permission to completely stop parenting the two boys, to let welfare pay the bills, and their alcoholism take free reign. At the end of the Christmas visit after their August 10th marriage, her father made his move.

"It's only right, Rachael. Goddammit, you're a woman. Women naturally know how to raise kids. I can't take care of no boys and you know your mother. She's, just simple like. She can't do it neither."

"But, Daddy ... ?"

"No buts. You see to it those boys are taken care of, or dammit, you're no good for nothin'. Now you take 'em. And remember, we love ya', Rachael. Your Mother does too."

Paul and Rachael returned to Norfolk with the two boys poking at one another in the back seat of the car. Though it was never actually talked about openly and honestly, Paul moved over and made room for them, naively thinking they would simply fade away in a couple of years, and he and Rachael could pick up there and start their own family.

But the two didn't fade away. Both were refused entry into the service and neither developed skills for the real world. They simply hung around and hung around while Paul Vincent paid their way.

Paul never suspected how truly obligated Rachael felt toward the two. Where Nick the younger mostly let life take place around him, Ben would demand from life by demanding from Rachael. Instead of appreciation, Ben developed a powerful sense of entitlement that Rachael seemed helpless to. Once Paul refused to provide an alibi to keep Ben out of jail and Rachael withdrew into days of what he now recognizes as manipulative depression. Blinded by his feelings for her, it took years for him to see her depressed state was simply a well developed ploy. Meanwhile, because her smiles were his reward, like Pavlov's dogs, he instinctively and unconsciously became an unwitting part of her obsession to care for the brothers.

Dr. Selesky had helped him search his early life for signs why he would accept he was to be used by Rachael and the boys. His mothers on-going comments—"a man should take care of his wife," seemed to jell with the themes of the John Wayne movies of those days, "strong silent men ignore their own needs in order to make women smile."

Paul mumbled to his socks. "You've been screwed by yourself …an angry mother, a damaged wife with an unbreakable nylon umbilical cord attached to her father and, a couple of usurious kid brothers."

"Pardon Master Chief?" The messenger leaned in to hear through the mumbles.

"Nothing." Paul said. "Just remember; flash bulbs never re-light. Sand dabs live forever and continually return to indulgent places where a stupid sailor feeds the hand that bites him."

"If you say so, Master Chief?"

"I'm like the damned horse who pulls the plow all the hot summer but has to give up the warmest stall to some non-deserving favorite, come winter."

The messenger, still at the doorway, threw Vincent an onomatopoeia. "Tick-tock, tick-tock, Chief."

"Tick-tock, shit. Wait a minute. I'm recapping something."

During Vincent's first tour as Swift Boat skipper in the Mekong Delta, Rachael and her brothers had become bolder and bolder about excluding him from their lives. Upon returning from Vietnam in early 1967, she was distant and cool toward him, a manifestation of her guilt and fear. Five months earlier she had sneaked four thousand dollars of their savings to Ben as a down payment on a cheap workingman's bar now tagged as *Ben's Bistro"*. She, or Ben, had also forged his signature on the loan arrangement. Once confronted, she simply dared Paul to do anything about it.

Paul's rank was forcing the messenger to feign patience but he was turning his hat nervously around and around in his hands. Paul stood up and reached for his khaki shirt and the messenger reached for the doorknob. Maintaining balance, Paul forced both feet at once into the brown oxfords, still laced from the night before.

"Tell her I'll be up …shortly."

"Aye aye, Master Chief."

As soon as the messenger left the small quarters, Vincent flicked off the shoes he had just crammed his feet into, undressed rapidly, stuffed the previous day's wrinkled uniform into a net laundry bag, flicked on the shower and immediately stepped into its cold rush. He wasn't sure why he was cleaning himself up for her but he couldn't stop the process.

Barely drying himself, he pulled underwear, socks and a freshly creased set of cotton khakis from the metal closet at the foot of his bunk. He turned to the small mirror over the single sink and ran his *Norelco* over his face. Because only one of its two shaving heads worked, this process took an impatient filled extra few minutes. Promising to clean the shaver later, he brushed his teeth and, with a small comb, organized his short brown hair. He looked at his reflection in the mirror.

"Man, you look truly crappy." His brown eyes seemed puffy and ringed with circles of fatigue and confusion. His normally tanned complexion seemed pasty, his curly hair needed trimmed at the neck.

Turning back to the center of the room he took fresh service ribbons from a top drawer and snapped them into place above the left pocket of the starched shirt. He rubbed his brass belt buckle with a tissue, wiped his hat's insignia on his shirtfront and fitted the hat on his head. He decided against wearing a tie, optional to the winter shipboard uniform, shined the toes of his shoes on the back of his trousers and turned to the full length mirror on the inside of the metal door. Although his uniform was very neat, it didn't seem to hide he was thinner than his usual 170 pounds.

"You look like a chicken in eagle's clothing." He said to his image. His Chief Petty Officer's hat with the eagle and two stars of the master chief insignia suddenly felt heavy. With a practiced move, he pitched his head forward. The hat slipped off and downward. He deflected it with a balled up fist, flipped it with a right knee jerk and caught it, insignia up, squarely on the toe of his extended right foot.

"Well." He flattered himself. "Stand by, Rachael. Least I can still manage the important stuff."

CHAPTER TWO
Who is Rachael, Really?

Summer and winter the sun warms the deserts to the east of San Diego. Late each day the warmer air rises, drawing clouds of cooler replacement air from the Pacific ocean, over and through the city. Overnight, often, mist, some fog and pockets of moisture slide inland and hang at the coast and in some valleys, insulating the earth until the determined morning sun evaporates the mist. About half of the days of any year the sun is unable to dissolve the overcast until mid-morning. On those days, the moisture enriches the soil, soaks into the coastal plants and gardens and adds crispness to the air. The result is that nearly any San Diego morning is cool, pleasant and promising. A common San Diego greeting: "Ahh, *another* day in paradise"

"Yeah! But don't tell the tourists it's like this alla' time."

Paul Vincent stepped onto the topside deck of Truaxe. His focus on meeting Rachael was so distracting he didn't notice the beauty of the day in his favorite city.

"G'mornin', Master Chief."

He answered the greeting of the Officer of the Deck with an automatic return salute and a head nod. He followed the pointing arm of the messenger, took a few steps, turned a corner and saw Rachael. It was like standing in front of an unpromising refrigerator, a once inviting dish, now stale.

She was looking away, lighting a cigarette. From his angle her profile, her right side toward him seemed different. There was slightly inflated flesh below her eyes. Her hair seemed shorter and tangled looking. Its usually noteworthy glistening color seemed washed out, yellow and sticky. An attention getting part of her, the lips in which he once saw beauty were carelessly smeared with lipstick that was too bright. Her normally sky-blue eyes were surrounded with thick mascara modeled for her by the bar crowd. The powder blue flyaway jacket he had brought for her from Saigon a year earlier was pulled over her shoulders. She clutched the cigarette to her chest and he saw that she, not usually a fashion victim had nonetheless stopped wearing a bra. It didn't work on her body. In the morning chill her nipples outlined against a white blouse that looked rumpled. Her skirt was too short for her sitting position and a ragged web of a snag in her right nylon distracted from her very shapely legs. She seemed to be someone else sitting there on the dark blue canvas chair. She looked empty, he felt empty.

Though standing very still, his heart began beating as though he'd sprinted topside. A myriad of anxiety bumps formed at his neck and crawled down his back, chilling his blood, causing a shiver and forcing a deep breath.

The feelings confirmed something. "It's better when I'm away from her." He thought. "Be careful." His racing heart calmed just a little. A new tranquility was filling in. At that graphic instant it was again clear he was no longer in love with the woman before him.

Selesky's words, "do not feed the hand that bites you" flashed from his memory as he greeted her.

"You wanted to see me, Rachael?" He tried to be business like, so out of character between them.

She turned her head slowly in his direction and looked up with eyes like a wounded deer's, to focus inside of his as though searching his brain for indications of the impact of her being there.

"Oh, Paul ..." Accompanying the fluid like words, her body posture slowly slumped, shoulders forward. Her eyes changed modes from searching his to pulling at him. He spoke to maintain control.

"What's do you want, Rachael?" He liked that his voice sounded calm.

"Oh, Paul." She repeated the sighed greeting, her head cocked to one side. "Everything happened. This and that ..." She shrugged her shoulders in a dramatic exaggerated move. "I feel so bad inside." She shifted to an open outright whiny sound. "I need you, to help me."

Facing a major weapon, her helplessness, he bit his lip to keep from talking, to keep from tricking himself.

She moved her shoulders slowly in circles, positioning them for reaction. "I'm ok, but not really." She looked directly into his eyes again. "Can we go someplace private?"

He searched her eyes as she had his only seconds before. Hers flicked quickly away, lacking her usual confidence. Caution shaped his answer. "No privacy on the ship. We havta' meet here."

"Whatever." She flicked the cigarette carelessly into the air. It cleared the side of the ship but scattered sparks against the concrete pier inches from a fuel-line-connecting valve. He looked about hesitantly. The messenger who had told Paul of her arrival stood close by, listening.

Paul locked eyes with the young sailor. "Git," he said. The man looked struck, snap-turned and left the area.

Rachael was now staring at the deck, pouting, but this alternate weapon appeared so contrived it, like the helplessness ploy, fell flat, no clout.

" For the first time, I think I see you as others see you, Rachael. A true view."

"What?" Uncertainty was all over her face.

She shifted to still another major weapon; crying without restraint. Her breath gasped in sobs and huffs for air. Sailors coming to the ship for the workday were walking by the strange scene and looking. Embarrassed, he wanted out of there. He moved close so only she could hear him and spoke through involuntarily clenched teeth.

"Rachael, why *are* you here? My attorney says not to talk to you. You've lied, forged my name ..." She interrupted.

"You wouldn't call me ba-ck." The whine was too exaggerated, as in a cheap movie. "I'm wor-ried. Your things are set out at the ho-use. It saddens me. When you pick them up, it'll be em-p-ty there?"

She cried more. Caked mascara oozed downward. He heard shoes scrape on the steel deck and looked up to see his Commanding Officer, Captain Clifford, and the ship's executive officer, Commander Griffith looking at him. He turned to salute as was the custom upon the first meeting of the day, but both officers dropped their eyes, pivoted and strode away. Embarrassed, he turned and growled at Rachael.

"You didn't come here to cry like this and talk about my things."

"No. I didn't. I need something that no one else can do." Her face suddenly gained credibility. She touched his hand with only a finger and his earlier chills returned. His heart raced as in an invitation to run. Panic motivated his words.

"Look, I'll call later. I'll arrange to come by for my things. We can talk then." He turned to leave.

Her eyes locked on the back of his head. Her voice again rolled smoothly. "Don't go, Paul. Please? Listen?" He turned back to her. She looked away and down. He had to lean in to hear her.

"It's Ben. He's been taken to jail, arrested." She hesitated. "For …this and, and, he didn't do anything wrong." Without making eye contact she rambled with a difficult to understand story about Ben and his wife's involvement with some back room gambling in the bar. He let her talk. History was repeating. Ben needed help, but this time her pouting, helplessness, tears and pleading had no impact. Selesky had been right. He was there to serve her family.

"Rachael, stop all this." But he knew she would play it out.

"Oh, Paul! Ben was in jail and we needed bond money. A lady we know paid it but she needs the money back before her husband finds out. Five thousand …before Truaxe deploys. I know you can get money. Benny can't stand being locked up. He'll go crazy. Bunny is crazy already, and …"

"STOP! … ." He shouted, but calmed quickly and again spoke through clenched teeth. "There's nothing I *want* to do." He wondered candidly: If she needed the money before Truaxe deployed, was the lender's husband a Truaxe sailor? Who would lend Ben five thousand dollars under any circumstance?

The story held his attention. He pictured her mind racing, confused that he wasn't already holding her in his arms, making it all better. He braced against another gambit. She looked at him but then quickly away.

"Maybe you are right about, you know … " Her voice trailed off.

He crunched into the bait. "Right about . . ?"

"You know, …you know …what this is all about." She shrugged again, stalled, then finished the sentence: "A baby." She glanced at his eyes for a quick surveillance, and away again. "Maybe I'm …lonely when you're at sea. We could reconsider this, that …you know." She selected words that normally pulled him in, but nothing was happening.

She tried a new tact. "I could love kids. Help us, help me now, I'll …"

"Say what you want to say, Rach. Spell it out."

She straightened up in the chair, put her hands on her knees, pulled her shoulders back and focused her eyes on the bridge of his nose between his brows. Words tumbled out rapidly: "I want to come back to you. Have your baby as you've always wanted." Her composure slipped, she looked away again. Her tears flooded and ran freely. Her shoulders shook. She was compromising herself once again for the brother.

With a returned chill he agreed again with what Selesky had been saying. There had *never* been a true Rachael. The drunken father had manipulated her into life as the substitute parent for the two brothers.

"I come up with five thousand dollars to keep Ben out of jail, and you and I could have a baby?"

"Yes."

"You'd give your life away for Ben?"

She looked away but the side of her jaw formed the word he barely heard. "Yes."

Paul had grossly underestimated such father-power. What had been so menacing, life threatening and endangering in the old drunk's power over her?. He'd always seen the man as a soggy graham-cracker of a person, a dirty automobile with "wash me" on his sides.

Paul had been too distracted, too innocent of such raw social ploys. Her father's early life message that she was to 'take care of the boys' had literally been a command that Rachael surrender any self-identity. For eleven years he had been married to the caretaker of Ben and Nick, nothing else.

He pulled her from the chair and held her close. He was sure she thought she had won, but he knew she hadn't.

"Yes. Oh, yes, Paul." Her flooded tears, her mucus voice and her body pressed against him usually ended all his resistance but she sensed something wasn't right. He was too tense.

She tried one last time. "If you ever loved me. If you could love a child of ours, you'll find a way to get the money." The soap-opera statement was emphasized by new shakes of her body.

He spoke into her sticky yellow hair. "Rachael, you go back to Ben and, tell him my position, will you?" She leaned back and watched his face with concentrated hope but feigned adoration. Her open hands reflexively stroked his arms up and down lightly. He took her chin between two fingers and spoke directly into her eyes. "I know Ben sent you here. I know you hate failing him. But, if he has any questions about why I haven't given in to you? Get a dictionary, the two of you look up the word: D-I-V-O-R-C-E." He spelled it slowly for her. "I want one."

She flipped her head in a borderline manner, literally shaking tears away. "You ass. You high and mighty ass. You cause all this trouble then you run. You promised to love me, you swore to love me, but look at you, running away."

There, he thought, is the truest Rachael he'd ever get to know. He turned away, toward a nearby hatch to escape below decks.

She screamed above the din of the vent noises. "You are the worst of men!!" Her voice caught in a sob, but centered again. "I'll never divorce you—N-E-V-E-R!" She stepped to above the open hatch and yelled down at him. "The world would be better without you." Paul glanced up to see the O.O.D. taking her by the arm.

"NEVER!" She yelled one last time.

Below decks, his thoughts still sorting, he sat on the edge of a large metal stowage locker and let his heartbeat slow. Rachael had tried her magic wand on Paul, but found the batteries dead.

"Really over now, Paul?" Abie Lake was there, patting his shoulder.

"How absolutely different life really is from what we think life really is." Paul said into the air.

"I have no idea what the fuck you jes' said, Chief."

Paul shook his head and looked tense. Abie backed down. A couple of men who had seen the Chief on the quarterdeck with Rachael came down the passageway. One stopped the other and pointed. Both turned and went away.

After awhile, Abie commented: "Return to a scorned woman and she'll sharpen her claws on you."

Paul rose to his feet and faced his friend. "Definitely over now."

"Over? Shit. Watch a man whose tryin' to forget an ex-wife and you'll see 'im walk in front of a car or off the side of a ship."

"That'd make her happy. You hear her? Her world would be better without me?"

Abie stroked his chin with thumb and forefinger. "I think she meant all men be dead. If there wasn't no men, you know, lots less crime …and," he broke into a laugh. "A whole lot more fat women." The silly laughter drew a smile from Paul.

"Yeah, laugh, Abie, but the chips are down. . '

"When the chips are down, just means the Buffalo is empty." Lake sputtered, very pleased with making his friend smile.

Paul, smirking, said: "I'll come up later, Abie."

"I'll make coffee and we can sit around and consider tradin' in all women."

"For what?" Pal seemed hopeful there might actually be a choice.

"Velvet soft gloves?" Abie jerked a half-clenched fist back and forth and grinned.

"The garb of a monk?" Paul said with gloomy resolution.

"I ain't getting' invested in no vestments. Too much like a dress. You gotta' get further away from women than that even."

Both men were still smiling as Abie pivoted to leave.

"Hey, Abie?"

"What?"

"It's harder than hell to leave someone you once thought enough of to marry."

"I'll take your word on that. I'll never have ta' do it."

As Abie left, Paul was intercepted by Lieutenant Stumpf and three of his radiomen who had been out of sight but waiting for an opening. In typical and likely necessary male fashion, they all ignored the obvious struggle of Paul's.

"Can we get down to the business of getting this ship off to Vietnam?" Stumpf asked with a wiggle of his glasses.

The men all had good questions. His ability to answer them symbolized a return to professionalism, the depression replaced by resurfacing energy. As Lieutenant Stumpf put it;—"You're a damned good sailor, Chief Vincent …get sailoring."

And he did.

For the next two days he seemed to be his old highly respected, top performer self as long as he worked on the business of pre-deployment and readiness. However, the lifting of the Rachael distraction exposed in Paul Vincent a dim but foreboding sense that his long suppressed Vietnam anxiety was about to return.

"Jesus, Jesus." He exclaimed aloud. "Will life ever smooth out?"

With exactly five days until the ship deployed, he knew he had to get up to date on the war. Just because he had failed himself for eleven years he could not fail in Vietnam because of it. He needed his confidence to return. He could not rely on luck at all. Working on the communication tasks with his men, some obviously suppressed feelings surfaced in the form of an internalized and judgmental male voice.

"You were lucky the last time, you know. You didn't actually fight. All you did was train the Vietnamese. All you did was maneuver the Swift Boat in and out of the deltas and those confusing, twisted and smelly rivers. You never even pulled a trigger. The ARVN's did the real fighting. The men you lost were Vietnamese soldiers, not American. Made it easy to forget, until now. Or, have you really forgotten, or is it all simply stuffed away, ready to flood out again? Was it skill or dumb luck that brought you back alive and well?" The voice shut down but Paul spoke aloud.

"Does luck run out?" He quickly scanned but none of the others seemed to notice what he had said.

Rationally he knew this trip he'd be safely at sea in the Gulf of Tonkin. The Truaxe would not be concerned with the Mekong Delta and little towns like My Tho, nor with the running tides around the canals on the disordered edges of the Plain of Reeds. He felt a little calmer. This trip there would be no cursed overpowered but undermanned little boat for him to worry over. He felt relief. There would be no handful of under-eager, under-aged, under-trained Vietnamese soldiers depending on him to stop their war. He began to feel quite calm now..

"Relax, Paul. Relax, it'll be a breeze this time."

He pulled a lined yellow tablet from his desk and listed priorities for the trip, some global, others more to the point:

One—Accept the divorce actually has real value.

Two—Accept that Vietnam will dominate your life for the next seven months or so.

Three—Speculate that if and when there is time off from the war, there may be time to explore a new future, *perhaps* in Hong Kong with Cynthia.

Four—Get your mind totally free so as to not jeopardize the lives of anyone while in the gulf.

Five—Get specific and get busy. Get a senior technician to proof the maintenance report worked on all night long and get it to Lieutenant Stumpf, right now. Schedule a shipyard crane to have the antennas cleaned, today. Get the Navy Electronics Lab to check their transmitting range patterns, today. Send a memo to the C.O. letting him know you would be happy to train as underway Officer of the Deck on the way to Vietnam. Make sure Lieutenant Stumpf brings the crypto publications up to date, today. Insure all department heads concur with the internal routing guide so incoming messages find their way to the correct officers, tomorrow first thing. Have the 1st class radiomen make up task group call-sign and frequency assignments for Yankee Station and the gulf and conduct individual and watch section training in their use. Re-check everything with the supply clerk and the electronic techs. Can't run out of spare parts, or teletype paper, can't run out of fluid for the copy machines, nor pencils, nor paper clips nor dots for all of the I's.

Make a list, check it twice. Do all men have up to date security clearances? Has the C.O. signed the list approving the officers he wishes to have message releasing authority? Are the correct batteries for the emergency boat radios on board? Do you have both NATO and S.E.A.T.O. radio-frequency crystal allowances? Can the operators in C.I.C. use the challenge and reply codes? Have the patch-board switches been properly color coded to reflect the new remote position installations? Do the O.O.D.'s know how to trigger the voice encryption devices on the maneuvering nets? List the details and follow through on them. Details, follow through. Details, details. This is what you do, Paul Vincent. You're a Master Chief Radioman. You are taking a ship to war. People are counting on you.

"Jesus, people are counting on me, Abie, an' here I Am. I just find out I lost eleven years. I got enough work for six crews. Goin' to a shootin' war I want no part of. Don't know if I'll even see Cynthia. Wonder if I'll ever have children …"

"You'll have children. And I'll toast that all of your children have wealthy parents."

"I'll never have children, Abie. Hear me."

"You bellyache like a spoiled prince."

"There's sour mash, with acid thrashing around in my guts."

"Like an ulcer bleeding out, Chief?"

"Bad marriage bleeding out."

"Uh!"

By mid-afternoon Paul Vincent was beginning to feel more like he'd finally taken charge of his life. He walked out onto pier four to telephone Rachael and arrange to pick up his things and to schedule one last appointment with Doctor Selesky. It was not that he felt he needed additional counsel from Selesky, it was more to bid the man farewell and thank him for his objectivity, guidance, patience and friendship.

CHAPTER THREE
Sea of Luzon, December 1967

On the same day Paul Vincent walked out on Rachael in San Diego, Navy Lieutenant Michael Borrelli made one of many radar navigation checks on nearby land. Just several minutes before first light, as conning officer, he was navigating the U.S.S. Preble toward Subic Bay on the western coast of the Republic of the Philippines. On this check, peering into the scope, something different caught his attention. There was a new white blip against the flickering green background. Just five miles to the east, less than a mile from the beach was a clear indicator of a surface contact. He was sure it hadn't been there a moment before.

"CIC, Bridge. Lookit' that contact at 043, nine thousand yards."

"CIC, aye."

Bending again into the inverted funnel light shield over the radar repeater screen, Borrelli wondered why he'd missed it earlier?

Just aft of the bridge, in the combat information center, the CIC Watch Officer located Borrelli's contact on his own radar repeater and tracked it. Almost instantly, he jerked into practiced action.

"It's a god-damned sub." His comment alerted the inattentive CIC watch just in time to see the contact disappear from the scope.

"Anyone see that?" He asked into his intercom.

"I did. Went down like a sub."

The ship's telephone buzzer tweaked Captain Eric Delafield, Commanding Officer of Preble out of his sleep and wide awake, in micro-seconds.

"What is it?"

"Possible submarine, Captain."

"Go to ASW. I'm on my way."

By ship's alarm signals, the OOD ordered the crew of Preble to Anti-Submarine Warfare stations. He then increased the ship's speed to flank, changed course to intercept the contact and yelled into the voice tube leading to the lookout stations.

"Lookouts. Scan dead ahead, report anything you see. Might have a sub at periscope depth."

In a back corner of CIC, the alerted sonar operators could not identify anything on their scopes or headsets because Preble had turned nearly into her own wake. The churned water caused sonar signals to echo and re-echo false patterns. While one operator intensified his previously relaxed search, the senior operator immediately reversed the audio tape file and replayed the past several minutes, looking for something they may have missed. Harold Long, the ship's chief sonar tech entered the sonar area just as both operators spoke at the same time.

"Got one."

"Got what?"

"November class."

"Tell the bridge."

"Bridge—Sonar. Contact. Warship—submarine."

After a quick exchange of messages with Commander Naval Forces Philippines, (COMNAVPHIL) Preble learned there were no friendly submarines known to be in that area. After several minutes of tracking, comparing their SQS-23B PAIR sonar data to a stored file of sound tapes, the senior sonar man verified his first impression and made a report to the bridge and to the CIC officer.

"November class—probably pre-1960, pre-update. An old timer."

Captain Delafield stepped into the sonar area of CIC and spoke to Chief Long. "Are you sure it's a November?"

"Yes, Sir. We're sure. It was dead in the water, drifting downward but it has headway on now. It's a November class alright. Rattle-rattle-rattle." Captain Delafield drafted and submitted a high precedent sub-contact follow-up message report.

SECRET NOFORN

SUBMARINE CONTACT

A. SOVIET—NOVEMBER. POSITION 13.02N 118.12W PHIL SEA

B. COURSE 343 SPEED EIGHT

C. 45 PERCENT BURNABLE FUEL ON BOARD

D. ASW HELO AOCP (anti-submarine helicopter out of commission needing parts)

E. UNODIR TRACKING (unless otherwise directed will follow).

F. TWO MK 17 ARMED (nuclear weapons armed)

The contact was in the Philippine Sea just west of the city of Iba, 17 miles north of the entrance buoy to Subic Bay, a major U.S. Navy port and shipyard.

"We've got us a live one, Mr. Hardesty." The Captain spoke into the intercom to CIC and the bridge. "Let's get 'em."

"Damn! Nothing for months in the Tonkin Gulf, here we are in Subic's back yard, and bingo."

December 23, 1967 had been a routine day for the officers and crew of the USS Preble until the sub contact.

"Two goddamned hours from the end of 740 miles of ocean, an' this happens."

"I was actually lookin' forward to Subic Bay, twelve days rest, Christmas an' all."

"Me too. And some badly needed maintenance."

The crew had been starting to relax, anticipating to the balmy nights and hot days of Subic and of the liberty city of Olongapoo. Half way through their seven month Vietnam tour, it had been thirty-seven days since their last rest port.

Until the contact, there was not much to do in CIC except watch for ships, mostly fishing boats crossing their course, and keep the SPS-10 radar tuned and operating so the officer of the deck could use it for navigation. But the relaxed state was suddenly ended. They had a live one.

The November class *'podvodaya lodka atomnaya'* (nuclear powered submarine) was the first class built by the soviets. An older almost experimental ship built between 1958 and 1960 at Severodvinsk shipyards, it was easy to identify by sonar. The unsophisticated hull shape, not teardrop designed and with many free flooding holes in the outer casing, combined hull noise with a noisy and clumsy reactor to provide an easy to read underwater profile. Chief Long had said it best: "Rattle-rattle-rattle."

With the executive officer conning the ship, Captain Delafield was free to monitor the sonar and CIC information. He spoke as he leaned over the CIC officer's display position, "So we've got us an old November, Mr. Hardesty?"

"Absolutely, Cap'n—A bonafide widow maker."

Because many proved to have serious radiation leaks, the Russian sailors dubbed November class submarines 'widow-makers'. The leaks caused enough Soviet submariners to be injured by radiation that special hospitals had been set up in the USSR to study the cases.

"Maybe she's in trouble in there." The captain speculated. "Broken down? Reactor failure?"

"Wouldn't be the first one to die out here."

Lieutenant William Becker, the ship's intelligence officer, flipped the pages of a book marked Top Secret. "Novembers are in trouble no matter where they go, Cap'n. It's behavior here suggests here a potential for nuclear contamination."

"Quote the source and inform COMNAVPHIL of your suspicions, Mr. Becker."

"Aye, aye, Sir."

At the operations office of COMNAVPHIL Lieutenant Commander Peter Klein was shifted into action. He immediately alerted COMSEVENTHFLEET, (Commander Seventh Fleet, Western Pacific) by teletype and because communications were solid with Hawaii, was able to inform CINCPAC (Commander in Chief Pacific) and, because the ionosphere was exactly right, high frequency communications reached the pentagon by way of Naval Communications Station San Francisco (NAVCOMMSTASFRAN) at Stockton California.

Within eight minutes of Preble's first message having reached COMNAVPHIL, contact alarms sounded in the pentagon war room. The duty admiral for operations picked up a red telephone and informed white house operations. The duty State Department Representative notified the Philippine Embassy by telephone. Because there were no secure telephones to the Philippine embassy, prearranged code words were used.

"Good day. Please pass to the ambassador. SEATO. POTLUCK. SEVEN."

"What?"

"Is the ambassador in?"

"Yes. But napping."

"Wake him and tell him what I just said."

"Potluck, Mr. Seato? Today? At seven? There is no potluck today."

"Just tell him, please ...and I mean it."

"Very well, Sir.

On a golf course in Texas, the Emergency War Orders Officer, the ever-present officer who carries the daily nuclear attack codes, briefed president Johnson. The president moved quickly to his car and picked up a telephone. Voice encryption devices hidden in the car's body whirred into action as did a system of telephone relay signals. His voice was moved over lines to the Air Force transmitter sight near Dallas/Fort Worth and switched immediately to the Naval Communications Station San Francisco. Within seconds he spoke directly with the pentagon and with the staff officer at Commander Pacific Fleet in Hawaii.

"Go for it, or not, Mr. President?"

"I need more information from the Filipinos, Captain. How much time do we have before that thing is in international waters?"

"Minutes, Mr. President—five or six."

"If I'm not to you in four minutes, scrub it all and track the thing, clear?"

"Nothing in four minutes, scrub and track, that's clear, Sir."

"The way she's underway now, she wasn't in there just for a rest."

"I agree, Cap'n. Likely they been droppin' someone on the beach , or pickin' someone up."

"An' us with a busted helo."

"Put a boat in the water?"

"No. No time to slow up."

The ship's helicopter could have been over the original position of the contact within three minutes to look for proof of surface activity. A boat would take twenty minutes at least. Without that information Captain Delafield was only guessing.

"To COMNAVPHIL, Mr. Becker. Remind them of helo failure and let 'em know we're chasing the sub. Recommend air recon of that area. They'll either do it or not, but I believe the recommendation is sound considering the goddamned sub is well underway now."

"Yes, sir."

In the humid early morning heat, sweat rings started to appear on the Captain's khaki underarms and in the center of his back.

"Arm the Octuple, Mr. Harrington."

"Armed, Sir."

"Send the crew to general quarters."

"Aye, Aye, Sir."

With those orders, every man on board tried to do what combat sailors must do. They stuffed their real feelings, entered a practiced state of concentrated denial of fear or anxiety, fixed their thoughts on their job and quietly hoped everyone else was doing the same. One of the most complex real-life games in the world, sub versus destroyer, was playing out and this particular game had two very experienced players, Captain Eric Delafield of the frigate Preble and Captain Betov Nikolayev of the Soviet November class attack submarine, *Pedrokli.*

Captain Nikolayev leaned over his crowded, poorly lighted chart table and cursed. With the American coming down on his submarine, he knew he had to get further into the Sea of Luzon and into international waters quickly.

"All normal on the dive, Sir." His diving officer reported the status each minute of any dive.

"Very well." The captain murmured. "Have the word passed to prepare for battle stations."

As more men crowded into the small conning area, Captain Nikolayev removed the heavy coat that had felt good only minutes before. The sub had been cool until then, having spent the night some 80 feet below the surface where the water temperature centered around fifty-five degrees.

"My sweat is self-generated, Mr. Medkolonovich." The Captain spoke to his Number One officer. "We took a risk, we are caught."

"It was important to deliver the two men today though, Captain. No one can blame the trying."

"Chancy but feasible. That's how it looked earlier. But now … "

The surprise appearance of the American ship had forced a decision. Scrap the mission, or take a chance that the American sonar men were napping. His ECM officer had advised him as they lay on the bottom only thirty minutes before that the repeated high pitched swooping sounds they could hear passing over their hull were from an American SQS-23 type sonar, in sweep mode. They had calculated the American was not seriously searching. The swooping sounds neither increased nor locked on to their 110 meter hull as it lay slightly tilted near the sandy bottom.

"We chanced the American sonar man was playing with himself …or napping, or both. We were wrong."

Considering 28 years as a submariner, Captain Nikolayev had played the odds. He was hoping the Americans would not recognizing his hull as it gently raised to the surface, discharged the raft, and returned to the 88 foot bottom.

"I am hoping they are looking, if looking at all, for *horizontal* movement submarines."

"Its a chance, Captain. It's a chance. If their operators have not recognized our reactor noises while we were dead at the bottom, they are asleep. But, if you want to chance it …we have only to get to international waters."

"They'll just harass us then."

Harassment from a determined U.S. Anti-Submarine Warfare Frigate with a sonar like the SQS-23 or 26 model is terrible punishment. Each sweep of the piercing electronic signal slamming against the sub's hull resonates a racket stronger than a hundred decibels of clanging bells. A noisy street corner generates 80-90 decibels.

"Crank up the decibel levels. Put their fuckin' heads in a fuckin' bell and ring it 'til I say stop."

Some destroyer-submarine chases have lasted for days as Soviets attempted to outrun or outlast U.S. antisubmarine ships through the cold war years. Many subs, the older types, not designed to go deep enough to avoid the blasting noises, have been forced to the surface simply to rescue their crew from the ear ringing exposure to the shattering hull noises. Or, some eventually surface simply to replenish oxygen, their purifiers overtaxed or broken down. Now and again, but not often, the Soviets have been able to shake the American sonar and escape. To Captain Nikolayev, slipping away to international waters only to be harassed by Preble was not a real sense of having escaped.

Only thirty-two minutes earlier the Russian had quietly released seawater ballast and eased to the surface. No sooner had they surfaced into the moonless darkness than the ECM officer verified what he was afraid they might find. His devices revealed the Preble's surface search radar *was* being used for navigation and though it passed over them three times, it now locked on to their 90 foot long steel tower.

A voice had called up to the open bridge from their jury rigged and crowded ECM station. "Radar locked on us, Captain. They may see us as a fishing boat."

The captain sighed with resignation. "A fishing boat that goes up and down?" They were caught.

"Get those two up here." Nikolayev had commanded.

The two men he had picked up weeks earlier from a small boat near Haiphong harbor scrambled to the open conning tower bridge. One of them stopped to thank the captain but Nikolayev shushed his strange sounding English and waved him on to hurry as someone might shoo a cat.

"Git, off my ship. Hurry. Go fast."

Inflating the black rubber boat with the pull of two cords, the men quickly hooked a man-sized plastic bag to an oarlock and pushed the boat over the side. They dived into the choppy water without a word and were climbing into the raft as Nikolayev pulled the hatch over his head ten seconds before water poured across his gently submerging sub. Just then the first rays of blue tinted daylight spilled over the area.

"These are terrible moments, Captain, are they not?" The Number One officer was pale and frightened. His first time under attack.

"This is fate, Mr. Medkolonivich." The captain grunted. "If we weren't making these missions that break international law, we wouldn't have these kinds of troubled moments."

Mr. Medkolonivich didn't know how to reply to such an unlikely critical statement from his commanding officer.

WHAM RRUUNG, WHOOOP. WHAM, RRUNGGGG WHOOOP! The SQS-23 sonar had them dead on.

"Rig for patrol quiet." The ECM officer ordered into his hand held telephone.

"Yes." Nickolayev smirked. "Patrol quiet in a steel tube propelled by a thrashing machine with something from hell banging on its sides?" Again Medkolonivich was confused by his captain's sarcasm.

All hands beneath the ocean were struggling for any protection they could find against the violent noises. Cotton was quickly passed around. Men swallowed and re-swallowed and stuffed the cotton to protect delicate inner ear balance. Eyes squinted involuntarily or glanced about nervously, sweat appeared on foreheads but palms remained dry and cold. Each man counted within his own tensions, timing to the impact of the next sweeping bang.

"All normal on the dive, Captain." The diving officer yelled the disparate remark.

"Very well." The captain yelled back. "We must *rush* for international waters." Turning to his navigator, the captain sent him fighting for elbowroom at the small chart desk jammed into one corner of the 4 by 4 meter conning tower. "ETA international line, please."

The diving officer, the captain, the ECM officer, two periscope operators, two telephone talkers and a weapon's control officer were elbow to elbow in the ridiculously small space. It had been two years since his ship had been tracked by a U.S. destroyer but most remembered the experience. Many faces, already pale from lack of sunshine took on a pasty glow like that seen on a corpse. No one spoke unnecessarily. From practice and a sign of dedication they all tried to outwardly repress their anxieties. Some men wore nervous smiles but even with mouth corners turned upward, the fear shone in their eyes.

"Nine minutes to international waters, Captain." The navigator yelled. However, fearful the distracting noise might hamper his mathematics he went right back to the chart to double check his estimates,

"VERY WELL. THANK YOU."

"All normal on the dive, Captain."

'WHAT?—WHAT?"

"ALL NORMAL ON THE DIVE, SIR."

"VERY WELL—VERY WELL."

"We've got a positive I.D., Cap'n Delafield. It's the *Pedrokli.* Hull number 61. Last tracked August, 66, off Adak."

"Mr. Becker. Inform COMNAVPHIL. We've positive I.D. We're within Filipino coastal waters. Under SEATO directive 10-10, we can attack in the P.I.'s behalf, without their okay."

"Aye, Aye, Sir."

"They're moving now for sure." Sonar reported. "Range 4 thousand yards, 000, One five zero feet. Course possibly 340."

"Ready two mark seventeen's, Mr. Harrington."

"Why are we arming the nukes?" A mess cook telephone talker asked of a senior petty officer.

"It's S.O.P. to arm them when the target is confirmed hostile. Don't shit yourself."

"Isn't that asking for it?"

"Listen, Dummy. What if he throws one first?"

"Oh!"

Mr. Hardesty, as CIC officer, calculated the Russians would be in international water in eight minutes. Within five minutes the Preble was sitting right on top of *Pedrokli*, the SQS-23 on full bang. They anxiously awaited COMNAVPHIL's permission to attack.

On *Pedrokli* all hands watched the clock tick as they tensed for any sign that a homing weapon had been released by Preble.

"Jesus, I'd hate to be in that tin can." Lieutenant Becker was speaking with Lieutenant Borrelli. "They've gotta' be listening for a homer on 'em."

"Yeah, they know we got 'em."

Intelligence information was clear. Once a U.S. homing torpedo was launched, there was nothing to do but wait, feel your life go by within the privacy of your thoughts and brace uselessly for the sudden crushing end as, depending on the submarine's depth, near a quarter-ton of pressure per square inch is released into the hull and onto every person present. What is it like to be crushed to death? All submariners wonder. On *Pedrokli* , some wondered if it would be worse than the sonar noise banging into their very souls.

"Two minutes, Captain." Both ships advised their C.O.'s

"One minute, Captain."

At COMNAVPHIL the clocked ticked to the last second of the four minute wait. "Release the message to Preble, Mr. Klein."

"Aye, Aye, Sir."

"DO NOT ATTACK. REPEAT—NOT ATTACK—MAINTAIN CONTACT—TRACK AND ADVISE."

Captain Delafield seemed very disappointed. "Tell the crew, Mr. Becker. There goes Christmas in the P.I."

"Yes, Sir. Standby for a moan."

COMNAVPHIL took the Christmas rest away from Captain Eric Delafield and the crew of Preble, but gave the lives back to Captain Betov Nikolayev and the crew of *Pedrokli*. But, with the sonar on full lock, it was not a high quality life that was returned to them, but it was life.

Captain Nikolayev's squinting eyes reflected the overwhelming discomfort of the noise. Because of the extreme disadvantage, it was difficult to express the relief they felt over not having been attacked. Out of a frying pan, they were surely still in a fire.

He yelled to his diving officer.

"No attack. We are safe unless that man up there is an idiot. Go to 280 feet when depth permits. Make turns for 28 knots, course 352."

"Destination, Captain?"

"We go over to Yulin, the Chinamen's naval base at Sama on Hainan island and get the Americans to go away."

"But we'll go right through Yankee Station, Captain."

"We have no choice. Evaps won't hold up much longer than that for fresh water and the purifiers will be no good after 35 hours."

"Yes, Captain."

"Walk about Number One. Tell the crew they have my hearts strongest feelings. Make due best they can. We should be there in 30 hours."

The two years since last attack had eased the memory of the intense pain of the hammering sonar, as women forget the pain of childbirth. Captain Nickolayev's eyes watered, his jaw tensed and locked as he finally got around to stuffing cotton in his ears. A distracting headache developed. He was very aware he was too old for this type of duty. Looking around at his frightened crew he sincerely felt pain for them. These men had been closer to him than any other humans, ever, even closer than his busy father and his aloof, angry and overworked pipe smoking mother on their farm near Vitebsk in the western USSR called White Russia. These men were his closest family, his family of the vulnerable steel tube.

Obedient to his orders, to his mission and to his steel family, he took his submarine into the Luzon Sea. Doing so he moved into an existence as hostile as outer space might be.

"We are in trouble here, Mr. Medkolonovich. With the noise of the American, we'll be unable to hear another submarine coming at us."

"Is like driving auto blindfolded, Captain. Hoping to stay between the fences and hoping others see us first."

Knowing he would also have difficulty receiving the USSR submarine guidance signals with Preble's sonar banging on them, he was afraid for navigation safety. The Captain sided up to his navigator and peered with him at the unsure track lines laid out on the chart.

"We are forced to dead recon, Captain."

"How are chances that we run aground on the Paracel Islands?"

"I question the chart's accuracy under the best conditions, Captain."

Nickolayev turned to his ECM officer. "Do we know who is chasing us?"

"Only that it is a frigate of the Coontz type. Perhaps King, Dewey, perhaps U.S.S. Preble. Is good new sonar, for certain."

Preble would be met sooner or later by another U.S. ship, one with more fuel. The ships would share their Russian as a pride of lions share a kill. Before they reached their destination, *Pedrokli* would likely be practiced on in a near sadomasochistic scene with as many as six to ten of the menacing sonar. Could his men take it? Could he take it?

Sliding down the damp cool bulkhead to rest on the deck for the long voyage under punishment, he patted Lieutenant Medkolonovich's hand as a father might. Nickolayev hoped aloud: "Americans and us. We all go to the symphony. No symphony people will ever do anything stupid—to start a real war we have to fight from this trap of an old submarine."

The young lieutenant leaned back and closed his eyes trying to recall an accurate memory of Mozart's symphony number forty.

Now miles from where they left the sub, the two men were frantic. Only twenty minutes earlier they had been dragging the small but heavy boat through the surf when they realized Preble was tracking the submarine they had just left. Wheezing for breath, they both seemed scared. The larger man panicked.

"Leave it. Run to the trees." He gasped in English. "They'll launch a helo after us."

"No, fool." The smaller man said. "They would of by now. They don't got no helo."

"Look" The big man pointed. "They're chasing our sub."

"Maybe, maybe no. Pull your end."

"We should run?"

"Stop. Dammit. Do as planned." Two men hurriedly cut into the rubber boat, deflating it. They opened the large plastic bag and dumped its contents onto the sand. Taking off their wetsuits, they lumped the clothes, fins, plastic bag and the deflated boat into a pile.

"Git changed, fast. Case they get help."

From the pile on the sand they selected fresh clothing, flashlights, ration tins and shoes. They took several minutes to dress and divide up the contents of two large envelopes.

The larger man looked toward the sea and the now compact outline of Preble.

The smaller of the two men continued to make decisions. "Dig. They might come and look later. Safer this way, to follow our plans."

Using two folded shovels from the bag, they started to dig a large hole in the sand a few feet from the surf's edge.

"Shit, heavy."

"Look, clams."

"Fuck clams."

"Worms on my legs, yecht! "

"Water comin' in, shit."

"Too shallow here. Move back twenty feet."

"Fuck it, keep diggin'."

"Move back twenty feet." After twenty minutes of very strenuous work on a second hole attempt, they buried everything except what they carried. With their residue now three feet deep, they left no sign the sand had ever been disturbed, Following the last of their plans to the moment, the smaller man carried the two shovels to the waters edge and threw them as far as he could into the rolling surf.

Returning to the edge of the jungle and to the larger man, he announced, puffing some, "Headin' south now."

"Yeah." The second man was also still panting. "I'm out of shape—but I'm glad to get out of that friggin' sub. Whew! Stink. An that stuff they called food?"

"Yeah."

"OK, I'm headin' north to meet Nagsaya and that bunch. In that outfit you sure look your part. Have a good trip."

"Sure."

Checking a small map and compass, the smaller man headed into the jungle below some cliffs as the larger man walked north on the open beach.

"Watch for planes."

"Yeah, Yeah."

CHAPTER FOUR
The Tailor Loft

Annie's European accent always became more inflected when she tried to be persuasive. "He's not only not Chinese, and not from Hong Kong, he's a *total* bloody outsider. Can't possibly perceive of our politics and, I furthermore envisage, he is fat." Her voice trailed off.

"So what? So he's fat. So he's an outsider."

"Don't be obtuse, Shaman. If an outsider comes to Hong Kong and attempts to alter even one ...*anything*." She threw her hands into the air and stalked across the room, away from Shaman. "Hell, you know ...the story. . the covenant. "

"But that's a stupid wives tale. And what can *he* change anyway?"

"No-no, not wives tale." Au-yeung, the old Chinese man raised a shaky hand with a crooked finger, spoke up, and defended Annie's position. "If outsider comes to Hong Kong, tries to change anything, change even one small rule?" He brought his thumb and forefinger within a hair of one another.

"I know, I know." Shaman interrupted. "It's panpsychism, however. Valueless."

"Pan whatism?" It was Star, the lovely Indo-Chinese woman speaking up with a curious smile.

"Panpsychism." Shaman answered quickly. "Voodoo 101. Every physical thing has a psychic aspect. As I said, bullshit."

"Not bullsheet." Au-yeung almost yelled pulling his two bony fists upward to stress his adamancy.

Bobbing his head from side to side mimicking a schoolboy reciting his parent's latest order, Shaman scorned Au-yeung and Annie's concern..

"If any stranger changes even one small rule." Shaman openly mocked Au-yeung. "*Everything* that could possibly happen to anyone involved with him, will happen. And ..." he turned to Au-yeung, entwined his fingers and emulated a Boris Karloff ghostly voice. " ...they say, they will all die a violent death." He dropped his hands to his sides and expressed his most skeptical look. "And that's not a wives tale?"

"NO!" Au-yeung spoke nervously. "Was first noticed over three hundred years ago. Is now most prominent of the unspoken rules."

Shaman laughed openly. "Horse-pucky, Ay-yeung."

"It still makes *me* worry." Annie continued.

"But he's a mature sophisticated man of the world, this Polav."

"Oxymoron to say 'Russian' and 'sophisticated'. I for one am nervous about this venture." Annie folded her arms and turned away from the group, her way of announcing her position was one of devil's advocacy. She was waiting to hear more information.

Shaman reached for her, touched her shoulder. "Russian or not, I see him as sophisticated—smart. And he's been paying us very well."

"And he pays in American money, too." Au-yeung said.

Annie turned quickly toward Ay-yeung. "Now you side with Shaman?

"No side. You correct about danger, he correct about money."

The four of them: the Europeans, Annie and Shaman, the 69 year old Chinese man, Ay-yeung, and 'Star', the beautiful Indo-Chinese woman, all stopped talking for a moment. As they reflected, Star lit a cigarette. Shaman dropped into a dusty chair, oblivious that it soiled his camel hair overcoat. Annie turned to the small corner stove and opened her coat to allow the warmth to reach her very shapely body. Au-yeung turned to the window.

This was usually how their meetings went. Each openly provided opinions on one of Shaman's plans, then deliberation took place. After deliberating, the serious personal contemplation followed. Shaman would drum his fingers silently and wait. Annie would appear distracted, Star would pace and smoke, Au-yeung would stare out of a window.

It was two days before Christmas, 1967. On this day in other parts of the world, Paul Vincent was walking out on Rachael, U.S.S. Truaxe was preparing to deploy to Vietnam, Captain Delafield on U.S.S. Preble was settling his crew for a long chase of Captain Nikolayev's Russian submarine and the rest of the world prepared for the holidays. In Hong Kong, in this sunlit but chilly loft over a dusty smelling tailor shop on Hankow Street in the Kowloon district, the group of four held a quiet and secretive meeting. These four, who had known one another for years, were discussing the arrival of their guest for the afternoon, the Russian named Polav.

Au-yeung looked out of the window and over the bay toward Hong Kong's main island. "Four and a half million people here." He mumbled, but all could hear. "I remember when less than half million."

"What's your point, Au-yeung?" Shaman was impatient. "You distract us."

"My point?" Au-yeung turned arthritically slow to face Shaman. His voice was soft but slightly crackled by age. "Most of people just work here, and live here. Some come to play ...foolishly with women, gamble, opium. Some, Shaman, willing or unwilling, maybe like your Russian, come to fall in trouble. Not knowing rules, they try change things here. Annie correct. How English say? Covenant? Yes, covenant. Covenant of violent death, is true. You reject covenant tradition with *American* words ...how you say—horses-pucky?"

"Don't be so afraid of strangers." Shaman seemed unsettled by his old friend's insistence. "I know the chance of discovery increases every time we add anyone new to our circle, Au-yeung, but it's time for changes."

"Changes?" Star spoke up with vigor. "I theenk ve' lucky ve' manage vhot' ve' hab' as it ees' now." Her native French and her second language, Vietnamese, did not combine well to form discernable English, but English had become the common language over their many years together. They hardly noticed one another's accents. Star pointed to her face with one red tipped finger. "I? I vorry."

Shaman tried to calm her. "I'll worry about what we manage, my Dear, Mo ... Star." He almost called her by her real name."

"See? Why I worry?"

"Please, I'll worry for all of us."

Star stood dramatically with left hand on hip, her right elbow held shoulder high, her right hand pressing against her lips. A long cigarette jutted from the fingers. She drew in deeply, held the breath then exhaled both smoke and words. "So, you will insist we host this new person then, this person with this funny name."

"It's a code name, Star …code named 'Bell'."

"You and code names. I am still discomfortable over this. " She spun herself to the right and placed her back to Shaman. The entire group stared at her. From either back *or* front, she looked much younger than the forty five years she claimed. Her silhouette was hourglass and only a very picky person would say she was slightly overweight. Today her dark haired page-boy was covered with a black and gray tam that matched the checkered wool pencil skirt, black cashmere sweater and three inch heels. A filmy gray scarf was knotted close around her neck. With the heels, the scarf, the tam, her skillfully applied makeup and dark lipstick, Star offered a purposeful fantasy to the world. Shaman had teased her often that all she needed was a high split in her skirt and perhaps mesh hose to look campy French enough to have stepped from a Gene Kelly movie. But Star knew what she was doing. Half French, half Vietnamese, the image she projected enhanced her outside profession and the group's purposes.

Knowing full well they were looking at her, she purposefully stepped in front of a dirty but sunlit window and silhouetted the side of her face and body to the group. The glaring contrast concealed the expression on her face but all could see the outline of smoke curl from the cigarette tip and an elongated funnel of smoke explode from her lips. She turned then and faced them, both hands on hips, appearing defiant, but quiet. This was Star's epic but standard way of giving in to Shaman.

Eyes shifted back to their leader.

"As before, I've thought this through. I wish everyone to simply meet with Polav, with an open mind."

"As with Star, I'm uncomfortable also, Shaman, but willing to listen." Au-yeung, almost seventy, pointed one slim and slightly blued finger toward Shaman, but not in a threatening manner, simply as punctuation. "I must remind you. We've let no one into the circle since Annie, late in '62. It's been five years."

"I respect that." Shaman said but there was a touch of patronization in the comment.

Au-yeung lit a slim cigarette with an American Zippo lighter, clicked it shut with a practiced flick and blew smoke into the room. He tried swallowing a cough but sputtered and made it worse. He walked the length of the large loft, coughing openly, unable to talk for nearly a minute. The others, their shoulders pulled in against the growing afternoon chill, waited for his fourth or fifth coughing spell of the day to pass.

Au-yeung, whose artist shop in the tourist district was a front for the organization, had been working closely with Shaman's group since early 1961. He'd always been conservative, cunning and a good judge of money and how to use it. His store had been invaluable for washing their incomes. Recently he had become ill, but refused to tell his friends how ill or what kind of illness. They watched him lose weight over the past few months. He was now very thin even for an older man, but he wouldn't answer any direct questions about the weight loss, his constant coughing nor his seeming loss of energy. Since his illness, he'd needed more money for hospital and medicines and for more paid help at his store on the main island. Annie, Star and Shaman had already discussed in private that perhaps Au-yeung's illness might influence his judgment or even cause him to take unnecessary chances for money.

"We'll not be letting anyone *really* in, Au-yeung." Shaman threw finger quotes around the word "in". "No one is becoming a member of our inner circle. The Russian has simply asked us to consider the two offers. Now hear me again. Offer number one? The ongoing proposal to pay cash for information we gain on when the Americans are planning to quit in Vietnam."

"This is different from what we've been selling him."

"Yes. He wants no more equipment capability, weapons capability ...so on. Just, when are the Americans leaving?"

"The second offer is the man, Bell?" Star still seemed skeptical.

Shaman was patient with her. "Yes, Love. Secretly meet, hide, debrief and develop a new identity for Bell, who is to arrive soon by ship."

"And then we simply sneak this man out?" Star's question was more like a statement of impossibility.

"Yes. And we can do it."

"You feel pushed, Shaman?" Annie asked openly. "The Russian has been paying well lately, correct?"

"Correct."

"You hate to refuse him for fear of offending?"

"Correct."

Annie turned to Star. "You're afraid we're chancing safety for money?"

"Also correct." Star's response had a snap to it.

Annie turned back to Shaman. "Are we risking our standards a little, perhaps? Letting this man Polav know details about our group?"

"Risky? A little, Annie." Shaman rubbed his open palms together and smiled. "But my standards, although they include some slight risks, remain high." He raised one eyebrow, and tapped his head with one index finger. "I feel it is safe."

His confidence caused everyone to wordlessly slip back into the contemplation mode. Shaman leaned against the light gray vertical boards of the unpainted wall and waited.

He was a handsome, well-groomed man, 55 years old, and although his family had left him very strong financially, money wasn't all he needed from life. Shaman liked heady excitement, the kind that comes from the chances one could take in what he often described to the others as a supposedly cooperative but actually an adversarial society. True excitement came only when he was cutting an edge near risk, risk he would indulge constantly and tease and skirt around. He'd organized this tailor loft group to be the working unit of his need for risk taking. While he did it for the fun, the others appeared to be doing it solely for the money.

Operating secretly and selling selected privileged information to the highest bidder, Shaman saw his group as soldiers of fortune who never bore arms. Anyone else would see them as international spies, not with a 'cause' one could see beyond money.

The need to bargain with Polav played to Shaman's need for risk and adventure. He leaned in to convince the group.

"Polav represents interests who hunger for advantage, and we have the easiest access to providing that advantage. How long the Americans are to remain in Vietnam to be exact. We need literal …objective signs that the U.S. is *seriously* making arrangements to pull out, out of the war." He looked from Annie's face to Star to Au-yeung, awaiting signs of approval.

Seeing mostly blank stares, he kept talking, explaining his views as though teaching grade school social studies. "Moscow thrives presently because the Americans are up to their red-necks in Vietnam. Their President Johnson is spending so much on the Vietnam war, the U.S. has less for defense of Europe. So, Russia has it easy keeping up the arms race."

"Ah-hah." Star came to life. "But, if they thought U.S. was pulling out …"

Annie took over. " …out of their million plus dollars a day Vietnam … "

"Polav's people …" Shaman interrupted, " …will have to obligate more rubles for their own war machines …"

Annie touched Au-yeung's arm. "Rubles that are scarcer and scarcer, needed for grain, for coal—to keep the people happy with Lenin's theme."

"Yes, Yes. I understand this" Au-yeung said pointing to each person, then out a window toward Hong Kong proper. But, do we, do you. . . . and the girls in the city have access to that knowledge?"

"Yes-yes, my friend." Shaman came back quickly. "The U.S. conceals much from the Russians and Hanoi, not perfectly, but rather well. But they do not conceal much from themselves"

Annie took over again but spoke in a patronizing broken English as though it would take that to get Ay-yeung and Star to follow her. It was something she did unconsciously when concentrating and everyone had learned to accept it. "Soldiers who come Hong Kong, R and R? They know more than they know they know."

"Yes, yes," Shaman liked that Annie seemed in favor of the idea. "Focus on types of forces coming in. Types of transports piling up."

Annie dropped her feigned accent. "Find out how much of the actual war is being turned over to the ARVN's and at what rate. Is the U.S. romancing Laos or Cambodia to support the ARVN if the U.S. were to leave?"

Shaman took over. "If so, what is the price they are paying? Look for signs of the U.S. turning major decisions of the fighting over to the ARVN. Turning ships over, airfield control, harbor operations, any signs of leaving."

"So, we need visiting ship numbers and types." Star joined in with an—'I am now taking specific notes'—attitude.

"Yes. Especially information on transport ships, cargo haulers, *Air America* heavies, 707's not rigged out for passengers. Beginning to take machinery out."

They all took a moment to digest the idea. Finally, Shaman spoke, calmly. "I believe we can do this … "

Annie touched his arm. "All we have to do is …" She stopped, halted by the lack of any concrete idea of exactly how she was to proceed.

"Shake a bit of pretty ass at them?" Au-yeung laughed a dirty-old-man laugh that ended in a coughing spell but caused the others to smile.

"Details later." Shaman shrugged. "A little booze and a promise of women like Speckle."

Annie struck a grinning coy pose, index finger indenting her right cheek. "Or like me?"

"There are none like you, except you, my Dear." Au-yeung looked at her longingly as he made his comment.

Shaman faked a leer and twisted a non-existent moustache. "You have certain selected higher-ups to work, Annie."

Getting the American servicemen on R and R to brag about themselves and their work had become easy for Star and her girls. She used the lovely Speckle from Laos, the adolescent looking Chinese women Ping, Beebe, and Ay-yeung's daughter Mae Yee Chen, the Canadian blonde, Luann who also worked at Au-yeung's art store as his 'girl Friday', and the Italian looking Eurasian, Sorrel, in their game of games. A few drinks, a little feigned hero worship and the promise of closeness from these beautiful woman caused many Americans to open up without realizing they were doing so.

"Oh." One of the women might say in expertly simulated naiveté. "I read story 'bout navy war? Russian submarine no one able hear coming in water. They bad people."

"Bullshit, honey. We can hear anything they've got from fifty miles out. We can even tell when they ate last with the gear we've got. Never worry 'bout it. Now how 'bout you and me …?"

What one sailor said on any one subject was just a disengaged piece of some overall picture. Shaman was the expert on joining the seemingly superfluous bits into meaningful intelligence. Even the most innocuous comments of some careless soldier, sailor, marine or state department employee were carefully memorized or taped and passed on to Shaman by bar girls and whores throughout Kowloon and Hong Kong Island. The resulting intelligence envelopes delivered to Polav by Shaman became worth more and more to Hanoi and to the Russians. The envelopes coming back to Shaman became thicker and thicker. In 1967, Au-yeung's art shop had cleansed over U.S.$750,000.

"That's moving a lot of Jesus on black velvet, Au-yeung." Annie would joke.

"No, no. Elvis Presley on black velvet now."

Annie seemed to like some distraction from her relatively routine daily life but she was also afraid that some day, doors would burst in, armed police would explode into their lives and cart them all away, or worse.

Annie, an exceptionally beautiful and exciting looking woman worked the scheme differently than the others. Where Star, Speckle, Ping, Beebe and the others worked the bars, nightclubs and whorehouses, Annie had her own contact points. She worked the Anglican churches, the U.S.O. dance hierarchy, the charity clubs. Not being accustomed to tricking or being tricked, she originally felt she could never pretend to enjoy being with someone while surreptitiously steering the conversation to subjects she wanted information on. She actually learned the trade by listening to tapes of Star and Speckle working on men.

"Just get a little piece of the pie." Star would say. "Shaman will bake it all, later."

Once Annie learned technique, she became an expert.

"So." Shaman wrapped it up. "Get anything we can on the U.S. turning the war over.

"Use alla' girls then?" Au-yeung asked. "I can send Beebe, Luann and Ping soon. They almost finished with what they do now."

"Wait." Annie looked about the tailor's loft as though some enemy might be listening. "Don't use real names."

"Sorry." He patted her hand to amplify his apology.

"Picture the headlines in Nebraska should we get caught." Shaman said as he held an imaginary newspaper in front of him and imitated an American accent. "'Wha' lookee, hear, Blanch. Beautiful oriental woman gives up everythin' for life with rather plain and unexcitin' man from Nebraska, who just happens to work for the CIA'." He laughed aloud, his need for excitement being fed.

Still smiling, Shaman surveyed the group with his eyes. "So, everyone know what we need here?"

"Yes, yes. Mind read the world." Annie grinned.

"More of different information, only sooner." Au-yeung kidded.

"Me an' my girls are back to being the saddles again." Even Star managed a smile.

"Call Polav the Russian up here, Au-yeung."

Polav arrived in the loft. Shaman seemed nervous through the introductions but the stranger seemed calm and at ease.

"At last we all meet." He said. "Mr. Shaman has told me so much of all of you." He took Annie's extended hand and continued in a rich and thickly accented English, flagging him a eastern European. "Ahhah", he sighed to Annie. "As beautiful as Shaman has promised. And I hear, as smart as beautiful." His outdated stereotyped sexist phrases from older men fell harmlessly from these women.

"They'll never change, sexism is about the only sex they have left." Annie would joke privately later.

Polav turned to Au-yeung. "And here, the wisdom of the group. Very happy to meet you, Au-yeung. I know of your beautiful art shop."

Turning to Star, he held her hand in both of his and patted. "Beauty, cunning and leadership all in one lovely person. Mademoiselle Star, I am honored."

One by one the worldly group relaxed seemingly charmed by Polav.

When small talk was completed, the Russian sat on a large wooden box, ceremoniously lighted a dark cigar, snuffed the match with two thick fingers, stuffed it in his coat pocket and leaned forward, hands on knees, obviously ready for conversation. Shaman slid his shaky chair near Polav and lowered carefully into it. The others stood in a semi-circle as Shaman began.

"We are totally in agreement to stop providing information on U.S. capabilities, Polav.

And ... " Polav interrupted him by raising one hand. He calmly looked about the loft, pointed from corner to corner and asked: "Is this safe to speak as such? So bluntly?"

"Of course. For six years we've used this loft. But, would you rather go to another location? Out on one of the noisy piers, or, a loft down the street is also available."

"Nyet-nyet. Too much fuss." He took several short puffs on the cigar, looked at its glowing end and spoke. "No more stairs today." He smiled and spun the cigar hand in a circling motion. "Continue, Shaman. Pardon my interruption."

"I continue. You now want precise information on when the U.S. is pulling out of the war. We assume to continue the same prices, the same exchange points, and so on."

"Yes! Very good, Mr. Shaman, very good." The Russian seemed pleased. "Now, on the other issue. The Bell issue?"

"Tell us while we are together, Polav, why you need our organization at all for this Bell business?"

The large older man put his hands out, palms up, raised his bushy eyebrows and looked from side to side. "Ladies and gentlemen, I am alone here. Our consulate has nyet Komitet Gosudarstvennoy Bezopasnosti ..."

"What is that?" Au-yeung asked puzzled by the Russian phrase.

"KGB." Shaman provided.

"Yes." Polav shrugged his shoulders and raised his brows again as if to indicate: 'don't ask me why there is no KGB'. He continued, speaking slowly, deliberately, as if with practiced training. "Some necessary informal agreement with the British and even the forthcoming New China government. We cannot chance angering either of them." He turned and looked directly at Annie.

"So, my pretty girl. My Soyuz Sovetskikh Sotaialisticheskikh Republik has no covert organization here. But happenstance is bringing this man in here before long, and, his exit is sealed behind him. I cannot compromise my consulate's agreements with local governments. I turn to you as friends and as profitable business partners, to handle this for me."

Shaman rose from his rickety chair and strode to a nearby dusty window. He looked out over Hankow street without seeing. He spoke to the window and to Polav. "Do you know this man personally? This Bell?"

"No. Only by reputation, my friend." Polav hoisted up from his awkward seat on the edge of the box and stepped the few paces to stand beside Shaman. "He has been a valuable infiltrator." The cigar wiggled up and down as he spoke. "You will know more yourself when you debrief him."

"How will he contact us?" Annie asked.

Polav turned quickly. "We have coded words." He answered. "He is to get to Macao where my people will identify for him whomever you wish to be his contact man. Bell will speak of 'bells' to the contact person, and then, he'll speak of 'traveling'. He has freedom to construct his own opening questions around those words. It works all the time."

Several more questions were answered just as quickly by Polav but the conversation stagnated when Annie mentioned prices.

"You ask a fortune, my good lady." Polav turned to Shaman. "You take advantage of my situation."

"I don't know. I worry." Shaman feigned. Turning to face Annie, Star and Au-yeung, his expression not visible to Polav, Shaman made a familiar grin that told his colleagues they should follow his 'worried' lead.

"This bothers me too." Annie agreed and folded her arms against the chilling air in the loft. Star said nothing but pulled her shoulders forward and also folded her arms.

Polav turned from the window. "It is not worry you have, it is hunger for money. Is it not?"

No one took up his challenge. After a long minute of eye exchanges but with no variations in facial expressions, Polav broke into a practiced grin. He spoke, but his pronunciations seemed to suffer.

"Very well, very well. I veel give you da' price but you must tell me this day, you are *da*, or *nyet*." He scratched between his brows with just his middle finger. Annie wondered if it was an unconscious western 'fuck-you'. However, Polav's scratching evolved into a forced laugh directed toward Shaman.

"In asking for aid here, I anticipated reasonable consideration. Maybe I counted too much on our comradeship, our history." He smiled toward Annie. "I expected, how you say? as the Americans say: Favored nation status?"

Annie smiled.

Polav then turned to the old Chinese man. "It is an easy task, Au-yeung. Get Bell in, get what tapes, papers, information he might have, to me, then get him out. You are organized for that simple task?"

Au-yeung pursed his lips but said nothing.

Polav turned and nodded and spoke to each of the four, in turn.

To Au-yeung: "Take a vote, wise man."

To Annie: "You are hard bargainer."

To Star: "There is room for a smile here, the money is good."

And finally, to Shaman, curtly: "I'll wait outside, thirty minutes."

The aged Russian adjusted his heavy topcoat from one arm to the other, then invited Shaman to hold it for him. Shaman opened the huge garment. No one spoke while Polav shrugged into the coat and stepped to the banister at the top of the loft's wooden stairwell.

"I need to know in thirty minutes." He belched loudly and without apology. Pushing the flared bottom of the topcoat close to his knees with one hand, he grabbed the wooden railing with the other and peered downward, measuring the small steps leading from the loft. Grunting every other one, he disappeared from view down to the tailor-shop proper. Tina, the wife of the shop owner glanced at him from her job of applying small sparkling beads to the collar of a dark blue cashmere sweater. She nodded but without a smile. None of the other workers so much as looked up as Polav passed through and out into a slight stench of fish in the afternoon Kowloon air.

The four remaining in the loft waited into the third minute without speaking. Annie watched Polav from the window.

"He's outside. Standing there, puffing that smelly cigar."

"You are correct, Shaman. We worry too much, I think." Au-yeung took a shuffling step, stood with his fingers interlocked at his waist and spoke freely. "I dislike him some, but I do agree with him. Easy money."

"Polav is such a spy for a spy." Annie said, shivering affected disgust. "He looks like one, talks like one, acts like one." She walked to the small coal stove in the corner of the room and fanned her opened coat back and forth. "And he's fat." Shivering even more, she shrugged the coat off her shoulders to allow the stove to warm the tightly fitting beige woolen dress. Ay-yeung's eyes cornered to her trim body with clear admiration and more. Sensing his eyes on her, Annie impatiently jerked the coat back onto her shoulders, cape-like. Au-yeung seemed oblivious to the rejecting move.

"Annie, Annie." He smiled and spoke through his cigarette yellowed teeth, "You are so lovely, why do you worry? What does a spy really look like? He pays very good …and in American green dollars. So he belches. So he's fat?"

"He has a smell." Star offered. "I don't theenk fat Russians wipe their asses clean. Huh, Annie?" It was easy to tell when Star was being funny. She wasn't this time.

Annie ignored Ay-yeung's comments, didn't answer Star either. Instead she stood quietly in contemplation. Her pause was enough to alert Shaman.

"You'd like to think more about it, Annie?"

"Yes, but he's insisting thirty minutes."

"That's a bluff." Shaman speculated. "We are the only game in town."

Star stepped to the stove beside Annie, dropped the nub of her lipstick tipped cigarette to the rusted plate under the stove and crushed it with the toe of one fashionable shoe. "You theenk to agree, Annie?" She asked. "I am thinking maybe also yes."

"It all seems safe enough, Star." Annie turned her back to the stove and for direct warmth, again shrugged the coat free of her shoulders. "I'd feel better with an agreement that *we* set everything up. *We* organize it all, passport and all, and, I feel very strongly," She paused until the three accomplices looked directly at her, "that we can dump this Bell person at any time, without question if we so much as sense there is a dollop of danger." She spun back to face the stove.

"You think as I think." Shaman said as he moved close to the stove next to Annie. Au-yeung also moved in, putting one arm around Star, the other around Annie's waist. Standing thus, as they had a hundred times in the past, the four discussed the where, when and how of it all, for *more* than the thirty minutes.

Polav returned puffing up to the loft. He made a pretense of resisting because of the prices but gave in after twenty minutes to, as Shaman counted on, the only game in town.

Shaman was to arrange for Bell's passport with existing but shaky Kowloon contacts. Everyone agreed Annie should hold the passport, making her the core of the exchange.

"Is this more involved than you'd care to be, Luvs?"

"No, Shaman. I'll do it.

If a phony passport was found on anyone, Annie, with her spotless and conservative reputation could most easily be believed by authorities.

"Yes, inspector." She imitated a dowager type. "Was on the seat of the tram. Intended to turn it in, weeks now."

"Of course, Madam." Shaman held a mock monocle. "Thank you, Madam."

A drop-off/pickup was arranged. Using a simple but excellent crypto system supplied by the Russians over two years ago, Bell would be furnished with the encoded telephone numbers for Shaman's Central District office on Pedder Street, for Annie's home telephone and for Star at her hotel. As a last resort, Bell was to contact Au-yeung in person at the art shop, asking to buy a painting titled *American Liberty Bell.*

Whoever made first contact was to arrange for Bell to meet Annie either at the Tin Hau temple in Aberdeen, Monday through Saturday, or at either the Mercy or State hospital Sunday tea dances.

After agreeing the group of four could drop Bell any time they felt threatened, Polav eventually left the loft, but because of the high dollars promised, was not smiling freely.

After fifteen minutes, Au-yeung followed Polav down the stairs but took a different route to the Star Ferry for the return ride to Hong Kong proper. Star also went down the stairs but took a seat in the tailor shop and began what appeared to be a long visit with Tina and her husband, Lom Quon. Shaman and Annie left the shop together. As pre-planned, they walked north instead of toward the ferry landing. Huddling in their coats against the cold ocean winds, they looked like any European tourist couple checking the shops. Shaman seemed truly pleased.

"This Christmas might be our last one away from the city for quite awhile. We'll be very busy you know. Au-yeung gave me the latest on contact arrivals today. Without any increase from the new efforts, you have five regular contact men arriving in the next two months, Speckle, three. Star her usual several."

"I can't believe I have five, Shaman." She ran two quick steps to catch up with his longer strides.

"The list is in my pocket, but I recall …that Jefferson from the U.S. submarine. Ansley from Army Intelligence. The Turkish guy."

"Ansley and the Turk means I'll have two in the city on the same days. I hate that."

"Are you worried with two the same days?"

"Shaman?" She sounded frustrated, unsure. "What do I do if Bell arrives in the middle of other contact days."

"Get creative." He quipped, not looking at her. "Write to them, delay them. Do what women always do, say you're on your damned period."

Annie breathed heavily from the pace he set, her nose shading pink from the wind. She tugged at his arm. "Is this going to get out of control?" Her disgusted overtone grabbed his attention. He stepped ahead of her and turned to face her. Walking backward and sideways, he suddenly sounded pleading.

"I, I haven't meant to overload you … " He backed into an elderly Chinese couple and scattered their packages. He tipped his hat, apologized, "Duibuqi-duibuqi"—and caught up to Annie. "It'll be alright. I'm sure. We've …"

"Never mind, Shaman." She laughed but it was forced. "It'll be alright, maybe. I believe I just need to rest up for it all."

"I'll help manage it all, Dearest." He squeezed her gloved hand, fell in beside her and beamed at her, an indication he wanted to shift from work to play, from worry to ignore. "And let's start that wonderful rest this weekend."

Annie sighed and snuggled close to him, put her left hand in his overcoat pocket, hooked her right hand to it, stared straight ahead and became quiet. He didn't seem to notice her withdrawal into deep and private thoughts.

After another half block, at Nathan Road and Humphrey Street, he paused to hail a taxi. Waiting, he smiled and nudged her attention. "I like going away with you for this weekend." She returned his smile and covered his hand with hers. When he looked away to wave for an approaching cab, the smile left Annie's face. When he looked back to her, the smile appeared again. When he looked away again, her smile went away. It was that way throughout the weekend and had actually been that way through the last few years of their relationship.

CHAPTER FIVE
Readiness Through Training

While Paul Vincent thanked Dr. David Selesky for support and later had dinner with Abie Lake and his wife, Captain Robert Clifford kept all officers aboard Truaxe for what he called, an 'emergency' meeting. With deployment less than a week away, Clifford had been in the wardroom all day sifting through pages of incomplete training forms. Despite that he knew better and regardless of his father's concentrated warnings, he had truly neglected his ship's training close to the point of no return.

"Shit." He whispered almost inaudibly. The white-jacketed steward's mate who was setting out coffee cups, water beakers, yellow pads and pencils readying for the meeting, heard the under-breath 'shit', tensed and moved away from his Captain. Clifford pushed back in his chair. The cigarette that dominated his face wiggled up and down, its filter clamped between grinding teeth. The drifting smoke caused his eyes to reflexively squint. "Shit-shit," he repeated, and snapped a pencil in two. Leaning his head way back, he squeezed his eyes tightly closed. A long ash tumbled down his khaki shirtfront unnoticed. "Shit, Shit, Shit. I've done it again." The steward quickly left the wardroom for the nearby pantry area.

When under pressure, Robert Clifford would slip into prolonged periods of daydream and fantasy, a personality flaw he never could master. For the past five months he'd been daydreaming about how well his new command must look in his record, how pleased his wife and father must be with his professional standing. He'd been fantasizing about the recently visited romantic ports of call which included the sixty day trip around South America and through the Straits of Magellan, about being respected and revered as Captain, about perhaps becoming Chief of Navy Operations someday, or even Chairman of the Joint Chiefs of Staff. An unflawed command of Truaxe could pay off within two years with an assignment to a pentagon staff, first step toward the admiral stripe. Family tradition would remain intact and perhaps, just perhaps, his retired admiral father would judge him more favorably.

After promising himself and his father that he would not slip up with this new command, there he was, sitting in a wardroom facing a self-generated mess. He had called the meeting to set up crash-program plans that had pulled him out of similar messes before: Catch things up while finding someone else to blame for the neglected training. To add to the pressure within, he'd made a hasty decision to send a message report to the Commander Seventh Fleet declaring Truaxe trained and combat ready to arrive on station in the Gulf of Tonkin in three weeks.

But he knew Truaxe wasn't ready.

Kicking his chair back from the table, Clifford stepped into the adjacent officer's head. Alone in the small polished space, he addressed his six feet, 190 pounds in the mirror. "You monkey fuckin' stand-up fool." He splashed water on his face, moistened and pocket-combed his short blond hair and noticed his pale blue eyes were sitting in inflamed whites. He leaned on the stainless steel sink with not very tanned, but muscled arms. "Someone will catch on to you. These nuke sailors are smart bastards."

Re-entering the wardroom to face the meeting, he heard his father's words. "Pure blind luck has been on your side too long. Some day you're going to royally screw something up."

Married, two nearly grown children, the son of one recently retired admiral, the grandson and nephew of two others, Clifford wanted to have the navy calculated to his advantage. He struggled constantly to keep his performance competent but inside he raged with fear and suspicion near paranoia. The movement of his eyes that others interpreted as active intelligence actually reflected his internal state of nervous anxiousness.

Many things that did work for Clifford, however, had brought him to where he was in the navy. He was an excellent navigator and ship handler, could get men to produce, for whatever reason, and, he was a gifted and respected mathematician. In navy graduate schools, he was known to have a remarkable memory for numerical pattern details and complex engineering methodology. He was also somewhat superstitious and sentimental. His crews in the past seemed to like that part of him and his other human side; collecting good luck mementos and bits and pieces of shelf cluttering paraphernalia from every port of call.

As captain Clifford grew older, his retired father, whom the family referred to as "Our Admiral", was living more and more vicariously through his son's career. Our Admiral's cronies, who pushed golf balls around the course at the Miramar or Coronado Air Stations in San Diego, often cringed when approached by the proud father. It took at least the first four holes to be updated on the latest concerning young Robert.

"Well, my boy had dinner with Admiral Rickover last week. Rickover says. (blah-blah)."

"Well, Robert's ship's been chosen to show the flag in Rio during the change of ambassadors there. Ambassador Fallen says to Robert … ".

"Now Robert's been tellin' me 'bout some new gear …usin' satellites? A new …well, never mind. Real classified stuff you know."

Our Admiral, who Clifford's wife secretly called a "wizzled American version of Jacques Cousteau", visited his son's home often to talk about his son's career and to re-talk his own. With bony finger pointing or the petrified snake cane he'd discovered in Thailand shaking in the air, the old man with white thin hair plastered close to his pale scalp and who seemed frail to everyone else, could reduce Robert to stammers with a simple flick of a phrase.

"Well you handled that wrong, again."

"But, b-b-but, F-Father. I, I, I."

"BUT? But doesn't cover no bread. I handled that problem when I had command of the Thetis Bay. Do it my way." Our Admiral felt he guided his son, advised and encouraged him. In reality he did little more than bully the man. Though unasked, Our Admiral also influenced the officer transfer section in Washington to send Clifford to duties the father felt would enhance the career of the younger officer. If Clifford objected, something he did less and less over the years, Our Admiral would explode.

"God dammit! What do you really know? My experience can be yours. Look at my successes and match 'em." Every interaction with his father seemed to leave young Clifford's ego resembling a piece of bruised fruit but of course, none of that information ever spilled out on the golf courses.

Clifford's wife, Melinda of the Smith-college-eastern-seaboard-finishing-school-set stayed away from the mood swings caused by the embattled father-son relationship as she stayed away from most of Clifford's professional life. She loved her two teenage children and treasured the social life that ranking naval officers and their wives could enjoy. To Clifford, who never quite understood children, his two seemed like intruders who came and went and patronized him as they asked for more money but seemed openly disrespectful of his profession.

"That's what kids do today, Robert. It's the anti-war thing. They still love you."

"Sure, yeah," he would say. But he didn't *feel* loved.

He grew to leave the family portions of his life to Melinda.

In his official jacket in Washington, because of or in spite of his father's influence, his son was recorded as hardworking and dedicated, a man heading somewhere near the top. In mid 1966, the navy honored him or his father's wishes, with command of the hottest new navy prototype, the U.S.S. Truaxe, DDG(N)-35.

Clifford telephoned immediately from Norfolk to San Diego.

"I've got me the Truaxe, Dad, How's that?"

Our Admiral hid any emotional clues by simply grunting.

"That new nuke powered destroyer, father. A one of a kind ship of the line." Feeling full of himself, Clifford flaunted the new command. "Six cuts above anything *any* Clifford's ever commanded."

Aware of the special nature of Truaxe, our Admiral couldn't actually snub the teasing comments. The sleek guided missile destroyer was driven by two of the latest General Electric D2G nuclear reactors. The father side of him wanted to praise his son, but his almost vulgar competitiveness wouldn't permit it. "Getting a command's one thing. Keeping it is another, Robert."

The telephone lines chilled for several seconds but the younger officer's enthusiasm was not easily neutralized. "She'll make an unofficial 45 knots." He was whispering unconsciously and ridiculously. Both knew they were passing classified information over a common telephone line. "Like a Coontz class destroyer leader, Dad. You know, the DLG-9 ships? Almost the same hull, only nuclear."

"That's real nice, Robert." His father's envy didn't conceal well and Robert rubbed it in, But what do *you* know about nuclear power?"

"I'll be schooled. Admiral Rickover doesn't make mistakes. "I'm the ship's experienced handler, my exec, a commander named Arnold Griffith who I haven't met yet, is the Exec. He's a nuke engineer type since high school. Academy, class of 54, P.G. school nuclear physics and propulsion. He was propulsion officer on the frigate, Truxtun and before that, nuke engineer on the Enterprise. And also, Dad, for balance we've got a second specifically trained nuke officer. Some Commander named Merideth Deiter. An ex-submarine type. Him an' a core of enlisted operators have been with the ship's reactor since it was first activated in that G.E. plant in Idaho, late '64 or so. He's a serious engineer. Remembers everyone's name, never forgets a combination to a safe or someone's telephone number. You know the type."

"Like Ed Gibbons, C.O. of Kittyhawk?"

"Same sort."

Dad's detailed knowledge was becoming outdated and Robert rubbed it in a little: "She's the first destroyer with tactical data systems for weapons and air control. Runnin' silent and runnin' deep doesn't do it at all any more. If conditions are right, we could punch out Rusky eardrums at three thousand yards. An some of the missile are nuclear capable, I am sure."

"You got a helicopter on board?"

"Yep," He said boasting even more. "UH-2C. Kaman, Seasprite. I hear the crewman's put a gattling gun on her."

There was a pause, then Dad continued. "Where'd they get the name? I don't know no navy hero named Truaxe."

"Guy named "A. Bradley Truaxe". Navy physician from San Diego."

"Well, you got the Clifford name to live up to. So don't let us down, you hear?" And he hung up the phone.

Once off the telephone, despite that the conversation had been filled with the familiar one-ups, Robert sat immediately down and penned the first of a series of expected letters to his father. Much like an actor trying to get the *New York Times* to say something nice about his performance but trying to appear as though it didn't really matter, Clifford junior proudly gave his father information he was sure would be taken to the golf links.

Dear Dad.

Please, not so much worry from you about getting the ship ready. I know what I'm doing. Plenty of time yet.

This executive officer? Arnold Griffith. He appears to be a tough, demanding and serious officer. Truly tall, dark, handsome and athletic looking. He's 36, a bit more formal than I prefer. He never calls anyone by their first name, usually addresses them by 'Mr.' or by their rank: "Commander This", "Lieutenant That". He wears a necktie with his uniform even at sea where I don't require it. He's a stickler for regulations. Seems a bit vain too. Checks his appearance in any mirror he passes. Met his wife, Barbara, but he seems uneasy around her. A sorta' Philadelphia money type. Maybe drinks a bit too much too. No kids. He told me he was in line for a command of his own but requested Truaxe as X.O. Dedicated USN type?

Had our second bomb-threat yesterday. We're getting used to the anti-war nuts doing all they can to slow down progress.

It'll be good to be in California soon, even though we all know where we'll be taking this show boat right after the first of the year.

Affectionately, Robert

Truaxe had been designed from the keel up to be an extended range escort for the nuclear powered aircraft carrier Enterprise. The frigates Truxtun and Bainbridge had preceded Truaxe as Enterprise's escorts but the navy had grown to recognize other uses for those two ships. With pressures building in the Middle East there was a move to convert Truxtun and

Bainbridge to be classed as special cruisers. Their nuclear propelled steaming ranges would permit them to act as flagships for admirals with large navy staffs who could stay aboard for long periods in remote parts of the world. As part of the long-range plan, the smaller, quick and capable Truaxe was the first ship built to actually take over the Truxtun and Bainbridge jobs. She wouldn't be considered doing that job until she took station as escort in the Gulf of Tonkin near the end of January, 1968. The navy was pushing Clifford to get her there truly ready for duty.

It was 6:30 p.m., the evening meal was over and he was seated where he had spent most of the day being briefed on readiness and briefing others on his expectations. He was re-learning another wise saying Our Admiral had warned him to never forget. "Now Robert, readiness is only achieved through training. Do not neglect it. Every man must be able to do his job in the dark or blindfolded, one hand behind his back, *and* … . do someone else's job at the same time."

Clifford similarly ignored the apprehension expressed by his executive officer, Commander Griffith, right after they had left Norfolk. "On training, Captain. I suggest we get on it heavily. Lean on the men hard …drill, drill, drill. Then, let up when they know what they're doing. That builds respect for themselves and for you."

Commander Griffith entered the wardroom, took a seat next to Clifford, but didn't open conversation. Clifford dismissed the Supply Officer, Lieutenant Commander Becker from a brief one-on-one meeting and asked him to stay for the next. Becker looked at Clifford, looked at his wristwatch, looked at the overhead, sighed deeply and plopped into a chair with a trapped expression on his face. A dozen or so other officers straggled into the wardroom. Most squinted initially against the bright lights but continued to squint against the room's one major shortcoming, bad air. With a low overhead and what proved to be inadequate ventilation, cigarette smoke pressed like *Velcro* against their eyeballs. Clifford was one of the heaviest smokers and while almost everyone squinted, no one openly complained.

"What's this meeting about?" An ensign asked the gunnery officer.

"Training, I hope. We've got to make a training readiness report to COMSEVENTHFLT—Today or tomorrow."

"Readiness? Training readiness? Are you joking?"

"I have a feeling it's crash program catch-up time."

"I have a feeling we're about to be fucked without lubrication."

When all three of the fifteen-foot green-felt-covered tables were filled, the captain coughed a loud throat clearing crack. The room came to order.

To his officers, their Captain was a difficult man to understand or to follow. After over six months with him, few tried to do either. One moment Clifford could be all smiles, closeness and friendly, the next moment stern faced, distanced and threatening. Few pretended to understand what action stimulated which mood but everyone sympathized with anyone trapped in the wrath of a Clifford mood swing.

He was not a stoic secreted ivory tower skipper. He claimed to Our Admiral to be involved in everything on his ship. He walked the decks almost daily and talked to everyone, officer and enlisted alike, often becoming inappropriately included in the network of people who passed new jokes throughout the ship. This over-involvement and his remarkable memory for complex figures and nomenclature kept him micro-managing many small shipboard details even though he missed some important major events. His officers were kept off-guard, never knowing what insignificant job he might suddenly require them to divert attention to.

"Lieutenant Hicks? Ya'know those spotter cards for the lookouts? You can't tell a Perry class FFG from a Knox Class DE. You know that? Better change that, today. Hear me?"

He would receive a polite "Aye, Aye, Sir."

"Mr. Lukarmo? Those cooling fans in the crews compartments? They interfere with the television reception. Ya'know, crackle-crackle noises. Chief 'lectrician says they need some kind of in-line filters. You know that? Better get on that. Hear me?"

Another polite "Aye, Aye, Sir."

He could explode over the unimportant details yet be almost flippant over things others considered very serious.

"Mr. Stumpf? Come to my office."

"Mr. Stumpf? This letter to Training Command? Just 'cause you didn't get someone to this KG-59 school, I ain't sendin' this letter."

"B-but, Cap'n. I got no maintenance …man for the KG-59, and it is complex equipment."

"Hear me? Do what you have to do …"

"But …"

"No 'but'."

"Mr. Valentino? Come to my office."

"Mr. Valentino. This letter to our bosses askin' for a qualified OOD to ride west with us? Bullshit. We'll train our own."

"Pretty short anyone even near qualified, Cap'n."

"Put yourself on watch."

"I'm on watch, Cap'n."

"Put the executive officer on watch."

"He is on watch, Cap'n."

"Dig deeper. Put that Master Chief on watch. We beg no one for help."

He would not acknowledge the helpless disappointment reflected in those 'Aye, aye, sirs'.

As soon as coffee was poured all around, Clifford coughed again, grunted and looked around his wardroom.

"Are we all here? Where is Mr. Harper?

"Transferred. Remember? Left yesterday, Sir." The answering officer had to speak loudly over the hum of the near useless exhaust vents.

"Right. Forgot! Where is our Master Chief? Wasn't he invited, Mr. Valentino?"

Commander Valentino, the ship's Operations Officer was Paul Vincent's Department Head. Lieutenant Stumpf worked directly for Valentino. "I let him go ashore, Captain." Valentino said, flat and with a chill in his tone. "Personal business."

"I saw some of his personal business this morning on the quarterdeck. That's trouble. Know anything 'bout that, Mr. Valentino?"

"No, I don't." Valentino offered. "I'll brief him on this meeting tomorrow, Cap'n."

Clifford grunted, then increased the amplitude in his voice and addressed the entire room. "Listen up. The more I hear about ship's readiness the less I want to hear. We're in trouble on *this here ship* and I want it put to order." Clifford raved on, finger pointed and sweeping from one blank faced officer to the next, referring over and over to 'this here ship.' He, like many professionals, always referred to his ship in this mocking manner. The saying, 'this here ship' is heard throughout the navy and cannot be accurately traced. It adds or detracts something and follows some unwritten rule that only the commanding officer can refer to his ship as 'this here ship'.

"I want you to know, only a busy physician in a demanding private practice has more to read on a daily basis than does the C.O. of a warship. In addition to my regular duties, now I have taken personal charge of the training of each department, each division—down to the last swingin' dick on this here ship, and I'm pissed about that. I want to walk out of here tonight with the exact, I say *exact* detailed proposal for in-depth, down to the last man training. It's been too mishandled—I want watch station bills up to date now, TONIGHT! I'll check them personally at 0700. If I hear we still need a school for someone, or some guys head is the wrong shape for an Oxygen Breathing Apparatus to fit air-tight, or one o' the new kids doesn't know a fire alarm from a collision alarm, I'll be after that division officer's ass. I'm sick of waiting for you people and getting nothing for my wait."

A neurotic teacher was berating a room full of junior-high-school children for putting on a poorly performed Christmas play they hadn't been permitted to rehearse for. They were deadpanned, helpless, most pulled into self-protective shells. They made no eye contact with one another, not wanting to see their fear or disgust reflect from the eyes of others. Clifford, protected only by his rank, was performing one of the ceremonies this society designs and encourages: He was misusing power. Like the parent over child, umpire over player, raging husband over terrified wife, shrew over milk-toast husband, police over citizen, boss over vulnerable employee, any bully over any frightened victim, Clifford was *demanding* rather than *commanding* respect. He was holding others responsible for his own shortcomings. He was yelling 'do as I say' but implying powerfully, almost openly, to not call him on his shortcomings, or things could get much much worse. Protected by his rank, blame-deflecting belittlement of his officers was something Clifford had always done. Unfair, yes. However, no one can break this USN unfairness screen because the fear is too great and the system doesn't permit it. A captain has too much power. Court martial, restriction to quarters, ridicule in front of peers, control of career chances. This built-in fear prompts an erroneous assumption in the navy; that no matter what a commanding officer does or says, he does so for good reason. It is the job of his officers to accept there is good reason, pretend they understand the good reason, further pretend there is not a better way to handle it, support him and obey without question. While blind faith is required for God, Alla and Jesus, C.O.'s may well outrank even that threesome.

History tells only two stories where the captain had been wrong. Many men in many wardrooms surely compared their Captain's ravings to Captain Queeg and the strawberries on the U.S.S. Caine and to Captain Bligh and the cat-o-nine-tails on the H.M.S. Bounty. How many other ships have been out there under the command of a truly crazed officer, helpless underlings passing their time to get away? How many officers sit there biding their time until *they* can be the C.O., until *they* can use that power? How many others, fine people, have left the navy because they could never picture themselves in a position of command, to be hated by others as much as they hate their commander?

But maybe Clifford truly knew something the younger officers were missing. Perhaps his purpose all along was to force them to think and take the initiative. Going down the eastern coast of South America, instead of using the calm waters for gunnery and helo training, Clifford had insisted on an extensive and time wasting initiation ceremony for crossing the equator. "Imperium Neptuni Regis must be honored," he would say over and over. Perhaps he knew the ceremony would meld the crew on 'this here ship' in some special way known only to those in command. Many wondered then, had they somehow missed a clear signal to take the initiative, to be *real* officers, take charge? The minds in the room where whirring.

Their Captain complained and threatened for several more minutes, then simply stopped talking. He took a large bite out of a biscuit he had saved from dinner and, while chewing, made circle motions with the biscuit toward the exec seated on his right. With his mouth full, he said "Take o'er R-nee."

Griffith nodded toward Clifford and with a practiced click-click, opened the black leather briefcase he always seemed to have within reach. He removed several stacks of neatly paper clipped pages of training reports. The officers instantly picked up their pencils, arranged note pads and readied for Griffith to speak.

What is it, Clifford wondered immediately, that caused Griffith to command that kind of response? Respect? Fear? The man did look sharp, Clifford noted. Although it was late in the day it wasn't unusual for Griffith, in his role as super-officer, to have shaved even for an informal working meeting like this. While the officer has a dark facial appearance, his cheeks and chin had that white outline heavy beards reveal after shaving. This night he'd failed to wipe the shaving cream well enough. A small dab poked out under the lobe of his left ear.

Clifford watched Griffith arrange the reports in front of him, focus his scanning vision a few inches above everyone's head, and address the group. His opening comment was a direct shot at Clifford.

"Looks like we've gotten the attention we've all longed for, Gentlemen." Clifford missed the shot, the others didn't. Griffith took another. "I guess this evening's real question asks simply if it is too late to forge a warship out of this fission driven boxcar?" Twenty pairs of anxious eyes darted toward the Captain but immediately relaxed. The Captain seemed preoccupied with his biscuit.

Griffith referred to his 3 by 5 cards.

"We rate 356 men, we've got 299. Thirty-three have actual experience as destroyer sailors. Of the twenty-two officers, six are destroyer experienced. Ship built on the east coast? Most men *with* experience are Atlantic ocean experienced, not Pacific. Only twenty-seven men and thirteen officers have sailed the western Pacific. The only Chief Petty Officer to have Pacific destroyer experience is Master Chief Vincent. Our personnel officer, Mr. Beauford, has offered his first born child for some trained men ...but ...no. We have a lot of work ahead of us."

The few signs of appreciative laughter were tempered by thoughts of the amount of work about to begin. The focus changed from griping about what they already knew, to an extremely detailed seminar. Every division officer was required to coordinate with the training officer exact times when particular men were available for specific types of needed training. Yellow pads flurried.

Most were astonished when Clifford told them he had already notified the Commander of the Seventh fleet that Truaxe was trained and ready.

A naval by-word, actually likely a by-*law*, is to respond to the phrase and to the idea of 'readiness through training'. It is likely the first captain said it to the first crew on the first ship ever. "If we train, we'll be ready, gentlemen". Hence: Readiness through training.

A ship is either 'ready for duty, or not. Extensive records are kept at command headquarters keeping tract of which ship is qualified and in which areas. Reports are exchanged among trainers as to which talents, schools, or qualifications were missing from which ship, and what was being done to fill the requirement. On and on, over and over, the navy trained through courses, schools, study guides, visiting training teams, 'underway training groups', in port instructional teams, and more.

One young officer turned to one another and whispered. "We're ready? Readiness through training? We've had no training."

"What?" Clifford snapped at the cynical mumbles. "You think we'll not be ready? Not for a millionth of a thought do you think that. We WILL be ready."

At Griffith's steering, an extensive letter was drafted to Captain Edward Gibbons, Commanding Officer of the U.S.S. Kittyhawk, the carrier Truaxe was deploying with. Griffith also suggested Captain Clifford personally visit and ask the Kittyhawk skipper for cooperation in what he would say was just some extra training to round off the final edges, but, which would actually be most of the crew's first real hand experience at working closely with another combat ship. Clifford could only agree to the common sense problem solving suggestion.

Watching Griffith take over and work under pressure, Clifford, for the first time, felt uncomfortable around the man. He sat back, watched Griffith, and reflected. Who is this man? Really?

During the trip around south America, Griffith had seemed content to keep pretty much to himself. He only left the ship when the Captain insisted he do so, usually in the name of public relations.

"Mr. G. I need official U.S. representation in Rio tomorrow at that embassy welcome ceremony. Valentino is too quiet. Come along and be entertaining and sociable. And, I need similar help when we get to Valpariso. Also, for Valparaiso? Anyone in the crew who speaks Por'ta'gee?"

Griffith would show up on the quarterdeck in either his uniform, or in gray trousers and navy blue blazer with a "Truaxe" insignia on the breast pocket. He would go ashore with the C.O., do the PR stint and return as soon as he could. In Valparaiso, he came up with two crew-members from Rhode Island who spoke Portuguese.

From the outside it appeared the Captain and his executive officer had a perfect, albeit somewhat formal professional relationship. On Clifford's side though, he felt both pulled toward and shoved away by the man, usually at the same time. Griffith was never openly contemptuous toward the Captain but he wouldn't laugh at Clifford's jokes, not even the funny ones. He never asked Clifford a personal question nor did he ever discuss his own personal life beyond a brief introduction of his wife at a stuffy officer's party upon commissioning. Although he always rendered a snappy first meeting salute, he never accompanied the salute with a verbal greeting. He would never volunteer information to ease a problem Clifford was dealing with, but he was quick to cooperate once asked. In a letter to his father, Clifford stated: "I can't get a real feel for Griffith. Something I can't understand slips through the cracks toward me—a mystery resentment of some kind."

Griffith also kept most of the crew-members off stride by being private, formal and demanding. His mechanical looking grin included an arrogant peculiar sneer within it. Senior Chief McCullough, the ship's Chief Yeoman, worked the closest with Griffith on a daily basis.

"I swear, Paul, that bastard acts as though he knows how often every man on this ship jerks off, and to what theme."

"Yeah." Paul agreed. "Like he's privy to some potent secret of the universe?"

"A secret he's determined to keep but hold us accountable for."

Vincent was empathic. "Every time I've spoken with him I walk away with this question mark over my head."

"Like that freakin' black briefcase? It's the las' thing he locks up at night. Takes it out first thing in the morning."

"Dorty peektures, perhaps, Mac?"

"Dorty ladies underwear, perhaps."

"Nah, he's too Mr. Clean for that."

"Beneath every Mr. Clean, there's sumptin' dirty."

The training meeting broke up officially at 11 p.m. At 11:05, Paul Vincent was returning from his 7:30 meeting with David Selesky and his 8:30 dinner at Abie's house in southeast San Diego. He had first stopped by Selesky's office to say goodbye to the man who had stood by him through the attempts at marriage repair and through the separation. He wanted to express appreciation for the several favors Selesky had volunteered but had trouble saying it right out. When Paul had been hastily sent to Vietnam the first time, Rachael had complained of being afraid in their inter-city apartment. Selesky had intervened to get her moved into navy housing, even stretching a point. As an M.D., he certified she was pregnant so she would qualify for a two-bedroom house. She had lied to Selesky privately, saying she wanted the extra room as a baby room to surprise Paul, but it was always intended as bunking space for brother Ben, his wife, Bunny and their two kids. Nick, the tagalong younger brother plopped on the living room floor as often as not. Paul felt obligated to Selesky for having been helpful, but felt embarrassed that Rachael had tricked him.

"We both learned from her didn't we, Paul?" Selesky joked as the two men stood with hands clasped in goodbye.

"I've learned from you. Show me a liar I'll also see a cheat and a thief. She turned out to be all of those. But I've learned most from your insight. I owe you, David Selesky. I'll not forget I do."

"You only owe yourself, Paul. Helping you was my job."

Paul couldn't accept the comfort and nourishment he had so valued from Selesky could simply be tossed off as 'his job'. He had never felt so important to anyone in his life. As he turned to leave the office, the two hugged impulsively and both were moved to near tears.

"Well, look at us." Selesky said.

"Yeah, look at us.

"And remember, Sarah Barkley's gone to the trouble to arrange for you to pick up your stuff the evening before the ship leaves."

"I'll be there, and, maybe see you in Westpac."

"Maybe."

They spontaneously hugged again. It was the first time Paul Vincent had permitted that kind of closeness with a man.

Taking that warmth with him to dinner at Abie Lake's felt real human.

"Only reason Vera Veronica Robinson ever married me, Paul, was so her name would be Veronica Lake like that blond white beauty Clark Gable was always chasin' in them old movies?" Abie teased his attractive wife.

"Oh, Abie, quit." Veronica stepped up to behind her husband's chair and put her hands over his eyes. "I married you because you're as rich and warm as your creamy frosting skin … " Abie pulled away and smiled. '

"An 'cause I make you tingle all over."

Veronica rolled her eyes but smiled.

Paul had known Abie since 1961 when they had served on a minesweeper. Albert Blake Lake, signalman second-class was from some place in Kansas and bragged to have been the only black kid in his high school. "They'd give me the football to run with 'cause the lily whites on the other team was afraid I'd rub off on 'em."

"Don't call me "Albert" and don't call me "Blake" an' don't call me "Lake." I hate 'em all. Call me "A", "B", like my mother did."

"Abie?"

"No, I'm not Abie Hoffman. "A", followed by a "B".

No one could handle a name like an "A" followed by a "B", so "A-B" became Abie, like in Hoffman. Abie gave in over time.

Abie also claimed he had never seen more than a basin full of water before he joined the USN. "I hate water. I don't drink it 'cause fish fuck in it an' I don't swim 'cause I got no gills, but, I don't mind sailin' over it 'cause they pay me ok and it keeps me out of Kansas."

Raised in Steubenville, Ohio, when Blacks were 'Colored People', neither Rachael or Paul Vincent held prejudices. Over the years, until Paul's marriage became strained, Abie and Veronica had often visited for dinner with him and Rachael. The couple also came to know Ben and Nick and became aware of their power over Rachael, hence, over Paul.

"You should'a slapped them kids around in the beginning, Paul, you wouldn't'a had this trouble."

"You don't hit kids, Abie."

"Oh yeah? If God didn't want us to slap kids, why'd'e give us arms with hands on the ends."

"Kids are great, Abie."

"Watch one of them pabulum breaths for five minutes and what do they do? Shit on you, spit on you, or spill somethin'." Watch a six year old for five minutes they'll jeopardize their life or someone else's at least once."

Veronica, who was a bank executive would tease Abie about being only a second-class petty officer after some 15 years in the navy. He was at least three promotions behind his age group. She also accused him of being a follower.

"So ten years in rate. You know, Veronica, that makes me probably the best and most experienced second-class signalman in the navy. See, when you see it that way—you feel prouder, right, right? Get lemons, make lemonade. Right, right? And damn sure I'm a follower. Leaders get yelled at too much. Now you listen, Veronica. The navy says my I.Q. is 100. 100 is average, right smack in the middle. That makes me not smart—but not dumb either. In six years I'll have a pension, you'll still be countin' other people's money. Who dumb? Who, I ask, is dumb?"

Veronica would just shake her head but would also smile. She loved the man, and knew that many thought well of him, including Paul Vincent.

That first dinner without Rachael had only been a little awkward. As Paul cheek-kissed Veronica good-bye, she hugged him very hard and said two things that seemed important to her. "Paul, you'll get over Rachael, she wasn't really for you" And, "I'm counting on you to watch out for my Abie in all that ocean, you hear me?"

"Not a problem, Veronica."

Heading toward his stateroom at 11:05 p.m., Paul could hear loud voices coming from the officer's country passageway. He stopped to listen.

"Now say that again, Mr. Griffith. So I have this right." He peeked in through a small port. Captain Clifford was holding a cigarette with thumb and forefinger almost touching his cheek near his eye. He kept wiggling it. Ashes flicked toward Commander Griffith. The flicking seemed intentional.

Griffith addressed the Captain formally and stiffly.

"Simply stated, Cap'n, I repeat. For you to jump those officers for your own lacking seemed outright unfair."

"Me? Lacking?"

Griffith became pleading. "Look. The emperor wears no clothes in this matter, Cap'n."

"What's that mean?"

"You are naked, but there isn't anyone to call you on it." Considering the challenging content of the statement, Griffith seemed composed. "I didn't even call you on it …and I'm embarrassed by that. I sat there like the rest and let you blame, when we've had no leadership on training."

"No leadership?" Clifford exploded. "No one can say I'm not leading. Can't call *me* on *anything*." He then seemed to whine. "Thank somebody I'm aware how behind training is. You hadn't caught it." He attacked again. "I am *not* the one's been shirkin' duty. Training really is behind. And, where have you been, Exec?"

"Trying to get your support. *That's* where I've been. And you know it."

Clifford became tense-faced. He leaned forward and dragged each word out precisely as though speaking in cadence: "If you have been such a hot shot trainer, Commander Griffith, how come we've not gotten Chief Vincent ready for the officer of the deck post at sea yet?" He then shifted to rapid fire assault: "He's the onla' one close to qualify' not countin' Stumpf. Where you on *that* ? Do I hav'ta break in Chief's myself?" He shifted back to cadence clarity: "Or, Mr. Commander Griffith, are you ready to stand double O-O-D watches yourself this trip?"

Griffith backed away a step. "I didn't *want* Chief Vincent qualified. I want to serve on a *quality* ship. That's why I want *officers* as conning officer. Safety is the topmost component of quality. We'll be safer with officers. I though you'd support that." He became whiny. "I don't want some Chief who can't keep his personal life together handling this ship while people are sleeping below the water line."

"No guts, no medals." Clifford was openly rude.

Griffith ignored the crack. "If you would have let Commander Valentino send that letter …we'd have a new conning officer now … But nooo—we'd look bad. Can't look bad. We could run aground due to lack of training, but we'd damn sure look good doin' it." He boldly mocked Clifford. The Captain missed it.

"Damn straight we'll look good. Do I have to monitor all details? Dammit I'm not crying to the bureau because you didn't see the O-O-D shortage. That is that."

"If I were captain … "

Clifford cut him short with a yell. " …WHICH YOU AIN'T." Then quietly: "but please continue."

Griffith backed away. Clifford goaded him. "Go on, if you were Cap'n?"

Griffith's composure faded but he tried to stay forthright. "If I were, I would have written the letter …for training help, an O-O-D." His voice cracked and softened. Power shifted strongly to Clifford. Griffith struggled to continue, " … I would have been more supportive of training. Tonight's scene …including this one, would not have happened, Sir."

Clifford's jaw tightened. Already beating himself up over this, he was not expecting this blast from Griffith. His face grew red.

"Now you listen to me. As my exec, you couldn't get officers to get training organized. Who says you'll *ever* be ready for a command?" With that remark, he turned the discussion to his final power weapon, the fitness report he penned for each officer each year

Griffith backed down, his eyes closer to showing an emotion than Clifford had ever seen. "I'm sorry, Cap'n." He said. "But I was …just very concerned about training, safety, the ship's welfare and morale."

"An you fuckin' well better be concerned, X.O." Clifford left for his own cabin but turned and took one last shot. "I don't want this emperor clothes shit to go anywhere. Not one bit further. I want active support by you on training. If there's *any* sign I'm not getting that—there will definitely be a letter to the bureau from me, but it won't be about training—it'll be about you. IS that clear?"

"Yes, Sir."

Paul Vincent left the area flustered by the infighting. He didn't want the senior officer pedestals to tarnish right in front of him. He wanted to serve in a navy where the leadership was locked in step, confident, capable. This power clash worried him.

After leaving the exec, Clifford went to his quarters and spent several minutes at his desk reminding himself, promising himself and reprimanding himself. He was restless and nervous. He would not, could not, let himself get so far into his basic flaw again. No one had come that close to calling him out before. He was glad he had backed Griffith down, even if it strained their professional relationship. Our Admiral had often said: "You can back anybody down. Everyone has a weak spot." Griffith's appeared to be his career, his vanity.

Our Admiral had reminded him over and over that subordinates are there to learn and to serve. Clifford just took the philosophy too far.

He smoked two cigarettes and jotted an impulsive note to Our Admiral about how his officers had let him down. Afterward he sat with his feet on his desk, lost for several minutes in self-pity. After several more minutes his mood swung. He made a mental note to make things better tomorrow, especially with Griffith. He could hear more of Our Admiral's advice. "A long deployment is no time to start peeing contests with the second in command."

CHAPTER SIX
Women Take Care of Their Own.

Darkness was well wrapped around San Diego by the time Paul Vincent was thanking David Selesky and Clifford was yelling at the officers in the Truaxe wardroom meeting. At that same moment less than half a mile away from either man, Rachael Vincent sat her third drink of the evening on the glass topped coffee table and answered a quiet knock on the front door of her rented navy house at 3405 McCandless Boulevard. For the last few months, evenings would have found her already at Ben's Bistro tending the bar or waiting the few tables, but the gambling charge had closed the place. Brother Nick, not handling the turmoil of Ben's arrest had headed north, supposedly on a job search. Since Paul Vincent had refused to provide money to pay back the borrowed bail funds, Ben was working part time as a table filler in a Chula Vista card room promising each evening he would make a killing that night and have the needed money. Bunny was waiting tables at the Rancho Steak House in nearby National City near the San Diego Naval Station, which left Rachael to watch their two children, Little Angie, 7 and Rebecca, 5. Steady drinking helped her cope with it all.

The children stopped their dollhouse play as aunt Rachael opened the door to three women standing on the porch, their makeup and facial expressions skewed by the glow of the shielded yellow bug-light above the door.

"Yes?"

"Rachael Vincent?"

"Yes?"

"I am Barbara Griffith, this is Celica Domansky, and this is Ruth Thomason." The taller woman spoke through bluish lips. "Dr. Sarah Barkley was to have called you?" There was just a slight twang to her voice. Southern accent? Rachael was a little drunker than she wished she were. The woman was talking again, and looking puzzled. "We're the officer's wives." Rachael looked blank. " From your husband's ship?"

Rachael *had* taken a call from Doctor Selesky's co-therapist, Doctor Sarah Barkley a few hours after Paul had left her standing on the Truaxe's early morning quarterdeck, but she'd completely forgotten it. Yes, Sarah said some officer's wives were to visit her. Was that tonight?

"May we come in, Mrs. Vincent?"

"Pardon? Yes. Please do." She stepped back while the three well-dressed women entered the small living room. Rachael wished she had straightened up earlier.

"May we sit?"

"Sure. Surely. Yes." The three women lined up on the small couch. Rachael's memory returned then. This was something about Paul coming to pick up his things.

"May we smoke?"

Rachael sat her drink glass on the glass-topped coffee table and picked up an overflowing ashtray. "Yes, Yes, just a minute." She left the room with the ashtray and returned almost immediately with two unmatched but clean ones. No one spoke. The two children had returned to their dolls. The three visitors were all smoking. Rachael lit a cigarette. The room filled with smoke. No one spoke. Rachael's drink glass condensed a ring of water onto the coffee table. She picked up the glass and sipped from it. It dripped freely down her front. Barbara Griffith offered her a handkerchief. Rachael dabbed at her front with it, then impulsively wiped her mouth with it. No one spoke, but six eyes got wider as lipstick smeared the white cloth. She handed it back to Barbara. Barbara didn't accept it. No one spoke. Rachael wiped at the coffee table water ring with the handkerchief, but for only a second or two. She stood up, stepped back toward the kitchen, threw the handkerchief toward Barbara Griffith and cried out through a drunken haze..

"Leave me. Leave me alone. Get out of here."

Angie and Rebecca abandoned their doll play and froze. The one called Celica was immediately on her feet and touching Rachael's arm. "We're here to comfort you. Please!"

Ruth joined her beside Rachael. "See what we might be able to do. Make things better now."

Barbara stood and spoke softly. Not in the yellow light, her lips were no longer blue looking. "We're on your side here. We know of the divorce …divorce plans, Mrs. Vincent. May we call you Rachael?"

No answer. Rachael stood frozen. Then her lower lip pulled upward and tears surged. Celica clenched a hand to Rachael's upper arm.

"We'd like to call you Rachael."

The one called Ruth took over. "We understand from talking with Sarah Barkley, the counselor? And Doctor Selesky? That your husband—well, Master Chief Vincent wants to come by and pick up things, things he'll need on the trip. Night before the ship sails?"

"Whatever, yes." Rachael sniffled loudly. Barbara retrieved the handkerchief from the floor and handed it to Rachael.

"It's alright that he comes by?"

Without asking, the one named Ruth took Angie and Rebecca by the hands. "We'll just step outside for a few minutes, girls, while Auntie Rachael talks." Patronizing, she directed a look toward Rachael. "Little people —but big ears you know."

Barbara and Celica remained with Rachael. Barbara spoke.

"He'll pick up his things, leave the car to you, the title signed. Mind if I make us a drink? Where's it kept? In the kitchen?" Walking toward the kitchen, Barbara spoke over her shoulder. "He'll leave the car key and his last key to the house on the kitchen table. He would prefer you not be here, naturally. Oh, I've found some Scotch. You too Celica?"

"Yes, lightly."

Celica pulled Rachael to the small couch. "In case you don't want him here alone that night? We're offering to be here to support you. We've done those sort of things before, Rachael."

Barbara Griffith came into the living room with four drinks in bar-like cocktail glasses squeezed waitress-style between her two hands. She clanked them to the glass coffee table and picked one up. Rachael took one. Ruth took another. The fourth started an immediate ring on the glass.

Rachael broke down again, sobbing loudly, her gaze moving from one woman's face to the other. To Barbara: "You just don't understand."

"To Celica: "I have no money … Paul's fault."

Back to Barbara: "My brother has no money to help. Paul's fault too."

Ruth came back into the room with the two nieces. Rachael intercepted her gaze. "Paul won't help me. No one will help me."

Back to Barbara Griffith. "What am I going to do?"

No one spoke.

Within three minutes all four women had finished their drinks. Within three more minutes Celica Domansky and Ruth Thomason went out the door. Within two minutes Barbara Griffith had mixed two more Scotch and waters and was sitting on the couch next to Rachael, patting her hand and saying "there, there, there." Rachael Bristol Vincent pressed her face into Barbara Griffith's shoulder. Her lipstick marked the pale yellow collar edge

"I'm so lonely. I'm so hurt." She sobbed.

"I'm lonely too, Rachael."

Rachael leaned back, away from Barbara so as to see her face. "But, you're an officer's wife. You're smart. You're pretty."

"And I'm lonely too, Rachael. Very lonely."

The two women held one another, breathed whiskey breath into one another's faces and cried for several minutes. Angie and Rebecca watched, then went back to doll play. Angie fixed imaginary drinks, Rebecca passed out imaginary cigarettes. Within three minutes they were pressing two of the dolls together and mocking tears. "But you're pretty. But I'm lonely too."

The little girls were very pleased to be playing grownup.

CHAPTER SEVEN
No Kiss Goodbye

January, 13th, 1968, the night before Truaxe's early morning deployment to Vietnam, Paul was at the McCandless Street house. The overfilled leather suitcase and carry bag he set on the front porch had been Christmas gifts from Kurt and Cynthia three years earlier. He had told Rachael he'd won them in a shipboard raffle. She had smiled at how lucky he was. Guilt had tinged viscerally over the years of lies concealing his affair and the guilt was slow to wash away despite the turn of events. The lying days were over, but the lies in both directions had hurt the basic trust of the marriage. He thought of Selesky's saying: 'show me a liar, you'll also see a cheat and a thief.' I've already lied and cheated, he thought. When will I steal?

He stepped back into the empty house to telephone for a taxi and with two solid rather final snapping sounds, flipped the car and house keys to the kitchen counter. He took one last look around. Rachael insisted that playing the radio constantly was one way to make a robber think someone was at home. Nat Cole's peaceful tones filled the living room with a promise often made, often broken. "*When I fall in love—it will be forever …*" Paul choked back a surprising shot of sadness tears.

He shook his head, checked the back bathroom for an old shaver that might be better than his existing shaky *Norelco*, not there, and headed for the door.

Rachael, Ben, Bunny and a woman he didn't recognize were standing in the front doorway looking at him.

Rachael spoke. "Well, the non-husband sneakin' around the non-wife's house. Steal anything?" She'd clearly been drinking and the biting anger still gushed from their encounter on the ship. However, he was impressed by how little it impacted on him. Even her appearance fell flat. She had on a skin-tight blue wraparound dress with a plunging neckline that gapped open too much. A tired black purse hung from her shoulder and her blue shoes were slightly off color. Her makeup was too pronounced, her eyes glassy from drinking, her words raspy. He had once been pulled to any sound of hers but now her voice grated poisonously. He cringed, fearful she could slug up inside of him, feed on his insides, empty him and leave a hollow shell. His face displayed his repulsion. Hers turned stock white. They were immediately back to a thousand and one other nights of drunken exchanges.

"Let's not, Rachael. I was told you wouldn't be here." He headed for the doorway.

"By who? Sarah Barkley? She your new girl friend?" Her sneering voice imitated a spite-filled twelve year old. Then she changed approaches. "Just wait." She struggled to present sober but it wasn't working. "Just want ta' tell ya' one thing." Her head weaved just slightly. "See, 'm not, you know, yelling or anythin'." She had a look on her face he knew so well—'I have drunken things to say right now and your job is to stand there and pretend I am brilliant.' He hated the embarrassed feeling the scene caused front of the stranger. He turned to leave.

"Wait." Rachael called and took one step toward him. She stopped but her perfume reached him. She still wore *Moondrops* . 'Damn', he thought, 'I've tired of everything that is her.'

Ben stepped nearer, his eyes looking Paul over in detail. He stood beside Rachael but didn't speak. He looked the same as ever, like someone who just published a *robber's guide to major cities.* The off-green polyester double-knit suit had several snags down the left trouser leg. The jacket hung open, his belt was cracked around the buckle and he had dribbled something, not necessarily from dinner, down the green shirt-front. His burnt-red tie was draped over his left shoulder. His hair gushed out in all directions. He glared at Paul and he also seemed a bit unsteady from booze, or, considering being out on bail, from life.

Bunny stayed in the kitchen but she too peered directly at Paul, grinning in that way she did only when she'd been drinking. He had never disliked Bunny. Attractive but not real personable, she was sort of a hologram. To Paul, she always seemed unhappy, like a cat with new drapes but no claws to shred with. Abie's wife, Veronica referred to Bunny as 'a rose without perfume'. Overall, however, she was all right to be around and seemed to try to be a good mother. He could never understand what kept her with Ben. Bunny continued the hollow smile and actually waved a few fingers. Paul waved back without thinking. "Where the kids?"

"Overnight sitter."

The unknown woman stepped forward, smiling.

"Hello, Chief Vincent?" She spoke boldly, percussively, like a Bob Fossey musical number. She was dressed expensively but trendy in a short skirted navy blue suit with a white collarless blouse. Purse, shoes, earrings and some little stitching on the jacket all matched. Paul saw her as out of place with Ben and Rachael, a sort of 35 year old Ivy-League-take-charge-type on a mission of some sort. She had to be one of the officer's wives from the ship. He was very curious though. Interwoven with the Ivy League propriety was a feeling that if this woman invited you in for a drink, it would end up bed and breakfast.

"I am Barbara Griffith." She stepped three paces toward him, her hand outstretched. "I'm president of the Truaxe wives club, the ombudsman here to help Rachael through this unfortunate … " Paul instinctively reached his hand to meet hers. Before the fourth pace, the Ivy League facade gave way to reality. Barbara Griffith's drunken knees buckled. Her eyes rolled upward; her arms flailed; the purse flew. She fell against him with an air-lost grunt. Intuitively he grabbed for her but caught only her jacket. She banged her head against his hip-bone and slid down his front, dropping the last foot or so in free gravity. Her jacket slid off her arms and ended up in his hands. She smelled strongly of the saccharine presence of rum and coke.

Any favorable expectations he might have had for Barbara Griffith scattered like startled birds. The woman who was volunteering to mediate the separation and divorce had been out drinking with one of the teams. He felt tricked by the scheme.

"I'm out of here, Rachael." He said, and headed for the door.

"'Outta here'?" she mocked him. "You and your hippy talk. You're outta' here, ok?" She took two steps toward him and Paul thought she might attack him in some way with some weapon. Reading something in his face she stopped two feet from him. Barbara Griffith was upright again, steadied by Ben. She had a bruise growing on her cheekbone. Her expression was full Ivy League again. She spoke, ignoring she had just taken a drunken fall.

"Paul. May I call you Paul? Things don't have to be awkward." She pulled away from Ben's grasp. Her expression changed from Ivy League to one of surprise. She swallowed impulsively but belched openly. "Whoops! Sorry." She swallowed again and put a manicured hand to her throat. "Wooo. I usually don't drink much, (belch) but Ben has been so charming. I believe I have drank … (burp) drunk, too much. Tonight? Please understand?"

Paul was stony faced, staring directly at her eyes.

"Chief Vincent." Thrown by his glare, Barbara Griffith wavered and fought for lost composure. She smiled directly at his eyes. There was something fascinating and unexplored about her but Paul couldn't break through to it. She then turned her body nearly 180 degrees without moving her feet and was looking behind her to Ben and Rachael. She swung back toward Paul like a weighted door. "I've spent a lot of time with Rachael and Ben … " Her voice trailed off, then re-started, "Oh yes, with Bunny too." She repeated the body turning motion, this time peering hazy-headed toward Bunny who was still visible through the kitchen door. Bunny looked quickly away from the woman's gaze. Swinging back to face Paul, Ivy League continued.

"They're holding no ill feelings that you are divorcing. All they want is for everything to eventually iron out, so everyone has a better life."

"They? They? Am I divorcing a committee?"

"And we need money to come in … Tell him that." Rachael sounded like a child hiding behind a skirt hem.

"Oh yes!" Barbara continued. "Money should be understood before you leave tomorrow."

"I earn it, they use it? Is that what you mean by 'understood'?"

"For sure, Paulie." Ben ended his silence. "You owe Rachael for wife support."

Paul didn't respond.

"And in talking about money, Mr. Vincent." Barbara Griffith stepped inappropriately close to him, her face inches from his. Bad breath and bad manners combined in a belch. He backed away waving his hand as a fan.

"In case you didn't know …" Although Ivy League seemed to be picking each word carefully, most were slurred. " …though, I understand—Rachael has tol' you. I am the pershon', that, who gave, err loaned Ben and Rachael the, I might say, sorely needed, five thousand dollars. Now, Mr. Vincent. They tell me it has something to do with money that you owe people … (squelched belch) Right?" She didn't wait for an answer. "BUT …but, but—they said you have access to money and … " The astonished look on Paul's face locked her throat.

Paul's eyes caught Ben's until they held, then caught Rachael's. He looked toward Bunny who was in full tears standing in the kitchen doorway. His gaze held hers also.

"What the fuck is going on here?" Paul's voice was soft but with anger clearly close by. Barbara Griffith's head snapped upright as though hearing the 'F' word for the first time ever. She backed stumbling towards Ben. Ben put one arm around her waist.

Words began to tumble out of Ben's face. "Now you'll see the biggest liar in the world go into action, Barbie. Just watch. You'll understand why we had to leave this ...why I've had to help her all these years."

Paul spoke in a single unchanging tone. "Fuck you, Ben."

With a squeak from her voice, Rachael rose to the toes of her high heels and scurried down the hall toward her bedroom. Breaking into tears she bumped and scraped against the walls as she moved. Paul repressed a reaction to follow her.

After letting out a gasp of her own, Bunny ran after Rachael.

Ben Bristol stood still. He'd never seen that look dominate Paul's face. His drunken brain had been overanxious to impress Barbara Griffith, causing him to break a rule he had always suspected existed: "You can play around the edge of it, but *never* openly lie to or lie about Paul Vincent."

Rachael had run, Bunny followed, Ben looked fear-filled, and Barbara looked lost. Paul knew immediately what had been going on in his absence. They had somehow convinced Barbara Griffith that Ben was the backbone of the family, the man-in-charge around the household. Barbara Griffith was getting some sobering new information.

"What am I missing?" She asked, turning to Ben. "What's going on I don't know about?"

False bravado being better than no bravado at all, Ben continued his bluff. He ignored answering the question that would cause him trouble and addressed Paul directly. "Nothing to say, big shot?"

"Not to you, no-shot." Paul turned to Barbara and shook his head with disbelief. "You really don't know, do you?"

"Know? What don't I know?"

Paul broke the deception. "About Benny boy's arrest. The money they beat you out of, Mrs. Ombudsperson, went for B-B brain's bail."

Barbara Griffith seemed instantly sober. "B-B brain? Bail? Jail? Over what?" She turned to Ben. "Is this the truth?"

Ben Bristol had many faults but four major ones ruled his chaotic life. He failed to learn from past experience, had trouble understanding the present, thought everyone else had the same difficulty with reality as he did, and he believed any mess caused by one lie could be eliminated by another.

"Now you see what we've put up with, Barbara. Paul's crazy. Been protecting him for years. He sees a psychiatrist. Afraid if the navy found out, Rachael's life 'oud be ruin't. Now you see why she couldn't have a baby with him. He's too crazy."

"Ben's a piece of shit, Mrs. Griffith." The words came out of Paul more as factual information than to insult. Paul turned directly to face her but had enough sense to stay formal. "As for you, Mrs. Griffith. I'll not mention what I've seen here and I think I've seen plenty. But you be careful what you believe—*especially*, if you start making any kind of statement about me to my ship. You hear that well?"

"Don't threaten her." Ben demanded. "Or, or, I'll …take you out this second." Ben tried upholding the facade.

Ten years of Paul giving in ended that second. Reprisal suddenly seemed logical and very necessary. He covered the five paces to Ben's face in less than a second. Ben shoved Barbara Griffith into Paul and tried to turn and run. With his left hand, Paul caught Ben's right shoulder and jerked him spinning back toward face to face. Paul's right hand was flying before Ben's face had come all the way back around. Fist met forehead—"Thud"—and Ben dropped like a water filled balloon. Something also snapped inside Paul's fist but he took a quick breath and refused the pain.

Barbara Griffith made her second ungracious trip of the evening to the carpet, this time folding forward in a crumpled swoon.

"Rachael—Bunny—Get in here." Paul's voice was very commanding. Ben stirred on the floor. He raised to his hands and knees but stayed there, his head hung low, the premature bald spot in the rear center of his head showed clearly. Barbara Griffith moaned.

"Rachael—NOW!" Neither of the women had ever heard this commanding voice from Paul.

The two women appeared in the doorway. Rachael held a small automatic in her right hand. Paul saw it but he knew three steadying facts. Rachael didn't know how to load the thing. She didn't know how to cock it. She didn't know how to release the safety.

"Drop that now, God-dammit." His order carried a powerful conviction. Rachael became entranced. Bunny slapped at Rachael's hand. The gun fell to the carpet.

Ben dropped to the floor again and moaned. Paul motioned with his head that Bunny was to go to him. Barbara Griffith rolled over onto her back on the carpet and stared upward into Paul's face. She tried sitting up but became more glassy-eyed than ever. Relaxing backwards, her legs splayed, her skirt slid up. Her panties showed, white, cotton, clean looking.

She raised her head and actually spit at Paul. The spittle pitched halfway down her front and plopped at the beltline of her dark skirt. He reached to help her to her feet but she struggled against him, flailing one fist. Pulling on her one arm, he managed to slide her onto the living room couch. She sat there blank faced. The bruise on her cheek from the first fall now had a partner across her chin.

Paul stooped and picked up the automatic and yelled into the air. "NOW …" He said, and with practiced flicks insured the safety was on, pressed the release, caught the loaded magazine and slipped it into his pocket. He then jerked back the slide. There was no round in the chamber. "I'm outta' here," he finished

He turned. As he left, Ben was struggling to his feet with Bunny's help. Rachael was leaning against a wall, blankly gazing at him. The very baffled Barbara Griffith sat on the couch holding her fingers pressed into her disarranged hair.

He walked out of the front door. He heard Rachael's voice following him weakly. "Paul? Paul?"

"Don't feed the hand that bites you." He said clearly into the night air.

Paul grabbed his two bags from the porch and walked to the corner pay phone to call a taxi. His right hand would not close around the suitcase handle. As he fumbled for change and dialed a number, his body shook with a brief uncontrolled chill, a delayed reaction, he sensed, to the pistol held by the unsteady Rachael.

He telephoned the taxi number pasted in the booth then waited and paced in the cool night air. Nearly thirty minutes passed. His right hand was puffy across the fingers and behind the knuckles. He called the taxi number a second time and complained to an insincere voice. He waited another ten minutes. Just as his cab appeared, two forms came out of the house he had just left. It was Ben, with Barbara Griffith. They got into the car Paul had just returned for Rachael. He heard Ben's voice break the late night quiet.

"I'm just takin' the lady home, Bunny. Just go to bed." The doorway went dark at the house.

Paul slipped into the cab. "Follow that car, Cabbie."

The driver laughed aloud. "I've always wanted to do that."

They trailed Ben's erratic driving to a small motel twenty minutes north on Pacific Coast Highway under the noise of planes landing at San Diego's *Lindbergh Field.* Paul's driver darkened his cab and pulled across the street from the motel. They watched Ben enter the windowed registration office where he remained for several minutes. They watched Barbara Griffith in silhouette apply makeup and brush at her short dark hair. Ben returned, eased the car into a parking area and got out. He had a bottle in one hand. He opened Barbara's door. The two of them, arm and arm, kissing as they walked, entered room seven on the ground floor. The lights went out inside the small room almost immediately. Paul instructed the driver to leave his lights out and park in the motel lot. As the Cabby parked three stalls away from Ben's car, Paul wondered; where does this woman keep her scratch pole? She is real troubled to be spending part of the night before her husband's ship deploys, fucking a man who lied to her, took her money under false pretenses, and was made a fool of in front of her. The fact she *was* spending part of the night with Bristol convinced him the woman, bottom line, could be real trouble if left off a leash.

'Wait here, Cabby," Paul said handing the man ten dollars. "If you drive away, I'll understand, but, I'm going to need a ride out of here in about five minutes."

"I'll wait."

Paul walked across the parking lot and into the motel office. He showed 67 year old Billy Brand both of his hands. Paul had the 32 automatic, now loaded, in one hand and two twenty dollars bills in the other. "Take me to room seven."

Billy Brand had retired from the navy enough years ago and worked in the hotbed motel business long enough to know harmless trouble from real trouble. The jerk of a man with the black eyes he'd let into room seven a bit ago seemed like harmless trouble. The two twenty dollar bills seemed like harmless trouble. The thirty-two seemed like real trouble. Billy Brand took the two twenty dollar bills from Paul. "I'll walk with ya'," he said. "That way I'll not loose my keys to ya'."

"Okay." Paul followed Billy Brandt outside and the several yards to room seven. As Billy held the key at the lock he asked Paul, "You t' shoot anyone?"

"No."

"Didn't think so." He unlocked the door. Paul stuck one hand in and took a chance at finding the light switch. It was there. Two shaded table lamps burst to life illuminating two very flushed bodies and two shocked frozen faces. Paul flicked the light switch on and off three times, then left it on. Stepping one pace into the room he kept the gun in plain view and leaned back outside of the motel doorway. "That's enough with the camera." He said into the air. "You get now." Billy Brandt, quick to see the play, turned and hurried off.

Paul turned back to the bedroom scene as both Ben and Barbara struggled with their clothes. He spoke directly to Barbara Griffith. "I hoped you'd have good sense, now I know you don't. I have photographs of you and needle-dick here fucking away. In one year from now, after I'm transferred from this ship or after your husband goes out of my life? I'll destroy the negatives. Do you have any questions about your part of this deal?"

Barbara Griffith wouldn't look at him but instead sat frozen on the edge of the dingy bed, her eyes covered with both hands. Bristol's hands were actually shaking as he buttoned his shirt and connected his worn belt.

"Last chance, Mrs. G." Paul said. "This is my career here. I will do whatever I have to do to stop this malicious bullshit, including show the pictures to my Captain, and to your husband."

"There won't be any trouble, Paul." Ben said. "She won't say anything to her husband, right Barbie?"

"No." Barbara said quietly. "I won't say anything." Paul walked away.

"Where to?" The cabby asked. Still worried, Paul decided to watch the motel for a while. He wondered if what he had done would be effective. The driver left the lot but parked barely out of sight in a shadow. He tuned to soft music. Within twenty minutes, a taxi pulled into the motel. Barbara Griffith walked from room seven toward the cab. Ben stood at the door of the room. "Barbara, wait now. No use bein' like this." Without looking back she left in the taxi.

"Well." Paul said aloud. "Let's go back south. Naval station."

"That driver will report his destination over the radio in a minute." Paul's driver volunteered.

"No matter." Paul said. A few minutes into the ride Barbara's cab reported heading for a Coronado address.

"You want I should write it down?" The driver asked.

"Not really." Paul said. Coronado was enough for him to know she was likely headed home to Commander Griffith.

"You got that; leavin' tomorra' look, Chief. Are you?" The driver asked.

"Yes, we leave tomorrow."

"I got outta' the Nav 2 year ago. Engineman. You goin' ta' Yankee Station?"

"Likely."

"Been there. Done that. G'luck."

Once aboard ship that night, his fist thumping pain, Paul headed toward his quarters. It was 11:05 p.m.

Once in his bunk he found that while his body slept, his brain would not. Electric dreams flashed the faces of Rachael, Cynthia, Commander and Barbara Griffith, Ben and Bunny, all the players in the drama that his life had become. The faces mixed and flashed against jungle grass and trees and the smells of hot wet soil and air. Yes, they were all going to Vietnam with him.

CHAPTER EIGHT
Baby Killers

At 0700 the morning of January, 14th, 1968, Paul Vincent was having his right fist wrapped in a plastic splint-like bandage that wound from mid-arm to fingertips. When the corpsman started fitting a sling into place, Paul stepped back.

"Is this overkill?"

Chief Corpsman Frank Bellefontaine leaned his head forward and popped the roll of tape with his teeth. "Hell of a lot of blood under there. Just playin' safe. If we wasn't gettin' underway I'd shoot you over to the dispensary for x-rays."

"Overkill."

"Not over-fuckin'-kill. You'll maybe wear this as long as a year. You're dumber than an armpit to not wake me last night or go to the Naval Hospital at Balboa. May have a broke Trapezium or Pisiform." Looking disgusted with his friend, Bellefontaine spun away on his stainless steel stool and got busy straightening up. "Do the daily soaks I'll line up. At best, this hand is going to be about as effective as a marshmallow bullet for some time coming."

"Let me try it without the sling for a day or so. Paul asked.

"Look, if you've punched someone, you've macho-ed yourself into some serious trouble, hand wise." He said smoothing the last of the tape into place. "Let's look at it everyday and do some soaks, more so when it starts hurting."

Bellefontaine slipped off his stainless steel stool and finished stowing away the things he'd used on Vincent's hand. Vincent pulled his right shirtsleeve back into place and tried flexing his fingers.

"Ouch! I really did it, huh, Frank?"

Bellefontaine looked back over his shoulder. "Look, you're thirty-three, yer' not 'vincible. Who'd you hit, anyway?"

"Some other Chief Corpsman who wasn't telling me what I wanted to hear."

"Oh."

Twenty minutes later, without fanfare, Truaxe set sail from the 32nd Street San Diego Naval Station and eased slowly into the bay and under the graceful curves of the practically completed arching bridge from mainland San Diego to the small city of Coronado on what was called North Island. They left two men on the pier that would miss their presence for sure: Fred, from the *Meal a Minute Canteen Service*, and Alfonse from the *Fleet's Ready Dry Cleaners*. They also left ninety watery-eyed wives and children waving from the concrete of pier four.

Paul stood in the crisp air on the signal bridge and watched the people fade into his distance. He turned away and into a practiced mindset for sailors, the letting go of home, hopefully to focus on the trip.

Looking forward and aft on the now familiar decks of Truaxe, he could see several men in their dress blue uniforms standing alone or in groups of three and four, watching the shore go by. Abie walked up to Paul and addressed that mixed message that comes with being in the navy and going to sea.

"Why does this feel so good and so bad at the same time?" Not waiting for an answer, he turned directly to Paul and asked a new question: "What you thinkin' of?"

"I'm thinkin' maybe the wrong person across from you at breakfast is better than no person at all."

"You're harder to follow than a ballot proposal. Let go o' that woman."

"At least you had breakfast with Veronica. She's waiting for you to come back."

"Yeah, I had breakfast all right. Bran flakes."

"But it was *your* wife, *your* bran flakes."

"Bran flakes aren't yours, you jes' rent 'em."

Abie genuflected over-graciously, left Paul's side and went below to take care of the bran flakes. Vincent stayed on the bridge and watched the San Diego business district slip by to starboard. They gradually passed the Broadway pier at the foot of downtown and within a minute were alongside the one hundred year old museum tall ship, *Star of India,* the city's tribute to man's history and accomplishments at sea. It lay moored in lapping water at the foot of Ash Street. Paul exchanged waves with an old man who stood on the bow of the *Star.* The apparently ancient mariner held a pipe in his teeth and nodded slowly over and over toward Paul's eyes, as though comparing eras. Truaxe, steel hulled, aluminum decks and masts rumbling confidently and defiantly to the sea under nuclear power. The *Star of India,* iron hulled, wooden decks and masts, laboring once a year to sea straining under canvas. Master Chief Vincent turned to a signalman manning a signal light.

"A hundred years from now, B-Buck, you think Truaxe'll be moored like that as a tribute to man's history and accomplishments at sea?"

"Huh?"

As Truaxe passed Lindberg Field National Airport, Paul got just a glance between buildings of the Ben and Barbara Griffith motel. Further past the Naval Training Center, fishermen and women waved from the rough gray rocks of restaurant row on man-made Shelter Island. From the port side of the ship, from the seaplane ramp at the North Island Air Station, the roar of three double-ended helicopters lifted off heading south to Ream Field in nearby Imperial Beach. The noise made normal conversation impossible.

"Imagine having a ship-full of those noisy bastards?"

"What?"

"IMAGINE HAVING A SHIPFULL OF THOSE NOISY BASTARDS?"

"CAN'T HEAR YOU, THOSE BASTARDS ARE TOO NOISY."

"Right."

As the three helos headed south and over the Hotel Dell Coronado, the sun burned through the morning haze.

"Left standard rudder."

Clifford turned toward open sea and increased speed to nine knots. Passing the submarine base at Ballast Point, two of the black nuclear bulks dipped their colors to half-mast and immediately to the top again, an early morning salute and a bid for good luck. Captain Clifford, Griffith, Paul Vincent, the lookouts, the OOD, and others on the bridge rendered a salute in return to the sub's traditional recognition. It was navy doing navy that morning.

The military dead in the Fort Rosecrans National Cemetery and the life saving Point Loma Lighthouse appeared on the ship's starboard side as they neared the breakwater buoys.

"Secure sea detail, Mr. Griffith. Set the regular steaming watch."

"Aye, aye, Sir."

At the breakwater, about twenty sailboats were lined up as though waiting for Truaxe to come by. Some had out drag anchors, others had their sails dropped, flapping uselessly. Some Truaxe sailors anticipated a civilian fare-thee-well of some sort. Others knew better.

"Here it comes." Clifford said. "Pass the word on the phones—no reaction to this."

"Aye, aye, Sir."

As Truaxe drew even with the first two boats, two large banners were hoisted, one on a mast, the other spread between two of the boats. Any expected exchange of good-natured waves was quickly altered as a volley of middle finger salutes and anti-war hoots defined the true purpose of the rag tag flotilla. One banner read "PEACE" in neat blocked letters. A second banner, recklessly spray painted red on white caught in the riggings. You could barely make out the word "MU-DER—S".

"Murderers?"

"Yeah, that's us ya' know."

A woman pulled a multi-colored tee-shirt off and waved it over her head, yelling something. Her bright orange bra top came off next, her breasts shaking in the morning sun. Several binoculars were raised. One lookout reported—"nothin' special."

Barely intelligible words floated over the water, "Baby killers . . murderers ...baby burners ..." That surprised some of the naive, disappointed others, frustrated most, and dramatically disturbed some of the younger first timers. Following Clifford's order, however, all hands topside stood mute and motionless, keeping their feelings to themselves.

On impulse, Captain Clifford grabbed the topside P.A. microphone. "Attention to port." All hands topside faced the sailboats and stood at attention.

"Hand, salute." Clifford ordered. All hands snapped a salute in the direction of the sailboats. This was responded to by almost unanimous middle fingers from the boats, some stiff armed Hitler salutes, some crotch grabbing and at least two bare bottomed "moons."

Abie had just returned from his bran flakes duty and picked at his anti-war boss. "Doing their part for peace? Mr. Stumpf?"

"People handle their frustrations in different ways, Lake."

The dimly heard charges continued over the wind noises ... "baby killers" . . toward the ears of the Truaxe men. " ...murderers ...war mongers."

"At ease." Clifford announced. The men dropped their salute. Many went immediately below decks.

Almost past the small flotilla, Clifford's tension was too much. His face reddened as he spun around and jerked his ball cap from his head. "Jesus, who the fuck we fightin' for?"

"Let it go, Cap'n." Commander Valentino's calming message didn't take.

"Are they really not aware we are trying to be ...to be ...leaders ...of a worldwide battle against communism? For some sense of freedom?"

"Bob Dylan tells them, 'never follow leaders' ... Cap'n." Stumpf offered.

"Who the hell is Bob Dylan?" No one answered. He turned to Stump. "Okay Mr. Under Thirty ...who the hell is Bob Dylan?"

Stumpf summed up the frustration with one clear sentence. "One of *their* leaders, Captain."

Clifford starred into Stumpf's blank expression, turned his head but not his eyes toward the OOD and displayed his lack of frustration tolerance.

"All ahead flank."

The quickly answered engine bell kicked Truaxe rapidly toward thirty-eight knots, a speed highly illegal in this part of the bay entrance. The increased torque plowed a formidable wave behind the ship. Clifford turned his gaze from Stumpf's to the sailboat row. The boaters saw the wave coming and waited helplessly. Some grabbed lifelines, life jackets and one another. A twelve-foot wall of water heaved into the group of boats and sent them hurling, bobbing and pitching. At least three bearded and long haired men who tried to stick it out cross armed and stiff legged, were pitched off their boats. One boat overturned in the 56 degree water.

"There's a 'finger' for you, fuckin' hippy jerks." Clifford yelled, but his words were lost to wind noises.

Commander Valentino held his glasses on the scene. "I see three life jackets come up from that overturn, Cap'n. There's another."

"Long haired bastards." Clifford spoke through clenched teeth.

"Two boats alongside them now, Cap'n. They okay, looks like. We'll hear about this one."

"Got hair roots for brains." Clifford persisted. No one on the bridge looked at the Captain. Most looked away from the sailboats. A few faint cheers made their way to the bridge from elsewhere on the ship. A few boos also floated in.

Clifford placed his hands firmly on his hips, looked off to the starboard, west, and spoke into the air. "Slow to standard speed, OOD. Make course 270." Everyone seemed to wait and watch as the ship slowed and the bow turned away from the sailboat mess now lost in the sun's glare on the choppy water behind the ship. Shadows of its own superstructure fell onto the open bridge as the ship settled on its course toward Hawaii. It was suddenly chilly on the bridge.

The Captain spoke again, but quietly this time. "Mr. Griffith, I want all department heads, division officers and the Master Chief in the wardroom in fifteen minutes. Officers on watch, excluded."

"Purpose, Cap'n?"

"Training meeting, what else? Those assholes just shot morale to hell and we gotta' do somethin' right."

Overhearing the comment, Mr. Stumpf spoke up. "They were just protesting, Cap'n, against the war." He sounded whiny.

"They should support the serviceman."

"They do, they've friends in the war …it's the war they hate, not the men in it."

"Come along and fight it then. Protest somewhere else, get a job …"

" … You think they're wrong to protest?" Stumpf's face looked flushed.

Clifford stopped his momentum for a moment and squared in front of Mr. Stumpf. "Dammed right they're wrong, Mr. Stumpf. Damned right, they are wrong. I know it."

Stumpf's face became redder. "If someone's against a war …and we won't let them peacefully protest." He put his hands to his hips, spun, walked away and remarked back over his shoulder. "What the hell they supposed to do? Start a war over it?"

Clifford looked at his Communication Officer's back, glanced back into the glare around the protest boats, kicked a toe lightly against a stanchion then looked out over the bow toward the west. "Go below, Mr. Stumpf, okay?"

"Aye, Aye, Sir."

CHAPTER NINE
I Am the Captain of the Ship

Pardon Me, My Training Slipped"

Over two thirds of the officers entering the meeting asked Vincent who he'd hit. He ran out of smiling answers and moved the splinted hand out of sight.

"Did you get the diary out, Mr. Beauford? All 280 aboard? 22 officers? 19 Chiefs?" Clifford never forgot numbers.

"Mailed just before sailing, Captain, all aboard."

Ensign Sycyckp, a crew cut burly-armed large-chested athlete of a man, who the crew secretly called Ensign Suckup, leaned into Chief Vincent. "What's the diary?"

"A ship gets underway, S.O.P. they mail a report, a dairy. Anyone received, transferred, or over the hill since the last diary, goes into a computer in San Diego. If we sink, the navy knows who went down."

"Oh joy."

Captain Clifford shifted some papers and looked about. Nodding to his Master Chief he asked with unofficial seriousness: "Who you hit?"

"Root brained hippy, Cap'n." Clifford smiled. Even Paul Vincent knew which side his bread was buttered on.

Addressing all present, Clifford then made three quick comments: "We rendezvous with Ed Gibbons' Kittyhawk in three hours. Because of the training, it'll take six days to Hawaii. I hold everyone personally responsible that all goes well. Any questions?"

All questions stayed behind protective masks. He turned the meeting over to Lieutenant Hicks, the Training Officer.

"Tomorrow's plan of the day lists times per exercise. Lieutenant Commander Corrigan? Please have the helo ready for replenishment exercises and for rescue at sea drills, 0740. All OOD watchstanders will make at least four approaches to a body-buoy … "

"If you need a real body, I have a man I can spare," a standard quip.

The exec spoke up quietly. "We're lucky to have Kittyhawk. Captain Gibbons is doing us a big favor. This opportunity has fallen in our lap … "

Clifford boomed in. "An I don't like it necessarily. Nothin' falls in your lap that you eventually don't have to have dry cleaned." No one laughed. "So, look good out there. I don't want Kittyhawk sailors seein' us as a bunch of god-damned weekend recruits sailing an out of sync half-sunk whaleboat around some bum-fuck reservoir. Ya' hear?" The exec winced at Clifford's vulgarities and took that unofficial summary as a signal to adjourn the meeting.

From that moment on, Clifford was involved in and micro managing every aspect of the ship's routine and of the exercises. He was either in his observer's chair on the starboard corner of the bridge wing, monitoring a scope in CIC, on the main deck close to the drill scene, in his 'sea cabin' adjacent to the pilot house and CIC or, at the furthermost, only seconds away from giving his attention to whatever was happening at the scene of the drill. If it was an engineering drill he was on the boiler flat, a communication drill, he was in radio central. On the two occasions where they fired five inch anti-aircraft rounds at target sleeves towed by Kittyhawk planes, he was in the gun mounts monitoring the skill levels. On one of the four Surface-to-Air missile shoots he was so close to the launcher he embarrassed himself by singeing his eyebrows, lashes and the hair on his arms. The blonde eyebrows were hardly missed but the beet red face lasted well into the third day, reminding everyone of the error in judgment at the highest level.

The navy leadership rule, "praise in public, criticize in private" was somehow reversed in Clifford's order of authority. During the many man-overboard drills to recover a body-buoy, Clifford, sun glasses in place and hat pulled low watched his OOD's try to learn. The words he used for encouragement caused sweat rings to appear under many armpits.

"Too much rudder, *AGAIN*, Mr. Stumpf."

"Mr. Lukarmo? What you been smokin'? You ran over him—you've killed him." Pieces and chunks of the home-made body floated to the surface aft of the ship, having been chopped by the spinning screws.

Another attempt. "That poor soul just changed water wings for real wings. Didn't he?"

Another attempt. "I can only tread water a day or so. Don't look like no rescue today, Mr. Dougherty."

Clifford had never served aboard a combat ship equipped with a helicopter deck and he proved to be a bit shy of the roar and rattle that comes with that new territory. He disliked that the pilot of the Kaman Seasprite wasn't a solid naval officer, continuing the rivalry and envy seemingly ever-present between combat ship sailors and naval aviators. He complained to Lieutenant Commander Corrigan, the helo control officer.

"That Lieutenant DiNoble? That pilot? I jus' don't like his attitude. He's a kid. He's got an appetite for excitement that he feeds with MY helo."

"He seems like a good enough and serious pilot ...his men like him."

"Yeah-but-yeah-but ... He takes a mile before I even given him an inch."

DiNoble and his gunner's mate, Randy Hill, and two mechanics, Murchie and Novack would tense Clifford's jaws when they repeatedly called him "boss" instead of "Captain" and by referring to Truaxe as a boat instead of a ship.

During the helo's takeoffs and landings Clifford seemed to be most animated. Without ceremony he would yell his anxiety over the ship's topside P.A. system.

"Now stay away from those rotors. I want no headless sailors on my ship." Next landing. "This ain't Disneyland. Get those spectators below decks. A ball of fire if that thing goes in." Next takeoff. "If that helo buys the farm, busted blades'll kill everyone within sight or hearing. Now, git' below."

Or he would caution DiNoble over the air-tac radio circuit whenever the weather was even slightly threatening. "It's pretty dark, the light's glare. This's a little target now Lieutenant, don't be in a hurry to get here." On a windy afternoon; "The wind's blowing like its looking for someone it can't find. And there's rain clouds backed up like planes at O'Hare. Now if you wanna' make that big landing deck on Kittyhawk 'stead of landin' here ...you just go right ahead and do that."

Never knowing when Clifford might appear, the crew started referring to him as 'the shadow'.

"I was at a urinal when the ship took a big roll to port?" Said Ensign Lasky at lunch, "And there was The Shadow, eyes like blue-marbles: 'Take a good aim there, Ensign, take a good aim'."

Data Systems Technician Second Class Foley: "I'm all alone …so I thought. Just finished over two dozen meter-checks inside the computer? Wasn't seein' what I wanted so I started them over again? This voice from behind me scares shit out'ta me. 'When at first you don't succeed there, Foley …go go again?'—It was the Shadow."

Just before turning in each night, Clifford would make a written statement in his Night Order Book, the traditional directory used to remind OOD's of scheduled course and speed changes: "When in doubt about anything, call me right away," he penned in sloppy cursive.

During daylight, any time he left the bridge proper, he would remind the OOD in a firm tone, "Remember, Officer of the Deck, I am always on call."

By the end of the first day's drills the word had spread on Clifford's renewed interest. It inspired the crew to try harder. Paul and Abie noted the change.

"He's outta' his lazy state, Chief."

"He's simply showing us he's a good skipper."

"The early bird gets the worm?"

"Sorta' like that."

"Well, the second mouse gets the cheese."

"I like the early worm remark better."

"An inch worm tryin' to be a foot worm?"

"Shut, Abie."

"Shut what?"

" Shut UP. That's what."

"If you mean 'shut up', say 'shut up, Mr. Boss even though thas' not too polite."

"Shut, Abie." Paul repeated.

"Well, if you wanna' say 'shut' instead of 'please be quiet, Mr. Lake', after all, you are the Master Chief, and I guess. . "

"For Christ's sake, Abie … Shut the fuck up." Paul bleated.

"Now that's a 'shut' I can understand, Boss." Abie replied seemingly very pleased with himself.

In the morning of the second day, Vincent was called topside to a bright and sunlit bridge. Lieutenant Commander Dominic Valentino was on the bridge wing with Captain Clifford, Commander Griffith and Lieutenant Stumpf. None were smiling. Valentino motioned Vincent to a corner.

A second-generation Italian from Boston, Valentino had none of the stereotyped exaggerated hype or extreme body language attributed to eastern seaboard Italians. He was the opposite; calm, straightforward, an accurate judge of personality and with a keen but not destructive sense of humor. Vincent liked the man who was also the kind of staff officer admirals looked for. A Henry Fonda movie type; cool, easy going, and never missing the details.

"Chief. Seems you're on to become a qualified conning officer, Captain's wishes." Valentino touched Paul's arm and looked left and right as someone might before offering privileged advice. "An' I say, go for it. Make your mother proud and when you park your yacht later in life, the boys at the Mission Bay Yacht Club'll buy you a drink. No?" Moving to where his back was toward the C.O. and X.O., he continued, quietly. "I just want to let you know there is not *complete* agreement about bringing you up here as OOD."

The comment renewed Vincent's memory of the late night argument between Griffith and the Captain he'd overheard in San Diego. "I believe I know part of this scrap already, Mr. Valentino."

"Listen, Chief." Valentino spoke softly. "Don't run from this. You do it. It'll be fine. It's just a bit of rivalry near the top." His eyes rolled slightly toward the other officers.

"I don't believe its just a bit o' rivalry." Vincent cautioned. "If there was a hall of fame for people who dislike Master Chiefs, especially me, Commander Griffith would be their honor guard."

Leaning toward Paul and taking any sign of a smile from his face, Valentino said, frankly. "Look at this. We are short two OOD's. Me, Corrigan, and the exec are standing the watches, four hours on, eight off and I'm doubled up 'cause I'm up here navigating evening and morning stars and LORAN positions. Mr. Stumpf is breaking in and so are you. First one qualified relieves the exec per protocol. I still get to do four on eight off. Next one qualified puts the rest of us in a neat four section watch, four on, twelve off. Want me as a friend?"

"I have no argument against helping, Commander. I just don't trust …"

"Hey, you're smarter than half the wardroom people. The Cap'n is pushing you for a commission. Quit the shit. Step into officer's country."

Though roundabout and spoken softly, it was an order.

"When do I begin?"

"It's already certified you're a qualified OOD, leftover from that mine sweep. You've only to become familiar with the Truaxe book."

"I've studied it already."

"Well, shouldn't be too difficult." A subdued giggle cracked in his voice. "Mr. Stumpf is doing it." Vincent's nervousness about moving into the ship's family of OOD's remained on his face.

"C'mon Chief, lighten up. This is a long trip just starting." Valentino turned mischievous, complete with open grin. "If you really don't want the OOD job—just ram this thing into Kittyhawk." He then poked Vincent's ribs lightly with an elbow. "Let me know ahead of time if you decide to do that—fair? My quarters are below the waterline."

Paul got in the last word: "Aye, aye, Sir."

One of Lieutenant-Commander James Corrigan's collateral duties was to stand his share of the OOD watch at sea. He was a 'mustang' officer, one who had worked his way from the enlisted ranks. Having been passed over twice for further advancement, sort of a signal to retire when ready, the rank of Lieutenant Commander was as high as Corrigan would reach. He was a hard working officer with twenty-eight years service, but like many mustangs, he begrudged enlisted men breaking into officer's territory without jumping through all the hoops he had. Underway Officer-of-the-Deck watches had always been considered officer's territory until recently as the navy looked for jobs for their Master Chief's, their cream of the enlisted stars.

At Captain Clifford's order, Corrigan reluctantly became Vincent's OOD instructor. The experienced man's juvenile-like resentment slipped through some of his instructions. During course change or engine order, he would comment openly: "When I do something, I want to always see you watching me." If Vincent had a question, Corrigan would preface his answer with: "I answer only good questions. Don't waste my time with those bad ones."

For the first two days it took vigorous pushes by the C.O. before Corrigan gave Vincent fair opportunity to maneuver alongside an object in the sea or take Truaxe into a course to recover the helicopter or the ship's launch. Also, when Commander Griffith was on the bridge, it seemed Corrigan would find some petty errand to send Vincent on, to keep *him* off of the bridge.

Despite this lack of real cooperation or encouragement, Vincent still did quite well. By the third morning he discarded the hand splint, but too soon. Several times during the day he drew the hand back quickly from painful knocks and bumps.

"Thought this would be easy, Chief?"

Corrigan never seemed truly impressed with Vincent's progress even though by the sixth watch together there wasn't much left to show or tell. Vincent would suggest he take his own watch, but Corrigan refused to report enough progress to the exec for final approval.

For four days the business of training went all day and well into the night. If "iron men" were called for on wooden ships, as the old-navy saying goes, *smart* iron men were mandatory for Truaxe. The electronic equipment and the nuclear power plant demanded intelligence, education, specialized training and a lot of skilled time devoted to sophisticated maintenance and operation. Truaxe was still a ship of the line, however, one that also required ordinary and specialized seamanship skills. On non-nuke ships the navy crews divided into three factions. The 'deck apes' handle seamanship skills, the 'snipes' run the engines and machinery, and the 'bridge pussies' manage the electronics, navigation and communications. On nuclear ships, a fourth faction 'nuke babies' run the reactor plant.

Regular sailoring skills, line handling, manning guns, passing ammunition, transferring stores and food, cooking, cleaning, boat handling, rigging, rust and corrosion control and any other manual labor tasks were considered deck ape jobs. Most bridge pussies, snipes and nuke babies looked down their noses at those jobs, and at the men who did them. These petty jealousies and prejudices were part of day-to-day interactions and spilled over into the rigorous parts of the training. It was going only fairly well.

While lessons *were* learned, many were learned the hard way. The bridge pussies, snipes, nukes and deck-apes were all eager, but most were unsure of themselves when it was necessary to cross into one another's worlds to cross-train or function in another faction area. The more experienced techs tried to fake their seamanship expertise and the more experienced deck apes pushed them to perform. The unfolding mish-mash of experience, resentment, disparate IQ's and on again off again levels of enthusiasm resulted in a standard new outburst pattern from Clifford. When anything went wrong, his already red face would deepen a shade, he'd smash his brimmed hat to the deck, or fling it to a far bulkhead, and scream: "Jesus fuckin Christ, really?"

There were two broken arms, two severe lacerations and uncountable bruises caused as men tried to man battle stations within Clifford's three minute limit. During a firefighting drill an inexperienced seaman charged a three-inch fire hose to full stream instead of fog position. The water force rammed an unwary technician's face against a piece of machinery knocking his right eye completely out of its socket.

Slam went the hat, cracking its black shiny bill. "Jesus fuckin Christ."

Lieutenant DiNoble flew the man to Kittyhawk for medical treatment.

A seaman named Don Malkin lost all four fingers of his right hand when a two hundred pound hatch slipped from a techs' grip and fell.

Slam went the hat, a piece of the bill flew into space. "Jesus fuckin' Christ."

Lieutenant DiNoble flew Malkin to Kittyhawk for medical treatment.

Foley, a Data-systems Technician second class was a man who refused to see himself as an egghead. He also refused to admit he didn't understand the basics behind block and tackle rigging for replenishment of stores. When a rig was swung between Kittyhawk and Truaxe to practice the transfer of sensitive ammunition, the second class got his foot caught in the eye of a line as it played swiftly out past a steel cleat welded to the deck. It severed his foot at the ankle.

Clifford's now dilapidated hat flew out of a doorway. "Jesus fuckin' Christ. Jesus, fuckin' Christ," was heard several times emanating from his sea cabin.

Lieutenant DiNoble flew Foley to Kittyhawk for medical treatment. The severed foot went with them in an ice wrapped plastic bag.

Salt water was known to cut through the dirt and produce a fluffy white mop within minutes when towed behind the ship on a piece of line. While he read a paper back book, a seaman deck ape tied six dragging mops to a thirty-foot whip antenna on the fantail. The mops flipped about, found one another, entwined and became a massive dead weight pulling on the antenna. It shorted a major transmitter to the sea, costing 20 hours of repair time and three thousand dollars for replacement parts.

"Jesus fuckin' Christ."

With three men flown to Kittyhawk, five more remaining aboard in molded casts or heavy bandages, Truaxe looked as though it had already been to the war.

Equipment also failed to live up to expectations.

The P.A. system barked: "Mr. Corrigan, come to the bridge."

Clifford waited, often chewing on his tongue, his battered hat barely balanced on the back of his head. "Mr. Corrigan, its just a fuckin' elevator. Why the hell can't we get ammunition from the magazines to the gun mounts?"

"Breakdown, Cap'n. Workin' on it."

Clifford walked to a small locker on the bridge, tossed his regular hat inside and retrieved a ball cap complete with gold Captain's 'scrambled eggs' embroidered on the brim. Talking to Mr. Corrigan, he fanned himself with the hat. "I don't see that elevator-fixing Gunner's Mate, what's-his-name ... ?

"McMartin, Cap'n"

"McMartin, right. He seems to just stand around and ...talk and lean on things."

"Well, Cap'n. We've discovered something. Sir, he's got ...alcoholic shakes. Didn't learn anything in that elevator maintenance school."

The ball cap sailed out over the side of the ship. "Jesus fuckin' Christ, we gonna' send him to Kittyhawk for AA meetings?" The question bounced off Corrigan's blank face. As he stuttered for a response, Clifford screamed: "Don't say 'yes' to that, for Chrissake. It's a freakin joke."

One of Commander *Griffith's* methods to motivate the crew was to publish a paragraph or so about training in each "plan of the day", the two page daily schedule of events that each crewmember is held responsible to read. One of Griffith's favorite catch phrases was to encourage "better training, better skills through *better man machine interface*". Lake summed it up after the fire hose accident.

"Sir, that man and machine sure interfaced okay. It cost him an eye ... "

Griffith did not see Lake's comment as amusing or informing.

Many interfaces with machines went wrong. A Mark Seven (MK-7) drill torpedo was launched to test control and targeting procedures. Mark Seven was the type of torpedo that once its batteries ran low, it surfaced and produced a bright orange balloon to signal its location so it could be retrieved, recharged and used another day. Late afternoon of the third day Lieutenant Stumpf was bringing Truaxe alongside to recover one of the hundred-thousand-dollar MK-7's. At first Clifford tried just to be a little advisory.

"Slow, Mr. Stumpf. Little right rudder, Mr. Stumpf."

Stumpf evaluated each suggestion too long before acting. The ship slowly loomed over the spent torpedo. Clifford moved in beside Stumpf, shifted from advisory to C.O., and fired suggestions at him. Under pressure, Stumpf became as skittish as a button-quail. Looking back and forth, side to side as though in a tennis match, he froze, but issued no engine or rudder commands.

Clifford screamed. "Right rudder. BACK THIS SHIP DOWN."

"Right rudder? BACK DOWN? Cap'n? Huh?"

The ship bumped the drill torpedo. "NO! NO!" The Mark Seven split a seam, "NO! NO!" filled with seawater, tipped and floated with point in the air for a few seconds "No! No! catch it." and then bubbled out of sight in three miles of dark ocean.

Clifford impulsively reached for his already sacrificed hat, didn't find one, snatched a ball cap from the nearest seaman lookout and sent it flying out over the ocean.

"Jesus, fuckin' Christ, Mr. Stumpf, really!"

Mr. Stumpf was told he was confined to his quarters until arrival Pearl Harbor.

The CIC air controllers had trouble intercepting Kittyhawk's 'attacking planes.'

"Mr. Lukarmo to the bridge." Bareheaded, Clifford tongue chewed and waited for the young CIC officer.

"Mr. Lukarmo? What the hell's wrong?"

"Well, Sir." Lukarmo unconsciously spun a ballpoint pen in his shirt pocket. "That new computer program uses different symbols than the men were trained with."

"So?"

A dark blue dot appeared on the pocket. "What used to be an attacking fighter symbol? That's now an incoming missile, a missile is now a weather balloon ...like that." The blue dot grew. "All different."

"They've changed the symbol program the week we deploy?"

"Well, no sir." He covered the inkblot with a fingertip. "Not exactly, sir. I misread something."

"Misread, Mr. Lukarmo?"

"We've been using the wrong, well ...you know." Lukarmo licked the blue dot from his finger tip.

"Jesus fuckin' Christ, Mr. Lukarmo." Everyone on the bridge put a protective hand to their hat.

Kittyhawk pilots delighted in sneaking in over and over with successful attacks on Truaxe. Lieutenant Lukarmo joined Mr. Stumpf in restriction to his quarters until the air controllers became more accomplished with the newer symbols.

"Jesus fuckin' Christ."

Previously ignored design flaws of Truaxe often came back into view like wrecking balls swinging on a crane. In order to replenish the reactor core every four years, there had to be a simple hoist access to the engine rooms. This was accomplished by the installation of huge screw in *Mason Jar*-like lids cut in the decks above the reactors. Rather typical shipboard interlocking expansion joints intended to stretch and relax as the ship rose and fell in waves were installed next to the jar lids, but they simply did not work. Senior Chief Hull Technician Baird explained it best to Clifford.

"Lookit' that expansion joint there, Cap'n. There it is, extended. Now, the ship takes a downhill run on this wave? . . hold on. There. See, not moving back. Just sits there, 'cept every once in a while it goes back."

"Just sits there. Doesn't go back."

"An' all this rainwater water on the deck? Supposed to run out through those scuppers over there?"

"Just sits there—doesn't run out."

"Yes. It swirls here in this little dip ... ."

"Through the jar lid ... .?"

"Into radio central and down into computer control and further into the nuke spaces."

A third ball cap spun out of his hand and over the side. "Jesus fuckin Christ."

"Yessir."

But Robert Clifford still had one eye on becoming an admiral. Admirals are supposed to make the navy function. If something is wrong, good officers fix it if they ever want to be an admiral. Complaining about anything would make any admiral look like he wasn't doing admiral real well. Do not look bad to the very admiral who was to recommend you for admiral. During the Truaxe shakedown cruises, especially the run around the horn where faults were to be observed and corrected, Clifford ignored many of them with a sincere sense he was making it easier for someone up the line. But, he accepted flaws neither his ship's budget nor his crew's experiences could manage.

The wrong seventeen-thousand dollar vent motors were installed throughout the ship's air conditioning and heating system. They had a basic blueprint flaw. Without any warning something in their design would let go and the vent fans would spin to run-away speed. Several broke free of their housings and flew into sleeping compartments or down passageways. One bounced off the computer in the CIC spaces and put aircraft control and coordination out of action for seventeen hours. In one case, a runaway fan ripped the uniform and several layers of skin from a night baker working in the main galley.

There was always seawater below decks because several topside hatches sprung their aluminum collars and lost watertight integrity. They were stuffed with rags during wet weather. Aluminum pins designed to hold steep topside ladders were rocked back and forth by daily use and by wave action. The aluminum wore through in ten to twelve days at sea. Steel pins used to replace them chewed away at the softer aluminum of the ladder frame. By the time Truaxe arrived in Pearl Harbor, most topside ladders had been replaced using the wood stored aboard that was intended for patching battle inflicted holes below the waterline.

With these built-in distortions, life went on aboard Truaxe.

In addition to breaking in as OOD, running the ship's communications center and all communication drills, Paul was required to spend additional time updating his Gunfire Support skills which he had been formally schooled on two years earlier. His year as skipper of a Swift Boat in the Mekong Delta put him ahead of the other bridge personnel identifying V.C. craft used to move troops and supplies up and down the Vietnamese coast. Clifford was pleased that Vincent had the skills. He ordered his Master Chief to school the lookouts and OOD's. It was difficult squeezing the instruction time in between regular duties, between everyone's watch obligation and the daily exercise schedule. Going without sleep, however, he managed six to eight hours a day until the trainees could quickly tell a Russian P4 aluminum hulled torpedo boat from the newer non radar reflecting wooden hulled P6's that the North Vietnamese were reported to be buying. With training video tapes and sketches he made, he helped the others learn to spot a fast attack *Shershen* class on a small 'OSA' hull with its four torpedo tubes instead of two. He was surprised the others had not already received that training somewhere along the line.

Each night right after eight o'clock reports, the captain held a wardroom meeting to check off the completed drills and to discuss readiness for the following day's schedule. Clifford, with his aptitude for numbers, was able to commit the complex drill numbers and schedule to memory and was impatient with anyone who couldn't do the same. The training officer took the worst beating.

"Dammit, Mr. Hicks. That C-121-C and D-313-EE was to be squeezed in at 1350 right after the E-303-EL and FL providing that 1020 helo exercise went off well." The chain-smoking man was right.

After five days of drill following drill, the crew cleaned up the ship, made ready for an executive officer's inspection and both Kittyhawk and Truaxe made course for Pearl Harbor now less than a day away. The chief got out of his men's way by retiring to his quarters to make a dent in the pile of training reports that seemed to have a life of their own.

Paul liked his quarters. Most Chief Petty Officers bunked in one of the two CPO quarters, nine Chief's forward, eight aft. Senior officers had their own rooms. Junior officers bunked two to a room while Ensigns, the most junior officers in the navy, bunked several together in what was called the J.O. bunkroom. When available, master chiefs' were permitted to use spare officer staterooms. As the only master chief on Truaxe, Paul had his own 8 by 10 foot room. That added some prestige to his position as senior enlisted man and also provided the privacy he had relished to get through the troubled divorcing days.

This afternoon, upon entering his quarters, he did something he'd been delaying. He replaced the smiling 8 by 10 photo of Rachael with a smaller one of Cynthia. The move resulted in a sort of empty feeling.

After the few days and nights aboard the ship, despite the hard work and drills, or because of them, a feeling of change was setting in over Paul. He'd smile more often, aware of things he hadn't permitted time for in nearly two years. He got caught up in small details of life again. He once said to Abie:

"I'm experiencing a …a poetic-like re-discovery of the world around me".

"A what? What the Hell you smokin'?"

He'd walk topside after dark just to be alone in the warmer breezes and smell the tang of heavy salted air. He saw order in the guy wires, antenna and masts silhouetted against the stars or moon. During the day he could appreciate again the uncontrollable eternal movement of waves, the swoop of gulls against the wind and when further at sea, of albatross flying for hours bare inches above the waves. He actually tried sketching again, something he'd given up when he'd married.

Lake offered his critique. "Looks like the pitchas' people with kids puts on the front of their 'frigerators."

"Quit, Abie. It's campy and it beats the shit out of depression."

"I ain't sayin' nothing to no Master Chief, friend or not, who I catch standing topside sketchin' or in the dark singin' selections from *Kingston Trio's Greatest Hits."*

Paul even tried to quit smoking but that lasted only forty-five hours.

Not two minutes after the word was passed that the executive officer's inspection had been completed, Paul was ordered by telephone to report immediately to Commander Griffith's office.

He entered with hat in hand.

Griffith motioned with a chrome letter opener that he should take a seat in front of his desk. His baritone was somewhat softened. "Master Chief. We should talk."

"Yes, Sir."

"Informally, perhaps." He ran the letter opener back and forth across the palm of his right hand, seemed to see his reflection in it and brought it close to his eyes.

"Yes, Sir?"

Griffith reached into a top drawer and pulled out a small mirror. Leaving the conversation hanging he inspected something barely perceptible in the crook where the flare of his nose met his face. He flicked with one fingernail at whatever it was that distracted him, tossed the mirror back into the drawer and again fidgeted with the opener, still watching his reflection. "Something isn't right in your life right now. Correct, Chief?"

"Pardon?" Had Barbara Griffith been talking?

"Listen to me." He tossed the opener to the desk and picked up a yellow pad, flipped some pages overleaf and spoke without looking at Vincent. "This was my first in-depth inspection since leaving Norfolk. This ship isn't clean, well maintained nor sharp. Except the nuke spaces. I was counting on you as a leader to keep the over-all levels on this ship higher. High as I would expect from any Master Chief. I'm *very* disappointed in you. Pinups everywhere, the tattoos, the books."

"Tattoos? Books?"

"An' radios on rock music, also. Those Rolling Stoners concert tapes?""

Vincent didn't reply.

"Yes, tapes." He picked up a pencil and launched into a story which, when being retold to Mr. Stumpf, Vincent could only recall bits and pieces of: "This awful music shrieking in the background, I opened their lockers and was hit in the face ...pictures of women naked as jay-hawks ...reminding me of raw steak sandwiches ...immoral values ...aspersion of the dignity of the image of young women ...and TATTOOS, on the men's arms, backs. You know. 'Death before dishonor'. 'Hard-fast'. Tattoos." He seemed very calm but he talked rapidly. "We must use logic here, Chief. You and I know anyone who gets one of those blue lined exploding naked girl pictures on his arm ...will regret it later on. Hate the navy for letting it happen. You see my point?"

"All respect, Sir. But I'm not ...aren't you trying to get the world to look your way ...in some way?"

"Trying to do right. The right thing."

"I can't always tell the difference, Commander ... " Vincent's fingers got busy throwing little quote marks in the air, " ...between the, 'right thing', and, 'none of my business'."

Griffith's expression grew very resolved. "Well you better well learn." He followed the comment by mimicking one of Clifford's eye-locked stare-downs.

Representing, defending or accounting for his men was not an unfamiliar role for Vincent. By happenstance and because he'd moved up in rank so quickly, he'd been in charge of divisions of sailors since he was just over twenty-one. Under these circumstances he knew his best position was to lay back and let the complaining officer dump as much of the issue as possible. The goal? To get it to all go away.

After Vincent agreed to see to it that all pinups would be removed from anywhere on the ship, and further insure that all personal radios which were tuned to rock or anti-war music would be confiscated and that no more novels would be seen sticking out of the back pockets of any man on board, Griffith seemed to relax some.

"I can't have my Master Chief not be interested in the control of morals, a code of conduct."

Navy regulations hold several paragraphs on morals and conduct. The navy defines lewdness quite clearly and lists expected values and expected sexual behavior of all men and women. Regulations aside, generally speaking, free expression by the use of pinups and tattoos is permitted in most quarters. Navy moral standards do not get real tough until someone and someone else actually begins what might be described as an in-depth sharing of body parts, whether hetero or homosexual, although the navy pretended (circa 1968) homosexuality has never existed over any water, anyplace, at any time.

Lieutenant Stumpf said it best one night during conversation in Paul's quarters. "Griffith and those like him? They interpret the filamentary threads of regulations and add thick ropes of their own beliefs, and erase any effectiveness."

"How'so?"

"Chief, no one wants to be put on report for petty violations. Hard working men are distracted from duties by having to be alert to the whims of the misdirected and not always so well meaning Griffiths. Remember Fleck, in Argentina? He couldn't get to that antenna maintenance you needed? The exec had him, and me, writing that dammed report on swearing."

"Oh yeah. On the impact of vulgar language …on morale?"

"Right. He heard Fleck tell Anderson to 'get the fuck outta' his way'? It took me and Fleck two fucking hours to write the fucking thing, and then. And then, Griffith circled spelling on Fleck's report."

When Vincent refocused, Griffith was saying something about the OOD watches.

" …if it wasn't for your personal life and now this new lax moral leadership." He stalled for a few seconds by looking away. " … I *might* just accept Mr. Corrigan's opinion that you are ready to be trusted. But no."

So, Vincent thought, it *is* personal. "Lax moral leadership we've covered, Commander. But, my personal life? Not clear."

"Your marriage. We all know you're getting a divorce." Griffith's face reflected an annoyed look, annoyed over patronizing this very senior enlisted man. "Rumor of scandal. Rumors are, pretty good on the ship."

"I have no idea what you're talking about …'scandal'."

"You're our …my, most senior enlisted man … " He started having trouble looking at Vincent. He dropped the yellow pad and picked up the letter opener again. "Something that distracts from character. Your divorce." He said the word 'divorce' as some describe a perverse act. He stood and yelled a loud statement. "GOOD MEN DON'T ABANDON THEIR WOMEN." He seemed to catch himself out of character. His voice quieted several decibels. He sat back down, began tapping with the opener. "This isn't a south sea island where women are property, to be misused …left alongside a highway."

A shooting pain abruptly distracted Paul. He'd been anxiously flexing and squeezing the injured hand since he'd entered the room. He purposefully relaxed the throbbing fingers and knuckles. The distracting pain lessened just slightly. Griffith was still talking.

" …so we're …afraid to have you as OOD."

"I see 'scandal' as a powerful word for a divorce, Commander" Paul said evenly. "Scandal? I haven't killed anyone. Who is saying what to you?" Paul shopped cautiously. Griffith stumbled for words. As Paul waited, he visualized the drunken Mrs. Griffith with Ben in the no-tell-motel, the clean white panties on the un-vacuumed floor, a lingering smell of yesterday's bodies, her legs in the air illuminated by headlights of cars on Pacific Highway and the flicking of the bogus flashbulb bedside lamp. Had Ben given Barbara even more misinformation after their night in the sack? Had Barbara told her husband of her drunken jaunt to the motel, as a vengeful attack of some kind? Should he ask Griffith outright if he knew his wife was a drunk who slept with someone who carried a card with him to tell what to do at an intersection regarding red or green?

Where was Selesky when he needed objectivity?

Griffith was finishing a statement. " …so, I don't miss much on my ship, Chief. Never mind how I learn things."

"But you believe I miss a lot, Commander?"

"Suit yourself on that, Chief." Griffith said, dropped the opener, grabbed at it but it slipped to the deck. He let it go.

Vincent now watched a personal ruckus of in-fighting click from view to view like a rotating kaleidoscope. Clifford's wish for him to be an OOD. Click. Griffith's early fight with Clifford over that subject. Click. Corrigan first acting crummy to train Vincent but eventually recommending him as qualified. Was that Clifford pressure? Click. Or his true judgment? Click. Anti-Griffith? Click. Griffith not accepting him as qualified, and blaming morals. Click. Calling a scandal over Vincent's divorce while his own wife was screwing Ben Bristol even though she knew Ben to be a liar. Click. Did Griffith know? Click. Barbara Griffith's five-thousand dollars to Ben. Click. Likely Griffith's money. Click. Again, does he know? Click. There had to be more to eventually come into view, so he backed off to await more information.

"Listen, Chief … Master Chief. This navy's important to me. I take it further than a lot of you people do. I'm aware of your divorce but I'm also aware you've got some kind of an in with Captain Clifford."

"Pardon?"

"He overlooks your deficits. He believes you're officer material but I don't see it." Griffith spouted opinion as though it were factual data, uncaring how he might impact on Vincent's sense of self. "You're not the officer material I am, or Commander Deiter is, Lieutenant Commander Valentino, Lieutenant Commander Corrigan even. Like Mr. Stumpf's not officer material …nor Mr. Lukarmo …you see?" Griffith was out of line with such personal opinion statements made to an enlisted man.

"I believe the Cap'n simply wants me to relieve the load as OOD, Sir. Not take over the navy."

"Wait now. I don't mind that he and I see things differently. He is the Captain. I'm not. But …mind you. I will be one day."

Click. "I'm sure you will be, Commander." Paul patronized and checked his watch."

Griffith's seemed to begin to reflect a deeper resentment toward Vincent. "Yes I'll have my own command. But first, I want to insure this is a privileged conversation."

"Privileged?" Paul gave a puzzled look. It is not common practice to have an officer-enlisted man 'privileged' conversation.

"That's what I mean. You have no education. You're *not* officer material."

"Pardon?"

"You're too uneducated."

"I've no *formal* education, no. But I know this ship, my job, I know the navy."

"You don't know the *officer* navy." Griffith snapped. "For instance, *privileged* means; secret. This conversation is to remain secret. It is an order." Griffith seemed again to be in a class struggle within him, straining to be one-on-one with a person he perceived as below his self appointed station. He rambled. "Captain Clifford and I see things from different angles … I can't let his . . ahh. . attitudes …our differences …cancel out my …ahh …hamper my …" The man delayed, then for the first time looked straight into Vincent's eyes.

Vincent finished the sentence, right on the table. " …your future?"

The man was trying to lobby for his help in managing things with Clifford, but he'd used bullying to do it, a tact that usually worked with enlisted men. Griffith new suddenly, Vincent *was* bright, he would not be bullied. Griffith acknowledged the awkward moment with just the slightest flicker of his eyes.

Vincent took the conversation back. "I'm not particularly sure how all this involves me, Commander. I have no intention of changing my life to be in the wardroom. I'm flattered to act as OOD, in fact, it's always been sort of fun to do so."

"It *can't* be *fun*." Griffith said evenly. "That's the difference I see. For you it is 'fun'. For *real* officers it is life and death duty and obligation."

Griffith got out of his chair again, leaned forward with both hands on the desk. "Chief, this is a very privileged comment I'm about to make."

Vincent said nothing.

"It's our job, as senior men to protect our Captain."

Paul let him talk.

"It's tradition also. We protect our C.O. from his inability, no, from his unwillingness to be err …from his refusal to be formal and responsible to the last letter …to model excellence …like that. We cover his deficits. It's important to me to have a command of my own, retire as high in rank as I can. Same as you, but I think for different reasons. I love my country. But I also want to retire …well off, financially well off. To relax, to travel …with my wife."

(To a motel off Pacific Coast Highway?)

"So we protect Captain Clifford from …?" Paul led.

"His flaws."

"You're afraid if we … I, let the command go slack …poor morals, ethics, cleanliness is next to …so on …"

"Right. It'll show in my fitness." He added quickly; "And in your evaluations. Need I say more?"

"We've regressed to one-upping here, Commander. What is the bottom line?"

Griffith sat back down. He fumbled the desktop for the lost chrome opener having forgotten it had fallen to the deck. His lips were moving slightly. Vincent felt the man was rehearsing a final statement. He managed to look Vincent in the eyes.

"Privileged, Chief?"

"If you say so, Commander."

"Bottom line? To protect ourselves, we must protect our Captain. From himself, from hurting this command ...which will hurt our careers. Enough said?"

"What d'ya need from me, Commander? Specifically."

"Get yourself in gear. Be USN. Square away your marriage. Model true U.S. for your men, responsible, practical, effective ...strong leadership."

"Like John Wayne, Commander? *Sands of Iwo Jima?*"

Griffith saw no humor.

The following morning a full paragraph in the plan of the day announced that all pinups were to be removed and all personal radios turned in to the ship's bos'n locker until Truaxe returned to San Diego. It further stated that a paperback sticking out of a pocket would be considered a uniform violation and that all hands were to register their existing tattoos with the ship's personnel officer. Any fresh tattoos would be considered an act of self-maiming and against navy regulations.

That announcement caused Arnold Griffith, Commander, USN to be nicknamed: 'Tough Toes Arnie'.

As Truaxe took station behind Kittyhawk to enter Pearl Harbor, Griffith again buttoned Chief Vincent on the bridge as he was conning the ship. Lieutenant Commander Corrigan was on the port bridge-wing observing the Chief from a distance. Captain Clifford was in his chair on the other wing watching the cloud-covered mountains of the Island of Oahu come into view. Griffith looked about and while smoothing his hair in the reflection of the compass repeater, whispered to Vincent.

"Our conversation that we didn't have? Went a bit further than I wanted it too, Chief, and I regret that."

"No need to be sorry, Commander. Things ... "

"I didn't say I was sorry." Griffith looked about the pilothouse and kept his whisper low but harsh. "I said I regretted it ..." He leaned in to where Vincent could smell his after shave lotion. "I regretted you weren't setting a better example." He stepped away but bounced right back. "That you didn't know intuitively the position we regular navy people are in with our Captain here."

Vincent's impatience showed. " I have a watch to stand, Sir."

Griffith ignored that fact. "Set an example. By example these younger men will begin to conduct themselves with better order—not be so offensive to be around."

"Aye aye, Sir." Paul said a bit too loud.

Griffith backed away and visually checked the posted station assignment against where Truaxe was relative to Kittyhawk.

"Seem far aft of station to me, Chief Vincent, Mr. Possible Future OOD."

Griffith had distracted him then belittled him for being distracted. Just as Paul turned to give an engine command to correct the station, the C.O. yelled in from the bridge wing. "OOD. Get this fuckin' ship on station with that fuckin' bird farm. I want no brown-shoe flyin' sailor to say we can't keep station."

"Aye, aye, Cap'n." Vincent turned to the bridge phone talker. "Increase turns thirty RPM." He turned to Griffith. "Is there anything else?"

Griffith, grimacing over Clifford's language made no reply.

Entering the pilothouse, Clifford seemed surprised to see Griffith there. He announced. "Mr. Griffith? I just told Mr. Corrigan, I'm letting the Chief here take Truaxe into Pearl Harbor. He's qualified. He can take his own watch when we leave port. Take yourself off the watch list."

Not consulting Griffith for an endorsement to qualify Vincent caused Tough Toes Arnie a flush of red. Griffith left the bridge without acknowledging what Clifford had said. Clifford looked at Vincent and smiled with childlike delight. Paul knew then, for sure, though several of the clicks of the kaleidoscope had clearer images, there were many meaningless designs and patterns still to be figured.

Helpless to it for the time being, he turned to the business of taking the ship into Pearl Harbor.

It's a twenty-minute ride from the breakwater to the hard right turn past the shipyard piers and then left past the submarine base. From there a straight easy glide toward what was called "Baker Docks" the last time Paul had moored there, but, since the U.S. had joined the international community using the newer phonetic alphabet, Truaxe was to moor today at "Bravo Docks".

The chief took it cautiously. "Right standard rudder, there."

"Right standard rudder, sir—Chief."

"Very well. Ease to ten."

"Easing to ten, Chief."

"Very well. Steer zero nine two. All ahead slow."

"Steady on zero nine two, Chief. —All engines answer—ahead slow."

"Very well."

Taking the captain's overriding suggestions only twice, he eased the ship against a light breeze and into the pier without a hint of a bump. Even though his khaki shirt armpits were ringed with wet marks he felt very confident by the time the last mooring line was in place.

Like a child checking with his teacher, Paul looked toward Clifford.

Clifford wrinkled his nose a bit, humorously, and patted Paul on the arm as both men headed off the bridge. "Ya' done good, Master Chief."

Some public relations type had been busy ahead of them. In the typical 76 degree sunny mid-morning weather, the ship was met by a navy band, a fairly large crowd of local staff officers, a Honolulu television crew, 8 or 10 Truaxe crew wives who had flown over, and fifty or more curious onlookers. Well-practiced plastic faced hula girls danced for the crew as the mooring lines were secured. The dancers then scurried around the ship in their skimpy sarongs, smiling and putting orchid leis around the necks of the officers, mostly ignoring the looks and comments, not any off color, of the enlisted men.

Because Truaxe was a new ship and a nuclear powered one at that, they were moored in prime space; pier Bravo-1, right across from the navy exchange store near the main gate of the famous old base. Paul had seen this sort of arrival many times. But each time, it was a good thing.

The ship received mail. There was nothing from Cynthia. Just a newsy note from Selesky.

Page 2 ....

Some more news. I saw Rachael shopping at the Navy Exchange Store three days ago and I sort of pushed myself in on her. She was with a Barbara Griffith? They seemed real friendly. She had to introduce me to Ben, so I finally got to meet your adversary. I understand what you mean about him. The kind of a man who when he has a three-way, the other two don't know about it. Right?

Oh yes, unless I'm stupid, and I'm not, Ben also seemed very friendly with Mrs. Griffith. Something going on there?

Also, I expect a call today about my own orders. I'll let you know as soon as I know. Sarah Barkley just passed my desk and sends her best.

Warm Regards

David S.

Where could the developing relationship of Ben, Rachael and Barbara Griffith lead to? On impulse he telephoned Rachael just to feel things out. They actually made small talk but she avoided direct answers about Barbara Griffith's presence.

"I don't know if her relationship with her husband is good or not. I haven't seen her since that last awful night when you hit Ben." According to Selesky, that made her a liar.

No, she had not received an allotment check, yes, Ben's bar was still padlocked. The conversation became strained and guarded. He later considered her politeness was part of some new plan, probably of Ben's, to get more money out of him. His hand started hurting again.

As he walked back to the ship after telephoning, Nancy Sinatra sang on some sailor's portable: "*One of these days these boots ...are going to walk all over you ...*"

CHAPTER TEN
Yankee Station

It was the fastest speed run transit from Hawaii ever by a U.S. warship. Watching the wake trail out behind the ship, Ensign 'Suckup' commented to Lake. "We're runnin' like we'll be late for the war."

Lake offered one of his usual one-ups. "Bein' late for a war is like bein' on time for a root canal."

On Wednesday, the 29th of January, 1968, at 1800, Truaxe sailed into the southern end of the Tonkin Gulf after only 5 days and eleven hours from Hawaii. They left Kittyhawk two days behind.

Abie Lake was the only man on board whose birthday was skipped as they passed the international date line, eliminating January 25th from their lives.

"This is like Vuja-Day." Lake complained. "What's happened before is happening again, only backwards. Goin' east in 1964? I had *two* birthdays."

"So now you're even."

Upon arrival with the seventh fleet, Captain Clifford secretly crossed his fingers and reported a radio courtesy call to the Fleet Commander and to his immediate commander, CTG 70.8, the task-group-leader-in-charge of destroyer-type-ship missions, that his ship was *Ready for Duty*, offering the ship to any mission within its scope. Truaxe was promptly ordered to relieve Truxtun of her job escorting Enterprise. At last, the nuclear powered Truaxe eased into station behind the nuclear powered aircraft carrier she was built to escort. There was a feeling of celebration as the two ships joined at 19 degrees north, about 108 degrees east on what was officially called "Yankee Station" but better known by any sailor as The Tonkin Gulf Yacht Club.

In 1968 it was okay to be a 'nuke' ship running with another nuke ship, matching speeds and endurance, setting new records. The major news magazines made cover stories of Truaxe joining Enterprise and the crew felt okay being part of these new experiences of men and machines. Clifford became so puffed up by telegram requests from senators and congressmen to comment on his ship's mission and viability he nearly slipped into his flawed state of letting things go on their own. But late that first night in the gulf, an overheard conversation brought Clifford to his feet. On the darkened *flying bridge* high above the conning bridge, he inadvertently overheard Paul Vincent and Lieutenant Stumpf.

"This war is like most of my relatives, Lieutenant."

"How so?"

"You never visit them on purpose. You hope they never visit you either, but if they do ...protect yourself, 'cause it could be *real* trouble."

Stumpf leaned two arms on the top rail and spoke into the night. Clifford could barely make out the words above the hum of exhaust vents and sea wind noises, until he cupped a hand around his left ear and leaned into the darkness toward the two men.

"And we are stuck, Chief. From my Dad's seat at CINCPACFLT? A bunch of powerful people want us out of the war, another powerful bunch want to stay in to improve weapons, train the army for what they feel will be a *real* battle someday in eastern Europe. We're in the middle here. Can't win, and better not lose. Over and over, Dad speaks of his fears over our country's poor leadership."

Clifford had heard versions of Stumpf's comments across the wardroom table and was only slightly surprised the officer was telling them to an enlisted man. Not aware Stumpf and Vincent were true friends; it was Vincent's answering comment that centered him.

"I have fears about leadership too, Lieutenant." Vincent said quietly. "Look at Griffith. The man's strange, weird acting ... "

"Yeah, like Will Rogers never met him?" Stumpf laughed at his own joke.

"For sure ... And the Captain ... ?"

"Yeah. Who is this man?"

"His need to be a star?" Vincent asked philosophically. "Seems like the kind who brings his own music to a piano bar. The wrong things seem important."

To Clifford, the comment wasn't offhand and Stumpf hadn't defended him. His self-esteem spun like an out of sync turntable. He practically jumped out of the darkness but his ego stopped him. He needed to hear more. He remained in the shadows, his fingernails digging into his palms. The son of CINCPACFLT and a combat veteran Master Chief were referring to him as a weirdo. He felt limp. Was the word out that far? He decided he could not hear any more negative comments. He turned quietly, made his way away from Stumpf and Vincent and climbed slowly down one of the shaky wooden ladders.

"Does the entire ship see me this way? The entire navy? I thought I caught training up pretty well. Those injured men? They could have been hurt anyway. Who's to know? I am NOT a weirdo, dammit. I am a *commanding officer*, and a good one. Look how they received me at the embassy in Rio, at the British Navy Office in the Falklands. Dammit, dammit ... " There were sudden tears in his eyes. "Wait," the healthy part of his professional side spoke up from deep within the core of whoever Clifford was at that moment. "I cannot rest on those fantasies. There's a war nearby. I can't daydream lives away." He snapped his fingers to signify some internal realization. His chest swelled, he put his hands on his hips. "But at the same time I can't let the bullshit remarks of some enlisted jerk ruin my day. I *am* the captain." (I am the Pope, I am the King, I am the God.)

He fumbled his key into his cabin door and stumbled inside. Before his rump even hit his chair, he was scribbling on a yellow pad.

"Dear Dad. . .

We're in the war now and I feel very alone, as they say, 'here at the top' ...a feeling I am sure you can relate to."

Back on the open bridge Stumpf and Vincent were still consoling one another, oblivious of having disrupted their Captain's world. Stumpf was looking at a star formation in the clear sky. Vincent followed his gaze. "Seems like a waste of time out here, Chief."

"I feel stagnated or something. I'm right back into a state of mind I used before in-country."

"Swift-boat state of mind?"

"Yeah. It's called denial." Paul liked he could use some of Selesky's psychobabble language.

"Being a sailor is just a job, like any other job? That kinda' bullshit?"

"You got it."

As a seventeen year old, for Paul Vincent, the navy had become a job, a place of employment, a way out of Steubenville, Ohio. "The recruiting poster had promised me some travel, adventure, excitement and a profession, Lieutenant. Compared to stackin' boxes at Greenberg's Grocery or shoveling slag in the Weirton Steelmill …it looked good. I was too naïve to consider that when I came into the navy for a *job*, that I was agreeing to be a *real* military man, shoot at someone, truly be in a fighting war. I'd seen too many movies."

"You and a thousand others, Chief."

"Since the swift-boat tour, I am really aware, I am a shooting sailor. All that stuff. "

"You're not in the delta, Chief. We're miles from the war."

"I owe myself this easier tour, L.T. I'll get through this alive, and maybe with Cynthia start the family I want later on?"

"Christ, Chief. We went from being uptight over the war's poor leadership to killin' or not killin' to calmly talkin' 'bout bringin' babies into this piece of shit world." He turned away. "I'm going below." The not so thin officer worked his way carefully to the same ladder Clifford used, and turned back toward Vincent. "Anyway, it *is* last day of January and we made it here on time. Off to a good start. The whole wardroom likes the sound of starting our tour here with that 36 hour TET holiday cease-fire. Even though some of the crew tell me the cease-fire is 'cause the V.C. are worried because Truaxe has arrived."

"It does seem that way, Lieutenant. We come, and there are no planned air ops from Enterprise for at least the next 45 hours. R-E-L-A-X."

"Hell, even Tough Toes Arnie managed a smile at dinner this evening."

"Look up imperious … "

"Find Griffith. I know. Night Chief."

"Night, Boss."

Late that first night, after Commander Griffith had turned in, the hidden radios played. *The Beach Boys* sang *"Good , good, good, good Vibrations."*

Truaxe and every U.S. ship in the gulf received the same high precedence secret message at the same time; 4 am, January, 31st.

"Saigon under attack. American Embassy under fire. Ambassador Bunker evacuated 0300. 12 V.C. battalions within Saigon. Multiple coordinated V.C. attacks throughout I, II, III, and IV corps proper. Bien Hoa and Tan Son Nhut airbases under fire. Hwy 1 south from

Go Vap to Thu Doc, hwy 15 and hwy 4 north and the entire Tan Binh Dist considered in V.C. control."

Updated reports arrived on Truaxe every few minutes in radio central and Vincent monitored the radiomen that were jumping to keep up to the message load. Four teletypes spilled out general communications and two special circuits followed the quickly developing air war. To interact on Yankee Station, sixteen voice circuits were in use in CIC and three on the bridge. High precedence message orders and advice came and went without a hitch. The supervisor of the radio watch, capable Radioman first class Pete Peterson, was very busy.

To his messenger. "Here's a Flash message. Cap'n's on the bridge. Send it up the bunny tube and follow it later for his signature. This is NOT a dress rehearsal or a drill. Get the fuck movin'." The messenger, Radioman seaman Andy Hyde snatched a hand phone, punched a buzzer to sound on the bridge and spoke rapidly into the phone … "Flash message coming up in bunny tube … 1 —2—3 NOW".

Peterson barked to a crypto operator: "Takes seven minutes to upgrade the setting on that box and we already know the Exec is coming here with an outgoing Flash. Get movin' get movin', be ready for him."

To Vincent: "Chief …two UHF transmitters went down and I can't get CIC to tell me which are their priority circuits. Call Lukarmo will you?"

To someone on the phone. "Look, I got me a war up here and you want me to tune in country and western? I, I can't get to it. What? Okay. Okay. I'll get to it."

To his watch crew. "Pies comin' up. Barny? Put some shit-kickin' music on number three and patch it to the galley."

To Vincent: "Lookit' this. 46 sorties in the air offa' Kittyhawk alone. We tryin' to kill all commies like that Pope who tried to kill all cats?"

"Looks like." (What Pope?)

Communication circuits quickly became overloaded in the rapidly moving situation. Not knowing what to expect, COMSEVENTHFLT ordered the entire Yankee Station team to general quarters and darkened ship, fearful the extremely well coordinated series of attacks in-country might mean the Chinese or the Soviets had entered the war.

"As unpredictable as grasshoppers." Stumpf commented as he emerged from special crypto with a secret 'eyes-only' message for Clifford. "Member, Chief? Douglas MacArthur thought they were bluffing also 'til three hundred thousand Chinese came over the Yalu river into Korea, 1950-51."

"You got three hundred thousand Chinese in your hand there, L.T.?"

"No, and don't call me "L.T.", Chief. I'm a lieutenant."

'Okay, I'll call you Lieutenant if you tell me you don't have three hundred thousand Chinese in that message."

"No, this is only a situation report on available allied nuke weapons in the area."

Ashore it was a madhouse coordinating U.S. retaliation. There were no accurate accounts of ARVN defense forces that could be counted on. The U.S. had long known of the corruption within the Vietnamese military, but the politics and sociology of the corruption was an intact part of the culture the U.S. had tried, but could not dent. The TET attacks revealed that while various Vietnamese district leaders received pay for perhaps 300 troops, they could field only 30 to 40 for actual defense. The remainder of the money had gone into the system's pockets over the years. The V.C. had infiltrated these so called defensive forces also, and therefore knew exactly where to snake through the outer rim of the city and avoid resistance.

Having been in the gulf for seven months, Enterprise was to be relieved by Kittyhawk and the crew was winding down. But, Kittyhawk was still two days out. Surprised by the turn of events, the experienced but tired crew of Enterprise pushed her exhausted pilots and worn planes in the air within thirty minutes of the original message in support of in-country forces. Kittyhawk was ordered to flank speed and to get her planes into the fight when distance permitted. Truxtun, who had been relieved by Truaxe early that day was ordered to turn around and return to station at maximum speed. The dragons, having begun to snooze for the TET holiday, were now awake.

At 3 p.m. on February 1st, Vincent was standing the OOD bridge watch when Truaxe received a Top Secret message. She was ordered to immediately receive a helicopter from Enterprise who would deliver some special charts and maps. The helo would also deliver three new crewmen who had just arrived on Kittyhawk from Subic Bay where they had been waiting for a flight to catch their ship, Truaxe.

By the time Clifford got to the bridge, Vincent had already turned into the wind and ordered the waiting helo to sling the men and maps down and get clear fast. The helo moved in, synchronized course and speed twenty feet above the ship's fantail. The experienced helo crew dropped a weighted pouch center stage on the deck followed within seconds by two frightened young cooks and a second-class engineman who were lowered to the ship by a practiced pulley-controlled rig. When the last lowered man, the engineman, let go of the rig, the helo roared, rose and was gone in a flutter.

A messenger ran the bag to the bridge.

As Vincent watched over their shoulder but also watched his ship, Lieutenant Commander Valentino, Captain Clifford and Commander Griffith immediately poured over the charts. They began to whisper.

"Truxtun to relieve us? Shit. We just got here." Clifford seemed confused.

Valentino offered. "We're fresh, they're not."

"We're faster, also." Griffith added.

Captain Clifford walked out on the bridge wing and spoke to Vincent. "OOD, come left to two-seven-two. Make maximum RPM."

"Course 272, max RPM." Truaxe was ordered off the cushy job of escort ship and into the real war.

As his ship headed West-Northwest at over forty knots, Master Chief Vincent was relieved as OOD to take care of his primary duties, communications. He stayed close to radio central and, as was an advantage for any radioman with Top Secret clearance, scanned through intelligence messages. Almost every U.S. or allied post in S. Vietnam was experiencing some sort of alert, attack or harassment. Viet Cong or North Vietnamese 82mm mortar and 122mm rockets fell everywhere and caught most U.S. and allied forces in the so-called holiday lull.

The only U.S. forces not surprised by a TET attack were those taking on the NVA at Khe Sanh in the narrow northwest corridor of S. Vietnam. The NVA had successfully tricked nearly everyone by pressing what appeared to be a siege at Khe Sanh, day after day of heavy shelling. That attack had been taking the attention of almost all U.S. effort for weeks prior to TET because President Johnson was sitting in the war room in Washington, head in hands, determined, as he repeated over and over 'not to be caught as the French had been at Dien Bien Phu in May of 1954.'

If someone were to look at Vietnam from outer space during those weeks, Khe Sanh would have sparked into the air like the brushes of an overworked generator. With most U.S. concentration in the north, U.S. Generals in the south were in a tizzy reorganizing available troops to prevent loss of important areas and thwart serious damage to airfields around Saigon.

Lieutenant Stumpf, because of his father's rank, was used to hearing of command decision and had grown up among and on the knees of high ranking military men. Reading the Khe Sanh reports, he murmured to his Master Chief. "Westmoreland's war, Chief. The most over-rated but worse general since Custer. I feel strongly for my father at this moment."

"But Westmoreland's in charge of the south right now, isn't he?"

"Isn't he? It'll take him, Harriman, McNamara *and* the Pres to make sure we lose this war."

Vincent did not like hearing such pessimism. "Are there any good guys?"

"Maybe Krulak, Victor the Brute ... Wally Greene who can't get an audience past the JCS ... " Stumpf's inside knowledge made it all too convoluted. Paul wanted someone to be truly in charge, respected, dynamic and confident and with the support of everyone around him. This type of thinking was obviously too idealistic for this war.

Leaving Yankee Station, where large numbers of U.S. ships could be seen on radar, Paul felt like they were leaving the *real* action for whatever it was CTG 70.8 ordered them northwest for. Just two hours away from their departure point, there were no other ships on short-range radar but the shores of N. Vietnam emerged ahead of them.

At sundown, Vincent and Lieutenant Commander Valentino were doing the sextant star navigation for the evening position. "It's so calm out here, hard to think all shit's broken loose just twenty mile in there, Chief. Like the eye of a storm, perhaps?"

"Perhaps."

"A hurricane with a *thousand* eyes is what my father calls this war, Chief. An eye for every person involved."

"Christ, who is this great observer?"

"Runs a fruit market in South Boston."

At 7 p.m. a lengthy message was received in radio containing the details of their Top Secret orders. Truaxe was to proceed to a point a few miles south of the city of Vinh, North Vietnam, near the rail line that follows the coastal highway known as route 1A. They were to secretly land a boat at that point, 100 miles north of the Demilitarized Zone which was then defined roughly at the Ben Hai River. At 0600 on the morning of the 4th they were to bring two CIA operatives out.

"Why us?"

"Well. Seems the ARVN's were to bring them out ...but the fuckin' Arc Lights had a hang-up ... ?"

" ...that's the B-52's from Guam?"

"Yep. A bomb rack stuck for just several seconds after a target, then rained eight or so two-thousand pounders right in the middle of an ARVN unit."

"Fuck me!"

"Killed every last ARVN ... "

"So the navy's inherited the pickup job?"

"You got it. Fuck-up's rule the war."

All of the message traffic concerning the pickup was Top Secret. To help the busy radio messengers, Vincent would hand-deliver many of the messages himself to the action officers throughout the ship. On one such delivery of a message to the captain, Vincent was jerked to his own reality.

"Chief? You been told yet? 'Bout goin' ashore?"

"What?" As if stopped on a path by a striped snake, adrenaline shot throughout Vincent's frame.

Clifford also seemed jumpy. "Because you're a conning officer and all. An' because of your power-boat work, an' you've been to gunfire support school and can spot from ashore, an' I hear you're a *good* spotter."

"What? Cut to it, Cap'n."

"I want you to pilot the boat ashore to pick those two men up."

"What?"

Unnerved by the strength of Vincent's 'what?', Clifford broke eye contact. His gaze bounced from corner to corner of Clifford's small but well-appointed sleeping cabin. "Griffith was to have told you." The comment was a blaming mumble and a self-pity curse at the same time.

In a new kind of shock, Vincent did not speak.

"Well ..." Clifford took off his hat and slowly rubbed his hair too-long with an open hand. He then inspected the hand as if looking for something. He tossed the hat on the sky-blue cotton spread stretched on his bunk but it bounced to the deck. Neither man moved for it. "You can have your choice of a signalman to take with you but we've already picked the engineman." Clifford went on. "The exec insists the new man who just choppered aboard has made similar runs. He's a small-boat engineman, anxious to be part of the mission."

Vincent's thoughts swirled. How could *anyone* actually *want* to go in-country in a small boat launched from a brand new duty ship?

Clifford broke into some philosophical rambling about the value of the mission to the CIA, to the TET defensive, to the war, and overall, how it applied to his personal sense of what he referred to as 'man's search for meaning', a sprawl of words he'd likely embezzled from some scholar. Clifford talked on and on but the subjectivity of his ramblings were worthless to Vincent's racing feelings and need for concrete objectivity. Going ashore in a rubber boat under the guidance and protection of Robert Clifford had not been part of any rational prediction nor possibility. Paul could think of no real procedure built into the system that would permit him to refuse the order, so he searched for a new one. Breaking into the captain's rambling, his words flew inappropriately into the air, exposing his fear without question.

"Wait, Captain. Wait!" He flipped his own hat to the dark blue carpet beside Clifford's. The Captain's eyes flipped wide open and locked on his Chief who was speaking with strength. "I can't do this—I made a deal with myself." He threw his hands in the air and plopped into a chair. "No in-country for me again." Sensible word selection was impossible. "This' bull shit, Captain. I've done my swift boating. Let someone else do this one."

Clifford was dismayed and seemed intimidated. Vincent was the man he'd overheard calling him a weirdo, a claim not rebutted by Lieutenant Stumpf. He flashed a quick longing for his father's stern advice. He needed to respond to Vincent's disrespectful plea and still save decorum. Nothing came. He decided to receive it as humor, complete with affected chuckles.

"Heh heh, yeah, Chief, let Mr. Stumpf fuck it up? Heh heh." Wait, he thought. The man already thinks I'm weird, now I'm giggling weirdly. He shifted positions. "I am the Captain, Chief Vincent. I am giving you an order." Now I sound like 'I'm taking my ball home 'cause he won't play fair'. He shifted back, determined to use adult to adult, man to man, professional to respected professional humor. "Well, this isn't the boy scouts where we vote on whether or not we'd go to sea on a rainy weekend—is it now Master Chief? Heh-heh." Dammit, he hadn't wanted that 'heh-heh' to pop out.

A wall of resistance still up, Vincent hadn't truly heard nuances in the man's responses. To him, fate was running a sneak attack. After liking his position on the ship: interesting, no threats, comfortable, tourist-like, and planning to be with Cynthia soon, change was coming all too fast. He felt jerked from a sound safe bed and pushed toward a pit with an angered beast waiting. His anxiety continued. His heart beat time with the flips of the wings of the butterflies in his stomach.

For almost a minute the two men's apprehensive out-of-sync breathing was all that could be heard in the cool cabin. Eventually, self-consciously, their looks were drawn to one another. Both were surprised to see an equally stunned expression on the other's face. An unspoken transfer of empathy popped through the surface of the tension in the room and spread like dye in water.

Clifford's thoughts zoomed: 'Command, dammit, command. The no-win is parcel to the job. You are responsible to the navy for the mission and you are responsible to this man for his life. You're in the navy. You signed the enlistment paper—now own it.'

Vincent's thoughts also galloped. 'You're a professional, dammit. The no-win comes with the job. You are responsible to the navy for carrying out the commander's mission and you are responsible to yourself for your life. You're in the navy. You signed the enlistment paper—now own it.'

The separate thoughts were equally sobering as each man struggled to return to his proper role. Paul leaned over and picked up his hat. Clifford lifted his own from the deck and placed it beside Paul's on the table. The gold embroidered *scrambled eggs* on Clifford's hat brim looked ostentatious and out of place next to Vincent's plain black brim.

"Humph." Clifford quietly moved his own hat to a high nearby shelf. He spoke nervously, talking about the mission in the way he felt a Commanding Officer should, but feeling very inadequate. Paul was also struggling with his role of listener, the receiver of orders, the one who is to do, or possibly, to die.

Paul interrupted Clifford once, his dry mouth causing numbing sounds in his words. "I'll take the boat in, soon." It was more a statement he had to hear from himself than a confirmation for Clifford.

"Yes, soon. Take the boat in."

Hearing the human process of his own voice and Clifford's mimicked answer, Vincent began to shift robot-like toward acceptance of the order and assimilation of its true meaning. Deep breaths began evenly pumping the adrenaline required to take apart the denial state he had unconsciously established on the ride from San Diego. The adrenaline soon accessed a part of his brain he hadn't needed since he'd commanded the PBR's in the deltas. With a long unused but once very effective ability, Paul Vincent faced his Captain as Master Chief Petty Officer Vincent and with a committed voice, itemized the questions whose answers would lessen his anxiety and optimize his ability.

"How much time do I have? Who's briefing us? When will the boat be uncovered for me to check it out? Where are the shoreline charts? How free will communications be? How will we be armed? How far away will Truaxe be for cover? Who we picking up? Are they injured? How'll we find them? Will I absolutely be the commander of this mission even after we pick up these people?" He watched Clifford's face change from casual listener to what he hoped was a capable C.O. Paul then added, "I'll take Abie Lake as my signalman and spotter and I want final say on this new man."

This was the first time Clifford had been this close to a war and this close to an experienced man who was suddenly preparing for combat. He became galvanized by two opposing feelings: admiration, and something close to fear-ridden intimidation?

Shocked he was supposed to have the answers to the rapid line of questions, Clifford was unable to centralize thoughts. Impulsively, nervously, he picked up the phone, dialed the bridge and in true practiced Captain's voice, transferred his nervousness to someone else.

"Bridge? This' the Cap'n. Have the ops and weps officer report to my cabin immediately."

Waiting, he shifted to an all smiles side and unconsciously began patronizing his Chief.

"You really want Lake, Chief?"

"Yes, why?"

"Seems one of those men who found a grade he liked in elementary school ...and stayed there."

"I want him. I know him well. This could be difficult in there."

"This'll be a piece of cake, Chief. The air cav and the marines'll have this offensive cleaned up in two days—we'll be back on Yankee station taking it easy on plane guard." Paul made no reply. "These CIA pickup operations go on all the time over here." He stepped behind his desk and sat down, looking over Paul's head into the room, he repeated. "Piece of cake."

Vincent was only dimly aware of Clifford's time-passing comments. He pulled a yellow pad from the desktop and busily searched his memory. He needed an up to date copy of challenge and reply signals, radio with fresh batteries and a backup, waterproof covers for the chart, a gun-fire control coordination chart, cipher codes, fresh water, perhaps medical aid kits for the men ashore and arms and ammunition. Should they take the Chief Corpsman, Frank Bellefontaine? He cursed the navy, the ship and the Captain. The ship had not trained for this type omission.

Watching what appeared to be Vincent's confidences grow, Clifford felt an internal melancholy promise that this would all go well and he would be commended for the job. This was his first real chance to shine during a time of war and he began taking credit in advance. In college it's 'publish or perish', in the military it's 'do or die'. His happiness was in Vincent's hands and he was very aware of this symbol of dependency. For Clifford it was 'Vincent does well or Clifford's admiral hopes die'. Unrehearsed words popped from his mouth.

"Four generations of sailors, Chief. Four big ones. I'll be the fourth admiral too, you bet."

Paul reeled by what he saw as Clifford's transparency. "I go in-country? You think of admiral?" It was a cutting challenge of rank.

Clifford backed off. "Huh? No. I think I misunderstood something you asked, Chief. I was rambling a bit wasn't I? Waiting for Mr. Valentino and Corrigan to get here. I'm running a bit nervous too, Chief."

"Nervous isn't good enough, Cap'n. I've got a hell of a list of unknown's here. I'm apprehensive."

"Over what?"

"I think we were okay ...we could fart around on plane-guard, Cap'n. But this is different. This is my life on the line."

"C'mon. Piece of cake."

"NO MORE CAKE." He snapped loudly. Clifford was again intimidated. Paul saw it and calmed himself.

"Sir." He tried calming but the anxiety controlled him. He couldn't stand what he saw as Clifford's arrogance or ignorance. "I'm worried about ...plain old ability, Cap'n."

"Ability? Whose ability?" Clifford's heard weirdo again.

"The crew's true ability to help in a real emergency." He stared at Clifford. There was a knock on the door. Commanders Valentino and Corrigan entered, ending the charged conversation.

CHAPTER ELEVEN
Three Men in a Tub

"You comin' or what, Abie?"

"Watch the navy's hottest signalman for five minutes and he'll take the toughest job."

"Let's take advantage of the remaining daylight."

Spread out on the fantail next to the ship's flashing new updated version of the Kaman UH-2C twin engine, twin seated, gattling-gun equipped Seasprite helicopter, was the unremarkable looking flat-black 18 foot neoprene raft chosen for the trip. The raft, a Mk-9/AL Spotter Boat, one of two on board, was equipped with a thirty horsepower *Seahorse* motor with a three horsepower toy-like battery powered affair as backup. The boat smelled like a tire store.

Snapped into place by heavy plastic clips along the sides and back of the boat were several oars, a fishing kit, fresh water army-type canteens, two watertight storage compartments and four very outdated M-1 carbines, their wooden stocks dented in several places.

"Plenty of bullet clips tied to these straps, Chief." Lake announced into the air.

"Clips? Clips!?" Seaman Abalar, one of the gunner's mates helping square things away mocked Lake. "Clip's is what your ol' lady puts in her hair. These are *magazines*. Ammunition magazines. Whooee!" He blew into the air in disbelief. "You gonna' go into a shootin' war with 'clips'? I should be going."

Lake looked picked on.

Under the rear seat were two watertight compartments which, Vincent learned, held two battery powered UHF/VHF A.M. radios. Under the three wooden platform seats were six inflatable life jackets. Two compact A.M. handie-talkies were sealed in floatable plastic bags."

After looking the raft over and looking over the side at the choppy gulf water, Abie asked, "Why the hell don't they send in the Kaman copter?"

"Look up 'confusing' in a dictionary ..."

"Ah know. See U.S. Navy orders ..."

Lieutenant Commander Corrigan supplied the answer over their shoulders.

"'Cause every damned farmer near route one seems to be spotting for helos. Any chopper up north here means clearly there's a plane down—or, *someone* needs picked up. If the NVA doesn't get the chopper, they get the waiting men. So, tsk tsk. We send a low profile boat. This one. Question answered?"

"For a simple question you get the meaning of life." Lake mumbled to Vincent.

"Pardon, Lake?"

"Nothin', Sir."

Vincent picked up one of the AM radios.

"Thos'is backup radios." He turned to the voice and saw a tall man dressed in dungarees and black ball cap standing on the deck at the end of the boat, making a "V" type peace sign with his right hand. "Hello," The pasty faced tall man said. "A'hm Cecil Tuckah." A twang of hill country slid into the air with each word from the man. "A'hm the guy what dropped in outta' the skaa' a few hars' back, jes' in ta'hm to take yew 'an him on a boat rah'de."

The accent was so distracting, Abie and Paul looked to one another to keep from laughing. It didn't work. They turned away from the white freckled face and grease covered hands, but the voice didn't stop.

"Hey, don' y'all hide away. I take a bit o' gettin' used ta'." They turned back to the voice as Tucker jump-skipped into and out of the rubber boat and arrived on their side. He extended to Vincent the same hand he was wiping with a grease-grayed rag. "Cecil Tuckah."

"Tucka?" Paul asked.

"No, it's Tuckah. T-U-C-K-E-R, Tuckah."

"Oh." Lake jumped in. "Tuckah, like in 'fuckah'?"

Handshakes concluded, Tucker scratched his nose with the back of his wrist and pointed to the boat with his head. "Good motor. Ah' also checked out them radios. They both work good." Cecil Tucker, second-class engineman. Friendly, twangy, twenty-eight years old, eight years in the navy, the last two at various 'Nam commands said he was from a "waad spot inna' road" in southern Kentucky, and 'l'il navy motors was his 'specialty'. He looked like he'd be the quiet confident country type. Confident, country was all right, but he was *not* quiet.

Vincent had Lake and Tucker further check the boat and re-stow the needed equipment while he planned strategies with LCDR Corrigan. As Vincent took more and more charge, he pulled his two men into the detailed planning and Corrigan eased into the background. By midnight the three men slated for the boat felt organized, familiar with the boat's equipment, and connected with one another.

"Hope we screw this up a bit." Tucker said at one point. "If we screw up they'll send us back to Yankee station to fall in line. Do somethin' right and this navy seems to go out of the way findin' somethin' new and new and newer 'til they find somethin' you *can't* do."

"Because?" Abie was learning that as long as Tucker talked, he worked.

"Because? Because then ya' fit in with the overall fucked up rest o' the people in this bog puddle outfit."

"Do it right or not , and some officer will rub the shine offa' you?"

"You smart and fast for a colored boy."

The comment brought Abie upright from stowing some food kits. His voice became threatening "Okay, Tuckah … Listen. I'm not sure why ass holes sound more like ass holes when they've got a southern accent, but you qualify. You from the south, I ain't. If you fightin' a civil war. I ain't. I used to be colored, now I ain't." His voice shifted to less threatening, almost amused. "I'm creamy chocolate, actually, but my wife prefers callin' us all 'black'." Then back to threatening. "If you think you're one up on me 'cause you're white …think again. If you could spend one Saturday night as a black man in Southeast San Diego you'd never want to be white again. So, 'til you do that …and unless you think you can weld me to the deck with one punch, knock off the colored-boy shit."

Tucker stood upright beside Abie but extended a head taller into the semi-darkness. He wiped his hands with his favorite rag and jammed it into his back pocket. He reached up just fast enough to cause Abie to flinch just slightly, and touched the black man on the end of the nose with one finger. He then licked the finger-tip.

"Christ woowee. I almos' called you a nigger. I wonder what *that'd* set off in ya'."

"'Nigger' ain't so bad …its 'colored boy' rassles my huckers."

Paul and Abie decided they liked this new man, Cecil Tucker. He'd tested their humor and they'd passed. They liked the way he handled the engine, the other equipment and handled the argument with Lake. They were also comforted by his reported in-country experience. With three hours still to kill, they were so filled with adrenaline they elected not to try for sleep.

"Paul … Chief? Some mail came in that helo pouch." Lake handed Vincent's two letters to Tucker who passed them over one by one, reading the returns.

"Looks lah'k an attorney letter. That's one of them guys they bury twelve feet deep when they die? 'Cause deep down they nice people."

"Give me the letters, and stop the stand-up routine."

"An' this one smells good and is from …" He studied the address carefully in the glow of his red flashlight. "A Cynthia Howser. You know her?"

"He sure does." Lake chimed in. "He gets a letter from Miss Universe and I get none from my Veronica but one from some place in New Jersey, threatening me if I break the chain."

Vincent clicked his fingers, Tucker handed him the letter.

In the red light he found that Cynthia and Kurt had actually flown on to France, but had promised more letters to keep him up to date.

Being so late at night, Tough Toes Arnie had long been in his bunk. Many illegal radios were quietly tuned to AFRS Saigon. Vincent hummed along with *"The Lovin' Spoonfuls* " old hit,—"Summer in the City." He found himself thinking of Cynthia.

At three a.m. Vincent shook the two men awake.

"Shit, I haven't been up this early since I stayed up this late."

"Shut up, Abie. In the boat."

The men were loaded down. Webbed belts held a Colt forty-five each, several spare magazines, a USN regulation survival knife, two hand grenades and a flashlight. They all carried a good pair of binoculars on wide neck straps. Vincent packed two charts, recognition signals and communication authentication codes in a plastic bag. With clearance from the OOD, they lowered themselves into the rubber boat, first Tucker who started the little battery engine, then Lake who was balancing a can of *Coke*.

"After the war I'm comin' over here and gather all the 'luminum from the bottom of this bath tub gulf. I musta' threw five hundred o' the things over the side myself."

Out of the darkness, Clifford appeared and leaned over the rail. "You organized, Chief?"

"I'm organizing this shit we're carrying." His preoccupation sounded like resentment. The Captain stepped back three paces.

"I'm sure we'll be back on Yankee station tomorrow. Back to plane guard and rest … "

"That an order we've received, or a guess, Cap'n?" The earlier resentment kept spilling out.

"Educated hunch, Chief. Best I can do." He backed away three more paces. "See you shortly after sun-up for pick-up. We'll be at 10 miles so don't hesitate to call for help if you need. Weather states no rain. That's a blessing." Paul was running out of patience listening to the man restate information from the earlier briefing.

"Hey!" Lake interrupted from the darkness thirty-five feet below. "It's hard holdin' this thing 'longside."

Clifford backed off even more and offered a little salute as Vincent tossed his poncho down into the boat and went over the side onto the unsteady rope ladder.

"Check the radio first thing." Clifford said nervously. He then stepped to the lifeline and stared down into the darkness. "You men truly ready? You get some sleep?"

Vincent yelled back as his feet hit the soft bottom of the raft. "We're fine, Cap'n." But then mumbled to himself, "Enough, enough."

The faces above evaporated into the darkness as the three men settled into the semi-cramped boat. Vincent tested the radio by telling the officer of the deck they were clear of the ship's side. Within seconds, right next to them, the Truaxe engines pulsed into full power. As water swirled under their boat, the barely visible gray sides of the ship moved away. They rocked gently then bobbed hazardously as the ship slipped away into the darkness.

"Gawd, this thing flip-flop's over" Tucker drawled, "I'll be walkin' water like Jesus."

"And the *alleged* virgin birth?" Lake asked.

Vincent interrupted. "Start that *real* motor, Tuck. Two guys in there are waiting on us."

"An' who the hell else is in there?" Abie asked the darkness.

Tucker spoke as he jerked the starter cord. "Whole bunch o' little farts in there who don't bathe too often, but who'll …" his words were lost in the snapping sputter and the runaway wail of the high performance motor.

"Jesus. Too loud!" Vincent yelled tapping Tucker.

The engineman moved quickly. He flicked both hands over the engines housing, twisted a dial, fondled two extended rods and the noise cut way back. Moving the dials more, Tucker reduced the engine noise to a confident sounding rumble. Then he finished his sentence. " …who'll not be real happy seein' us come into their real estate without a pass."

He pulled his rag out of his pocket and turned to Vincent. The chief could barely make out the man's face, but it seemed scrunched up by concern and confusion. "Who the fuck unset my motor? You?"

"Whaddaya' mean?"

"I had it tuned quiet-like. That roar coulda' been heard fer' twenty miles."

"But who's in there to hear us?" Abie asked with a worried voice.

Lieutenant Cao checked his foggy-faced watch as his company of men jumped onto the dark highway from the two derelict Peugeot trucks.

"Press on." He warned. "We have four kilometers to go and is nearly sun-up."

"Lieutenant, we'll never make it in the dark." Sergeant Theu complained as the men organized into a column. Lieutenant Cao located one of the many paths the farmer's oxen use to get from the high plain fields to the lower ones near the beach.

"How can we say quit." Cao tormented his sergeant. "We try to make it."

It had been just over six hours since his City Guard post had received the weak radio message telling of the time and location of the U.S. pickup of two spies. Cao had been busy ever since. He had located the two old trucks and with a promise he would soon have two CIA agents and perhaps the pickup boat team, talked his supply officer out of some strictly rationed gasoline. He encouraged a radio operator to ask Haiphong H.Q. if torpedo boats might intercept whatever U.S. ship had dropped the boat off. He enjoyed offering command decisions however unlikely they were to be listened to or carried out.

Lieutenant Bien Cao of the NVA regulars had taken duty with the 'city guard' after three years in the south, fighting ARVN and U.S. advisors. City guard duty was considered a well-deserved rest for valuable officers who had proven themselves. Lt. Cao knew though, in three months he would be returning to the Quang Duc and Lam Dong sections of South Vietnam for his third year long tour. His generals, under the sound advice of such determined revolutionaries as Ho Chi Minh and Pham Van Dong insisted that after their soldiers were rotated home for rest, they would return to fight only to familiar battle areas, not be placed in new zones where they would be as confused as the often rotated U.S. troops were.

"American biggest mistake is putting men back to U.S. after only one year." General Xuan Bon Song was known to boast in meetings of his officers in the north. "Just when officer or soldier know area and know what to do and how to do, they replace him with new face, new brain, no history. Do not make same mistake." He warned.

General Xuan Bon Song had been fighting the North's mission since 1954. He had watched the Viet Cong strength grow from a handful of uncertain Viet Minh guerillas to where, by 1968, they boasted an organized strength of over 50,000 with some 68-70 battalions in place and over 35,000 back-up support forces, not counting at least 25,000 trucks and drivers . Many now feel that had the U.S. not entered the war, the Viet Cong political and national spirit may well have dwindled from lack of support. But Ho Chi Minh knew U.S. intervention would stir the same strong sense of Vietnamese nationalism called upon to defeat the French. He also had patience to wait out a prolonged war. Through extremely gifted international probing and with the help of the inept South Vietnamese government, President Kennedy fell for Ho's trick. The Americans, by helping S. Vietnam, would really help Ho gather support.

Excited since receiving the alert message, Lieutenant Cao wanted to again be part of the war. Although his wife and children were glad for the City Guard duty, he hated just sitting around each day where the only action was to count and report to Haiphong the number of B-52 bombers that flew in almost daily from Guam.

"Double time. Double time." He ordered. The men, most of who were new recruits or recuperating wounded fell in line and struggled to keep up to the motivated Lieutenant and his veteran sergeant.

Sergeant Theu puffed up to beside his Lieutenant after several minutes of running. "Who we exactly expect find at ocean?"

"Who we find there?" Cao inhaled strongly and looked at his sergeant with an intensely concentrated face. "Americans. The enemy."

As recommended in the operation's order, Vincent shut down the purring motor when they were a little beyond one mile from shore. Lake and Tucker quietly paddled them in toward the beach while Vincent scanned the shoreline. The two agents, Hinkle and March, were to make a pre-dawn pickup signal, four dashes of a light. It was 5 a.m. It would soon be light enough to see the daytime pickup signal: four white patches displayed on bushes. He kept the glasses to his eyes.

As the daylight increased, the inland seemed to be as the charts had promised. The men could just make out a series of low jagged hills about four hundred feet at the highest, divided by narrow rain-washed valleys. With more daylight, several well-used paths could be seen among bushes and small trees making their way from the hilltops downward to several cultivated areas on the lower hillsides. The area was not as isolated looking as the men anticipated. At the shoreline itself, now less than a hundred yards away, forty or so yards of beach sand gave way to shadowy rough scrub brush and then to richer looking plant life back on the hills. A loamy smell breezed out to the boat. In the warm morning, Vincent felt a chill settle in around his shoulders.

It soon grew too light to see a flashlight signal, and, there were no white patches. Vincent hadn't considered the agents wouldn't be waiting.

"Chief?"

"What, Lake?"

"I read that a man never hears the bullet that blows his brains out."

"Shut up, Abie." But the damaging thought had been planted.

"Chief?" Abie again.

"What now?"

"Did you know Vietnam was here before you found out where it was?"

"Dammit!" He said aloud. "Shut it up, Abie." He found it necessary to shake his head again and again in order to break through his resentment. "I'm right back in the middle of a fuckin' shooting war I thought I'd ever see again, so shut!" Lake became quiet. With no verbal outlet for his anxiety his face became very strained, his eyes squinted, his lower jaw stuffed out and upward, awkward looking.

Tucker had stowed his paddle. Letting the light surf move them ashore, he held his glasses to his face. The small boat skittered onto the sand at 5:50.

With no sign of the CIA team, Vincent wondered how long they should look or wait.

"Fireworks Zebra, Spot One, Over."

"Fireworks Zebra, Over."

"Arrived home, no parade. Advise, Over."

"This Fireworks Zebra, wait on station. Out." It was the Captain's voice on the radio. Clifford seemed concerned enough about the new mission to have stayed awake and on top of it.

"Sheeit." Tucker moaned. "We stay in here long, we hav'ta eat C rations."

"So?" Lake bit.

"Taste lah'k late-August road kill."

Following Vincent's motions, the three men dragged the light boat over the sand and into some brush. Vincent searched seaward but could not see Truaxe.

"Should see smoke at least." Tucker offered looking to seaward.

"Tuck." Vincent said flatly. "It's a nuke. No smoke?"

"Oh." Tucker deflated some. "Where the fuck is it then?"

"Must'a taken it farther to sea to escape being seen …now that a longer wait looks possible.

"Christ, look at that." Tucker yelled, pointing as he dropped to the ground. "How the fuck we miss them?"

About a hundred yards inland and two hundred yards south were several civilians entering a very large terraced rice field that covered the size of two football fields. The three men ducked behind the brush, Vincent quickly counted. "Twenty five of 'em. Look like farmers."

"Yeah. I see nothin' but them dark cottons. " Tucker reported. "Coupla' splotches o' color here and there."

"Kids, too. Some."

Most wore the funny little lampshade hats that seemed standard issue among the farmers in Southeast Asia.

"Damn." Lake growled as, following Vincent's motions, the three belly-crawled carefully toward better brush cover. " I smell worm farts."

"Hush it up, Abie." Vincent ordered using a rushed new word. Then: "The farmers must've come down a tree covered path."

"Don't look la'ke they seed us, yet."

The civilians were nearly all in one clearly defined field and soon fell into order, stooping over and weeding along the terraces in neat masses of what appeared to be yellowish young rice. Though the binoculars didn't allow Vincent to make out faces on the farmers, darting jerky movements could identify a few children.

Vincent flipped open a small book and ciphered some numbers. "Fireworks Zebra, Spot One. 25 farmers in a field 200 yards south of point x-ray. Observing. No contact. Over."

"Fireworks Zebra, roger. Out."

Vincent tried to superimpose Vietnamese faces from his past on the farmers ashore thereby making them less of a threat. It didn't work.

Abie commented naively. "Don't they know there's a war on? They just hoein' like nothing's happening."

"This is their farm, dumb ass." Tucker dug at him. "Farmers farm."

"You should know, Hoopie."

"I'm not a Hoopie. Hoopie's are from West Virginia, no shoes, think welfare is a job, and gots two brothers named Bubba."

"Well, double Bubba," Abie said calmly, lifting his glasses again. "You got your information someplace."

"Just people, Abie." Vincent reminded. "Doing the best they can."

Tucker again started scanning in other directions. "Where those G-men? Fuckin' feds could screw up a carnival."

"Don't know. Keep looking." Vincent picked up the radio. "Fireworks Zebra, Spot One." He pulled the cipher codes from their pouch and encoded a few simple signals, basically asking the Captain if perhaps the boat crew should stay low for 24 hours in case the agents had been delayed because of the increased TET commotion on the inland roads. Clifford acknowledged then took several minutes to reply.

"Spot One, Fireworks Zebra. Ref your last. Negative. Does not fit the big picture."

Fireworks, Zebra. Roger, out."

Abie lowered his glasses and looked at Vincent. He seemed truly nervous. "If we don't find 'em, if they got sucked into some NVA gun barrel? And if we get sucked into the same barrel? How's *that* fit into the big picture?"

Abie had always kidded him about the 'big picture'. During his swift-boat tour around the Plain of Reeds, Vincent had seen enough of the war to forget trying to see a big-picture. He saw instead, a certain rock and a hard-place the Vietnamese were between. The tremendous damage done to working people by the corruption of the loosely democratic Vietnamese government, which he called the "rock", *and* damage from the cruelty of Ho Chi Minh's men who wanted a communist type power-base, which he called "the hard place."

"What the hell we doin' here anyhoo, Chief?" Abie had asked.

"We Yanks want those people to have a right to vote for their own rock or hard place, Abie. That's what the war's about. The Vietnamese right to choose."

The big picture had always been discussed in the navy as though it were some tremendous idea off in some university or in the Pentagon. Most sailors sort of assumed that someone in authority had it; the President, Vice President, Secretary of State, surely the Chief of Naval Operations. When a mission or job resulted in feelings of frustration or annoyance, someone was always heard to say: "Well, someone knows how this fits into the big picture". That statement seemed intended to make everyone feel better but it also seemed, to Vincent, to keep people from questioning specifics.

As a gut-reaction, he had suspected, then decided most influential people on both sides were simply acting and reacting their leadership roles hoping, as Vincent did, that someone above *them* had the picture. He thought of President Truman and 'the buck stops here'.

"Christ, Abie," he said out of the blue. "Can you imagine? The absolute end of the big picture is with President Johnson?"

Vincent noticed Tucker staring at him. "You bitter, Chief? You seem uncertain."

"Me?" Where did that come from, he wondered? He ignored the question.

Vincent had scrambled from the streets of his small hometown to his position of respect in the navy by never acting uncertain. Coming up through the ranks, if uncertain about a next move he would simply get composed and barge ahead as if he never had a doubt of what to do. Half the time in the navy he was learning a job at the very time he was officially tasked to do it. He liked what Admiral Halsey was famous for saying, "When you are in command, dammit, command." But he worried now, because he'd also heard Clifford say it.

Lying in the sand he felt tired, sweaty and itchy in his khakis, a black USN ball cap and gray sneakers. The binoculars were heavy in his hands, the forty-five, the extra magazines, the charts and the canteen felt huge at his side. His Ben Bristol hand thumped anew, almost as bad as the night he'd hit the man. At that moment, the mute acceptance of extreme discomforts, the uniforms, the language, feigned bravado and now the return of the hand pain and churning fear, all seemed ridiculous. With a further chill out of context with the heat of the morning, he was hit with something very clear. He was not invested in the war. He was also no longer invested in the navy or in being a Master Chief.

"Rachael wasn't Rachael? Shit, I'm not even me."

"What, Chief?"

"Nothing."

He rolled over onto his back in the coarse sand and finger-roots of the brush. "Is this fair to Tucker and Lake? I don't want to be here." He was unquestionably aware he was treading time, like water, until he could be away from the war to be with Cynthia. How could a woman change his whole life in this way?

The radio startled him, "Spot One this is Fireworks Zebra —report, over." Vincent didn't move. Lake grabbed the microphone.

"This is Spot One. Over."

"This is Fireworks Zebra—last search of area, depart in fifteen minutes. Over."

"Why not depart in *twenty* minutes, twenty-*five*? What do they know on the ship?" Vincent asked into the air.

"Hey. Chief? I work for you, remember?"

Vincent again shook his head to concentrate. Was Clifford worrying primarily about his admiral stripe as he gave commands about the mission, even the order to depart?

"Tucker, go north, Lake, go south. I'll go inland here. Be back in 12 minutes and I mean that."

"Whafo?"

"Look for signs of the CIA team, that's all. And get back here."

He then mumbled.—"I've got the big picture, not you."

Twenty minutes later they were rowing the small boat out into the Gulf. As they moved through the small breakers and into smooth swells, Vincent and Tucker kept checking the farmers but saw no changes in behavior.

"I doubt they have a radio, Chief." Tucker projected.

"I also gamble, Tuck, this far north, if they see us, the farmers will see us as locals or the NVA. I hope."

"I hope so too. I feel helpless as a fundamentalist Viking."

"Hey." Abie said, sloshing one hand over the side. "The water's warm as pee."

"Next time," Tucker said, jerking a hand away from the black boat sides. "But there won't be no next time accordin' to the Cap'n, ah'll brang a fuckin' aig and we'll fry it on the rubber sides of this boat."

Well clear of the beach, Vincent told Tucker to start the engine. He reported to Truaxe they were heading out for rendezvous and pickup. Tucker unrolled a poncho and drew it around his blanched white arms. He seemed nervous and unsettled despite his crack about the eggs.

"You drive, Lake." Tuck shoved the motor handle toward Abie. "Lemmie' help the Chief here look fer' them CIA's. Hell, don't know what you boys 'ud do without 'ol sharp eyes bunny hunter lak' m'sef protectin' ya'."

"You shot Thumper?" Lake sounded disgusted.

"None o' that Disney shit. I ate Thumper too. An', I'd eat Snow White if I had a chance."

Lake took the motor. Vincent was glad to have Tucker's energy on lookout. "Goddammit, Tucker." Lake whined. "Quit. You sloshed around enough to where there's too much water in here to get comfortable." Lake steered with a hooked arm and tried operating the little hand pump to draw water from the soft bottom.

Tucker tipped his ball cap. "Fuck you very much, Abie. Here, Chief. Look to the rah-gt, ain't thet sumpin' or somebody I see movin' in those hills?"

Lake looked quickly and agreed. "Some new kind of shit on those paths up there."

Vincent looked but saw nothing new. Tucker rubbed the binocular lenses quickly with his shirttail and shifted from a sitting position to where his knees were in the soppy water. He locked his arms tightly against his sides. When his gaze was steady he became very excited. "Sheeit." His face turned whiter than even his normal pale.

Abie saw something too. "That curly path, Chief, like a slim road on the southern side of that center hill? See em"?

People dressed in dark outfits were snaking hurriedly down a high path. They were still well inland and appeared to be jogging, almost running along the winding trail in the ultimate direction of the beach. From the distance they looked like upright worms, but no contrasting colors showed in their clothing and they were fairly evenly spaced. All three men knew the truth at once.

Vincent ciphered. "Fireworks Zebra, Spot One. Movement ashore. 25 to 30 personnel at coordinates 410-50, two thousand meters from the beach. Likely NVA. Over." He was breathing heavily.

"This Fireworks Zebra, roger … Observe and advise. Out."

The Chief tried not to think of the lack of real training back on Truaxe.

Tucker, the man who promised he'd be at home in-country seemed very tense and nervous, surprising the Chief. Lake was animated. "I ain't trained for this kinda' shit, Chief." He kept the boat heading seaward with one hand and gazed ashore with binoculars with the other. He threw an Abie-ism into the air: "Stand still for two seconds—around here you could get shot … "

"They don't appear to see us." The Chief hoped.

"Tuck … I don't want'em hearing a motor noise out here. Put the 'lectric in place."

"No." The refusal surprised the chief. "Bad idea. We gotta' git outta' here."

"Shut it off. What's the matter with you?"

"But." Tucker looked to the Chief, then ashore. Then back to the Chief.

"Off—dammit." Vincent snapped. Sweat exploded across Tucker's forehead. He swung his hand against the slide control, shutting the motor off.

All forward motion stopped immediately.

"Alright." Vincent had to re-evaluate Tucker in the anxious moments. "Turn on the electric." He commanded.

The sudden quiet and the loss of forward motion caused Vincent to feel even more vulnerable in the broad sea. He could hear a Java Rice Sparrow screech, then a Macaw sound from the trees ashore, then a distant train whistle. He decided the only thing that had kept the patrol from hearing their motor was absolute luck, perhaps only the patrol's running footsteps.

Where Tucker looked white and motionless, Lake's nervousness came out through his mouth. "I see twenty five little people . ." He mocked the breathlessness of an announcer from a B grade thirties movie. " ...comin' off the mountain ...are twenty—maybe twenty five ...no, twenty eight slanty-eyed little jerks in baggy suits lookin' like the army of Egypt, with jerkweed hats, little fungus covered hats! Some have helmets on, Chief." His voice became serious. "They *are* regular army. An' I see two 50 calibers and a mortar maybe, or two." He checked the coordinate map, shifting from nervous buffoon to a more settled gunfire support spotter. "Count twenty eight regular army, Chief."

Through the long glass Vincent could tell they were a patrol but doubted the farmers had called them in. The farmers, he decided, would not have stayed in the field if they knew a shooting fight was about to happen this close to them. He cautiously relaxed a little and ciphered a message.

"Fireworks Zebra, this is Spot One. Twenty eight to thirty, I say again, 2-8 maybe 3-0 armed uniformed personnel at 410-52, moving seaward ...a kilometer from the beach. They do not see us. Over."

"This is Fireworks Zebra. Two mounts at ready, Over."

Vincent felt a jolt of anxiety. The only way Truaxe could have *two* gun mounts to train on the patrol was if the ship were sideways to the action. If she were coming in at high speed to pick up the boat, only the forward mount could be available for firing.

"This is Spot One. Did you report, TWO mounts available. Over."

"Affirmative. Ready to fire. Over."

"This is Spot One. We are vulnerable. Request rendezvous for pickup. Over."

"This is Fireworks Zebra. Negative. Will wait hull down on station. Report coordinates for salvo when ready. Over."

Coordinates? Was the crew *really* ready to take on a mission such as this?

"Didn't count on this kinda' shit, Chief, did we?" Abie sounded truly afraid.

"Get that damned electric going, Tucker."

"A'hm tryin', I AM ...tryin'"

"Why Clifford keepin' the fuckin' ship at sea, Chief? Somethin' we don't know 'bout?"

"Don't know, Abie. Shit, I don't know."

"Wonda' if'n those troops in there got our CIA folks." Tucker's voice was also halting. He, like Lake, seemed very upset.

"The motor, Tuck, the motor." He watched as the Southerner fumbled trying to hook two battery clamps to the terminals. It finally buzzed into life. The quiet motor didn't do much more than make it easier to keep the bow pointed to seaward.

Vincent scanned the horizon for Truaxe but still could not locate her. The glare on the water from the low-level morning sun turned the sea into a giant reflector.

"Guess what, folks, " he reported with the first positive discovery since leaving the beach. "We've got a Yahooty on our side."

"What's that? Abie asked.

"Yahooty. Remember basic seamanship? Sun glare makes us one of a million shadows. We're camouflaged by it. So feel better now." It was almost a command. He felt just a bit better with the new knowledge, and Truaxe burst in.

"Spot one, this' Fireworks Zebra. Request coordinates. Over."

Abie looked seaward to locate the ship.

Vincent readied his two men. "Okay, this is gonna' be a shooting war, folks." From the overall tension and from squeezing the microphone button, he felt strong pain return to his right hand. From habit he cursed Ben Bristol's hard forehead and immediately flashed a memory of Rachael. Hating that, he flicked his head as if shaking the correct slide into place. An instant scintillating visual of Cynthia appeared in his thoughts, erasing Ben and Rachael. Cynthia, great breasts, he thought with shallowness.

He shook his head to concentrate on the chore at hand.

CHAPTER TWELVE
Call for Fire

Shit! Shit! Shit!" Clifford kicked a signal light stand. "First real job in a real war and we botch it."

"I didn't think Vincent was the man to send in there." Griffith's spoke with a straightforward 'I told you so'.

"You don't like him 'cause he's divorcing his wife." Clifford said matter of fact. Pulling a toothpick from his mouth, he added, "He's the only real experienced man in the god-damned crew, Griffith."

"Should have sent an officer in there."

"Who? You? Smiley Valentino? Forgetful Lukarmo? Checked-out Stumpf? Give me a break. Vincent's been over here. He knows what to do. Tucker's experienced also. The CIA's fucked this up, not my men."

Griffith stood mute, brushing at his uniform front.

Clifford again grumbled at Griffith. "What if I've already lost the CIA agents? Forfeit our men too? The boat?" He turned away and half mumbled. "Too chancy for them waiting in there in this daylight this far north."

"What's more important, Cap'n?" Griffith back-peddled the attitude in his voice. "I mean. Look at it this way. Those CIA agents were doing something big for the war, most likely. I think it's worth a gamble ...to gamble our men. Leave 'em in there for now." He raised both hands, palms out and made a face like a bad used car salesman caught pushing too hard. "Don't hear me wrong now ...gamble for the chance of getting the CIA."

Clifford looked at Griffith but gave no reaction to the recommendation.

"What I *really* mean, Cap'n," Griffith said in a patronizing near whisper, "is, get the CIA men out or your first mission *is* a bust, lost crew members or not."

"*My mission?*" Clifford almost yelled. "It's *our* mission, Arnie? That's why I'm worried."

"Maybe ask CTG 70.8 for instructions?" Griffith's question was really a second recommendation.

"What? Ask the teacher? This is a ship. I command it." Clifford shifted to an almost fatherly grin. "We'll pull this one out with something" Then he barked: "with *something*." Then he softened again. "Never worry, Mr. Griffith." He turned his back to his executive officer and became very busy scanning the horizons.

Griffith sat his brief case on the chart table. He seemed rattled. He peered at the navigation chart before him, made some measurements, checked his watch, 6:30 a.m., and punched the button to the intercom to CIC. "CIC? Exec here. At the boat's best speed, give me their ETA, ten miles from the shore."

"Aye, aye, Sir." There was a pause of several seconds. "Ah, Sir? What *is* boat's best speed?"

Griffith's anger flared. "O'boy." He sounded disgusted. "Don't you have that information in there? Tell Mr. Lukarmo ..." His spirits dropped. He whined into the intercom. " ...that's critical information—GET IT NOW." He banged the button closed with a hard strike, jerked the hand back and shook it.

The captain touched his arm. "A bit snippy are we Mr. Griffith?" Leaving Griffith standing there rubbing a stubbed finger, Clifford headed off the bridge. "I'll be in my cabin exec, if I'm needed."

"But, what are we doing here?" Griffith seemed very confused.

"OOD knows. I've given him instructions while you were goading Lukarmo. You need a separate briefing?"

Tough Toes Arnie's jaw tightened. Clifford left the bridge.

Lieutenant Bien Cao and Sergeant Con Theu reached the field a few meters ahead of their scattered patrol. At the approach of the uniformed men the farmers looked to one another with worrying, questioning faces. Not wanting the tender plants damaged, some of the older farmers moved to meet the soldiers at the edge of the rice.

"You have been here all day?"

"Yes, since soon after sun."

"Then you see two Americans on highway, on paths, on beach? Anywhere?"

The farmers looked to one another.

"Did you see a boat, any kind of a boat? Or helicopter?"

The lieutenant's face showed frustration and stubbornness. The peasants appeared afraid, off stride. One of them called to the others in the field.

"Anyone see two Americans, on beach?" He pointed toward the beach. "Or see a boat?" He pointed towards the ocean to the east. "Or a helicopter?" He jabbed one finger upward several times.

In unison the crowd in the field rose upright from stooped positions. Some wiped their faces. All looked uncertain, their heads turning back and forth to see if anyone had the information. No one spoke.

The remainder of Cao's sweating patrol arrived in rag tag order. They looked grim faced and fatigued. The children who had been scurrying around outside of the field's edges gathered to see the soldiers.

"I saw a boat." One child spoke up. "Over there. A black boat with men." The young girl pointed more into the air than toward the gulf.

Cao pulled ancient binoculars from a worn leather side pack and quickly scanned the ocean. Squinting, he tried again and again to see against the powerful sun glare. Frustrated even more, he turned to the little girl. "When? How long ago you see the boat? How many men?"

The child, only 5 or 6 was startled by the force of his words and by Cao's intimidating appearance. She shuffled to her mother and hid behind her knotted skirt.

"Tell me! Tell her to talk to me, now." With shaking pointing fingers, Cao commanded the humbled mother.

"Go easy." An elder cautioned. "She's only a child."

"You let spies get away right in front of you. We've been hunting them. You let them get away?"

"But ...no. We were working. We weren't looking." The old man was pleading, trying to shift to a mode of reason.

The butt of Cao's AK-47 came up and caught the old man in the groin. With a shocked gagged sputter, the elder folded to his knees in the foot deep water.

"No" A woman screamed and dived towards the fallen old man. Sergeant Theu followed Cao's move and smacked the woman with his war-worn MAS rifle.

The farmers panicked. Some reached for the two fallen friends, several started running away from the soldiers.

"No!" Cao shouted to his weary men. "Stop them. Stop them, stop that running one." With one hand he pointed his Ak-47 in the direction of one of the younger men who was now running full speed across the rice field, water flying ahead of each flailing footstep.

Recruit Gia Dinh, on his first mission, 15 years old and anxious to do well, mistook Cao's pointing the Ak-47. Gia raised his French MAS sling rifle and followed the man for only two seconds. Cao shouted: "No, NO!" But too late. The trigger was pulled, the running man pitched forward with a splash and was instantly, except for his rice straw hat and the heel of one floating foot, hidden from view under mud churned water.

With shrieks and screamed words, the band of farmers burst away in several directions. One older farmer grabbed at the rifle of young Gia Dinh and pulled on it. It discharged. The old man clutched his stomach and dropped to his knees in front of the young soldier. Surprise infected both men's faces. In shock, Gia let go of his gun and fell backwards into the water. Another young soldier, protecting Gia, fired three rapid rounds from his 9mm British Sten Gun into the kneeling old man, killing him instantly.

"Stop this! Stop thhiiiiis!" Shouted Cao amidst the screaming, but his words were inferred by his confused patrol as "Stop *them!* Stop *them!*" Twenty five rifles and machine guns opened fire immediately toward the running peasants. Cao's plea's were lost to the noise.

Within seconds it was over. Only three of the farmers, including the scattering children could be seen above the muddy waters.

In the spot boat, Lake hollered. "Oh! My God!" just as Tucker cried. "Chief, Jesus. That's a murder in thar."

There were no bird sounds from ashore. Puffs of blue-black smoke squirted upward from the soldiers and evaporated. Bodies crumpled beneath the rice plants. Slight rattles of the weapons could be heard beneath the sound of the wind and the slapping of the swells against the rubber boat.

As his brain recorded the bloodshed, Vincent stood bonded to the boat floor, his pained hand twitching the radio microphone with every shot seen ashore.

"We're next." Abie yelled. His voice snapped Vincent to life.

"Fireworks Zebra—Spot One. Hostile fire ashore. Regular army fired on what seemed to be unarmed civilians in a field. Children and adults murdered, some children still in danger. 300 meters from Spot One … Wait. Out." He groped for reasonable thought. "We can't do a fucking thing he said into the air and into the open mike." He released the button and his ship was immediately on the air.

"Request instructions. Request briefing. Over."

"This is Spot One, wait. Out."

Lake was so out of control he took a swing into the air and lost balance, toppled over the side into the gulf water. In one motion Tucker jerked him immediately back into the boat, his own binoculars still trained on the uniformed soldiers who were scattering all over the field. Now and again a puff of blue smoke would rise in the air and the three in the boat would hear a faraway crack. Vincent, shocked, drew a long calming breath and re-surveyed the people who remained. On this look, he couldn't sort a single farmer or child from the group at the field edge.

He stood then, locked in disbelief. Tucker also seemed immobilized. Squatting on the boat bottom, his face was blank, no clues to his thoughts. Lake tried to stand in the boat but continually fell to one knee, shivering as though cold. "I wasn't ready for this, Paul. I'm sorry, but I didn't sign up for this." He dropped Vincent's rank, their long friendship taking precedence during the anxious moments.

"Nor I, Abie." Vincent said quickly. "Hang in there. We'll sort this out."

"Sure. What. Yes, why. Chief, sure." Tucker seemed to be capable of only one syllable at a time.

"We've gotta' talk to them." Vincent said, but his words didn't reflect what his mind was putting into order. "Tucker, pull in that putt-putt and stow it. Lake, throw out a drag anchor." Vincent's mind started clicking along the way he liked it. Ring the soldiers with gunfire from the ship. Prevent them from escaping via their trail and push them down to the beach. Then, *capture* them.

Was it crazy enough to work?

"Fireworks Zebra, this is Spot One. Hostiles …" But even as he was about to give the command he'd trained for hour after hour by shooting at target islands, rafts and fifty gallon drums, he was stopped by a memory he promised to always process at this point in any battle, when possible. A general's guidance from the U.S. civil war jumped into his thoughts. "Not even the finest war plan survives first contact with the enemy." Paul Vincent swallowed and re-swallowed that thought, but went on with the plan.

"CALL FOR FIRE." He yelled into the mike. "Coord 400-40. Report when ready. Fire for effect. Over."

Fireworks Zebra…roger 400-40, firing for effect. Standby …ready with two mounts—Over."

"This is Spot One … Fire. Over."

"This is Fireworks Zebra—wait—out.

"Wait?" He starred at the small radio, helpless.

"This is spot one, Fire. Over."

"This is Fireworks Zebra—casualty—wait—out."

A casualty? Something had gone wrong aboard ship. A misfire? No. He had said a casualty. The word is loosely used in gunfire to describe everything from a broken trigger to an explosion in a magazine. He instinctively looked seaward. No trace of the ship could be seen. He looked back ashore. The NVA were making their way toward the hill trail.

Suddenly—"This is Fireworks Zebra. Shot. Over."

They could hear the round of five inch 50 caliber hiss overhead and to the south of them. A THUMP followed when the explosive round bombed into the rain soaked earth of Vietnam. Vincent couldn't see where it exploded.

"There." Abie cried pointing south. A smoky cloud appeared slowly, dimly, far beyond the top of a hill. The round had been poorly coordinated aboard ship.

"Help me do coordinates, Abie." Vincent balanced the coordinating map, the radio mike and his binoculars.

"400-33. Tell 'em, Chief." Lake barked.

Vincent yelled into his face. "NO, GODAMMIT, NO. DON'T HIT 'EM. Just barely overshoot 'em ...some close rounds, bring 'em down to the beach." His voice was composed. "Pay fucking attention, Lake."

Abie looked quizzical for a half second then nodded, more composed. "Sorry, Paul. I've got it now. I hear you now." He looked at the coordination map for a second then back to Vincent. "Don't give 'em coords, Chief. Tell 'em up or down."

"I've gotta' get on the same planet first." Then, over the radio. "Fire again, over."

"Shot, Over."

Again the round hissed overhead. This time it exploded dirt and debris two hundred yards beyond the intended coordinates.

"This is Spot One. Down two, left ...one. Over."

Until it took shape, if it took shape, trying the plan without actually telling Clifford was taking a severe risk. It had to work, he thought.

"What if they rain one in on us?" Tucker looked very nervous.

Vincent spoke to his worried man. "Fingers are for crossing, Tuck. Do it."

"This's Fireworks Zebra. Casualty cleared. Will improve now. Shot, Out."

Tucker didn't calm. "What the hell we gonna' do if they DO surrender? Ya' better git that ship in here."

"This is Fireworks Zebra—casualty—delay, wait—Out."

Something wasn't right on the ship. Full minute ticked by extremely slow. The soldiers were jogging toward their trail, heads searching for the source of the explosions. Vincent's back and front was soaking from nervous sweat.

"Shot." called the voice from Truaxe.

The spinning hiss came but the dust explosion was much higher than even before, a mile beyond the troops.

"What the fuck kinda' shootin' ship I git' myself 'signed too? Git that ship closer in heah." Tucker's head jerked from shore to sea, back and forth.

The soldiers were scrambling toward the path they'd entered on, about 300 yards inland

and to the north. Intense cooperation was needed from the gun mounts. He felt he'd better bring Clifford and the ship in on his plan, in case it was just too far out of limits.

"Fireworks Zebra, this is Spot One." He called calmly. "For C.O.—Plan ring of fire and capture. Hostiles vulnerable now and can be cut off from escape path and forced to the beach. Fire salvos left to right! Same elevation and stand by. Further, request Fireworks Zebra proceed to scene ASAP. Over."

"This is Fireworks Zebra. Negative to that plan. Fire directly on the troops—now. Acknowledge, Over"

What to do? Lie?

"This Spot One—acknowledged." With his heart thumping, he disobeyed the order and reported coordinates that followed his plan.

"Roger—Salvo, eight. Shot. Over."

Tucker screamed. "You disobeying an order? Chief?" He threw his hands into the air. "What the fuck kinda' N-A-V-Y am I in' here?"

A hiss blew past the spot boat, then another and several more. Hell was about to rain in on the soldiers who were in a rumpled string sprinting beyond the paddy. The smell of the burning munitions and powder drifted down to the three men in the boat. 100 yards ahead of the running troops, sand and trees jumped into the air in a pattern of THUMP THUMP THUMP THUMP. The shots blew the edge of the tree line away, perfect. The entire group of running figures stopped in their tracks.

"This is Spot One. Left 300. Salvo. Over."

Quite a few seconds passed.

"This is Fireworks Zebra. We have a hang fire mount 52. Proceeding max speed your location. ETA one five minutes. Awaiting your declaration of helo safety. Over."

"Ain't safe, Chief." Lake said. "Some of those jerks are still armed in there and that still may be two 50 cal types those two men are luggin'."

With a hang fire on mount 52, the aft mount, Clifford was forced to train the mount safely seaward and wait a prescribed amount of time to see if the faulty round would fire. With only a forward mount available, it was just as well he head toward the action as stay sideways to it.

Vincent advised them of the possibility that the enemy had 50 caliber machine guns with them.

Clifford turned to his exec. "50 cal. Those pilots worry 'bout those guns?"

Griffith picked up the telephone to the helo deck and spoke directly with Lieutenant Salvador DiNoble.

He turned to Clifford. "Pilot says since a battle called Ap Bac, in '62. The V.C. bring choppers down all the time with 50's, Cap'n."

"Shit. Keep him aboard. I ain't losing my helo."

The next salvo sang in over the boat. THUMP THUMP THUMP. Off to the right a big tree burst into flames. The soldiers saw this and started running back to the left, heading south and nearer to the sandy beach.

The next salvo made a big curtain of exploding wood and sand not twenty five yards ahead of the fleeing men. Two lead soldiers dropped from the explosion and stayed down.

"We killed one, Paul."

"Too close, too close. Shit." Into the mike: "Left 100. Salvo, repeat."

" ...Roger. Shot. Ten.. Out."

There was no leadership among the men ashore. They scattered more, some running toward the beach, others to the right, north. All they knew is that someone was storming war on them and they had no idea from where.

"Oh fuck. This is gonna' work, Chief. Oh! Fuck me." Abie cried out.

A new salvo tore the terrain ahead of the scattered main group. All of the group pounding from north to south stopped in their tracks. A smaller group started running north again.

"This is Spot One. Hostiles splitting into two groups. Can you give me two mounts. Over."

"Negative on two mounts. Hang fire. Proceeding to your area." It was the C.O. on the circuit.

"This is Spot One. Roger. Need second mount ASAP. Over."

"Understood. I have one mount available. Out."

The captain was experiencing his first combat action from the blind end of a radio speaker on a ship out of visual range. Vincent knew Clifford would continue coming toward the shore at this time, one mount or not. His need for involvement and control would win over Vincent's need for tactics.

Again Vincent requested two mounts. Again he was refused.

The next salvo landed pretty far back. Three of the eight rounds again landed over the top of the hill, the remaining five scattered over a two hundred yard area, too erratic to be effective.

The troops ashore reacted unconsciously to Vincent's plan. As they edged towards the sand, the blasts were farther away. They'd mostly reached the beach and most were sprinting northward, a few running south. A small group simply stood in one place directly inshore from the spot boat. Vincent split the gun's mission and threw four rounds ahead of each running group after cautioning the ship to be more accurate. He got even poorer results. The north rounds fell almost into the larger pack, dropping several men and splitting it into two smaller groups.

"Paul, we killin' men in there. This ain't workin'."

"Shut it up, Abie. It's bad shooting." About fifteen men were still hauling it northward. Now two groups were heading south, one about fifty yards ahead of the other.

Tucker shouted. "Thar she comes, Boss."

They could easily see Truaxe well under the horizon. White smoke popped out of her bow with each shot of the salvos.

"Pappy, those fuckers in there 'er just runnin' now. This is all fucked up." Lake seemed overwhelmed.

"We should quit," Tucker screamed. "we should stop."

"We should WHAT?"

"Quit shootin'." Tucker seemed more frightened than excited.

"Fuck you ... " What had happened to the rock of a man he'd left the ship with?

After two more salvos, pure fright driven fatigue took all running spirit out of the men ashore.

"There ain't a rifle among 'em, Chief." Lake called out as he inspected with his binoculars. "No one's got a gun."

"Git that helo in here now, Chief." Tucker urged strongly. "Let *them* take over this."

Ashore, Lieutenant Ben Cao pulled his uniform shirt off and then his skimpy gray undershirt. He attached the undershirt to a dropped MAS rifle and with tears of failure in his eyes, waved it in the air.

"There's a flag, Chief." Lake yelled excitedly pointing to the most northern group.

"This is Spot One. Unarmed and panicked hostiles are grouping on the beach directly inland of us." He felt capture of the troops was an obvious choice for the captain and would be easy. Bring the ship in close to frighten them further. Send a launch ashore and round them up.

"Recommend helo monitor roundup and surrender of enemy troops. Certify helo safety. Over."

Intimidation would be easy for Lieutenant DiNoble and Randy Hill. From the Seasprite, fire a few rounds of gattling gun into the water and demonstrate that, if necessary, they could instantly gun down the group. Vincent again picked up the mike. "This is Spot One. Total passive surrender can be had within seconds of the helo arriving on the scene. Over."

Vincent watched for signs Clifford would accept his recommendations. Nothing. The ship was approaching rapidly but the helo did not lift off.

The very calm voice of the captain crackled over the radio. "Spot One, this is Fireworks Zebra. We have visual contact, we take target control. Out." Vincent helplessly relinquished control, unable to tell if Clifford showed signs of agreeing with him.

Without command responsibility for gunfire, Vincent was suddenly left with too much adrenaline, too little to do, too quickly. He gasped for breath, his mind wondering how his fanatic idea would evolve. As he tried to take it all in, he felt both confident and competent. They hadn't found the CIA men, but they had a grand prize for their troubles.

Truaxe was charging in bow on now, at flank speed. She carved through the water throwing tons of ocean to either side of her contoured bow. As she turned in an arch to the north to avoid hitting the spot boat, the sea-toss exploded against her anchor housing high on the bow. Rainbows curved and flickered in the resulting spray. Vincent felt somewhat overwhelmed by that particular view of the power he'd held in his hands only seconds before.

Impulsively, Vincent again pressed the mike button. "Fireworks Zebra, this's Spot One. Recommend use helo for roundup and to force surrender. Over."

Again the Captain's voice crackled over the small speaker. "This is Fireworks Zebra. I say again. WE TAKE TARGET CONTROL. OUT."

The gray mass of the ship pounded past only thirty or so yards from the boat. As her swollen wake approached, the three men gripped for handles and were tossed like children in the surf on an inner tube. Truaxe shuddered and heaved like a dinosaur as her powerful engines backed down to pull her to a stop parallel to the shoreline. Just then the helo twisted like a leaping ballerina off the afterdeck, rotors clapping in the sun as she gained altitude and speed. She slipped sideways and was over the beach in a few seconds. The 7.62 millimeter mini-gun was obvious sticking passively out of the left side of the plane's nose. The gun, designed to strafe ground troops, could put out a stream of bullets timed to strike two to three feet apart and could cover a football sized field in just two seconds, hitting everyone in the area. One display of that firepower ringing around them and the soldiers would change politics. Vincent felt sure of that. Lake felt sure of that. Tucker nodded his agreement.

Vincent could see the headline or the cover story on *Time* magazine. "Ship captures foot soldiers".

'SHIT SHIT—CALL 'EM—NOW." Tucker screamed.

Looking towards the ship for a moment, the three men in the boat saw balls of white smoke blurt from the ship's 5 inch mounts. Crack/crack/crack/crack, over and over again. Vincent gazed in disbelief. Though his mind recorded what his eyes saw, it did not process him into any sort of movement.

"Call'em. Goddamn you." Tucker grabbed Vincent's arm very hard.

Jerked out of his trance, he shoved Tucker backwards and yelled into the mike.

"STOP CEASE FIRE, OVER."

Vincent turned to the beach but he needn't have. He knew too much about the brute of the five inch gun to doubt the scenario. The beach was ripped into a new form. The soldiers, in sheer terror, were literally running in circles. Truaxe was walking five-inch shells right up the beach from left to right. The shock waves and blast sounds reached the boat, thump, crack crack, thump thump, as the explosives bombed into the midst of the Vietnamese.

"Stop." He said into the mike.

"Spot one, this is Fireworks Zebra. We have fire control . . .do not use this circuit—OUT." It was the exec's flat voice on the radio.

Vincent felt revolutionary confusion. His heart beat dutifully but very hard. His stomach burned as though from coals. His emotions drained, he dropped to his knees in the boat and gazed at his ship now almost dead in the water, two hundred yards to the north. The firing had ceased, smoke from the mounts dissipated. Everything seemed too calm, out of perspective. The morning swells caught the ship under the fantail, lifting her in gentle rolling motions. A gull squawked once from a distance pulling Vincent's eyes ashore. Three Cormorant-like birds flew from the hills and glided to the ground, screeching as they wobbled in among the exploded bodies. The only other sound above the gentle breeze was the downwind buzz and flap-flap of DiNoble's helo as it hovered near the beach about a hundred yards north of the fallen Vietnamese.

As everyone watched, the nose of the helo dipped forward. The quiet little craft moved quickly toward the troops as a dragonfly might glide over a pond. Flames squirted from the chopper as it made a long slow turn and Randy Hill's gun ripped several hundred rounds into the beach. Nothing moved except the flying sand and the jolted clothing of the fallen men. One of the cormorants thrashed away, screeching. The others disappeared into the rage of bullets, bodies and sand.

Dead of feelings, Vincent's mind slowly assimilated the gruesome truth. Five-inch cannon and a gattling gun had been used on panicked, weaponless, and worst of all, surrendering people. Personally compromised beyond any ever, something reshaped inside of Paul Vincent. If Clifford truly represented his navy, he could not be part of it. If Clifford was somehow a fringe idiot, that might be different. He could understand then, a renegade had somehow penetrated his navy, to be sorted out, court-martialed, jailed—even executed. He had to find out which was the truth.

Ashore the chopper again hovered. The tree line was burning in some places. Hugh gaps of sky could be seen where trees had been. Craters were scattered all over the beach, some now filling with brown seawater. The soldier's remains were slumped on wet sand like laundry bags strewn on a loading dock. The black feathered bodies of the two Cormorants, wings splayed, lay just inches from one another. The moment called for some kind of releasing scream but it hung dry in Vincent's throat.

"Up your asses, motherfuckers." Lake yelled and stuck his middle finger skyward toward the ship.

"Chief, we gotta' git some dope on this one." Tucker said evenly. "Them fellers out thar'." He pointed towards the Truaxe. "This whole nightmare seems like a fuckin' dream." His words seemed to describe every thought as it passed by. "An' you Yanks' is s'posed to be the decent men heah?" He looked like the kid in the 1919 news clip when the Chicago White Sox cheated in the world series. "Say it ain't so, Joe, say it ain't so."

Abie patted Tucker's shoulder, but said nothing. Tucker touched Abie's hand.

"I don't know. I don't know." Is all Vincent could say.

As they readied to be picked up, Vincent's heart continued to hammer. Adrenaline gushing, he felt strangely different and was asking questions he'd always left others to decide. Why were they in that strange country in the first place? Who was deciding what was right or wrong? Why had the soldiers killed the farmers? Weren't they harmless, unarmed? Why had Clifford killed the NVA? Didn't he know *they* were harmless, unarmed? Is this war reaching its intended goal for anyone? What was the goal again? Anyone remember?

"I feel like a fucking hippy." He said aloud.

"Wha … Paul?"

"Nothing … Abie. Nothing."

"We traveled a long way jes' ta' ring the bells of a bunch of poor idiot Vietnamese, Chief? You agree?" Vincent ignored the man.

Tucker started the gasoline motor and steered the small boat toward the pickup point. Climbing up the rope ladder, Paul Vincent knew he was going to confront Robert Clifford, but not sure how to do it. He wanted an explanation of some sort, clear, correct, guilt free and wrong free.

"I'm going to talk to the Cap'n." He announced to Lake.

"Oh, shit." Abie said.

"Hey," Tucker joined in. "Yer' actin' like some kid who missed a nap."

CHAPTER THIRTEEN
Mutiny?

As the three clamored off the shaky ladder and onto the ship's main deck, several men tried conversation with Vincent. He pushed them aside, vaulted the steps of the wooden ladders three at a time and headed to the fourth deck and the bridge. At the third level, a strong arm hooked its elbow through his.

It was Lieutenant Stumpf.

"PAPPY!" He yelled. "Cool it." His voice softened but was still insistent, "cool it down," but also uncertain, "please."

"What happened back here?" Paul asked, almost hoping for an answer that would make all the conflicted feelings disappear.

"Don't ask. Nothing went right."

"Why'd he murder those people?"

"Chief—wait. He's just an order-following future-seeking puppet … "

He pulled against Stumpf's grip. "I'm gonna' confront him."

The lieutenant put a second hand on Vincent's arm. There was a new look of adamancy in his usually unremarkable chin line. "No! This'll do no good for anyone. Don't be stupid."

"He killed 'em."

"Fuck you, listen to me. If those troops killed our CIA? Clifford'll feel justified. He may well be right."

"It makes a sticky ball in my gut." Vincent said, looking away with the new thoughts about right or not right.

"Besides, here on the ship? Nothing went right. CIC operators fought, fist fought, over your ranges and bearings. Guns crews panicked. Two men ran from mount 52 during rapid fire, terrified. Mounts broke down again and again. Kolb's hands are all burned, something wrong in mount 51."

"Doesn't seem to justify the shelling of the NVA, of the gattling gun." Sweat darkened Paul's khaki shirt almost completely.

"The crew hand carried ammo five decks. Dropped a VT down a ladder."

"I was in enemy territory."

"They mishandled a hang-fire, endangered everyone."

"I saw children die."

"Goddammit, Vincent …*these are children on this ship.*"

The piercing comment slowed Vincent and forced him into a series of flashing new thoughts comparing children.

Stumpf continued.

"Pappy, listen. We're good-cop bad-cop at the same time."

Vincent's shoulder slumped. "Why can't I accept that this is how war is? I'm asking for empathy. I'm getting philosophy."

"Fuck empathy …philosophy. Fuck you." Stumpf's face reddened. " Look at reality. Just …" He stopped talking and forced-calmed his voice. " …let this go. You're heading on twenty years navy. Save this 'til another day."

"No!"

"But there are dozens on that bridge who'll support Clifford." Stumpf warned.

He hadn't thought of support or non-support. "How can anyone support that …?"

"From here, we did what we are supposed to do; kill enemy forces. Don't you see?"

The two men looked at one another for several seconds. Stumpf relaxed his grip. Vincent spun and grabbed the ladder rails. "Comin' or no?"

"Paul?" Stumpf seemed very surprised at his chief's lock-in anger. "What the hell did you think would happen in there? A walk in the sun?"

"Don't insult me, Lieutenant."

Stumpf walked away but turned back. "You're seeing now what I've known for years …watchin' all; this navy shit."

"That's not navy what we did." Vincent said and started up the ladder. "That was murder in there. No other way to see it."

"Just wait for the right day and time. This is NOT it." Stumpf said. He backed away and stood there, hands in pockets, his head nervously shaking from side to side. Vincent turned and went up the last ladder to the bridge.

Arriving on the bridge level, he forced himself to stand, wait and observe. The ship was moving directly into the morning sun, east, at thirty knots, rising and falling evenly on low swells. He had to shade his eyes with one hand and hold a ladder rail for balance. Most of the battle station crews were in the process of being relieved by the regular watch section. There was no usual chatter. The men were looking mostly down at the deck, not at one another. Many still had their pants tucked in socks, sleeves rolled down and collars buttoned, a standard *general quarters* defense dress against chemicals and heat. Most seemed tense.

The Captain was standing on the starboard side of the bridge-wing, sun-glasses in his hand, sweat rings on his underarms and down the center of his back. He was initialing a radio messenger's clipboard. Lieutenant Commander Corrigan was standing near him reading over his shoulder, an insincere grin too pronounced on his face. The exec was near the pilothouse door, looking aft with binoculars, right through Vincent. His briefcase was on the deck beside his right foot. Griffith was the only one still in his helmet and un-inflated life jacket.

Handing the clipboard back to the messenger, the Captain noticed Vincent. He began a smile that erased when he saw the Chief's expression. With a deep breath, he looked away, lifted his hat from his head, smoothed his hair with one open palm, replaced the hat, turned to face the Chief again and wiggled a forefinger, signaling him to come closer. Propelled by the need for answers, Vincent took his first controlled step and started his first uncontrolled sentence.

"I can't understand you." He said directly to Clifford. "Fucking murder back there … " He was next to the Captain whose jaw dropped, lips quivered and whose face passed through several expressions. Corrigan stepped aside and looked very puzzled at Vincent, his eyes now overly creased against the sun's glare. Vincent didn't stop but was speaking now without a full breath.

"What the hell am I in the boat for if you throw away my carefully planned decision." His breath was gone. " …throw away all I had gained in there? I had that plan working … " His voice broke from emotion. He breathed in and lowered its pitch. "You murdered in there … I want no part of it." He had mistimed his breathing. The last three words were expelled with a gasping sound. He felt silly.

A voice like someone rubbing fish scales backward grated in from behind him. "Chief. Back away from that." Vincent ignored it.

Clifford's right eye began to tic. He turned away and looked out over the railing, a time honored method of dismissing someone.

For just seconds Vincent seemed to calm and regroup. All those within hearing waited. Vincent's feelings remained strongly unsettled. His legs locked but he held a signal light stanchion for balance against the even rise and fall movements of the ship. He would not be dismissed. He hoped Clifford would not hide behind rank. "I have a right to an answer, Cap'n."

Clifford didn't move nor respond. Vincent waited. Corrigan broke the silence with a calculating reminder. "C.O. owes you no explanation." The man was right but Vincent still did not let go.

Vincent's left hand shot to Clifford's right shoulder and pulled him around face to face. Clifford reacted quickly, automatically and defensively. He chopped Vincent's hand away. Both men's faces progressed through dissimilar expressions. Spittle flew into Vincent's face as Clifford choked on his own saliva and though trying to speak, managed to only utter several unclear noises.

He stopped trying to talk. He looked away, wiped his forehead with an open hand and seemed to calm. He tested his uncertain voice again. "I'm the Captain, Chief. I, me." The words came out as a child's might when reminding a friend that it was 'his ball' and the game should go 'his way'."

A radio messenger burst onto the bridge wing and took two or three steps toward the C.O. He noticed something amiss and stopped in his tracks. Lowering the message board to his side he became one of the dozen or so fascinated witnesses.

Clifford spoke again but again had trouble getting the sentence started. "I determine … I judge … I'm responsible …ultimately …who gets killed around here!" Unsurely, he repeated, "who gets killed around here." His voice lacked sureness.

"Those soldiers, they were surrendering." Vincent also seemed to falter.

Clifford's voice evened out. "You hearing me? I decide who gets killed …not some man in a boat who over rides, OVER RODE, my order—LIKE YOU DID" He thrust a more confident face into Vincent's and searched for more words. "I make those DECISIONS. NOT YOU." Vincent backed away from the man's hot breath. Clifford, now confident appearing turned away and spoke into the air. "I decided who DOES get killed. Those gooks killed the CIA team—I am sure. A team I was, you—was …you were …responsible for getting out."

"They killed the CIA? That's what I need to know. A reason, a something."

Clifford turned back to him. "THEY MUST HAVE KILLED THEM." Where are they, if not killed? Clifford felt in control again as Vincent *seemed* to quiet. The roll of the ship caused a sudden 'bang' from the unattended swinging pilothouse door but no one changed his attention to check on it. It banged again, slightly

Vincent took two steps toward Clifford, and looked into his face to speak.

"NO!" Clifford screamed. "NO!" He jammed his index finger into the Chief's chest, pocket high, very hard. Once, twice, a third time so forcefully it drove Vincent back on his heels. They were so beyond military decorum there seemed to be no stopping. Then, Clifford went too far. He leaned into Vincent once more with one finger and pushed. No one could tell exactly why, but Vincent pitched backwards. Perhaps the push itself? Perhaps a slight tilt of the ship's deck in the swells? Maybe partly an instinctive flinch? Whatever, Vincent fell backward. His back struck the edge of a signal light. A sharp streak of pain shot through his shoulder blade. "Ahhh!"

Instinctively, as the night with Ben Bristol, 'fight', not 'flight' responded. Vincent's open right hand arched through the air and smacked Clifford's left cheekbone. Clifford's head snapped across his right shoulder. He stumbled backward, flailing his arms for balance. The Ben Bristol sprain stabbed Vincent's hand with agony, but even then, impulsively, Vincent and others reached to grab the Captain. Clifford's frantic hand closed on Vincent's sprain like a clamp.

"Ahhh!" Vincent jerked away from immediate pain, letting Clifford fly backward through the other grabbing hands and to the deck. Vincent pulled the sprained hand close and favored it.

The Captain was quickly pulled upright and balanced himself. His cheek glowing red, his jaw remained at an awkward angle for just a second. He turned his fists into knots. On male-automatic, several arms pulled both men away from one another. Vincent, whose right hand would not close, dropped both hands to his sides. Clifford relaxed his fists, wiggled his jaw back and forth and also dropped his hands. Abruptly, both men seemed calm. The arms released them both. Clifford stood silent, rubbing his face. Vincent slowly opened and closed his thumping right hand.

"What the fuck, Chief ..." The grating voice from the back of the group broke the anxiousness.

"Shut up." The exec ordered into the air.

Clifford started to speak but Vincent, slower and calmer than he thought he could be, interrupted him. With an ascorbic touch having crept into his voice, he spelled out his question again. "Why was fire control taken from me while I had the best information? I was going to capture them, get some answers—find out about the CIA ..."

"Fire control is ultimately mine." Clifford spoke as calmly as Vincent. "I decided the scheme was too crazy ...chancy. " He sounded in control again.

Vincent was getting the one-on-one conversation he had hoped for but that fact had become lost because of the slap. However, because no one, including Clifford and Vincent seemed willing to gather the energy necessary to access the implications of a man striking his commanding officer, the 'slap' was being ignored at least for the moment. The two professionals were measuring one another.

"You are well out of line, Vincent." Corrigan's surprise comment disturbed the fragile world of understanding Vincent hoped was building with Clifford.

"Stay out of this." Vincent was so curt it sounded like a warning. Corrigan surprised even himself by backing off. His shoulders shrugged involuntarily. Vincent continued.

"Tell me something of value? Did you have some specific intelligence from the gun-line commander, Cap'n?" As Vincent continued with his questions he had immediate afterthoughts. (That was a clear question—he should answer.) Clifford said nothing. (Be assertive and draw respect.) "D'you know something 'bout why the NVA fired on the farmers?" (How could he possibly know that?) Clifford said nothing. "Can you say something that will make me, an' my men feel better about what we just did in there?" Clifford said nothing. (Too pleading, too like a high school debate question. Be stronger, objective.) "That shouldn't have happened, Captain." He continued softly. (Now you're scolding a child, be careful.) Clifford said nothing.

"Dammit," Vincent continued. "If there was a danger, I'll sure accept that. I'm not asking you to explain your actions, of course not." (Christ, it sounds like I am.) Clifford said nothing. "I have men to explain to." Clifford still said nothing. (And it's embarrassing to have a nut for a C.O.) "Say SOMETHING." (Please—Please.)

Like kids at a playground after school, the two men were faced off, hands at their sides. Clifford remained silent but the onlookers backed into a circle as if on some united response to an unseen signal.

Clifford could have ignored Vincent forever. He could have simply told him to 'shut up.' With the wave of a finger he could have had the man literally dragged to the ship's tiny brig. Everyone waited for a commanding move against Vincent's insolence but Clifford surprised everyone by staying in conversation. "I have a lot of intelligence you're not privy to. I made the decision, that's all."

"Be specific." Vincent spoke too fast, too demanding, causing Clifford's mood to shift back to exasperation. His mouth opened but closed quickly. His right eye began to flicker. "There was hostile fire on that beach. You r'ported it, Vincent. I took 'eh ... 'propriate action." He pushed his hand into his shirt pocket and came up with a toothpick. He pointed it at Vincent. "I don't ...want to hear bullshit about what happened before I got there. I followed your advice. Then, when I see hostiles, I take hostile action." He seemed pleased with that line. He repeated. "I see hostiles, I take hostile action." He put his hands on his hips and spoke directly toward Vincent, toothpick now wriggling with each word. "Now I don't want to hear anymore about this."

It was the final comment everyone was waiting for. Clifford stepped toward the Chief and stood less than a foot from him. "Now, let's stop this." It was almost a whisper. Then he shouted into the air. "OOD? Clear this bridge of everyone except those actually on watch."

Anyone not truly needed rapidly disappeared down ladders. The radio messenger even left the bridge, his board unsigned. The exec snatched up his briefcase and obediently stepped inside the pilot-house, joining those who were suddenly very busy with their duties.

Vincent wondered if anyone consciously had the ship's control during the hassle.

He and Clifford then stood alone. Facing his silent Captain, Vincent could only helplessly but intensely fear that his own stupid reaction to Clifford's finger punching aggression now fogged the original point. He was no longer a respected co-professional intellectually questioning a Captain's judgment. Now he was a hotheaded enlisted man irresponsibly out of control. That prompted a sudden chilling thought. Was Clifford so clever as to have set this all up as he saw the truth of what happened ashore? Did he anticipate that frustrated adrenaline would prompt Vincent to slap him, thus distracting everyone from the NVA deaths? Was Vincent grossly underestimating this man, or was Vincent ridiculously paranoid?

The seconds ticked away. No one spoke. Clifford seemed miles away, staring. After a long time he turned to the Chief and again whispered so no one else could hear.

"Master Chief, Vincent?"

"Yes, Sir?"

Clifford leaned in close. "Let's, for now, see this as …as …you …over-reacting …in some serious way." He paused to let his words make impact. "Those bastards, by your own report, killed some thirty civilians. And that's what we are here to prevent. "

"Are we sure they killed the agents?"

"No, I'm not sure. So what? You didn't prevent murder from the spot boat, and I guess we couldn't prevent it from where we were." He stuttered slightly. "But …b-but. They'll never d-do it again." He stalked away, hands jammed into his pockets, rambling on about his 'decision'.

Hibernating into professional safety, Clifford was justifying the killings as some kind of official revenge. The argument seemed so logical Vincent found himself studying whether or not revenge was a valid premise.

Clifford turned back toward him. "Look. This is a warship in a combat zone. We are both sailors, Chief. We do what we have to do. I have to sift through this. Go below now, report to my cabin tonight, 1930. "

He had shifted from outrage to 'fair' again and promised to give it more thought. Not having any idea where he stood, Vincent turned and walked toward the ladder. He did not say, "aye, aye, Sir."

As he grabbed the ladder rails, Griffith was standing around the corner. His voice stern, he touched Vincent's arm. "I told you … I couldn't count on you to protect us from him."

Astonished, Vincent started to defend but Griffith turned quickly away just as the Captain called out: "Exec? Mr. Griffith? Where you at?"

Griffith stepped around the side of the pilothouse where he could be seen. Clifford spoke with a commanding tone.

"I want a semblance of order on this here ship. We've got spaces to clean up …ammunition inventory to get to 70.8 for replenishment. And, I want this ship cleaned up, and …tell the supply officer to have dinner on the fantail tonight. You know …steaks, hamburgers, some good greasy fried potatoes, so on. I don't give a shit 'bout his regular menu."

"Aye, aye, sir."

CHAPTER FOURTEEN
Vincent Regroups

Chief …why'd ya' not listen to me?" Stumpf asked elbowing his way into Vincent's room.

"I did listen. You just didn't change my mind."

"Well, you're in a world of shit." With an irritated puff of nostril air Lieutenant Stumpf pulled his hat off by the bill and stuffed it under his left arm. Lake removed his ball cap and stuffed it in the back pocket of his fresh dungarees.

"If you'da come with me." Vincent tormented. "You'd know the real story.—Close the door, Abie."

"They say you punched him." Stumpf said, balling up a fist.

"Pollard saw it all from the signal bridge." Lake followed. "You hit *each other.* "

Abie took the only chair and fidgeted with a box of paper clips taken from the desk-top. Vincent dropped down onto his bunk, leaned elbows onto knees, chin into hands and waited to see what he might learn. Stumpf hooked his hat to the doorknob and leaned his back next to it, arms crossed. The rush of water against the outside bulkhead of the quarters and the gentle rise and fall of the deck suggested the ship was still heading east, riding smooth against very low swells.

"Look, Pappy. Let's start this over. Clifford may *look* like he lost it when he fired on those troops, but I'll offer he had a good reason —or … "

"He'll *think* he has a good reason …"

"WAIT! … . OR … I repeat, OR." Stumpf said impatiently, "he's makin' one up right now." He pointed a finger at Vincent. "And …it'll be a USN reason …one that'll fly, and one that'll cancel your shit with him today."

"What I did wasn't 'shit' … I resent that … "

"Quit being so friggin' defensive and just listen to me!" Stumpf insisted. "Confronting him so blindly was shit." He spoke with conviction seldom seen in him by Vincent. "You should'a waited. You know that. Should'a made a case against him. Used the whole picture. Fr'instance, I listened to the circuit monitor tapes and he'll notice later. You never reported the white flags."

"No shit?"

"No shit."

Abie jumped in. "I told *you* 'bout 'em, Paul." The paper-clips slipped from Abie's hand and fell to the deck. "Shit!" Tumbling with a roll of the ship, paper clips slid across the tile in a three square foot area. Lake dropped to one knee.

"Wait, Lake." Stumpf stopped him with an open hand. "The flags were seen by the crew on the ship …up close, I'm sure. The spot boat not reporting them just gives Clifford an edge." He put his hat back on his head; finger pushed his glasses into place and started waving his right hand. "Wanna' know what I think? Objectively?"

No one spoke for a moment. Abie started gathering paper clips. Paul went into hindsight. He was beginning to see the substance of Stumpf's earlier advice. He could tell he was going to get Stumpf's opinion on navy infighting and system manipulation without actually asking for it.

"Listen, a Master Chief slaps his Commanding Officer. The C.O. should put him on report. Right?"

"Right." Lake, paper clips between his teeth, answered for his friend.

"The Master Chief, a career sailor ...he'll fight. Justify his actions. Right?"

"*Rimmft.*" Lake echoed through lips clamped on paper clips.

"And that defense, after today ...will have to be that you are crazy, which you aren't." He held a hand up to hold Vincent's interruption back. "Or, the Chief's emotional reaction to unjustified killings. Which it is ...was ... "

"Makes sense." Abie offered losing several paper clips from his lips..

" ... AND, a court martial board will wonder: Why does a Master Chief with a spotless record hit his C.O.? Because the C .O. shot enemy troops? No. That's what we're paid to do ...and, the Chief's been in combat before, in the Delta ..."

Lake touched Stumpf's arm, stopping him. Mumbling, "Mait a mimute" he spit most of the paper clips back into the box. He also spit out: "An Pappy didn't punch anyone in the Delta." He lifted one eyebrow toward Vincent. "Or did you?"

Vincent didn't answer.

"He didn't." Stumpf continued. "He punches when he sees something terribly wrong. Now the kicker. Why did the C.O. order the gunfire if the Master Chief, who was the C.O.'s eyes, told him not to?"

"Because, technically, the Chief never told him they were surrendering."

"Right ...it confuses the already confused." Stumpf rested his case by re-folding his arms.

"Confused me." Lake said as he put the last paper clip in the box and returned to his chair.

Lake circled the box in the air. "It all goes 'round and 'round." Vincent pulled the paper clips from him and set them on the bunk. Lake continued. "Cap'n can say, technically, it was the Chief's fault that he killed the NVA?"

"E-G-'zactly." Stumpf burst on. "For now, Clifford's knows. If he puts you on report he'll face a board of inquiry. If he doesn't put you on report he'll face having to convince the exec, Dieter, Corrigan, Lukarmo and other USN lifers and ass-kissers why he shouldn't ...and one of *them* might start an inquiry themselves ...a get even ..."

"So you figure," Lake asked, "The Cap'n's aware he's in'na a corner and he'll look for some way to protect himself?"

"Fuckin' a' ditty-bag, Lake." Stumpf said, using an enlisted man's boot camp phrase, "Way I see it, Chief, there are no bendable-enough navy rules to permit you hitting a Commanding Officer, him wrong or no. I offer he'll try to get you to understand why he has to write you up but that you should accept a Captain's Mast …not a court martial. He'll try to get you on his team. Get you to fold over. Offer to protect you …maybe save your rank …transfer you to a shit job somewhere …restriction to the ship …something you can buy."

"Woah!" Vincent moaned. "He's taking a chance I'll not insist on a court."

"Yes he is. And if you do? He'll stack the court with officers on his team, likely. He'll find 'em."

With a flick of his thumb toward the forward part of the ship, Vincent referred to the earlier conversation with Stumpf. "I appreciate you're not sayin' 'I told you so', Mr. Stumpf."

"I was just about ready to say that, actually."

Vincent wiped his face with both hands. "I'm to meet with the Cap'n after chow."

"An' who else?"

"He and I, I guess. Hadn't thought …"

Stumpf looked flustered as he grabbed the doorknob. "I got the next OOD training watch. I gotta' go."

Lake got up with him. "Me too." He turned to Vincent. "Sorry you got the skipper on your ass, Chief. Tucker's got the exec on his. Glad no one's on mine."

"Why the exec on Tucker?"

"Don' know. We were back aft just a bit ago squaring away the boat, testing the radios, drying things out. Griffith was there. I went for some rags and he and Tucker was kinda' arguin' over somethin'. You know, yellin' at one another but not with loud voices."

"Tucker's no match for Griffith." Vincent turned to their Lieutenant. "Could you look into that, Mr. Stumpf?"

"He's an engineering division man."

"He's no match for Griffith. And I might need him on my side later on."

Stumpf nodded his head up and down several times. "Surely, Chief. I'll take a look."

After Stumpf and Lake left, Vincent felt the depressed feeling ride in like a familiar tide. He'd opted for a peaceful cruise on a Yankee Station destroyer but got a battle centered rescue boat instead. He'd wanted simple answers about his Captain's wrongful aggression but had used aggression himself. He wanted time in Hong Kong with Cynthia but had likely jeopardized that with his hot-headedness toward Clifford. As he undressed to shower he felt totally in the power of the navy and, being stuck on the ship, felt a sudden kinship with the Edward Hale character he'd read about as a child. "Man without a country, that's me."

Nearly naked on his bunk, self-pity took over. "Where the hell is Selesky when I need him?" He pulled off the last sock. "Where are Kurt and Cynthia, for advice …before it goes too far …if it hasn't gone too far already?" He balled the soiled trousers, damp shorts, socks and all into a knot and tossed them toward the laundry bag. He missed.

He lay back on the pale blue cotton spread and gazed at the mass of white wires that transited through the overhead. He let his mind reach for better times. Thoughts moved to Cynthia and Kurt, his citizens of world politics, his social protocol managers, international diplomacy experts and elaborate financial schemers. With their education, he a psychologist from some University in Rotterdam, she in her second year of medical school, and their sophistication born of exposure to the world, they could understand what he was enduring and likely provide good insight. He wanted to be in their living room again on Victoria Peak and tell them of the huge once in a lifetime risk he'd taken. They'd laugh at Stumpf's phrase 'world of shit', but they'd also understand its meaning. He wanted Kurt to disappear eventually, as usual, exactly at the right time so he could take Cynthia into the deep oriental bath, be calmed by her, then end the night by making love with her.

His mind ran with thoughts of their history. He was twenty-five, she twenty-seven when they'd met eight years earlier. She had become part of his life whenever he was in Hong Kong over the ensuing years. Visiting again and again, they had fallen in love—or something close to it. He had spent nearly six months time with her in the early sixties when he was stationed there for shore patrol duty. He'd visited ten days in 1964 on an inspection tour out of a cushy shore duty job with Commander Fleet Air Hawaii. During his '65-66 Vietnam tour he'd managed three, two-week R and R visits to her. Now, mid-February, 1968, although letters substituted for realness, it had been almost 19 months since they'd touched one another.

True he had considered leaving Rachael for Cynthia before, but he always stopped himself, passively waiting for more signals of what was correct or right. He'd found some of the signals in Selesky's objective reasoning—'if you didn't know Rachael, would you be looking for Rachael?' . He breathed deep and heard some inner voice.

"Even without Cynthia, you fool, you'd have left Rachael to be away from the hectic life with her and the bar, a life without children, a life of too much drinking, sneaking money, the gambling, the low-lifery." As he climbed off the bunk and grabbed a towel, he convinced himself the inner voice had to be right but his thoughts stayed within the history of it all. He plopped back down on the bunk, folded his arms and reflected to the night in Selesky's comfortable office when he told the man of his seven-year on again off again affair.

Selesky had seemed un-shocked as Paul talked of Cynthia's impact on him from the first meeting when he was just another sailor in Hong Kong. He'd first met her husband, Kurt, at a tailor shop where Paul was buying a sport coat for himself and something to surprise Rachael with. He immediately liked Kurt, drawn in by his European accent and his relaxing charm. Within an hour he was at Kurt's home high in the tram area above the city. Paul almost refused the invitation. His experiences in sailor towns throughout the world suggested Kurt was likely homosexual and that eventually Paul would have to thwart a gay pass. But even as he had those guarded senses, he also liked the man.

Vincent had said to Selesky: "That June night was the first time I actually felt like I belonged someplace."

"What was so special, Paul. So different? So right?"

"Don't know. We sipped cool drinks, played two games of chess on a veranda overlooking the city. That's all. A large, gray brick home. Big trees shade it. I mean real trees, Idaho trees, Colorado trees. Probably like hundreds of other houses over the world, but something makes it different. It's peaceful. It's on Victoria Peak, above Hong Kong proper."

"By that tram?"

"Yes, not half a mile from it. A veranda connects to the living room at the right side of the house. Gray-blue carpets, gray-blue walls, intricate carving in the woodwork surrounding the living rooms walls …not oriental carvings …no. More like woodcut art, something I'd seen at the Gritty in Venice. The veranda goes around back of the house where it's screened in alongside three large bedrooms. From the bed or in the showers? You can see clear over to Kowloon. Out on the veranda, you see right down into the harbor, the ferries, ships, cars on the roads, the lights and crowds of Wanchai and the Central District."

During chess, Paul stumbled with Kurt's accent. Referring to the chess game he once said: "Give it a go, Auslander." He learned that while Kurt had been born in Holland, his father was an exporter who had taken his family to London. Kurt's accent resulted as British-English laid over Dutch. —"Don't trollem angst over it." "Let's waller a cuppa'?" However, while speaking with a primarily English accent, he didn't say 'matey' or call anyone 'guv', his unfamiliar phrases would confuse Paul again and again.

Many would consider Kurt a handsome man. Mid-forties, with a full head of mostly sandy colored wavy hair that if examined closely showed some dim graying evenly spaced. His hair color and his light but slightly pock-marked complexion reflected his Dutch roots. "Ringer ringer of a move, Paulie." He was so stereotypically European that if he smoked with an ivory tipped cigarette holder or put a monocle in his eye it wouldn't surprise Paul. "Bloody well take that to your Queen." But he didn't smoke, or use a monocle. A tailor they both knew once referred to Kurt as the 'kind of Brit who after speaking to you for three minutes, can tell what you do for a living and how much your house is worth'.

At around ten p.m., the chess game had been interrupted by a snappy tat-tat of heels on the veranda's oak decking. Cynthia came onto the pleasant light. She was Paul's age. That surprised him. He'd expected Kurt's wife would also be pushing fifty, a bouffant, a bit heavy, a little overly made-up, corseted perhaps. But she wasn't and that immediately and consciously changed the focus of his evening.

"One minute I was relaxed, just pleased with life and with myself. The minute she came into view the evening changed into something else. I felt captured …no, distracted, distracted, David. That's a better word. "

"How so?"

"Her just walking into view? Somehow made a promise of some sort. Even though she could have just murdered seven old ladies. A promise that somehow …if she were in my life, life would be better. No, not just better. Complete. Thorough. Absolute. Know the feeling?"

"Well. I've never *fallen* in love, Paul. But I've stepped in it a few times." Selesky laughed. Paul didn't.

"Where Kurt was this conservative, near formal guy? She was more alive. She was dressed in summery things. Full skirt, off the shoulder blouse, like a country girl, sort of, but not really. I could see why they matched. Kurt, a handsome man. But Cynthia, Christ. By any known standard throughout the world, was exceptionally, David, hear me …*stunningly* beautiful.

"Stunningly? You were stunned? Why do we say 'stunningly, Paul? What's it truly mean?"

"Look up 'beauty' in a dictionary? It'll say 'see Cynthia Howser'. About five-five, a little shorter than I like. Shoulder length hair. Dark and shiny with flickering flashes, shimmering although not totally black. Dark-brown eyes. Warm looking, almost too large, but they fit a, I'll say it …they fit a *flawless* face. Her complexion? captivating clean, a wonder …"

"A wonder?"

"Somewhere between southern European olive smoothness and northern European translucence. That night? Her cheekbones would flash a touch of natural color when she smiled. And all the right *other* stuff. Small waist like it was pinched in on purpose, but wasn't. Breeder hips. And breasts …too much?

"One on her back, for dancing?" Selesky laughed. Paul didn't.

"I was never one for breasts …more a long-leg man. But her? Large for her body, but I discovered something."

"Your mother stopped nursing you too soon?"

"David …no." He scolded. "I discovered that great breasts on a woman you're already crazy about? It's like discovering the airline ticket you have to a place you're already happy about traveling to is first class, not tourist." Selesky stayed in his scolded mode.

"It doesn't matter, David, really. If she'd not had breasts? I would have still taken the package as it came and loved the 'no breasts', or the small breasts. But they do come with her, it was like—like."

"A perk?"

"Beyond perk or perky," Paul smiled. Something . . something, very 'her'."

His first sight of her attractiveness on the veranda had brought Paul to his feet that evening. He stuttered through the introductions but could not stop staring. He was too obviously captivated, but couldn't seem to control it. While shaking her warm hand, something succinct passed between them.

"Something moved, David. Transferred, not just from me to her, but, she sort of—gasped when I touched her hand."

"Gasped?"

"Something jumped, uh, involuntarily …from her to me.. I felt it, she felt it but Kurt seemed oblivious to the reactions."

"Blind …gay …burned out on her, all three?"

"She settled into this large chair with Kurt for several minutes, right across from me." Vincent smiled to Selesky, acknowledging the pleasure of the fantasy of infatuation he was describing. "I could smell her perfume, her presence changed the temperature of the veranda. Kurt wanted to continue the chess game but I was …well, I check-mated a pawn, twice."

"Brain in head of dick?"

"No, somewhere else, somewhere new. The two of them chatted, house talk, in English, for my benefit. I had the feeling German-Dutch was common for them. Their voices fascinated me. Her British accent altered somewhat what I later learned was natural German. She asked Kurt at one point 'was the post late that day?' I had that feeling any words she spoke should be inscribed somewhere, on stone."

"Boy, you're like a kid to wet concrete."

"Iron flakes to a magnet. For instance, he asked her to pick up the dry cleaning the following day …and I saw him as this cruel sadist forcing her into some sort of protracted slavery. See where I was?"

"Rescuing? Saving the damsel in distress."

"Wasn't I ? If she'd'of wanted her car washed, I'd'a licked it clean."

A gray cat she addressed as 'Puss' had moved onto her lap on the veranda. While she scratched the cat's ears, she kept looking at Paul but would jerk her eyes away whenever he'd catch her looking. Pleasured by his internal response to her presence that night and to the visual thrills she extracted from him, he was also nervous about it.

"I had no idea what to do with it, David. It was a rush of rushes."

"Rush of testy testosterone?" Without waiting for an answer, Selesky broke into an off key tune, crooning like a piano bar patron. "There's a line between love and fascination, that's hard to tell …on an evening …when you're horny."

"Fuck you, David."

To Paul, the veranda became empty and sort of cold when she excused herself. Kurt stayed glued to the chess game and made small talk but Paul became restless, over-sipping his drink, over checking his watch. After twenty minutes, Cynthia reappeared from a side door. She looked different in a ponytail, fresh makeup, an unquestionably tighter black skirt, black heels Rachael called 'pumps', a small bag in her hand. He became powerfully drawn sexually.

Although the details still swim unclearly in his mind, within an hour of their first meeting and without awkwardness, he found himself being shown the city of Hong Kong by this stunning and polished lady, sans husband Kurt. Twisting and winding over Barker Drive toward Old Peak Road above the Central District, she had stopped the small sports car at a turnout and immediately threw open the door.

"Her voice was electric in the air." He mimicked an excited child as he described her to Selesky. " 'Come with me! Come with me. See the lights'. She said. Elated, eager, just because I was there, it seemed."

He paused to think but Selesky urged him on. "Yes, yes."

"She was out of the car in an instant, me following. There she was, this surrealistic iridescent sight … "

"Surrealistic? Iridescent? How does a woman glow?"

"From her face." He answered quickly, from his memory. "The lights from below us aglow around her face and hair. Colors soft, pastel …like in a large bath bubble. A magical place." He said with a sigh. Though Paul had never expressed this private part of him aloud, it seemed safe and somewhat necessary to talk of these feelings to Selesky.

"Iridescent?" Selesky seemed doubtful.

"To lead me to a wall at the edge of the overlook where we could see the lights below. She took one of my hands and, 'snap', David, as on the veranda, 'snap', a bolt thrown, a lock clamping shut. It got her too. Her hand stopped at her mouth, fist folded, like this."

"Adultery is for adults?"

"Sort of. We stood at the wall looking at the lights. I was sixteen again, two kids at the Swing Haven Dance at the high school in Steubenville. You know; what's next? Who starts?"

"That edge of rejection versus bliss?"

Still holding hands, side by side, the two had positioned themselves against the waist high wall and gazed awkwardly without seeing out over the city lights. Charged expectations filled the air between them. Cynthia eventually spoke because she could not remain quiet.

"I don't know if I have a desire to point out night sights to you … ." Her voice trailed off. There was a smiling and teasing hesitation and an unsure catch in her accented voice. " …or if stopping here is … . is …simply because I'm …too distracted by your company to trust driving all of the turns correctly."

Her comment broke the screen and released the suspense for both. They kissed for several minutes, soft breathless kisses that lasted for moments. They languished deliciously in one another.

"I remember saying to her. 'Christ …and you're married." Those words described everything that was going on with me.

"But, so were you —married, I mean." Selesky reminded.

"No I wasn't then. But I was pretty well engaged to Rachael, sort of. I wore a ring now and then."

"She stepped back, David, lifted my hand, rubbed my ring with two fingers. 'So are you.' She repeated it three or four times. It sobered the minute. I didn't correct her or try to lie. I watched the ring become some sort of a barrier to the …runaway craziness."

"It would."

"She leaned against me and sighed. At that instant, David, out of the blue? Out of the black? All that had ever existed between Rachael and I." Sadness overtook him as he spoke.

"What, Paul. All that had existed … ? What?"

"Was somehow changed …forever." His eyes glistened, then flooded.

"Why is that so sad?"

He sniffled self-consciously, stretched his upper lip and suppressed the tears. "I didn't want that." With one finger he flicked a tear from the inner corner of each eye. "I didn't want to be reminded that a marriage to Rachael might not be good, would become empty, flat. Could a great pair of boobs tear it down …like so. Was I so shallow?"

"So while you felt good with Cynthia, you also felt sad?"

"Very. My ability to stay, be content …with Rachael? Was over. Simply because Cynthia … "

"Because Cynthia, what?"

"Just …because. No more. No less. Just, because she was, what she *is*."

In the lights above the city he had pulled her around to face him. There was some promise present as he held her shoulders in his hands and looked at her face. She smiled openly, no secrets, no coyness or shyness. He wanted more of whatever it was that was surfacing that night. By the wall on the hillside above the city he voiced to her what he was feeling. "Never before like this." He said quietly.

"Nor I." She answered with a smile. "Never before."

"And, David. I had no idea if that was really true for her. Not really. I didn't know her. All I knew were the new feelings. I was trying to describe something to her I couldn't describe. But for all I knew that was something this lady did every other night …right?"

"Understand."

"But then she said: 'You've just change everything in my marriage'."

"How do they know to say exactly the right thing?" Selesky offered with a grin.

"I ignored her comment but yet I knew, David, someday." He became withdrawn into new thoughts.

Selesky gave him a moment or so, then: "Someday?"

"I'd leave Rachael for whatever it was I was experiencing with Cynthia. Funny, Huh?"

"But not necessarily from Cynthia, right?"

"Right. I wanted that fullness with Rachael, the feeling of love? Of whatever I was having with her. We drove down to the Central District. Abandoned her MG. Didn't even lock it. Left it at some restaurant parking lot just so we could be closer to one another. You know, the gearshift and brake in the way? We walked to dinner at a restaurant called Frenchie's."

"I know the place."

"Yes. She, she spoke French to the owner. He knew her and Kurt. She ordered a dinner which …huh, I can neither remember the name of, or forget the taste of. Truly. After that, we had cocktails at Landaus' on Gloucester road. Know the place?"

"Don't think so."

"In the taxi's between, 2 a.m. probably, she directed the drivers in Chinese, mind you. German, English, French, Chinese …she amazed me. "

"What of Kurt?" Selesky asked.

"I asked her that, twice. All she would say is that Kurt was fine. And I was to stop asking."

"Must have been a legion of questions darting through your mind. Who is he really? Why did he permit his beautiful wife to go off in the night with a stranger? Would you be robbed at any minute for your millions? Were they really husband and wife? Was he homosexual after all, trolling with her as bait?"

"I had very little thought outside of her, David. We danced close to each other until real late. A small place off Hennessy Road. I was beginning to know her and thought nothing more of him."

"Shallow sort, you."

"Shallow? I was captured. Besides speaking several languages, she had …she had *substance*. She was a trained O.R. nurse, 'sister' she called herself, British I guess. And, in medical school, working to be a physician. Too much. Did not want to stay in Hong Kong forever. Kurt's business kept them there at the moment."

"What he do, this husband, Kurt?"

"Banking …she said. And a diplomatic rep for several Balkin and North African countries …you know, visa business, money rates, touristy things …and adoption procedures. Boring. She seemed stuck with him. . "

" You want to *think* she was stuck with him."

"Right. She seemed to be. Her parents were gone, no brothers, no sisters. I wondered mostly why she wanted to be with me?"

"That's your Steubenville low self regard. Why would anyone but some jerk want to be with you except a rather flawed Rachael?"

"At dinner, David. We didn't 'eat', we 'dined'. We also danced, floating dances among over-dressed people and I felt out of place in uniform." Selesky imagined the scene as Paul went on and on. "We exchanged life stories like so many do on first dates. I felt like a charged capacitor just watching her, listening to her, touching her."

Paul and Cynthia had returned to her car by taxi that night. It was three a.m. and she asked him to drive the M.G. Although it was on the 'wrong' side of the road and the steering wheel on the 'wrong' side of the car, he managed it well as she directed him to the eastern end of Victoria Park while she freshened makeup again and added a touch of perfume.

"What is that?' He asked when the gratifying aroma found him.

"*le Shocking*", she replied snapping the small top back onto the dauber. "Elsa *Schiparelli* makes it. My favorite."

At the park entrance she motioned he should park near the quiet swimming pool, closed for the night. They walked, touched and talked in the dim glow of lights from the nearby city. They passed two other couples on the warm quiet paths. He led her several yards to the grass among tall trees. She went willingly. Soon, not another soul was anywhere close to them.

They lay on a blanket taken from the car and in the deep cool grass became oblivious of anything or anyone. Within minutes, he lifted her skirt, kissed her and as they kissed he touched her gartered thighs. His first purposeful sexual move electrified them.

"My fantasy sailor in this fantasy park." She whispered.

"Just follow me." He smiled to her.

She murmured 'yes', playfully. She whispered words close to his face and kept kissing his face, touching his eyes and mouth with fingertips.

"I want to make love with you—here." He said. "Are we safe here, Cynthia? "

"From?" She asked.

"I don't know, Chinese rowdies?" He half joked.

Her breath caught. "It's safe. We're the only rowdies here." She rose and stood in front of him. A smile glistened on her face, she ...

RRRUUUNG! ! RRRUUNG! ! ! Vincent was ripped from the past to the drama of his present. The black telephone screeched from its metal box on the bulkhead above his head.

"Paul? Abie. I'm on the bridge. You sleepin? How you doin'?"

He lied as he sat up straight, getting his bearings. "I'm good. How you and Tucker?"

"Fine. I'm still numb, I guess. Everyone is buzzing about what happened. Wahoo."

"Wahoo what, Abie?"

"Do a number on a Master Chief and he'll get even."

"Abie. No jokes, please. Seen Tucker again?"

"Yes. Onna' fantail a bit ago for chow. Said he an' Tough Toes weren't arguin' ...jus' talkin. Seems fine now."

"Good."

"Hey, Hey. You know what Tucker told me 'bout them CIA guys?"

"What could he know about them?"

"Well, Tuck says, the exec says—'bout the time you and me and Stumpy was talkin?

DiNoble and Hill, in the helo? Under new orders from 70.8 they sweep in lookin' for the CIA and what?"

"Talk."

"They fine' 'em, blown to hell."

"What'd'ya mean,—'blown' ...?"

"Dead. Two guys, Hinkle and March. It's them alright. But they was blown to bits by, guess what?"

"Talk, dammit." The telephone grew sweaty in his palms.

"By likely, our own shells. Way back a couple o' miles. Those overshoots must'a got 'em."

"No shit, Abie?"

"No shit, Chief. Now everyone from the mounts is talkin' 'bout guilt and murder and all. Blamin' you and me for callin' bad coords."

"Shit. Blaming? The mounts were off, Abie."

"But the men are dead. They gotta' blame ...it's the American way."

"Why hadn't the CIA people called us? Where had they been? Didn't they have a radio?"

"Stop. I don't know shit 'cept what Tucker and Hill says. They said they had no radio with 'em. Everyone is speculatin' crazy over it. But they are dead. They in the meat locker in double B's.

"An' this came from the exec via Tucker?"

"Yeah. He wasn't chewin' him out. Jus' tellin' him this kind of bad news."

Vincent showered in a thought-filled trance and tried napping again, tried getting his thoughts back to Cynthia, but his mind stayed current. His sleep filled with tossing bodies and repeated THUMPS of the five-inch rounds. Eventually sleep became impossible. He paced. In a pique, he tried kicking the steel bulkhead but it seemed too childish. Anticipating more trouble, he wanted to write all the facts down clearly but couldn't find the focus. Surprising even himself, he wrote to David Selesky.

January 6th, 1968
Tonkin Gulf
Dear David

Today has seen an extension of me that I first saw the day I knew I could no longer take Rachael's demands. Some things are 'right' some are 'wrong', and I have a right to my own version of which are which. Today I saw I could not accept wrongs committed by my navy under the guise of 'right', simply because the navy has the power, and the authority to be "right", and my ignorance over what it takes to truly decide 'right'. Today I saw a lot of innocent people die. Your counsel was correct. My 'magic carpet made of steel' is not the harmless one Guthrie sings of. I can no longer deny as I used to, that ships do kill real people from long distances over here.

Something changed in me though. I don't have a word for what changed, but it changed. Rachael has accused me of having the navy as my God and today I think I would agree that at least it might be my religion. My priest screwed up today and killed some troops who were trying to surrender. Some of us are having trouble with that blatant misuse of power. There are parts of me that want to cry as a child might and other parts that want to attack as a man might. I've done a little of both.

I can't figure this change in me. I'd have to write forever if I started to list the things I've seen wrong and ignored before in my life. Suddenly now, I can't ignore the wrongs. Maybe the 'flower children' do have something to say?

Rachael always asked me why I stayed USN. It was clearer then. Now I'm not sure. It has certainly been fun—until suddenly its not. So, I may have to leave the navy. I can't tell all of the details but I may not have a choice.

In addition, I got a confusing letter from Cynthia that leaves an important question in the air until she and I can meet. Something about an old letter of mine, not answered. Something important to do with her decision to be with me. And, because of illness in the family in France, she might not be in H.K. when we arrive.

I'm aware this note is scattered and cryptic, but I needed someone to dump toward.

Good luck on new orders. Look forward to seeing you again.

With warm regards

P.V.

Re-reading the letter he was glad he had Selesky to reach to although after writing he felt limp and somewhat without energy. Sitting at his desk he noticed he felt less anger toward the Captain. He almost understood how Clifford felt he had to mop up a scattered mess—a mess Vincent had made. Maybe if his own messages to the Captain had been clearer, his plan tighter, it would have been different. Maybe the Captain felt as let down by him as he felt let down by the Captain.

CHAPTER FIFTEEN
Honor? Or Cynthia?

At 1930 Paul Vincent took the sights and thoughts of the stirring day to Clifford's closed door. His shave was fresh, khaki uniform pressed, shoes polished and hat in hand. Seriously questioning, not Clifford, but himself, his throat was tight, his heart pounded like a one cylinder outboard motor. Had he been wrong up on the bridge to soundly judge the man in charge? Had he simply come to a place where he could no longer stomach a killing war? All confidence seemed shoved aside by Clifford's earlier whispering comment that he'd 'over reacted'. Had that been simply a meaningless mood swinging remark by the captain, a reminder the day was typical of war, an indication of forgiveness, or a hint, as Stumpf implied, of a possible Court Martial or Captain's Mast? He took a long deep breath and then two more before he knocked at the C.O.'s door, trying to make the knock sound confident.

From behind his desk Clifford nodded to an empty chair but Vincent decided to stand just behind it. The Captain seemed like he was trying to be professional; distanced, aloof, but the tic near his left eye was active and caused mini-flicks of his lash and trifling wiggle motions of the skin beneath his left sideburn. His hands were constantly moving. He touched and re-touched his eyelids, rubbed his nose with one finger or dug into his right ear. He was smoking a newly lit cigarette and shifting through the nervous behaviors, touch, rub, dig, puff. The aloof professional posture didn't carry very far.

Holding up the cigarette hand, palm out, he cleared his throat and spoke with the deep drone of a funeral dirge, speaking over the sounds of the rushing sea pushed against Truaxe's hull that came through the single open port on the Captain's left.

"Master Chief P.R. Vincent." He said formally. "I've spent the entire day reviewing … " He intermittently glared at Vincent but would not hold eye contact. ". . reviewing the pertinent details of today. I'm convinced that what took place was the result of a complex combination of fatigue from overwork and little sleep, for which I am responsible, distraction caused by your current upheaval at home, for which you are responsible, and …" He paused to rub the tip of his cigarette against the inner edge of a typical brass ashtray found throughout the navy, fashioned from a 5-inch shell casing. "some possibly, over-reaction to the powerful stimulus of fear, ahh, fear generated from being in the boat—and, that's human nature and …" He paused again and checked the end of the cigarette. " …there may also be some, ahh, some misplaced anger over unconnected events, something I know nothing about …and maybe you don't either. . you know. I've had a lot of psychology courses. Unconscious stuff on your part, anger, disappointments …prejudices." He again raised one hand, palm out and pushed his cigarette into the ash filled shell-cashing and rubbed it back and forth to snuff the embers. He impulsively sniffed his fingertips and resumed talking, his eyes either gazing at Vincent's chin or an inch above his eyes.

"I'm not exactly sure why, but I felt this here ship might be in …harm's way if I followed your optimistic plan." He had pulled in his shoulders, half bent his wrists and Vincent felt sure the man was taking the term, 'harm's way' from a John Wayne movie. "Coming in with the ship, I too became aware of white flags." Clifford continued. "I waited for you to verify them—a report that never came. That worked on my nerves." He put a second hand in the air to hold Vincent back. "Dammit, if you weren't seeing the flags, or if you saw them but didn't think …" He snapped his fingers and begun to speak in spurts. "The exec agreed with me. If you didn't think the flags …important enough to report …then …you may have made other …basic mistakes. I became, ahh …wary, yes, wary, of you bein' in charge."

Vincent took an overdue deep breath. Clifford thought he was starting to speak.

"Wait!" Clifford again used both hands to block any comments. His eyebrows drew together in a squint. He took a few seconds to dig an ear. "Listen, I considered your recommendation. Lowering boats, making trips back and forth ferrying prisoners. Hostile waters. Vulnerable to attack, too vulnerable."

"We could have used the helo for reconn. "

"Please … I am the captain. I can't recall the exactness—but it was there, mind you."

"What was there?"

"Worry. Worry was there. It had an impact on command decision." Clifford made 'command decision' sound like something that happened independent of him. The Captain withdrew into deep thought, slowly cracking all ten knuckles, one at a time.

As Vincent forced himself to remain quiet and wait, his eyes were drawn to a series of walled shelves filled with trophies and knickknacks. Framed letters, a photo of Clifford and Admiral Zumwalt, another with the current CNO, still another with Lieutenant Stumpf's father. His Naval Academy parchment, his master's degree and other post-graduate certificates surrounded the shelves. Several molded ship and squadron emblems in little lean-to stands were tapped fast to the shelves to prevent them from falling in rough seas. A velvet board displayed service ribbons and his lower rank souvenir insignia. A tarnished five-inch 50 caliber shell casing lay on the Captain's two-seater blue covered couch. He could picture it on a living room shelf someday, engraved, "Combat. Vinh, N. Vietnam, Feb, 1968. U.S.S. Truaxe DDG(N)-55. Robt. Clifford, Commanding."

Clifford was also quiet but had started a second cigarette. He continued to pick at his ear with purpose, again examining the end of his finger for residue. He poured a cup of coffee from a silver wardroom thermos and took an agonizing delay to add sugar and cream. He didn't offer Vincent coffee.

"Maybe I felt you weren't really the in-charge person I originally counted on you to be …maybe."

Vincent interrupted. "Wait a minute, Cap'n …"

"You wait! Our first combat action should have been something simpler but it wasn't. I counted on you. It's tiredness, overwork, worry, faulty equipment, things going wrong … "

"Poor training." Paul took the shot he'd been holding back. The only acknowledgement was a quick eye-to-eye contact, then a very rapid shift away.

Clifford continued. "Happenstance things …led to your breech of conduct." Earlier he had called it an 'over reaction'. Breech of conduct implied formal punishment was in order. Vincent's training-shot remark seemed to shift Clifford into an attack posture and Paul regretted making it. If he'd have stayed quiet he would likely be walking out of the office shortly, hat in hand, but all troubles behind them both.

"Breach of conduct is serious, Master Chief."

"Captain?" Paul said, unable to be passive. "You put me on report for breach of conduct and I scream bloody murder."

"Just a goddammed minute. There are officers on this here ship who are sure Master Chief Vincent's the real problem. Called in shells that killed the CIA team."

"The ship overshot …poor training … I'm sure the coords I called in are on the circuit tapes."

Clifford went silent. Vincent drummed fingers on the chair back. Clifford went off in a different direction. "Commander Griffith for one is confident you can't maintain loyalty to your family …you can't maintain it to us or to the navy. How true is that? Don't answer."

Clifford spun out of his chair and paced about three steps, as far as the small room permitted. He crushed his new cigarette in a second overfilled ash-tray and turned to Vincent. This time he spoke loudly from his standing position, finger pointing like an angered parent. "When a Master Chief takes a punch at his commanding officer, the man is sick. This morning this ship operated efficiently … " He slowed down as though hearing his erroneous statement. " …albeit closer to the action than we've been thus far. The men did their jobs—ahh, as expected, ahh—almost" He softened more. "The officers did their jobs, but Vincent here fucks it up because of the heat of the kitchen and maybe too much exposure to that heat? I might point out here, had you reported the white flags in a prompt and responsible manner …things would have ended up differently. As it was, without that report? I went in there with MY ship thinking I was attacking hostile troops, who may, in fact …have even been attacking my spotter boat …and I HAVE CIRCUIT TAPES TO PROVE IT."

Stumpf had been right.

Clifford continued, but calmer. "See, many believe you are the problem, the sickness, aboard Truaxe." Vincent started to counter but Clifford's hands flashed up again. "AND" He said loudly. "I'm telling this Master Chief right here," His finger still pointing stiffly, " …senior officers want your spotless ass for what happened today …and I'm afraid for you of the consequences of that and …"

"AND." Vincent stepped to the side of the chair he'd been leaning against.

"And, Cap'n. You have to also be afraid of the consequences for *your* ass, should mine go into a sling over this." Vincent's heart leaped to his throat. This is not what he'd anticipated. Where did his respect for the CO go? Would someone swing a fist this time?

Clifford stood there and mindlessly hand spun his swivel chair a full 360 degrees. He dropped into it and spoke, evenly now, carefully selecting words in the same manner used against Griffith that night in San Diego.

"Now just a God dammed minute, Chief. Our purpose tonight is not to hang you, nor anyone. It's to unite, to reconstruct events that created ...the moods ...that resulted in your ahh, over-reacting burst ...shall we say, burst of anger on the bridge? But, I haven't been able to actually do that. I want any problems fixed so not to hurt anyone in future ops under similar circumstances. I want them fixed by agreement between you and me."

The word 'agreement' did not catch Vincent off guard. Stumpf's predication was accurate. Vincent waited for Clifford to offer the Captain's Mast and a protected sentence. The mood swings, so obvious during the meeting thus far, caused Vincent to openly concede something he'd denied for months. Captain Clifford was a very worried or a very disturbed man.

"Mr. Griffith, Mr. Corrigan, Mr. Deiter, that nuke engineer? The CIC officer and some others? They're encouraging me to court martial you." He was cold again.

Vincent took a chance. Trying to sound friendly, he spoke for the first time in even tones. "You between a rock and a hard place, Captain?" It came out venom filled.

"Huh? I don't like the question ...an' I don't understand it either. What do you mean?" As Vincent started to answer, Clifford held up one hand and blocked him. He spoke, philosophically. "Fault, personal fault, is not the issue here. We can't exactly erase what's happened. Everyone in this war had a hand in the chain that took us to where we were earlier." He rambled unclearly. Vincent waited. "Ultimately, officially, the responsibility is mine. I'm admitting ...an error or two may have been made other than by you. We have inexperienced gun crews, unpracticed spotters. Hell, I counted the forward mount fired 66 rounds in under six minutes at one point when you called 400-33 and 401-44, before that last casualty." He paused for an instant and his eyes became bright. "Yes, that's it ..." he said as though he'd just had a revelation. "*Errors* played a part in the events ...on my ship ... OUR ship." He stopped and rubbed the inner corners of his eyes with thumb and forefinger. He spoke again quickly. "But I am not admitting to any of them myself. I'm not sure anyone can admit to or claim or pin blame exactly ...errors happened." Vincent thought of a bumper sticker he'd seen —'Shit Happens'—.

Clifford's mood continued up and down like the bow of the ship. He was pithy looking, then a sudden friendly smile on his lips. He wasn't talking Captain's Mast any longer. He seemed to be trying to say, without saying it exactly, there was need to forget it all, a need for a whitewash. The man was super-squirming in a triple bind. Clifford's responsibility for poor training could be proven as the cause of the overshoot that killed the CIA team. Despite Vincent's non-report, he admitted he had ignored white flags, so he also owns the killing of surrendering NVA. And, the officers Clifford mistreated over the months were likely all waiting for a chance to get even. But, as he still had ultimate control over the officer's careers, his tact suddenly came clear to Vincent. Clifford felt he could bluff the officers, but wasn't sure he could bluff the Chief. Any feathers in his cap over the battle, in fact, any *future* feathers, were, it seemed, in Vincent's hands.

"Cap'n, if a year ago I would have created an incident to bring a court martial to me I would have accepted your decision and passively assumed I had erred." Clifford smiled just a tight corner of a smile, but still had trouble meeting Vincent's gaze. "But there is a double bind. We each are in one."

"Oh?"

Vincent chose his words carefully, fearful of the lost objectivity of another mood swing. "You are being pressed to court martial me for my actions. I can't blame the exec and the others for wanting that. They want to preserve what you often refer to as good order and discipline." It was a conscious patronizing statement.

"True." Patronization worked.

"However, if you court martial me for the slap, someone will wonder why a master chief with my record slapped his C.O. Am I correct?"

"I hadn't thought of that." He carried an expression as though he truly had *not* thought of that. .

"Really? In order for you to prevent that question from being asked, you can't court martial me."

Clifford's nostrils flared. "Be careful, Vincent." His eye flickered, his fingers squeezed and pulled at his earlobe. The mood had swung again.

It was then Vincent felt a cold chill pass through his body. Something besides the unfairness of the shooting was controlling his responses to Clifford. A lengthy and honest court martial, which Paul would have to insist on, could likely mean not seeing Cynthia when the ship went to Hong Kong. Vincent found himself willing to be part of a whitewash, but for all the wrong reasons. He was willing to gamble his career where he knew Clifford was not, but he was not prepared to gamble seeing Cynthia, which Clifford didn't know.

"You caution *me* to be careful, Captain? Both of us may be walking on the blade edge of our careers. Don't deny it." He paused and then repeated what he now knew was only a bluff. "If you are wondering if I'll scream injustice if you court martial me? Yes, I will. I *will* gain support in a court martial from what I'll have to say."

Clifford went silent and also became expressionless. He turned from Vincent and fumbled with a lightweight khaki jacket hanging against the bulkhead. He pulled a pack of cigarettes free of a pocket. He fumbled for a match. Vincent waited, his heart pounding.

Drawing deeply of the first puff of the third cigarette in less than ten minutes, Clifford seemed to be delaying the moment. He resumed picking at his ear.

"Chief, we've spent a hell of a lot of time trying to put this here ship into a working machine of some sort. But it hasn't worked. The crew hasn't melded into a team. Not as we've both seen on other ships. There's a distance between command and the men. There's no spirit. I've known it since commissioning. It may be as simple as so many men are here only to avoid an army draft—unhappy men, their lives interrupted." He took time choosing his words, looking at the Chief for the first time as he did so. Ignoring any direct comment about the ship's lack of training, he seemed to be saying 'we've got trouble, right here in River City' and seemed to want Vincent to join him.

"I've got to do some convincing of some others, Chief, but I think our problem of earlier today is only a symptom of an underlying trouble."

There, Vincent thought. He's opened a door that others may accept but he's not sure I'll accept it.

"A sneaky low grade virus has gotten to most of the crew, maybe me too, obviously to you. Its like we're all a little low, a little dysfunctional—yeah,—dysfunctional. Good word for it." Clifford became animated, finger pointing, shoulders hunched. "Chief, listen to me. I believe a series of lectures might be the answer." He was smiling, talking rapidly. "Convince the others that we need to cement relationships, make 'em normal, bring in the ol' can-do spirit … "

"Pardon?"

"I can convince the others there is a universal morale problem that just came to its head through your actions …you know. Your breach of conduct being just an indicator of how badly the …ahhh, dysfunction has progressed. Do you UNDERSTAND me, Vincent?"

"Divert attention from our squabble to some sort of lecture series?

"I can't undue the past, Chief. But I can keep both of us from being hurt by it."

That was as straight to the point as it might get. Vincent said nothing.

"There is life here, Chief. Personal futures. What are you after, an apology of some sort?"

That stopped Vincent. "I don't know, Captain. I need something from you. Respect? I've lost respect."

"For me?"

"Yes! No! I don't know, Cap'n. I don't know if I have enough respect for *anyone* in a leadership role to where an apology would help today. These are all new reactions I'm having. Before today, if anyone would have told me I'd be after a naval officer for killing a listed enemy—I'd' of walked away from them."

Clifford sat again and folded his hands on his desktop. "I'm sorry about this morning …today, Chief Vincent. What can I say?"

Vincent didn't answer.

"I'm a sailor" Clifford continued. "I went in shooting enemy. Don't make me wrong for it. Not now. I'm doing the best I can in here." He was closer to being human than Vincent had ever seen.

"So you want to go to the lectures?"

"And don't see it as a diversion, Vincent, dammit. Even though its the only way I can think of to get the others offa' my back …our, backs. I think lectures could be designed that would point out how sailors have changed over the years, look how you've changed. Dammit man. Roll with me a bit on this."

"I'm trying."

"The world is a new place filled with new technologies. Men have to shoulder responsibilities in a new way.—blah, blah. You know what I mean? What the new way is, I'm not sure. Manual labor is lessening but maybe the sophisticated demands are causing sailors more trouble, and we, in command, aren't aware what it takes to lead these new technically oriented men. I sure as hell must not. You seem to know these men better'n I do. You could identify the issues, actually put the lecture series together. Use anyone you want to talk about morale, the war, the anti-war feelings, talk about command decisions and so on."

"Errors happened—command decision, happenstance—breach of conduct—dysfunctional crew, distance between command and men. These are all subjective terms, Cap'n. You're saying something like 'rain' had suddenly come down, or 'a plague' had struck. Something uncontrollable."

"Doesn't it seem uncontrollable to you?" Clifford demanded. "You hit me."

"You pushed me first."

They both reeled from the childlike exchange but neither chanced letting free the silliness of Vincent's remark. Clifford leaned back, made a distasteful face after a cold coffee sip and poured from the silver thermos again. This time he sat a cup near Vincent and filled it.

Paul's mind tracked rapidly. Lectures actually could hurt no one and although the crew had been propagandized since commissioning with lectures on racism, sexually transmitted diseases, leadership, communism, financial responsibility, illegal drugs, moral issues, homesickness and the like, and had spent almost the official required hours in on-the-job training, what good had it done?

"Maybe lectures are an OK idea, Cap'n." He said without getting too enthused. "But if I can see through them, others will also. Can I count on you … "

" … Goddammit, man …" Clifford leaned forward and interrupted. " …there's nothing to see through. I have command power on my side." He stopped as quickly as he started. His face changed from beet red to pasty white. The rock and hard place hit him right in his career. Master Chief Paul Vincent was either smiling at him, or smirking.

"What?" Clifford spat out. " What? Are you laughing at?"

"I'm not laughing. It's just that …we are stupid." Vincent leaned forward and addressed the captain straight on.

"Listen, you are afraid of your …for your career over this crap between you and I. I'm not. I'll tell you that straight up. The only reason I'm going along with your needs for the lectures …is because I don't want to be involved in a court's martial and be restricted to the ship in Hong Kong. I want to meet a woman I know who is waiting, and talk about marriage."

"So why the smirk? What am I missing?"

"If I wasn't so anxious to see a woman about a marriage? See the picture?"

Clifford stayed blank-faced.

"I would lay my career out to stop such as you. But I won't jeopardize my chance of seeing *her,* just to get to you."

The room chilled again. Vincent took a chance. "You pushed me first."

Clifford came right back.—"I hate your haughtiness, Vincent."

"You hate something, but it isn't about me."

"I hate that whole woman story … "

"You hate that your command, hell, maybe your whole life, like mine is out of control, something like that."

"I hated that plan you had, to capture … "

"What now? It would have worked and you'd have gotten no glory."

"The exec is right about you, Vincent. I hate what you stand for."

"No, no, Captain Clifford." Vincent spoke slowly. "You hate that what YOU stand for, all this right wing navy shit, is being overtaken by better sense."

Clifford balled his fists, his face showed an expression close to defeat. He spun away from Vincent. His hand moved rapidly to his left ear. His eye twitched again. He filled his cup again and again took a long time to add cream and sugar. The chief locked his own eyes at the back of Clifford's head, ready to have full eye contact when he turned again. His stomach stabbed a pain he recognized as likely an old ulcer scar, and he reminded himself he couldn't blame Rachael nor Ben for this one.

"Chief, I'm mighty tired tonight." The Captain spoke softly as he turned back to face Vincent. He paused but didn't seem to want a response. "It's been a bad day. To be honest, this is the worst day of my life, of my career. It's a bad day when the chief smacks his commanding officer in the full view of everyone on the bridge. Its bad day when an entire crew goes nuts or is declared sick …as I have just declared them. Its a bad day when we have to sit here like coyotes, chewing at one another's guts." He snapped a pencil he had been holding and dropped the pieces to the desktop. "Before we met, I met with the officers involved. Corrigan kissing ass, Griffith attacking your morality, Deiter … I couldn't tell what Deiter wanted. He, like you, seemed saddened by the deaths of the Vietnamese, soldiers and civilians alike. But him and Valentino? I find them to be the kind who declare a moment of silence when a fucking light bulb burns out." He stared into his coffee. Vincent waited.

"I don't want you to say another word, Chief. For some reason I can't put my finger on … I've let you have more rope than I've ever given anyone …especially anyone I outrank." Clifford slipped into his good-guy face. "I guess I respect you, maybe. I don't know what to do with you. You're going through something agonizing in your guts. I know you've got marriage troubles but don't we all? Now this new woman …rebounding maybe. Hell, maybe that's it. Maybe you're crazy and it's truly not me." He let his head shake from side to side. Vincent, through his own confusion and worry actually felt sorry for the confused and worried man.

"Vincent, you may not believe that we need one another …" He paused. Paul Vincent let it stand. "We need to cooperate with one another for survival." Clifford changed subjects and tempo and continued, slowly. "You are not to talk to anyone about our conversation—ANYONE! If you do, you'll live to regret it more than anything you've thought about regretting. Is that clear?"

"Yes. This was *very* personal. I have no need to talk about it to anyone, Sir."

"Very well. You're in a spot and I'm in a spot because of it." He acknowledged the double bind for the first time. "Yes, I hate the way you said it, but I do want to divert it from us. You may not think so but my main reason is to keep this ship operating on the line, here in Vietnam. That's my navy duty."

Vincent fought back a challenge to that. Clifford continued. "Before tomorrow evening? I want your agreement to my lecture plan. If you disagree, I'll take my chances."

Vincent knew he was dismissed with the bluff as a last shot. He stood and collected his hat.

"Cap'n." He said carefully. "Separate from everything else, the slap, our fighting today and arguing tonight? The way I attempted resolution today was wrong; yelling, swinging at you, was inexcusable, Cap'n. As one man to another, I apologize for that. If you're thinking of my well being here tonight, I appreciate that. If you are thinking of yours, I understand that also. We're stacked against a lot of odds right now."

He extended his hand to the captain because it seemed to be part of the apology, like the only thing left to do after being so personal.

Clifford calmly studied him as he might a navigation chart never seen before. He opened his mouth just a little and let the words come out. "Its a lot of odds, Chief." His voice was calm and even. "But we'll work it out. I have to live with the deaths of the CIA men and now, through your eyes, all those other men too." He reached his hand across the desk to meet Paul's. "Good night, Chief." There was a very slight but real smile on his face.

"Goodnight, sir."

The most peculiar personal interaction either had ever experienced ended at that point.

CHAPTER SIXTEEN
Not So Secret Secrets

The day after the failed mission, instead of being ordered back out to Yankee Station to relieve Truxton as plane-guard, Truaxe was handed over by her task-group-commander for assignment as close in gunfire support. Clifford felt he was being punished by COMSEVENTHFLT for not bringing out a live CIA team.

"Missile ship with a powerhouse sonar and they got me as a slave to jarheads and dogfaces. Least he should put us on PIRAZ patrol where we could use these new radars, control some aircraft and be part of the flashy stuff."

Two companies of the Third Marines were fighting the NVA's 325th Charlie Division in the hills east of Khe Sahn but near the gulf. They needed more artillery. When not needed there, the ship's five-inch 50 caliber guns and helicopter were to assist U.S.S. Henry B. Wilson provide gunfire support for the First Air Calvary who were jammed in just below the DMZ.

Abie updated Paul. "That Henry B. Wilson? That DDG number Seven? They're the ship that plays that *Magnificent Seven* music over their topside speakers when they alongside for fuel. Dun da da dun, da da dun, da da dun dunnnn. Like the movie."

"You been in the sun a lot Abie?"

"Just reportin' the facts, Pappy."

Gunfire support meant days and nights steaming as close as a mile from the beach, firing into the hills at unseen targets chosen by Army spotters usually in helicopters. Clifford voiced his discontent.

"Air Cavalry? Flyin' horses? So I get a bunch of dogfaces tellin' me I just shot a bad shot? This's Vincent's fault."

"No one's 'fault', Cap'n." Cdr. Valentino tried soothing his boss. "This is where we're needed ...that's all."

"Yeah—bullshit."

Now and again Truaxe used its own helo for reconnaissance or target spotting. On one such trip, DiNoble and Hill became gulf heroes-of-the-day when they pulled two downed U.S. pilots out of sure capture by a V.C. company. Clifford wallowed in the congratulations. Abie remained philosophical.

"Even with the hero stuff, Paul, this NGFS stuff is like childhood all over."

"How so?"

"Eighty five percent of what we're told is stuff we don't want to hear an' the stuff they want us to do is boring, scary or causes ear aches."

"Terrible, Abie. Terrible. I'll make arrangements for you to go ashore tomorrow night. A leisurely evening with the CIA, the Jarheads ...the Air Cav?"

"No! No, white boy. My department of common sense tol' me not to join no army or *any* outfit that carries their bedroom on their backs. In the navy? I got three hots and a cot, and no one is close enough to shoot me with a rifle."

On the day after the slap, as ordered, Vincent sent Clifford a detailed report of how the mission was seen from the spot boat. Within a day of that, Clifford submitted his routine battle report to CTG 70.8. No interpretive details or subjective descriptions are permitted within the format of a battle report message, only facts such as: the actual location, prevailing weather, time of first contact, time shooting started, time it ended, U.S. equipment or personnel casualties, if any, enemy casualties and body count, if available, identification of enemy weapons, enemy forces by company, division or regiment, and, estimated number of rounds fired. This information became colored pins on charts throughout the gulf, in-country and on postered walls in the pentagon.

The numbers also surely became part of General William Westmoreland and General William DePuy's 'war of attrition' fantasy that was being argued against by General Brute Krulak, USMC and others. In the early sixties, the two 'General Bills' projected the U.S. could out kill the Communists and take apart their willingness to fight, although the French had failed with a similar tactic. In early 1966, Marine Corps General Brute Krulak did some simple math after watching 230 Marines die in four days in the Drang Valley. With two and a half million troops available to the north, and a kill ratio of 1 U.S. or South Vietnamese soldier to 2.6 NVA, it would hypothetically cost a million U.S. and Allied Troops to wipe out the communist forces. No one at the president's level heard those realistic figures until late '67 when certain of the president's protective 'yes-men' faded from favor. In 1968, there were still *some* attrition fans around.

"Hell, Paul, even a dummy like me knows if you get a lotta' people killed and cost a lotta' money in a war. People back home'll soon say 'quit that'. French did."

"U.S. never lets the French teach us anything. We have to learn this on our own."

"We let the French teach us how to fuck with our face an …"

"Hush'it'up, Abie." Paul used his new 'shut-up' word again.

As is traditional, Clifford followed his message report with a secret personal letter to CTG 70.8, a letter Senior Chief McCullough, the captain's yeoman, shared in confidence with Paul. Although safely behind Vincent's quarter's door, and aware he was violating security basics by sharing the secret information, McCullough whispered. "Lemme' read some of this to you, Paul."

"Go, Mac."

"Cap'n managed to make the lucky discovery of the NVA appear to be his personal intelligence effort." McCullough turned to the letter's second page. "Clifford says … Quote: Realizing no enemy ashore could detect the spot boat against the Yahooty effect of the AM sunlight …"

"He referred to Yahooty?"

"Yep."

"The shitbird. He had me explain the word to him when I used it."

"He took almost everything he's said from your report …made it his, added some fantasy. He is clever. Now listen." McCullough returned to the report: " 'As CO, I ordered the boat to remain close in and not only look for the CIA agents, but to also search for NVA activity.' End the quote." Mac flipped further through the pages. "Now, later he says. 'aware the spot crew was minimally combat experienced, I brought Truaxe to within one-half mile of the beach to personally lend my experience to the gunfire spotting effort'."

Paul took the report from McCullough and quietly leafed through several pages. "He's told no outright lies ..."

"No, but he didn't say the NVA were surrendering at the time they were so called—'taken under fire'. Said nothing about three casualties to the gun mounts, or the overshoots."

Paul had more questions as he skimmed the letter. "Did he ever acknowledge the type of fatal injuries to the CIA men?"

"No. Page nine or so." McCullough took the papers and located the page. "He simply stated they'd been found dead ...the result of explosions, quote: not unlike land mines or artillery, un-fuckin' quote."

"He mention his Master Chief smacked him in the kisser?"

"Of course." The neatly uniformed bearded Senior-Chief-Petty-Officer returned the letter to a yellow folder which had a bold red 'secret' slash on it and dropped it into a plain folder which he tucked under his right arm. "That, my friend, is the latest from the memento collector."

"Thank you, Mac. Who *is* this man we work for?"

"Mind over matter, Paul. In his mind? He's all that matters."

"Not funny, Mac."

"Tell me 'bout it."

Although Clifford had directed Vincent make an appointment to discuss the lectures, he stalled his Master Chief into the third day.

"He's shut me out, Mr. Stumpf. Maybe Griffith, Corrigan ...are convincing him to hang me."

"Can't tell from wardroom gossip. Tense quiet during meals."

"I'm worried."

"I'd be worried."

"I'll get him movin' with a memo."

M E M O R A N D U M
9 FEB, 1968
FOR: CO ONLY
FROM: COMMAND MASTER CHIEF
SUBJECT: LECTURE SERIES.

1. FOLLOWING CONVERSATION IN STATEROOM—HAVE BEGUN STRUCTURING OF LECTURE SERIES. RESPECTFULLY REQUEST C.O. BRIEF X.O. AND DEPT HEADS OF SERIES TO PERMIT SCHEDULING COOPERATION AND SPACE IN PLAN OF THE DAY.

V/R

PAUL R. VINCENT
RMCM USN

Within an hour of passing the memo to Clifford via Chief McCollough, Vincent's telephone rang.

"Chief? You free to talk right now?"

"I'm alone."

"Good. That memo of yours? Let's drop lectures for now. May not need 'em. The best weapon we have right now? You and I go on as nothing ever happened. I want us to chat on the bridge, as before …chat. I want us to show good, eh …whaddya'call? Public relations—yeah, good P.R.—make sense?"

Paul stalled, assimilating the new tact.

"Listen." Clifford continued. "One thing is, I'm still C.O. here. Looks like …not putting you on report shows something. Shows …being part of a C.O.'s job is to display an ability to, quote, understand …trauma of battle, and so on. Hear me?" He didn't wait for an answer. "You felt some battle pressure that resulted in you unloading on me, but I *understood* … understand? Shows all concerned that I, and you, can …ahh, sorta' …accept these things during combat …and we shake 'em off and go on. Is this clear?"

Getting to Clifford was not as important as getting to Cynthia. "You do good guy. I do …what do I call it, appreciative enlisted man?"

"Goddammit …this' a suggestion more than a order, Chief." Clifford sounded a little whiny, manipulating. "Wish you could see it that way."

"Aye, aye, Sir." Vincent closed the book.

"An' Chief? You been in radio lately? Know 'bout the new orders?"

"No, Sir."

"We goin' into Hong Kong—R and R and show the flag."

"Thank you, Sir." Vincent hung up his telephone and was suddenly as apprehensive as an overextended stock agent two minutes before the bell. Truaxe was heading for Hong Kong. Would Cynthia be there?

"*Hong Kong* means WHAT?"

"*Fragrant Harbor*, no shit. Say' so in this tourist book."

"Fragrant as fish shit."

"Look up 'stink' in a dictionary …? Ta-dah …"

Approaching Hong Kong from the southeast, the pervading smell of fish and rotting things initially flares everyone's nostrils, but the human sense of smell is kind. Within ten minutes of passing between Green Island and Stone Cutter's Island, all noses seem to adapt. The crew becomes less distracted by the odors and more interested in their libidos.

"Gimble? I understand they have women like no other in the world."

"They also, dumb fuck, have VD here God hasn't even named."

"Use a rubber. An' don't call me 'dumb fuck'."

"Rubber's don't stop this rot, Walsh. It's like stickin' your dick in a fan blade."

"Ooowee!"

"Chopped carrot disease?"

"Ouch …quit."

"Well for me, you two …" First Class Petty Officer Bernard LeMot, the kind of sailor you'd expect to see in a library, spoke to the two first timers. "I take a chance *U.S. Rubber Company* has good products. I'm goin' ashore. I'm gonna fall in love 'til the end of time, or until Friday or jes' until we get underway."

"Whichever comes first?"

"Oh, I'll come first."

As usual the crowded harbor of the inviting city was a photographer's dream, but a Captain's genuine challenge. Bells clanged, whistles tooted everywhere. The local boat traffic, the junks, ferries, the water taxis and sampans all *seemed* to play a game of intimidating the larger ships into changing course or speed. The crowded waterway gave Clifford a chance for a public display of ship-handling skills and he held Truaxe steady all the way to prime anchorage just a hundred yards from the British Navy pier.

"What's that?"

"Where?"

"There?"

"Ask the Master Chief. He'll know."

"H.M.S. Queen Elizabeth."

"Laying like that? Upside down? What the hell?"

"End of an era."

Abandoned, bottom-up and rusting, the Queen lay in the shallows off Kowloon like a rotting bloated red whale. Once she had been the most advertised proudest ship in the British Commonwealth. In 1968 she was a derelict, abandoned even by the small company that had purchased her to use for coal carrying. Half way around the world from the homeland she'd once represented, she was a sign to all who used the busy port of how the British domination of the oceans had slipped away from them and how soon the lease on the land would expire, and Communist China would take control of all the British had accomplished in the area.

It was just a lucky break they were entering Hong Kong and not still on the NGFS mission. The U.S. was pressed for a supportive show of force in Hong Kong and the combination Kittyhawk-Truaxe had been selected mostly because their sides were not yet rusted from extended deployment.

"Seems funny to take us from the war just to act as show-boats, Master Chief."

"Not show-boats, really. British asked for support."

"Support? By us spendin' money over here?"

"No …read the news now and then, will you Abie?"

Since Mao-Tse-Tung's cultural revolution two years earlier had given almost unlimited power to his red-guard brigade, the guards threatened, now and again, to come over the border into Kowloon, the busy and industrialized mainland suburb of Hong Kong. Supporting the

British, the U.S. would often send in a heavy show of force to help intimidate the guards. Because Truaxe was new and nuclear, the navy also took this opportunity to show her off to the British Royal Navy Office in the city. Also, the 'slap incident' had, by rumor, spread to CTG 70.8, and mixed in with the loss of the CIA team. The 70.8 admiral was advised that a breather would be good for the crew, a chance to calm and regroup. Whatever the real reasons, all were very glad to be out of the forthcoming monsoon rain and unknown missions.

Meanwhile, Clifford was showing anyone interested that he could understand Vincent, forgive and forget. His behavior suggested all concerned should drop the subject of the 'slap'. His general attitude about the ship's own weapons having killed the CIA men seemed to be: 'war is hell'.

Once anchored for the generous fifteen-day Hong Kong rest, the ship gave way to a regimented hubbub as everyone not actually in a duty section scrambled to get their work out of the way to go ashore. By the time Paul cleared from radio it was past 5:30 p.m.

In his quarters, he dressed rapidly, anxious to find out if Cynthia had returned from France. It was the time of year temperatures ranged from low fifties to high sixties and the U.S. followed their British host's tradition. They were to wear dress blues. Vincent had not worn blues since Norfolk, years ago.

He shook the double-breasted gold buttoned uniform out of the storage locker and pressed it smooth with practiced hands. He put a new white cotton cover on his hat, tightened the stretch band and buffed the black bill. He fastened the rows of service ribbons into place, checked his money supply and headed for a liberty boat.

Lieutenant Stumpf buttonholed him.

" ...and there's some khaki-clad trouble makers in that wardroom besides Clifford who'd like to see you run over." Stumpf nervously buttoned and unbuttoned his left shirt pocket as he warned Paul.

"As if I didn't know who?"

"I won't say any names, but their initials are Griffith and Corrigan and probably Lukarmo." A faked sort of *Oliver Hardy* grin played over his face. His glasses slipped down his nose, a nose wiggle moved them back into place. They slipped again.

"Clifford thinks he can hold them back, Boss"

"Can't trust that. Look up 'sneaky' in a dictionary ..."

"'Clifford'?"

"Also see, 'Griffith and Corrigan'. Walk the chalk-line or you'll walk the plank, Chief. They're liable to ...you know, find a reason of their own to write you up."

"I'll be careful."

"It's divided the officers. In the wardroom, this damn ship is worse than the *Bounty*."

"Go ashore, Mr. Stumpf. Get a girl friend."

"Got one back home. True to her."

"A little warm body might relax you. There are some beautiful women over here."

"Mine's not exactly an 'aw shit', Chief. I'll wait. I'll leave my sex outlet to the *alleged* wet dream." A smile went with the remark.

In the liberty boat, the view of the city from near the water enthused Paul. More and more taller buildings had been built on the bedrock foundations of the main island and the skyline was beginning to rival most major cities. In the late day, lights were beginning to outline some of the more distant shapes. You could hear traffic noises; engines, horns, trolley bells and voices; a policeman, boat crews, an old man hawking a local bar, a paperboy, all yelling over the noise of the boat engine. Near the pier the purple streaked bilge water of the harbor was as dirty and filled with floating refuse as ever; decaying fish, foam cups, a gray mop head, pieces of rotted rope, tar balls and grease covered bottles sloshed against blackened concrete pier sides. At least once a day a body floated up somewhere in the bay.

"This' where they make television commercials to call attention to environmental waste in the land of the big P.X." Vincent quipped. "Cheaper to make 'em here."

"This place makes me change my 'never take more than one shower a day no matter what' position." Abie seemed overwhelmed by the filth.

"Phewee!" Tucker wheezed. "Reminds me of my granddaddy's outhouse."

"You bunk in it?" Abie would not let the Southerner alone.

"Lemmie quote the Bible, Lake. 'People who live in grass houses? Shouldn't throw matches'."

"Let me quote *Henry Miller.* 'Fuck you."

With Kittyhawk in port there was a crowd of liberty boats at the fleet landing. Vincent's enthusiastic liberty party had to lay-off for several minutes. He looked up toward *her* house on the hillside to the left of the familiar lights of the last Tram Station on Victoria Peak. Many times in the past she'd stood on the high veranda and watched his ship anchor, the liberty boats spill ashore.

"From my veranda, Paul ..." she had pointed out to him. " ...the liberty boats look like water beetles scooting about a pond."

Was she there now, looking for him?

Bumping the dock broke his daydream. He stepped ashore after almost a month at sea, the brief time ashore in Vietnam not counting.

The thirty or so men from the boat broke into groups of threes and fours and headed down the pier toward Harcourt Road in the west end of the Wanchai district—bars, souvenirs, dance saloons, tattoo and tailor shops, whore houses, hotels and anything else that catered to the sailors. Only one thing would cater to Vincent: A call to Cynthia.

He shoved Lake and Tucker into a spotless taxi and pointed them toward the Kowloon ferry. "See you tomorrow, maybe. Or the next day. Watch your money. Stay clean ...stay safe, stay sober."

"Yeah. . yeah, Pappy, let go."

The closest phone was in the shore patrol office behind the police station, five minutes over the walking ramp that crossed Gloucester Road. By the time he arrived there it was well into dusk. Most passing cars had headlights in use and the night air exhaust smells mixed with the stinky harbor smells. Just as he stepped to the entrance door, two timer-activated spotlights flicked on above the black on white *Shore Patrol* sign.

Next to the long counter in the S.P. office, the husky frame and pleased voice of Eddie Monk greeted him with open arms and "welcome, welcome, welcome."

Monk, a big man with eyes like two cocked guns had been an undercover naval investigator with the Shore Patrol office since before Paul's 1962 six months tour with him. Working together, they had become good friends.

With warm handshakes they pulled into Monk's office as they did each time Paul visited, to talk of what they called 'male bullshit', the Honk Kong days of years before and other things men do to hang on to a friend. Monk plopped into his creaky chair behind a worn wooden desk, grinned at Vincent and picked at the few scraggly hairs that seemed to always peep from the deep cleft in the exact center of his chin.

Though Eddie Monk was the kind of guy you'd trust with your kids, his office was a beaten up dreary place at night and probably the same in daylight. A terribly scratched wainscoting separated stained lower walls from the dreary white upper walls of a neglected damp-smelling room. Seven scarred wooden desks, twelve unmatched heavy oak chairs, mostly swivel, four floor lamps with dented shades, several mismatched filing cabinets, five telephones and a hat rack that would have been a Goodwill Store reject made up the furnishings. Five decades of busy Hong Kong police and Shore Patrolmen had scratched and chipped the furniture. Worn floor tile and a fourteen-foot ceiling combined to cause a hollow sound in the room to match the hollow feeling building in Paul Vincent's chest

"Good to see ya', Paul. Though I know you'd rather be chasin' Cynthia down right now than talkin' to me ..."

"Not before I get re-Hong-Konged, Eddie. How is it all?"

"Same ol' same ol'. Fights, drunken threats, bloodied faces, arrest vans, sailors complaining of being robbed, hookers complaining of being stiffed, wide-eyed drunks, arrested weary-eyed hookers. Sailors get younger. Hookers get older. Prices go up."

"Still the same."

"Yeah, sailors break the rules like there's a universal law they learn life the hard way."

"I hear drugs are more organized."

"Yeah. A few new rules because of the drugs. Some pocket searchin' of some men. We find drugs regularly. Hash, pot, speed. Other'n that? Rules remain: Don't fall in love with a lady of the night. Never go anywhere alone. If you screw, take a penicillin pill, or two, use a rubber, or two. Wash up and hope. Never show your money. Keep your billfold inside your underwear, against your dick. Don't wear a wristwatch with a stretch band. Never get drunk where you can't tell what you're doing. Never argue with anyone, over anything, at any time ...no matter what. Same old rules. "

"Same rule breakers?"

"Up a bit. Same percentage of spoiled brat mamas boys, but, these angry-angry draftees are really something to deal with. Sort'a 'fuck-you, authority'. I'll be dead in a week anyway."

When rules were broken they seldom cost anyone more than a chipped tooth, a chunk of pride and some money. Rarely was anyone seriously injured. Now and then a new strain of VD would pop up. A minesweeper with sixty men aboard left the city in 1966 after ten days liberty. Within seven days, fifty-one of the men had an active venereal disease. Once during his 1962 tour with the S.P.'s, Paul arrested an outraged sailor who set a hotel on fire when a whore laughed at his sexual ability.

"She kept calling him 'spaghetti dick' ."

"Not a compliment."

It cost the navy a few thousand dollars and cost the sailor three to five in a federal prison.

After talking old times until they felt re-connected, Monk pulled himself away. "Use the phone. Call her from here. Shut the door, come out when you've finished. It's only seven-thirty and I work 'til midnight."

428-9330. The telephone he'd called a hundred times in the past for a hundred meetings. This time, his hand was shaking.

Mia answered. "No! No! Mr. Paul. No Cyn. No Cyn. You San Degogo?"

"No, I'm in Wanchai, Shore Patrol, Eddie Monk's."

"No Cyn. She go, stay go. Tell me tell you—no Cyn. I know Mr. Monkey number. I call. But, you call back three days." The old woman sounded extra-hyper, somewhat out of character but Paul couldn't get details from her.

Three days?

An eternity.

He felt cheated, wounded. A rage of unfairness overcame him as it would a spoiled child. He wanted to strike out. But the part of him that had been part of him since he was fourteen or so reached up and grabbed his attention, to get him out of the blues. Distract from the rage, distract from the loneliness. He walked down the hallway, explained the Cynthia situation to Monk and spontaneously invited him out on the town. Monk begged off.

"Ol' married man now. But you go." Monk's rejection piled onto the Cynthia rejection. It showed on Paul's face.

"Christ, you've got it bad. Look. I can't be with you tonight and you've got three days to wait. Tomorrow? Get S.P. duty for the ship. Take part in a drug raid with the local police and S.P's. Like the old days." The invitation smacked of something familiar and it could help distract one more day.

Vincent dropped into a chair next to Monk's ancient desk. "I'm gonna' sit around here for awhile, Eddie, Okay?"

"You are a dismal poster boy for 'ain't love grand'? Do what you have to do, Buddy. I have work to do down the hall. You can have my office.

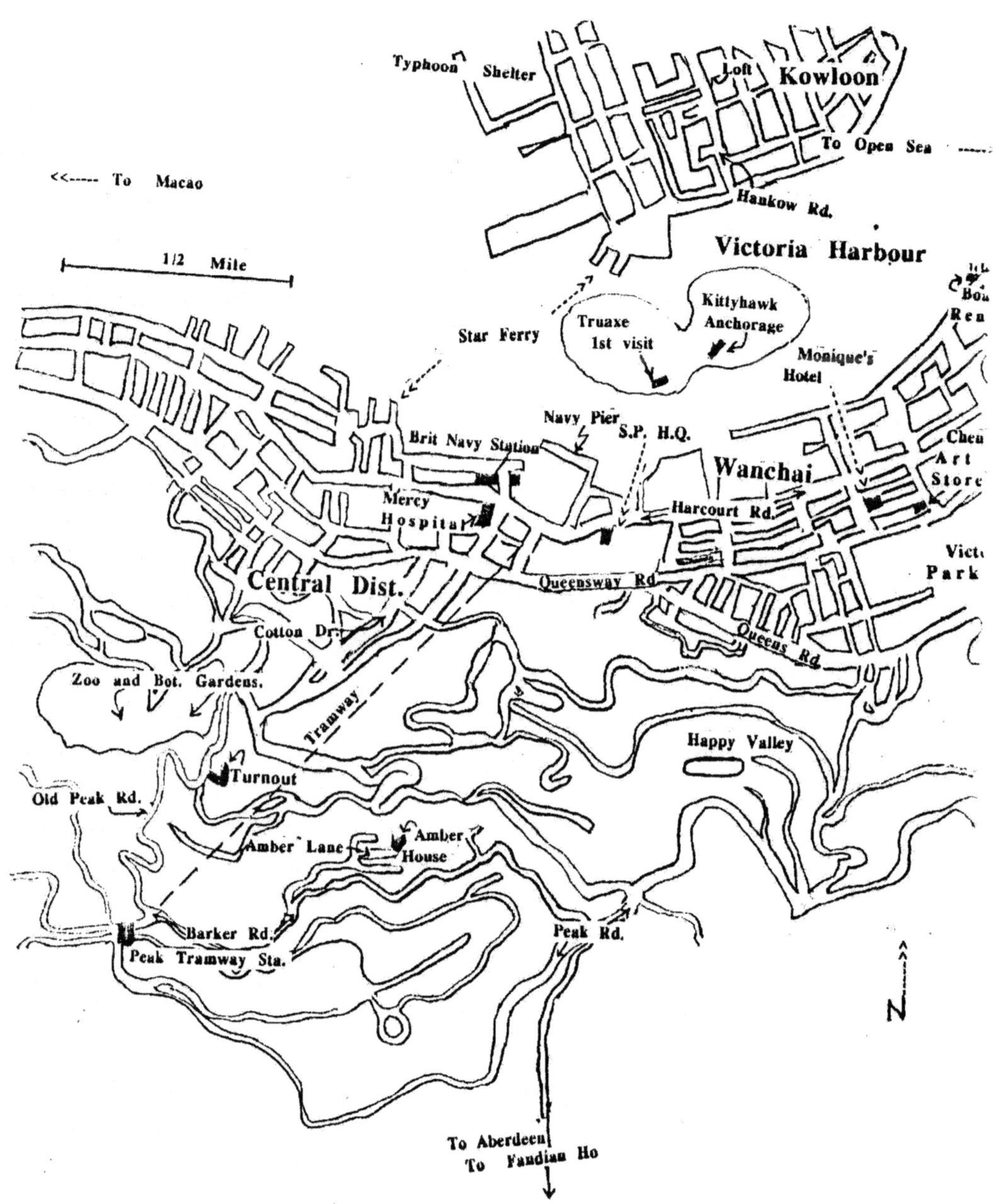
Typhoon Shelter
Loft
Kowloon
To Open Sea
Hankow Rd.
<<----- To Macao
1/2 Mile
Victoria Harbour
Star Ferry
Truaxe
1st visit
Kittyhawk
Anchorage
Monique's
Hotel
Navy Pier
S.P. H.Q.
Brit Navy Station
Mercy
Hospital
Wanchai
Harcourt Rd.
Art
Store
Park
Central Dist.
Queensway Rd
Queens Rd
Cotton Dr.
Zoo and Bot. Gardens.
Tramway
Happy Valley
Turnout
Old Peak Rd.
Amber Lane
Amber
House
Barker Rd.
Peak Tramway Sta.
Peak Rd.
N
To Aberdeen
To Fandian Ho

CHAPTER SEVENTEEN
Who is Cynthia, Really?

Pacing in the high ceiling office, Paul's footsteps echoed between worn green tiles and the tired green wainscoting. He looked into a stained mirror above an old but spotless sink and agreed with Monk He looked dismal.

He reached into his billfold for Cynthia's San Diego letter and skipped to the last paragraph for its rush of pleasure. "I have a new Wai-da tucked away, especially for our first evening. When packing, I ran across our tape measure. I have placed it safely next to our bed."

Strong and opposite feelings ran through him like opposed rivers, pulling, rushing, swirling. Childlike disappointment would give way to covetous but saddened longing. The desired sexual rushes he wanted were too fleeting, or seemed too shallow for the compelling moment. He stepped to the chest-high window and faced the darkness outside. Seen through a courtyard at the side of the Shore Patrol. building, the streets were busying with nightlife. While the city seemed full, he felt empty. While he craved warm welcome, the lights outside made threatening cold shadows. Thoughts of going out, looking up some Truaxe sailors for company gave way to feelings of unsettled impatience. None of his friends, Abie Lake, Monk, Lt. Stumpf, not even Dr. Selesky back in the states truly understood how important this visit was, how critical to his life it was to know exactly where Cynthia would fit in now that his marriage to Rachael had gone from 'till death do us part', to 'we are parted, Pal, so die'. He was concerned at how focused he'd become on being married and starting a family. He worried because it placed his happiness in the hands of someone else, a woman at that. But, at the same time it felt right.

"They can't know Cynthia like I know her." He said to himself. He tried counting the days he'd spent with Cynthia Howser to compare them to the number of days with Rachael. The first time he'd met Cynthia they had spent six days together. He turned sideways and wrote a '6' in the mist on the inside of the window facing the street outside Monk's messy office. A year later, seven more days together. A few months later, seven more. The column of figures grew on the window. 6, 6, 7, 10. Ten more days in 1963, or was it eleven? In 1962, as chief in charge of Hong Kong's shore patrol, the job Monk has now as a civilian, he actually spent more time with Cynthia, six months, than he had with Rachael, four months. He added the days into months, divided, multiplied, confused them, started over. In the end, he decided he'd spent 225 days with Cynthia over seven years, and, he was shocked to see, only 980 with his wife, Rachael. Where did the other time go? He quickly flicked the finger on the window mist; seven years are 2,555 days, less 225 with Cynthia, and 980 with Rachael. "Christ" he said aloud, "Of seven years, I've been at sea, or in-country Vietnam or elsewhere over three and a half. No wonder Rachael screams neglect."

When he later explained the messy window to Eddie Monk and what the figures revealed, Monk showed that part of him that always surprised Paul.

"The window?" He said, "according to Edward Fitzgerald's touch, is '*The Moving Finger writes, and having done so, moves on.*'

"Who?"

"A writer. I think he actually said somethin' like: '*not all your Goodness or Wit shall lure it back to cancel half a line, Nor your tears wash out a word of it.*"

"So? The meaning?" Paul refused to interpret.

"It means the figures are the truth, dummy, accept it. Move on." Monk said as he walked out.

Paul huffed at his reflection in the smeared window. Will it fade with Cynthia as it did with Rachael? 'Maybe the longer you're with a woman' he thought to himself, 'the less you find her exciting'? He then spoke out loud as he looked around the room. "You're out of control and this office doesn't help matters. Get out of here, now."

Reaching for his hat from the desk, he saw a movement in the corner of his eye. His own face again peered back at him from the window.

"Rebounding from Rachael?" He asked the face in the glass. "That why you want Cynthia so much? You going to die without the pleasure of either of them?" The thought of pleasure caused him to wonder; 'this isn't pleasure I feel. Nor is it pain. Is *pain* the opposite of pleasure? Or, as with love, is the opposite to have no feeling at all?'

"Go, find pleasure," he thought. "End this pain, this no-feeling. Be with someone else. Distract. She understands you see other women when you're away from her. She understood you married Rachael to have a baby. If she understood *that*, she'll understand anything you might do tonight. Do it. Go to Monique's."

When deployed on a ship and lonely, when hurting, when mixed up or out of control, Paul, as with many men ended up with a woman. "Dependent male crap" Lieutenant Stumpf heckled him. But Paul Vincent rationalized the sex distracted from his woes. He could shift his mind to a sexual state and the next thing he knew, a bad day was made into a better day. An older San Francisco hotel call-girl once reminded him. "Sex is better'n dope. Sex starts at marvelous and goes up. Dope'll eventually let you down."

Cynthia's voice seemed to come from the steamed window. "Sex just the excuse for you to bring someone close?"

He spun away from the window but returned quickly. "Cynthia? Kurt? In the glass?" He said half seriously. "Where are you when I need you?" Realizing he spoke aloud he reached over self-consciously and wiped his breath from the window. He smiled at the confusion, denied he was crazy, recalled the block letters that flew from his mouth with Rachael, reminded himself he hadn't been drinking so he *must* be crazy, but denied being crazy again.

His next words were close to a whisper. "Cynthia?" He wanted to be in their living room again above the tram on Victoria Peak on the road called Amber Lane. He wanted to eventually undress Cynthia, uncover her fantasy body and let it dictate the levels of excitement. He wanted to take her into the deep oriental bath, soap and suds her, hold and touch her, have a strong erection, make love and be both excited and calmed by her being there.

Suddenly there were mixtures of smiling images in the glass. Fragments of his and her past pushed and shoved to center stage. One vigorous memory after another dislodged from storage and came to life in the reflection as a fresh moment.

"After we made love?" She spoke words from one of her earliest letters. "In Victoria Park that late night? You took away a piece of my heart, Paul Vincent." It came out 'Pool Vinzant'. "Taking my heart was fair and unfair at the same time. You didn't know it then, but you gave me my handsome sailor in the park, on a blanket in the sweet grass. A fantasy I'd had for years and years and was safe to do with you. I love you. See what we have caused?"

When she spoke of love in those early days, he had scoffed. Love could not happen so immediately, he insisted. He believed *true* love was something you experienced only after struggle and sacrifice. True love was a process, a longing that carried a vague internalized promise that fulfillment would come tomorrow, or the next tomorrow. Selesky had laughed at what he called Paul's martyr model.

Cynthia spoke from the glass, pushing Selesky into the background.

"How do I love thee, Paul? Let me count the ways. One inch, two inches, three inches, four." Her teasing words, though thrilling at that past moment caused what she called 'being in love with him' to radiate as something else. Intense and blinding passion, yes, ardor, yes, fantasy fulfillment, yes, but love? He didn't believe so. The acquisition had been too easy, no struggles. She had become, he felt, as so many other women, simply an aphrodisiac.

After he returned to the states he pretended it was to go no further than letters. However, he found himself manipulating the Naval Manpower and Material Analysis Center in San Diego to send him for a six-month shore patrol tour to 'study the impact of illegal drugs' on the navy enlisted man. They bought it.

Arriving in Hong Kong in October, 1962, he delayed meeting with the true object of the trip until he was well installed in his job of organizing and monitoring the visiting ship's shore-patrolmen and lining up drug enforcement police contacts. It took only a week to learn the ins and outs. He hoped the dryness of the assignment would eventually be balanced by her nearness.

As he and Monk became friends that first week, he had confessed his feelings. "Here I am. Dating Rachael in the states, talking marriage, wanting children, being led about by my crank. Going to hell for sure."

"You ain't the first person to put good sense on the line for a woman." Monk seemed reassuring. "Just hope God grades on a curve. Since Moses was so perfect, the rest of us barely deserve much more than to go to hell."

The reassurance was taken away.

"Hey." A voice pulled him to reality. "Hey, Paul? You okay?" Eddie Monk jerked him back to the wainscoted room. The memories crashed around him leaving a diminishing erection.

"Anything I can bring from the *Galley Stove*? It's a new restaurant just over here."

"Huh? No. Nothing for me, Eddie, thanks."

Paul returned to the window and peered out through the courtyard to the streets where the darkness dominated and passing cars were now simply flashing lights. He tried to be calm but an unsettled anxiety was poking through any attempt at level thinking. About to turn away and again head for Monique's, he was stopped in mid-turn by the reflecting power of the unexplained. A smiling image of Cynthia's face echoed from the window more alive and unmistakable than any fantasy image had ever been. Their eyes truly met. She laughed. Her blouse fell away. His hand reached for her but jerked reflexively away when instead of touching cold glass he felt the smooth side of her neck. Delicately, she feigned a pout, pointed one hand toward him and motioned for him to touch her again. He did, but when his finger met the glass there was a noiseless powdery detonation ending with several commingled images pushing and shoving for center view. In seconds, he was watching her say goodbye to him as she had the first time he left her.

"Write to me, Pool Vinzant." Her windowpane face repeated the 1960 statement. "Also write to Kurt. Please!" His non-plan had been to leave Hong Kong and never see her again. Too awkward to manage a romance from long distance, she would likely fade from memory, he decided. He should find an *unmarried* woman to bring the same strokes of lightning charges. Rachael was to have been the one.

He told her "This is too awkward, you with a husband."

"Oh?" She tormented, "the nights of love fade so quickly?" But, were those tears he had seen in her eyes as they said goodbye?

"Let's just go back to our own lives." He offered.

"You are part of my life now. You *must* write to me, to *us*."

Though nonsensical, he wrote to them. To her, he wrote of playful romance and surface talk about his life in the navy. He knew she loved her work so he read about medical school, medical ethics, existing goals for cures of diseases. He wrote about what he read, addressing his letters to 'Doctor Cynthia Howser'.

To Kurt, he included sprinkles of what he could come up with on business and worldly matters, usually taken from Time Magazine. He and Kurt also continued an on-going chess match by mail, "Pawn to King's four—take that jab."

At that point the windowpane began to wiggle like a windblown pond. A touch of his finger settled a new scene into place. It was her voice again coming from the glass or from some madness of his loneliness. She was reading her first letter to him.

"When we touched on the overlook? I can't undo that touch. Once you learn one-plus-one is two? You can't unlearn it."

In the window, it was suddenly 1963 at the Fandian Ho, their secret nineteen-thirties runaway hotel in the Aberdeen section of Hong Kong. Fandian Ho was the place where they actually learned to be free with one another and where he learned to laugh and enjoy her body *and* his own at the same time. To not take it all so seriously, although at times it seemed *very* serious.

"How do I love thee, Paul Vincent? Let me count the ways." She shifted to a sing-song. "One inch, two inches, three inches, four. Five inches, six inches, seven inches, MORE?" Her shallow teasing words though sexually thrilling when she said them only furthered his belief that what she called 'being in love' with him represented something else. While bored and flicking channels on a Sunday morning, Paul had once heard a cheap-suited preacher speak of '*Primordial lust*' and 'the heat of the loins'. He believed that is what he had with Cynthia, and had to scoff at its effects and keep his sense of *correct* and *incorrect* in line. Later, after he and Rachael began to think of marriage, he had to contradict Cynthia's love for him even more to keep his goals with Rachael from being tainted.

"True love is something you experience after struggling, after sacrifice and longing." He told Cynthia during his second visit, 1961.

"You're wrong Paul." She insisted. "You and I have found love." With a pointed fingernail, she traced the hands on the face of his Timex watch. "Each moment is love. This one, and this one." She rose from the bed and pulled a thin sheet after her. It was something she did to distance herself for a moment.

"I don't deny you to look elsewhere." She said. "I do disprove howevah' when you do deny *us*." She made the complex sound so simple. "Just acknowledge our love, Paul. It will care for itself over time."

Truly made uncomfortable by her comments, he asked: "Why is it so important for me to acknowledge this love, these moments?"

"Listen, dummy." She said with mock sternness. "It gives me value. Like medical school gives me value." She poked his shoulder with one extended finger; "I'll do no theatrics now. Howevah', Paul, when I'm faded, fat and greedy looking? I must know I had value beyond simply my looks, beyond the fact my appearance churned men. I must know I was loved."

"Oh?" His 'oh' was flat, not sure he could manage taking on loving her. It seemed such an important responsibility.

"Remember, Paul. I didn't even know I had the *need* to be loved, until I met you."

"I'll practice loving you." He said awkwardly, wishing she'd drop the subject.

"It's tough to be in love with someone who is ten times zones away." She whispered leaning in close to his ear. "But try, damn you. Simply try?"

"I'll try." He answered.

"Of course". She said.

Paul returned on the fleet Minesweeper, U.S.S. Firm, the flagship of Mine Division 72, Cdr. R. D. Reinhart, Commodore, with Lcdr Lee Baggett, Jr., commanding. Though he had a wedding day set with Rachael he couldn't control urges to telephone Cynthia. Things seemed different when she answered his afternoon call. First, she insisted they not tell Kurt he was in the city.

"I can't do that." He said. "It clashes with the honesty of the past. He and I have a friendship. Shit." He continued. "I told you this would become impossible."

Then, once at the Fandian Ho where she said she would explain everything, she avoided talking about it and instead hurriedly pulled him into an afternoon-to-evening of body-pounding sex. Thirsting for a sense of strong connection, she insisted on staying in her clothes, actually pulling panties aside while they made love. At one point she rubbed his face all over her skirt, her garter belt, panties and hose. "Initialized by your sweat for when you're not here."

Later, resting, she admitted hating the double standards around their affair. "You and Kurt can be fast friends forever." She said. "But you and I …no? It's not fair."

"We're fast friends, Cyn." He said, looking about the destroyed bedroom. "For God's sake lady, what do you want from me?"

"I want you to love me, damn you. Not just fuck me." She cried openly. He felt cheap even though it had been her who set up and pushed for the wild sex.

"That's why I write to you." She explained. "I want …someday, someday, for you to love me." The impassioned honesty from the strikingly beautiful woman both flattered and overwhelmed him. He battled a strong desire to give in to her, but didn't.

"Someday." He stalled. "If it's meant to happen."

Her hand stung a slap across his face. She pushed away, yelling, her accent strong. "Daresay you patronize me, evah, Pool Vinzant." Her truth stung, as had her open hand. He quickly apologized and reached for her.

"I did not mean …to patronize." She knew he hadn't. 'Someone who truly loves you', she had rationalized many times, 'would never *purposefully* hurt you, 'evah'.

"Someday, Paul." She said, touching his reddened cheek. He said nothing because he still believed he could not let something permanent come of the affair. He was to marry Rachael and start a family, with order and good sense and purpose.

The windowpane replayed his first meeting with Mia who Cynthia described as her friend, her housekeeper, her handmaid and surrogate mother. It was the third night of the 1961 trip, the first time they made love in Cynthia's bedroom.

"She lives vicariously through me, you know. I've told her about you. She wants first hand approval."

Mia came into the large quiet room at Cynthia's first pull of the bell-cord above the pillows. Dressed in a tightly tied but shapeless chenille robe that once had been bright green, Mia showed no surprise the two lovers were in bed. Under five feet tall, very slim and bony, Mia seemed to be somewhere older than forty and younger than seventy, surely with more past behind her than future remaining. Paul watched the special old woman ignore the odors of sex, the trousers and socks, the bra, garters, and skirt on the floor, and the beard-rubbed red cheeks on Cynthia. She went about sort of on automatic. Paul wondered how regularly this scene repeated itself, and with whom?

She served a tray of hot tea, brandy and small sugar cookies. She then brought great soft towels and piled them in the bath next to the raised tub. She glanced at Paul often and he saw protective inquisitiveness in her toothy smiles. She delayed leaving by pouring more tea and eventually, without a hint of recognizing it as amorous evidence, picked Cynthia's clothes from the floor.

"That's all we need, Mia." Cynthia said eventually.

"No, Missy. Fix pirrows." She leaned over him and fluffed the pillows, smiling all the while. She smelled slightly of curry and hard milled soap, but not offensive.

"Mia? 'Nuff." Cynthia said, finally. Mia giggled, then nodded. It was a giggle of a friend's pleasure as she backed toward the doorway, palms spread against her thin thighs, mocking, genuflecting, eyes locked on Paul.

"Goodnight, Mr. Paul, G'night, Cyn." She left a last smile and stepped from the room.

"Sin? She calls you 'sin'?"

"No." Cynthia pushed with a playful open hand. "It's C-Y-N, she calls me." He pulled her close and encouraged her to lie against his chest to snuggle. She soon took his returning erection in her hand, wanting this to be the time for him to guide her down his body.

"We'll alter it now to S-I-N." He said with gentle touches in her hair.

"I've never learned this." She said.

"I'll teach. You learn." He cuddled her head in his arms and pulled his groin up toward her waiting mouth. "Relax with me." He said. Though he was a willing instructor and she a willing student the lessons nonetheless took way toward dawn.

The next day both of their sexual appetites continued uncontrolled, fanned by the fact Kurt was in Manila on a five-day business trip about exchanging yen for Dutch marks.

After morning sex, she admitted she would rather stay in bed all day but they were committed to a lunch at Frenchie's with several hospital friends, people Paul was beginning to know and to like. "We'll come back right after." He said, stirred by her open desires.

"And never leave bed again."

Just as lunch began she complained to Dr. Scott Salisbury-Baker that her throat was sore. Paul panicked a little as the thoughtful man picked up her butter-knife, motioned with it as a tongue depressor and insisted he look at her throat. Cynthia looked at Paul but didn't break a grin. She leaned over the lunch table, faced the Doctor and opened wide.

"Bit of redness, I see. Have you been yelling? The races perhaps?"

With another flicked glance toward Paul, she replied. "Well, I choked some on something last night. Perhaps?"

"Perhaps. Nothing serious." Scott said in a somber tone. "Watch it a day or two."

She nodded to Paul and began her salad. Later, back in her bedroom she asked, "Did I go too far? Think they talk about us?"

"Yes you go too far and yes they talk about us and now get over here and take your punishment."

She confronted the 'something' again.

In the park, while horseback riding during a summer rain, she did what she often did, even though he'd asked her not too. She talked about intimacy in a non-intimate place.

"You're a good catch, you do sex good, Paul Vincent."

"I've practiced since I was a kid." He joked, uneasily.

"Paul, stop! Listen! You are sensual the way a woman loves." She reached from her horse and squeezed Paul's muscled arm, hard. "You're one of those blokes who I know could kill *me*, or kill *for* me ...but, like this horse? Would never use that strength to hurt me."

He felt he would never understand women's interpretation of sexiness in men. "You like the cut of my jib?"

"Your jib is just fine." She said tossing her head to flick rainwater from her eyes. "But, the strength, the safety …is the truly good part." She dug boots into her horse and bolted forward, leaving Paul to look up into the raindrops to yell after her.

"So you love me 'cause I could kill you but I don't?" She pulled her obedient horse to a half-turn and yelled back at him.

"It's not that simple, simple. It has to do with …" She frowned openly, jerked the reins into a turn-away and yelled. " I guess it's a woman thing."

He caught up to her, and, blowing rainwater away from his mouth said; "I like your woman things." He reached over and traced a curled knuckle down one thigh. The outline of her garters pressed into view through the wet cotton. She flicked at him with her riding crop:

"Do men always think with their willy?"

"Only when our willy is with us."

She neck-reined the horse off to the right and into a gallop. She hoped Paul heard what she *tried* to say about him, about love, and about how much she wanted to be with him.

Later that same trip, after taking two days of final exams for an advanced medical course, she seemed preoccupied. Eventually, Paul pulled her to him. "What is it? "He asked. "The last time you withdrew from me I ended up with a slapped face." She broke eye contact.

"Over the last few weeks, I've been examined, as part of a course at hospital? We give blood samples, take x-rays and some of the newer scanning x-rays. We examine one another, and …" She exploded tears and looked away.

"What? What is it?" He was alarmed.

"They followed through with more tests, but yesterday. But it's no go."

"What is no go?"

"I can't have," she struggled. "ever …ever. A baby. Never." She cried heavily then. Wet tears and her Schiparelli perfume combined on his blue wool winter uniform and mixed an aroma that would always remind him of the helpless-hopeless tension he felt at that moment. Afraid to speak he held her and listened while she filled it all in. "You talk so much about marrying someone and having babies." He remained quiet. She spoke between sobs. "As long as you were unmarried …there was a chance for you and me, someday?" He remained quiet. "But now … I know not, Paul. And Kurt wouldn't understand about this loss. So I'll not tell him. He'd make some crack: 'surely with enough money in it, can they do a womb transplant Cynthia?"

He held her often during those seven days while she grieved the loss of the babies she would never have with him, or with anyone. Kurt misread her grief.

"What's with you, Cynnie, luv? Can't find the exact dress you want?"

She and Kurt saw him off three days later. By the time she waved to him at the pier, she had pressed her grief into a small corner of herself where it no longer showed. Paul wondered what else might be pressed into that corner, so well hidden behind the smiles.

He had to lean forward in Monk's squeaky chair and shake his head to avoid replaying his own tears from that day—the day Cynthia dramatically referred to now and then as 'the day being a woman was lost to me.'

A few months before marrying Rachael, Paul flew to Hong Kong on a boondoggle inspection trip working out of the Commander of Fleet air communication in Hawaii. Cynthia had only a day notice before he arrived and he was only there for 47 hours. The hurried atmosphere made them both snippy.

"You don't answer all of my letters." She said while lying on the bed.

"Yes I do."

"No, you don't." She said with a snit.

"I do."

"You don't. Don't argue."

"I'm not arguing."

"Yes you are."

"No I'm not."

"You are."

"Not." He calmed. "I think I do answer all letters. But there's a chance, I guess." He gave in.

"You missed one for sure." She smacked.

"What letter didn't I answer?"

"You know which one." It was an accusation.

"No I don't." He said, confused.

"Yes, you do."

"I don't."

"You do."

"Don't."

"Well …maybe you don't." She softened. "There's an ever so slight chance you didn't get it. But, I think you did."

"If you send it, I answer it." He felt certain again.

"No you don't."

"Yes I do."

"Don't."

"Fuck you." He said, and meant it.

"Yes." She said and meant it. He held her hair in his hands, his mouth pressed tightly to hers. He bit her lip and without saying much at all fucked her, very hard way into that night.

Later, by unconscious motive, Paul sent a photo of himself taken at the beach, by Rachael. He hadn't noticed the ring showed on his finger. When he telephoned to arrange his next visit to Hong Kong, Kurt heard one half of Cynthia on the phone.

"I'm with Kurt, here. Yes. On the veranda. No, only cold at night thus far. We'll watch for the big number seven ship, in the bay, on the twenty-ninth. And Paul? There's a new ring on your finger in the snap." (Oh shit—he thought) "You've married your Rachael. I, we …understand, of course. Fully understand. Of course. You love her. It'll be right. You have someone now, to start your family with. Of course. Kurt is smiling and sends his best. Of course. Send a snap of her, please. May we all meet, someday? Of course."

He shook his head again and spoke to the windowpane. "No more pain, Cynthia. Please? I see the struggles. Has it been love all this time, as you said?"

The windowpane voice shocked him—"Of course."

After a 1963 visit, his first since marrying Rachael, he joined Cynthia in making his first adulterous love. On the return trip to California, his conscience forced him to telephone from Hawaii. "Cynthia, listen to me." He said over the buzz of the Pacific cable. "I love your letters and I feel love for you …"

She interrupted. "So sweet to ring just to tell me so …"

"Cynthia." He said sharply. "That's not why I called. I've called to talk about reality and us."

"Us?"

"We."

"That is my reality too, Paul."

"No, it's fantasy. It's pretending neither Kurt nor Rachael exist. It's dancing 'til dawn. It's spending money on things I could never afford on a continuing basis."

"But, it would be different if we …"

"No." He insisted. "It's fantasy. Please hear me?"

"Is that so different from you and … ?" Controlling her tears, she would not say Rachael's name.

"She and I do *real* things," he said not meaning to be as cruel as his words represented. "We're getting her brothers out to the coast and into jobs. We're making sure her old father is comfortable. She's looking for work here. We have a future."

"Are you happy doing that, Paul? With your future. Truly happy?"

"Of course." He said. "Of course."

"And shall we still write as before?"

"Of course." He said. "Of course."

"Then we'll still write."

"Of course."

"Go away." He said to the reflection. "No! Wait! Stay. Please stay."

He picked up the heavy black phone, untangled the thick cloth cord and telephoned Amber Lane again, 428-9330. There was no answer. Mia must have gone to sleep.

Arriving for a brief R and R in 1964, he had faced the awkwardness that letters seemed to avoid quite well. Despite being engaged to Rachael he still wanted to make love to Cynthia, and, what do you say to a truly friendly man whose wife you want to sleep with? Even while visiting Eddie Monk he believed he could ignore that Cynthia was in the same town.

"Guilt …ahh, the gift that keeps on giving. I understand." Eddie Monk said at the time.

"That's not all of it, Eddie." He said. "I feel good I'm staying away from Cynthia and Kurt. I'm married now. Staying away combats the guilt. Rachael will be coming over in two weeks. I want them all to meet. I have this feeling I'll be able to lock in more with Rachael once I prove I can be true to her."

"Wow!" Monk exclaimed. "Tie a hamster to your brain, you'd wear it out. I hear more rationalization, imagination and justification in there than I've seen in most dictionaries. I see and I quote Charles Churchill—'Guilt in his heart and famine in his face'?"

Paul walked away.

Even though she said she would make the trip, clear to the last minute, Rachael didn't come to Hong Kong. She bought luggage for the trip, and described getting ready and packing, in letters. She made plane reservations and sent him copies. She stopped her mail and had someone lined up to water the plants. Then, within hours of the trip she called and canceled. Listening to Rachael on the telephone that night he was first surprised, then within microseconds, confused, disappointed, and finally —rejected and sad. When she cancelled, something happened inside of him that he didn't consciously acknowledge for some time. Monk said it best.

"Whatever has been preventing you from considering Cynthia as the one-and-only woman for you stopped doing its job the day Rachael refused to come to Hong Kong. I watched you change."

Monk was right. That was the day he phoned Cynthia but reached Kurt instead. The reflecting window unfolded to the day of the call to Kurt. Monk had reminded him as he picked up the phone. "Francis Quarles reminds us: 'Judge not the play before the play is done'."

"Fuck you."

"Cynnie is on errands, Paulie. Let's spin off to Happy Valley, wager the horses, have a bit-of-a-bite . We can ring Cynnie by five." His accent and word selection pulled Paul immediately back to the friendly days. He had long ago stopped asking what Kurt felt about his affair with his wife. It never came up, and it didn't seem as if it ever had to. He felt true fondness for the man.

The lunch at Happy Valley lasted into late afternoon and went well. It was a typical day with Kurt. "How is the navy? What's new? Who's winning the war? Is Admiral Zumwalt as brilliant as Newsweek Magazine reports?"

At 3:30 p.m. the weather turned too cold to enjoy the betting. Kurt insisted on early dinner as a way to stall until 5:00 p.m. A woman who seemed to know Kurt well stopped them as they entered a club on Wong-Nai-Chung Road.

"Kurt, can I join you?" the attractive middle-aged Asian woman asked in clipped English. "I've missed my ride and I'll wait now for my friend."

"Of course, LuAnn. This is Master Chief Paul Vincent, USN. Long time friend of Cynnie and mine."

Paul clock-watched as time crawled, finding it difficult to make light chat with the stranger who kept the conversation revolving around talk of the navy, to cater, she said, to

Paul. Kurt was able to answer many of her questions about Paul's coming and going, Paul correcting him only now and again.

Near the end of the meal a smiling Kurt walked LuAnn to the restaurant door when her ride appeared.

Returning to Paul, he finally telephoned Cynthia from their table. "Hello, Love. I'm late-lunching at the club with someone you know. I also have an ill-timed meeting this evening and must be in Kowloon by 8:00 p.m. You and this someone could perhaps come with? Do the shops whilst I meet?"

The fact that her voice was on the telephone only inches away jerked him to new feelings and his heart raced in response to the closeness. The reflection in the window again joined the memory, complete with her nurse uniform; white cap pined to her hair, a blue cape over one shoulder. When Kurt handed him the phone, she said: "Meet you? Yes. Yes." She shouted, her accent churning thrills in his chest. "On Edinburo street, on Queen's pieh' neah city hall. I'm meah' steps from my cah. And no guilt, Pool Vinzant. Kurt owes me a fortnight with you."

Every time she'd used that phrase in the past, they ended up with days alone together. The comment charged him. Kurt took the telephone.

"We'll be right there, Love, Bye." Kurt smiled. He seemed genuinely pleased that Paul and Cynthia should be together.

She arrived at the ferry landing in twenty minutes, innocent looking in the uniform. She wore no makeup but he saw the small gold earrings he had given her were in place. "She's cut her hair." He said as she approached.

"No." Kurt supplied. "Rolled likely, under the hat."

Holding her hat with one hand against the breeze she moved her eyes to his and walked quickly toward him, smiling at first but then, with sudden tears she fell into his arms. The aroma of newly dabbed *Shocking* floated around him and opened every memory pore. It took only seconds to stir his desire to the point it reached when they made love in Victoria Park.

"Oh, give the poor man a kiss, Cynnie." Too bizarre for Paul to show his real feelings in front of Kurt, they exchanged simple lip pressing promises of what was to come. Cynthia immediately turned to Kurt and kissed him a similar kiss.

"Thanks eva,' eva' for finding him again."

"How could I stop it, Cynnie?" Kurt said through a strong smile. "He blew in today and took over like a winter storm." To Paul, the remark joined the file of subtle comments that were pressing him to believe, at some level, the man disapproved of everything they were doing.

In early 1965 after he returned to the U.S., she wrote about that night, using Abie Lake's address as pre-planned. The window again reflected her face and the words pulled a smile from his face. "At the ferry when the wind came up and Kurt put us off from making the trip to Kowloon? I couldn't have planned it better." Paul leaned back against the wall of the darkened office. His active memory brought him the cold wind and the rest of the scene from the ferry landing in the bay. "Will you stay the night in Kowloon?" She yelled to Kurt over the sound of the ferry whistle.

"Likely stay with Chenny." He answered through cupped hands. "I'll ring you later at Amber Lane for sure." He said.

With a smile and a hat tip, Kurt joined the huddled crowd as wind blown waters thumped the heavy double-decked ferry against the pier.

"Not to worry over him." Cynthia said as she waved good-bye to her husband. "We'll go to Amber Lane. That's what I want."

A married man in those days, Paul tried a new contrivance to justify being with Cynthia

.

"I learn about women this way." He said to Monk. "I take the feelings back home and enhance what I have with Rachael."

"Bullshit, Paul. Plain bullshit. Bull-double-knee-deep-shit."

Monk was male honest-accurate. Rationalization only spooned more to the plate to feed the knowledge that his marriage to Rachael was not going as well as he pretended to himself and to others. Regrets of not having gone originally with Cynthia's demands for committed love came up more and more often, but always with contradictory feelings. He and Cynthia talked about the conflict now and again.

At Amber Lane when Kurt was in Europe visiting his father, the two of them were in the kitchen simmering the broth down after cooking a pot roast, as Cynthia said; 'the old fashioned way, in a pot'.

"I loooove cooking with you, P.V." She declared. "It is sooo homey, thoroughly touches a bit I miss with Kurt."

He also liked it. "With Rachael, cooking is always 'get it out of the refrigerator, into the pan, onto the stove, heat until ready, then down the hatch. Burp!"

"Burp?"

"We should have sailed off together on a tramp steamer, moved into a hut someplace, and cook together, huh?" He wondered aloud as he snapped fresh asparagus.

"But we didn't."

"I'm not a wealthy Kurt?" He speculated. "Is that some of it?"

"I'm not a fertile Rachael. That's *all* of it ..."

While Paul's finger absently pushed termite dust around on Monk's window ledge, the scene of Cynthia surrendering her blouse in Victoria Park wedged into view. Thrilled at being a voyeur to his own memory, he was as immediately awed and carnally spellbound by her breasts in the window scene as he had been that night when he first saw and touched them. He had stumbled for words that night in the park. "I never knew there could be such ..." The sentence would not complete itself until he found a word for the experience. He finally realized that night—he could not touch her breasts and talk and think at the same time nor did he want the moments so divided. He had to take his hands and eyes away from her before his breath returned and before all the words available to him from all the languages he had ever heard, could be sorted through. Soon a word did tumble from his lips to finish the sentence. Caught in the moment, he uttered; "I never knew there could be such *glory*."

Cynthia Megan Howser's chest had been leered at since she was fifteen. Other men saw 'tits' and 'knockers', 'boobs and chi-chi's,—this man saw 'glory?'

His childlike fascination moved her and awakened an innocence long slept. The woman who brazenly set out to seduce this handsome man earlier that night when she first saw him with her husband, retreated, replaced by the desire to be innocent and be loved in that innocence. In that distinct and elegant first time feeling, she covered her breasts with her hands.

"What?" He asked.

A tear-filled blush broke through her voice. "I don't know."

"Going too fast?" He asked also caught up in the innocence.

"No —yes—no."

He took her wrists gently in his hands. "Let me see." He asked, "Please."

Drawn in by the glory-fantasy she allowed him to lift her hands. In the dim light of the park the tanned flesh contrasted with the untanned. Her breasts were as though lovingly surrendered from a larger idealized woman and fitted imaginatively into place on her smaller body. As she watched him watch her, her areola softly flushed and both small nipples swelled. He felt her wrists pull against his grip.

He released her wrists.

"I'm …" She again covered her breasts with her open hands.

Immediately aware of her transition, he retrieved her blouse from the grass and draped it over her, covering her.

"Better?" He asked.

Her arms went up and around his neck.

"Nothing was more innocent and beautiful than us that night." He said to her face in the window.

"Nothing *is* more innocent and beautiful than us." Her face said in return.

As she dressed once at the Fandian Ho she looked in the mirror, cursed at what she saw and revealed more about what a woman with her figure deals with. "Kurt says my body looks like an explosion of leftover parts."

"What?" Such a comment seemed unlike Kurt.

"I'm too provocative, even in street clothes, he says."

"No shit?"

"Yes. He said I should be appreciative that he's married me." She was almost crying. She mocked Kurt's voice: "Cynnie, Dea'h. Is that gown not a trifle sketchy for Malcom's dinner?"—"Can't Tina sew together something that perhaps would conceal your bazookas bettah', my dah'ling?" That seemed out of character for Kurt but Paul couldn't see any reason for her to lie about it.

"The man's a fool." He soothed.

"I know, I know …" She said. "I didn't choose this. My mother was built like I am, even at age fifty when I saw her last. Chest, no waist, hippy. Kurt says I dress to be stared at. Not true, Paul."

He felt a no-win coming. "Wait." He said. "I stare at you and you smile."

". That is different. I'm being a fantasy for you. I like it that now and then my figure reminds you a rib must be missing." She looked with a smile.

"Conversations like this," he admitted, "make me wary.

"It is that safety feeling I have that you never seem to understand. I have it with you and I don't with Kurt, with others."

"Oh."

Throughout the Shore Patrol tour he learned more of Kurt.

"He prefers me dependent and beautiful, but not titillating. I'm to be social and agreeable, but as he says: 'Without abundant profundity, please, Cynthia'."

"Profundity?" Paul needed the meaning.

"Depth." She answered. "Kurt cannot stand being one-upped by a *mere* woman. He is quite engaged by his own ideas, you know."

"Why do you stay with him?" He finally asked the question he held since the first night. She paused and Paul wondered if she was rehearsing an answer she believed would be acceptable. "He has, shall I say, certain holds one me."

"Holds?" Was it money? The lifestyle. Was she *truly* shallow?

"Long story, Paul. I owe him. I owe him for now. So I stay, shallow and dumb."

"Dumb, you're not., Shallow, well, maybe?" He put both arms up and ducked to complete the tease.

"Shallow?" She mocked. "Moi? Perhaps I am, at times. I am afraid at times if I let go of him I'll just fall away into nothingness," she said with a shrug of her shoulders, "and crash on the rocks."

"Fall away? Rocks?" Paul took a chance. "Perhaps you'll fall away and glide, *fly,* not fall. Fly to someplace really really good?"

She responded quickly: "That an invitation, sailor boy?" The straightforward remark disarmed him. He looked away self-consciously. He'd meant the remark only to carry his overall feeling that she might likely be better off on her own, finishing medical school, not so controlled. He had not meant it as an invitation. He'd forgotten again, his importance to her. His face reddened.

She rescued him by making believe it had not been said. "Kurt and I pretend." She continued.

"Pretend?"

"I pretend he's the most important thing on the earth, and he pretends I'm not pretending. We go our own ways, mostly." She turned to the mirror to dismiss the incomplete subject. He watched her image in the reflection as she dressed, smoothing each cup into place around each breast, snapping the back clips seemingly without even thinking about the complexity of the garment. He tried to pretend with her that she was not provocative in modest street-clothes, as Kurt had charged. On the other hand he felt: no matter what she put around the arched waist, the great breasts and rounded hips, she could not *appear* unassuming. It was difficult to stop his estimation that she existed for sex alone. She *is* provocative, Paul decided; and she knows she is. At least, he re-thought it. 'I know she is.'

To support the desired illusion though, he said she wasn't provocative and she pretended he wasn't pretending.

There was a tap on the glass and a knowing smile from her reflection.

"Of course." She said with a slight smile.

"That afternoon in the rain in Aberdeen?" She referred to the summer of 1966. He was on R and R from Saigon. "Now *that* was romantic, Paul Vincent." They had been at Ocean Park near Aberdeen and while walking back to the Fandian Ho became caught in a summer rain. They waited impatiently under a balcony by a restaurant but when music came from inside, he coaxed an umbrella from the surprised hand of an old English-looking gent, pulled her into the street and danced with her in the warm downpour, humming and spinning her and also spinning the umbrella, *'singing-in-the-rain'*. He placed an imaginary flower in her soaked hair and for several minutes spun her sensually but with balance on the shining cobblestone side street.

"The old gent and the two Chinese women snickered and called me 'fa-shao nupengyou.'"

"What is that?" he asked.

"'Fevered girlfriend', more or less. Even strangers know you warm me."

CHAPTER EIGHTEEN
Wai-da Becomes the Center of Life

In Monk's lamp lighted office the erection that resulted from the cobblestone dance night mixed with the discovery of Wai-da and the stronger retention of love that followed that discovery. He relished the erection it brought but he also felt wrong about it. He wanted the seriousness of missing her to be symbolized in a more gentle way. There has to be, he thought, some exceptional keepsake to represent how differently he felt toward her than he had ever felt toward any other woman. In late 1966, quite by accident, he discovered it.

Kurt was away on one of the many trips and Paul was in for R and R from Vietnam. With Kurt gone, she and Paul again lived as though they were husband and wife. She cooked, he cleaned. He even ran the vacuum cleaner, washed Kurt's Humber sedan and did the deck windows once. He usually felt very at home in the fancy surroundings. Only now and again struck by pangs of conscience;.

He waited and watched one evening as she dressed to go to dinner. A small tag on her dress caught his eye.

"What's this? W-A-I-D-A?"

"Wai-da? Pardon?" She said, and blushed deeply. He pushed for the blush.

"What is it." He teased.

"Nothing, nothing." She said. "A Taiwanese clothing kind-of word. I forget exactly."

"You're blushing too much to have forgotten."

She pulled a sweater from the dresser drawer. "Okay, here. And no laughing. Here, Wai-da is on everything of mine."

"Wai-da?" He read.

She turned back to the dressing table and began opening hairpins with her teeth. 'Click'. "My Taiwanese seamstress, who Kurt calls tight-assed Tina? She makes all of my clothes". Years ago she said, 'W-A-I-D-A' was her *special signature* for extra-special clients." She 'clicked' a pin and slipped it deftly into her hair. Another followed, click, slip.

"Her trademark?"

"I thought so. I didn't think much of it. You know how my shallow side likes to feel special." She cocked her head, shifted her shoulders, locked her teeth and spoke in a mockery of refinement. "I felt quite upper class Brit, sort of." Click. She turned to face him, holding a pin in mid-slip. "Mia came from doing laundry one day, two bras in her hand." Paul watched the poised hairpin. Cynthia laughed nervously in reflection. " 'This not good, Missy Cyn.' Mia tells me. 'Why not?' I ask, half listening."

'Wai-da is Taiwanese word, Missy Cyn.' She said to me. I assured Mia it meant I am 'special', but she blasted right back at me, in sort of a cackle—*'Shuangren bu hao-wai-da,'*.

"Translated?"

"Well, *roughly* translated—'wai-da is double not good to put in a brassiere."

"Industrial strength?" Paul chanced the crack.

"Moreso," she said. "And, no gloating, Paul Vincent. It means sort of, 'the biggest ever'. But more like 'and still growing' ...such as in tidal waves and billowing clouds,"

"Oh." He said, truly amused. "Could also be the Taiwanese word for—'glory'." He said, softening it some.

"That," she said with a knowing smile. "will earn you at least one night with the Wai-da lady."

He picked his hat from a table and readied to leave. "So the Taiwanese have a word for my favorites?" He said approaching her and covering each breast gently with his open hands. "My wai-das?"

Cynthia smiled self-consciously. "Yes. Your wai-das." They kissed.

Stepping back from the kiss, she slipped the last pin into her hair, stood with legs slightly apart, hands on hips with shoulders pulled back to extend her bust, "will you take this Wai-da lady to dinner?"

"What can I say?"

Later, in the car he learned that wai-da must represent Tina's resentment toward the wench with the big chest and big bucks.

"Mia dines out on it." Cyn said. "When I get huffy with her? It's 'yes, Wai-da madam—right away, Wai-da madam'. You angry also wai-da, wai-da."

And so 'Wai-da' became their *special word of endearment*, representing the difference their love for one another was from any other love, anywhere. Their hearts were wai-da for one another. Her eyes were wai-da as was her love for him. "Kiss me wai-da, Honey." His muscles and cock were wai-da to her, "Ohh, wai-da baby-baby." Her warm arms and nighttime cuddles were wai-da—'Wai-da closer, snuggle in' he would say when they slept.

Holding her arms wide outstretched and pushing her chest out as a child might when measuring its love for a parent, she would say: "I love you, *waiiii*-daaaaa, Paul Vincent, thissss wai-da much." Representing their love, it touched his heart. On the erotic side, wai-da could be electric..

When in Subic Bay once, he had a Filipino silver smith make a very small set of earrings with their letters "w-a-i-d-a" dangling from small clips, and kept them hidden away for months. When he eventually slipped them into place beneath her dark hair, Cynthia spilled quiet tears over the symbols and stayed tightly in his arms for several moments.

Wai-da became clinched in as their special trademark. When around Kurt and among people their love affair was secreted from, Cynthia would get Paul's attention and make a mini-wai-da gesture by slowly opening and closing her thumb and forefinger.

When she'd say goodbye as his ships left, her open arm wai-da gestures would stop traffic.

Once between his visits, she was longing for the erotica with Paul. To play to his fetish-like attraction to her breasts but likely also to one-up Tina, Cynthia had the seamstress sew what she and Paul later referred to as a *super-wai-da*. With a straight face and the same tone she might use to order a dozen of handkerchiefs, she instructed Tina to copy her regular bra but pad it an additional inch or two at the tips.

"I'm told many women pad their bras, Tina, is that so?" Tina didn't answer.

"I want to be in on the trend. Make it of fine linen."

Cynthia enjoyed one-upping Tina's Wai-da one-up.

In the window, her wai-da smile gave way to a new image. It became the night of their argument in *Frenchie's* restaurant only 22 months ago. As before, and as she was wont to do, Rachael had decided at the last minute to not join Paul during his second R and R from Vietnam.

"I cheat on my wife to be with you. You cheat on your husband. It's like infidelity is all the rage this war season."

She put her fork down and he watched her cross her arms over her dark blue coat-dress, the one with fifty white buttons. "We don't *cheat*. That's an ugly word."

"Its the truth, dammit. When I'm with her, I think of you. When I'm with you, I never think of her."

"Not true." She whispered so the diners couldn't hear their argument. "You're thinking of her now. I don't mind. Think away."

He whispered also, but hoarsely. "I feel guilty because I prefer you."

"I don't believe in guilt." She said and began nervously pulling on the top button of her dress. "It's too … American."

"Don't be so …so …"

"Banal?" She cracked.

"I don't even know what *banal* means, Sounds like a word Kurt uses."

"Means 'tasteless.'"

"That's you then, tasteless, like this dinner." He put his fork down. "I hate the guilt."

"You talk as if Moses were sitting behind us, watching all the time." Her hands went to her lap and squeezed the napkin. "This really too difficult for you?"

"What?" He asked, confused.

"Being with me?"

"Yes …no! I don't know. You trick me. Don't ask that." He sipped red wine to stall for thoughts to clear any guilt away. Nothing came. "I need more control of the guilt."

She grabbed his hand across the table and dug her nails into his palm. "Must guilt win over us?" She seemed upset then and also, too, too serious. "Must someone else's rules take us from one another?" Her voice became loud. "Can't we just live the wai-da moments?"

"That sounds trite to me." He said and regretted the crack immediately.

"Fuck you, Pool Vinzant." Others looked at them. He self-consciously gathered his hat and walked out on her. He'd gone a stubborn block before he realized this terrific and beautiful woman was following him, cursing quietly, carrying her shoes, and also hating the whole scene. She followed him into a small park not far from her car. The night was heavily scented. "Jasmine in the air." She said, hoping his mood had ended.

"See how you are." He boomed, letting his mixed feelings rule.

"Is this what life is for you, Cynthia? Jasmine? The correct dinner? The *moments*?"

Her face flared red. She faced him head on, hands on hips, shoes held on fingertips.

"Will you please understand, Sir?" She pleaded, stomping one stocking foot in the grass. "You married someone else. She's refusing to give you the baby you married her to have. You've been to Vietnam. Tomorrow you go back to that horrible place where even bakery trucks have tail gunners. I've had you for merely six days. I pretend I'm having a night out with my man as though we'll go home to our children, talk of the mortgage …of vacationing … " The tears broke through. "Damn you, Pool Vinzant … I've begged life for these kinds of fucking moments and I'll take them anywhere they come." He had again forgotten how much she loved him.

She pulled the shoes up to her chest with both hands. Her voice calmed. "I know you have trouble it being only for the moments." She said to his dumbfounded look. "I'm sorry I relish them so."

He inwardly tried to see it her way. "I understand some of it, Cyn, about the moments business." He said, taking her shoes in one hand, her hand in the other. "I know I sound old-fashioned …but I need to believe whatever I have lasts, it won't end. But hell, we can't even *start* it. We're both so married."

She stepped in front of him and stopped him from walking away. . "Lasts, end, start, married?" She checked off each word with a wave of a hand. "Don't they all show up in each moment, one at a time?"

That stopped him and added to the feeling that perhaps he *had* failed her, and himself. He turned to Monk's window. "You're so fucking clever tonight, window. Tell me its not a tricky no-win. Women who are fun and alive at the moment, that's Cynthia—can't offer a future, can they? Woman who promise a future can't laugh or be alive—that's Rachael." Cynthia's splendid but unsmiling face looked at him from the windowpane and her voice flowed, firm, and clearly.

"Listen again, Pool Vinzant. I not only laugh with you, and at you, you've laughed with me, and at me. I have a longer and more struggled history with you than that fucking Rachael bitch. She has truly failed you. Turn the years back-to-front. We are *in* the future you said, in1960, we'd never have. When we met? We had a future coming that you refused to even examine with me. Our future is still unwinding today …" She pointed to the face of his watch, a Bulova Acutron she and Kurt had bought for him. " and this moment, and this one, as you sit and wait for me. Now don't say 'no future' to me evah again. " The window went blank and black. He leaned his forehead in his hands and let quiet tears grieve the lost years.

It took a quick walk outside for a few moments before he truly convinced himself he was not truly crazy. He recalled Selesky telling him that at times, our minds must re-trace our lives and re-file happenings in better order. Was that what was taking place?

He returned to Monk's office, sat down soundly in a squeaky swivel chair and almost pitched over backward. Catching himself on the desk corner, another early letter forced its pages from a waiting recall file and spread its words across the black window, in deep cream letters. The March, 1963 'night of the pill', long before she'd learn of being unable to become pregnant, the 'night of the woman' took its place. On her bed in her bedroom he had moved between her legs, desperately wanting her. She raised her hips and hugged him with full arms, ankles clinging to him. Smiles covered her face. She had read and plotted extensively about the new birth control medicines and convinced her long time friend the solemn and dignified Doctor Scott Salisbury-Baker (who knew she still dated Paul Vincent) to write the prescription. The doctor had suggested discreetly, a slight smell of clove from his breath: "It might improve sexual spontaneity with your husband, My Dear."

"Of course, Scott." But Cynthia was anticipating just a certain moment with her sailor.

When together finally, the tension reached that certain inevitable point and she spoke through sexual gasps, trying to say it as she had rehearsed it for weeks while waiting for him to arrive on his ship..

"I have the new pill." Her words were just as she had wanted them to be. "You can come in me, now."

"Truly."

"Yes. So so truly."

He came within seconds of her invitation and they were both very pleased with themselves.

Leaning forward from the squeaky chair he picked up the heavy black phone, untangled the thick cloth cord and telephoned her house again. 428-9330. Again, no answer. Mia must know it is he she is ignoring.

Monk poked his head in the room as Paul set the heavy phone in its cradle. He took one look at Paul's gloomy expression and stepped inside.

"You look like hell."

"Sorting things out …thoughts racing "

"Sorting it out, once and for all?" Monk played out a smile.

"Something like that." Paul tried smiling but it didn't form.

"There are two tragedies in life, Paul. Georgie B. Shaw said; 'one is to *not* get your heart's desire. The other is to get it'."

"This Shaw fellow must've been following me the last few days."

What he really needed jumped back into his thoughts. At the Kowloon Hilton one night she'd stood by the side of the bed, naked, recovering from just having brain-jarring body-taxing feet-locked-to-the-bedpost sex. Their sweat glowed on both their bodies.

"My God that made me rubber-legged." Her face was flushed, her breath barely returning from the orgasmic lurches. She slipped off the bed and dizzily stepped for the bathroom, grinning as she walked. Words hissed from a sucked in breath. "I forgot this part." She said.

"What part?" Her comment dimly pulled him from his afterglow.

"Some*one* is running out of me. A *lot* of someone."

His afterglow clicked off. Rachael had always hated his semen, treating it as something that leaked from a bloated-busted can.

"Should we go back to rubbers? To pulling out?"

She turned and smiled toward him. "Not evah! What goes in must come out. It's sooo …male. Sooo, …something …sooo … "

"Primal?" That word described a lot of her feelings about sex with him. She could let go of every part of her personality at times except the primordial sexual side, and just let it run. He remembered being very pleased to have found her.

"Primal." She agreed

The memory of the 'introduction of Willie' slipped into place like a 3-D slide in a hand-held viewer. Getting dressed to go to dinner, she was leaning against the doorframe of the bathroom dressed only in panties and bra, snapping dark hose to dark garters. He was still on the bed, freshly showered, still naked. She seemed happy, bemused. He liked that while she wore the newer pantyhose to work, to shop and to school, she stayed with the garter belt and stockings when they were together.

"Wait." He said, watching her dress. "Those look like boxer shorts."

"No, dummy." She said stepping back and looking down, snapping the waist of the thin white garment with small open leg holes. "These are tap-pants, open, more airy, not as snug." She took up a pose in a fighter's stance. "Not boxer shorts, unless you want a punch. After tonight? will you take this pair with you as a memento?"

"To add to my collection of things that go snap in the night. Of course."

"Of course."

Paul daydreamed aloud. "You're my dream come true, you know?"

"The way I understand it?" She teased. "I'm *any man's* dream, I just came true for you. This isn't the days where an ape man with a club wins by chasing his woman into cave number sixty three. I carry my *own* club. I nominated my own man this time. I didn't just settle for the ones who wanted me."

"Why me, for God's sake?" The classic question from low self esteem"

"Because, Pool Vinzant. I've told you again and again. You, sir, are safe. And I want you because you're safe."

Kurt had been safe once to her, she'd said. Now Kurt was *something else.* Now Paul had become safe. What was 'safe'? Would he soon become 'something else'?

Pacing some, he poured biting coffee from Monk's steaming pot, let it burn down his throat, and tried to take the room into his past. She'd been with him in that same room back in 1962.

"Oh, Paul. It's too shoddy here for you." She had wanted to see where he worked. She laughed a sympathy laugh. "These old wooden desks."

He had felt a little embarrassed in the run-down office that night with her. He tried making it all right. "Frees up a steel desk for front line duty." He quipped. "I'm here for six months, Cynthia, at the most. Its worth it to me to have the time we want."

Her face became serious. "I know it wasn't easy for you to find duty here, but, I am, very ... " Her voice caught, uncharacteristically. He pulled her to one side of the room. Sensing something had gone wrong, he asked; "What is it?"

"Nothing ...now ... "

"Does this office spoil the image?" He was hoping he was joking.

"No, dummy." A smile flashed but melted quickly into uncertainty. "Can't you see? You came here, for me. I am so …pleased …no, not pleased. Yes, pleased, but that's not all." She spun away from him, stiff-armed fists at her sides. "Oh! Fuggit, Paul … I am …" She turned back toward him and her face changed, the smile returned, this time with a self-conscious touch. As one might expect in a Dickens story, she curtsied ceremoniously, "I was …*struck silent* when I found you wanted to be with me,"

He also was struck silent also by her confessional statement, but he forcibly repressed happiness tears over it that night because it went in the face of his plans with Rachael. However, anything repressed eventually bursts forth and in the quiet S.P. office, standing alone, he cried for several minutes over loving her, missing her, loving the memories, loving even the sadness of the moment without her.

Eventually, calmer, he picked up the telephone but just held it. He didn't dial.

"How do I love thee, Paul Vincent … ? Let me count the ways …"

He had told *her* once, while dancing, that he loved her. She'd pushed back from him a little surprised, and looked directly into his eyes.

"I'm apprehensive over that …some." She practically mumbled.

"Apprehensive? I doubt that." They'd had a few drinks and he was feeling confident, non-threatened and not guilty. He used his cowboy accent she always seemed pleased with. "Welper', I fergot, ma'am. This be all fer the moment fer you."

"That's a bloody saved up brown stamp, Paul Vincent."

Unanticipated anger slipped through. The accent dropped. "Truth hurt? You're the '*only* moments' lady." Discomfort of that first argument colored his voice as he spoke but she wouldn't be pulled in by his anger. She moved in close again, continued dancing quietly, moving with the dance and against his body. When she finally spoke, her voice was very calm.

"You're missing it, now, cowboy dummy hick from Steubenville. I say 'tis the moments, yes, perhaps. But only because …as it is …" She let the sentence trail away, but he wouldn't.

"As it is …? As it is *what?*"

She turned and tried to break from the dance but he held her wrist tightly, spun her back to him and looked as her eyes filled with tears. He finished the sentence for her. " …that's all we can have?"

The facts had stayed the same, but the feelings had changed with the times. It was at that instant he felt true love for her. "It's more than just the moment now, isn't it?" He said into her eyes. "It can now go on and on?" It wasn't a question.

"It's changed everything. It's ever more safe promising with you … "

He sipped Monk's terrible coffee, his thoughts locked on her word 'safe'. It had dumbfounded him when she'd said it, but he'd sorted it out over the years. She'd responded to his caring by feeling 'safe'. Rachael responded to his caring by demanding far more caring. Cynthia saw his kindness as safety, an open door to feel loved and safe. Rachael saw his kindness as weakness, an open door to unlimited taking. With Cynthia, he could be himself. With Rachael, he had to be what she wanted him to be.

He'd first noticed the freedom of being *himself* with Cynthia when they were at dinner one evening with Kurt and their friends. He'd made a well intentioned remark about the growing war in Vietnam and had offended some of those present. She neither ran from him nor jumped in to rescue him.

Later. "You take me just as I am, don't you?"

"I have no agenda for you to follow, Paul Vincent, if that's what you mean? Just be you."

Rachael always seemed to have something hidden behind the stated or the obvious. No wonder he went to so much trouble to get six months near Cynthia. With her, he could be Paul Vincent just as he comes out of the bottle, without guessing her moods, her desires, without having to be responsible for her feelings or reading her mind.

"Other women always seems to keep some secret side to them, to be guessed." He mumbled into the air.

"If you mean Rachael? Say Rachael."

"Yes, Rachael. A sad side I can't get to know. With her? There is no foreplay. Its lights out, after dark, man on top, in and out, repeat as required, no talking. Heaven forbid if anyone makes a body noise."

"No smiles? No looking? No pointing?" She teased.

"No anything. With you ...foreplay seems to begin at first meeting."

"My Christian name was to have been 'Coitus'. I think the minister advised against it."

"Film at eleven."

"Details at eleven ...twelve ...one ...two, three. Let me count the ways, Wai-da."

He was suddenly anxious to get out the door. He couldn't mask the teary eyes so he waved at Eddie Monk from a distance and reassured him he'd stop by the following evening ready for Shore Patrol.

For now, however, he was following his needs to a place he'd gone to on other trips, mostly before Cynthia but also, but less often, since knowing her. He was heading to Monique's, for some effective distractions.

When lonely, the presence of someone, almost anyone stopped the loneliness and, the sex when it happened, distracted from general woes. Perhaps it is just a guy-thing where, left to its own ability, testosterone can justify getting some sperm to some egg, any egg, real or not, hidden behind a condom or behind some chemical, or not, or behind a diaphragm, or not, at any drop of a reason, or not.

Until he'd tried to focus in Monk's office, he hadn't admitted to himself how the unsettled divorce, the crash-programs to get the ship deployed, the injuries and hassles over training, the possible lawsuit over the bar, the potential loss of the house in Virginia, the botched boat mission, the dead CIA agents, the fight with Clifford, and the latest, the frustration of Cynthia being out of the city, had taxed him. He was fighting off his need to hold and be held by just any woman. He wanted that to shift to only Cynthia now. Staying with her images in the window helped make that possible.

Tape-measure-night toyed with the nerve endings in his groin causing the pleasantness of an erection to grow against his leg.

"Can I ask you for something only you can give me, Cynnie?"

"Sounds like something I shouldn't tell Mummy."

"Something I want with you …fantasy stuff."

"I can hardly wait." She'd risen to her knees on the bed, naked. "Love it when you're …" She took his erection in her hand. "when you come up with stuff like this …"

"I want to measure you. You know: bust—waist—hips?"

"*Playboy* gatefold stuff?"

"Its 'centerfold'."

She clamored out of bed and he was immediately afraid of being rejected. He was about to take away the request, but she turned and faced him with hands on hips, her right hip tossed higher than the other. Mocking Sophia Loren style, with just a touch of butchered Italian accent, she invited:

"How' you like a' measure me, Beeg Boy?" Carnal energy gushed between them.

"Definitely, certainly." He rose to his knees on the bed. His erection swung in front of him like the mast of a busy crane. "Can you tell it seems like a good idea from here?"

"Decidedly, verily." She said, peering.

He turned on his knees to follow her as she walked around the bed, reached into and rummaged through some things in a small night stand. He dropped to his stomach next to the perfumed drawer.

"Whoops." There was a small automatic and several bullets in the drawer. She picked the gun up. "Bedroom toy," she said without smiling.

"I take away the request."

"Ahh-hah. But I have a request." She pulled the small pistol out of its holster and smartly cocked its slide. "Are you ready, Sir?"

His face conveyed confused amazement. She laughed at his expression and returned the gun gently to the drawer.

"I'm like my cat. I get distracted easily." She stepped back a pace and posed hands on hips, one leg forward.

"Kurt and I?" She spoke evenly. "He takes me shooting at the range. He says I'm a good shooter. You know how men are. Safety and all that? They love to flash their nine-shot penises about."

Paul regained himself when she reached back into the drawer and came up, not with the small gun, but with a fancy oriental porcelain case, much like a make-up compact.

"Ah-hah, here's what I searched. Better toy." She drew a gold-colored tape measure from the little case and draped it over his erection.

"Measure me." It was almost a command.

He took the tape and borrowed Selesky's line. "Adultery …is for adults."

He measured her and she measured him and they rolled on the bed and played with the measurements. The tape measured in meters and centimeters but he adjusted quickly, said the right 'ohh's' and 'ahh's' over her dimensions and she blushed appropriately. While measuring his erection she feigned a swoon. They hugged and giggled. Show me yours, I'll show you mine. They laughed like children behind a barn and then eventually fell into one another's arms. She closed her eyes and smiled. He kissed her face, her neck her breasts. She opened her eyes and her legs and watched his face and loved him. He entered her willingness and watched her face and loved her.

Cynthia, Cynthia, Cynthia. He could not shake the images as they continued to tumble into view. Once as they walked into the hotel room at the Fandian Ho, she had screamed. "Hurry, Hurry. No teasing. Go down on me." She'd held his head, his hair, tightly. She screamed, pushing against him.

Later, holding and cuddled, she'd laughed at herself. "Sometimes? Even immediate gratification isn't fast enough."

In the sail boat, after dark, anchored off Stonecutter's Island she had asked coyly, patiently, but with breath shallow. "Tease me, more. Tease you, more." She'd opened her wraparound skirt. "Keep me right here, at this delicious place." He worked his way down her body, slowly and easily. "Delay my gratification ...kill me with it." He went down on her, for a long time.

Once they'd talked of marriage as they smoked mild hashish, his first, in her bedroom. She was standing naked at her dresser, fixing her hair. The "M" word had scared both of them.

"Married?" She toyed. "Could you be with me forever? I'm very vain."

"You've got a cute ass."

"I roll the cereal box wax paper down tightly to keep the cereal fresh."

"Do you hang up the towel after use?"

"No, but Mia comes with me as a package deal."

"I read books."

"I send thank-you notes for presents and dinners from friends."

"I owe a bunch of those."

"Are you aware", she continued, "I'm the kind of woman who never eats anything softer than her tongue ..." Then, with her hairbrush she pointed toward his erection and laughed. "Except some times." Turning to face him she balanced on her toes, arm akimbo. "Also, I won't go anywhere I'm not dressed right for. I seldom go anywhere I cahn't wear veddy high heels ...and," She feigned a shocked surprised look. "I never swim anyplace that isn't chlorinated." The word came out 'cloordinaded'.

"I'm not real bright, actually." He'd confessed in return. "I believe the government makes food appear magically in the markets."

"You know? So do I."

"I like dogs and will want one in the house."

"Cause of the unconditional love they give?"

"There is no unconditional love. Well, maybe for kittens and puppies and new babies, but not between adults."

"There is too, Paul Vincent." She mocked disappointment.

"Is not. There are always conditions waiting in the wings. You'll eventually want something I can't give. I'll want something you can't give."

"Yes, but. Don't get serious." She pulled her hair from under a fastener and refused to address the serious point he made. "Life's ups and downs should never interfere with a couple's ins and outs."

"I have trouble with cats." He said as hers crossed the bed.

"Ohh? My mother once said … 'if a man can't love a cat, with its autonomy. He can't love a woman with hers'."

"One can't say 'mother' and 'autonomy'."

"Also, I want a man who can talk rough but who hugs soft."

"And I want a Madonna who has the moves of a whore."

"I also believe that if you want to put a bag over my head and screw me as if I am someone else? That's Okay."

"As long as it's a designer's bag?"

"Of course." She stuck her nose into the air, it came out 'av 'kahse'.

"For a stuck up, hoyty toy, bitch type, you love fucking."

"I love …" She smiled with a sideways glance. " …what you said. But … I also think …seeking pleasure from the AB-normal makes pleasure from the normal, more difficult."

He pulled away from her breasts where he'd left stubble-rubbed redness between them. "Me too." He managed. " …but, I don't pretend to know one from the other."

"Nor do I."

"So," Lying on the bed he put the back of one ankle on one raised knee and crossed his hands behind his head. "You're wondering if I am the man you could let our children spend weekends with after a divorce … ?"

"Cute, Paul. But we'll not divorce. I'm not one of those women who will want to talk when the rugby game is in overtime."

"But you're adventurous. You dance in the rain, you screw in a boat at night …you shoot a pistol."

"But I'm not …*very* adventurous." She dropped into the padded wire-backed chair at the dressing table and spun it toward him, leaning an arm on its back. "Really. I'm not very adventurous, sailor boy. I'm homey, I want children, I think." She laughed cautiously. "Although I don't know what we'd do with them. I may want them just to have a captive audience?"

"Monk says some Brit said a Brit and an American marrying … 'will always be divided by a common language'. Something like that."

"Rathah?"

"Rather."

"Potahtoe."

"French fries."

She stopped fussing with her hair and locked eyes with him. It was before her bad news about being infertile. "I'd have your babies. Does that worry you?"

He was sobered by *her* sudden seriousness.

"Some. Where would we call home? San Diego?" He wouldn't stay serious. "Hong fucking Kong?"

"What's Montana like?"

"Too cold. Hawaii's too hot. Hong Kong is too many rats in a cage. See, I too, can be complicated."

She began brushing her hair. "You've killed the theory that complicated men have erection trouble."

"You've killed the notion that women with boobs which have their own zip code have no brains." He motioned her back to the bed.

"What's a 'zip code'?" she queried, sliding in beside him.

"Something wonderful when it has to do with boobs," he said, running from the joke, "but even though you've been spoiled and your zip code's spoil me," he continued, "I'd consider a fifty year test of having you in my life."

Standing in a robe at the side of the bed, she reached down and took one of his fingers in her hand. "We've said the 'M' word, didn't we?"

"Yes, we did."

But it had all been lost to the hashish except for bits and pieces that floated into thoughts now and again.

The taxi slid to the curb at Monique's.

CHAPTER NINETEEN
Monique's Place

"If you look up British colonialism in a dictionary," Paul told Stumpf, or anyone who would listen, "It'll say—'see Monique's bar, Hotel Lu-Sur Kuoche, Hong Kong."

At 9:20 p.m. he stepped into that Lu-Sur Kuoche on Wing Lok Street between where Bonham Strand splits into east and west. No matter the hotel's formal name, actually more Taiwanese than Chinese, the place was known internationally by the name above the door to the bar, 'Monique's'.

The interior of the hotel looked just as he had remembered, warm and wooden, something from a late 1930's movie. The large lobby was quiet. An oak bladed ceiling fan turned overhead even in winter and mixed the subtle smells of the bar, the rich odors from the nearby dining room, the cigar smoke of men and the cologne of women. The result was the stereotypical essence of a Charlie Chan movie.

Paul expected to see the regular desk man, Dartmouth behind the shined wooden front desk but instead an older Chinese man was there. Paul asked for Dartmouth. "He be in Sata'day" the old man said but didn't look up from his pencil work.

An old European gent sat in an easy chair reading a newspaper that was as carefully creased as the trousers of his gray whipcord suit. Paul guessed him to be an old colonialist, perhaps on speaking terms with Lord Mountbatten, surely with Sydney Greenstreet. The England of Kipling was still in the hotel though no longer in all of Hong Kong.

The entrance to the bar was off to the right, its door hung with a beaded curtain. Inside, a second wooden fan turned above like a slow rotor. An aged Chinese bartender greeted him with just a slight nod. He climbed a bar stool and sampled a local beer, the first in months. The tart flavor cut the salted dryness from his throat. The Beatles—*'Lucy in the Sky with Diamonds'* came into the bar from hidden speakers.

Usually Hong Kong nightlife starts very late. The bar was unusually empty except for himself, the unobtrusive old man, and three Chinese women who were sitting at a small table against the wall under the polished wooden staircase to the second floor. Eight or nine leather covered bar stools were lined up and waiting to do their thankless duty for the evening. The ten or so rich wooden tables were also empty except for a small candle centered on each of them. Lights from passing cars flashed through two large stained glass windows on the street-side wall. To Paul, it was an intimate room. He had spent many peaceful evenings there but had never brought Cynthia. He immediately wished she were there.

In the bar mirror Paul could see the three Chinese women leave the corner table where they had been chatting. Just before they reached the stairway that led to Monique's quarters above, one paused and shot a quick giggling glance at him. He recalled her face from the past but not her name. He smiled into the mirror and tipped his glass in the direction of the three obvious hookers who were readying for a night of the trade. The one he recognized clasped her hand to her mouth to cover a new outbreak of giggles, then struggled up Monique's steps, hampered by extraordinarily high heels.

There was commotion among the beads of the doorway. Captain Clifford entered the room, his eyes resenting the darkness. Griffith was behind him defending against the beads. Two British naval officers followed, hats tucked under their left elbows. The beads had barely stopped swinging when Lieutenant Stumpf parted them with his balding head, one hand covering his glasses. Two more Truaxe junior officers followed behind him, Ensigns Hanson and Merryweather.

"Over here, Griff." Clifford led everyone to a center table. They hadn't recognized Paul.

Just as unexpectedly, some crewmen from the ship came through the beads laughing, joking, as alike as a group of mustached cops. Tucker, Lake, Boswell, Abalare, Froman, Jackson.

"Chief!" Abie spotted him. They all crowded around. Clifford's crowd noticed also. In seconds everyone was standing and chatting, except Griffith who remained at the table. Paul left the bar stool and gravitated with the group toward Griffith, but not on purpose.

"My records fucked up." Tucker announced to the X.O. The Southerner had been drinking.

"No, Tucker." Griffith seemed in pain being buttonholed by the drunken man. "The diary entry had a mistake. Your SSN was inverted. I've already taken action to fix it. Until then, borrow money someplace—from Lake here."

"Fuck you very much, Sir." Tucker's drunken and disrespectful thank you was not well received by Griffith who turned away abruptly.

"C'mon, Exec." Tucker continued. "You tunin' away imply you jes' too officerial or sumptin' to put up with our common shit?"

Lake grabbed Tucker, spun him toward the beaded doorway and spoke to Griffith with a little drunken curl to his own voice. "Whoops! No offense, sir."

He turned to Tucker and pushed not too lightly. "Let's git' outta' here."

"Good idea." Paul encouraged.

"Thought you was seein' Cynthia the lovely tonight, Chief?" Tucker grinned like a schoolboy, resisting some as Abie pushed toward the door.

"She's not here, as feared, Tuck … "

"Sheeeit." Tucker was still loud. "Wanna' come with us guys? We're just playin' along."

"No, I'm fine."

"Hey." Boswell whispered hoarsely to Vincent. "This an officer pussy palace?"

"It is."

"Really?" Abalare seemed surprised at that kind of discrimination.

Tucker turned to Paul. "Officer pussy is clap invested—infested." Turning back toward the room, he put one hand on Vincent's shoulder, one on Lake's. "Let's go down to Tiny's. They's havin' a blue light special. This one gal is sooo ugly … "

"How ugly is she?" Stumpf encouraged.

"Well," Tucker turned to the Lieutenant. "She's so ugly she works in a dark corner. But got this great sexy voice .... a real dick twitcher." The tipsy gang laughed among themselves. "She earns a living doing strip shows for the blind."

Laughing and yelling, pushing, shoving and hat flipping the group of enlisted men exited through the beads. Tucker's head immediately poked back through. "Made me laugh so hard the tears ran down ma' leg." Someone jerked him from beyond and he was gone. Two beads bounced and trickled across the shined floor to the carpet edge. The room was again quiet. The music had shifted—"*Will you still—me, will you still—me, . . when I'm sixty-four.*" Beatles still.

The officers returned to their table without inviting Vincent. He returned to the bar. A few minutes later he saw a good silhouette clicking seductively down the stairs. He continued looking into the mirror, his back to the room. It was Monique, a beautiful European woman in her late forties. She was looking at him but didn't acknowledge he saw her in the mirror.

She wore a form fitting pearl colored mandarin mini-dress under her bobbing spray of short brown hair. Her legs were sleek in pearl adorned nylons and heels. She had not lost her magnificent trim figure, the promise of breasts, well contoured hips, her stomach flat and carried taunt. She was lovely and Paul was very pleased to be looking at her.

The men at the table were also watching the scene. Watching the table of officers Vincent decided he wasn't the only man who could get pleasure from the visual presence of a beautiful woman. His libido stirred, then stirred again. Cynthia's face interchanged or blended with Monique's. He didn't want that reaction but it was there.

He suddenly felt wrong to be flirting with his vulnerability to beautiful women and blamed the turncoat fate of Cynthia's absence. If he stayed with Monique, let his male bullshit libido run, he would be punishing Cynthia in some convoluted way. He didn't wish to punish her.

"No!" He thought to himself. Do not start with Cynthia the patterns with Rachael. He had been sexual with many women through his married years. He had rationalized it as 'simply wanting sex', 'something men do'. But he also wondered if it might be some petty passive-aggressive punishment to Rachael for not being as passionately open as he longed for. He knew it was judged by many to be immature, sophomoric, may be even immoral at some level, but he wouldn't stop the patterns then and it looked as though even the promise of Cynthia would take extra effort to stop the patterns now.

Taking a sip of beer and blaming his sexuality he immediately knew he was doing what Clifford had done on the ship's bridge. 'Errors had happened' with Clifford. 'Sexuality was happening' with himself. A familiar carnal intensity was shouting to him that anything with two legs and a vagina was life's' promised fulfillment. He knew it was a crazy game but knowing it was a crazy game was what made the game crazy and worth playing. With a prayer that the future with Cynthia would develop and be filled with understanding, especially from himself, he allowed her face to superimpose over Monique's. His let his libido run on male automatic.

The sight of the lovely French woman approaching the waiting man had been choreographed by nature and projected in fantasy again and again over time. She did not look older than before. She looked mature, yes, seasoned, yes. Definitely more evolved to the world around her than the younger bodies without heads he had so often coveted. She looked good. She'd cut her hair in a shapely page boy which framed her sharp features beautifully. The set of her shoulders and head showed a quality he hoped could be seen in himself. She too was someone who had survived the vicious unpredictable streets since childhood yet it seemed she permitted the softness of the person to show through. As she left the carpet her heels clicked on the marble floor. Their eyes met in the mirror and shared just a sip of mutually intoxicating silent dialogue.

After the exchange, she paused uncertainly. She turned and smiled in the direction of the crowded table of officers. Vincent swiveled on the stool and towered over her. "Monique." He said. Just her head turned toward him and she smiled in a genuine way, decidedly glad to see him.

"Hi, Paul-guy." It came out 'Pool-kuy'. They joined hands. Her nostrils became a little flared and her small breasts rose against her dress in waves that marked her breathing. She seemed as excited and pleased as he.

"I would have recognized you anywhere, Monique. You are very beautiful, as ever."

"*Ma foi, mon ami ?*" She seemed truly pleased and shifted to English. "Coom' eento' ze' room weeth me, Paul. Ze' coffee and *compte rendu.*"

What could he say? "j'aimerais" he remembered. She seemed pleased.

"Oooo, j'aimerais—you 'vould like." She teased. As they fractured both French and English, the seven officers eyes were glued to the scene. Not understanding much of her French, he had long ago learned to ignore her use of the words. She never held him responsible for understanding them. Now and then he would sneak in an '*oui* ' or '*non* ' or beg her '*de trop-de trop* ' (too much too many) but she didn't require him to learn.

As the embattled Master Chief disappeared behind the door with the beautiful mistress of the most famous officer hotel in the city, there was pleased and displeased commotion at the table of officers.

"She wants a bloody green card?"

"He's moved right in. Got something going I surely can't see."

"He shouldn't be here. He should'a gone to Tiny's."

"Hope he watches his billfold."

"I've a feelin' he don't need no billfold here." Stumpf offered.

In a room adjacent to the bar was her office. They sat close together on a small loveseat. Her crossed legs were intentionally exposed to the thighs by the cut of the skirt. They hugged. She said a few words about his new Master Chief stars, about how long it had been. She began chuckling, open with the enjoyment of being with him.

"Paul, I joost love it when you come here. I have excitement weeth you I swear it to be the true." Her butchered English was tricky to follow at first. "Ohhh, you silly man-Paul." They were both suddenly animated." You play so well the sailor meets girl. *Le style, c'est l'homme ...* How many times we do that?"

"Ten—Twenty. Ten years? More?"

"Ah-hah. You are such a sailor-boy." She rubbed his hand and then kissed his lips, quickly but not too quickly.

"We drive the officers 'quisitive I theenk."

"Those guys out there? From my ship."

"You in Hong Kong fast with your ship, Paul."

"How'd you know?"

"*C'est la vie.* Men from ship here since noontime. I know everything, every sailor story. I know Captain out there, from other ships. And funny man, commander with satchel."

"Griffith."

"Yes—he from other ship—in way past. Always satchel."

"How are you, Monique? You look real good."

"*Le tout ensemble?* I am good, I theenk." She lifted one magnificent leg and turned her foot back and forth. "Still can wear the come-fuck-me shoes. I still need the *Kotex*." She laughed. "My top still bigger than 'round my ass. *Tant mieux* in ziz' business." She laughed aloud, took a cigarette from a nearby table and took the conversation to business. "You want lady tonight, correct?"

Monique made a living catering to men's needs. She winked at him and rubbed his groin, coaxing an area that had already been coaxed by his wai-da reflections of Cynthia and by Monique's approach down the stairs. She smiled a knowing response. He felt very shallow.

It had been over ten years since Paul had been sexual with her. But he always asked, and she always said 'no'. "You and me? Tonight?" He hunched his groin as a salesman in a polyester suit. "Wanna' fuck, Babe?" She returned the hunches and shook her breasts rapidly back and forth. When the chuckles receded, she said, "I have my quirks and …you play well. But, you have the …the *…non de guerre …*"

"Huh?"

"The Dutch lady, no?"

"But, she's not in Hong Kong tonight. I just want to be with someone"

"Oooo!" Monique looked truly concerned. "Dutch lady find out you here? Would be trouble?"

"Maybe, maybe." Monique's sudden sense of propriety didn't seem to fit. "She's in Europe. We tried meeting this trip, but no luck on our side. I am only human, Monique." She changed then, noticeably.

"Ah, then, I see. Paul-boy. *Sans peur et sans reproche* ?"

"Huh?"

"The cat away …the mouses …?"

"Something like that."

Talking of Cynthia pulled some desire quencher into the room with the impact of a bucket full of class A guilt. Being sexual seemed suddenly out of line. "Sleep with me tonight, Monique? Just sleep."

She stood up from the couch. "No, I cannot. Not tonight." She snuffed her cigarette in a desk ashtray. "My *l'homme* now. Not understand you and me." She seemed suddenly distanced.

"Is he a good guy?"

She managed a smile again and pulled back into her hostess role. "'Ees better than the corner of the washing machine ...vibrating away."

"Does he not take good care of our Monique?"

"I no longer change my life over fifteen centimeters of meat." She laughed.

"Ah hah."

"Now maybe twenty one centimeters?" She held her hands the appropriate distance apart and laughed aloud. " ...maybe. But, no more of me. For you, tonight, for old Shore Patrol times, I am offering you *sans doute, sans pareil*, one of the beautiful delicacies of Hong Kong ...she will sleep nicely with you ...*tant mieux*.." She stopped for a moment as though thinking of her sales pitch, then added: ". . delicacies of the world. For that matter."

He sat back in the comfortable office of the old hotel as she played out the description that caused his imagination to run. Though his intense desire had surely lessened, it hadn't died completely. Who, what, was this woman she was offering to him?

"Waiting on the other end of the phone, not five minutes away is the delicacy I mentioned."

"Well, let's get calling her."

"Rasha ...is her name ... "

"Rasha?"

" ...but for reasons that will be obvious to you, she is known as 'Shampoo'.

"As in hair?"

"As in hair, *mon ami*. Hers and yours ... " She shook with laughter.

"Expensive?" If she could be at Monique's within five minutes, she was operating from expensive territory.

"*Au contraire* ... Not the first time, Paul-boy. *A' bon marche'* ...She's like a fine opium seller ...she give you the initial taste of sweetness for, ahh, let me see." She pulled his billfold from his inner jacket pocket, flipped through and took some bills and held them up. He took two tens back from what she had taken. She reached and pulled one of them back.

"Quality, is expensive, even when the price is cut." She said folding the bills tightly. He watched his forty or so dollars slip under her watchstrap. "Like opium ..." she repeated. " ...and," she smiled again. " ...she is finely grained, of excellent quality." Then she added quickly, the standard lie. "Beside that, she had medical check today."

He kissed her full on the mouth. She returned the kiss with controlled passion, the kind of passion one shops around for but takes home with them. "He's a lucky man, Monique."

"You be in room seven in twenty minutes you will be the lucky man. Take shower. She will come in with her own key. *Cherchez la femme* ."

"Cher what-la-what?"

"Look for ze woman."

As she picked up the telephone and waved him out the door, she called after him, '*gardez la foi*'. He recalled that phrase: 'Keep the faith'.

As Paul walked through the bar to get the key for room seven, the seven officers were on there feet readying to go to the dining room for a late evening meal. Griffith stepped in front of him and asked quietly.

"Was *that* the woman?"

"Pardon?"

"The cause of the divorce?" Griffith's eyes were icy.

"C'mon, Griff." Clifford spoke up, tugging at the sleeve of Griffith's coat. "The Chief is taking care of himself."

"An' doin' bloody well by it too." One of the British officers chimed in. "That Monique's no piece of fluff ya' know."

"Sure … " Griffith didn't appreciate the man's positive comment.

Clifford shot Paul an eye roll. The two British officers stood by, listening, but pretending not to. Stumpf tried to change the subject. "Chief, we have good communication with Yoko, from the ship."

Griffith ignored him. "If that woman's what you're trading …for a quality American woman, Vincent … " That crack took Paul close to disclosing what he knew about Griffith's Barbara.

"Sir …" He started, but Clifford must have felt a Vincent explosion coming.

He stepped between Griffith and Vincent. "Never mind now. I want my dinner. C'mon now, Griff …" He pulled at the exec's arm. Griffith turned with Clifford but kept talking as he moved off.

"Your message is clear, Vincent. No wonder the crew … American men are in such sad shape. If *you* are a model … " The words were lost to the clicking of the beads. Stumpf shrugged his shoulders and turned to follow Griffith and the others. Ensign Merryweather leaned in to Paul.

"C'mon, Chief. He's a guy horribly mislead by the promises in the Rockwell paintings." There was a strong odor of booze on the man's breath but Paul still liked being understood.

"Thank you, Mr. M."

"Compared to the exec. Scrooge was just a very misunderstood man. Let him go."

"He's gone." Paul managed. " …but probably to buy a velvet Rockwell someplace."

Paul watched the beads end up in hopelessly tangled knots. One of the Chinese girls from the corner table stepped over and skillfully untangled them, a businesslike look on her very pretty face.

Distracted by sudden fatigue, perhaps by the interaction with Griffith, perhaps by a developing moral sense he'd hoped for, his libido suddenly took the night off. He no longer actually cared to meet the well advertised Rasha-Shampoo. "Maybe better." He thought. "Maybe I'll just spend the night with her. Play cards, talk … God, I hope she talks."

As he showered in the plush bathroom he thought more of missing Cynthia. As he tried rubbing himself rosy with a rich towel, which didn't work, he knew, despite any love for Cynthia, being with Rasha would likely be comforting even if only by being a distraction from the loneliness. He caught up in his argument of what was 'right' and what was 'wrong'.

If he walked away from this moment because of some 'supposed to' obligation to his love for Cynthia, he would walk away lonely and unhappy and likely, at some level, resent Cynthia for it. If he stayed with Shampoo, he would carry guilt and confusion over the violation of the 'supposed to'. It was a no-win that society had brought to the human race when it decided sexual monogamy was to be the revered symbol of man and woman's commitment to one another.

"Putting you in a room with a pretty hooker is like asking the mouse to guard the cheese." He said to his reflection. " Inspecting his body in the full length mirror he felt uncharacteristically pleased. " Or the snake to hide the bird's eggs." The top half of him was brown from shirtless hours on the Truaxe main decks in the afternoon Vietnamese sun. The lower half was contrasting white. He laughed at the image. "Two guys glued together. The top half, where the brain is, true as a second blue moon. The dick half, ready to lead the pack of lost souls straight to meet Rasha, the shampoo experience." He flexed his muscles. Rachael had always said he was 'skinny'. He insisted he was only 'slim'. In the mirror, he curved his arms again and flexed his belly firm. His muscles were wiry and taut, his cock looked large and youthful with its half erection. He decided he was full bodied enough. Most past lovers seemed to adore his physique. One three-dollar Steubenville hooker had once said to him at age seventeen: "You ain't a heavy weight, Paul boy, but you got a hell of a hammer and a pile drivin' ass." He wasn't sure why that pleased him but he never forgot it had been said.

He heard the door open as he hung the towel.

Monique had not lied or exaggerated. Rasha was oriental but not just Chinese. Her face was a mixture of something and something else that might have been disproportionate or ugly on some women but it all worked for her. She was heartbreakingly attractive and his breath caught, and caught again. He stood naked, eyes locked on hers. She was in white, a long dress of some shiny material with a lightweight matching jacket. Her perfume had also entered the room and overtook the lingering smell of his shower.

"*Moondrops,* " he said.

"Yes." She seemed pleased. "You like it?"

"Yes." He lied. It was Rachael's perfume. He hated that.

She stepped toward him. "Hello, Paul." She said in three crisp syllables. She seemed to have no nervousness at all but acted as anyone does who is in his or her element. Balancing with one finger on the back of an overstuffed chair, she was standing like a stork on one leg and removing the high-heeled shoe from the other. She dropped the shoeless foot and bent forward for the second one. The shoes off, the skirt of her slinky two-piece outfit touched the carpet.

"Not talking?" She asked.

It took effort to find words. "Hello yourself. You are stunning—everything Monique said …is true."

"Monique talked of you also. You are a handsome man." But then she laughed.

"Pardon?"

"You always meet stranger in such formal attire?" Her 't's were slightly clipped and there was a slight roll when she used 'r' as in 'strangers', 'formal' and 'attire'.

"What?" He asked. She pointed at his nakedness with an up and down finger. Nakedness seemed to fit with this woman.

"Paul? I'll undress for you, and you watch me. See if I do it correct, Paul." She used his name again and again, her slight accent very enticing.

"Watching a meal prepared right in front of me. Please do it."

She removed the light silken jacket from one bare shoulder, then the other. With her back to him, she peered over one shoulder and with seasoned moves dropped the jacket to a chair. Her hair, freed from the confines of the jacket, was everywhere. To emphasize it she kept her back to him and shrugged her shoulders, waved her head from side to side. Her hair tossed in heavy flint black swirl as he believed only Asian hair can. It settled below her waist. Thin blue streaks flashed around her as light tried to find its way into the mass. He stepped close to her and flicked at it with his hands and lifted heaps of it again and again. She let him touch her, turning around and around as though modeling, the hair flowing over her shoulders, pulling across her throat.

"Monique said you've been to sea for years and years and years. And I can tell so." Her hand brushed his erection. He again felt very wrong. Inside of him, a conscious that had been testing values most of his life took its first real and rather final form right there on the spot. It surprised him as much as it did her.

"Rasha." Her name sounded contrived. It was not 'Cynthia'. "I want to have dinner in the room with you, talk, just be together. Is that ok?"

"Oh! Monique thought … "

"Monique was wrong. Is that ok?"

"Yes …is ok. I understand. VD afraid?"

"No." He felt cowardly.

"There is the Dutch Lady?"

"Christ, does everyone know of the Dutch lady?"

"Dutch lady—You feel bad with me …over her?"

"Suddenly yes. Maybe my conscience?"

She stepped back two steps and said: "Conscience is not bad thing." She then went to a known dresser drawer and brought out a deck of cards. "Instead, I tell your fortune. Is okay?"

"Is okay."

She dropped down on the bed and spread cards in front of her. He slipped his trousers on and tucked the half erection out of sight. "What have I been before, Rasha? Where have I been?

She curled her legs in front of her and covered her front with her hair. "The cards say …ahh, the cards say …" She looked at his face with a feigned sigh in her voice. " …you have been a man without love before. Am I correct?"

"Oh shit!"

Late that night, vision-flashing dreams hampered his attempts at untroubled sleep. The aggression in the rice field and the anger with Clifford and Griffith kept brain cells firing in anxious cycles. He tossed and re-fought the bridge battle with Clifford. His body was tense, alive with aggression. In the troubled bed the perfume of Rachael was there but the tormented dream turned to a dream of Cynthia. Her touch, her hands, her mouth so warm. It was suddenly good to be a man, alive, in bed. Just as anxiety can be the enemy of the erection appearing, an erection and its purpose can also distract from disquieted moments, especially in a strange bed. But, her body was too light on his legs, her shoulders too narrow, the hair he held in his fingers was not wavy. Too heavy and too long. The warmth though. The delicious warm mouth continued to move. It had to be Cynthia. He wanted it to be Cynthia.

Why does this pleasure need permission from without?

He reached for her and pulled her up to him. She rose and turned willingly, laying on her back, opening slender thighs.

"Please." She gasped. She had been with a hundred men, but she was gasping for breath. Is it this good because he said 'no'? Others had said no, and she let them go easily? How is he different?

Without words, he moved over her body. Her legs closed over his back, high, near his shoulders. She lifted masses of her hair over his back to caress his shoulders, his face, his eyes.

It's not her.

Her arms closed high around his neck. Cynthia? No. Wrapping her hair around his neck, she pulled him to meet her kisses. Her lips were not full enough. He pushed into her and she parted wet but different.

"Ohhh." It was almost a patronizing acknowledgement, but her hands settled against the front of his thighs not around his shoulders. It was not the closeness promised. But he couldn't stop.

Move this way, and that. Search, it'll be there. The feeling will be her. She was too slender …but Cynthia became slender. 'The woman without reasons brings the medicine I need.'

She sighed deeply, once, once again and adjusted to move with him. Within seconds, she removed her hands from his thighs and returned to caressing him with her hair. She was too breathy. . but Cynthia became breathy.

He wanted Cynthia's breasts against his chest …but there were only small breasts. It was too wrong. He ignored it by lifting away.

"NO!" She cried out and moved against him. "It's —good, ver' good." He moved into her over and over as though he were detached and watching from afar.

Her head spun in the passion as she came.

How is he different? How is he so very exciting and different.

He was the Dutch ladies man. That is why.

"It wasn't right." He sat on the edge of the bed in the darkness and smoked.

"Was not wrong. Do not blame me."

"I don't blame you."

"To me? It was…. but no matter." She got out of the bed and stood in front of the window, open to the cold night air. She drew a sheet around her body, tucked it tight and folded her hair again and again to the top of her head.

"Will you come back to bed?" He asked.

"Do you want me to?"

"Of course."

He awoke to bird noises above traffic noises and dim voices. Remembering her, he let his arms slip across the sheets of the bed in both directions before he opened his eyes. She had left in the night. He opened his eyes to the bright room. It was also cold. The window had remained open all night and explained the bird noises. He heard water splashing and remembered there was a fountain in the garden below the room. He slipped out of the plush bed and into the chilled air. Pleasant after shocks of Rasha passed through his body and he took a moment to sit and recall her and to wonder about himself. A new set of values, given away within minutes of arriving.

A little note on the table beside the bed said 'with love, R'. The coquette's signature white panties were next to the note. He gathered them in his hand and squeezed them. "Why could you not have been here instead of her?" He asked himself once again the question that formed so many times in his thoughts: Why does this pleasure need permission from without? He'd once asked Selesky: "If A loves B, why can't A rejoice in B's fulfillment from C?" As Selesky would say to him: "You ask old questions in new ways. Get out of your head, Paul. Don't question your dammed feelings, accept the sons-a-bitches for what they are."

Only two days until Cynthia arrives. "Why could I not have waited?"

Several people were already in the patio area after Paul showered, dressed and wandered downstairs to a needed breakfast. The trees over the tables had been skillfully laced enough to permit the morning sun to warm the lattice walled garden. It was very inviting. People sat grouped at small white tables on rolled wire chairs with spotless quilted pads, quietly talking, reading and watching one another come and go. White jacketed waiters, mostly Chinese served British breakfasts of knockers, beans, eggs, heavy biscuits, tea, thick European coffee and other things that usually talk-back an hour after eaten. Small brown and yellow finches hopped among the legs of the diners, quarreling and snatching crumbs. A large yellow cat lay on a warm stone bench, every muscle except those in his eyes ignoring the birds, for now.

Clifford and Griffith were at a center table. They each had a newspaper spread in front of them. Where the Captain's uniform looked a little mussed, his shirt obviously on its second day, Griffith was creased, crisp and smooth. Paul wondered if the two had stayed at Monique's and if so had they slept alone, or, like he, intended to sleep alone but weakened. No, he thought, they couldn't possibly have shared one of the willing beautiful women between them. No, the only three-way he could see either man involved in would be a light bulb.

Paul headed for a corner table but Clifford saw him. As on the bridge wing the day of the slap, he wiggle fingered Paul to their table. That seemed to jerk Griffith from his newspaper.

"Mornin', Chief. Sleep well?" The Captain seemed truly pleasant. Or, was it PR for Griffith's sake?

"Yes. And you?" There were times he liked the man.

"Did fine. Called the ship already, everything's fine there. All communications circuits stayed in all night."

Paul nodded to Griffith. Griffith grunted, sipped his tea and scowled openly.

"That woman from the bar was asking for you." Clifford said.

"Which?"

"*That* woman." Griffith spat out 'that woman' like someone might refer to 'that snake' or '*that* child molester'. "That proprietor woman."

"Monique?"

"Thin disguise, Chief." Griffith leaned into coffee.

"Pardon?"

"She asks us where you are so we'd think you hadn't slept with her?"

"God as my judge, Commander, I did not sleep with Monique." He relished that it was the truth.

"Will you two quit the moral sword-fighting? This is Hong God-dammed Kong. Every man to himself here."

"Humph."

A waiter took Griffith's attention, something about a telephone call he was trying to make to the states. Vincent looked at Clifford with a 'what the hell you doing with this man around your neck' look.

Clifford shrugged his shoulders animatedly and answered openly although Griffith couldn't overhear. "He's like a cat, Chief. Always on the wrong side of a door? Whines. Bitches. I can't shake him."

A bright yellow scoop necked dress brought Monique onto the patio. A bulky white shawl pulled around her shoulders framed her hostess smile in full operation. She spoke briefly at a few tables; laughingly flicked away several hands that patted toward her bottom, then rescued Paul for breakfast.

"*Zaofan* Pool Kuy? My girls and me?"

"*Oui, Merci.* " Vincent tried to be as international as he could in front of Griffith. He wondered if Rasha would appear for breakfast. He stood.

She turned to Clifford with a smile. "Hello Captain. I hoping you sleep very well." To Griffith. "Good morning Mr. Satchel." She smiled at him. Griffith curl-lipped her cheery greeting provoking an anti-male look from Monique that would have put a stereotyped suffragette posture to shame. Turning to leave with Paul, her shawl swished Griffith's newspaper, sunglasses and change to the ground.

Clifford took an openly crude shot, but laughed as he did so. "Feel your balls fall off, Arnie?"

During breakfast Monique read from a lined telephone note pad. "Paul, listen: Tell Master Chief Vincent he was cleared with OOD his ship's S.P. officer for that evening." Monk really wanted his company, Paul thought.

"What you do S.P.? Where you go?" Paul brushed her off politely, "Chasin' sailor drunks, mostly."

"You go Hong Kong police, or Mr. Monk and them?"

"I don't know, Monique."

"You do drug raid? Like old days?"

"Monique? Drop it."

"True you not go back Vietnam anymore? War over soon?"

He ignored the question.

Monique told him in confidence, her face serious and concerned, that the evening before, after Griffith had gone to his room the Captain had cornered her. "He is troubled man. He drunk too much las' night."

"Did he talk about the ship? The navy?"

"Non. Mal du pays … ."

"What?"

"Homesickly, I theenk you say. He talk of wife, of children and of father. All Americans hate father?"

"Did he sleep with a woman?"

"No. Say *n'importe* . He too drunk anyway."

"Did the other officer have a woman?"

"No, he sleep with satchel." She laughed.

"Will Rasha be here with the others?"

"No, she stay away. You know why?"

"What do I know?"

"You know. She fall for you, fella'."

"Gimmie' a break, Monique."

"No. You see."

Several of Monique's women joined them before she could order breakfast. "Thees' *coterie,* my girls? Sans Rasha? Is LuAnn, Is Beebe, Is Ping." Paul missed a couple of the names. There was something vaguely familiar about LuAnn but she seemed shy and would not make eye contact.

"Creme de la creme. You agree, Paul? You seen 'round the world"

Tipping a breakfast champagne glass toward her and the women, he patronized his friend, "I agree, cream of the cream, Mony." But he did not truly agree. Set it up any way you like, to him, Monique's hookers, regardless of how stylish they tried to be, came across as hookers. Slightly too much make-up, their dress a touch too revealing, a skirt an inch too short, hair one hue beyond acceptable. Colors not quite complimentary. Most of her women had come from the deep mountain villages and lacked formal education. No matter how she tried to groom them, except for rare exceptions such as Rasha and Monique herself, their basic undersocialization peeked through the finished product. He felt anyone walking onto the patio could identify the table full of women as professionals. But, overall Paul enjoyed being with them.

"What other ships coming Hong Kong, Pool Kuy?"

"Ohh, two other carriers down there. Sooner or later."

"I have trouble telling when ships coming in." Monique complained.

"C'mon. You know more about ship movements than the pentagon."

"Non—ademi. We need to plan business."

"Yes." One girl touched his arm. "Please tell."

"My sisters are in Macao with children." Another said. "They can't pay money come Hong Kong if no work Hong Kong. When ships come? How many? How long stay?"

"Can't you ask the newspapers, the tourist bureau? Surely they know what ships come when."

"Not 'til too late."

"I hear minesweeper 339 is not for war." The Macao girl said touching his arm. "I met many men from that ship."

There had been a scandal that a minesweeper captain ordered to search civilian sampans for V.C. supplies was letting them pass from the north to the south.

"I don't know." Paul said sipping his champagne.

"I hear what you call *Market Time* mission is now Vietnamese navy job. Is true?"

"Why you care about that shit, Monique?"

"Lotsa' customers minesweepers. I like wooden-ship men. It true they go back states?"

"The crews did, yeah. Some. Some stayed to train the Vietnamese. The smaller sweeps."

"Ohh, not good." The Macao sister moaned. "Vietnamese not come Hong Kong R and R."

"My ship'll be back in June, I understand, but you know how that is."

"War still go forever?"

"Forever, I guess. It's hard to find a formula for peace."

One Eurasian thirty-year-old who had very good complexion and terrific facial features but who had ruined it all with orange hair spoke up as she stirred heavy cream into her coffee. "Formula? Take war? Take away all parts that kill people? What left is peace."

"I salute you." The glasses tipped again. He felt a bit of an early morning champagne buzz, but let it grow.

One Chinese girl, all of sixteen, rubbed Vincent's thigh and teased him, talking in Chinese, softly, as she might a night time date. Paul hardly noticed the attention but Monique snapped at the girl. *"Bu, Bu-hao."* Then turned to Paul. *"Duibuqi."*

"What? Speak English."

"Excuse her. I think she been talking to Rasha." Monique turned to the pouting girl. *"Mei Guanxi. Ni hui shou Yingyu ma ?"*

"What?" Paul asked.

"I told her you forgive her. And she to talk in English to you."

Most of the women seemed aware something had gone on between Paul and Rasha the night before. When the Macao girl started some good-natured kidding about Rasha and Paul, Monique shushed her. The girl back-talked Monique and some Chinese and French he understood fell out of the rapid exchange of gossipy chatter. He heard 'Cynthia' and '*affaire de coeur*', and other unlikely references for a Macao hooker to make. Monique's burst of French was too rapid for him to follow but the girl's responses were halting, easier. "Rasha—*les cheveaux mpl*', a reference to her hair—'*le sexe*' which was international and '*faire l'amour Rasha* ' he knew to have something to do with him getting it on with Rasha. Cynthia's name came up twice again and the sixteen year old kept cupping her hands in front of her own small front, asking; *"Duo da?' zher?* and making 'woo-woo' sounds. The scene pulled a feigned laugh from

Vincent that stopped it all. The women all giggled then and even brought Monique back to a calmer state. Paul felt uncomfortable with the candid references to Cynthia but didn't say so. He took a big drink from the last of his champagne.

"Not talk about Dutch lady to Paul now." Monique warned.

"I should bring her by here. To meet everyone." He teased them.

"Not a good idea now. Not a good idea." Monique was straight faced.

"Why not? You gossip over her. Let her meet you, have a chance."

"This not a good place for Dutch lady." She was stern voiced. "Small city here." She rattled off some rapid Chinese and all of the women began taking last bites of breakfast, draining glasses and gathering their things.

CHAPTER TWENTY
Swish Slosh Swish Slosh

Paul Vincent had been on several raids during his shore patrol tour. So, as he took a sidearm, a flashlight, a whistle, a Billy club and a white-on-black 'S.P.' arm-band from the trunk of the unmarked car, Monk briefly skimmed over the strategy."You're going to like my two helpers. They replaced Pliesse and Pevac? One *is* a bad motherfucker and the other one is worse." Monk introduced all around.

"Master Chief Vincent, meet my right and left balls ... Tom Tie, and Tex-Mex."

Tie shook Vincent's hand. "If we are the balls, that makes Monk the prick." He said with a smile.

"Makes me the asshole?" Vincent said, compelled to be on the humorous good side of this twosome.

Tom Tie was a six-foot four-inch two hundred and fifty pound hammer of a man. While friendly and soft spoken, he gave the impression those were just impressions. He'd been a small town cop before the navy but felt bored and too restricted. With two-year limits to Shore Patrol duty stations, his life had the number of changes he needed to keep it interesting. After ten minutes of chatting, Vincent decided if there was a club for capable but threatening people, Tie could well be its doorman.

Emilio Esplanade, the second man, was a Texas born Mexican who had ten years naval service as an engine man before he found his way into navy law enforcement and stuck there. He wasn't as tall as Tie but his biceps and chest muscles stretched the wool uniform material.

"He said he hates his name—'Emilio'. And we voted against—'Esplanade'." Monk said.

In a sing-song—"So, you call me Tex or you can call me Mex."—the big man displayed an easily likable grin and shook Vincent's hand with what felt like a flesh covered callused piece of movable iron.

Monk outlined the strategy.

"As in the old days, Paul, we'll be going off-shore from Aberdeen. Police after some drug traffickers, likely some Mafioso Triad rejects, small time. U.S. sailors will be around ...likely."

"They take the local thuggees, we take the sailors?"

"Yep.' Monk confirmed. "The raid is on a hotel in the Bay, off Apleichau Island. Don't know if we've hit this particular barge before, but twice now we've hit some shit out there."

"How so?"

"The Triad in-fighting seems worse. Even less internal control than a year ago. Tie here shot one of the nameless geeks a couple months ago. If he hadn't, I'd'a taken a bullet."

Vincent looked at Tie who was busy trying to read his wristwatch in the dim light.

Vincent hadn't counted on a life or death way of passing an evening. He was afraid, however, if he backed away this late, he was over reacting to the residue of the spotter boat incident.

"Oh boy, I come along for a night cruise, and find I should'a stayed in my bunk?"

"Lighten up, Paul. We're with Lieutenant Han of the Royal Hong Kong Police." Monk assured him. "He's thorough."

What time we meet Lt. Han?" Tie asked."

"Ten p.m."

"It's ten now."

The four men moved off in the chilly night to meet the local police on cobblestone Quomoy Lane just below Brick Hill. From where they walked, they could see down Quomoy Lane into the Aberdeen Harbor area and out toward the industrial buildings of Apleichau island just a quarter mile away. They were in the touristy Aberdeen district, a twenty-minute drive from the city's Central area. Paul felt good to be there, only three blocks from the Fandian Ho. With thoughts of the Fandian Ho, thoughts of Cynthia soon followed. On the hill above Aberdeen, he swallowed a thrilled feeling but managed to push her out of his mind.

It had rained earlier and runoff streamed through the gutters from the hills above. Wet streets reflected lights from the harbor.

Despite the earlier drenching and the water dripping from buildings, the waterfront of Aberdeen was its usual crowded self, nearly as crowded as mid-day. The shopping tourists had long disappeared but the night-life crowd was in full force surging from bar to bar or waiting to catch water taxi's to the three floating restaurants dominating the inner bay.

Lieutenant Han and three others from the Royal Hong Kong police sloshed an unmarked car to the curb twenty yards beyond Monk's team. The four small plainclothes men approached Vincent, Monk, Tie and Tex-Mex under a light on the damp street corner. Although Vincent had known of a sergeant named Han during his Shore Patrol days, he had never been on a raid with the man.

In damaged English Lieutenant Han did the introductions, then, realizing Vincent was new, felt a briefing was in order. Everyone leaned in politely as Han spoke, his little frame jerking nervously from side to side, his breath puffing mist into the chilly night. He was easy to like but his whispered English was difficult to follow.

" 'Kay, Monk, Chiep? . . the pran is to take seberal small boats, five, six men each. Just show …er, ah …surprise. My men? They do rots—sorry—lots times. 'Kay?"

"What do I do exactly?" Vincent asked.

"Jus' ride arong, keep out of way. When we get sailla', we set sailla' aside an' …you …watch 'em. They give t'ouble, is …is, ahh, onny time I want you hep. 'Kay …kay?"

" 'Kay." Vincent said. Monk smothered a laugh.

"Now, Mista' Monk, Chiep? We afta' two men in special. We know on boat tonight. We find them. Oders …oders we may not take in, maybe take in. Depend, kay?"

"*Kuai chun juanr.*"" Monk said mocking a 'can-do' spirit.

Vincent didn't follow. "What? Kuai chun what?" He insisted, nervously.

"Piece of cake." Monk reminded him.

"Not accurate." Han said. "Kuai chun juanr is more like Chinese jelly roll. When you 'Mericans tell Chinese like I speak Engrish, we do good talk alra time, yes?"

"Ohh!"

Han stepped away with his men, his head shaking to express—'how do I get these people in my work?'.

"I think he's playing it up some for your benefit …kay, Chiep?" Tie remarked.

"You say 'piece of jelly-roll' an' accuse *him* of drama?" Tex-Mex jabbed.

"We do get pretty bored with this, Paul." Monk added. "There's a lot of politics in these raids that we Yanks are excluded from. Royal Police make a major bust on a Triad family or Dragonhead once or twice a quarter. That makes a headline splash, but mostly, on a daily basis? Drugs are ignored."

Tex-Mex spoke up as he polished his flashlight lens on his coat sleeve.

"Where life follows art? Politics follow drug money."

"Sex, drugs, rock and roll." Tie added.

"No rock and roll." Monk corrected. "Sex, drugs and ching-chang music."

"So for some reason important to somebody, we raid a floating barge of a hotel tonight." Vincent summarized. "Two guys to be singled out, the rest played by ear. "

"Still want to come?"

"Yeah. Cynthia's not in town. Beats a slow night on TV." He meant he'd rather be on the raid than take another chance falling between the legs of Rasha or someone like her and falling even further into guilt.

After several minutes, Vincent was assigned to a small sampan with Tie and six local police. He looked them over in case he had to spot the good guys later on. When he sat back to relax something suddenly jerked him upright. The last time he went out in a small boat, the world had been blown to hell all around him. His heart slipped into a higher gear and even slow deep breaths didn't seem to calm it.

"You okay, Vincent?" Tie asked.

"Me? Yeah. Why?"

"You're puffing some."

"A little out of shape." Vincent defended. "Still smoke some."

"That smokin?" Tie said. "That's sure natural selection in action. Dummies are eliminated by dumb behavior. No helmet on a motorcycle? No seat belts? The smart survive …dumb die out." Then he added. "No offense."

"Offense taken."

An old man, wrinkled and considerably bent over was the pilot, navigator, helmsman and source of propulsion of their fifteen foot long unpainted boat. Moving slowly but with purpose, the old man pushed the boat from the dock with the tip of a long oar, stepped to the small platform at the rear of the flatboat, fitted the oar between two worn vertical risers, and started moving its flared end left-to-right in the water. With a complicated series of strokes passed along over centuries, he moved them through the stagnant smelling channel at three or four knots. They fell in behind three other raid boats. Moving smoothly, they made their way into the first channel that was nothing more than an open space between row upon row of anchored sampans and junks tied side to side to side to side.

It was colder over the water. Everyone became silent.

Vincent checked each sampan as they passed. Almost without exception he could see someone, an expressionless someone, starring back. Man, woman, child? He couldn't always tell.

"This light and this peacefulness reminds me of the beginning of the gondola ride … *Pirates of the Caribbean* …"

"Yeah …" Tie interrupted. " …just before the boat drops into the *pirate's den?"*

"Thanks a lot."

The quiet remained but some night water noises and thin music from one of the floating restaurants made its way to them. Insects buzzed in and out of hearing range. An unseen fish slapped in the water. The smell of fish—flavored smoke and of hot fishy oil permeated the air. The rhythm of the old man's paddle swished and sloshed behind the boat.

For ten minutes they alternated from channel to channel, swish, slosh, swish, slosh. The rows of colorless sampans began to appear even more alike as they slipped past them. Vincent still looked for faces. He still saw them. One old man stood in the yellow light of a lantern, chop-sticking food into his face from a small can. He stared at Vincent with no discernible expression. Mist rose from the can and from his breath. Two round faced children peeked from under a canvas cover at one point, their blank stares reflecting the powerlessness of their station, not the happiness of childhood.

They made a graceful turn and passed Magazine Island to their left. The open water of Laimma Channel lay before them, sprinkled with dim lights of floating hotels, homes and barges. Immediately ahead lay the well-lighted restaurants.

"I've been here six months." Tie whispered to Vincent. "Never been on one of the restaurants."

"A touristy ritual." Paul said. "Chose your fish or lobster from the holding tanks alongside. Have a couple drinks while the food is cooked."

"All tourists?"

"Not really. Locals come in after 5 a.m., breakfast eaters …so on. Never stops."

Close aboard, they passed the *Tai Pac* restaurant. Mostly well dressed diners were at tables behind large glass windows, chatting, drinking, eating. The ching-chang music tinkered its way over the water, lingered as they passed, then mixed with music of the next restaurant in line.

Swish slosh, swish slosh. They moved past the last restaurant, now more than a mile from shore. Ahead they could make out only four dimly lighted barge-like craft, at anchor.

"The Switchblade Hilton." Tie mused.

"Where are we now?" Vincent asked, squinting into the night.

"Mile off Waterfall Bay, give or take." Tie guessed. "That's Green Island lighthouse flashing ahead to the right."

That gave Vincent his bearings. He'd been in the area before, sailing with Kurt and Cynthia.

He pushed thoughts of her away for the tenth time in ten minutes.

He recognized lights on Lantau Island flickering dimly seven miles ahead of them. Now and then off to the side he could spot one of the other sampans passing in front of lights ashore. They approached to within twenty-five yards of the last barge on the right of four look-alike barges. The other boats swished in from all sides. From the quiet appearance of the hotel barge, it looked as though their surprise had worked. All men pulled flashlights and at some given signal covered the barge with varying intensities of beams. The lights started some commotion. Two men broke and ran from the topside deck, down a ladder to disappear through a small doorway near the bow. Vincent, imagining hordes of gunmen starting to shoot at them as though in a television drama, felt like a sitting duck the last few seconds before his boat touched the barge. He was glad to get from the boat to the barge deck.

Tie moved in beside him. "Pull that side-arm and cock it, Chief. Han comes on like Charlie Chan but this looks like serious business."

"Shit." Guilt or not, he could have been sitting in the bar at Monique's.

Vincent pulled the navy issue Colt-45 from the holster, jacked a round into the chamber and released the safety. He pointed the piece into the air, feeling awkward. His heart began the same beating rhythm he'd felt in the spotter boat. "Shit," he said aloud. Real fear registered within him.

By prearranged plan the Chinese officers positioned themselves at the doorways that led below decks. Vincent could smell richly cooked food.

Lieutenant Han appeared beside him, his revolver drawn.

"Chiep. Take one man, go with these Chi and Aloo. They gonna' kick doors. You help, kay? If 'Mericans, you take in charge ...kay?"

"Kay. Kay." His heart was almost audible.

"Two 'odda men, come me. ' end barge ... Kay?"

Monk and Tex-Mex followed Han. Vincent fell in behind Tom Tie who fell in behind the two Chinese officers. The officers pulled their revolvers and stepped inside a doorway near the stern of the barge. Immediately there was the strong smell of opium mixed with sweet marijuana, spar varnish, cooked food, some perfume, and a touch of dampness.

It was very quiet. Vincent could smell Chi's garlic breath mix with Tie's after-shave.

"Least it's clean in here." Tie murmured. "Some of these barges? You need a tetanus shot just to walk aboard."

They were in a narrow soft-carpeted corridor about 160 feet long, almost the entire length of the old but well-fitted barge. Evenly spaced small doorways led off both sides of the passageway. Above each door was a small fixture with a dim bulb glowing more orange than white. It was difficult to tell if anyone was further down the passage.

The two officers stopped at the first richly enameled doorway. Well-polished brass figures indicated it was cabin B-9. One officer knocked hard and called out in Chinese. "*Fandian fuwuyuan.*" Paul searched for the key to the memory files containing the Chinese language skills he'd developed during the six months with Monk's S.P.'s, but there was no ready access.

"*Room service.*" Tie provided. "More or less."

No one answered the door.

They waited a few seconds. The taller officer turned to Tie.

"*Lai erzi, shuang.*" Tie pulled back and kicked the door before Paul interpreted the remark. It snapped a latch and flew inward. The two officers dived into the room. Vincent pointed his pistol.

Four men, dressed in muted colored cottons, sat on the floor inside the dimly lighted but richly carpeted room. They gazed dumbly at their intruders. No one moved. Two active pipes were burning.

"*Ypeum.*" Aloo said. Lingering smoke stung Vincent's eyes.

One officer took four handcuffs from his belt and snapped the four men together and to a thin vent post. None of the smokers spoke.

"They seem hardly aware they're bein' cuffed." Vincent commented.

"Stoned …as Mount Rushmore." Tie offered.

Vincent nodded agreement.

"Zombies." Chi said. Vincent wondered if he was speaking English.

Back in the passageway there were voices further down. Another pair of officers was working their way toward Vincent's group, banging doors and kicking their way inside. He heard Monk's strong voice.

They repeated the scene in the next shadowy room where they found two young men, age's twenty-five or so, also dressed in workingman's cottons. There was also a very thin, stark naked, perhaps forty-five year old woman with them. They'd been smoking together on pillows. The two officers had to help the stoned women into her smock. They cuffed them in same fashion as the first four, no resistance, passive acceptance.

The third room appeared empty when they first kicked their way in but the familiar smell was strong.

"*Ypeum.*" Aloo repeated.

On a small table were several freshly served dishes of food. Aloo took a piece from a plate, turned to Vincent and spoke rapidly. "*Ni xihuan chi zhongguo cai ma ?*"

Tie interpreted. "You like Chinese food? The man's offering you a …some part of a chicken …" Tie picked up a bit of the food and smelled it. "Alleged chicken." He laughed.

Officer Chi stepped to a cabinet built against the far wall, and kicked its door. It snapped open. A leg and arm came out, then a body. A slightly built man slithered out, followed by another. More handcuffs, some hollering in Chinese and they were out the door to the next room.

Lieutenant Han was with them again.

"Chiep. Got two salla' boys on top. I take ID caad and Liberty caads. They from Truaxe ship. Heah'." He stuck two USN ID cards into Vincent's hand and was gone.

"They won't go far without those." Tie offered.

After two more smoke filled rooms, Chi lead them out a side door for a gulp of fresh air. Suddenly there was some scuffling on the upper deck. Vincent heard yelling, then a gunshot from a revolver. After more yelling from several voices, there were several gunshots from different calibers. The two officers pushed Vincent back into the passageway. Feeling like a target to anyone who might shoot from the ends of the passage, he dropped to the deck. Tie dropped beside him facing the opposite direction.

Vincent's heart was hammering. From outside, one of the Chinese yelled several phrases. Tie interpreted for Vincent.

"If anyone opens a door down there? Shoot right away." He pointed both ways in the passageway. "It won't be a good guy."

Paul's temples pulsed. He was ready to fight. He jumped to his feet and with the barrel end of the forty-five, rapidly smashed three of the closest dim light bulbs.

"Good move …get down." Tie was also very tense.

There was more yelling in Chinese, outside. He could sift out Han's excited voice.

The light changed at the far end of Vincent's passageway. The door was opening. Two forms jumped in through the door and dropped to the deck at Vincent's end of the passageway.

"Shoot." Tie ordered.

Vincent pulled off two rounds and heard one slam against metal. His gun jammed. His ears, punished by the shots, refused to hear anything. Vincent fought to free the fat unfired forty-five round that jutted upward from the pistol's ejection slide. "Fuck."

Tie spun his direction, fell against him and pulled off three rounds.

"Head down." Someone yelled in English. Tie then squeezed off several more shots. Like in the spot boat, the gunshots were both bone-chilling fearful and adrenaline rushing.

"*Xue, Xie …wei … Lai wang.*" A screaming voice came from the end of the passageway.

"Don't shoot!" Tie yelled. "Someone's been hit …stomach. Its not a cop."

Two Chinese officers tripped over Vincent and Tie and ran toward the voices.

"They nuts, Tie?"

"No Fight's over. Someone hit down there."

At that instant there was another scuffle above them and once, then again, something heavy hit the deck. A body? Two bodies? The door opened at the far end of the passageway and several flashlights brightened the area. Vincent recognized Chi, Aloo and two other police who had been in his boat. Two men lay on the carpet, two officers bent over the bodies.

"Chief?" Han appeared at the doorway. Vincent felt baby-set.

"Yes, Lieutenant. Right here."

"You 'kay, Chief?" His 'Chiep' had cleared up.

"Fine. What happened?"

Han spoke several phrases in Chinese then switched to English.

"We got men we wanted, Chiep. No one hurt upstairs." He forced a laugh. "Dummy upstairs shoot wrong way." He seemed to be fighting for calm.

Han pointed to Tie's forty-five. "You belly shoot them people?"

"Yep."

"Tlade …sorry …trade me gun or you make report on bullets." He pulled the forty-five from Tie's hand and exchanged his thirty-eight revolver for it. "Take it. I make report. I shoot in dark." Han left.

Paul was surprised by Han's move. "A new sort of diplomatic program?"

"Less politics this way."

Han's voice crackled back into the passageway. "No one else left on boat but dummy smokers. Help round them up, prease." He seemed calmer.

"Right." Tie said. "Gotta' finish what we came for. It'll be easy. Those shots probably sobered everyone."

Vincent put his forty-five in the holster but left it unsnapped.

As directed, he, Tie and the two officers went down a second flight of narrow steps to an equally well carpeted and somewhat lighter deck. "Fancier floor, high priced rooms." Tie said.

"This really safe, Tie? My blood's still pumpin'."

"Me too. I shot those two … I can't stop thinkin' 'bout it."

"Was tonight the same as the last time? Out of the blue like that?" Paul asked.

"Always in the dark it seems." Tie said as though thinking aloud. "Han just accepts it. Life value seems different to him, to them, maybe."

"Will there be trouble over the shooting?"

"No, Chief." Tie said real direct. "There's no ACLU here."

Vincent couldn't tell if his remark was a tension relieving crack or a serious comment on the state of Hong Kong human rights.

Following the lead of officers Chi and Aloo, the two distracted U.S. servicemen resumed the knock and kick ritual. They found three men huddled in the first room. Two in the second. They ran out of handcuffs.

Chi knocked on the next door midway in the passageway.

'Say, hey. What is it?" A strong American voice answered.

Chi looked at Tie and stepped aside.

"Police and Shore Patrol. Open the door."

"Yeah? And you'll also sell me some excellent insurance?"

They waited five, six, seven seconds. Tie took a deep breath, drew his leg up against his chest and let it fly near the latch. It cracked but held.

"Wait a goddamned minute." The voice hollered.

The Chinese officers seemed threatened by the voice of an American who didn't sound drugged. When they both pulled their weapon, Vincent and Tie followed their lead.

The door opened. A narrow-waisted blond man, slightly taller than Vincent, stood holding a towel partially wrapped around his waist.

"Whaaa?" His expression announced pure off-guard surprise and fear.

"This is not room service." Tie said moving toward the man. The blond stepped backward into the room. His eyes on Tie's gun, he became torn between raising his hands or holding the towel. He saw Vincent's drawn forty-five and Chi and Aloo's revolvers. The towel dropped. His hands went into the air.

"I …did hear shots. I *was* awakened by shots. Was I? Shots?"

The room was small, like the others but was better lighted and furnished more like a European hotel room. There was a second man lying on the bed, partially covered by a white sheet, his back to the room.

"Watch these two." Tie said and pointed toward a narrow white painted door at the far side of the room. Pistol held in one hand, he kicked that door open, looked into the room but stepped right back out. "Toilet. No one there."

Vincent looked around for the signs he was learning to recognize. "No opium. No pipes, no papers, no smoke, Tie."

"No women either. But women could'a run out, taken the drugs with'em, after the shooting. Won't get far."

"But look here." Vincent said.

Hanging from hooks on the back of the door was a jumble of shirts, ties and dark blue uniforms. Two gold stripes on the sleeve of one jacket, a lieutenant, three stripes on the other, a commander. Two officer's hats lay on a table near the door. Four black oxfords stood side to side against the foot of the only chair in the room.

"Sir." Vincent said. "I represent the navy here. Get dressed."

"Shit." The man said and with the look of an extra ticket holder on an oversold flight, dropped into the chair. He started to whine. "We've paid the bill, in advance. You've no right to … Further, I'm a naval lieutenant …" He looked at Tie. " …and let's not forget that."

Tie's confidence and composure was intact despite that he'd just shot two men not twenty minutes earlier. He seemed to know exactly how to handle himself. "I can't tell who you are—not from what you have on. Jes' git your clothes on, cowboy."

"Don't 'cowboy' me."

"Don't delay *me*. "

Vincent, as senior man carried out the ritual for arresting an officer. "Sir, I am Master Chief Vincent, U.S.S. Truaxe. I'm T.A.D. with the Hong Kong Shore Patrol …on assignment with the police. You are being taken into protective custody. If you cooperate, you will be turned over as fast as possible to the shore patrol officer. Sir, if you remain silent you are ahead of the game. This here is Petty Officer First Class, Tie, and he is permanent shore patrol in this city, and, he knows what is going on. Any questions?"

The lieutenant looked blankly at Vincent.

"Do you understand me, Sir?"

"I hear you. So what?"

"You've been formally warned not to come to these barges. These Chinese officers are conducting a drug raid here. You'll likely have some explaining to do to the shore patrol officer."

"Is this guy on drugs?" Tie asked.

"No."

"What's his name?" Vincent asked.

With nervous movements, the lieutenant lifted a pair of trousers from the door hook and slipped them on. He dropped to the chair and reached for socks. Fussing with them, he motioned with a flip of his head toward the man on the bunk. "He's not on drugs. We were pretty drunk when we fell in here for some sleep some time late yesterday. DAVID …" He yelled toward the bed. " …get up." He turned back to Tie. "If anything, he's faking it right now. We've been up partying for two days."

"Why out here?" Tie asked.

"I'm not talking anymore, cowboy." He said defiantly at Tie.

"Get him moving." Vincent urged Tie toward the man in the bed and then reassessed the scene. Two booze glasses and some sign that two people had taken a meal earlier that day. Of twenty-five or so cigarette butts in the only ash tray, none had lipstick marks on them. No perfume in the air, no hair pins on the bed but there was a mark on the shoulder of the one in bed that looked like a 'love bite'. There were two overnight shaving kits, not much bigger than camera bags and not unlike those carried by many sailors who come ashore for a day or so. A comb, some matches in one ...cigarettes, tooth brushes. No drug equipment.

No wonder there were no signs of women, these two had slipped out to the barge to be safely away from prying eyes.

Tie caught it at the same time. "Let's get these girls movin', Chief. There may be more Americans down the row." He spoke with a sigh but without a grin. Neither man flinched at the 'girls' remark.

Tie pulled the man on the bed to a sitting position.

"Here, David." The blond Lieutenant tossed trousers, shorts and socks to the bed. The other man looked foolish sitting there naked with his head in his hands. He had a stubble of beard growth and his thin hair was a mess. Clearly in view now, it was an unmistakable love bite on his upper shoulder.

Suddenly—more recognition. The fine hair, the way he tossed his head. The man looked directly at Vincent's face and the unknown jumped to startled understanding.

"David?" Vincent asked, surprised.

"Oh NO!" The lieutenant gasped.

The man on the bed sighed. "Yes." He said. He blinked his eyes and passed one hand over his face in an upward direction that smoothed his hair.

"Little fucking navy we have here?" Tie seemed amazed. "This guy from your ship, Chief?"

"No, David Selesky, M.D., a psychiatrist I know, from San Diego."

"Well, no shit."

Vincent couldn't connect the sedate and serious mindfulness of the man who had been so dedicated to Rachael and him to this lump of a man with a hickey on his neck in a drug barge in a back harbor channel of Hong Kong.

Selesky pulled on his shorts, tried a smile toward Vincent but it erupted into a strange sounding laugh.

"Nothing's funny, David." The Lieutenant said. "Get dressed, let's get distanced from this."

"Hang on, Patrick—I'm working on it." He started on the trousers.

Poker faced, Chi and Aloo rattled a line or two in Chinese and stepped out of the room.

"Hao, hao." Tie said, waved them on and turned to Vincent.

"They'll continue without us, Chief."

"Right." Vincent felt better alone with the two Americans.

"I can't find my eyes." Patrick announced.

"Look in the shaving kit." Selesky seemed alert to the Lieutenant's problems.

"They're not there. I looked."

"They ARE in there." Selesky countered, getting stronger. "You ALWAYS put them in there."

"C'mon, girls." Tie repeated.

Topside the air felt free again. The two American officers looked especially uncomfortable as they stood in the muted lights, curious flashlights playing on their faces. Han was there with four more sailors. Two seaman from Kittyhawk and two petty officers from Truaxe.

Vincent pulled Han aside. "Those sailors on drugs?"

"No, no drugs, Chiep. Ladyman I think, like the two oppicers. . I think."

"Ladyman?"

Tie was right there. "C'mon, Chief. Nudge nudge, wink wink." He said with a grin.

"Naby tough on that, I theek. They pay few dolla' and hab a no one care room."

"What do you think about it, Han?" Vincent asked.

"'Dey better 'dan opium peo'ble. Better dan' dat."

"I'd rather be into dick than into some of the drugs I see around here." Tie sounded matter of fact.

"Like pussy on a stick." One of the other sailors said. Everyone fell silent.

Vincent turned the two seaman over to Tex-Mex and asked Tie to deliver the Truaxe sailors in the morning. The men from his ship didn't seem to recognize Vincent in the dark and in that unlikely place. Neither Monk nor Han seemed to have any investment in what Vincent did with the two officers.

Ashore, he walked with Selesky and the lieutenant, Patrick Balkin.

"I don't get it. I hate it, don't like it, can't deal with it." Vincent said.

"Least you're up front." Balking forced a laugh.

"Paul, Listen. This is rough, I know … " Selesky fought for words. "I once told you my relationship was different …from most. Now you know. Just let us go on about our business."

"Wow!"

"Wow, What? Just walk away. No one is hurt here." Balkin was pleading but with a firm sense of an entitlement to be heard. "Ten to twelve percent of the navy is gay."

"No shit?" Vincent seemed amazed. He turned to Selesky. "That true?"

Balkin kept the stage. "The truth will set you free, Chief. But on the way it sometimes beats the shit out of you. Wake up and smell the jock straps … "

"Patrick." David said. "Slow up. Don't be so crappy …"

"Look, this kind of thing …could cost you your career." Vincent struggled for understanding.

"Why cost us anything?" Selesky asked. "This is who we are. Does who you are cost you a career? Cost you anything?"

Patrick chimed in. "*To bottomless perdition there to dwell?* Look, I'm not given to mendicancy—but, is that what you want?"

"Perdition? Mendicancy?" Vincent's lack of formal education showed.

"Eternal damnation." Selesky said, but Balkin took over.

"And begging. Want us to beg? Say so" He had a slight Brooklyn accent, covered over by quality education. "Your virtue is a vice here, Chief." He acted proud but fearful.

"Are you attached to Kittyhawk? Here locally someplace? You up from 'Nam?"

"If you don't know where we're from, it'll be easier for you." Selesky was right, and, he owed the man.

"How soon can you two be out of Honk Kong?"

"Ten minutes?"

"I told you in San Diego that I owe you, David."

"I'll hold you to that—but not with demands, Paul. Please hear that. You were in a bad way. I helped. We're in a bad way. You can help."

"Ablution is actually a given, Chief Vincent." Patrick said firmly. Vincent wasn't sure what 'ablution' meant. He waited. Patrick continued. "We can undermine anything you might assert." He seemed full of new energy.

"We can? How so?" It was David who asked the question.

"Combine the separate elements, David. We are attached to Naval Investigator Service office, of Yo'kus'ka. Technically, we're on R and R—but by definition, never off duty. I'm not generally manipulative of Master Chiefs, but with these circumstances I'd be compelled to preserve our chosens by insisting that the good Doctor Selesky and I followed some suspicious sailors out to the drug barge ...in the line of our never ending duty. You simply blew our cover."

"Good one, Patrick." Selesky seemed pleased. "No drugs on us. We would pass a urine test ...have a history as a drug investigation team."

"No shit? N.I.S.?"

"No shit." Patrick pulled out a badge. It *looked* official.

"Why'd you wait 'til now?"

"Observing for bias." Patrick said as he stuffed his badge back into his coat pocket. "Holding back our hole card, one might say. You, guns and all—came on like Buck Rogers. I was frightened ...shitless in there."

"Me too, Paul." Selesky added. "You must admit, guns and all . . Christ. Those two armed Chinese officers ... "

" ... And that ape with the pistol."

Vincent was surprised that anything could disrupt the logic of anyone as together as he felt Selesky to be. Selesky spotted it.

"I've tarnished the pedestal with this, haven't I?"

"Sure have."

"It's more comfortable off the pedestal, for me, okay?" Selesky said. "I'm human. We all are. As Vonnegut says: '*we are what we pretend to be*'. Let this all go."

"Whose Vonnegut?"

"Some guy who realized we are what we pretend to be." Vincent was beginning to like Balkin's wit.

"Who are you guys pretending to be?"

Selesky jumped right in. "A doctor, in the navy, with someone he loves …and with you, someone he also loves, but in a different way. I'm pretending to be respected by you, for our history as doctor and patient, now as friends …like that."

He owed the man. "Go on." He said. "Tonight never happened."

Selesky gave him a bear hug. Patrick Balkin shook his hand and grinned. "David has said you're one of the good ones, Paul." The two men turned to walk away. Selesky stopped and swung back.

"Wait! The woman! Cynthia! Have you seen her? Is it all ok?"

He'd remembered her name. Selesky began probing with good questions and Vincent was telling everything, as though he were a patient again. He filled Selesky in on Rachael's last try for money, Ben and jail and the motel night with the exec's wife, the killing of the NVA troops, the slap of Clifford and the PR ploy, Griffith's attitudes, Cynthia in France. He talked for twenty minutes with David's encouragement. He became teary eyed once, surprising even himself. He sputtered something about hating the war since the spot boat incident. Selesky stood and listened with a hand on his shoulder.

"Maybe this is the one, Paul, that teaches us war doesn't work … I hope."

"Who's Cynthia, rather, Cynthia who?" Patrick asked directly.

"Cynthia Howser, right, Vincent?" David remembered. "I'd like to know how it goes with her." He turned quickly to Patrick. "Give me one of your cards." Patrick fumbled and came up with one.

"Here. Write to me, to us, care of this address. Let me know what comes of Cynthia. Don't you rescue anyone now. Your life is already a soap opera."

The two men walked away toward the lights near the bay. Monk's car slid to the curb next to Vincent. "Home, James?"

"Home, James."

"Gad. That lieutenant swallowed a dictionary." Monk offered.

"You heard all the conversation.?"

"Yeah, no problem. I just want to get you back so I can look Tom Tie up and see how he's handling the shootings. He struggled terribly over the last ones."

Vincent felt a shudder of his own as he thought of the bullets flying in the narrow passageway.

One more day until Cynthia's arrival.

CHAPTER TWENTY ONE
Letters, We Get letters

The following day, several bags of mail arrived aboard ship. One concerned Cecil Tucker.

February 12th, 1968
From: Enlisted Personnel Distributing Office, Pacific, San Diego, California
To: Commanding Officer, U.S.S. Truaxe (DDG(N)-55)
Subject: Tucker, Cecil (n) 298-37-8891 EN2, Diary Entry

1. Diary entry 1070 Dated 31 January 1968 listed subject man. No record EPDOPAC. Trace and advise.

"R'aht thar'. Ma' SSN's still wrong. Dam't' all." His accent and his excited state made him difficult to understand. The Personnel man in charge of the crew's pay kept staring from the SSN in the letter, to the SSN in Tucker's service record. "Until they git me in theah' computa' correctly," Tucker continued, "Mr. Carter won't pay me."

"*Can't* pay you."

"*Won't* pay me. He got money. Tell someone ta' git a message out to EPDOPAC."

"Well, when the exec isn't too busy, later, I'll see what I can do with it. Maybe I'll know somethin,' err, something by tomorrow ... "

Tucker snatched the record from the man's hand and stormed up the passageway. "I'll see the exec ma'se'f dammit. Had 'nuff red tape and no action."

"But, but, but." The clerk watched Tucker's back disappear up the passageway. He turned to other work, mumbling something about 'stubborn red-necks.'

Forward, in officer's country, a stern faced and puffing Cecil Tucker knocked on Griffith's office door.

"Yes?"

Tucker barged his way in and shut the door behind him. Two steward mates, cleaning the passageway near the office heard strong words exchanged inside and while they agreed there was loud discussion in both directions they also agreed the aluminum door blocked even a pressed ear's efforts. The precise words of the exchange escaped understanding.

After twenty minutes Tucker blew out of Griffith's office and stomped aft, still red-faced, still angry looking. The scuttlebutt-spreading steward mates thought enough of the dimly heard scuffle to mention it around. Master Chief Vincent heard of it.

"You and the X.O. clash over something, Tuck?"

"Sorta'. Ma records fucked up and ah' cain't git no pay, still."

"I'm told you and Griffith went to battle."

"Who says?" He seemed alarmed.

"Stewards."

"Oh?" He looked out over Vincent's shoulder. "They jes' heard him chewin' me out for botherin' him with my small potatas, thas' all."

"Need anything from me?"

"No, X.O. says he'll git a letter out correctin' it all."

"He won't send a message to fix it?"

"Say's cain't send no message on low priority shit."

"Not fun to be broke in Hong Kong. Need money?"

"Kin use a dolla' or so." Tucker's eyes seemed to light up.

"Forty do it?"

"Forty fine, Chief, 'til ah' git paid—'preciate it."

"Just pay me back, Tuck."

Arnold Griffith stacked his two personal letters on top of the pile of official ship's mail. The top letter was in his wife's handwriting. A second letter, addressed to him by typewriter, had no return address. He sat that one aside.

January 28th, 1968

Dearest Arnie

It was bad enough you didn't come ashore the last few days before leaving. I've received no letter from you even though I know you stopped in Hawaii. I can't believe your needs take things that far. I am lonely. I'm not special to you anymore. I feel abandoned by you. I can't live this way. I can't accept this is a marriage any longer.

Please understand—I want a life and you haven't given me one for nearly two years. I hate saying this—but you knew it was coming. I've met someone else. His name is Ben Bristol. His brother in-law is on your ship but we're not saying anything to him or his wife. You no longer care for me, and this person makes me feel special and that I count for something.

I'll never say anything about you to anyone. Ever. I'll get a quiet Nevada divorce. Not you, nor anyone, will find us.

Barbara.

P.S. I've taken $5,000 from savings. That's all I'll need.

"Abandoned?" Griffith flashed on the word. "I've used that word to chastise Vincent. 'Men don't abandon their women ..."

Arnold Griffith rolled the letter into a knot and tossed it through an open port. It plopped into the gray harbor water and floated. He kicked a chair, raked his hand through his hair and flung his arms about in exasperated helplessness.

"I loved her …" He spit the words out dramatically. "She can *surely* wait just a while longer. I've got a life mission duty here." His face puckered involuntarily and tears flooded from his eyes but he made no sound of crying. "Bristol? There's no Bristol on the ship. Brother-in-law? Could be anyone." He was ranting. "Can't she just wait a little while longer? I'm almost ready."

Trying to regain his composure, he stacked and re-stacked the official mail. The typewritten letter fell into his lap. He tore it open.

Dear Commander Griffith
We met once at the ship's party. I almost feel like I know you but actually I only know your wife, Barbara. She and I have become friends, but I am worried about her. She has been dating my married brother. Yes, I know this might be a shock but there is no other way to tell you. I believe she is only dating him because she is lonely for you. She has cried with me about you not wanting to be with her. She's explained you don't like to come home anymore. But you are really wrong about her. She is a good woman and will only break up Ben's marriage if she continues to see him. He is a happy married man.
Could you please say something to her but please do not let her know I told you? And most of all, do not tell my husband I've written you. Some things must remain secret.
Rachael Vincent.

"VINCENT?!!!! He haunts me." Griffith became purple-faced. "I can't lose Barbara, not at this important time." He gasped aloud. "I've haunted Vincent openly. Is this his way of getting back? No. Couldn't be." He stood and paced back and forth. "I've tried so hard with Barbara." He couldn't grasp why she couldn't be more patient, more understanding just as everything was close to ultimate fruition.

Rachael Vincent and Ben Bristol? He met her at a ship's party in Norfolk where Barbara thought she was 'rather sweet'. That was she on the quarterdeck with Vincent a day or so before the ship left San Diego. He met her earlier too, in the company of Ben when the ship arrived in San Diego. While he thought there was something attractive but naive about Rachael, there was something classless about Ben. His clothes smelled of stale barroom smoke, his breath like an ash tray. Griffith's had recently overheard a piece of gossip about this Ben. Who had said it?. What was it? Oh, yes! Ben had trouble in his business, some scandal about the police, a plea for money from Chief Vincent. Money would be his power over Ben, he felt.

He grabbed a pen and pulled a Truaxe letterhead page from a drawer.

Dear Mrs Vincent /or/
Ms. Bristol, whichever you prefer.
I received your letter ref my wife, Barbara, today. I agree with you, there is no good

way to tell a man that his wife is having an affair or is leaving him. I appreciate your concern and your insight that the affair may only reflect Barbara's loneliness for me. I admit our marriage hasn't been all it could have been lately, but the story is too long. In truth, Barbara is acting too quickly. Our long-range plans will soon blossom. She is too impatient.

I would greatly appreciate anything you might do to stall Barbara's leaving me. Enclosed find my check of good faith (and for expenses) for $300. There is a separate check for $300. Please pass it to your brother, also for expenses, if you believe he might be persuaded in some way to be supportive of me in this cause. I am not bribing—I am being realistic. Barbara may just need to be wined and dined, kept distracted to wait for me. And, you said it would be a shame to break up Ben's marriage. Any future for him with Barbara is uncertain. A lonely woman, Barbara, runs to an attractive man, Ben. I understand how it can happen but I also know Barbara—she will regret her actions later. Please understand—this is very important to me. As you suggested—this is our secret.

Sincere regards—

Arnold Griffith

Intuition guided his words as he wrote, read, re-read and re-wrote the pleading passages. Somehow, he felt the money would attract both Rachael and Ben but it took over an hour before the letter had the exact flavor to depict just the right amount of 'hurting sailor husband,' with a touch of naiveté and an invitation that 'a U.S. naval officer would likely be appreciative of their efforts'—perhaps with more money later.

"Ahh! Good, good." He spoke aloud as he sealed the letter. He then telephoned Clifford for permission to go ashore early, a standard protocol.

"Anything wrong?" Clifford questioned.

"No. It's personal. I've got to telephone San Diego."

"Anything I can do? Barbara all right?"

"Well, it concerns her …she's all right." He broke down to Clifford. "It's my marriage. I think she wants out."

"Nooo?"

"YES." Griffith whined. "And Vincent is involved in some way."

"How the hell could he be involved, Arnie?"

"You'll see, he's involved. But later. I'll sort this out if I can get to a telephone."

"Do what you have to do, Arnie."

"Thank you. Thank you, sir." Then he added. "I'd like to meet you for dinner tonight, Cap'n. China Fleet Club?"

"No. Not for me. Too stuffy for me, too Brit. Same with the British Officer's club I'm goin' back to Monique's."

"That place? Again?"

"That's where I'll be. Nine p.m."

"I may see you there, Cap'n."
Griffith grabbed his black-brimmed uniform hat and headed for the quarterdeck.

Dear Paul
This is not an angry letter. Just you should know the allotment you started has not come yet and I am short of money. BB has talked Barbara into extending the bail loan but the police padlocked his bar and we have no income. I know you hate him and I'm not asking for him. Can you wire us some money as an advance? I'll return it when the allotment comes.
Also, BB and Bunny are having problems. That Barbara woman flirts with him and takes a lot of his time, mine too. I think he flirts back just to have the bail money. You not lending us the five thousand will probably cost Bunny her marriage, but I don't want to holler at you any more.
Barbara's husband doesn't write to her. I think she wants a divorce. I also think she has her eye on BB and his bar, now that he owes her a favor. He'd be quite a catch, you know. I Can't have Bunny and BB at odds. I'll end up with their kids if they break up—you know how dependent Bunny can be. Is there anything you can suggest? You always cared so much in the past, I hope you haven't pulled totally away.
Please understand about the money.
Rachael.

The letter was too reasonable for Rachael and he found it necessary to read and re-read it, searching for where interpretation might be necessary. She asked for money. He expected that. He couldn't tell if he was slipping into his 'P.V. to the rescue mode' or if it was truly a reasonable request. He wrote out a check with the feeling it was like shooting one last bullet into an already lost war. He enjoyed knowing Ben was failing her but he did not enjoy knowing his money was surely feeding Ben.

Rachael was likely up to something that didn't show directly in the letter, he figured. She had total domination over Bunny so she couldn't really be worrying about that. However, if Ben came in with a woman Rachael couldn't control, that would be a difficult adjustment for her. Rachael seemed intimidated by Barbara Griffith's classy facade. She would not want her to have a strong position with Ben.

As he sealed the letter, he laughed at Ben for likely pretending affection to stay out of jail. He laughed at Barbara, having an affair with a creep to protect badly managed money. He had a smile over Rachael having called Bunny 'dependent.'

"Takes one to spot one." He mumbled, and was glad there was an ocean between them.

Dear Rachael.
Enclosed is my check for four hundred (blood from the turnip). I hope it helps out, and I also hope the allotment begins next month on time (so I don't have to feed Ben directly). I also hope Ben irons out the bar trouble so you can all get back to work, with life returning to normal (whatever that is).

I know nothing about Barbara Griffith worth anything, other than she seemed pretty drunk that last night when I was there (and she falls a lot, bruises easily and she's fucking your brother). Please, do not get me involved. I don't get along well with her husband (he's out to eat my guts alive as it is). Also, I agree, it would be a shame for Ben and Bunny to break up, two kids and all (although it would likely benefit the kids to have new parents). And, I know what you mean if you had to take the kids on (you didn't want a child of your own let alone of your brothers). I support your need to move Barbara on (if she hangs around you'll lose control of Ben).

I am glad we can be sensible and I'm sure you appreciate I was able to, once again, help out. (The old ploys still work don't they?)

I'm standing OOD watches (you couldn't care less). Maybe I should have taken that commission years ago when it was offered (you would have had more money for Ben). It's fun to play officer of the deck (but what do you know about playing anything?).

I'm in Hong Kong, earlier than anticipated (big deal, you never wanted to come here). It was both fun and exciting to see some of the people I knew from my tour, the one's I wished you could have met, but didn't (because you didn't want to take time for your husband's life). I'm waiting to see others, later (you'd shit yourself to know who and why and what we do that you and I never did). I've met with Eddie Monk (he still thinks you're a jerk). Went on a drug raid, sort of for old times (old times, something we'll never have now).

Here's a surprise (in case you're still reading). I met Doctor Selesky here in Hong Kong, you know, the one we thought might be sweet on his assistant Doctor Sarah Barclay? Well, forget that. He's gay, and the navy doesn't know it (you couldn't care less, but then, maybe you are gay and that's been the problem). I discovered him and another guy during a drug raid on a Samsei barge. Imagine that? (Imagine anything?) I let him go because of the friendship, (something I don't think you calculate) but I think the friendship will end now. Nothing in common and all that jazz (somewhat like you and I?).

I still regret our errors (regret I didn't see them years earlier).

Hope all gets better there (so I don't have to support you for very long). My best to Bunny and the kids (likely the only truthful feeling in this letter).

Paul

Sitting on the ship in Hong Kong, the smells in the air and the familiar noises the same as 1966 and last year, he could not stop the rejected feelings from replaying. A bolt of impassioned anger toward Rachael passed through him as he sealed the letter.

"You can have my money, Rachael—but not my trust, nor my real care, ever again." As he put his hat on his head to go mail the letter, he thought. "Whew, sounds rather soap opera-y." Then he wondered as he walked, if she could ever do anything that would regain his love or trust?

He walked aft to the starboard passageway to drop one woman from his life into a mail box to free him the time to find out if the other woman was in the city. Mailing the letter he noticed commotion on the fantail near the quarter-deck. The Captain was there with Lieutenant Commander Valentino, Lieutenants Hicks and Beauford and another officer, whose back was to Paul. Valentino saw Paul and motioned.

"Here's our Master Chief, Mr. Balkin." The name rang in just as the officer turned. It was Patrick Balkin, duffel bag and suitcase beside him. Their eyes met. Balkin did a strong face grimace and shook his head from side to side to communicate to Vincent to pretend to not know him. No one else noticed the signal. Balkin stepped forward and extended his hand, his face out of view of the others. The grimace returned: (You don't know me.)

"Nice to meet you, Master Chief. What's the name, again?"

"Vincent, Paul Vincent." For the moment, he agreed to follow Balkin's silent request as Valentino explained Balkin's presence. "Mr. Balkin is the replacement conning officer we've asked for. He'll be in the operations department. Maybe take over communication officer duties so Mr. Stumpf can move to CIC."

"Oh? Welcome Mr. err ..."

"Balkin, Patrick. My pleasure to be aboard."

"Yes."

Vincent felt truly 'one upped'. Balkin had put one over on him the night before by not mentioning Truaxe. Now, Truaxe had a homosexual communication officer who was the lover of a homosexual friend who had counseled him over a heterosexual marriage. He didn't know what that might mean. The questions kept coming: is a high percentage of the navy really gay? I guess 'if you are in to men, go where the men are'. Were they obvious if he knew where to look? Do homosexuals have secret signals to one another? Could you not tell by looking? Balkin wasn't swishy in a stereotyped way. Neither was Selesky. Neither is Clifford. Is Clifford homosexual? Griffith? Deiter? Does it really matter? Where is Selesky anyway? Had Selesky and Balkin lied in other ways? Despite the number of questions, answers were very scarce.

He telephoned radio, determined everything was satisfactory there, snatched his black-brimmed uniform hat and returned to the quarter-deck to go ashore. He needed to find out if Cynthia had returned.

Captain Clifford opened his last personal letter, of several.

Dear Son,

Just a note. Rumor here in San Diego is that Truaxe isn't doing very well. Seems the C.O. Kittyhawk dropped Bill Mackberry a note—something about low training status on Truaxe—something he observed while in company. Did you use Kittyhawk for training backup? If so, always stupid. Never saw a brown-shoe carrier C.O. yet who wasn't out to put a surface fleet black-shoe officer out of the running for admiral.

Also, what's this about morale problem aboard? Whose writing letters home? That secretive exec of yours? Never liked that man. Fill me in.

Also the club is buzzing about some classified mix-up on a CIA pick-up over there. Who messed it up? Do you know? It doesn't sound like a rumor.

The TET affair is a chance for you to shine over there and don't mess it up. Whatever you do, stay on plane guard or better yet, PIRAZ or some other aircraft-control duty. Stay away from NGFS duty or that CIA pickup duty. That's for common tin-can sailors.

If you can keep from it, don't be going off to any hot liberty ports until you look as though you've earned your ribbons, rusted some.

And don't get drunk ashore—you talk too much when drinking.

Mother sends her love.

Dad

Griffith's call had interrupted Clifford long enough for the content of Our Admiral's letter to burn a hole in his stomach. After giving Griffith permission to go ashore, the Captain swallowed a heavy throat lump and sat with a tear close to the surface. The letter was simply another reminder he'd likely never get it right. To break from the teary-eyed state he stood, said "fuck me" quite loud, grabbed his black-brimmed uniform hat, called the OOD to ready his launch, and he too, headed for the quarter-deck.

Griffith, Stumpf, Vincent, Tucker, Lake, even the new officer, Patrick Balkin, and others, were waiting to go ashore when Clifford arrived for his launch. Griffith, standing next to Tucker was grim-faced and kept starring at Vincent. Vincent tried lightening things with a bit of humor.

"I hear you and Tucker discussed politics and relatives today, Commander." He could instantly tell Griffith wasn't buying small talk. He tried anyway. " ...but you prevailed." Without a word Griffith turned his body away from Vincent and the others, crossed his arms, rocked slightly on his heels, and looked toward the city. The rejection burned through Vincent.

"Well, you sure say the right things." Stumpf moved close and whispered. "Must I re-remind you? Watch *out* for that man."

Clifford interrupted the awkwardness, perhaps consciously.

"OOD? Everyone can ride in my launch. No use waiting for the liberty boat to return. Damn bird farm boats probably hogging the fleet landing."

'Aren't I a nice C.O.?' Stumpf whispered to Vincent as they boarded Clifford's personal launch.

In the boat, Clifford spoke over the resonating sound of the motor.

"Chief? Like you to have dinner with me, a few of us, tonight. Monique's." The no-win flashed in P.V.'s head. Refuse and go against the PR program. Accept and delay happiness if Cynthia is in the city. He tried showing a disappointed or surprised expression.

"I have an appointment, Cap'n. One I must keep." He noticed Balkin and a couple of the others paying close attention to the conversation.

"An APPOINTMENT, huh?" Clifford gave Vincent the time honored and subtle 'never refuse an invitation of the Captain's look'.

"Old friends. Known them for years." This was too awkward already.

"Bring them along." Clifford seemed tense. The PR facade was slipping. Vincent feared Clifford's mood might swing, jeopardizing everything.

"If you insist, Cap'n. It would be easier if I could …bring my guest."

Clifford broke into a big grin of a smile. "Good, Good. Really. Bring anyone you'd like to dinner. That'd be fine."

"Sure, sir. What time, sir?"

Clifford's smile seemed forced now. "Nineteen hundert or so? No …too soon. Nine or so, better. That'll …is fine. Good. Good." Most others in the boat seemed to relax. Griffith stayed well distanced from it all.

CHAPTER TWENTY TWO
The Best of News, the Worst of News

At 6 p.m. Paul dialed 428-9330. It barely rang one ring before Cynthia picked it up on the living room extension.

"Yes?" Her voice filled him with anticipatory longing.

"It's me, and I'm in the city."

"Thank God and more!" Looking nervously over her shoulder, the beautiful brunette kicked the telephone cord ahead of her and carried the coveted conversation through the French doors to the veranda. She put the base of the telephone on the railing, ran the free hand through her hair and spoke anxiously to Paul. "I can see your ship clearly anchored out. All day I've been watching liberty boats come and go. Each ring of the telephone was … "

"Meet me."

There was a sob, but not a happiness cry.

"What is it?" He asked.

"It's dreadful." Instantly her voice was a harsh whisper. "I need you, now. Kurt's reversed himself. *Everything* is coming apart." The way her words tumbled out, the strong accent, word choices, sounded like Cynthia, but the whining 'rescue me' sounds were more Rachael.

"Wha'dya'mean 'need me'—'reversed himself'—'everything's apart?"

"It's not *US*, *we've* not changed …but I'm frightened. Kurt's changed." Her voice dropped to where he could barely hear her. "I can't say it all on the telephone. Where can I meet you?" There was a shiver in her voice.

"I'm trapped into dinner with the Cap'n tonight."

"*Before* we can meet?" She dropped the guarded whisper.

"No, of course not. You, me, the dinner." He paraphrased the long story of hitting Clifford and of compromising himself in order to see her. Pacing as she listened, she only half-heard the troubled tale.

"I don't understand all of this. I can't say much."

He heard an airplane. "Are you on the veranda?"

"Yes."

"Is it Kurt you're hiding your voice from?"

"Yes."

"Must you hang up?"

"No. But he's watching through the window. I'm pretending I'm speaking to Candice, but it's so cold out here he surely knows I'm up to something."

"If you hang up? I'll understand. You can reach me at Frenchie's until eight thirty then Lur-Sur Kuoche at nine p.m … ."

"Monique's?"

"Yes. I can't ditch this dinner thing. If I haven't heard from you by nine, I'll be back to Frenchie's, I'd guess after ten thirty."

"I can't wait. I'll get away. The dinner? Is it really proper for me to be theah? Seems perhaps to be a men only affair?" That instant he loved the accent.

"Its proper. You're necessary, actually. We'll get in—get out. I hate this. Please understand."

"I understand, but so much is happening. I have terrible news to pass on."

"Cynthia, tell me. What the hell you mean in your letter about an 'unanswered letter'? 'A coward's way out'?"

The phone went silent. "Cynthia? Should I come up there?"

"No! No! No heroics, Sailor. Not here." Her voice seemed frantic. "Not now." Then calmer "I'll explain it all." The whisper returned. "The letter too."

"In Frenchie's, soon?"

"The soonest is by eight. I've got to shake away from Kurt."

"I hate this." He said. "I wasn't counting on ..."

"Just see me, be with me." She interrupted. "Please? And no questions right off?"

"No questions?"

"Not right away, questions. I need to see you. I'll be in white, new." She sounded momentarily happy. "And underneath ... ?" She forced a playful voice but it was too strained. " ...new undies I bought secretly and specially. You'll love it." Her seriousness returned. "Just love me?"

How could he not?

In the taxi on the way to Frenchie's, she swam into his brain. He'd never heard her sound truly frightened and that frightened *him.* The taxi sped past the Shore Patrol office where two nights ago he'd spent the evening in reverie with her. He was amazed he had repressed so much about their affair. But, as he'd learned recently, anything repressed eventually bursts forth. In the quiet taxi, her face reflecting in the window, he suppressed a growing sadness. A voice came from the taxi window. "How could you ignore a glorious love that is this strong?" He looked. There was no face for the voice.

Wearing dress-blues he nervously stepped into Frenchie's and checked his hat and gloves. It was 7:50 p.m.

The restaurant was still the habitat of the hanger-on European aristocracy in Hong Kong and normally protected from casual tourists and curious military visitors by an unspoken pretense of being a private club. Only because the Howsers had introduced him had Paul grown to be accepted by the socially conscious crowd who chose to ignore he was 'common U.S. Navy'. Over the years, Kurt and Cynthia actually taught him to not be intimidated by the wealth.

"You pay your way? You owe no one anything. Screw everyone, and take what you pay for."

Tonight the place was, as usual, crowded with tuxedoed men and gowned women causing his uniform to stand out. Some faces familiar to him nodded his way but only for seconds. He stood on the three step riser facing the main dining area, the dimly lit bar to his left, foyers for *dames* and *messieurs* to the right. He lit a cigarette and despite the unresolved anxiousness with Cynthia, couldn't suppress a slight smile. He was very pleased to be in the place.

Frenchie's reminded him of the Kitchi Gammi Club in Duluth where he'd visited only once with distant relatives. There was also a touch of the La Valencia Hotel above the cove in La Jolla, also not unlike the left and right sitting rooms of the Gritti Palace hotel in Italy. The nineteen-thirties had been the hey-day for Frenchie's but because of appreciation by enough followers the atmosphere and style survived well. Polished hardwood was everywhere as were expensive gold fittings at the bar, the telephone cabinets, *le garson* and *maitre d'* stations. Accentuated by grand wingback chairs, the oval-shaped linen-covered tables set on islands of sparkling marble divided by curved path-like lanes of majestic carpeting. Well-chosen elegance continued in the imposing crystal light fixtures suspended on thin gilded rods spaced evenly from the domed white ceiling. They cast subtle light on seemingly indifferent guests. These were older people mostly, older money, conservative but all with the private and well-protected wounds. It was a small, private and cross-protective society. Some brought their wife or husband while others brought whomever they wished with the assumption that no one would interfere, ever.

The owner, Frenchie, approached across the dining room, reading glasses in one hand, the other hand extended, an open smile on his slightly flushed bearded face. Though round around the middle, the fifty-something man in the gabardine tuxedo seemed to float up the three familiar steps.

"Ahh—Chief Vincent," The world's most gifted greeter clasped Paul's hand and immediately noted his second star. "No! no! Lookee' here, lookee here: MASTER Chief Vincent. Congratulations, it is great to have you back." He peered over Paul's left shoulder. "Alone?"

"In a few minutes—Cynthia … Mrs. Howser. I'm sorry I didn't telephone ahead."

"*Pas de immediatement important.* Will you be wanting their …her, regular table?"

"More privacy tonight, Frenchie."

"Of course."

At two minutes before eight, a nod from Frenchie motioned him across the large statue and palm lined dining room. Only a few of the well dressed looked up from their meal. While Frenchie held menus, a pair of formal waiters fussed Paul into a table behind a chest-high polished wood barrier. His host spoke as he handed the Chief a menu.

"From the ribbons, I see you've been to the Vietnam. You seem …ahh, how I say, Master Chief …"

"Nervous?"

"Yes, you seem so. But I hope all is well between …" His eyes rolled up and toward the door. Paul knew what he meant.

"We'll work it out, Frenchie. This privacy helps."

"Yes."

From where he sat he could raise his head slightly and see the riser. Early diners were arriving regularly in two's and four's. Restless for answers to resolve the earlier conversation he watched impatiently for the familiar figure in the promised white dress. As Frenchie greeted the guests on the riser and escorted them to tables, Paul caught snatches of conversations from the outgoing hospitable host. He heard German, Italian, some French and some Baltic language, but mostly English. People caught Paul starring. Some seemed distracted by his frequent check of the riser area. He felt conspicuous in dress blues.

He sat back out of view but couldn't see the riser. He moved his chair slightly. It grated on the marble. He lit a cigarette, his eyes scanning for her presence. Too many faces, arms, bodies, black ties, dinner jackets, yellow gowns, blue dresses, no white one. Too much laughter, glasses clinking, and now, music began from a stringed trio in a small alcove. Where was his fantasy lady? Two couples stopped to chat at a table, blocking his view. One of the men wore a turban, used a cigarette holder. Paul snubbed out his cigarette. Go outside; meet her at her car or at her taxi. Move the turban couple. He rose to leave. Has she been in a car accident?

There she was, just below the riser not twenty paces away. Not smiling, she stood quietly, looking for him. Her hands held a small white evening bag. Frenchie stepped next to her, bowed and smiled. She gave him her hand. He pointed her toward Paul. She quickly looked in his direction. Their eyes met.

She was almost too lovely to take in or to consider all at once. Dressed in white as promised, she cast an iridescent glow against the darker panels behind her. She wore a white cape that rested on the tips of her shoulders but a white scarf of some magic kind that only she could find dominated her appearance. It made its way in smooth contours, swirling like a drape from her left shoulder around her throat and tightly then around her head. Her face, framed Madonna-like, reminded him of and drew him to her extreme beauty. Unnoticed by him or her, diners were beginning to watch the handsome sailor and the stunning woman.

He had to touch her. He worked his way across the hushed room, oblivious of the colony of onlookers. Not touching anything but her waiting hand he backtracked his steps, across the room to behind the barrier. *Shocking* filled his head and followed them. Once behind the barrier, he kissed her. There was an absolutely correct pitter-pat of applause from several smiling diners. Both he and she smiled self-consciously and as he held her chair, the others, just as correctly, turned their attentions back to their own lives.

Once seated, she shrugged slightly. The cape fell away. Below the Madonna scarf, her breasts floated in the bodice of the dress. He smiled down toward her and touched her cheek with the back of his hand. She had truly dressed especially to please him despite whatever had drawn the fears expressed on the telephone. The smile of pleasure that emitted from his face gave her permission to feel dignified in her appearance and not the usual self-consciousness prompted by Kurt.

"Thank you." He said into her eyes. "You are perfect."

She rose, stood beside him, touching his arm. She whispered, nodded her head just slightly and smiled. "Every woman wants moments just like this one."

"I can't just sit here with you." He said and glanced about for Frenchie.

"Nor can I." She grabbed his hand. "Come, this way." She led him toward the back of the restaurant. Frenchie was there immediately.

"Inside …my office. You are alone."

The door clicked shut and clicked again. The small purse fell silently to the carpet as they kissed for the second time.

"I can't think." He uttered.

"Nor I."

"Don't"

"I won't … Oh Paul, kiss me to die." With muffled noises for words, he guided her with open mouth to a corner of Frenchie's office and an opened roll-top desk lighted by the green radiance of a banker's lamp. He pressed her against the desk with just enough force to topple the lamp. Its bare bulb projected their shadows boldly onto the beige walls beyond them and onto the ceiling above.

He put his hands on either side of her skirt.

"Now I'll say hello to you." He said with a new deep kiss.

With a flurry of smooth and confident movements he lifted her to the edge of the desk while her cape, his jacket and her white tap panties dropped to the floor at his feet. She lifted her legs around him. One garter unsnapped around the curve of her buttocks as he pushed solidly into her. The other held. Her mouth clasped onto his. Their memories choreographed the moments that followed.

Straightening herself she laughed. "Think Frenchie knew we'd do it in his office?"

"I think he was afraid we'd do it at that table. Remember the others applauding us?"

"Were we that transparent?" She turned to him, blushing. He took her in his arms. Her blush disappeared quickly, replaced by a total loss of color.

"What is it?" He asked.

"I have to tell you … "

There was a knock at the door. Her body tensed.

"Yes?" Paul asked the door.

"Is I, Sir, madam. Frenchie." His voice muffled by the thick wood.

Paul looked to Cynthia. Her tenseness loosened slightly. She smiled a fixed colorless grin.

"Come in, Frenchie." Paul invited.

"Je me suis enferme' dehors." Frenchie's French confused Paul.

"What?"

"He's locked himself out." Cynthia said reaching for the door. "Let me."

The perfect host entered with a bottle of champagne tucked in his arm and two glasses balanced from the tips of extended practiced fingers. If the smell of sex still lingered in the room, Frenchie handled it well. Paul saw Cynthia's foot brush the white panties under the desk.

As their host poured champagne he jabbered to Cynthia and at one point, with a click of his fingers, "oh yes," pulled a pair of beige driving gloves from his pocket. Bowing just slightly he offered Cynthia the gloves.

"You'd telephoned about them last week? You were correct. At the table where you and Kurt dined Tuesday, with the *charge' de' affairs* of the *Saudi* consulate?"

"Frenchie. You are such a dear. Thank you for finding them."

"My pleasure of course." Turning to Paul. "Would you prefer dining *le bureau*, Master Chief? Or *la salle s manger ?*"

"Le bureau?"

"The office, Paul. Here?" Cynthia interpreted, smiling. "Or the dining room?" But it had not been solely Frenchie's French that distracted him.

"You say Cynthia left the gloves last Tuesday?"

"Yes, Tuesday." Frenchie's smile froze when he saw Vincent's troubled look. He looked toward Cynthia. Her expression said 'no-no.' His look turned to one of artificial disregard. "But I could be wrong? Could I not, Mrs. H?"

Cynthia's eyes again flashed alarm but her voice was calm.

"We've been in Europe …until just last evening."

"Europe? Last evening? No. Yes?" He reflected the helpless expressions of a person who had done something very wrong but had no idea what it was. He even checked his fly to see if it was open. "My memory, Paul. Forgive my memory. Must have left the gloves weeks ago. Seemed like just yesterday . . .like Tuesday."

Borrowing the phrase from Cynthia, Paul said: "'Of course', Frenchie," and added. "Not by choice, of course, but we dine elsewhere tonight. Not by choice. Political. Navy. You know."

Frenchie then borrowed Paul's 'Of course' and used it several times as he backed out of the charged air of the office.

Paul turned immediately to her. "What is this? What don't I know?"

Cynthia backed away from him, the expression was frightening to her, one she'd never seen on his caring face. "Wait. I must explain." She said. But it was too late to explain.

Paul Vincent's mother and two brothers discovered early that when he felt tricked, he showed true anger. Anger, he learned over time, was a physical thing that overtakes someone when they don't have coping skills for whatever it is that is happening. He had never developed coping skills for being lied to or tricked.

At age four his father had deserted them but his mother lied about it, swearing to Paul that his father was very ill and was in the front bedroom of the small house on High Street in Steubenville. Paul and his brothers were to play quietly near the kitchen stove during those winter days and to sleep on the mattress while mother came and went to tend the ill father. One of his earliest memories was that he was suspicious about it all. Without really knowing why, he waited until his mother stepped next door during the afternoon to talk with a neighbor. Telling his brothers to wait, he slipped quietly into the bedroom where thick cheap expansion blinds let in very little light. In the darkened room he slid his small arms onto the cool bed and walked down its one side, feeling for the father, across the bottom, feeling for feet between the wooden spooled bars, and up the opposite side, again, searching for a person. There was no father lying ill in the bed. There was no one there.

He returned to the warm kitchen and played with his brothers and kept his new information to himself. He never understood the lie. He distrusted his mother, and likely a lot of other things from that day on.

When at age six he uncovered Santa Claus, he waited for his mother to return from work and confronted her openly. "What else do adults lie to kids about?" It was then he learned, the feelings of 'anger' and the activity of crying real tears were related. Selesky reminded him "anger and tears are on opposite ends of a continuum for us when we face tough things. Some people cry, some show anger, some do both at different times."

Paul cut his hand while working as a delivery helper at Greenberg's grocery and Doctor Vukovitch, who had delivered him thirteen years earlier, told him through whiskey smelling breath that he needed stitches in the hand. His mother always referred to Doctor Vukovitch as a saint of some sort and Paul was ready for excellent care.

"If it'll hurt." Paul said, as bravely as a thirteen-year-old can be. "Tell me, Doctor, and I'll get ready for the hurt."

"It won't hurt, boy. Now gimmie' that hand." With his mother holding the hand pressed to a linoleum tabletop, the half drunk Doctor put four stitches into the knuckles of the thirteen year old, without anesthesia. Paul walked home that night with the thumping hand jammed into his winter coat pocket. He would not talk to his mother. He lay awake all night with the pulsating wound beating time to the building question: Why do people lie? Why do people lie? Why do people lie? Helpless tears ran freely between bouts of anger."

In the ninth grade, Mr. Greer, the principle of the High School ordered Paul to the basement of the school, behind the furnaces. He told the boy to drop his trousers. Touching Paul's privates he talked nervously about erections and 'feeling good,' embarrassing and confusing the adolescent. When Paul told his mother, she accused him of making it up to cover for poor school grades. "He's a school official. They never do anything like that. Shame on you." He then nervously turned to someone he trusted. Carl Keefer was the friendly Boy's Department Director at the YMCA on Fourth street. He knew Mr. Keefer would help him with the confusion over Mr. Greer.

"We just won't tell anyone about this, Paulie boy." Keefer said, offering Paul a stick of chewing gum. "This is just our secret. Understand? We can't be accusing Mr. Greer now, can we?"

Later that year when suddenly and without publicity Mr. Greer disappeared as the school principle, Paul was able to look Keefer in the eye but Keefer couldn't return the look.

By the time he left Steubenville for the Navy, he saw clouds in the motives of most adults. He built a dam against the trickery that overwhelmed him as a child by pushing the confusion's into crevices of memory where usually they remained generally unremembered. But, Frenchie's' glove comment jerked the thinly protected barriers immediately away. The near forgotten sores of tricks and lies bled again. Cynthia, of all people, had joined his confused mother, Mr. Greer, Carl Keefer, Doctor Vukovitch, Rachael, Ben Bristol, Griffith, Captain Clifford, even David Selesky and Patrick Balkin—the group of those who lied.

"Let me explain," she repeated.

"Fuck you," he said. The anger over being lied to showed clearly. Any explanation was useless. He couldn't bear that his special Cynthia revealed she too had hidden plans and motives. Tears from the opposite end of the anger fought to spill forth. He hid them from her by turning away.

"Can't I even try to explain?" He didn't answer. He walked to the doorway and grabbed the polished knob. Her hand touched his elbow. Her perfume slipped unfairly into his brain.

"Wait, dammit, Paul Vincent. I'm not an evil person. I'll *not* lose you over this. You listen to me. You owe me to listen."

He held the doorknob, struggling with the uncovered hurt. He spoke to the door. "What can you possibly say? You've said I was safe for you to be with. Did you think I didn't also need that safety?"

She grabbed his arm and jerked him face to face. "Jesus, do you forget everything so easily? Is there no understanding in a man who just made love? I've hurt you, Paul but I didn't want that. I'm not out to get you."

"Feels like you are. I've changed my life for these moments."

"You selfish bastard. So have I." She spun away from him. "Can't you see? It's the letter has caused all of this ..." Turning back to him she dug her nails into the sides of his neck and screamed, "DON'T YOU SEE?"

He lifted her hands away, pushed them to her sides and gazed with squinted eyes at her flushed and fearful face. His neck burned and dominated the feelings. She moved one hand to his arm. He pulled away from her grip but she had faith it was an involuntary move.

"The letter. *That* letter? The 'coward's way out letter' I referred to? You can't have known of it, but I thought you did. I only found out today you didn't know." Her words were nonsense to him. He turned to face her and she saw his tears for the first time. His expression said to talk, but that it had better be very good. She shivered reflexively.

"There has been a terrible thing done to me, *BY* me, truthfully by Kurt. A mistake to you ...to both of us, my letter."

He put his hand to her lips. "Start again."

"For years now, since '62, I am sure." She looked down. "Can I say this? Here?" She shivered again. The shiver quivered her voice. She walked to the desk and drew the cape back to her shoulders. "You'll not believe me."

"Perhaps."

"All right." Exasperated she walked to within two feet of him and faced him straight on. "Listen to me. I'm looking direct to your eyes. Believe me. I've learned, Kurt has not been all I've thought him to be." She reached for his hands but he held them away. She crossed her arms, pulled the cape up close to her throat. "Years ago, right after you left visiting? I wrote to you, at your ship. I asked you ... " Her voice faded. He recognized her expression, the one that flashed when she was embarrassed.

"Tell me." He took her hands then.

"In that letter, I asked you if you would not marry Rachael—for me."

"What letter?"

She pulled away. He watched her press eight fingers against her forehead. She looked down. "You never received the letter."

"But ... I would have remembered ... "

"Wait!" She snapped. "Let me ...finish."

He backed away.

"I said if you would leave Rachael, I would leave Kurt."

"That was in your letter?"

"Yes. And when you told me just weeks ago of having left Rachael, and asked me to consider being forever with you, such a nice way to ask me, I went to Kurt, to tell him I was leaving him. He became," One finger curled against her lips. " ...what?" Her hand moved into a fist beside her cheek. "Hostile? Yes, no ...furious actually. No. *More* than even furious, he became." Her eyes caught his as the right word clicked. "*Enraged.* Truly enraged. He cursed me and then cursed you. I tried talking but he cursed more, then laughed, crazily. I was shocked." Her voice calmed considerably and she continued. "Somehow, I think ...stupidly. . he knew I'd leave him someday ...for you. A foolish childish thought, yes, that he would just stand by and let that happen. But his rage was so surprising, so out of character."

"Cynthia. I've always thought it was trouble. Us ...fooling around. I suspected he was *pretending* to be all right with it ..."

"I was misled also. Until today. He yelled. He said your recent letter was 'merely your loneliness calling out' ... 'divorce loneliness, asking me to comfort you.' He insisted you were simply rebounding, but not to anything we've had, but to what you think we *might* have. He said we would tire of one another without his money."

"Fuck him ...and his money."

"Wait! He tripped himself." She said. "He said you refused to leave Rachael before for me, and would likely not leave her this time."

"What?" Paul lost track.

"He couldn't have known you refused me," she said, " ...unless you'd told him you'd gotten my letter and refused me."

"I would not have done that. I didn't know you'd asked me."

"Of course," she agreed, "he could only have known I asked you to leave her ...and you refused me in some way, if he had read my letter to you. If he had intercepted it somehow."

"He admitted it?"

"At first no. But I'd caught him and he knew it. At first he led me to believe you had received it, and rejected me by not answering. I asked him then, why was he so concerned if you had rejected me once? That's when he told me all of it. Laughing, insanely. You had *never gotten the letter.* He had stolen it."

"This is craziness ... "

"But don't you see?" She said taking both of his hands, "I thought you *had* gotten the letter. I had no bloody way to know he was selectively intercepting my letters. For years. He took them from where they waited for Mia to take to post. Steam them open ...letting some go on to you. I challenged him that he was lying about that. He laughed at me, detestably. He went to the safe, in bravado but crying also. He threw a blizzard of letters and papers from the safe. Several of my letters to you fell to the floor. I was ... Paul ...dumbfounded. He took one letter from the pile and threw it at me. It was the actual letter I asked you to leave Rachael with, May 14, 1962. He grabbed it from my hand. Ruthlessly cursing me and cursing you, he paced crazily back and forth, rubbing his hair, waving the letter, reading the letter aloud. He mocked my love for you."

"Wait, Cynthia. Wait." She wouldn't wait.

"I thought you had refused me. It's clear now. You know it all." She let go of his hands and looked at her small watch. "And we must leave for the Captain's dinner. "

"Fuck the Captain. Wait. Why would you think I'd refused you? Why did you not question my not answering?"

"My own stupidity caused me to think you'd refused me. If your answer was to be 'no', I told you to simply ignore the letter. I didn't want to receive an *actual* 'no' from you in writing. Foolish of me. We were to go on as we had, meeting whenever we could."

"Oh fuck!"

She re-took his arm. "Okay, Okay. It was a foolish childish love-sick stupid way to arrange it. That's why I called it a coward's way out. But I was so …hopelessly romantic, and, afraid of the 'no'. I wasn't sure of the power of your feelings to Rachael. When you didn't answer it after a month, I was broken hearted—but I." She hesitated, and then became very matter of fact again. "I think I simply denied it all. I …just went on."

"I gave you no way out in my letter from San Diego."

"That's what I said. You gave me no cowards way out." She folded her arms under her breasts and turned from him, speaking into the air. "After awhile I pretended I hadn't sent my lettah', evah! That you hadn't seen it." She turned back to his eyes. "Sometimes I believed it myself. I had never, not once, not for an instant, dreamed you hadn't received it."

"I never knew."

"Of course you didn't know. Damn him, Paul. He's tricked us pitifully. He later took advantage of my sadness." She was crying freely now.

"Took advantage? How?"

Her mascara ran. He touched her cheek with his handkerchief, shifting Kurt from the caring and friendly man to this new role of planned deception. She took the handkerchief.

"I can't tell now. Not now. We'll talk later, by ourselves. Someplace, just you and I …the clock is moving. The dinner? The Captain?"

"Is the worst out, Cynthia? Now?

"I have more to say … I need more understanding …from you … "

"Jesus! Kurt. He …he seemed to never mind you and I. Somehow … "

"He lied all along. He hated it, he said. Hated me …and you."

"This is awful. If only you would have questioned my not answering the letter? Oh hindsight's curse. I would have left Rachael. I know that now."

"No! Oh God, Paul." She became very energized and backed away from him, still crying openly, shocked, anger within the tears. "Don't ever say that." She stepped back to him and shook his shoulders. "Pretend, with me. I've never sent my letter. Your letter is the first time either of us asked the other. Please!"

He pulled her close. "I understand."

The lie over the gloves had become lost in the new and startling knowledge. He felt close to her again and the closeness cloaked the earlier trickery. His anger raged toward Kurt, but, even in the anger there were other feelings.

"The years he's pretended and denied? Must have been awfully painful for him."

"At first I felt that way about him." She said. "But I have no sorrow for him now. He's done things, evil things that will take away any feelings of sorrow. "

"I can't believe he's deliberately hurt you …or even me."

"I understand the shock. I had to spin out of that also. He should have told me, years ago that he couldn't permit us, you and I. I would have listened perhaps. But no, he chose a sweet, so sweet revenge over both of us. Have you forgotten the lie about last week that Frenchie blew open?"

"The lie. Yes. Why the lie?"

She stepped away from him and picked up her small purse form the floor near the door. Returning quickly to the desk, she flicked under it with one high heel and scraped the white panties into view. "These cost me over a hundred Hong Kong dollars." She said smiling and pushing them into her small purse. "Now, take me to the dinner. The clock moves so fast and you said we can't miss it."

"I hate this."

"We can do this. Put Kurt away for now so we tend to your trouble with the captain.. I'll explain it all later …the lie. Just don't hate me. I've never been out to get you …evah." She took his hands and pulled them against her breasts and kissed his lips. It was not a sensual move. Duplicating the need for closeness that surfaced their first night by the wall on the overlook, it was just a furtherance of this night's renewed closeness.

"Can we make it through this, Sailor?"

He tried to smile with her. "We'll make it through this, Wai-da."

In the taxi on the way to Monique's he pushed away the feelings that while his own life was filled with troubles, he was once again comforting a troubled woman.

CHAPTER TWENTY THREE
The Captain's Dinner

Despite the anxieties of the evening, during the taxi ride, as in the past, Paul adjusted the position of her skirt to what he called 'subtle-tease-position-number-one'. In 'number-one' her garter snap is visible, a hint of thigh, but no panties in view. Subtle-tease-position-two and three were generally reserved for the ride home or to the Fandian Ho. Two: Garter tops, with an outer thigh and slight panty view. Three: Garter tops, at least one unfastened, inner thigh view—panties in his pocket. *Everything* is off key this evening, he thought. *She* has her panties in her purse from the cavorting at Frenchies.

Paul struggled with the myriad of feelings. Being extremely glad to be with her was off-balanced by her story of Kurt. Taking in her beauty and letting sexual arousal fly freely was held back by the unknown discussion coming up with Clifford. Being with her had advertised one thing: *happiness*, but delivered another, *turmoil*, like a bait and switch sale at a hustle store for used lives.

At the curb near Monique's, Cynthia double-checked the garter that had let go in Frenchie's office, and pulled her skirt down and into place. By the time the uniformed greeter reached for the taxi's door in front of Monique's, Cynthia had renewed herself to where she was confident and seemed calm.: "I'm not wearing panties, Sir," She said flatly, then with *a* 'what's a person to do about the bad help we get these days' ring to it, added "these garters were to be the stress-tested variety."

"Next time?" He helped. "We're to ask the sales girl if she's tried them."

She nodded agreement and took his hand. He touched her arm. She looked into his eyes and took a very deep breath to keep all the feelings in line.

"I scarcely know how we are managing this." She said as she rose up from the taxi seat and stood beside him. A trace of *shocking* followed her from the warm car into the chilly night.

He grimaced as he paid the driver and said: "I'm embarrassed I'm putting the navy ahead of you tonight. But that's …"

"Paul," she rescued, "we cannot predict these untested things. Look at me." She forced a laugh. "I feel like that *Gone With The Wind* woman." The taxi crunched away in gutter litter. Paul put on a quiet Georgia accent:

"Y'all means 'Missy Scarlet'?"

Fidgeting with her purse and cape clasp, she looked up and down the neon-heavy street. "Put off troubles until tomorrow?" She said. "That's me, isn't it? Deny that everything has gone to hell?"

Paul said, pulling off one white glove, "Selesky says we deny the crap until we have energy to deal with it."

"Cynthia *Denial-Crap* Howser." She smiled. "I'll change monogram on the towels."

"Remind me to tell you about Selesky." Paul said with a finger snap.

"Is it good?"

"It would have been surprise of the month, if you hadn't had yours all saved up."

He took her hand. The doorman moved ahead of them and waited under the shiny brass letters *'Hotel Lu-Sur Knoche,'* over an equally shiny brass-framed doorway. He had one hand on the opener, the other palm up. Cynthia stopped walking.

"This dinner tonight?" The doorman dropped his palm. "I can't pretend to grasp the power warlike chaps have over one anotha', but this dinner liaison sounds like you could end up damaged?" Her accent seemed strongly evident.

"Perhaps, darlin', but I think not."

"You're here' to nurture your Captain's troubles toward you, true?"

"You got it." He tugged her hand and turned for the door. The doorman's palm went up again but Cynthia stood fast against Paul's tug. The palm dropped. Paul faced her, removing his second glove.

"Why have me here? I know its first night and all. But aren't we looking a bit like little Paulie can't be away from Mummy?"

"Two agendas tonight that we know of. Clifford's still is trying to undo tensions between him and the other officers over the slap ..."

"Agenda numba' two?"

"As you Brits say, Clifford's 'number one,' Commander Griffith, has the idea I've left a wonderful warm nurturing woman, Rachael, for some twit from Hong Kong who wants her hooks into me for a U.S. of A. green-card, okay?"

"What's with Griffith that he's after you?"

"I'm not sure. I know his wife is having an affair, complete with sex in second rate motels with Rachael's stupid brother."

That popped a snicker from her face. "With Benny? Really? Oh? Lovely, Paul. And does Griffith know all this?"

"Not that I can tell. Griffith's a real plastic 'no feeling's' sort of a man, from the outside."

"Though you have this one-up on him 'bout his wife, do you fear consequences because of his rank?"

"Somewhat. He acts imperious about my divorce, about you and I yet he can't keep his own wife at home."

"So I'm to be ...?"

"Just be, y'know ...flexible. I don't know what else is on for tonight. Dinner is to be with Clifford and Griffith, Mr. Stumpf probably, Corrigan, others, I'm not sure who all. I'm hoping it's just a contrived show of good faith, bury of hatchet, and so on." He started toward the door again. The palm went up.

"Bright and witty then? Or cheeky?" He liked that her sarcasm had returned.

He stopped and faced her again. The palm dropped. "Bright and witty, please!"

"Virginal and innocent?"

"With that body in that dress? These guys aren't dead, Cyn."

"Bright and witty, I can do. Let us address virginal anything, later …at Amber Lane."

Paul tucked his gloves inside his hat, placed his hat under his left arm and took both of her chilled hands. "Amber Lane? I didn't think that was a possibility, considering …"

"Kurt has gone off to Chenny's, to Kowloon to pout, and more."

"I remember a gun in a drawer next to the bed." He tried a laugh that ended in a stuttered moan.

"Shh. We're denying, remember? I elect not to cry any more tonight. I want my disposition to match this dress."

She moved quickly toward the door. The door opened, Paul did not notice the man's palm. *"Suan ku la duzi' doufu ge …"* A stream of unflattering Chinese warmed the air as the door closed behind them. Paul didn't notice he had stiffed the doorman.

In the inner lobby several conventionally dressed couples and singles were coming and going. Some sat in the alter lobby off to the left, in twos and fours. Almost everyone seemed taken by Cynthia's cape, Madonna scarf and piercing heeled appearance. Where men scrutinized her openly, women glanced furtively, but glanced again. Paul checked his hat and gloves and habitually reached for her cape.

"By the by." She said quietly through a smile. "We're being monitored by everyone." A touch of seldom seen self-consciousness flashed on her face.

"I've noticed.

"I've dressed for *you*, Sir, not for the world heah.' I'll keep my cape in place until my nerve improves. Even the crowd at Frenchie's struggled some with this dress …understand?"

"Of coahse'." He mimicked her accent and took her elbow to guide her toward the dining room. "I want this to be nice." He managed.

Eager to share this favored place, he ignored the curious faces and without actually pointing them out, hoped she would admire the colonial touches, the European architecture, the fine furniture pieces, the *Bogart* air, the incongruous softly played rock-and-roll music. He wanted her to beam as she often did when he showed her something from his world. Something was different, however, and she knew he noticed it.

"I'm really fine." She said in response to his questioning look. "The denial isn't as locked in as I would put forward. I'm also a trifle self-consciousness, perhaps. I'd ratha' it were two hours from now."

She studied the lobby with purpose, even stepped to the beaded doorway and inspected the dim bar. Two British naval officers came out of the beads and startled her. They stood to read a menu poster supported on an easel but it was clear they were checking her over.

Turning her back to Paul, she spoke and turned for him to remove her cape. "Screw it." She said in a soft voice, turned her back to him and added; *"Nous voici donc a Monique's"*

"English please?"

"So this is Monique's." With a shrug the cape fell into his hands, the imaginations of the onlookers confronted the reality. Responsive comments drifted to them. "By jove." In a provocative and alluring sense, she was easily the most beautiful woman to have ever walked through the doors and there was some apprehension that she might erupt over the top of the sculpted bodice of the dress. Conversations momentarily stopped in the lobby.

In the noticeable quiet, Paul saw an unsmiling Monique looking straight at him from next to the registration desk. She jerked her eyes from his. Puzzled, he walked toward her. "Monique?" With an exaggerated hip wiggle, nose in the air, she walked quickly right past him and off to the left into the dining area. "What?"

Dartmouth, the registration clerk he'd known for years skittishly looked away and busied himself with paperwork. Cynthia saw the odd scene but didn't address it as Paul turned back to her.

At that instant two British officers came out of the bar beads and walked past Cynthia. One said to the other: "Jolly best looker since the continent, Sean."

"I agree with that guy." Paul said quietly, taking her hand.

Suddenly several uniformed Truaxe officers steamed into the lobby from the dining room. Commander Griffith led the way, then Corrigan, Lieutenant Stumpf, Commander Deiter, Patrick Balkin also, and Ensign Merryweather, with a couple of others. Captain Clifford was not among them.

"This is the gang for dinner." Paul touched her elbow to begin introductions.

Commander Griffith accepted the first introduction with a cold nod you might expect from someone who doesn't leave a reflection in a mirror. Commander Deiter offered a polite 'how-de-do', Corrigan stared at her décolletage, but, most of all, as each officer was introduced, they said the proper phrases, walked on by and clustered inside the front entrance. Lieutenant Stumpf sauntered in close to Paul, took Cynthia's hand, gave only mini-seconds to staring, and then expressed how he looked forward to meeting the 'Lady from Hong Kong.' He then whispered to Paul "The world went to hell in the dining room a few minutes ago. Captain Clifford chased us all away."

"What."

"He's waiting for you … Both of you. He's now scrambling to get a smaller table."

"Are you serious?"

"Chief, hear me. Griffith messed up the invites. We ate early, without you and Clifford. We assumed you both stood us up. What do I know? Something about Griffith saying 1900, Clifford said 9:00 p.m. Who's to know? Now he's promised to meet us at *The Diggers*, that officer's watering hole off Lockhart Road, at eleven p.m. Personally, I'm heading back to the ship."

Griffith, Ensign Merryweather and Balkin circled back to Stumpf under the pretense of hurrying him. Balkin pulled Paul aside by the arm and whispered.

"As you astutely described to David and me, it's very political on Truaxe. I'm playing follow the leader for now, but we've got to talk on board." He nodded to Cynthia, "I sincerely hope we meet again and wish the best to you both."

"Who is that? He's handsome." Cynthia whispered.

"Part of the Selesky story. Details at eleven."

Meanwhile, Griffith came out of the *Dracula* character, stepped back from the door and made small talk with Cynthia. Paul caught the tail end of. " …and, I repeat, I apologize for being a chapter from *Bell, Book and Candle*, Ms. Howser. I'm sure we'll meet again. Good evening for now."

Merryweather's homesickness spoke to Cynthia. "Look, ma'am." He said with a hat tip. "You are just too lovely to plain walk away from without a comment. You've caused me to miss home. My wife is also very beautiful."

"Thank you. Thank you."

"Well." Vincent said as they watched the officer's snake out into the cold and now rainy night. "Now what?"

"You warned me to be flexible."

Two well-dressed Oriental men standing by registration turned and spoke in Mandarin directly to Cynthia. Though one of them smiled, the words didn't sound friendly. Expensive look aside, Paul saw them as street-wise higher-ups, Triad type men who would have a weapon hidden strategically somewhere on their body. Cynthia seemed to totally ignore their remarks and stepped quickly close to Paul.

"I have a bad feeling." She said.

"Coupl'a jerks. What'd they say?"

"It's not them. I shouldn't have come here …"

"My ship's gang was a bit too coarse? Okay, maybe even cheap. Sailors stare at floating cleavage … "

She said, looking nervously around. "It's not that, at all."

"You're right. You're upset … " He again took her lightly by the arm. She pulled away. "Can I take you someplace to wait for me while I speak to the Cap'n?" Even as he spoke, however, an internalized warning voice stopped his sudden need to pull her out of there. There was something new in her portrait, more going on than bouncing off the officer's stares and the major fallout with Kurt. What is it? He asked inside.

"The dinner idea is gone to hell here." He said touching her arm. "Let's see the Captain. There'll be an explanation …then, in-out, we'll get on our way."

She turned to face him. Her face muscles seemed fixed.

"What?" He asked, and suppressed asking "*NOW* what?"

The officers and captain's odd behavior, there was also something about Monique's behavior, Dartmouth not speaking to him, the two Chinese thugs speaking openly to her. He pushed for a laugh. "Maybe this place isn't just a military version of Frenchie's."

"Comparing Frenchie's to Monique's," she said, "is like jasmine to sewer gas." She said, and again turned her back to him. "Time to return my cape." She moved into the cape and closed it tightly at the neck with one hand. "This dress was okay at Frenchie's," she said, "but not here. This is moah' like a watering hole fa' people without left wings. Drink, dine and who cares. Agree?"

"You got it."

"I imagine, if someone disappears upstairs with a …you-know, no one says anything?"

"Not openly. But I'm sure there is in-house gossip." He spoke from experience but hoped it showed as speculation.

"I can't see the fun here, not in the state I'm in, Paul. Does your Doctor Selesky have any tips I can use on strengthening my denial?"

"Tranquilizers, a few. Martini, perhaps. Home, being held close."

"Which are we closest to? Wait! Don't answer." The remark came with a touch of a second forced smile.

He knew it was no good to try to talk her into having a feeling that just was not available to her under the circumstances. Leading her into the dining room area, he said: "We'll be in and out of here before anyone you know sees us." The dining room greeter broke that wish immediately. "G'd eve'n, Ms. Howser." The 110 pound stoop-shouldered Chinese man spoke raspy but understandable English. "Fine to see you here again. I trust Mr. Kurt is well?" Turning to Paul as though favoring a stiff neck, he asked in a haughty sort of way: "I'll take your hat and gloves, Master Chief?" Stiff necking back to Cynthia: "Your wrap, Madam?"

Surprised by the man's familiarity, neither Paul nor Cynthia moved or said a word.

"This way then, please." His face expressionless and with a toe-in limp, the small man led them through the short hallway to the headwaiter's station. "Wait here, please, Ms. Howser, Master Chief." He handed Paul two menus, turned and was gone.

"I don't know him, Paul." Her surprise was much like when she'd discovered she couldn't stand the taste of an American hot dog.

"He knows your name." Paul said matter of fact but her face said 'no comment, please!' She dropped her small purse and Paul picked it up.

"Love?" She said, "I've bungled this. I can't stay here."

"He's from some other dinner house, Cynthia." He said. "Be reasonable."

"It's not just him knowing my name. That was just the overkill. It's more, much more. I'm so sorry, but." She looked directly in his eyes, but had trouble holding hers there. "It's about what I have *not* yet told you."

Dread overcame Paul. "There's *much* more to the letter story, isn't there?"

"Yes …*a great good deal* more."

His coping mechanisms were grossly strained. "Christ, Cynthia, there's one inquisition here already."

Her eyes became widened, she gripped his arm with strong fingers and spoke between stiff lips and closed teeth. "My tenseness is deserved. You're not listening to me. I cannot pull this off. I want to …run." She grabbed his right arm. "We should run."

"But … I don't understand …"

A hand touched Paul's left shoulder. "Master Chief?"

"WHAT?" He asked—too loud, as he jerked—too fast.

Captain Robert Clifford stood there, startled, but also startling them. He grimaced, grabbed Paul's left arm and spoke rapidly. "Come with me, quickly."

"Wait!" Paul jerked his arms inward and broke the grips of both Clifford and Cynthia. "What?"

"I been lookin' for ya'. We gotta' talk." Clifford's eyes were glowing, his face was red.

"Wait!" Paul said.

"Oh, yes." Clifford noticed Cynthia and ignored Paul. "And this is your friend … Miss. . Miss …"

Cynthia clasped a hand on Paul's arm and repeatedly squeezed it. One, two, three. He interpreted her signal that he was to straighten up, begin it all again.

"Cynthia Howser, please meet Captain Robert Clifford." He said.

Smiling beautifully she repeated a rapid succession of light squeezes to Paul's arm that he discovered said: "Watch me do this." With a clever and seemingly practiced series of moves, she inhaled deeply, deftly dropped one shoulder which floated the cape to one hand, took Clifford's hand with the other, caught his eyes in a manner to melt a heart, murmured four complimentary phrases about him, his ship, his navy and his country, and within seconds, completely captured the man's full attention.

Paul was excessively impressed. He'd never seen her use charm to that degree on anyone at anytime for any reason, except, of course, on him. He caught her eye and peered: 'well, aren't you something?' She grinned back: 'aren't you glad I'm on your team?' She was suddenly a different person from the pleading Rachael-like woman who begged to ruin a moment ago.

Clifford dropped her hand and stammered. "Please, come join me …please?" The man was pleading but Vincent was ready to beg off and leave.

"Captain? I understand dinner is off."

"Yes. No. Follow me, please." He consciously looked directly into Cynthia's eyes. "Both of you, come." It sounded demanding. Clifford stepped ahead of them into the large and crowded dining room. They followed. Paul touched her arm as she walked slightly ahead. With her cape over one arm, her appearance turned heads in their direction but the two of them hardly noticed.

"You okay now?" He asked.

"I'm okay. Your Captain is not okay." Clifford had surged way ahead of them.

"The way you changed back there? Now we know why men fight wars over women."

"I'd lost sight of the importance of this meeting. I'm back now."

"But, you said there's more to the letter story."

"More, yes. But later. Like on the telly and as you say, Paul 'details at 11'. When I saw that frantic man …knowing he is your Captain? I have to re-focus."

"What is this 'more later'?"

"I'll simply tell you later."

"There's nothing 'simple' tonight." He said. "I'm afraid for you. Why am I?"

"Don't be. I think we're fine now."

"You *think* we're fine. *Think?* Why wouldn't we be?"

She slowed, very in control compared to when they were in the outer lobby.

"Here, give me your arm." She directed. "Be a true escort, in the British sense."

"But you hate the way they treat women."

"Like trophies? Not so bad under these circumstances."

He stopped her for a minute and let Clifford go even farther ahead. "I've never felt us like this. Something is between us."

She displayed the first truly tranquil look he'd seen since they'd entered Monique's. "*Nothing* can get between us, Paul, evah. Not now." She led him with one hand toward Clifford. Just before they caught up to the Captain she looked back but didn't stop walking. "I love you, Pool Vinzant."

"But … "

They found the Captain standing by a large cluttered table, holding a drink in one hand and arguing with a waiter. Clifford handed the unsmiling man a few folded bills. Cynthia looked at Paul with a question mark. Paul addressed Clifford. "Captain, I just spoke to Lieutenant Stumpf, in the lobby. He said …"

"They're assholes." Clifford long-necked toward the lobby entrance, and then sipped from his drink. Some diners were looking at them curiously.

"They." Vincent continued. "Lieutenant Stumpf said you wanted to see us."

"He said that, did he? I assumed you weren't even coming tonight."

"The dinner was at nine, Captain. We're on time.'

"Really?"

Cynthia stepped in. "When you first walked up to us, Captain, you said something to Paul. You said, 'come with me, quickly. We've got to talk', correct?"

"Perhaps. Maybe … I … "

"What's going on, Cap'n?" Vincent asked.

"I'm sorry, Chief. Look, I'm sorry to both of you." The waiter appeared and ushered them to a table set for three in a small raised alcove behind and overlooking the main dining area.

"A hurried table for three?" Cynthia said. "My word, Deah'." She clipped her accent strongly, joshing at the man she hardly knew. "You surely *were* expecting us, I see."

"Yes. Well … Yes … Sort of …"

"Captain. The officers said you chased them away, to meet them later at *The Diggers*."

"They said that? It must be true. True, I chased them away. They wouldn't listen to reason."

"What reason?"

"They didn't *want* to work out the problems I feel exist. They had dinner early. Said they'd remembered the invitation as 7:00 p.m. Said they thought it was just you and I and Ms. Howser here. Griffith knew better, for sure." He fingered the waiter and without asking, ordered brandy for three. "That early dinner was a complete disregard for protocol."

"A simple mistake, Cap'n?"

Clifford was staring down at his brandy. "Huumph, to Griffith. An' who the hell's that Balkin guy? Why'd we get him?"

"To hell with him." Paul said. "Listen, Sir. If the object was to get Griffith and company to see you and I model something positive, hell, we're doing it right this moment."

"Sort of. Let's have dinner now." Clifford managed. "They've all left, I am sure. But, I can tell them later we had dinner."

"All things considered, I'd like to beg off from dinner. "Paul said evenly. "First night together and all."

"We are going to talk, Vincent." His mood took a long turn, bad. "First night or last night. I don't give a shit."

Cynthia excused herself and quickly was up and away from the table, purse in hand, cape left behind. The Captain was on his feet.

"Where she goin'? I offend her? By God, Chief. That's an extraordinarily beautiful woman. I know you want to be with her. She comin' back?"

"I think she's insulted. We'll likely be leaving, Cap'n."

"Shit, shit." He was a little drunk. "You runnin' off too?" He ordered another brandy. "I need you with me, later."

"Wait a minute. I'm to be part of the scene at *The Diggers?"*

"I thought …" Clifford was suddenly having trouble tracking.

"After everyone has a face full of booze?" Paul said. "Is *NOT* the time to do PR"

"I thought," Clifford tried again, "when they had dinner without us? I sorta' thought we'd catch up to them, Chief. But you are right. I don't want to go to *The Diggers*. Hell, I don't even want to go back to my ship. Hear me?"

"I don' understand."

"You heard me. Someone purposefully designed the evening to where you wouldn't have a chance, Chief."

"Pardon?"

"I'm being pushed to court martial you." Clifford said quietly.

"And you can't do it, can you?"

"No. I can't and I won't. They want me to. Corrigan, Griffith, some others. They know it's my decision and I told them I wouldn't do it."

"*Couldn't*—do it." Vincent reminded, strongly.

"God, you can be an asshole, Vincent." Clifford said sucking in cigarette smoke.

"I'm sorry, Sir." Paul said. "But, sounds like anything of value coming from this evening is ruined, agree?"

"No, something's going on among them. That's why I meant it when I said I might not go back to my ship."

Cynthia returned to a silent table and sensed the tension. Her thoughts spun. If this is the tempo of the evening, I'll soon see this man I've chosen manage life as it comes. But, even if he comes with me tonight, what I say later might cause him to *reject me before this night is completely over.*

Paul sensed her tension. His thoughts also spun. If this is the tempo of the evening, I'll soon know if she can accept how I must deal with the pressures unfolding here. To insure *we* have a future as a couple, I have to insure I have one without a court's martial. What I do might cause her to *reject me before the night is completely over.*

Clifford reacted to the tension. If this is the tempo of the evening, Clifford thought, his basic flaw is exposed and naked. If I court martial Vincent, he'll get me for the shooting and that'll cost me my admiral stripes, or more. If I fold to that pressure, I'll lose face with my officers. The word will leak out, and that too will cost me admiral. Griffith has rejected me, now Vincent is rejecting me. The navy will *reject me before the night is completely over.*

"We'll have one drink with you, Cap'n." Vincent said assertively. Nodding and pointing, Vincent signaled the waiters. Two of them appeared and cleared away the setups.

The Captain ordered still another brandy for the three of them though Paul's and Cynthia's glasses sat two deep on the table.

While the waiters cleared the table, Cynthia looked at Paul and chanced a whispered "are we having fun yet?" It was suddenly more important to hear her unfinished feature story than support Clifford's need for PR order and discipline. He'd take a chance he could manage the disturbed Clifford at another time.

"Captain, sorry this didn't work out." He got up from his chair. "She and I have got to go now."

"Wait. What? Why?"

Cynthia put a hand on Paul's arm, pulled him back into his chair, and took over. "Similar to yours, Captain, our previously well planned lives have taken an unanticipated turn we positively had not planned for. Being here at one point in support of you and Paul was important enough for me to forgo my troubles, our troubles. Howevah, we can't forgo them in favor of too much brandy and some senseless broken protocol." She followed her statement with a look that asked silently 'is that clear enough for you?'

Clifford turned back from his brandy. "Look, there's something good between you two. Right?" He put both hands into the air in an 'I don't judge anyone' pose, then reached for the brandy with those same hands. He hadn't heard a word she said.

Cynthia creased her brows. "I am a devoted sort," she said to Paul, "but this is a bit ridiculous …agree?" Clifford, leaning forward, elbows on the table, cradled the brandy in his palms. "Amber color," he said, then turned to Cynthia. "God woman, you stand up for him don't you? He's got you, hasn't he? Hell, I have nothing. My wife refuses to come over! It's not even the money. Melinda merely invents excuses. I say 'merely,' but she never does anything 'merely'."

He broke into a rambling monologue about his wife and family that switched to become a diatribe about Vincent and the ship, about Vincent handling men, Vincent being a good communicator, about being a good OOD—'the best, the best.' Cynthia offered polite attention while checking her watch.

" Paul likes your navy." She said when he slowed.

"Paul? Paul is it? Paul R. Vincent … 'navy-liker'." He turned his face from her to him. "Y'know?" He laughed. "Vincent? Can I call you Paul?" He laughed again, a somewhat brutal snicker. "I see something in you I don't see an over abundance of among enlisted men.

Paul looked at Cynthia. She shrugged and the shrug said: "I'll give this a moment more if you wish." Clifford sensed they were leaving and spoke up. "You can't leave, you guys. Listen! You and I have the same minds, the same abilities …" He looked at his upturned palms.

"And?" Paul said trying to move Clifford along to a point of closure.

"And …you've used yours different than I. Better, wiser. You get jobs done."

"Brandy's talking."

"Don't be embarrassed." Clifford insisted.

"I'm not embarrassed, Captain. We have to go."

Clifford looked at Vincent's face, then to Cynthia. "You've got it all, Vincent. Don't you? Shit. I don't have anything, 'cept maybe a universally cold wife and a university' bastard father." He turned to Cynthia. " …the navy work seems easy for Vincent, here. Hassles roll off his back." He brought one finger into the air toward her. "He advertised you as an astute and interesting woman. Are you waiting for him?"

"You mean tonight? Or for the future."

"Both …either."

"Both are correct. But." She pointed upward, Clifford followed with his eyes. "I suspect a man-to-man conversation is hanging over the table …"

"Man to man?"

"Awaiting a clearance that shan't be granted until I'm gone. Is it true?"

"Maybe, Ms. Cynthia. Has he told you of our recent ...incident?"

"A taxi ride outline."

Clifford hunched his shoulders and pulled his brandy closer. He looked around to see who might be within earshot. A waiter stood nearby looking bored. A lone moth landed on the table, bounced against the hot candleholder and fell to the tablecloth.

"Dead." Clifford said. "Lookit' that. Dead. Right?" He turned slightly and faced Vincent. "Like those rice paddy people?" Then he threw it right out. "What the fuck those NVA's do that for?"

"That was my question, Cap'n."

"It was them who set off this chain for us. Over this stupid fuckin'—s'cuse my French,—war, ma'am, Cynthia."

"It's a bad war, Captain Clifford." Cynthia agreed.

"Please call me Robert."

It changed to Robert and Cynthia and Paul. Soon it would be 'buddy' and 'Honey' and 'Pal.' Vincent signaled the waiter and motioned for coffee all around. He learned from Rachael's drunken crowd that it didn't sober them but it often kept them from falling down. He did not want to end up Clifford's nightlong care-taker.

"Let me 's'plain somethin' t' ya' two." I hate a war we fight over principle. Ethics, religion and that shit—s'cuse my French again—I like a war where we go after someone's STUFF. Those were the good wars. Land, gold, water rights ..." he burped. " ... Rape and pillage, well ...not rape, Ma'am." He was off on a Rachael-like drunken lecture. Vincent nodded to move to the door. Cynthia agreed. Clifford was still rambling. " ...and its a crushin' strain t' hold the whole ball o' wax together."

Cynthia mocked him openly. "It's lonely here at the top?" Clifford didn't hear her, or it didn't sink in.

"This path to admiral's been laid out for me since I was in'na womb." He stuck his thumb in his mouth mocking an infant. "That's what I want. Admiral number three—number four, in the family pack ..." He leaned back in his chair, lost his balance, caught it, and said, "Perseverance is what it takes."

"Mr. Stumpf said it takes obsession, Cap'n." Clifford wasn't hearing.

"I almost got the navy licked but this fuckin' super Chief here?" He shifted his gaze to Cynthia and curled one hand slowly into a ball and looked from it to her face. "He'd feed on a man's heart while it was still beating." He leaned back in his chair and open handed himself on the cheek, hard. "He slaps me." He leaned back to Cynthia. "My father's slapped me. No one else."

"You've had too much to drink, Captain."

Clifford was tugging something out of his shirt pocket. "Listen to this. You'll love it, I know." He unsteadily but carefully unfolded a wad of toilet paper. "I saw this in the men's room at the China Fleet Club and wrote it down. Now listen ..." He moved the paper back and forth to focus in the candlelight. "The U.S. Navy is composed of incompetents ...leading the unwilling …to do the unnecessary …now catch this part …on behalf of the ungrateful.' Whew!" He tossed the paper table-center. A corner of it struck the candle flame and began a slow burn. Paul balled it into a knot and dropped it into an untouched brandy glass. The brandy ignited. Clifford immediately placed an open palm over the glass and snuffed it out. He examined his palm, said nothing, and continued talking.

"That says it, huh? Incompetents, unwilling, unnecessary, for the fucking ungrateful, 'S'cuse my French. Which am I, Vincent? Which are you, Vincent? Which are you, lady? Don't answer. "

"During the firing incident?" Vincent replied. "I saw you as the *incompetent* leader, Cap'n. Yes. And I was *unwilling* to fire on the V.C. The farmers deaths were totally *unnecessary*. "

Clifford counted three fingers with the tip of a thumb. "Incompetents, unwilling, unnecessary'." He said. "Wanna' try for 'ungrateful'?"

"Me maybe." Vincent offered, not mocking the man. "Maybe you."

"You're both wrong." Cynthia spoke authoritatively. "The Vietnamese who asked for U.S. help originally? Perhaps are the ones most *ungrateful* ."

'Woah, lady. You are a tough one. But, the graffiti has a point …"

"It's ancient angry graffiti, Robert." Cynthia affirmed. "Simply that. A provoked soldier on R and R. Don't be a simp. The words of the prophets are *not* written on the walls of the loo."

"Don't talk down to me, dammit." He flared. "Listen, lady. God, that's quite a dress. In my career? Throughout my career? I've backed everyone down who called me on my shit. That fucking Griffith's got some cross of some kind to bear …but he tried to bully me one night in San Diego and I backed even that sly fucker down."

"He called you on screwing up training." Vincent confessed. "Said if we weren't trained …someone would die. I overheard it."

"You did?"

"Yes."

"And I backed him down, right?"

"You blackmailed him with a fitness report …"

"Never. You misread, misheard." He turned back to Cynthia. "I backed down the mucky-muck Griffith. He's weak … "

"I don't see him weak." Vincent said, curious about the reference.

"Vanity? It says 'Arnold Griffith'. That's his weakness. Afraid for his career and his image. Everyone has a weakness, Vincent. What's yours? Can't stay away from women?" His remark quieted both Cynthia and Paul. "What?" Clifford demanded. "No weaknesses? Is he afraid of me? No. Afraid for his career? Hell no. He calls me incompetent …and slaps me. He even jeopardized seeing you …and lady, I admire him. I wouldn't jeopardize seeing you."

"You're still in college, Robert." Cynthia said for shock value. "You still relish power over reason."

"Power over reason? That's a buzzy sentence. There is no reason left. I've shot my wad, and, and, you know what, lady?"

"I know you start sentences before thinking, Sir." She said. "Also, Captain, you seem very drunk, struggling with something." Cynthia seemed to still hold compassion for the man.

"I don't give a damn if I've shot my wad, or what you think." He pulled away. Cynthia picked up her purse. Unaware of a tradition that was playing out in front of her, she turned to leave.

"Cynnie, hang in there a minute?" Paul said sharply. "We don't walk away and leave a damaged man who is also in command of a U.S. warship."

"Skipper?' Paul asked. "I'm taking you to bed, upstairs." He tugged Clifford's shoulder. Clifford didn't flinch or withdraw. His mood swung, softer.

"I'm not in control anymore, Vincent." His head waved from side to side. "This war has killed my career." He dabbed his eyes with a linen napkin from the table. Paul looked around. They were the last diners. The waiters were out of sight but surely aware of the emotional scene.

"Look, Those hours I spend in my quarters are nothing but crying jags. I tell Griffith my eyes are red from a cold. What's he know?"

"You are clinically depressed, Robert." Cynthia made a valid diagnosis.

"Depressed? Yes. The same thoughts go 'round and 'round in my head." He dropped his head and waved it from side to side.

"You've jumped through all the right hoops to get something you thought you wanted? But the game has no real prize at the end, has it?" Cynthia concluded for him. "

"Huh?"

"No real prizes, right?"

"Maybe."

"But tonight you see it has no real value anymore." Cynthia continued Paul's line. "Right?

"Maybe."

"Welcome to the club ..." Paul grouched.

"Club? We goin' to *The Diggers*? What club?"

"What club? The, navy-life-is-bullshit, what-the-hell-good-am-I, is-this-all-there-is, mid-life-crisis-is-really-mid-life-opportunity-club. That club." Paul said, proud he was able to put it all in line.

Clifford sat quietly for a few seconds but he was too drunk to access anything of psychological value.

After almost a minute, he said direct to Cynthia. "Griffith's urged me to saddle Vincent here with the boat trip, but denied that later. In my quarters? I watched his mind work when he was getting ready for the boat trip. Vincent here turned off everything except getting ready for that mission. I admired him. Shit. I wanted to be like him. But with him ashore my heart got pounding. Going in on that gun run with you calling the shots?" He turned to Cynthia. "I was afraid I wouldn't do what Vincent wanted."

That shocked Paul.

"Vincent here wanted one thing, Griffith didn't agree. CIC and the intelligence officer, that Valentino? Kept asking me what to do. I was trying to think clearly, don't you see? I fucked up that shooting. I think I killed those men ...unnecessarily." They watched him swallow hard and fight back tears.

Paul and Cynthia stayed silent and noticed the music no longer played from hidden speakers.

"I was coping 'til you came along, Vincent. One day at a time I could keep my thoughts lined up. You wanting to capture those V.C.? That was the kinda' things I dream of. But it was too big, too much to cope with." He began to whine as a child might. "I'm a small coping person. I know that. Dad knows that. I pretend I'm not …but … "

"You're too tough on yourself." Cynthia offered. "They didn't elect you Captain because you're a fool."

"They don't elect, lady …you pull strings. You cheat on scores, on inspections, on tests. Any string you find? You pull. Incompetents and unwilling, remember? For the fucking ungrateful. My father's bowed and scraped for me. I know he has. That's why I'm Captain."

"So what?"

"If the word gets out on the killings? We killed those CIA agents? I'll never be promoted to a staff job. Never get my star. That's what."

The practiced waiter returned and silently refilled Clifford's coffee cup. Clifford sipped from it and pulled his head back, examining the contents of the cup. He set it down and picked up a nearly empty brandy glass. He drained it and made a soured face.

Vincent tried to think of Selesky's empathic cool even sentences. "So you never get stars. Is that so important to you?"

"It *IS* me, godammit …until you came along." He swung his arm backhanded and sent glasses, cups and a candleholder flying to smatter against the nearby wall. Clifford's gaze followed the mess.

It was ridiculously beyond decorum but Paul tried to recover it all. "Wait. We'll be home in a few months. You'll get the stars. No one's out to stop the stars. Hell, we'll be home soon, we can all relax, away from this war."

"I hassle at home. I never relax. My father's on my ass. Melinda's on my ass. The kids want money money money. She and the kids are some of those up-noses who think there's no life east of the Coronado bridge." He leaned toward Vincent and whispered. "Tell you what I'm gonna' do? Catch me a first class airliner, tonight. Go to Kansas someplace …someplace where they don't know what a ship is. Wait!" He sat upright, ignoring the mess on the table and the crunch of glass under foot.

He turned to Cynthia. "Can I pull it off, lady? Can I really continue to make 'em think I'm okay? That I'm not too, out of it?" He tried to focus on her through his drunken haze. "Do you? Do you?" Surprised by his direct question, she struggled for something to say. He jerked his eyes to Vincent.

"You tell me, Vincent. You know every-fuckin'-thing …you fuckin' know-it-all." The pressure transferred. Vincent tried.

"We'll go back to the ship, Cap'n. Everything will be okay. We'll go back to plane guard duty and just play the game by the rules."

"Good thought, Paul." Cynthia tried to help. "Robert, you're pulled one way by traditional navy thinking, pulled an opposite way by new feelings. Am I right?"

"You're the know-it-all." His comment was smart mouthed, but his eyes were locked to hers. She kept trying.

"The new feelings question the old ones, correct?" She sat back in her chair again. "You and Paul are actually very much alike right now." Vincent bumped her elbow.

He saw no humor in the comparison but he saw immediately how she had played Clifford's card of admiration for Paul.

Clifford's brow furrowed. She'd gotten to something in him. She took advantage of the calm to break the pattern at the table.

"We all need sleep. Let's continue in the morning, breakfast. Approach the new day with new … "

Clifford stood up and leaned frontward against the table. It skittered under his weight. He was embarrassingly rumpled looking and red faced.

"You must promise, right now, you'll stand by and let me take you to Captain's mast, Vincent." He nearly fell forward. "Fuck you if you don't. I'll not court martial you over the slap. Not that. Just some harmless, non-judicial punishment . . to, to …" He stood upright and tried looking about the room, but kept losing his balance.

"To save your damned career?" Vincent finished.

Clifford stared at Paul but, hopelessly drunk, his eyes were not focusing. "Where's that Griffith?" He cried out. "Let's tell him."

"Paul?" Cynthia had her purse in her hands. She'd had enough. "He's too drunk for knowledge."

Paul stood next to the weaving man and signaled the waiters.

"We've warmed and kissed his bum for nearly two hours … If there's a man in there someplace … ?"

"Well, I can't tell if the man, the drunk or the nut will eventually emerge." Paul said. "I wish his father were here tonight. Sounds like he's part of the shit we're seeing."

Monique was there with three of her waiters. She was as stern faced as when she ran from him in the lobby. Cynthia pulled her cape from the back of her chair, stepped back and became curiously very alert.

Paul addressed Monique. "Can you take care of the Captain?" He asked. Monique locked eyes with him, spread her legs until they pressed outward against the light slim maroon skirt, and took a strong pull on her cigarette. "*Pourquoi, Paul, c'est la vie.*" Seeing the questioning look on his face, she switched to fractured English. "Soch ees' the life of a drunk." Smoke came puffing out with the words.

Clifford put up a little verbal struggle but slowly gave in to the firm grips of the waiters who stood holding him, waiting for orders. Monique said nothing. Cynthia spoke.

"Take him to room Twenty-three." She said to the waiters. The three started maneuvering Clifford toward the door. Monique looked icily both at Paul and at Cynthia where her eyes swept the scarf and her bosoms.

She smirked "everyone to their own taste". Paul, confused, asked why she was so snippy.

She looked at Vincent but tossed her head toward Cynthia. "*Demander Hollandaise femme.*" She spit.

"What?"

"She said to ask the Dutch woman." Cynthia said without affect.

"Why ask you. How would you …?"

"Il ne comprends pas correspondance toute le monde?"

Cynthia responded with confidence. *"Ici on parle English tant mieux, mon ami, Paul. Quand meme, mot juste*—Fuck you, bitch."

The 'fuck you, bitch' Paul understood. "What the hell you saying? Monique? What's she saying, Cynthia? Goddammit, SPEAK ENGLISH." He yelled.

Cynthia was busy fastening her cape in place as she spoke to Paul. "She says you should ask *me* why I have …connections …connections here. Could order the waiters to room so-and-so. I told her, for your sake to speak in English. I also told her to get fucked."

"Monique? Cynthia? You know each other?"

"Oui."

"Yes."

Confusion reigned. He had years of intimate history with both women. To find them linked in some way spun his projective imagination. He almost bolted, but something stopped him. ""Either of you, tell me." He demanded. "What the hell's going on here?"

Monique spoke slowly. "The Dutch lady …ees. . the trouble here tonight." She pointed toward Cynthia. "Ask her what is going-g on."

"I'll ask her nothing." He said thus displaying where his alliance dividing-line lay. He put out one hand to Cynthia. "Let's get out of here."

Monique did not become passive. She stepped in front of Cynthia and, in legs spread stance with hands on hips, spouted. "Ask heem' who he slept weeth' last night?" The open violation of trust took Paul off guard. He looked immediately to Cynthia for reaction. She was impossible to read.

"Listen Monique." Cynthia said in an even voice. "I expected better from you. He knows nothing of this part of my life, as yet. You are cruel and you are unfair. I explained on the telephone to all of you why I had to be here tonight."

"Le shoc, maadam?" Monique's comments were still bitter. She lost him as she switched from English to Chinese, to French, back to English. "Go ahead. Ask sailor who he slept with last night—*nu pe'ngyou Rasha—le femme le plus rapid.* Balcony fountain room."

She did not lose Cynthia, who mumbled offhanded as she reached for Paul's hand. *"Noir le coeur."* She said directly to Monique's face. (Black hearted bitch.)

"Ask heem." Monique pressed. "He keessed me also, een' *le bureau.* He asked me to sleep weeth him. I say *non.'* Monique's double betrayal stupefied and humiliated Paul, but her comments also betrayed something between the two women. Cynthia's face was tense as Monique continued to expose him. "My girls saw Dutch lady's man come from number 55 ship, two days ago. Rasha pay me for stay hees' room, if he come here. Thirty dollars U.S. from her, forty from him, later. How that?"

Cynthia tossed her head proudly, dropped Paul's hand and closed the space between her and Monique's flared nostrils. In caustic monotone, she unloaded. "Listen, you incinerated star; THAT rundown on my man is nothing. You count for nothing and you've told me nothing. You can't get between us, because you *are* nothing. If he kissed you, he kissed no one. If he slept with Rasha, he slept with no one. Get the picture?"

Monique withered for just an instant, and bounced back weakly. "I am not 'notheeng'."

"Listen, catch on, learn it. You do not impact. You are no one ...and you hate that ..." She turned to Paul. "We should leave now."

"How? How do you know her?"

"We must leave now." She repeated, then stepped close to him to whisper: "I will tell you everything ...tonight. I'm sick of the charades of my life."

Despite Cynthia's strong remarks, Monique would not completely deflate. She shifted to Paul but pointed with a shoulder toward Cynthia. "Cynthia *apporter, . .le plus grand le soutin-gorge le sein la robe. ... Lu-Sur Kuoche* ." Monique's too-rapid French was filled with infection. "Ask bitch-lady that, Pool, kuy." Her English was venomous.

Cynthia replied calmly. "*Non, Non, Monique. Mauvais mentir* " (bad lie).

"What?"

"Step back, Paul. This has bottomed out at school girl prattle. She said I've worn this dress here to Lu-Sur Kuoche. That is a lie. I just got it from Tina. Monique knows that."

"How does she know that?"

"Later. Please wait. Patience?" Patronized, Paul took a passive role but hated it.

Monique stepped in front of Cynthia again but now spoke softly, putting a hesitant hand toward her, as though to touch her. "*Dieu defends le droit., Cynthia leAnne. Jeu d'esprit, s'excuse.*"

"What?"

"She is saying she insulted me only as a joke that went too far. I don't believe her for a snatch of an instant."

"Ees correct. I error ...greatly. Please forgive me." She turned to Vincent. "You too, Pool kuy. For the old times? Excuse me?"

"I think you just killed the old times, Monique." He said.

"Pardon?" Monique said.

"*Pei de chose non.*" Cynthia answered for him, softly.

"What?" Paul hated being left out of the French. "What is being said?"

"I told her what you said, that her hatred is not so small a matter to be dismissed easily."

Cynthia pulled her shoulders back, held her head high and shot a plastic smile toward Monique. She said boldly and sarcastically; "Thank you for tonight's hospitality". The last of the Chinese waiters chanced a laugh. Monique glared at him but recovered. She nodded to Cynthia.

"You are ze' most welcome for my 'oospitaletee'." She said, looking very shaken. Whatever he might have missed in the language exchange, Paul surmised, it sure seemed Cynthia had prevailed. He was also now very sure these two had a connection, a relationship of some sort that was not changed even by the anger filled exchanges he witnessed.

A waiter handed Paul his hat and gloves. He tried not to feel numb. His world was pressing in on him. His captain threatened a court martial, or worse. Now, the woman he was blindly releasing his heart to was revealing too much newness, too fast. He could understand the childish coded letter becoming a jealous man's screw-up. Kurt being capable of cruelty was not setting well. Now, this biggest shock: Cynthia connected to Monique. What could that mean? At one end of the spectrum of possibilities, she was an owner, a silent partner to the seedy but lucrative business. Knowing how she and Kurt spent money, that was possible. At the farthest and worst end, he contemplated she was one of the specialized whores. Not possible. His value-center spun. His double-standard sexist-upbringing surged foreword. How could he love a whore?

"Paul?" She said his name but the usual melody was missing.

The room was empty except for their threesome and one waiter. Monique had backed several steps away and stood without expression. Her hands were folded against her taunt belly, thumbs circling one another.

Paul led Cynthia away through the nearly empty lobby and, as they reached the door, Cynthia gave the doorman a small card. "Ask *le garcon* to give this to *Madame* after we leave." With no room left for disappointments, Vincent jerked the card from the surprised man's hand. She had scribbled some French on it that included a telephone number, 428-9330.

"What is this?" Paul asked her.

She said, impatiently. "For Monique. The Captain is to telephone us in the morning." She was surely thinking ahead.

Paul returned the card and some cash to the doorman. As they waited silently in line for a taxi, the music from a bar next door swept onto the street with them.

Will you still love me, tomorrow, the Shirelles.

CHAPTER TWENTY FOUR
Conditional Love

After leaving Captain Clifford at Monique's, they took a taxi to Amber Lane but couldn't draw together. Paul was very plagued by all the recent events in his life. This most recent one, that his Captain was psychotic or alcoholic, or both, made it difficult to have empathy for how Cynthia's life was being hammered into new contours of its own over on her side of the taxi. While his own sense of himself and duty, honor and ethics was being reshaped, she was a woman who'd been presenting an image of being decent, moral and ethical, but who said she was about to openly tell him secrets she could hardly admit to herself.

"Everything's different in here." He said, ignoring the pressing issues as they stepped into her bedroom.

"Yes. Medication I think. You know; when depressed, go shopping?"

The 35 by 18 foot room had been completely and expensively redone in powder blues and white. The soft blue brocatelle edging of the white carpet was picked up everywhere; lamp shades, coverlets, pillow edges, the bedspread and in rich crown molding against the ceilings and repeated in the molding around the fireplace mantel. The same blue was also in the vanity and its padded, wire-back chair, and, in a huge wingback chair. Dried blue-white eucalyptus arranged in stark white vases beside the bed filled the room with a gentle spicy fragrance. The overall effect produced an inviting space, cool by color but warm by design. It was a room for sleeping, thinking, reading, for making love, *or* for having sex. He had all of those with her, in this room.

Duplicating many past nights, Mia delivered tea and cookies to the room but when Paul greeted her she smiled blankly and avoided his eyes. The ambiance being different from scores of other nights, Paul asked himself: 'How blind have I really been?'

Cynthia sat on the edge of her bed, Paul in the winged chair six feet from her. His jacket hung on one wing, his hat and gloves balanced on the other. Neither could give to the other beyond an exchange of weak smiles. Overall, both were silent for the first time ever when together. Selesky said once, very clearly: "When a couple is quiet? That is exactly when they should be talking."

"We should talk now." Paul said in response to Selesky's distant wisdom.

"Yes." She agreed. She tried a smile again but her lips barely expanded.

"Thank you." He smiled at her smile and tried to start the 'talk'.

"For?"

"For you. For walking into Frenchie's as you did. And, even knowing everything could go to hell at Monique's, you went there just to please me. And also ...thanks for the wisdom you used with the Captain."

She didn't answer directly beyond another incomplete smile.

"And with that?" He said, matching her semi-smile. "Tell me everything."

She shrugged her cape free. It slipped to the bed behind her. A deep breath lifted her breasts against the bodice of the magnificent white dress. "It's from a movie." She said following his eyes and referring to the dress. Crossing her shapely legs, presenting the band of her hose on one thigh, she stalled more. "Ava Gardner wore it. I knew you'd like it when Tina showed me a picture. I'll wear it a future evening." He wondered if there would be future evenings for them.

She flicked at a gold pin and unhooked the swaddling scarf. Dipping forward, she carefully unwound it from her neck and head, and then folded it neatly on her lap. Standing, she defiantly threw the scarf toward the vanity chair. It missed. The beautiful woman moved to the vanity mirror and shook her compressed hair free of pins. She fluffed at the unconfined locks halfheartedly, gave up and turned the small swivel chair to face him. He hadn't missed a move. To him, she released the most beauty into the air when seemingly unaware of her beauty.

"What?" She asked his smile.

"The moment. Wow!" His comment came out flat. He wanted to say something about how her beauty wasn't all that he saw, that it simply symbolized this great love he felt with her, but it was too soft to fit into the hard edges of the nights actions. The brief attempts to talk faded into his taking a taste of Mia's flat Asian tea.

She stayed on the swivel chair and faced him with her hands clasped at the front of her knees, fingers interlocked. "This is terrible. I feel squishy inside." Her words seemed without feeling, but they *were* talking again..

"Where is Kurt?" He asked.

"He was so distempered, he went to Kowloon to Chenny's, to his friends there." She became quiet again. He resisted going to her. He wondered what she was thinking though Selesky had cautioned him again and again against trying to read anyone's mind, especially someone you were sleeping with.

Is this the day I lose him? She wondered. She took a tissue from the vanity and crumpled it in one hand causing Paul to wonder —how many tissues were in how many traumatized women's hands in how many conversations in how many rooms in how many countries?

She spoke self-protectively. "Pool Vinzant." Saying his name was part of a stall for time or for correct words.

"Tell me everything." He urged and stayed in his chair.

"I thought I'd lost you when you found Rachael." It surprised him that she went so far back, to Rachael. "But you came back to me then," she continued, "I thought I'd lost for sure when we found I couldn't have a baby. But you came back to me even then, again." She spoke evenly, her accent's inflections faded into their familiarity with one another. "When you married Rachael? I thought again you would be gone forever, to start that family. But, no, you always came back. Now I'm afraid *again*."

"Of?"

She took a deep breath and it caught, almost a sob. "Listen to me. Then, you are free to leave if you wish."

He stayed quiet, braced to stay, but braced also to run.

"After Kurt stole my letter? Picturing you with Rachael?" softly clicking her thumbnail and forefinger, she searched for a word. " …was fucking maddening. Even though Kurt couldn't let on he knew I was reacting to your rejection that *he* caused, he was very kind to me. I see now I became depressed over it all. I grew dreadfully cold about love toward him *and* toward you. Before then, in conversations with friends, Kurt would always say love was actually a stupid childish thing. Though he said there was no such thing as love, I always silently disagreed with him. I felt *something* with you and decided it was love. But when you didn't feel it in return I became very mixed. When you didn't answer my letter, it became easy to sort of join Kurt's ideas that love was bullshit."

"That was about May, 62?" He asked.

"Yes."

"I never detected any changes in you."

" I kept my letters to you as always, light, frothy. Hope stayed alive for a while. Eventually, I gave in."

"Gave in?" She seemed different in manner and voice. He could not pull in all the thoughts and feelings it took to follow what it had been like for her, and still deal with his own anxious anticipation.

"I gave in to something Kurt had always pressured me for." Her eyes avoided his, causing him to wonder what could be so bad that she stalls saying it? She was obviously *extremely* apprehensive.

"I'm mortified, Paul." She said to the ceiling. "After I thought you didn't want me? I became, for him, a …an, agent. A spy." Her face lost its color. The words hung in the air between them. It seemed silly.

"Agent? Spy?" He repeated each word to allow them into the same part of his mind that she occupied. They didn't want to fit there.

"He made me, *made* me." She said with a Rachael-like, world-blaming whine. Then she changed quickly to common-sense, more like the Cynthia he knew: "I *know* I permitted it, but I was … I gave in"

She addressed the expressions that played on Paul Vincent's skeptical face.

"He is a spy, P-Paul." She actually stuttered. "Y-Yes, he's a b-banker. Yes, he assists some c-countries in diplomatic areas. But, but, but the real part of his life is to gather secrets, pass them on …for money, money, cash and jewelry sometimes."

"To whom?" Paul was exceptionally confused but kept his voice calm.

"To the highest b-bidder." She said, shuddering. ""Contacts. *We* get information. He passes it on."

"Who are 'we'?"

"Me, others, many …not too many."

Those few words brought previously disregarded questions to the surface and in microseconds, furnished each with an answer. Kurt's eager and easy friendship had been phony then, contrived. Him never questioning the obvious love affair with Cynthia: a ploy. The willingness to change plans anytime to please Paul's schedule? A trick. The expensive gifts, the quickly answered letters: patronization for favoritism. Casual conversation about the navy, always edging on classified information. It made sudden sense. Paul had clearly been entrapped by his own neediness for friendship with Kurt that led to Cynthia for sex and for love. The transparency of it all crushed his self-esteem. His pride weakened, he felt sudden but permanent damage to his whole sense of self.

He was on his feet. His hat and gloves toppled to the floor from the back of the wing-backed chair. He kicked the hat and sent it flying to crash and clear a vase and two framed pictures from a bed stand. "Fuck." He uttered. "Tricked ...myself this time."

Cynthia flinched but remained still, her fists rolled into knots of tension. Caught up in his hurt, Paul raved. "I've told the bastard about ship's manning levels. Not intentionally, just comparing the military to civilian jobs. We've talked about new gun-mounts while watching old war movies." From pressure of squeezing his fists, the Ben Bristol hand began to thump. "I won that bet comparing the French Mirage to one of our jets. He sucked me right in. I'm a common fucking traitor."

"No, Paul."

"No, Paul? Bullshit, lady. And you were the set-up. I put him on to those disbursing officers from that aircraft carrier. Remember? He made some joke later about some money-swapping scheme. Japanese yen for Hong Kong dollars and back to U.S. dollars. I wasn't sure the impact. Now I see. I was used beyond simply helping a friend." He paced near the French windows that led outside to the deck.

"We all were used." She hoped a meek reminder that she was also tricked could help him not feel so singled out.

"That brings a hell of a question to my mind." He said with hatred close to the surface.

"What?"

He forced his voice to return to calm. "Just say 'yes' or 'no', Cynthia. If it is 'yes,' I'll simply leave." Her eyes snapped to meet his. "Who was I in this?" He asked.

"Who were you? I don't under ..."

"Was I just one contact of many? Was the sex and 'I love you' just a game? I want 'yes', or 'no'."

Her hands flew out toward him. He got his answer: "NO, Oh! NO. NEVER." She too was on her feet.

"How can I trust this? How can I know?" He said, and then added with a flash of angry passion. "Son-of-a-bitch. Does *every* woman bring mistrust and trickery? FUCK me."

Both became locked in the pains of the moment. With self-esteem almost drained, neither could gather the beautiful feelings they normally brought to one another because of their love. Neither realized that comparing the beauty of the past to the turmoil of these moments is what caused this tremendous hurt. Tears ran freely from her but her hands remained locked in front of her. She was unable to move toward him. He seemed equally blocked.

"When we first met," She said shakily. "You *were* to be a contact. My first. Hell, I didn't know you. Kurt had told me on the telephone that you seemed nice, harmless, and a good place for me to start." Hating how cheap it all sounded, 'contact', 'my first', 'harmless', her voice was hampered by several involuntary sobs. "Way back before you and I met, Kurt openly solicited my help. But, I said 'no', too scary." She put her hands out to her sides and looked down at herself but then pulled her shoulders back, dropped her arms and locked her eyes on his. "Look at me. I may not seem so now but do not forget, Paul, I was a naive nurses-aid from a stonewall farm town in northern England. Kurt swept me off my feet, charming me and exciting my Mom with the idea of money and a sense of a nice life for me. I came to Hong Kong and was living the high scene before I really knew the man I was with. He made almost no demands on me as a wife. No budget to care for, sex was bad but only minutes a month. I learned about his real profession, a spy, so slowly …it never really seemed to matter. Over time I realized Kurt was politically omnivorous, usurious and very-very clever. He wanted me to be …to spy. I didn't even know what the hell he meant. He said it was for the money but it was *really* for excitement, his excitement. Please believe this."

"Tell me all of it." He pulled her over to the winged chair. She sat. He instinctively dropped to both knees on the floor in front of her and sat back on his heels. "All the details."

"I …it's so mixed now."

"Talk." He insisted. Could she tell him all, yet expect him not to run away?

"Just when I met you," she said straightforward. "I was *trying* to become a contact woman, for *his* sake. Oh hell, for my sake too. I wasn't anyone then. What would I do? Where would I go if I left here? I wanted to be a full registered nurse, not just a nurse's aid. He laughed at that, but I sneaked in the classes. Became licensed, worked in hospital. When he knew I wanted to be a physician, he teased me, openly. 'Day Dreamer', he called me. He gave me no verbal support. Would actually plan things to interfere with my studies, my homework, my working on research papers. I thought if I humored him about the spying, he'd not complain when I catered to the grueling medical school schedules."

The information swarmed into Paul's sharp mind and searched for companion files. There were none except for similar memories of Ben and Rachael's seedier side as it became known. He hated that this great woman, this Cynthia of his life was fitting into the same space with the contaminated remnants of his marriage. He became more saddened, listening further, he became numb.

"The spying was more like a child's game to me," she went on unevenly. "An unrealistic man's little boy game. I wasn't well read enough to know even what valuable information was. Paul, I wasn't even sure where Vietnam *was* at the time it all started. He assured me spying was easy. He would introduce me around. I pumped for certain military information. We had clue words. It seemed foolish to me but serious to him. You saw it in action the first night, on the veranda out there." She pointed to the deck, only fifteen feet away. "If he asked me a laundry and postal question in front of someone, that meant he wanted me to work on that person."

He remembered clearly the remarks about laundry and 'the post'. He also remembered telling Selesky he thought Kurt was mean for making her responsible for those menial chores. "Was I just one of many?" He again asked, dreading the answer.

"NO, I as-su-re you." She *whined*, very close to the tones Rachael used. "YOU WERE THE FIRST TRY." Her hands flew to her forehead and rolled into fists in what he saw as over-drama. "I need you to believe me, to believe *in* me." She dropped her hands and grabbed one of his. Hers were very warm. "You saw what happened that night." Her voice was pleading. He was confused again.

"I saw what?" He struggled for clarity. Her face mixed with Rachael's and with Ben's.

"You were there, dammit."

"Where?" He actually shook his head and blinked to get her clearly into view.

"That night …at the ovahlook, when we touched. Damn you, Paul Vincent, I fell in love with you." Her breath caught in gasps against the emotional moment. "In Victoria Park?" She threw his injured hand downward, rose out of the chair and stepped around him, to the edge of the bed and turned to face him. "Remember in the Park? That was special when you covered me with my blouse? You protected my shame over my breasts. You took me as I am. You gave me my life's fantasy sailor in the park. You've never laughed at me, evah! I felt different with you than I had ever felt with any man. I felt special and equal."

Her tears ran freely again as her words yanked him directly and accurately back to the evening in the park, so many years past now. He looked for but saw no faked attempt to present a pained expression or voice tone. 'This is NOT Rachael.' He thought. 'It is NOT Rachael. This is Cynthia, the one I came back to'

She again looked him right in the eyes. "I tell you the truth, Paul Vincent."

He had to believe her. He was all she had left. Was she all he had?

"When Kurt saw how stricken I was with you, he built a phony theory about it. He said I would feel like I was in love with *any* contact I made within reason. Said it was some psychological defense against helping him outright, a transference thing that happens in intense relationships. I wondered if he were right, that the love I felt would happen with *any* man I plied for information. He was always such a psychologist. I always forget he has a degree in clinical aspects, from Rotterdam. He said the excitement of spying likely turned me on. But often, some of his theoretical nonsense makes some sense. He manipulates soooo well. I assumed there was something to what he said, at first. Now I realize the spying nonsense is a primordial experience for *him*, erotic, sexual …basic, but not to me. Some out of control nonsense that rules him, and because of circumstances, ruled me."

"What a turmoil of thoughts." He said with true empathy.

"In here," she crossed her arms over her breasts. "In here, I knew. The life-long dream I have of love …is filled by you. It was *not* a stupid transference anything."

She stepped back a step and sat on the edge of the bed. "Girl met boy. Bloody damn shame for Kurt, but, bingo—bango. I fell in love. Do you see now?"

"It's coming together." He turned to face her again and said. "It was to your benefit to play along with his dumb-ass *theory* that you would fall for anyone. In jealousy, he might stop pushing you to spy so much, or at all?"

"Yes, and I was glad. The pressure was over to keep spying but I also had you in my life. I was like a schoolgirl with wet undies over you. I connived. I said I would practice getting information from you. He believed me. He encouraged me to keep writing to you because you were bright, had top-secret clearances as a radio person, and you know a lot about the navy."

"I have to believe this, Cynthia." He said to himself more than to her. "It's too crazy to be made up." Some humor sprinkled to the top of the tension.

"Goddamn right you believe it." She smiled too, and sprung forward from the bed and dropped to the floor in front of him. " I'm being more honest with you and with myself than I've been in years." She said. "I pretended along with him. It seemed harmless and it kept me hypnotized and vicariously close to you."

"You could have told me about it all, from the start."

"Quite so?" She mocked shock. "Be real. Like the first night? I should have said, by-the-by, I'm a bloody spy ...you'd of what?"

"Run." He said, and then added. " ...probably laughed."

"See?" She squeezed his right hand, the injured hand. He inflexibly jerked away from the pain. "No!" She cried out and fell forward against him. They both rolled to the floor. He heard the dress rip.

She rose to her knees and faced him. "You pulled away!" she said frankly.

He pulled the thumping hand close to his chest. "I hurt my hand awhile back. I just flinched."

She reached to softly encircle his neck with her hands and arms. "I thought you were pulling away."

"I'm not." He got to his feet. She was still on her knees. The rip in the dress exposed her entire left shoulder. She lifted the torn flap over that side. A ladder-run appeared below the knee of the hose on her left leg.

She reached her free hand up to him. "Please!" She asked quietly.

Everything was processing at once. He reached for her and lifted her against the pain of his right hand. She fell against him. As he held her close the splendor from the past emerged from the smell of her warm breath, the fragrance of *le Shocking* mixed with subtle odors of her body, the taste of tear-stained hair strands against his tongue as they kissed and re-plighting their troth. "I'm not going anywhere." He said. "I'm here for the long haul."

Reacting *from* the kiss and *to* the words, she pushed her face hard into his shoulder and neck.

"Mostly after we'd made love," she said quietly and evenly, "when you were caressing me, I tried hardest to tell you everything, countless times I started to tell. I pictured I could lay there, tell your safe chest, hear your heart race at first, then become calm again with *complete* understanding, of course. Naïve? Stupid?" She pulled back to see his eyes. "I knew I shouldn't keep a lie between us for very long. But it got out of hand as so many things do."

"I had no idea ..." He said, truly expressing his astonishment of the story.

"I had a premonition though, and Kurt warned me ...that if I ever told you, you *would* run away. You'd convinced me how you hated being tricked by Rachael and Ben, and ... I knew I was tricking you more every day." She flicked her face forward and pecked at his lips just to see if they were still there. Back, to look at his eyes again, she continued.

"I delayed the awful until it became more awful. Tonight, this moment, and this moment, is what I've dreaded for years and I'm here in it, and we're both still here, still alive."

"Still alive." He answered. "And, you were very right." He said, letting his feelings select the words. "I *might* have done anything in anger."

She put one hand behind his neck; the other grabbed his shirtfront. Her nose was running. She sniffed hard. She squeezed his neck. "I believe Kurt started to realize I was *really* in love with you. That it *wasn't* just a phase. He stole my letter then." A sob grabbed her breath. "He plotted for me to come unglued."

"And you did."

She backed away one step but held his shirt and neck. "Sort of. After I thought you didn't want me, I believed Kurt's love theory then. I said 'fuck-it', Paul. Hear the words? F-U-C-K IT. There is *no* real love. What I had with you was not returned. You wanted Rachael the bitch liar with the golden womb. I just became a nothing, Mia said."

"Nothing?"

"Mia said I was like a vase, bless her."

"A vase?

"Dropped and broken and dropped again. Glued and re-glued so many times I no longer looked like a vase." She hunched her shoulders in sort of a 'so-what.' "I became his spy almost because there was nothing else to do." She unconsciously ran a finger over his lips as she searched for words. "The feeling I had ...was something like—'you didn't want me for anything. At least he wants me for *something*'. Can you understand that?"

She stepped back and dropped her hands to her sides. The torn dress top slipped away again baring her flushed shoulder. She tried to signal honesty with a locked gaze to his eyes, but he looked away from her, into his own thoughts.

"How?" He said into the air. "What all did you do?" He wanted to hear she wasn't effective as a spy. He wanted to hear something he could forgive and forget. She pulled the dress top back into place and held it with one hand. "How were you involved? What did you do." He asked again.

"The group worked soldiers and sailors but mostly state department people coming in from Vietnam. The Anglican church, the British and America embassy offices and military officer's social set." She spoke rapidly. "Information intelligence, Kurt called it. It was easy because I worked at hospital. I know influential people. I talked. I listened. I learned the tricks from Monique, what type of information they needed, I learned information from Kurt and ...other contact people."

"But what did *you* do. Exactly, you?" She hesitated too long. "Wait." He said. "When you delay answering? I can't trust your answer. I'm trying to, but ..."

"I'm still afraid. Afraid you'll run."

"The long haul, remember." He reminded her with a soft nippy kiss above her lips.

She realized then what he was searching for. "Oh Darling, Darling." They had never called one another 'darling' before. She stepped away from him. With that move, Paul's male-female double-standard wanted to jump into play and make her completely at fault for any sex she may have had with anyone, but, her open acceptance of his night with Rasha took the edge from that kind of role playing false pride.

"How far did it all go?" He asked and the question threw him into more thoughts. Since knowing Cynthia, he had been sexual with his wife, Rachael, of course, and with some others when they were long between reunions. He just never admitted it openly or clearly. He knew Cynthia and Kurt had sex now and again but he accepted that because she played it as part of a duty, not of love. Try as he might, he was still near paralyzed by his double-standard thoughts that she might have been sexual to be effective as an agent. He asked her again, but stayed away from using the exact words: "How far did this go?"

"The work took a lot of time and energy." She said.

He deliberately used the exact words. "Were you sexual with these contacts?"

She answered quickly. "Does it matter?" The question ripped at him. He truly did not know if it mattered. She was too intelligent to not use her intelligence with them and with him, and, her intelligence was also her great beauty. 'Does it matter' was the best answer she could have given. It forced him to grovel where she must have groveled when she'd learned of Rasha, and of him asking Monique to spend the night. All things considered, and there were many to consider up to this moment, for the first time in his life he found himself dropping the double standard he had lived with for so long. He asked the deep insides of himself: 'Does it really matter who had slept with whom—under all of the circumstances, anywhere, anytime?' He stood up and paced without realizing he was doing so.

"I've got to think." he said and absently pressed a thumb and forefinger hard against his sinuses. "I've …got to think." He repeated, pacing.

"Please, yes."

He was testing himself and being tested by her. He turned to face her. She had returned to the wingback chair where she sat with both elbows straight, her hands jammed between closed knees, the residue of the tissue barely visible in intermixed fingers. Tears, touches of sweaty hands, and the roll to the carpet now grayed the short white dress. Her hair was an irreparable mess. The position of her arms slightly pressed her breasts into pronounced and floating cleavage. It was surely not a purposeful pose, he thought, but what if it was? Trust struggled to run away. Rachael used such ploys. But this was not Rachael who had lied about wanting a baby for years. But Cynthia had also lied for years. Distracted by the bawdy sight he wondered if she was that shallow to try to keep him pulled in by flaunting body parts. He wanted to blame her for having the power to distract him with her innocent posture. He recalled a derogation Kurt used with her, and spoke up: "Purposefully provocative?" The remark stung, her cheeks erupted red.

"Don't you *dare* think that." She jerked her arms to cover her breasts. "That groups you in with men exactly where I couldn't stand it. You know that, Damn you, Paul."

He tried to take it back. "I'm sorry. Please, forgive that." He vice-griped his forehead between thumb and forefinger. "Listen!" He said looking straight into her eyes. "You wanted understood? Understand me now. I'm crazy right now, with …all of this. I've been tricked before—Rachael—over and over."

She relaxed her arms again. "I am not Rachael." It was a gentle reminder, not an angered shot.

"Of course." He said, then turned from her, rubbed his hair with an open hand and paced again. "And I'm sorry about the provocative crack, I'm sorry."

"I know." She said evenly. "I knew you would be. It isn't you to talk that way, to me."

"No!"

"But, I have to tell you more, Paul." She said.

He stopped pacing and in order to slow down any new info said, sarcastically: "Who says I can *take* more?"

"You must know it all now." From surviving being truthful thus far, she was finding relief in that the truth shall really set you free and she immediately loved this freedom from the lies. With her new energy, she again braced for him to jerk away.

"I haven't been to France. I, we told you that because …" His expression stopped her voice.

His face was one of complete neutrality caused by the simple fact that all of his energy was given toward the shock of what she said, leaving no brain left to map out facial expression.

" ...there were others in town I had to see. People too dangerous to ignore. I couldn't see them and see you."

"You lied with planning, purposefully."

"The only purposeful lie. But remember the circumstances, Paul, think of everything. The letter theft. I really did not believe I was of any true importance to you. Don't forget that."

"Does that make it okay?" He asked angrily.

"YES!" She hissed, just as angrily. "Listen. I'm so ... I've made such mistakes. I'm being punished ..."

"Who should be?"

" ...and I should be. I may have let Kurt cause this, but I take the last blame. Please know how hard that is for me. I take complete blame for fucking up my own life, and for hurting you, the only source of happiness. Paul, I have been so crazy ... "

"You could have been with me since the first day?" He could not believe it.

"Yes."

"But ... I waited for you. I trusted ..."

"You slept with Rasha ..."

"Well, fuck me. Maybe I knew at some instinctual level ...?"

"Oh fuck you, fuck all of this." She snapped at him and burst up from the chair. "Do not try to come out on top of everything tonight with some 'instinctual' male bullshit. My lie was necessary."

"A necessary lie is an okay lie?"

"Paul, stop this. I had to see the contacts, gather money in. It truly *was* necessary. Even poor Mia lied to you on the telephone. She said I was terrible to ask her to do so. I saw she couldn't look at you earlier. My fault. She loves you also, Paul."

"I don't feel loved." His arms were crossed.

She walked to near him. "You know everything now."

They each paced some until they found neutral corners. She by the bed, he next to the wing-back. He reflected on the evening and gathered loose ends to see if 'everything' could be assimilated, filed into sense and then, accepted.

"Monique's role?"

"Her bar and hotel. Monique's was the primary place for contacts. Doesn't the CIA know that, Paul, or the N.I.S.?

"How should I know?" He responded, as he realized: "That was why you never would visit Monique's when you and I were out on the town?"

"Yes." The words were flowing easier. "They'd decided long ago my identity had to be protected, mostly to protect Kurt's pride and to support his ownership of me. I was to stay away from all the others in case they, the most visible, were ever *caught*."

"Asking you to Monique's caused you to break that rule tonight?"

"As far as I was concerned, after my fight with Kurt, the rule was dead. Monique is loyal to Kurt though. I'm sure she telephoned him about her and I cat-hissing tonight. Perhaps he warned her that I might tell *you* all of our secrets."

"Shit, Cynthia. How dangerous is that assumption? How crazy might they get to protect their secrets?"

"I am safe. I'll get the word out that I've said nothing, compromised zero."

"Cynthia." He said sharply. 'They could KILL you."

"Screw that, Paul. Besides, if dead, don't we just go back to wherever we were before we were born?" She tossed off any inherent fears of death.

Paul was stopped momentarily by her philosophy. "I can't actually remember before I was born, Cyn. Think that's how it is?"

"Of course." She snickered. "Let it go."

"But, then," He returned to the puzzle at hand. "Rasha and Dartmouth? How do they fit in?" He asked

"Rasha. Her inside name is Su-Lin Speckle. She telephoned Kurt this morning. Said she had slept with you last night or the night before. Kurt ruled it over me. I didn't want to know, true or not."

"That's why you could handle Monique's crack about me and Rasha?"

"Yes. It was old news. I'd worked it out earlier in the day. I'd betrayed you in some ways. Could I hate you for betraying me? I faked it well even though I'd like to cut Speckle's hair off and stuff it down her skinny throat."

"What can I say?"

"About them? Nothing. Not now. I never liked Speckle—Rasha. Her and her flashy seductive 'shampoo' shit. I can't respect Monique now. I did once because she seemed so …such a survivor."

"You were one-up on her tonight."

"The bitch. Her and her French crap. She's Vietnamese, mostly."

"What about Dartmouth?"

"Dartmouth? He's into something sexual and different. Kids maybe. He knows we do something that isn't exactly legal but he has no idea how far it goes. So, he plays our secret games and Monique overpays him. Other girls at Monique's are players in the organization, Beebe, LuAnn, Ping, Missy, Bonnie, some others. But minor players …mostly tease and arouse and get guys to talk into tape recorders at the bars and in bed. It's pretty easy to do."

"I had breakfast with them all at Monique's the other morning."

"They're always around her. Monique is very organized, with rules and covers and code words. Except, she doesn't know that Kurt has them spying on one another." Vincent's head jerked instinctively toward the window then to the door.

"Are we being looked at, right now, or listened to?"

"No, no, but …like the dining room greeter using my true name? That's a major breach of rules. We are never to use the group's organization for any personal stuff, no matter what. Kurt most likely had telephoned and asked him to report on us if we came in and he got caught up in it and used the wrong name."

"This is all pretty far out, Cyn." He plopped compliantly into the vanity chair and pulled her to his lap. Their body smells commingled again life-size: the tearful saline, nervous perspiration, the now faint but persistent residue of the *shocking*, his diluted after-shave all combined in a serum-like symbol signifying their closeness. Her sniffles continued. "I love you, Cynthia." He said of the moment.

"I can tell you must." She whispered into his hair. "You are still here."

He continued pressing her for clarity.

"True," she agreed. "I likely would not have gone to Monique's with you tonight had Kurt and I not fought. After it all came out I thought, bugger it. I couldn't deny myself being with you. Yet, I forgot how involved I was with the group. How important it still is to them, and how vulnerable they are now that I might betray them. Even Monique is off stride. She used my inside name once tonight, in the arguments—in French—'Anne'."

"Anne? Anne?" A distasteful look crowded onto his face. "Doesn't fit you. Too many names, I can't keep tract."

"I'll do that for us, Darling." She repeated the endearment. "But you need to know how far it has gone. Monique is very involved, as 'Star'. I know she's been pumping your Captain for years as he's come and gone. They call him 'Clifford the braggart'."

"You mean he's a spy?"

"No, no. He's just stupid. Monique calls him a dumb Indian, gives him dumb Indian names, like: 'Talks when drunk'. 'Dances with whores', 'Runs with scissors' Like that."

"She used to also pump his father, the high and mighty admiral? Said he was a sucker for a threesome with younger girls. Beebe and LuAnn mostly, they were fourteen-fifteen when it started. You imagine? They are in their thirties now. She's also gotten information from that crude idiot, Corrigan, and another guy from your ship ...a guy with a mixed up name, like a European tennis player—Sukanarmo, Lukanarmi? But none of us know Stumpf."

"Monique pumped me at breakfast the other morning, before I went out and discovered Selesky in the drug raid on the barge."

"Begging for information on ships to help the poor-but-honest madam know when to bring poor working girls to the big city?"

"Am I that stupid? Don't answer." With that day's early morning champagne masking the memory, he felt even more compromised.

"And David Chen?" She said bringing in still another person she had introduced him to. David Chen had actually transposed a photograph Paul had of Rachael into oils, a common Hong Kong money-maker that at times, as in the case of the Rachael portrait, ended up as some pretty good art.

"Chenny ...the artist guy? That's where Kurt is now?"

"Yes, his organization name is Au-yeung. He's the money person."

"That doddering nice ol' man?" He bounced his forehead off his fist several times, lightly. "He fooled me. Shit, you all fooled me."

"We've fooled a lot of people."

"It's that big? You have to wash the income?"

"Yes. He's one of the partners. Kurt, who is called 'Shaman', then me, then Au-yeung, you know as Chenny, and Star, that's Monique, we were the original governing partners." She dropped her head and let her eyes close for an instant. Locks of hair fell over her face. She brushed unconsciously at them. Tears had stopped but her face was flushed, the whites of her eyes streaked with red. She was still absently squeezing, pressing and kneading her hands together. The tissue had been crushed away. She looked much like a worried Rachael. "I must look a mess." She said.

He could not say anything personal at that moment.

"So Frenchie's glove story started it all coming apart?" He remembered. "Is he involved too, for Christ's sake?"

"No not at all. He's a friend …a true friend, is all. He knows I love you."

"Again, I don't *feel* loved."

"In January, Paul …when you wrote from San Diego and asked me to leave Kurt? I started pulling away from scheduled big-money contacts. That's when it became strained between Kurt and I. It ended when in anger over my not wishing to work, he told me he had stolen the letter. Now you truly know everything."

Vincent was suddenly still. She sensed it and sat still on his lap. The same centering force that surfaced in Clifford's office, the force that enabled him to go ahead and put the boat mission together took over. A reality clicked into place like when the ball in a roulette wheel finally accepts a certain number. 'That's how it is.' You may not like it, but it's the truth, run *with* it, or away *from* it. His mind was moving along in an objective mode that he recognized. He remembered her telling how she detested men wanting her just to want her. Yet, it looked as though she allowed herself to cater to that very thing. If she had tricked men with her beauty, and used them, she had also tricked herself, he thought. She hates any part of any purely primordial exchange between a man and woman, unless they are in love, and the lust expresses the love.

He urged her to her feet, joined her, leaned against the vanity top and put both hands into his trouser pockets. "I have questions before I can decide if it matters what all you've done, we've done. If I would have received your letter, and answered it, said I would leave Rachael? Would you have come with me to the States then, right away? Left Kurt?"

"Yes." She said. "Smartly. I swear it. I wanted life with you …however it would be. I knew you hadn't much money—but money had not bought me what you were giving me."

"If I would have *truly* received your letter and simply decided not to answer it …you would have had the same reaction you experienced by Kurt stealing it. Right?"

"We can't know that. We must go with what truly took place. Kurt was such a strong influence over my depressed state. I loved you but I also hated you for not answering me."

Distracted by the word 'hate', Paul wondered, if she would have expressed the hatred side of her feelings in 1962, where might he be now? Would he have compromised even more with Rachael? Found some safe bimbo to be with, some woman who could only talk about her hair and her next dress?

Cynthia took away his pointless wondering by again moving next to him. "Wait!" She said with snap. "Wait! I know now, Paul, because I know you better now. If you had *really* received my letter—you would have answered it, even to say 'no' to me. You respected yourself too much to be part of my childish game. And if so, we would have … I don't know. It was such a life-changing stupid letter. I hate myself for being so, so." She grabbed his face in both hands, her finger traced his lips again then she kissed him for several seconds. "I've ruined our lives by being such a hopeless cowardly romantic?

"Wait. Stop, Cyn." He pushed away from her and turned away. "When I asked you last month, to come with me. Did you tell Kurt you would?"

She spoke to his back. "Not right away. I was afraid. I waited until we learned Truaxe was coming in early and then I knew I had to tell him. That's what started it all. I told him I couldn't go on making contacts … I was too compromised then, too … " She looked away and searched for a word he might understand, " …dishonored?"

"By . . ?"

"By what I was doing. I couldn't do it any more. Soiled …dirty."

He turned to face her. "And he said what? Did what?"

"That's when he told me about stealing my letter, about his true feelings. I feel truly worthless now, guilt, shame …since the instant I heard your voice on the telephone." She rose from the chair and faced him. "We've been tricked, Paul, I've tricked us. He's tricked us. Do you see?"

She had trusted that Kurt knew best, and had been tricked. He had trusted that his navy knew best, and had been tricked. He'd trusted the doctor as a kid and was hurt by the stitches. Tricked by the pedophile high-school principal. Tricked by Rachael slipping money to her brothers. Selesky on the barge with Balkin and many more tricks. He understood being tricked.

" I see how it can happen." He turned to her and took her shoulders in his hands, his face again inches from hers. "My other question has no value now," he said. "I understand it all, Cyn."

Both of their faces were unflattering, tear stained and baggy eyed. He tried to smile, to transfer his better feelings to her, but his face wouldn't freely change expression from the one that reflected the weighty moment. Hers was equally unchangeable. They reached for one another at the same instant and pulled tightly together as they had so many times in the past. The kiss lingered exactly right. After a moment of holding, she asked the question to which either answer, 'yes' or 'no', would change her life completely.

"Can you love me, Pool Vinzant?"

He squeezed her very tight to keep from walking away. He had wanted only the beauty of their relationship but had been hurt by its circumstances. He knew this day's suffering would come to be part of the relationship, to follow it along.

He thought it had been love with Rachael because there were so many struggles with it. It had obviously not been truly love, for it was over now and he had no lingering feelings of love for her. Does this new struggle mean it's the same kind of love as with Rachael, also to be over soon? He felt alone and in a lonely world. Can he lose Cynthia? Can he be *that* alone? Can he be that alone knowing she too were alone? Something Selesky said jumped to his thoughts. "Any time, Paul, is a chance to regroup and start life over again with a new look—with new and tested values. Any time."

He released his strong hold and faced her eyes. Her eyes were wide, her mouth open, her head moving slowly up and down unconsciously prompting him. He looked at her eyes and his filled with tears.

"Yes, Cynthia Howser." He said. "Starting right now. Let's do this again."

"I can do that."

CHAPTER TWENTY FIVE
The Floor Disappears

At just after five a.m. Paul was awakened by Mia's hard whispering.

"Missy Cyn. Mister Paul. Wake, Missy Cyn. Telephone lady. Missy Cyn." Cynthia stirred on his arm. "What is it?" Fatigued from the explosive and revealing night, they had fallen into the bed at 3 a.m. and simply held one another. They awoke like two children too long in the back seat of a car. He was still in uniform trousers and T-shirt. She was in a half-slip, both hose were run from heel to out of sight. The white dress was in a bundle on the floor but Mia automatically picked it up as she coaxed her mistress awake.

"Telephone, Missy. 'portant, lady say." Mia's voice awakened Paul and at first he couldn't place himself. Without raising her head, Cynthia rubbed her palm over his beard stubble. Her face reflected surprise, then confusion, then recognition. "What angel awakens me?" She said, smiled a half-face smile and rolled away from him. She left a circle of moisture on the pillow where her mouth had been.

Sitting on the edge of the bed she pulled the telephone to her ear.

"Yes?"

He could hear a scratchy woman's voice barking short rapid statements through the telephone in her hand. Cynthia came wide-awake.

"Yes?"

Paul rose in the bed and caught Mia's eye. "Food, please, Mia, coffee?" She nodded, pulled her flowered robe tighter and left quickly, leaning forward, elbows emphasizing her haste.

Cynthia held the telephone to her ear and rubbed her eyes with her free hand. She listened to someone giving her extended instructions. "Yes. Now? No. Yes. What time? How many calls? What's the real source? Who all is there, Star? Can we trust this?"

'Star'? Who was Star? Monique? Yes. Hearing that name Paul moved into Cynthia's vision. She looked at him but looked quickly away. He nudged her, spread two hands palms up and shrugged his shoulders, 'what's happening?' She shook her head back and forth rapidly, impatiently. Sitting on the edge of the bed, the phone held to her ear by a shoulder squeeze, she shivered. He pulled the bed's blanket over her shoulders but she motioned for a robe from the closet. As he sorted one, bits of Cynthia's conversation with Monique pulled suspicion from him.

"Really?—I hate this—Kurt? At Cheney's. I don't know why he said that.—No, don't tell Kurt yet. Please! *Merci Oui. Merci. Bon jour. Oui.* " He slipped a practical woolen robe around her shoulders just as she slammed the phone into the black receiver, raised both fists shoulder high and shook her head back and forth.

"Bloody fuck everything. There's a recall out for your ship's crew."

"What?"

"You're going back to the gulf …today."

"Wait!" Paul was stunned. "That was Monique?"

"Yes!"

"You trust Monique on this?"

"She knows these things. After last night's fight, she would not lie over this. Too much history. The S.P.'s are beginning to search for your crew. I assure you—you're leaving when …" She kicked both feet forward away from the bed. "Fuck, when I need you the most. I, I … "

"Wait. Give me the phone."

He called the S.P. office and gave a skeptical police officer Cynthia's number and convinced him to telephone and wake Eddie Monk. While he waited for Monk to telephone, Mia re-entered the bedroom and helped Cynthia out of the robe, to undue her garters and remove her hose. All was going to hell but even within the hell he was stirred by Cynthia's nude body. Their eyes met, he smiled at her and nodded as if to say—'someday'. She smiled back and nodded, 'yes'.

Monk was on the line. Where he would not reveal details over the telephone, he suggested strongly Paul stop at the S.P. Headquarters as soon he could.

"Monique's intelligence was accurate, Cyn." He said softly. "The ship's leaving, likely to the gulf. I gotta' get to Clifford."

"We should shower."

"No time."

"You need one." She said. "Pheromones have shifted to body odor oh irresistible one. C'mon, shower. It'll be the closest I've been to a naked man in months."

"Ah-hah."

Still stunned by the news, they showered together in near silence. To him, she was a human Valentine. In that kind of love, despite the circumstances, his erection was automatic. In response to the erection and his touch, her nipples swelled. Without a word, he moved her to the side of the warm shower walls and slipped easily inside of her.

"Yes!" She sighed as one leg lifted around him and up.

"Yes!"

She gasped with him. "Come inside of me."

At that instant of orgasm, he inhaled noisily and cried. "I do want you forever."

"It *is* forever." She said softly into his chest, relishing it as he ground into her toward repose. "If you just believe it is." She whispered as she pulled back and looked into his eyes. "We have this moment, and … " Manipulating her vagina around him …she repeated; "and this moment."

He knew then what she meant by that.

While drying with heavy towels taken fresh from the warmer, both showed that having been sexual was terrific in that it re-declared their holds on one another sexually, and a little silly, in that it was the quickest quickie they had ever had.

"Someone pulls the rug from under us ..." He said.

"and the buggers also take the floor?" She joined him.

'So we fuck in mid air."

"Good for us." She said, pulling playfully at his half erection. She accentuated her frustration by snapping her towel against the wall as a middle-school child might.

"Let's get moving." He said. "I want to find some way for me to stay in H.K."

"God," she said. "That would be too good. Where should I drive you to?"

"I'll try calling Clifford, then I'll likely call the ship for details."

He hurriedly shaved with her leg razor and began to dress in his uniform. When he looked for his T-shirt, Cynthia said straightforwardly; "No. I took the T-shirt. My sleeping partner tonight in case you leave."

At that instant, Mia called in from the bedroom. "Missy Cyn, You wanna' me wash Mister Paul's undie-shirt and dry with dryer?"

"NO!" Cynthia yelled in reply and ducked out of the bathroom. Within 2 or 3 seconds she returned, T-shirt in hand. "She was going to wash this. Take away all the good smells? No way, how you yanks say, Jose?"

Touched by the thought, he yelled out loud. "Mia, where are Cyn's clothes from last night, from this morning." The little woman entered the bath, ignored they were both naked, and looked questioningly.

Paul nudged her out of the bathroom to where they located the soiled white dress, the ruined stockings, the scarf, the white bra, and the white tap panties. "Here." He said, snapping up the panties. "*My* keepsake."

Although the white shirt was quite wrinkled, under the double-breasted blue coat, most of the wrinkles were out of sight. With Mia helping pick at lint for two minutes, he eventually looked decent. With her watching, he breathed deeply at her panties with a smirk then tucked them neatly into the inside pocket of his jacket. "My constant partner 'til we meet again."

Hurrying with him, Cynthia dressed in simple jeans and flats, and stopped in front of her large mirror. She stood naked from the waist up, hands on hips, shoulders back. "Should I, Mia?"

"No, no." Mia said, hand over mouth. "Wear clothes."

"No, dummy." Cynthia said. "My new wai-da?"

She'd said in her letter she had a new wai-da especially made for his return. But, the return never really happened. Should they, could they under these circumstances still have the right to play the games they loved with one another, despite the disorder?

"Yes." She said.

"I'm a recovering sexist," Paul said as he slip-knotted his black tie. "But I don't want to recover too quickly. Wear it."

Mia pulled a folded white bundle of cloth and straps from a small bag in the dresser's bottom drawer and handed it to Cynthia; "For when Mr. Paul come back." Paul reached out and caught Mia's hand.

"Mia, I know about the lies. I understand. You love her and you had to help her."

Mia's small face flushed. "Mia so sorry, Misser' Paul."

"I understand. I'm glad you helped her. We are friends still, Mia?"

"Oh yes, Mister Paul. Good friends again." He hugged the tiny woman, her little frame strange in his bent over position. She returned the hug and added several back and shoulder pats from her little hands.

Cynthia broke it up. "Hey, you two." She said pushing her arms through the straps of the wai-da. "More hugging later. I need Mia's good fingers."

Mia stepped behind Cynthia and connected the hooks and eyes. Cynthia smoothed the generous cups over her breasts and turned to Paul. The erotic response stuck in his throat.

"Whew," he managed. "Each wai-da gets better."

Turning back to the mirror, Cynthia giggled. "Well, I'll never fall through an open manhole." Then, hands on hips, Cynthia self-consciously tested her friend.

"Well, Mia, what do you think?" Mia rolled her eyes, said 'you closer than you look,' then rocked her head and feigned a look that said: 'I don't understand why with your figure you would want to be even more so.' But, she knew why. Her mistress was aglow. Her man was aglow. Mia pushed a finger knuckle deep into one padded cup, "Wai-da for sure," she said, then giggled and handed Cynthia a white cotton turtleneck taken from the bed.

While she stood at the floor length mirror holding the sweater at her side, Paul stepped behind her, wrapped his arms about her as he had many times before, and for just a few seconds held her wai-da breasts. He pressed a kiss into the inner softness of the back of her shoulder.

"I love you, wai-da" He said, and the phrase pulled a thrill from her.

She whispered. "I know, wai-da. I know."

He stepped away from her. The fresh feel and scent of her in his mind, on his hands and against his body gave him something to take back to Vietnam.

Pulling the turtleneck over her head and tucking it inside the tight jeans, she looked into the mirror while Mia started flicking at her hair with a doubled sided brush. She turned sideways and pulled her waist in. "Looking at me and not seeing boobs will be like looking at the ocean and not seeing water." A good laugh came out with the words.

"Look like all sweatta' …no brains girl." Mia said and held Cynthia's head still to brush her hair. "Wai-da …is very nice to Mister Paul?"

"Yes, it is, Mia." He agreed. "So don't change her clothes ever again, please. And give yourself a raise, and give the wai-da maker lady a raise."

Mia tipped her head toward Paul for a flick of a second and tossed out a barely audible remark—"an' you have raise too?" She looked quickly away as though she hadn't made a sexually tinged insinuation and never would. Cynthia smiled in pleased disbelief.

Cynthia stepped from under Mia's brush and took a lightweight red jacket from the closet. Back to the mirror she decided the jacket accomplished what she wanted it to do. She turned to Paul. "It's okay *you* see this sweater today, but the world can only have glimpses."

Mia pointed Paul toward a tray of French rolls she had brought in at his earlier request. "Creative tooth decay," Mia said, trying one of Cynthia's jokes.

"Thank you, Mia." He spoke to Cynthia through the first two large bites. "I'm afraid Monique might awaken Clifford and upset him more. I want'a get moving." He washed the roll down with lukewarm black coffee.

"This recall could drive him further over the edge." Cynthia agreed.

"It could—let's get going."

"I'll drive you to Monique's first."

The telephone rang. Cynthia grabbed it.

"Yes?" She looked puzzled. "Wait. Who are you?" A long pause. "Yes, I remember meeting you. No. Not here." She looked at Paul and shrugged. Then, back to the phone: "S.P.'s said what? Yes, Chief Vincent's here. One moment, please." She put the phone toward Paul. She shrugged her shoulders, squeezed a palm against the speaker mouthpiece and announced: "It's the one who's against recreational uses for the human body."

"Griffith. How?" Puzzled, Paul took the phone. "Hello?"

"Master Chief Vincent? Exec here. I can't locate the Cap'n." Griffith sounded irritated. "According to the S.P. office, you know what's happening."

"What?" Paul pushed him to compromise the classified move over the telephone but he didn't.

"Is that the same woman you were with last night?"

"No." Paul lied, not knowing why he needed to aggravate the man.

"No? Is she with the Captain then?"

"Likely." He said to add to Griffith's confusion.

"Where is the Captain?" Griffith demanded.

"Why would you think I know, Sir?"

"The last I knew, Cap'n Clifford was with you."

"Yes?"

"Where is he, Vincent? Come alive."

"I thought the Captain returned to the ship last night." He lied.

"Where is this number I called?"

"I'm thirty minutes away. Is that all you wanted with me?"

"Chief Vincent. If you can put your hands on the Commanding Officer, you tell me where he is." He sounded very rattled. Why Griffith's hurry to find Clifford? If Clifford couldn't be located the exec would have to take Truaxe to sea, something Paul thought Griffith would relish.

The buzzy line went dead but the 'click' caused something to jump from obscure to clear. Vincent recalled the charged San Diego conversation between Griffith and Clifford, later amplified by Griffith's statement to him that he wanted a respected C.O. to sign his fitness reports. Griffith had to be torn between taking the ship and being a star himself or finding and supporting Clifford so *he* could become the star worthy of signing fitness reports. He explained it all to Cynthia as she completed her makeup.

"So you have a choice between Captain Crazy or Captain Entrails-eater?"

"Neither choice is choice." Paul mused and dialed Monique's. "And I can't forget what Clifford says about Griffith's vanity. I think that's at play in here in some way. Shit. Why'd I leave Steubenville?" The time-worn phone system again buzzed and hummed. He waited.

"Christ!" He said directly to Mia as he took another cup of coffee from her helpful hand. "Will Clifford keep that one threat he made last night."

Mia looked at him and screwed up her face. "No ast' me, Mr. Paul. No as't me."

"Which?" Cynthia asked flicking her compact open.

"He'd rather be in a first class cabin of some airliner rather than the Captain's cabin of the ship. Remember?"

"Yes."

"Maybe he's flown away."

The phone came to life at the other end. "Dartmouth? Paul Vincent here. Yes. You too. Listen. I need to talk directly to Captain Clifford. You know his room? Monique does. Hurry."

There was a pause.

"Goddammit, Dartmouth. Get the son-of-a-bitch on the phone or I'll reach through this line and grab you by your slimy limey neck."

Cynthia turned from her makeup mirror while Paul waited, hunched into the noisy phone. "Slimy Limey? Dartmouth?"

"Now that I know he's patronized a friendship to me over these years? I guess I'm just aching for an excuse to make his nose cartilage part of my fist, for just an instant."

"I love it when you're full of male bull-shit."

"Quit. Once I start on Limeys, you could be next—and by the way? You've got a great butt."

The phone buzzed and crackled. Cynthia moved close to him and pushed her hips against his, then snuggled against his arm. "Isn't there a way to alert someone that Clifford is disturbed?" His attention was on the phone line. Cynthia turned away without an answer. Someone picked up the line at Monique's.

"Captain Clifford's here. Who is this?" Clifford's voice was clear and energetic, surprising Vincent.

"Captain? Chief Vincent. Good morning."

"Yes. Chief. Listen. I want to talk to you 'bout las' night. We can meet for breakfast—for brunch. You name the place but not here and not the China Fleet club nor the British 'O' club. No naval places. One hour will be okay."

Clifford didn't know of the recall.

"Wait …not so fast, Cap'n. I want to meet you right where you are, in ten minutes. There are some things you should know."

"Not here." Clifford was stern voiced. "One hour. You name the place." Then he added, " …an' no women along."

"Captain. We haven't got one hour. Brace yourself." Paul cryptically told him the story. He also gave him the S.P. telephone where Griffith was waiting. Clifford told him to wait, to not hang up. He could hear him breathing against the mouthpiece.

"You okay, Captain?"

"Okay? Of course I'm okay. I'm heading out the door in five minutes. Meet me A.S.A.P. at the fleet landing."

Vincent reached out once more, stepping gingerly over the protocol boundaries that had been destroyed the night before. "Captain, we must talk about what was said last night."

"Not a word, Vincent. Not a friggin' word. Meet me at the fleet landing." The line went silent except for the fluctuating buzz. Clifford was back to pure and total USN.

They said good-bye to Mia after cautioning her to not tell Kurt anything about Paul. They hustled outside.

"Wait, Paul. Do this."

Cynthia insisted they lift the metal top from her nearly new 280SL coupe. "Everything is coming apart'. Your Captain is a loony-bells. Kurt is also crazy. You and I likely also qualify as mad—but lord, I'm not miss-spending this winter sunshine. I replaced a broken windscreen in this cah', and had it buffed for your visit. I want the sun on our faces. This could be our last hour for, for how long?"

She started the engine and put red-framed sunglasses to her eyes. As the motor warmed she grabbed a scarf from the glove box and flicked it over her head to tie at her chin. Its color matched her jacket and matched the car's faultless red paint, exactly. "Hang on, sailor man." She screeched the tires on the curved driveway and headed onto the road leading toward the swarm of the city. He grabbed his hat to keep it from lifting away. The car radio warmed up to *The Kingston Trio* singing a very familiar tune: *It Takes a Worried Man, to Sing a Worried Song.*

He snapped the radio off.

She maneuvered the right-hand-drive down the tram hill toward the fleet landing and Paul's speculative thoughts became crazy-making. Cynthia is an informer now. What do spies do to informers? Could Cynthia, who previously seemed so naive, control the world-wise street-wise Monique, David Chen and the rough looking Chinese men who hung around Monique's? Could Kurt control them all? Would he even want to?

"Okay, Lady love. What if Kurt finds out you've told me everything? How much danger is there?"

"I've been thinking about that since the recall. I won't tell him I've told you anything to hurt his organization. We said nothing in front of Monique to discount that. He'll believe I'm hurt over the letter. I'll lead him to believe ...something. I'll tell him you were hurt, devastated, over my lie when I told you we hadn't gone to France. You got angry and have left me forever. Said you were going back to Rachael, heaven forbid." She reached and patted his leg without taking her eyes from the road.

"Wait, Cyn. Lies and more lies? I don't like this. This isn't you."

"I know it isn't me. This is who I've become because I couldn't *be* me. Don't you see?"

"It's got me off guard."

"Paul, under this ...this ...shit? Underneath this facade, is me. What you're *hearing* is the survival me. This is the me I've learned to be over the past months. The *real* me is the me I've been these past few hours with you."

"Will you be able to put it all away, if we get away?"

" Surely. I like the 'me' you fell in love with. I hate this lying, frightened 'me'."

"So you are frightened."

"Only for the future. Frightened of how we sort this all out. Your ship is leaving. I'm forced to sort out and re-think everything. I'll need money, a visa. My passport is in Kurt's bank box. I'll have to wait until I hear from you, see."

"Is there danger?" He insisted. "Answer me."

"Some. Perhaps." She was truthful. "I'll not suffer for what fools do, I believe that. You've known me. Besides, we have no great choices."

"You *seemed* frightened last night while I held you." He said.

She put her hand on his thigh again. "Put away my tears from last night. Think *of* me, not *for* me, P.V." She used that rhyme with his initials only when she was pushing to be heard. "I'm not the kind of woman who cries when the tape dispenser becomes empty. I'm a big girl especially when life is working for me. With you back, it's working."

She looked at him and smiled. In the blowing scarf, the sunglasses, jeans and jacket, twisting the steering wheel to manage the vicious curves, she did look pretty damn capable. He forced himself to accept her self-confidence.

"It's hard for me to leave you in danger."

"This is not a movie, Paul. It's only danger if he believes I've told you of the organization. I'll not tell him that. At this time, despite the powerful disagreement, I am as vital to his work as he. Maybe even more valuable. He's behaved as an ass and he knows that, but he's not a stupid ass. The selfish side of him will not want me lost to the organization."

"Organization?" Paul parroted. "I hate this. Yesterday morning I was coming to Hong Kong to get this busty part-time nurse part-time medical student to leave her faggot of a husband for a life in San Diego working at a *Jack in the Box.* Now I'm going back to a war I don't want to be in and leaving the woman I love in some sort of a conspirator laden fucking spy ring." He lifted his palms into the wind above the car. He looked up in a mock prayer. "And GOD, she says not to worry."

She didn't take her eyes off the road. "Not to worry, really. We must deny, Paul. Please! You're going back to Vietnam, that's your world, is it not? I must trust you to be safe there. This is my world here. Don't you know? Trust me, I'll be safe." She locked the brakes for an instant to avoid hitting a slow-moving cart, then charged the accelerator again which jerked the car out and around an old man and his bicycle rickshaw.

Paul pulled his hat to his lap. "Denial, you say." He looked back to see if the rickshaw man was okay. He was. "I hope denial works now that I have to count on it."

They reached the bottom of the twisting road and headed east on side streets. They drove a few blocks in silence among heavy traffic. The early morning dampness off the tram road gave way slowly to the February sunshine she had hoped would come and the warming air burned in Paul's nostrils. When he looked at Cynthia again he saw tears blowing backward from under her sunglasses.

"You cry." he said. "I can't leave you like this."

"I'm crying, Paul, because I'm letting the tears come. My life is changing now. Like—I paid for this automobile myself, part of my shares. First big income I ever earned … " She faced him and nodded. " …albeit ill-gained. Now it's helping a Yankee ship recover its crew so they can continue a war I couldn't care less about." She turned and touched his hand, then impulsively rubbed it hard. "Why didn't I stay in London and marry some very proper … Christ, I almost said 'attorney." She let it trail off.

He leaned closer to her now that they were on level streets. "I liked what we did in the shower. Thank you, ma'am."

"You're welcome, Sir. And thank *you*. You've been such a nice guy." She teased checking over her shoulder.

"Nice guys finish last, according to Leo Durocher."

"Finishing last in sex is a good thing, Mr. nice guy."

That pulled a smile from him. "We'll do 'it' again. Soon I hope."

She frowned with him. "Until this morning? I'd forgotten how. I forget if its 'in' first, or 'out' first." She tried to laugh with him but it didn't work well. Each returned to their spinning survival thoughts.

Again she pretended to not be crying behind the glasses. The projected loneliness also choked back his breath but he breathed slowly, pressed a finger to his upper lip and pretended also that he wasn't crying. To feel close to her under the circumstances, he put a hand between her legs. She squeezed the hand with her thighs and managed a smile. He tried to return one but failed. Neither of them spoke again as the car moved through the early morning traffic toward the last place either of them wanted to go.

CHAPTER TWENTY SIX
Stop Whining, You Wanted to See the World?

When the convertible came to a stop in the sunny center of the fifty-yard square area, all eyes shifted to the shapely lady in the red jacket and to the alert looking uniformed man.

"Oh oh ... I'm getting sailor eyes from everyone."

"You're the last chocolate in the box."

"Hadn't thought of that."

As Vincent shut Cynthia's door, Lieutenant Stumpf meandered up to them, arms swinging slowly, a big smile on his face. Vincent noticed for the first time the Lieutenant was really putting on weight, his trousers too tight across his thighs, his face rounder than ever. Behind Stumpf, fifty feet away were the eyes of Captain Clifford and a group of officers; Griffith, Corrigan, Valentino, Patrick Balkin, Lukarmo and some J.O.'s. A few yards to the left of the officers, about thirty of the crew stood away from the shadows of the nearest building, where they too could catch the rays of the morning sun. Most were smoking and all were looking grim. Beyond them, another thirty yards or so, was the actual boat landing with several noisy crafts of all types coming and going. A mile beyond that point, in the crowded harbor, Truaxe sat at anchor.

Vincent saluted, Stumpf returned it but then tipped his hat to Cynthia and grinned. "Hi." He greeted her a second time. "Hello, Cynthia."

"Hello, Harry." He seemed pleased she remembered his first name.

"What are the details, Mr. Stumpf?" Vincent asked. Stumpf glanced toward Cynthia with a look that said 'she's not cleared to hear what I'm going to tell you'.

"She knows more secrets than the law permits." That statement was truer than Stumpf would want to know. "Tell us the story."

Stumpf shrugged his shoulders then looked back over one of them to see if he could be overheard. He couldn't "Well, looks like the V.C. shore guns close-hit two tin-cans, the Wilson and McCormick. Shore batteries east of Deo Ngang. Both ships hit bad enough." Stumpf squinted, wiggled his nose and bit his upper lip in a series of timed movements that caused his glasses to jump upward nearly a quarter inch and settle into a notch on the bridge of his nose. Looking over his shoulder again, he continued. "Running out of a night time shoot? Wilson went dead in the water." The glasses slipped from the notch. He ignored them. "McCormick tried taking Wilson in tow but the gulf was rough and they had trouble making it happen. They were still dead in the water at daybreak, yesterday. The cruiser Chicago's guns and some Air Force help silenced the shore fire." His voice quieted even lower. "Both ships lost some men." His shoulders shivered just slightly. "I know the communicators on both those ships." He stopped talking as if to punt to Vincent.

"So we go back?"

A quick finger set the glasses back in the notch. "Only us's goin' back right now. Kittyhawk will come later today." He rattled on with more details.

Vincent wondered if the crew could muster up enough 'can-do' spirit to go back to the line, considering the interrupted rest. Was there enough negative residue left over from his having slapped the Captain to keep the crew from concentrating on their jobs once back in the Gulf? Considering Clifford came apart at Monique's, would he relieve himself of command and let Griffith take over? What is a man's responsibility to tell 'someone' Clifford is mentally disturbed? Who could he tell? Griffith? It could get out of hand. Tell Valentino? Maybe, but could Valentino control Griffith? Was Patrick Balkin really N.I.S. or had that story just been part of a sophisticated and well practiced contingency plan kept at the ready by all navy homosexuals?

Cynthia was having similar thoughts.

"Harry?" He came aglow when she used his name. "How's the Captain seem this morning?"

"I donno'," he said. "Says he crashed at some hotel after leaving you two. His hands are shaking a bit but so are everyone's hands whose been boozing it up." He lifted his own hand and studied it. It wiggled a little. He dropped it self-consciously.

"Wait here, Cyn. Be right back." Paul left Cynthia standing next to Stumpf and approached the group the Captain was standing with. About halfway there, Clifford broke away from the cluster and intercepted the Chief, put one hand on Paul's elbow and drew him off to the harbor side of the nearby building.

"Chief, 'mornin'. Glad you hurried. Stumpf filled you in, I see. We goin' back to the yacht club, and I want to get movin' post and haste."

Clifford draped a hand on Vincent's shoulder and pulled him in closer. Even with his PR ideas, Vincent felt it was too buddy-buddy for a Commanding Officer and his Master Chief. As the Captain looked over his shoulder to insure no one was in hearing range, the smell of *Mennen* after shave and coffee breath blew past Vincent.

"Chief, I want to mention last night …once."

"Good. Me too."

"Well, you're not." Clifford shifted to sounding hostile. "As far as I'm concerned last night didn't happen. Let's say I got a little tight, drunk actually. The booze put a rattle up my ass. So, I did a little private blabbing off the top of my head. So what? Drunken nonsense. I was tired, it was late, the food was good, the brandy warming," He tossed his head toward Cynthia, " …the company excellent." He posed a grin, an incongruous request for agreement.

"You're embarrassed." Paul said.

"I am not."

"And you're denying how disturbed you were."

"I am not, and you're out of order."

"I'm not trying to be. Last night I was 'buddy-boy Paul'. I understand anything that was said last night was between you and I. Strictly confidential—private."

"I demand that." Clifford said strongly.

"Captain," Vincent started to plead, "you know the crew is upset. You've named them dysfunctional, error prone, so on."

"They'll make it. *Can do.*"

"That's not all there is to consider."

Clifford stared at Vincent's eyes but said nothing more. Hoping the man would listen; Vincent went on, trying to make a case. "Reconsider readiness, Cap'n. Let's go for a needed rest, few more days ...for you, for me, for the crew. Tell COMSEVENTHFLEET anything. Tell 'em we broke a shaft." His thoughts flew, anxious to keep Clifford's attention. "Wait, I know. Classify a message so the crew doesn't know. Tell COMSEVENTHFLEET we suspect a radioactive leak. That'll buy us the time to rest up, for everyone, including you. Dieter will go along, so will Valentino." The words hung in the air. Vincent knew then by the look on the Captain's face that he had misread something vital. The emergency recall had hung those admiral bars in front of Clifford's eyes once again.

"Chief. I'm going to say this only once. I don't like it when you refer to my officers by their last names only and not their ranks. I don't want another word about what has been said or done. We are taking Truaxe back to the line." He started to walk away but turned quickly back to face Vincent. His index finger pointed directly to Vincent's chest just as it had on the bridge during the incident. He spoke softly so as to not be overheard. "Am I perfectly, perfectly clear?"

He turned away from Vincent, not waiting for a reply.

"Wait!" Vincent called. Clifford turned, eyes squinted and mouth held in a phony looking tough-guy veneer.

"You're going to try to bluff it through? Okay, Cap'n. I don't blame you. I can help you."

"I need nothing from you except good communications at sea."

"You're retreating into the very shell you admitted last night was failing you."

Clifford bounded back to him in five paces, eyes wide. When he reached the chief his voice was so soft to keep others from hearing that it took away the anger. "Don't you push it, Vincent." He was almost whispering. "You're over-reacting again. You over-react easily don't you?" His eyes showed the anger as he grabbed at the skin between his nostrils.

"I'm not over-reac— "Listen." Clifford cut in, sputtering. "I'm neither drunk, nor ill, nor scared. You just don't listen well. I'm fine, but maybe you're not. I am the Captain here. I am the Commanding Officer." He spun and walked straight back to the group of officers and men. 'I decide who gets killed here' flashed through Vincent's thoughts.

Helpless at the moment, Paul walked to the coupe. Stumpf had since gone back to the group of officers. Cynthia was waiting alone in the ever-warmer sun and had removed the scarf, sunglasses and jacket. With her breeze blown hair she looked very sensual to him despite everything. Her smile told him she knew how she looked.

"See me?" She teased, but not in a tasteless or shallow way.

"I wanna' remember you like this, through all this hazy crap. You look real good to me, Cyn." He leaned and kiss-pecked her forehead.

She mocked his American accent. "I wanna' look fine too, but not here. Fun places agin', carefree places. The sailboat …"

"Daytime in Picnic Bay on Lamma Island." He said.

She provoked his desire. "And night time fucking in Picnic bay on Lamma Island."

"Frenchie's office again?"

"Frenchie's office agin' and agin.'" She put-on. "And the Fandian Ho with the solid angel bed and the over-washed ol' soft sheets and open winda' …"

"The sea breeze there …" He remembered.

"You at night, naked by the window. Big guy in silhouette."

"You naked beside me."

The approaching danger was too strong for the fantasy to continue.

"Clifford's holding back, isn't he?" She asked.

"Yes."

She continued the American use of words. "He's gonna' bluff it?"

"He's used to coping." Paul said. "Maybe he can pull it off."

Cynthia let all her thoughts out loud. "You're hoping last night charged his coping batteries? He's gotten catharsis by talking to us?" She stopped talking. She was simply wishing aloud. "I'm trying to make lemonade out of bloody lemons. He doesn't even look bloody rested." Exasperated, her true slang returned. "The King and this bloody rotted Yankee mess."

Stumpf took several steps toward them and called out. "Chief, when that boat that's leavin' now returns to the pier? We need you aboard."

"Aye aye." That cut their remaining time to ten minutes. Vincent looked the group of enlisted men over carefully then turned to Cynthia.

"What now?" She suspected something new.

"I'm wondering how much of the crew they've found. If we leave short handed, and he sees admiral bars …he's liable to lie about readiness like he's lied before."

"Pity he wants to match his father's rank."

"You heard him yourself …groomed since the womb."

"Men," She blurted, "always trying to please some elusive unpleasable fatha'. What's under the kilt of this fatha' power shit?" She used more profanity in the past hour than he had heard her use in the many years together. "Why don't you tell Griffith that Clifford is crazy?" She was very irritated. "I *hate* this helpless feeling I have."

Stumpf caught his eye again. He held five fingers in the air.

There was a squeal of tires turning on concrete. Before a black Humber taxi was completely stopped, Lake and Tucker tumbled out, arms loaded with packages.

Cynthia grabbed Paul's sleeve. "Don't be cheeky and chase me away just yet."

"It's Lake and Tucker. I have to touch base with them. A minute. "

"I recognize Abie."

She walked with him to where the two men were paying off the cab. They passed a group of hurrying Kittyhawk S.P.'s, possibly heading ashore to begin a roundup of their own crew. An over conscientious Chinese police officer walked up, tipped his hat and asked Cynthia if she would move her car. "But, we've no time, don't you see … ?" She almost exploded at the policeman, but caught herself.

"You talk," she said," … I'll move the car." As Vincent approached Lake and Tucker, Cynthia gunned the small engine and popped the clutch. Wheels spun and burned just a hint of a screech of rubber. She took the car fifty feet to the nearest building and parked it with a second slight screech.

"Well, well." Moaned Abie as he watched Cynthia is the car. "A rich lady in a rich car and they break a law a minute."

"Glad you can laugh, Abie." Vincent teased him. "Look around. Think about it."

Lake looked about. He saw the Captain, the exec, some unhappy looking crewmen. "Uh oh, no one is smiling. This is not good news," he mumbled. He pointed his head toward Cynthia. "If she's pissed off, which she is, and if you're here with the working class, which you are, there must be work lurking not far away."

"Shit." Tucker also caught on. He became very fidgety, looking around in almost a panic state.

As Vincent explained, the two men were struck quiet in disbelief.

"We was jes' comin' back to take this stuff 'board and go back to two honeys we been with." Tucker talked evenly but kept his neck scanning as if looking for some clue that it was all a bad joke.

"Yeah." Lake said real straight. "I got me a honey who ain't disappointed 'cause I'm the first black guy she's met with a little dick. Imagine, she asked me if my dick came in mature size." Vincent thought he was joking. He wasn't. His expression was deadpan. Abie continued. "Fuck, Paul. Tell 'em you couldn't find us. They don't need us anyway." It was a sailors standard last gasp plea when liberty was cut short.

Tucker put in his vote. "Hell yes. Tell'em, I'm jes' warmin' up. Got this little woman back at the Harrison hotel? Cherry,—catch that name? Is jes' yearnin' ta' learn more knot tricks from me. We're onla' a quarter way through the manual. When she grad'i'tates, in 'bout three days from now, ah gets to test her with ma' version of the flyin' fuckin' half gainer."

"Your brains musta' went out the end of your dick." Lake snapped. "A gainers not a knot, it's a fuckin' dive, you hoopie." Lake shoved at Tucker. The taller man pulled away and laughed.

"Sure as shit is a dive …muff type dive, ahh might add." He turned to Vincent, in sober voice. "We gonna' git more time inna' small boat out' inna' gulf?"

Paul hoped not. However, if there was to be another pickup boat, Vincent wasn't sure he wanted those two along. They'd come back alive from the first run-in but Tucker was shaky, Paul thought. "No details yet, Tuck. All I know is our country calls to you," he kidded, male bravado at the fore, "get your asses in gear to answer the call."

"Look, I gotta' make a phone call." Tucker scanned about for a booth.

"Who to?" Lake asked. "Who you know in H.K.?"

"Ah ah ah …mah' little honey …at the hotel. Don' want to stand her up 'case we come back. I like her outters' so much I don' want her hatin' my innerds'."

"Shore Patrol office, over the little bridge. Closest phone. But Stumpf's sayin' three minutes."

"Gotta' go for it." Tucker took off running, holding his hat on with one hand, his pea coat tails flying behind him.

"HEY." A voice from the pack of officers stopped Tucker. "Where you goin?" It was Griffith.

"Telephone ...ahh, Sir. Sick mother back home."

"No time. Fall in at the landing."

"But." Tuckers face reddened.

"I said—Fall in at the landing."

"Shit." Tucker mumbled as he straightened his jacket, "godammit," squared his hat, "this isn't right" and started a slow walk back toward Vincent.

"Screw this, Pappy." Lake said dropping his gray wrapped packages for emphasis. "This sucks. First, some kid snatches my watch right offa' my arm and runs with it. Now this shit. I don't wanna' go back to the line." There were no jokes, no humor in his voice. "Doesn't feel right. Hasn't felt right since that day."

"What day?"

"What day?" Lake was very upset. "The boat day, Chief Short Memory."

"Don't smart ass, Lake. We gotta' go back." Vincent wanted no more resistance. His own life was disrupted enough. "I have no patience for this either. You know I'm ripped away from Cynthia."

"When I eat my heart out, Paul. I'll take little bites for more pain."

Cynthia walked up to them. She had met Abie during Paul's minesweeper days. She stood next to Vincent and placed an arm around his waist. Lake, acting like a child who wasn't getting its way, rudely ignored the reintroduction to Cynthia. Vincent let it go.

Tucker addressed Cynthia. "You'all's Cynthia Howser? We talked 'bout you in the boat." He offered his freckled hand and shook hers as he would a man's.

"Yes, you're Tucker?" Cynthia seemed pleased.

"Yes, Cecil, like in weasel. Named after a poor relative ma' mother thought was rich." Cynthia laughed with him.

"Paul's told me about you, Cecil. Sorry you must leave so soon?"

Tucker laughed aloud. "This kinda' shit rings a bell with me. Been rushed in an out of more fun ports than an overworked travel agent." He talked on like a stand-up comedian trying to impress an interviewer. "It's women like you, Cynthia, what gives ugly women a purpose." She laughed some needed laughs with him. He continued the theme. "Without the 'aw shit' women, we wouldn't have no 'wow, look at her'."

When he ran out of stories there was an awkward moment. Tucker looked stupidly dazed and stared at Cynthia inappropriately. Paul touched Abie's dropped packages with a toe to distract from Tucker and try to cheer Abie. "What'd you buy, Abie?"

'Stuff for Veronica, skirts ...stuff." Lake pouted. "This hoopie talked me into it. Now I owe him a hundred bucks."

"Tucker?" Paul asked. "You borrowed the forty bucks from me on a full billfold?"

"I came across some money, Chief." Tucker seemed embarrassed. "I'll pay you the forty soon we gets' aboard ship."

Stumpf finger whistled and pointed toward the launch. Lake turned and left without a word, Tucker hastily said good-bye to Cynthia and followed Lake. When Stumpf signaled 'two minutes', Vincent pulled Cynthia to the building by her car.

"I hate this. When will our days come for sure?" She asked.

"The only thing I knew *for sure* was the last time I checked my I.D. card my name was still Paul R. Vincent."

"Hold me Pool Ah Vinzent."

Behind a stucco building off Harcourt Road in Hong Kong, the man held the woman. His tears mixed into her hair, her tears marked his jacket front. He could not leave without covering one point they had not discussed. Holding her close, he talked into her familiar smelling hair. "You've been selling my country's secrets. I don't know what secrets. What you've done might jeopardize me, my men, my ship. It could well be the cause of us going back to the gulf. I can't stand knowing."

She pulled her arms tighter around his back. "You may not be able to forgive it. But please try."

"I can't understand you selling out values, morals, ethics and people, simply because you thought I didn't love you."

She pushed back to arm's length and looked directly into his eyes. "It wasn't a conscious 'fuck-you-I'll-get-even'. It was more an unconscious surrender of the worth of everything important including people, a 'what the hell'. Believe my heart." The never empty spring again pushed tears to run freely from her eyes. "My spirit was broken, don't you see? I had no morals or values …people meant nothing, I meant nothing." She pulled close to him again but he seemed so tense she couldn't meld as close as before.

"I'll need some time to get used to this." He said.

"Dammit," she snapped, "there is so little time. I can't defend myself anymore." She pulled her head back and looked at his eyes again. "My wonderful love, don't talk about this now, please?"

"I'm going back to the line. How much danger has been added to my life and my ship's life—because of something you've passed on to who it is you pass shit on to? Hear my question?"

"Yes! Yes! Yes!" She beat a fist into his chest. "I hear your damming question." She was yelling. He grabbed her wrists, hard. She unclenched the fist. He relaxed his grip, pulled her close again. She spoke again, her words buried against his chest. "I have the same question, dammit. What if I lose you out there because of something I've done? Forgive me, Paul. Try to."

Some empathy he felt for her position rose again.

"I love you Cynthia Howser."

"I love you, Pool Vinzent." She breathed an almost silent prayer into his shirt. "Forgive me, I need to hear it. Forgive me."

"I love you. I know you didn't do it to intentionally hurt me."

"Is that forgiveness?"

"Yes, I know you never do anything *intentionally* to hurt me, or us. It just takes awhile for that knowledge to kick in sometimes."

He held her and cursed Kurt. In most circumstances Vincent would require a person to be responsible for their acts. At this time, however, as he held her in his arms he couldn't help but feel they had both been truly tricked by a revengeful Kurt. Of course, Kurt no doubt felt tricked by them.

He kissed her good-bye, quietly, gently, tenderly, knowing much would remain as loose ends until he returned and they talked and talked again into a few late nights.

He walked away from her but looked about to focus his memory on the details of the moment. He recorded the sound of traffic from Harcourt road. The stench of fish from the bay. The sloshing sounds from the bobbing of moored junks and boats. The winter sun now slightly too warm on his back, the impersonal gray painted dockside offices. He documented the red car that would claim her when he left, re-imagined the recent impression of her waida bra against him and the released smell of *Shocking*. He locked in the stickiness of her teary cheek on his, the soft warmth of the good-bye kiss—her hand sliding out of his.

He stepped down into the diesel-smelling launch and sat on the padded bench between Tucker and Lake. The motor roared and the boat surged away from the concrete pier.

Cynthia was fifty feet away looking directly at him. She'd placed the light jacket over her shoulders causing the sun shadows to enhance her figure. The breeze swept her rich hair in repeated motions. She was smiling but it was a brave smile, not a spontaneous pleasurable one. Her left hand was moving at the front of her belt, nervously. Her right hand hung limp at her side, long fingers dangling the car keys against her thigh. He clung to the sight of her. At the last instant, just before true vision was gone, she raised her hand and waved a little 'see-ya' wave, pivoted, and walked to the car. A chill surged through him. He had wanted forever with her. He wanted to watch the years pass over their faces. A strong shudder passed through him, as he feared he might never see her again.

A nervous looking seaman with a beginner's mustache and a childish face turned on a small tape player across from Vincent. A tape of *The Supremes* started with a flutter and a squeal, then evened out. Their smooth and familiar voices declared to him and to the world—*You can't hurry love—no you just have to wait. ...*" It got to Vincent and because he was the Master Chief and could get away with it, he signaled the seaman by running one finger left to right across his own throat. With a nod, the young man clicked the tape player off.

Vincent glanced one last look at the pier. She stood next to the red car.

Cynthia could not bear to watch the ship move away into the morning, her thoughts too full, her sadness too deadening. She decided it best to leave and stepped to the car. Out of the corner of her eye she saw the packages still piled where Abie dropped them. She gathered them into the passenger seat of the Mercedes to give to Eddie Monk to mail or hold. Just before leaving, standing beside the car, she looked one last time. She could barely see the launch a mile away. She pictured Paul sitting beside Abie Lake and Cecil Tucker. Abie so angry with Paul, Tucker so filled with awkwardness and strained humor. What had Tucker said when she teased him about leaving so suddenly? The remark about ugly women was sexist but forgivable considering his background. Memory cells flashed and ignited within her, "Bell?"—"Travel Agent?" He'd said "This kinda' shit rings a bell with me. Been rushed in an out of more fun ports than an overworked travel agent?"

"He used the code words and I missed them. Jesus Christ. Tucker is Bell." One palm absently cupped over a knotted fist pressed against her lips. Her thoughts poured out. "Did he really say both contact phrases?" Her hand unconsciously ran back and forth over her forearm. "How could I have missed them?" Then: "Why did he give *me* the code words? He couldn't have. How would he recognize me? My name? Been informed by Polav? God, I never dreamed Bell might be an American. I pictured him as a mean looking pock marked Baltic type. We'd promised the Russian we'd pull Bell out of here and to Europe, but there he goes to sea with my Paul." She ran to the edge of the now vacant landing. She could make out the anchor chain shaking on the near side of the ship, drawing up. She waved her arms above her head, but it was useless.

"No, Tucker was too strange acting," she thought, "he's no agent. Yet, it looked like he was looking for clues from me on how to get away. I missed it so he panicked for that telephone." Her thoughts slowed. "But—why should I care? I owe nothing to this Bell, if it is Bell. Not now. Kurt's betrayed me." But a new thought. "But, my Paul." Her heart pounded at an unfamiliar pace, a pace she hadn't felt for years. Driven by true concern, true love, she felt fear. Fear for life. Fear for Paul's life.

The ship had spun on its axis and was silhouetted from its stern against a misty horizon beyond the bay's entrance. There was a distinct wake behind it. She spoke to her anxiety. "Paul's sailing with an agent and doesn't know it. Oh God, they've even been in the pickup boat together. What might happen out there?" She was in panic but at the same time knew panic would not lend itself to resolution.

She ran to the red car and pointed it toward North Point and Quarry Bay where she hoped to get a boat. She spoke aloud as she careened the car through back roads. "I'll intercept Truaxe. Rush up alongside and scream … STOP, STOP. A SPY aboard. They'll stop. He won't be a spy. I'll be laughed at but not by Paul. He'll know I did it because I love him. We'll be safe …safe."

At Quarry Bay she slid to a stop in the muddy parking area at Wan's landing where she and Kurt often rented boats. Wan, his thin lips hardly moving greeted her as the woman who often came with the European man, Shaman.

"No boat to rent today, Miss Anne."

She pointed to one with both an English and Chinese rental sign on it. "Please, Wan. Take that one."

"No boat rent, Miss Anne." She thought he was kidding, some cross-culture humor gone astray."

"Hurry, Wan. No jokes now. Take me … "

" … Shaman telephone me. No rent boat to you."

"Wait …you misunderstand …" But the wispy bearded man in the blue coveralls turned away from her and busied himself with a small outboard motor tied to a stand. "Wan? What did Shaman say to you? I need a boat." But Wan was like a stonewall. She thought of other rental places, but they would be miles away.

Wan came back to life as she walked toward her car. "No good, Miss Anne. No good."

"What? What'd you say?"

"No one give you boat today. No one."

She sat in the red car and breathed deeper and deeper to calm herself. She thought as carefully as she could. Someone, probably Polav, had obviously, somehow, told Tucker/Bell how to contact her. No, too complicated. Tucker couldn't be the spy. I'm too upset. Wait. Could she find Polav and make sure? Could she trick him into telling her how to reach Tucker/Bell via the Russian's system of communications? How far would she have to go to find out? What lies could she use? Was Polav like other men? Could she use her body to get information from him? Would Kurt know how Tucker/Bell was communicating? Could she find out without alerting Kurt that Paul knows of the organization? She could lie again; tell Kurt she'd gotten Bell out of the city. But, had Kurt been watching her? Did he know everything? She had to chance finding out. To gain Kurt's confidence again, she knew she would have to convince him that Paul was out of her life forever. Could she do that?

CHAPTER TWENTY SEVEN
In the Tub Again?

Late afternoon the second day out of Hong Kong, Truaxe received a classified message ordering the ship on a new CIA team pickup mission. Vincent read the message as part of his duties as senior radioman. He decided Clifford would not want him in the mission's boat, but, considering Clifford's mood swings he couldn't be sure. He waited it out nervously and exactly one hour after the message had been routed to Captain Clifford, Vincent was called to the Intelligence Officer's stateroom.

"An' you've been nominated lucky guy." Commander Valentino soft punched Vincent in the upper arm. "Since you've got that nudge-nudge, wink-wink crack team already trained. Have them and the boat ready to be ashore at three a.m."

Vincent flipped on his denial lever, swallowed all contrary feelings, threw his 'professional mind switch' and began readying for the trip with his first comment. "I didn't figure I'd be nominated, Commander," He said, "but, in case I was, I've been thinking. I don't believe I want Lake along. He's burned out. Nothing' too serious but I wouldn't be comfortable with him along. Same with Tucker. He got unpredictable on me the last time out. I nominate Cutler, that other second class signalman and I'll take any engine man. You okay with that?"

"Sure, I'll double check the C.O. and X.O."

"Thank you."

Vincent immediately went aft. Just as he started inventorying the pickup boat, Captain Clifford cornered him.

"You got the word I see, Vincent. Best PR we could think of, my trusting you. For you to shine, me to look supportive?" At first Vincent thought the man was joshing but no, as the Captain continued talking his phrases seemed borderline paranoid crazy. Standing by themselves on the ship's fantail it was getting dark enough to make reading Clifford's facial expressions difficult. "Somethin's wrong with the officers on this here ship, Vincent." The Captain was breathing hard, hissing as he talked. "Sneaky wrong and I think its 'cause you been talkin' to them …about our conversation at that French bitches." Clifford pushed one finger into Vincent's chest.

"Wrong, Cap'n." Vincent stepped back but was stopped by a guardrail. Clifford glared at Vincent's face as, with shaking hands, he lit a cigarette. He leaned into Vincent and whispered again.

"*Someone's* been talking! People are avoiding me like I've got a fucking sickness! That Corrigan keeps squirming around me like he's had too much Kaopectate." He mimicked a child's voice. "—'you alright, Cap'n? You O.K. today, Captain?" Clifford dropped his *Zippo* to the deck where it bounced once and flipped over the side through a drain scupper. He exploded, kicking at the scupper. "See, what my life is like since that night?" He said. "I'm cursed by you, dammit. Even Valentino treats me like I'm a child. Where they gettin' the idea I'm … I'm fragile? Has to be from you. That new man, Balkin? He could use a personality transplant. He's followin' me like I'm his new best friend. I can't shake him, him and his questions. He asked me outright about our slap. Called it the 'incident day'. Where's that coming from? How'd he know? He just fuckin' came aboard."

"I don't know, Cap'n." Vincent said feeling helpless. "Someone else is talkin'. I've not said a word. I'm not your enemy. I go to bat for you. We are allies, remember?" He desperately patronized Clifford. "You took me into your confidence the other night. I respect that in a man."

"Confidence, shit. You and that brunette? I don't trust you. I just don't trust you."

"What can I say?" Vincent asked with a shoulder shrug.

"Nothing. I plain don't trust you. I see you as some liberal ass-hole out to fuck over the men in the trenches when it's tough. You an'. ..an' …top-heavy …" The sentence trailed away. Vincent tensed, fearing anything could happen. Clifford raged again.

"For all I know, that trollop is a commie sympathizer or worse." Clifford dropped his head and regrouped for a few seconds. Vincent stood mute. "Or maybe even a spy who took over your head." Clifford added.

'Commie sympathizer' was in vogue to be bantered about. 'Trollop' was an outdated and stupid word to use. 'Top-heavy,' a childish but cutting remark that in many man-to-man circles, asked for an exchange of punches. But Clifford was making it clear the conversation was not man-to-man. He was taking advantage of rank. Trollop, top-heavy commie sympathizer, Vincent could let go of, but 'spy' was too close to home even to come from a man who was raving. He nearly lost his own composure. In order to maintain, he jammed his hands into his pockets, swallowed hard and waited again.

Clifford flipped his burning cigarette over the side of the ship, violating one of his own standing orders. Vincent tried to center things with the man.

"I started all this Cap'n, with the slap. I apologized, and I thought you accepted. We've been making slow progress. Let's keep trying. I can't continue fighting with you like this."

"You can't? Screw you. I'm the Captain around here but …but. You feel like you're more in charge than I am?"

"No … I. . ."

"Shut … I am the Captain …furthermore …that Negro, Lake? He'll go ashore with you. I make those decisions, see? I want continuity on the boat team. Y'hear me?"

"But. I just thought …"

"No buts. Ain't no Chief tellin' me …" Clifford glanced up and quickly became quiet. A hatless crewman walked out onto the fantail and was kneeling near the pickup boat's equipment. It was too dark to recognize the man but he was close enough to overhear the argument if it continued at the same volume. Vincent, glad for the interruption stood quietly beside the Captain, thirty feet in the darkness from the hatless man.

Tucker's obvious lanky silhouette also came onto the fantail, but he kept his distance from the other man and went about checking equipment. Vincent and Clifford stood quietly, stiffly. They watched in dim moonlight as Tucker tested the electric motor, checked the several air pressure test valves with a small tire gage and finally, opened the radio packs and checked them out, likely with CIC. The hatless man who had been simply watching Tucker work, stepped over to him, took a hand held radio and spoke briefly into it and then walked forward with it, out of sight. One of the boat's bigger radios jumped to life, an obvious check from the hand held set.

After Tucker finished the equipment check and wandered off up the starboard passageway, Clifford put one hand on either side of Vincent, pinning him against the guard rails, and whispered. "Don't you violate even one small order ashore, Vincent. Not the slightest." Without waiting for a comment from the Chief, he turned quickly, and stomped away. Vincent ran ahead and stepped in front of Clifford.

"Cap'n. I respectfully request you send an officer in the boat with me. He can be in charge."

"Listen, Vincent." Clifford said. "An officer will be in that boat with you. It'll be me, on the end of the radio. I'm in charge. You follow orders."

He walked away without another word.

At two a.m. March third, 1968, Master Chief Vincent made his way through the ship to meet and be briefed in CIC by Commander Valentino. He was dressed in wash khaki's, black sneakers, black ball cap, and yes, on impulse he'd neatly folded Cynthia's white panties into his back right pocket.

He learned there were Russian and Chinese-made torpedo boats in the area and for safety, Truaxe was steaming in a darkened ship condition. There were no topside lights that could give away the ship's position, including navigation lights and international warning lights. In the darkened ship condition, whenever an outside door or hatch opened, an automatic switch turned off the lights in that room, to re-light when the door closed. Flash, on. Flash, off. Trying to read, write or work on a piece of machinery was difficult if a lot of people were coming and going to the outside decks.

At night, darkened ship or not, bright lights are not permitted on the bridge area or in CIC. The dim red and green lights used on equipment permit the human eye to remain dilated so watch-standers can make the best use of the dimly lighted chart desks and radar scopes and still be able to see out over the darkened water. Once the human eye is exposed to a bright white light, it takes several minutes to adjust to 'night vision'. Most sailors on watch protect their night vision once it has been obtained and it is expected that people coming and going respect that.

Coming from the below-decks lighted areas, it took Vincent several minutes to adjust to the darkened CIC. Valentino spoke before Vincent even knew the man was close by.

"Can you see yet, Chief? Come look this chart."

"I'll need a long briefing, Commander."

"That's an oxymoron, Chief."

"A whichy-what'?"

"Long—briefly … . like 'giantshrimp,' or 'military intelligence.' They cancel each other." Valentino's humor enjoyed a one up.

"What about a *complete* briefing."

"Okay, we'll do a short but *complete* …briefing." With a pair of navigational dividers, he pointed to the chart table. "Bend in to this chart, Chief." Talking slowly and evenly, Valentino did what he does best; make intelligence information make sense.

"One hundred miles north of the DMZ, just south and east of this small city, Ben Tuy, 18 miles directly east of Linh Cam, here," he pointed with the dividers. " …two CIA agents … " He pulled a small paper from his khaki shirt pocket and looked at it under the red light. " … Ronald Piper and Tom Hollander are waiting near the beach to be picked up. That's right here." He made a light "X" mark. "They've been inland for, I checked …fifty three days, living off the land. The CIA's job? Since about 1962 when Kennedy put 'em in charge of all paramilitary activity in 'Nam, is ta'gather intelligence on exactly how the Ho Chi Minh trail, that's here." His yellow pencil made an indiscernible line from the Laotian border, south. "where it goes into Laos, at Lang Mo, see, here's the DMZ nearby. It reappears in South Vietnam between Dak Bia, here, and Pleiku, that's here, …south of Kontum …" He rubbed briefly at the map with the pencil's eraser. "I hate a dirty map. "He said, then continued; "No one knows exactly which routes from the north are being used to supply which types of things to which people at which points. I mean food, engineers, equipment, and troops. We don't even know how much is carried further down the trail or how much is slipped overland, east, and carried south by boat. Piper and Hollander have watched these northern terminals for almost seven weeks. I'll tell ya' something extra."

"Sure." Vincent was impressed with the details of the mission.

"We once thought Rolling Thunder, that bombing mission of 300 days of bombing roads? would best serve if concentrated first on Route Twelve, here …see it? Comes in from Laos. Bomb it, interrupt food supplies, then bomb Route Seven from the north, to aggravate engineers and equipment, and, on this," the pencil traced another line. "mostly tree-hidden rail line between this point … Bai Doc Thon and, over here, Dong Hoi, where we figure troops are being moved south on the trains. We bomb like crazy but the stuff still gets through. CINCPAC and COMSEVENTHFLEET intelligence is anxious to know why. See, our French maps, which look like they were made on an Etch-a-sketch, told us there was only about three hundred miles of road from north to south, at best. And we've clobbered them all. I think I have a clue." Without waiting for a comment from Vincent, Valentino continued what was now an educational excursion.

"I figure, an' I'm probably not alone, that all Rolling Thunder has done is anger the Vietnamese. Now they're so determined to get supplies to the south, they've built a bunch of roads we don't even know exist. Y'know, pontoon bridges they float out at night, hide in the daytime …flimsy village buildings they cover roads with until night …so on. We bomb road "A", they use road's "F", "G" and "H" while we're busy keeping them from fixing road "A". I think. I'm not sure. But I believe Piper and Hollander will confirm such suspicions. Maybe."

"So you're saying," Paul asked. "Rolling Thunder strikes do not have enough clout to keep 'em from moving supplies south?"

"Looks that way."

"So we should be bombing the sources at the source? Haiphong? Hanoi? Hon Gay?"

"Maybe." He shifted the dividers to the northern portion of the chart. "Up here? Along the Red River? It's full of traffic …shipping. It has to be war supplies. Same on this river here near Lang Son, this too, the Cau River. But someone somewhere is afraid of something."

"What?"

"China maybe. The Russians entering this mess."

"Commander?" Vincent felt comforted by the informal conversation. He actually thought maybe someone, Commander Valentino, actually had the elusive big picture. "You have the same feeling I have? We aren't being permitted to go ahead and win this thing?"

"Huh! Who really knows, Chief. We're not winning it, but we could. Ask the White House. There are things we military types aren't supposed to be able to understand." He tapped Paul on the chest with the dividers. "But, enough complaining. Ours isn't to reason why …ours is just to …"

" …shut up and get in the boat?"

"You got it." Valentino tossed the dividers and pencil to the chart. The pencil rolled with the pitch of the ship. He caught it as it fell off the end of the table. "Now, go get that Piper and his buddy out. First though, see if your ol' teacher, Commander Corrigan, has any info for you on torpedo boats."

"Aye aye, Sir." Vincent moved across CIC to the weapons area where Commander Corrigan was waiting.

"The usual stuff, Chief." Corrigan editorialized as the two men gathered in one isolated corner of CIC. "70.8's intelligence feels there'll be a lot more movement inland because we've pretty well stopped the barges and sampans in the gulf." Corrigan sniffled, fighting a head cold. "We need to bring this Piper and Hollander out to find out where the movement is, exactly. But, be careful. I understand CINCPACFLT wants to send 'em back in later. However, if you end up inland two miles at this point." He pointed to the chart inland and south of Niem Island. "See if this village, A12, is really a vil. They seem to cover up for our recon flights. They're covering something."

"If we're getting recon into that area, how come evac pilots aren't picking up the CIA?"

"We want low profile on that path in, for next time. 'Sides, Chief, air support's just too busy what with the action continuing at Khe Sahn, Hue and now … Quang Tri." His pencil snapped against the chart, right between the words 'Quang' and 'Tri'. "Small boats been working best for team pickup." Corrigan continued. "No losses except the one's we lost last month, wouldn't you know?" He sniffled strongly and poked at his nose with a rumpled handkerchief. "Also, there's been reports of heavier than usual torpedo boat traffic but that's been up here." He touched the chart at Mat island, eighteen miles to the north. "They don't exactly have a mass of warships in the gulf …" he declared sarcastically. " …but they got a few torpedo boats as you know. We'll be alert in CIC. None of 'em will get close. There's an easier way to become president than being dumped into an ocean by a torpedo boat."

Vincent couldn't laugh with Corrigan's red-nosed smile.

"Look, Chief," Corrigan seemed irritated by more than the cold. "I understand you told Commander Valentino you didn't want Lake to go in the boat with you."

"True."

"I supported that when the intelligence team met. I figure if you're in charge, you should have the men you want. But the exec insisted … "

"Wait." Vincent interrupted. "*Griffith* insisted Lake go? I thought the Captain wanted him."

"No, but he supported the exec who also insisted Tucker go because he was the only small motor man aboard. Griffith said Lake was a good man and you guys probably just had a personal falling out. I figured you had your reasons."

"Lake seems burned out, seems angry. I don't want him along …but, I've been told he's going. I didn't even want to go myself …" Vincent backed away from a sneeze of Corrigan's, then added. "I'm burned out too."

"You're something … I agree. I was against you taking this boat in tonight, all things considered from the last time. But both the Cap'n and X.O. overruled me 'cause no one else has your qualifications, not even me." His comments were interrupted by intermittent sniffs of the runny nose. "That latest flap between you and the skipper really tested what I think of you anyway."

Vincent asked quickly, curiously. "What flap?" Did Corrigan know of Clifford's fall-apart at Monique's?

"What flap?" Corrigan seemed amazed. "You hit the man, dammit."

"Old news, Commander. Let it go. Also, I wish you would've won the argument tonight. I'm burned out but not only on this war, on this navy." Vincent felt a drive to unload and borrowed the ploy he'd learned from Griffith. "Is this privileged conversation?"

"Go ahead."

"I'm also pretty burned out on the officer corps on this ship, especially the last several days. Nuff said?"

"How so?"

"Well, its clear I have issues with the Captain. He's like a frog to me, he jumps with no regard to where he'll land. But I'm trying to manage that. You guys not showing up at that planned dinner was, was …a sabotaging trick …intentional, I think. By Griffith, maybe by you."

"Not true. Griffith's not after the C.O. Fact is if Clifford sneezes? Griffith brings a tissue. He simply and legitimately screwed up the time for that dinner."

"I can't agree, Sir." Vincent said, pushing the 'privileged' sanction. "You had to know something wasn't right. All the officers in the liberty boat during the invite knew the Cap'n's intentions. Explain that."

"Too much said." Corrigan lifted his peaked hat with one hand and wiped his head with the wrist of the same hand. "Conversation's gotten *too* privileged." He slipped his hat on using both hands. "You and I have things to complete some day, Vincent. But tonight's not the time." Corrigan tossed his pencil on the chart and, with a rapid series of hissing sniffs, walked away. On the next pitch of the ship the pencil rolled and fell to the deck.

Heart thumping from both the confrontation and from the anticipated mission Vincent gathered his chart and made his way to the other side of the crowded CIC to talk with the actual CIC watch officer. It was Lieutenant Lukarmo. As he spread his chart out to talk with Lukarmo, Corrigan called out to him from across CIC. "Hey! Chief?"

He turned, expecting to be berated despite the privileged caveat. "Yes sir?"

"Be careful out there."

Vincent was surprised. "Right. Thank you." Seems everyone has mood swings.

Lukarmo, as CIC officer, also briefed him. "Has been some PT action up here. Kittyhawk planes scattered them before dark but they're so small—tougher to track than mercury spilled down a steel stairway."

"That makes me feel good."

"We'll be watching good. Kittyhawk has some Rolling Thunder F4B strikes scheduled in over you at daybreak. Other than that, should be quiet. No Arc Light comin' in tomorrow. Typhoon at Guam too bad to get B-52's into the air." Lukarmo turned to a weather symbol chart for the area. "Weather from your men in radio? Tells us not much rain likely for the night. Plenty of high and low clouds, but no rain clouds worth seein'."

"No scratchin' from the *Crachin?*"

"Nope."

"When I was in the Delta," Paul made small talk. "It rained all summer. Some seventy inches they say. "

Lukarmo folded the chart. "Temp in-country where you are going was fifty degrees a bit ago, up to 92 by noon tomorrow, and damp. Ain't gonna' be no dust devils spinnin' on parched earth in there." He gave Vincent an 'anything else' look.

Vincent felt uneasy and told Lukarmo so. "Just put the word out, will you. Keep the watch on their toes. I feel defenseless in there in that rubber dingy."

"It's bein' back here so fast, I think. I feel sorta' out too. Like we're waiting around for something to happen."

"Yeah. Right. Let's keep it from happening."

"We will, Chief. Lighten up. Even the Captain's goin' easy. He told me he'd take the boat's radio circuit himself. He's got a handy talkie on his hip out there on the bridge right now. You get personal service."

"You've checked the radio's out?"

"Not yet. Soon's you get back to the boat."

"Someone checked them with Tucker earlier."

"Probably Corrigan, or the earlier watch."

"Listen, Lieutenant. Have someone in here, in CIC monitor the boat circuit, okay?"

"Yeah, sure … "

Vincent lost his night vision when he stopped by the galley for a sandwich before climbing into the boat with Lake and Tucker.

"Rub a dub-dub, Chief." Tucker jested as he started over the rail.

"An' all the King's sailors and all the King's ships … " Vincent cracked.

The radio on Vincent's hip came to life "Spot one, Wait, over".

A radar operator thought he saw low-riding blips on the long-range radar. Torpedo boats? Sampans? Swell reflections? Jitters? No one could tell. The mission was delayed. For thirty minutes Clifford peeled Truaxe through the area at forty knots. They confirmed no contacts.

Meanwhile, Lake was still protesting at the same force as when the launch pulled away from the pier in Hong Kong.

"I feel spooky, Chief. Greenberg tells me everyone was jumpy on watch in CIC tonight. What about THAT?"

"What about it?" Paul was fed up.

"A breakfast of consequences will follow a night like this." Lake shot back. "That's what Lieutenant Lukarmo said ...a breakfast of consequences."

"The poet officer just knows he can bug you ... Abie," Vincent tried. "Please lighten up."

"Never ate a consequence I can think of." Tucker threw in. "But, if'n we are what we eat, Abie, from what I saw in that H.K. hotel, that's what makes you a pussy."

"Fuck you."

No attempts to calm Lake were effective. He whined like an actor whose lines were changed at curtain time. Tucker told him to 'shut the fuck up' a couple of times. That didn't help. Vincent tried distracting him.

"Abie? Here, put this tape on your dog tags so they don't clank in there like las' time."

"Fuck you very much."

An exceptionally bright moon kept coming from behind clouds. Its intermittent light caused everyone's eyes to dilate then re-adjust, in and out. This resulted in poor night vision. The darkness, the unconfirmed radar sightings, the poor night vision, the fact Clifford was taking the radio and Lake's whining caused Vincent a sick gut feeling.

At 3:40 a.m. he felt the decks of Truaxe shudder and lean into a hard turn. They were either being diverted again to chase a radar blip or Clifford had started the run toward the beach. After a moment Vincent determined the course was west, toward the beach. He prepared to re-enter the boat.

"Chief." Griffith seemed somewhere between very official and very friendly. "We're going in now for the drop off ...if you guys are ready. But 70.8 has *officially* added that A12 to the mission. No matter the success of the pickup, but I know you guys will get those two men this time ...that village A12? Commander seventh fleet wants it verified—command post, or not. Understand?"

"I don' get it a'tall." Tucker spoke up."

Griffith's eyes jumped to Tucker. "I'm not briefing you," he snapped at the man. "Get down into the boat. The Chief will bring you up to speed later. And get rid of that Tonkin Gulf Hat."

Tucker mumbled something and went over the side with Lake. Griffith waited until both men were out of earshot.

"How the hell you ..." Griffith muttered. "Well ... Never mind, Chief."

"What?" Vincent asked. "Why'd you jump him? Why'd you insist they go tonight, against my better judgment. I think they're both burned out ...rattled."

"They are fine." Griffith said. "Just take command, Vincent." Griffith seemed nervous, like he had something to say but couldn't say it. Eventually he mumbled several phrases about Tucker being ignorant, butchering the language, and wearing an unauthorized hat. Vincent couldn't tell what was truly important to the man.

"Is this an official report of some kind, Commander? You're really building my confidence. I've got men I didn't want to have in the first place …now you tell me one is ignorant … What the fuck?"

"Don't use profanity, Chief." Griffith said. "Look, disregard what I've said." Griffith looked over the side and down into the spot boat then turned back to Vincent. "Where were we, Chief?"

"I don't know. Tryin' to talk about A12?"

"Yes. Pick up the CIA first. Go to A12. Take a look. Observe and report any activity on the roads or paths in the direction of A12. If the CIA team has already cased A12, forget it and get back out here. OK?"

"Uh-huh." Vincent clipped his acknowledgment short, did not include a salute or a 'Sir' in it. As he started down the ladder, Griffith stopped him with a hand to his shoulder. Vincent drove him back.

"Commander? Listen. Take your hand off of me. It's a bit tense here for me. My body is here. My heads back in H.K. I'm worried over this, over Lake, over all of it."

"And?" Griffith actually looked hurt.

"And? Leave us alone." Vincent slid quickly down the ladder leaving Griffith staring after him.

At water level everything seemed blacker. The wet rubber of the boat emitted its familiar inner tube smell. The water was more disturbed than it seemed from above, like desperate little water fingers trying to grasp the slippery sides of the spot boat and the nearby ship. High white clouds darkened only by their unusual thickness moved quickly across the sky and continued to block and unblock the moon and aggravate night vision. Vincent was uneasy as he tested the radio, hoping someone other than Clifford was actually on the other end of the circuit.

"This Fireworks Zebra, loud and clear. How me. Over." It was Clifford's voice, muted and flat.

Vincent suppressed a need to not answer, and confuse Clifford, but no. He borrowed a radio check quip often used in the delta among river and riverine drivers.

"Mark it Twain. Over."

"Muddy bottom. Out." Clifford surprised Vincent. He knew the standard response.

Clifford wasted no time moving Truaxe east to the waiting station. Within five minutes, even when the moon shone, the ship was completely out of sight as though beyond some imaginary horizon. Tucker started the outboard engine. It seemed exceptionally loud in the stillness left by Truaxe's absence. Vincent tapped the Southerner's shoulder and spoke above the motor noise. "Shut it down. Go electric tonight. Quieter."

Lake, doing his first autonomous move since climbing into the boat, put new batteries in the red reading light and made a circle on the plastic chart cover at village A12.

With just the electric for power, the small boat bobbed with jerky movements as Tucker pointed it toward the beach. As expected, more water sloshed into the boat than during the calmer first trip and it was different in other ways. There was no cheery prattle among the three men. Lake withdrew into silent anger and Vincent had trouble reading any kind of an expression on the black man's face. Tucker was also unnaturally quiet, sitting, clicking the radio microphone on and off and humming a pointless tune.

Vincent shifted his attention to the mission by shifting his binoculars toward the beach, but he couldn't see anything. "Wish we had one of those thermal image scopes, Tucker, like in school."

"Yeah, I don't unner'stan' all that near and far infra red shit …but I know I could see through those things in NGFS school."

"Tin Can navy won't have those things 'til in the nineties." Lake offered from his pessimistic seat.

The radio popped to life. It was Clifford.

"Spot one, Fireworks Zebra, Over."

"Spot one. Over."

"Spot one, Fireworks Zebra, Over."

The boat's radio wouldn't reach the ship. "Now what." Vincent said jerking the mike from Tucker. He keyed it and checked the radio dial faces. In the semi-dark it appeared there was an output reading to the antenna. "What's wrong with this, Tuck?"

"Wait. Donno'." He flicked on the red flashlight and turned it to the dial faces. "Acts lahk' no antenna, or onna' wrong freq."

"Spot one, Fireworks Zebra, come in. Over." Clifford sounded impatient. Tucker flipped the crystal door opened on the radio and flicked two switches. Vincent returned Clifford's call again.

"This is Spot One. How do you hear me. Over." He got through.

"Spot One, this's Fireworks Zebra. Been unable to raise you. Stand a closer watch. You're loud and clear. Standby."

Vincent turned to Tucker. "Shit. Was this thing off freq?"

"Maybe it got bumped." The man looked at Vincent with an exasperated expression. "I don't know. It's okay now."

The circuit crackled back to life. Clifford used shackle codes to cipher numbers: "Spot One, Fireworks Zebra. We ordered off station. Continue mission. Will rendezvous this circuit shackle alpha alpha foxtrot echo. Backup Shackle golf india kilo kilo. Do you copy. Over?"

Lake, now acting as he was supposed to, had deciphered the figures. "They'll be back at 0800—42.8 mgs backup freq, fuck, Chief."

"Fireworks Zebra, Spot one. Wilco. Over."

Now on their own, a new and steady white light distracted Vincent from ashore. It was not a CIA signal of dashes. He decided to take the boat north for a few minutes and beach it away from that light. As they sloshed along for another twenty minutes in near total darkness, Lake expressed what they were all three feeling.

"Hate goin' in there with no ship cover, Chief."

"Same here." Tucker admitted.

"Me too." Vincent said. " …but …"

"But, shit." Lake erupted. "That woman I was with in H.K? She say—Vietnamese people get real barbarian about spy shit. They go for entrails, and feed spy guts to the dogs. Says shit like that."

"You tell her you were a fucking spy, Abie?" Paul demanded and wondered if Lake's Hong Kong honey was one of Kurt's women?

"No. Just hypotheticalizing with her." Lake said.

"You've been reading too many war books." Paul said.

"Well, maybe so." Abie whined. "If today was a fish though, I'd sure throw it back, Chief."

The moon broke free of the clouds. The lapping waves reflected splashes of light to seaward.

"CHRIST! GOD! Oh, OOOHHHHH … ! It was Lake, peering and pointing. "Comin' at us, Chief. CHIEF … !"

Less than a hundred yards away a V shaped spray of water moved at great speed toward them. Truaxe? Vincent looked with his glasses. Tucker was up also.

"Oh oh! Ah' hear it." They were getting the throated whine of a high-speed engine mixing with sounds of the wind and water noises.

"Shee'it." Tucker yelled. "That ain't no Yankee boat."

The boat coming at them was low in the water. Vincent snapped his glasses to his eyes and found them fogged over from humidity. He wiped them quickly on his shirt-front and jerked them back to his face.

"Low in the water. A P-Six. A Moi boat."

"That us or them, dammit?" Tucker sounded panicked.

"Russian made. We've got trouble." While the Moi class wasn't a very capable boat to go up against an American destroyer, it was perfect for what it appeared to be doing. Paul Vincent's rubber boat was about to be rammed.

"Fireworks Zebra, Spot One. Torpedo boat bearing down on us north of drop point. Over."

No answer. Out of range?

He keyed the mike again. "Mayday, Mayday. North of drop point."

No answer. The boat came on. They could now see it clearly in the moonlight. The scene suddenly lit up like fireworks after night baseball. Tracer bullets from the Moi boat.

"Mayday, Mayday." Vincent called again. Bullets were being walked straight toward them. The Chief yelled. "IN THE WATER!"

The gulf was warmer than the air. Vincent's mouth and nose filled with salty soup. In seconds there came a smash, a whooshing noise and an immediate cracking sound, very loud. Pieces and fragments flew into the air. Some seemed to hang against the moonlight.

Vincent ducked under the water. The wash of the turning boat dragged at him. A brine taste filled his mouth. Something smashed hard into his back, low. It felt like an ax. Flashes of twinkling lights like stars were in his eyes. 'OH CHRIST!' He thought. 'Am I shot? My life ending in twenty feet of water off a beach I'll never see? I have no children.'

He got to the surface.

"I got 'em, Chief. Come hep' me." It was Tucker, yelling too loudly.

Vincent's leg hurt terribly but also felt numb. He pulled with his arms to swim but his clothes weighed a hundred pounds. His left leg stabbed more pain. He stopped swimming.

Where was that boat? Something bounced against his back and cut him. A piece of the spot boat was still holding air. He grabbed and found a floatable stowage section with torn and jagged aluminum strips. A plastic wrapped backup radio was there, someplace. He felt around for life jackets but found none. He held on and tried to breath. Lake's lunch sandwiches and a paddle floated past his face.

"Help me, Paul."

That was Abie's voice. Vincent wanted to care but couldn't. He needed to make the hurt in the leg stop. He thought; we must fend for ourselves. The raft section slipped away. He yelled out.

"Take care of yourself. I got trouble here."

He found the piece of raft again and draped his arm over it. His right shoulder wasn't moving right. He felt vibrations in the water. The torpedo boat was returning. There it was. He dived under. The heavy clothes were now to his advantage as he churned his arms to get deeper. His ears hurt, a good sign he was deep. He looked up. As the rumbling black boat swooshed overhead he saw its uneven darkness against the moon's wiggling splotch of light. He abruptly touched a soft mud bottom. His lungs burned. He pushed off from the bottom but not a good push. Fear flew through him. Looking upward, the surface looked just like the sky did, murky and shimmering. He fought for the top, every other kick flashed pain in his left leg. His right arm also ached. His head popped free. He dragged in half air, half water and sank back downward. Surfaced again, he blew the water away and rolled to his back. Rest. He floated with no thoughts, no feelings other than the pain.

The crushing hull of the boat was on him, right there, too quickly. He threw out his arms instinctively. The turbulence of the hull blew him aside like a rag doll. His legs crashed against the underside of the boat, his body tensed, pitilessly awaiting the slash of the propellers. His mind flashed 'I am dead'—'I am not breathing'.

The blades somehow missed him.

Or had they?

Every nerve began to scream an inventory. He couldn't think. "Maybe this is dying." He commanded himself. "BREATHE."

He wanted to dive deep again, to get away from another surprise of the boat but his breathing wasn't good. He rolled onto his back to rest, his legs bent at the knees, his hands moving just enough to keep him afloat. The utility belt with pistol, bullets, survival knife, binoculars and other weighty objects was too heavy. He unsnapped it and let it join the thousands of USN aluminum cola cans at the bottom of the gulf. Rest, rest, he commanded himself. Listen for the boat most of all. Listen. He floated for thirty seconds, forty five, a full minute. His breath returned. He watched the moon vanish into a thick black layer of clouds that left only a peephole in the sky. Cynthia's face floated through his vision. He tried to keep her there, to continue to rest. But no, something touched his head and he tensed in terror. He jerked his body in a splashing twist, to fight. It was Abie, floating face down. One hand became locked deathlike in Paul's hair. A survival reflex caused Vincent to slap Abie's hand away. Abie sank but Vincent followed him without question. Reaching about in the dark water he caught Abie's shirt with the Ben Bristol fist. It wouldn't hold. He struggled for a second grip. Changing hands beneath the black water, he caught Abie by the coarse stubby hair. The weight pulled them both down. Can't let go, he thought. His lungs were close to blowing up. He kicked and kicked again into the world of pain. A foot crashed against his chest. He began fighting Tucker for the hold on Abie. All three heads all broke the surface and Tucker, seeming very strong, crawled between them. Vincent felt more pain when Tucker propped a firm grip under his right arm pit. "Git Abie. Git 'em. Blow 'em air." Tucker was commanding, sounding very capable. Without question Paul squeezed Abie's nose and blew into his mouth, once, twice, again.

Abie choked and vomited a mouthful into Paul. He gagged, ducked under reflexively and washed his mouth. Up again he blew air into Abie, again, and again.

"Hurry. They might come back, Chief." Tucker was panting but he continued to hold the two men afloat.

"Am I doin' this right?" Paul asked. He tried to remember the class instructions. He was panicky.

"I cain't see ya'. Ah donno"!"

Abie seemed lifeless. Paul didn't believe he was helping him. He almost wished to hear the boat again, then he could let go with reason.

Tucker faltered, "Fuck, Chief, " and let go of both Paul and Abie. Lake rolled slightly and slipped away, under. Vincent snatched blindly and luckily caught Abie's collar. For a moment Vincent lay in Tucker's arms, Abie floating against his chest. He believed Abie to be dead. Did he want him to be dead? Resting, Vincent's breath slowly returned. NO! He *didn't* want Abie to be dead.

THE BOAT? Where is it? His mind scrambled to comprehend. He kept his head swiveling in the darkness like a radar antenna.

"Tucker?" The burning in his lungs didn't ease up as it had earlier. "Let's find that piece of the raft."

"You stay with Abie, Chief. I'll swim and look." They were both puffing heavily.

"Swim around my voice, Tuck. Look for life jackets too."

"You yell. I'll folla' ...the ..." he gasped for air. " ...sounds."

"Wait!." Vincent said. "Wait! I'll blow up my pants." Tucker held Lake as Vincent rolled forward in a fetal position, slipped his shoes off, let them go, then struggled out of his trousers. As taught in survival school, he pulled out all of the pockets, letting his keys, some change, his billfold, his favorite penknife and Cynthia's panties into view. He stuffed the panties into his upper right shirt pocket, tied the trouser legs closed with an overhand knot and swung them by the waist to catch air. His shoulder pounded pain but on the second swing the wet trousers caught air and expanded like a small 'V' shaped blimp. He squeezed the waistband tightly. The jury-rigged life vest held him afloat.

"Go!" He told Tucker.

Paul lay back, kicked slowly and held Abie by the collar, holding the expanded pants with the aching Ben Bristol hand. That arm began to tighten up and cramp. "Hurry, Tuck."

Tucker pushed away and disappeared into the night. Vincent yelled the signals into the darkness: "Now is the time ...for all good men ...to come ...this way ...to ...the boat. This way to ... Truaxe . . will be lookin' ...for debris."

In less than a minute Tucker yelled. "Ah found it." The two exchanged calls and worked toward one another. The trousers deflated slowly. Paul barely made it with Abie. They slid the injured man half onto a broken wooden seat in the small airtight section of the boat. They rested for several minutes without talking.

Daylight edged into the eastern sky. Vincent remembered Lukarmo saying sunrise was officially at 0617.

"Chief? Wh'are the navy? The ship?"

"No no, Tuck. Somethin's wrong. They. . . left station. We have until 0800 …before a check from them."

"We bein' swept ashore."

Paul checked the birthday *Patek Phillippe*, a gift from Cynthia. It was the watch engraved 'this moment, and this one.' It was waterproof and he'd surely tested it a few times over the three years while swimming. The second hand was moving. It was 6:20. Nearly two hours before Truaxe would check for them.

In the growing daylight he checked Abie. His friend's face was dull gray over brown, his lips colorless. A huge patch of messy looking blood covered his chest.

"Afraid to …to disturb his clothing more, Tuck. Make him bleed more."

"Look'it this, Paul. We really sweepin' ashore." They were being lifted and dropped by the surf. "We been hollering loud … " Tucker added. "They coulda' heard us."

"Quiet, Tucker. Now."

Vincent peered ashore from his disadvantaged point and pictured several stern faced and determined riflemen waiting in the mist-covered brush. He thought to push seaward but the surf was running well in.

"Got no choice, Tuck. We're goin' in." Hanging on to the raft piece, Vincent pulled his trousers back on. It would be bad enough just being without shoes in the rough countryside.

The plunges of the surf took all their effort for several minutes until they felt hard sand under them for just a few seconds. Floating again, they were swept inward further to tumble in the waves against more sand. There was a strong draw to lay still and rest.

"We gotta' move, Tucker."

"No. Ah cain't."

"Yes! We gotta' hide ourselves. The CIA team. Maybe they're well, maybe they've talked to the ship." In pain, they dragged Abie into the trees thirty yards from the water. Two of their lifejackets and other scattered boat parts floated ashore over a twenty-yard area. All of it had to be carried into the thickets where, after several trips, the two walking men dropped to the sand next to Lake.

Silent masses of gnats swarmed over them.

"Lookee this shit." Tucker whined. The sand where they lay was covered with two-inch long heavy bodied worms. Despite the worms and gnats, Vincent didn't move. His body ached all over from the crash, the swim and the crawl ashore. It was 6:45.

"This's trouble, Chief. NVA know we around." Tucker whispered, looking about.

Vincent thought of a book he'd recently read about Vietnam, something about 'Strangers in a strange land'. "We'll be okay, Tuck. Help me with Abie."

They propped Lake against a mound of sand. The injured man spoke. "Mama? Mama?" His jaw went slack, his eyes rolled, his head flopped forward like an object off a table. He looked dead. The two men moved quickly and probed beneath Abie's clothes. Paul pulled his friend's trousers down. His right leg was purple compared to his brown skin. The thigh-bone felt too close to the surface. "This leg feels like its exploded inside."

"He git' hit by the boat? Them, was bullets I saw too. He shot?"

"Don't know." A long deep gash ran from Lake's left shoulder down across his chest. You could see what looked like whitish crisscrossing muscle beneath the splayed brown flesh. There were clots of dried blood and glistening deposits of drying salt throughout the wounds. How much blood had he lost? Tucker flicked the slug worms away from Lake and made a ring of sand to deter them returning.

"Back there in Hong Kong, Pappy? Abie said it wouldn't be good in a boat agin'." Tucker had picked up Lake and Stumpf's private nickname for Vincent.

"Fuck that, Tucker. Lake's not a psychic."

"Not your side kick? I thought you were best friends?"

"I said 'psychic' …not 'side-kick'."

"What?"

"Never mind." Paul said and went back to tending Lake.

"C'mon, Chief. You don' look good y'self." Vincent was having less and less trouble with Tucker's accent.

"Look!" Tucker became alert. Several jet planes were coming directly toward them in a low formation. It was the Rolling Thunder morning strike going inland from Kittyhawk. It was doubtful the pilots could see them even if they were looking.

As soon as the roar of the planes passed, they both heard noises in the trees over the noise of chirping birds. Tucker moved toward the piece of boat and simultaneously slipped his utility belt off and flipped it to Vincent. Vincent jerked the forty-five free of the holster, cocked it and released the safety. The gun's clacking noise seemed very loud. Tucker, watching the woods over his shoulder, unclicked an M-1 carbine from the heavy fasteners on the boat part. There were more noises in the nearby brush, distinct branch cracking noises, branches flicking back to position after having been bent, all recognizable sounds.

Tucker came up with two M-1's, loaded. The two men squatted ridiculously, shoulder to shoulder in front of Lake, waiting for whatever was to happen. Vincent could hardly hear over his own breathing.

There were no more noises for several minutes.

"Ah cain't take this waitin'. A'hm gwin' ta' look."

"Wait. We go together. But wait." Vincent stood upright. Although his left knee hurt when he moved it, he decided there were no broken bones. There was a huge surface scratch down the right side of his back with the skin broken some above the cheek of his right buttock, but the blood was clotting. There was a deep puncture wound further down his buttocks, turning black and ugly blue, but also clotted. His right shoulder was very stiff and seemed to want to lock into position. The Ben Bristol hand was throbbing. Tucker had two bleeding scratches on his right forearm and a blue bruise growing on his right cheek near his eye but he admitted to no real pains anywhere. Tucker had also let his shoes sink away.

"Let's look around here now."

As the early morning chill and mist gave way to warm sticky sunshine, Vincent, stepping gingerly in stocking feet, led the way into the brush. Visibility was good through the low trees. Birds chirped as the two men spent nearly twenty minutes poking around the musty smelling wooded area. While they saw no one, they found scraps of paper, three emptied food cans with lids punched opened by a knife, obvious human feces, several old and discolored non-filter cigarette butts, some empty nine millimeter brass and a rain faded French language match box. They were fifty yards from where Lake lay.

Tucker tapped Vincent's shoulder and pointed ahead, "Jesus, look." his expression empty, his color white.

Tied in a standing position to two trees were two people in black coverall uniforms and toboggans. Shocked into fascination, Vincent and Tucker moved toward the bodies stupidly, without caution. As they got closer they both knew it was Ronald Piper and Tom Hollander. Tied to the trees by the neck and waist with thick brown wire, the faces were gray-white where they weren't splashed with blood. The midsections of the black uniforms shone brightly with not completely dried blood. Both men had been cut across the lower stomach as one might dress out a deer. One man's throat was cut. The other man's cheeks and jaw muscles had been cut away and removed. His lower jaw hung completely slack against the apple of his trachea. Both men's ears were missing. Their noses had been cut away and dangled by a thread of skin between their eyes. Their genitals had been cut off and were stuffed into one of the men's throats. One of the men's eyeballs had been carved out with a sharp instrument and lay on the ground covered with crawling insects. There was an overwhelmingly carious smell of body cavity, urine and feces.

Both Vincent and Tucker were shocked into silence beyond nausea. Like a puppet, Vincent took the survival knife from Tucker's utility belt and flicked the genitals from the mouth of the man. They searched the pockets and found nothing but the stub of a wooden pencil. Still moving like a puppet, Vincent removed the dog tags and verified their identity. Piper and Hollander, both Protestant, both blood type 'A'. He left one tag with each man and put the others on the chain around his own neck. They turned to leave.

"Wait." Tucker said, alarming Paul. Pointing down toward Vincent's feet he asked. "What size?"

Without a word they removed both pairs of black sneakers from the men. They walked away in worn, cracked and ill-fitting shoes.

Arriving where they left Lake lying on a parka, Tucker talked to the injured man as though he were awake and well. "Found them CIA fellas, Abie. Piper and that Hollandaise guy? They dead, Abie. Gutted spleens. Not too long. 'Bout forty yards in there is a clearing and a path. Lotsa' folks come and go heah'. I got shoes. Chief got shoes. Alla' God's children have shoes. They dead as hell, Abie, Buddy. Gutted."

Paul Vincent was similarly stunned by the condition of the two agents. The ordeal jammed him strongly against something he had been taught to leave to others. The molding and developing years of his life he'd been told that others knew best, smart men prevailed, important decisions were left to those who know what was right. Suddenly he knew that was simply the ridiculous and controlling rhetoric of people who needed followers. He was suddenly very angry that he'd lived the first thirty or so years of his life blindly believing such rhetoric. 'Ah!' he thought aloud. " 'Naive' does have a true definition; it's a synonym for ignorant."

The killing of the farmers by the NVA had been wrong. The killing of the unarmed NVA by Truaxe had also been wrong. The killing of Piper and Hollander was just as wrong. At some level now coming conscious, Paul began to understand the Vietnamese, seeing them now, partly as patriots, fighting several decades against a series of foreigners. He had sudden empathy for the little people standing huddled with their children, struggling to be free, looking off to some promise from the future when they could harvest their rice, worship their God and walk in their green land untroubled by occidentals. While he had empathy for their plight, he had no empathy for their methods. Facing Ronald Piper and Tom Hollander's mutilated bodies had shaken that image. For the second time in two brief months he felt betrayed by the people on both sides of a war he was trying desperately to understand. He could no longer leave his decisions as to what is right and what is wrong to others. "Good God, Tucker." He said. "I wish I could just be a simple follower.

"An' me too, Chief. But I cain't get them men from my eyes."

"Nor I, Tucker. Nor I."

"I kin' do a deer. But a man?" Tucker kicked at a grass clump and walked off, hands jammed into his pockets.

Like Tucker, Vincent couldn't imagine what might motivate such cruelty from nationalists of any vent. Ignorance, fear, entitlement, guilt, revenge? Twice now, he was disappointed that some powerful force could overtake humanness and make a life so valueless. As he stood listening to Tucker rave and looking at his ten year friend near death in the morning sun, something impalpable altered within him. The agents' deaths were wrong because it was murder. But it was right because they were spies and intruders. He couldn't understand why he hadn't always realized there are two argumentative ends to any spectrum. For every 'on the one hand', there's an 'on the other hand'. He struggled that what was wrong for one person was often right for another. Any matter correct was also likely incorrect when seen with another's values. One man's traitor would be another's hero. He knew also that instant, that most 'rights' and 'wrongs', for that matter, any idea that was 'supposed to be' or that was 'correct', was actually someone with power's arbitrary wish. He hated discovering that life was this complex. He liked the simple black and white he'd been misled to believe existed.

Tucker walked back toward him. Vincent spoke first. "Christ, Tucker, this has fucked over my thinking."

"Thinkin' does nothin'. Thinkin' won't carry Abie …"

"No!" He said aloud as he looked at his bloodied and broken friend and at the straight talking Southerner. The newly forming sense of what was correct or incorrect straightened

Vincent's strained back, caused the bad leg to hurt less, relaxed the stubborn shoulder and even permitted the Bristol hand to flex without discomfort. The real Paul Vincent was standing up. He turned and looked at Lake and Tucker with a renewed sense of ability and a staggering sense of responsibility to the two men.

In memory impulse he reached into his shirt pocket and transferred the prized but still damp-from-the-gulf panties back to his trouser rear-right pocket.

"Aw'right, it's 0800. I don't want to run into those motherfuckers who did Piper and Hollander. Let's get away from the gulf and to a better place, a place with better visibility. "

"Yes, Sir ... Chief."

As they dragged Lake, the water cans, the rifles and themselves into the jungle, Vincent clicked on the PRC-10 radio that everyone called the 'prick-10', a little heftier than a child's walkie-talkie set. He openly called for Fireworks Zebra. Nothing. Over the next thirty minutes he switched back and forth between the primary and secondary frequency. Twice he heard a dim signal from someone using the call sign 'Pink 113' but he didn't have the power to raise the man.

They heard nothing on the air as they settled further inland in some trees near a rocky knoll. A half-mile from the beach Vincent felt safer. Ground visibility was good in most directions, only some thin trees blocked part of their view of the gulf.

"We keep watching the ocean, Tucker. Can't miss the ship if it comes over that horizon."

"I will. I won't ...it will."

Between 0840 and 0920 Tucker made three trips to the stashed boat and carried supplies back to stack next to Lake. The pile eventually included another PRC-10, two tins of fresh water, two full canteens, two M-1 rifles with six magazines of eight rounds each, three grenades, two colt forty-fives with two magazines of eight rounds each. They also had two parkas, a 12 gauge *Very* pistol with four flares, some C-rations, several one quart sized plastic bags and one map of the gulf divided into NGFS coordinates. The first aid pack was gone from its storage compartment. Only Tucker had binoculars. They took turns scanning the horizon.

At 10:40 they heard footsteps in the brush. A patrol of brown and green dressed NVA regulars jogged down a trail not twenty yards away from them. Some wore backpacks; most had on beige woven pith helmets, not metal army helmets. Most wore tennis shoes but some had on rubber thongs which flapped noisily. One or more were smoking cigarettes and the familiar rancid smell of old tobacco carried to Vincent and Tucker. The patrol passed them, heading toward the beach.

"Let's go. We're moving further inland. That'll fool 'em."

CHAPTER TWENTY EIGHT
In Country

On Truaxe, Commander Valentino had to steady himself against the chart table as the ship leaned soundly to port. "I believe we have time to take the ship in there, Cap'n, pick up those men, get out again and still rendezvous for the firing mission by ten a.m."

"I don't see it that way." Clifford responded, also catching the edge of the table for support against a second large wave.

"Nor I." Griffith agreed. "Plus, what if 70.8 modifies our mission again and we're off station by that thirty five miles? Not a chance, right, Captain."

Valentino asked the obvious. "Can't we tell 70.8 we're doing it?"

"No, 70.8 seems firm about letting those men sit in there until later in the day. I ain't questioning the admiral's orders. The men'll be okay. I'm not real concerned because we can't reach them onna' radio. Their radio was messed up earlier—remember?"

"But they have backups."

"Vincent will be fine in there." The yellow pencil Clifford held broke under the pressure of his thumb. He didn't seem to notice, simply laid both pieces on the chart table. "Some o' you guys have been mistaken about Vincent." He slipped off his stool and walked away from the group. Over his shoulder, he added: "Hopefully, Vincent's located Piper and Hollander. Their added experience will help Vincent and his team." Stopping at the ladder that lead below, he spoke directly to the O.O.D. "I'm going down for a sandwich." Then he addressed Griffith and Valentino. "We'll pick 'em all up by 1700 today."

Valentino stepped to the top of the ladder and called after Clifford.

"With your permission, Captain. I'd like to brief the helo crew. Have them alerted in case we end up sending them in to bring the boat crew and the CIA out. As a last ditch, that is."

"Very well, Commander. Very well."

At one p.m., in-country, while waiting for something to happen, Vincent decided they could do more for Lake.

"I'm miserable from the salt, the sand," Paul said. "My crotch and pits."

"Me too."

Vincent picked up a handful of the plastic bags. "You watch Abie. I'll find some water."

"That stream we crossed?"

"Yes ...ten minutes, over and back." Vincent left Tucker sitting in the shade with the comatose Abie Lake. Walking and looking for the stream, he felt guilty. He didn't want Abie to die, yet he didn't want to die because of Abie. Clifford's words came back to him:

'I've decided who doesn't die, now I decide who does'. The thought he was anything like Clifford disgusted him. He was afraid their being alike meant he would eventually become as unstable as Clifford seemed to be.

After less than ten minutes he came upon the stream. He filled three one quart plastic bags, tied their tops together, hung them over his good shoulder and hurriedly returned to Tucker and Lake. Abie still looked colorless. The Chief took Abie's torn shirt, balled it up with his hands, poured water over it and began to wash his friend. He washed his face and arms, pulled his socks off and washed his feet. Without a word he pulled Abie's pants down again and cleaned him where he was dirty from runny bowels and strong urine. Tucker just watched as the man cared for his long time friend.

Later, Vincent made a second trip for water. He washed Abie's shirt in the stream, rinsed his own face and arms clear of salt and sand and carried back enough for Tucker to bathe. The walking, the carrying and washing movements seemed to ease the stiffness in his leg and shoulder and when he'd look at Abie, his own pain seemed almost deserved.

At 2:30 p.m., there was still no word from Truaxe nor any sign of a formal search and rescue on their behalf.

At 4:50 p.m. they heard a helo. Tucker ran to a clearing and scanned the sky. "Thar'." He called to Vincent.

"Quiet, Tuck. Shut up." He joined Tucker in the small clearing. About two miles to the south and slightly out over the gulf, a helo was circling. It looked like the Seasprite from Truaxe. The plane hung in one spot for fifteen seconds or so then moved inland for a mile where it slowed considerably and putted-in over the treetops. Vincent picked up the radio and called on every frequency he thought might be used by the ship's helo. No answer. He fired one of their flares but it fizzled from moisture and dropped short. A second flare was another wet dud, as was a third. At one point the helo buzzed directly over them. They could see Salvadore DiNoble in the pilot's seat but DiNoble didn't see them waving and jumping up and down.

In less than five minutes they were alone again, for the night.

"Show us where you searched, Lieutenant." Griffith nudged him toward the chart table in one corner of the darkened pilothouse. Griffith flicked on a red reading light and swung it over the table. A roll of the ship caused the lamp to swing back to where it had been. Griffith pulled a chunk of paper from behind the lamp's base, swung the lamp into position and jammed the paper into its hinge. It held steady above the table. Lieutenant DiNoble pulled a rolled chart from one of the zippered leg pockets of his orange flight suit and spread it on the table over the ship's position map.

"Here. We scanned between this point, Echo, and point Kilo." With a finger he traced a line on the map, upper right to lower left. Neither Griffith nor Clifford spoke for a moment.

Randall Hill, DiNoble's gunner's mate who was hanging close beside his boss, spoke up. "That's where we looked okay, Cap'n. No nothin' there. No people 'cept a couple of civilians and a ox in a field ...right here, coupla' clicks north of the original CIA beach point." He put a finger on the map north of where DiNoble's finger traced. "We also flew over this A12 vill. The gooks waved up at us. Saw nothing 'cept civilians though. Some animals."

"Well." Clifford mused. "We take a look at first light."

"Have to wait for the mist to burn off a bit. Can't see in, although they can probably see us." Truaxe took a particularly hard roll to starboard. "Ah oh …rock and roll." The four men grabbed the edge of the chart table and leaned into the roll. A door banged shut on the port side of the pilothouse, having slipped from the hands of a lookout.

"Sorry, Sorry, Cap'n …gentlemen … "

The officers ignored the door slammer. The ship righted again, but immediately, its bow lifted against a large swell.

Clifford turned to DiNoble. "Gettin' rougher out here." He pointed a finger at DiNoble. "DiNoble? You pick the time to go in …in the mornin'."

Vincent elected to stay where they were for the night even though the men had never felt so miserable. As the stars came out so did the masses of bugs. It became maddening. Tucker was bitching and swatting. Vincent covered Lake with a parka and despite the temperature cooling off for the night; Abie perspired heavily and seemed to draw even more bugs. They all fought ineffectively for sleep. Vincent heard screams and thrashing sounds as he tried to doze but couldn't tell if they were true noises or dreams. Once, for an hour, he sat and strained his eyes into the trees around them, anticipating a hoard of men coming bayoneting into them at any second. After awhile he slept, but awoke in fright over and over. He knew he might die if he rested, but he also knew he might die the following day if he did not rest.

Once he saw Kurt Howser in the trees with a gun held to Cynthia's head. He saw Ben Bristol directing the V.C.'s to his hideout. Corrigan's hooked nose expression judging him harshly. He saw Rachael laughing aloud and reminding him how his navy was treating him. Abie's face changed to Cynthia's face once, then to Griffith's. Clifford was yelling: "I decide who gets killed here" but Vincent was yelling back that *he* was deciding now, "ha-ha".

"You talkin' to me, Chief?"

"No …go to sleep. I'll watch."

He woke up once, cold but sopping with sweat. "Shit. I'm fevered." He took the last of the water and began a ritual of bathing his face and neck. Soon, hives from insect bites or anxiety covered his arms, neck, legs and stomach. Three feet away from him, Tucker also tossed, groaned and scratched. Abie continually moaned in his sleep and at one point cried out clearly. "Veronnie, your ass's too big for those pants." When Vincent moved to him, there was no sign he'd been alert or awake.

Time passed in and out but it passed. By morning Vincent seemed able to follow one logical thought with another but he couldn't tell if he was still feverish.

At 0620, he said. "Tucker. That plane. Its a YO-3, one o' them recon planes I hear, I think. They're lookin' for us."

The night before, after DiNoble returned to Truaxe without a sign of the spot boat team or the agents, Clifford appeared truly worried. He cursed Vincent, cursed fate, cursed the Vietnamese, the CIA, the rough gulf, the weather and his father. He sent a classified message to CTG 70.8. outlining the status.

O 040215Z Mar 68
FM USS TRUAXE
TO CTG 70.8
SECRET NOFORN
MISSION 301-03-68.

1. RECOVERY BOAT LAUNCHED ON SKED. TRUAXE CALLED FOR HIGHER PRIORITY MISSION 0540. BOAT ON OWN RECOG.

2. NO CONTACT BOAT SINCE 0540. DUE HIGHER PRIORITY MISSION UNDER YOUR DIRECTION, TRUAXE HELO DELAYED RETURN UNTIL 1750. HELO RECON FOR BOAT AND CIA, NEGATIVE. SUSPECT MISSION LOST.

3. UNLESS OTHERWISE DIRECTED WILL DETACH HELO FIRST LIGHT, HOWEVER, DISTANCE PREVENTS HELO RETURN TO TRUAXE. WILL VECTOR HELO TO NEAREST U.S. SHIP VICINITY YANKEE STATION WHEN PICKUP MADE/NOT MADE. IF NO CONTACT, WILL REQUEST SAR ASSISTANCE. WILL ADVISE.

Not more than an hour after Clifford released the message to 70.8, Truaxe received a message from COMSEVENTHFLEET on an unrelated matter, but a matter that caused Clifford great concern.

R 011223Z MAR 68
FM COMSEVENTHFLT
TO CIA / DEPT OF STATE / USS TRUAXE
INFO COMCRUDESPAC / COMACV / CINCPACFLT / NIS YOKO / NIS PHIL
SECRET NOFORN
INVESTIGATION 71-68

1. MISSION 267-02-68 TRUAXE. COMSEVENTHFLEET BEGINS FORMAL INVESTIGATION K.I.A. CIA OPERATIVES HINKLE AND MARCH, AT COORDS 09-MA 08-BW (SO. CITY OF VINH N.VIET).

2. COMSEVENTHFLEET INVES STAFF WILL BOARD TRUAXE FIRST PORT OF OPPORTUNITY.

3. FOR CO TRUAXE. PREPARE CASE INFORMATION PACKAGE IN ACCORD WITH SEVENTHFLEET INSTRUCTION 00121.3C, NOV 65.

"Investigation my ass." Clifford said clearly. "Those men were blown to hell, the NVA did it, and that's it. Nothin' to investigate."

"This is routine, Cap'n." Griffith offered. "I wouldn't expect much to come of it. I'll get busy on the prep package."

"But they kiss the asses of the CIA and Department of State? Why?"

"Probably just a paper drill to keep the politicians satisfied." Griffith egg-walked to prevent a Clifford tantrum.

"Dammit, Griffith, we got a war to tend to here. No time to be re-wishing history on this paperwork."

"Captain … The Chief Yeoman and I will take care of it. Never worry."

"Tha's no YO-3 flyin' in up thar, Chief. That's a newer helo. Maybe that *sprite*' thing off the Truaxe agin'?" Tucker was waving a green parka and yelling from a small clearing. Vincent, still afraid they'd be overheard, limped to Tucker, his left leg tight and painful again.

"Shut up, Tucker. Shut up." He called in a horse whisper.

At that instant, his left leg sunk into soft earth. A clear clean cut opened just above his sock, then filled immediately with blood. The alarmed Vincent yelled to Tucker.

"PUNJI STAKES." Then remembered they could be overheard. He whispered gutturally, "One got me."

His warning was too late. Tucker went down in a clumsy roll. The parka floated out and fell ahead of him. Tucker rolled to a sitting position and with both hands, clutched his leg above the ankle. From thirty feet away Vincent could see blood run through Tucker's fingers. Watching for more of the traps, within seconds he dropped beside the injured man. Comparatively, Vincent's wound was a scratch.

Tucker cursed into the air. "Oh, Mary Magdelana, ah'm cut real bad … "

"Bleed it, Tuck. Can you?"

"Yes. Yes." The big man's face grimaced as he repeatedly opened, squeezed and closed a jagged four inch tear on the side of his right leg. The punji had penetrated the narrow space next to the tibia, narrowly missing the artery and the calf muscle. "Hurt, hurt, hurt." Tucker repeated. It was a classic punji stick wound. A stick, sharp end up, buried to extend a few inches above hard soil. Hidden with brush, dead leaves or soft, sifted earth, the stick was to pierce the shoe or stab into an anklebone of anyone coming by. In the delta region Vincent had seen stands of punji numbered into the hundreds. When a suitable substance could be found, the sticks were often poisoned but the poisoning wasn't a scientific attempt. Often the only material found on a punji was human feces. In some areas it was the duty of V.C. forced or V.C. friendly civilians to keep fresh excrement smeared on the stands of punjis.

While Tucker squeezed his wound to force bleeding, Vincent pulled his khaki shirttail out and tried to fashion a bandage strip. It wouldn't tear easily as they seem to in the movies. He pulled at it clumsily with his teeth and with effort ripped a large piece of the material free. He jammed it around and against Tucker's wound just as the helo swooped in over them. Tucker looked at his leg, then up to the sound of the helo, then down, then up.

"I'll get the helo, Tuck. Hold the bandage."

Tucker pulled the torn shirttail tightly around the wound and rocked back and forth. "Thumpin'. Burnin' too."

The radio, laying twenty yards away by Lake, jumped to life.

"Hey—hey, this' Hunter three-two-one callin' you by. Over." It was DiNoble's New Jersey accent using a Search and Rescue call sign. Apprehension quickly gave way to hope. From the familiar voice, Vincent could picture the friendly Italian's face. He scrambled the short distance to the radio, his own punji wound burning and stinging but not bleeding. As he keyed the microphone he saw the dim outline of the chopper out over the gulf, to the east, below their eye level.

"This' Spot One. Loud and clear. You ocean side us 'bout a mile. Over."

"Hey—hey not so specific, Spot One. Dumbos every-whar'."

Hurrying back to Tucker and Lake and picturing big eared Vietnamese soldiers all around, Vincent began squeezing his own leg to promote a flush of blood. The helo noise grew louder. DiNoble was making a graceful swoop from the ocean below them, up the hill. If he continued he would pass right over them.

"Spot One …am taking a look-see … " He flew not more than one hundred feet directly over them. Randy Hill leaned out of the left doorway. Hill let a yard-long white object free fall to the ground. It crashed into the brush fifty feet away. Vincent scurried to recover it. DiNoble took the helo south, then circled about a mile to the west and came back.

"Hey guys. Achtung! Too bisky-risky to come in now. Eye-ball the Sprite. Over." Rescuing pilots resorted to any sort of double talk or slang they felt might work to confuse a listening enemy. Near the end of the war the NVA and V.C. had sophisticated counter-measure teams continually manning U.S. frequencies. In 1968, however, it was catch-as-catch can but still, many Vietnamese understood and spoke English and surely listened in on frequencies when they could.

'Bisky-risky' said enough: No safe place to attempt a pickup.

The chopper screeched back overhead. Randy Hill was pointing his hand in a southerly direction out of the opened doorway. DiNoble leaned the sleek craft over hard and slipped down very close to the tree tops. About a mile south he lifted into the air and turned hard to the east. A white smoke rocket shot straight down from the belly of the helo. The radio cracked to life.

"Goopers at the smoke. We're taking small arms fire right now."

They had to move in a hurry. If he could see the smoke rocket shoot downward, the enemy could have seen the white object come down by their camp.

Vincent located and returned the package to where Tucker waited by Lake. It was an M-16 and several magazines fresh from the factory, packed in a well-padded foam box. He flipped the openers and its top came off. The smell of freshly opened plastic filled the air and hundreds of little peanut shaped bits of foam spilled and tumbled away in the slight breeze. He jerked the weapon free from the packaging and turned to find Tucker leaning over Lake, his ear pressed to Abie's chest. The Southerner stood up and looked at Vincent sheepishly.

"Hard draggin' him an' hurryin', Chief."

"Is he dead?" His question sounded cold even to himself.

"I was jes' checkin'. Seems okay."

Vincent dropped down and tied a remaining piece of his shirttail to his own wound. "North." He said as he tied the knot. "They'll figure us to head for the beach."

The radio cracked again. "This 3-2-1. Taking Dandy Randy to a Steeler's game. We'll be the half-time show. Over."

"Roger 3-2-1, taking the Alcan highway. Out."

"We've got thirty minutes, Tuck, to get free of the gooks," Vincent reached down and gently crossed Abie's good leg over the bad one and tied his laces together. "Let's get."

"Gimmie that new gun. I kin' work it."

Keeping only the weapons, radio, canteen and map, they headed north through the thick brush. Every few minutes they'd switch sides on Abie who occasionally whimpered and once or twice made gasping exhaling noises. One of them had to always hold Abie's collar to keep his head from jerking too much.

In fifteen minutes, the three pressured men held up in a large group of trees.

"Wish to hell we were where these trees remind me of." Vincent confessed to Tucker.

"Whar' that?"

"San Diego, north of there. Avocado groves off Route 163. I like the dead leaves. Warning devices if anyone comes close."

"I wish to fuck we was in LACA. No leaves. All concrete." Tucker said.

"LACA? Where the hell is LACA?"

"L.A. You know. L.A. CA equals LACA. Whar' you from, Chief not to hear that?"

"C'mon, brush a clear place for us."

In a ten by ten clearing, they lay still on bare humid earth and waited for word from DiNoble. Fifteen minutes jerked by a second at a time on the *Patek*, 'this moment, and this moment'.

Cigarette smoke drifted into their nostrils. At that instant, leaves crackled not far away. Tucker gasped, "whoops" and put a hand over Abie's mouth. Someone was walking toward them in the grove.

Both men breathed deeply but quietly. NVA regulars were only one hundred feet from them, walking from right to left.

"Jesus, Tuck." Vincent whispered as he counted. "Eighteen—twenty—twenty five. Shit." The soldiers were strung out in a follow-the-leader pattern through the trees. You could hear their voices. Vincent's blood chilled as he realized they were within hearing distance of the men who likely brutalized Piper and Hollander.

Because of Abie, there was no way to run and both men seemed to know it. With an exchange of looks, they prepared to fight. Straining to see through the trees, Vincent pulled his forty-five out, slowly. Tucker armed the M-16 without the slightest rasping or clicking noise. Tucker passed a grenade into Vincent's free hand. The familiar weapon felt cold and hot at the same time.

They waited. A perpetual minute passed. Another. Vincent realized none of the NVA seemed to be scanning or searching. Rather, with rifles slung on their backs or tucked in an elbow crook, rabbit hunting style, they were strolling easily, smoking, and talking quietly among themselves.

"Stay down." He whispered to Tucker.

They lay quietly and monitored the expressions and movements of the NVA as they passed out of sight down a hill to the left. With a fierce jump in his chest, Vincent reached down and clicked off the PRC-10. If DiNoble had called just then, the NVA would have heard the radio.

When the last enemy soldier's leaf-smashing footsteps were finally out of hearing range, Vincent tried breathing calmly but the air caught in the fear in his chest. "They didn't seem to be searching." He commented. "Just moving to someplace."

"Yeah. Movin' for lunch before they look fer' *us*. Listen, Chief. If they tortured Piper or Hollander enough, which they did …"

Vincent interrupted, with a resigned tone. "They maybe told the NVA we were comin' ashore, and where?"

"Right. C'mon, Chief, how else that boat know when and where to ram us? They surely told the gooks to be lookin' fer' us."

"It—It's a wonder they didn't station men near Piper and Hollander, Tuck. It would have been simple to ambush us. But they didn't. Something else is going on …something …we don't know about."

"You readin' tea leaves, Chief? What you mean?"

They were interrupted at that instant by the sound of DiNoble's helo returning. "That's what I mean, Tuck. They could get us anytime … As you say—'small potata's'. They want the chopper."

"Fuck. Maybe we should stay away from it?"

"Stay here, forever? Bullshit. We'll let DiNoble know 'bout these troops down here and work around 'em. He's our only way out of this shit."

"A'hm tellin' ya', Paul." Tucker's head kept moving from side to side, peering into the trees. "I'm afraid we are out-thought … "

"So?" Vincent became flustered at Tucker. "What should we do? What's your idea?" He expected some sort of brilliant objectivity.

"Yer' still 'boss. We still alive. I'll follow you." Nothing brilliant came.

As Tucker grabbed Abie's legs, there was another crunch in the brush. They dropped back to the ground. Another small patrol of NVA was making its way from right to left through the same area as the earlier group. Six men in all, one carried a U.S. bazooka, a second man carried four or five unsecured rockets in his arms.. This group was also talking quietly and not scanning. Tucker held Abie's mouth. The NVA walked out of view within a minute.

"Gad." Tucker offered. "Makes you wonder who each of them men are."

"Want me to call 'em back and ask?"

"Fuck, Chief." I hear they workin' on a battery telephone in the states. Sayin' some day we'd all have one. Maybe by then the army see an enemy in a tree we could call 'em up and ask 'em if he had kids, and all."

"Tucker …listen for the chopper."

They waited another five minutes before turning on the small radio. At that exact instant Tucker announced, "Ah' hear the helo."

"I don't."

"None o' you radiomen have any hearing left after that Morse code dits it all away."

Vincent listened for a few seconds but heard nothing. Tucker was probably right. He switched the transmit side of the handie-talkie on, and whispered.

"Flapper this Spot One. Grand Central here."

"This' Hunter 1-2-3. Agree. Recommend make like Horace Greeley. Call you next quarter. Over."

"C'mon, Tuck. West."

They dragged Lake as quietly as possible. Abie's one heel on the ground dug a skid mark in the rotting leaves and soft soil and stirred the smell of rich earth into the air. After fifty yards, the shoe came off, the back part torn away by the skidding

"Shit."

"I hate it too." Vincent announced.

Tucker switched Abie's shoes and they began again the slow progress west.

"Me too. Next time I'm in-countra', remind me to brang' a stretcher ...two corpsman ...an' a passel of Marines."

The humor didn't work. The two men were so spooked, any new noise or movement engaged them. If a breeze rustled a tree, if a lizard scurried from their path, if a bird took off or a nut fell from a tree, they would drop into the brush, weapons out, eyes wide. After fifteen minutes of the slow progress, they discovered a small clearing Vincent thought would be big enough for DiNoble to drop into and lift out of. He called DiNoble. No answer.

After ten more minutes the helo buzzed quickly in over them and off to the east. Vincent pressed the button. "We Greeley two gridirons from you. Over."

"Wait. Want no F.O.D. Out."

"What's that?" Tucker asked.

"Pilot talk, Tuck. F.O.D., foreign object damage. He's avoiding bullets."

"Oh."

The helo sped in again from the east. Vincent smelled the exhaust as the helo passed over and veered north at treetop level until out of sight and hearing. The radio popped. "Got your county and your town. Lookin' for LaGuardia nearby. Wait! Out."

"LaGuardia Greeley of us a clicko' bitso'." Vincent felt moronic speaking in fractured language but the imprinted visual of the butchered CIA men and the presence of the strolling NVA intensified his dreaded fear of capture. He was being extremely cautious, 'clicko' bitso' or not.

The helo appeared in the east again. "Spot One. Anti-Greeley country blank of you. Thas' all they be. I'll Pinnochio for the fans on the air. Got me?"

"He's gonna' bullshit the V.C., Chief?"

"Right. I just hope we can tell the bullshit from the real shit." Then to DiNoble. "Roger, Pinnoch ... I'll tell Jimminy and Cricket. Over."

"Spot One, this' 1-2-3. Fuel a problem. Returning to base. Be back at twelve hundred. Over."

"Roger, twelve hundred. Will fire a flare at twelve hundred. Out."

"Roger, roger. Out."

"The NVA that stupid?" Tucker asked.

"We hope ...we just hope, Tuck."

Vincent grabbed an M-1, a canteen, the maps and one of Abie's arm pits. "Ready and unlock that fuckin' M-16, Tucker. We still got a mile to go. He'll be there and we gotta' be ready." A mile to the east was at least downhill most of the way, part of it back the way they just maneuvered. They would be crossing that NVA pathway soon. After a hundred yards, Tucker dropped to one knee and adjusted his leg bandage. Fresh blood sopped from it.

"Fuckin' thang' does smart, Chief."

"C'mon, Tuck. We'll be in a clean bunk in sick bay …two hours."

True to training, Vincent expected DiNoble to show up without warning and make believe he was picking the men up at some clearing far upwind from the actual clearing. Once he felt the NVA were biting, he would dart low to the trees and in a wide circle, move outside of NVA hearing range. Then, true to training, staying down-wind, his targeted landing zone between him and the NVA, fly to where Vincent waited and swing down for the pickup. All in all, they could chance taking less than three minutes from the time the NVA could no longer hear him to get to the ground, load the three men and get out.

Both men were puffing as they dragged Abie eastward and tried to measure a mile. On a slight down grade Tucker suddenly let out a yell and dropped his half of Lake. In a smooth swinging motion he upped the unfamiliar M-16 and pulled the trigger. Not thirty feet ahead of them two brown clad figures stood looking at them. The clothing on both of the men rumpled, jerked and erupted wet. The M-16 clacked empty. The two dropped as though someone had thrown life switches to the 'off' position. Tucker stood, frozen faced.

One of the figures rose back to his knees. Panic struck Vincent. The bantam-weight man looked directly into Tucker's face as he groped the ground for his weapon. The M-1 was still slung over Vincent's back. The forty-five still holstered. The Vietnamese man touched his rifle. Vincent jerked the forty-five free and pulled the trigger. Nothing. The man had the rifle shouldered. Vincent slammed the action back with his free hand and released the safety. A round fired into the trees. The man was re-cocking his own rifle. Vincent's gun hand pained from his smash to Ben's face. He put both hands on the forty-five and pulled the trigger again. The second shot hit bantam-weight. The rifle fired into the air as bantam-weight fell backward, his legs folded under him.

The corrosive smell of the gun's powder burned its way into the sinus above Vincent's right eye. There was a small slash on the knuckle of his right thumb where the forty-five recoiled. Neither Vietnamese moved. It was suddenly deadly quiet. Not even a bird could be heard. "Shit," Vincent snapped. Paul Vincent killed a man. His first ever. A blank tape slipped into place and started recording life from that new prospective.

He looked to Tucker whose face was still contorted and gazing blank eyed at the two dead men. From some automatic place, Vincent again took command.

"Tucker. Load that fucking thing." The big man jerked his head, looked at Vincent as though seeing him for the first time, then came to life. He loaded the hot M-16 and reached for Lake. Vincent unslung the M-1, cocked it and lost a round. He then hooked it awkwardly into the crook of one arm. He grabbed Lake's shoulder with the free thumping Ben Bristol hand. They ran ahead, but this time like frightened sheep, dragging Abie, caution gone, bullying their way through the brush, not hesitating for sights or sounds.

Vincent spoke as they ran: "We can be shot at any second." The terror was overwhelming. His lungs were burning, his side was aching as it did when he was a child and had run from stealing Mr. Reek's apples. Maybe a bullet would be a reprieve, at least a rest. Cynthia? Cynthia? Cynthia?

"What?" Tucker gasped. "What 'bout Cynthia?"

"Nothing."

They could see a break in the trees ahead. They luckily stumbled upon what had to be DiNoble's LaGuardia. It was quiet there. It seemed safe. Vincent keyed the radio.

"LaGuardia." He whispered.

DiNoble was right there waiting. "Roger … Pinnochio goin' for the field goal. I'll be landing by those two tall yellow looking trees on the north end of the clearing. Over."

"What trees? I see no yaller' trees." Tucker was panicked again.

"He bullshitting the listeners. Shut up."

"Oh."

"This' Spot One …roger. Be by yellow trees, north. Out."

"He'll be here right now, Tucker. He'll come in from leeward. Let's go."

They could hear the helos flap-flap sound as it lifted from somewhere to the east and south. Tucker and Vincent huddled conspicuously near the center of the small clearing, their backs to one another, Lake at their feet, hoping DiNoble could see them."

"Safe in there, Spot One?" DiNoble seemed hoarse.

They hadn't seen anyone in the brush. "Nothing seen." Vincent replied over the air. The seconds ticked past.

"Home for dinner, Spot One." The Italian sounded great.

There was only time for hope. Their hearts pounded in unison with the flap, flap, crack, crack of the chopper rotor and with the familiar smelling exhaust blowing wildly in over their heads. Just as they felt the heat of the engine blowing down on them, Tucker pushed Vincent hard enough to knock him down. Dirt scattered in front of them, some flew into Vincent's mouth. Under the noise of the helo, the M-16 was jumping soundlessly in Tucker's hand as the frightened looking man fired toward the trees.

"What!"

The roar of the engine over their heads made verbal communication impossible. Vincent looked about quickly, frantically, but knowing full well what was taking place. The NVA had troops waiting for the helo at every clearing for miles around.

"Look." Tucker yelled.

NVA regulars flooded through the trees fifty yards away, eight, ten, maybe more. Vincent could see they were being shot at but he couldn't hear the guns. More dirt flew, jammed into Vincent's face, his nose. He heard a bullet distinctly wing off of the strut of the helo just over his head. He loosed two rounds from the forty-five. Tucker was beside him then, flicking at the M-16, changing a magazine. Vincent rolled away to his left. Tucker fanned the gun into the trees and jumped to his feet.

They could now hear the shots that were coming in because DiNoble had taken the helo up. He glanced up in time to see flashes from the chopper's nose as Hill's gattling gun came to life. Tree tops exploded near the NVA. Large pieces of branches fell and scattered dust in the dense greenery. The NVA scurried to run. He could see one fall, then another. Someone screamed.

Tucker was running to the far side of the clearing, calling to Vincent.

"Git outta' thar'. Git outta' thar'." Vincent turned to get Lake but bullets sang into the air around him, hitting the trees beyond him, scattering the dirt next to him. His body jerked involuntarily, his feet lifted him in little jumps. "NO, CHIEF." Tucker yelled. "Let him go."

Vincent fell, and then rolled for the trees ten yards away. There were two Vietnamese soldiers not twenty yards beyond Tucker as Vincent rolled in beside him. Very panicked, he pulled the trigger from his kneeling position. The forty-five jumped in his hand but the round hit a tree five feet in front of him. Tucker's gun fired three rounds and clicked empty. One Vietnamese fell, the second broke into an arm-spread run-away. Vincent watched him go as Tucker made to reload the M-16. The running man suddenly turned, dropped to one knee and pointed a rifle directly at Vincent. Vincent pushed Tucker then dove to the right just as a bullet winged in over his head and split open a scraggly tree trunk. A sharp rock or branch stabbed deep into Paul's right buttocks, re-opening the wound from the boat. He got up and sprinted behind some leg sized tree trunks but toward the man, unconscious at the moment of new pain. The soldier had run a few yards farther but stopped again and from a stooped position turned his rifle toward Vincent. The man's rifle barrel banged against a small tree trunk. HE DROPPED IT. His face whitened. The rifle skittered downward through a bush, out of the reach of the alarmed young man. The soldier dove into the bush, grasping frantically for the rifle. He picked it up but DROPPED IT AGAIN. All the while, Vincent charged toward him. At the last instant the man abandoned his rifle, stood, threw his hands into the air and made a nightmarish sounding scream as Vincent twice pulled the trigger of the forty-five. With the barking noises the soldier spun fiercely as both bullets entered his chest one behind the other and blew the shoulder blade out of the man's back. Spread out in the leaves, dead, there was a hole the size of a volley ball just to the left of the man's upper spine. Vincent found himself shifting consciousness to full denial, to automatic combat military man.

It was dead quiet again but now the air carried a damp smoky smell. Vincent, gasping for air through his open, dry-tongued mouth, stooped beside the man. He was a little person, as most of them were. Blood burst from his distorted lips and mixed with bubbles, pink, not red. He was young but Vincent always had trouble telling Asian's ages. Maybe eighteen, twenty at best. His uniform was crisp, dirty, but new, as were his sandals. His ammunition belt still shone new leather or plastic. Vincent had now killed a second human being, an inexperienced soldier newly stationed from wherever they trained him if they trained him at all. If the young man had six months of exposure, maybe he wouldn't have dropped his rifle. Maybe he'd be looking down at Paul Vincent.

"Leave Lake now." Tucker was beside him, crazed. "They think him dead." He was talking in single syllables. "Cain't git him in that field. Git' shot."

"Okay. Tuck, Okay. Wait!"

The brush far off to the right jostled again and rifles cracked, whistling bullets through the still air. The two men dove into the bushes as several rounds rustled in over their heads and snapped into nearby trees. Vincent lay in the brush, reloaded and holstered the forty-five. He untangled the almost forgotten M-1 from his back. He then eased the grenade from his pocket and recalled how to arm the thing.

"Survive, Paul." He said aloud. "This is it here."

"We aint'a' gonna' make this, Pappy … " Tucker bellowed.

"Fuck you, Tucker. We *are*. Shoot."

A NVA soldier ran through a slight clearing ahead of Paul Vincent. Vincent tracked him with the rifle as though he were on a date, showing off, male stuff, shooting, at the arcade on the pier in Long Beach. He fired at the man. The man dropped.

The navy often said Vincent was an expert rifleman. They said that in boot camp and later at Boarder Repelling School after the Korean War ended. He'd qualified as 'expert' again while he served on the minesweeper and again while at NGFS school when he trained for the Riverine patrol duty. His minesweeper was called upon in 1961 to release and destroy a submerged field of WW-II harbor mines in a bay off the northern coast of Borneo. He was such an excellent rifleman, and even though he was a radioman, not a deck rate, the minesweeper C.O. used him to shoot at loosened contact mines as they floated to the surface. It had been easy. A passive blob of rusted metal floating and bobbing in the ocean off that foreign jungle coastline. Click, bang—BOOM. A pull of the rifle's trigger, click, bang—BOOM, the 16 year-old mine exploded.

Here, with a pull of the trigger, a life exploded. Once, twice, another time.

"Shooting can be good clean fun" the ad from the National Rifle Association said. He'd lain in the cool grass as a child learning to shoot his uncle's snappy little twenty-two rifle. Good clean fun. Today there was nothing good nor clean, there was nothing fun. He could hardly see the target enemy from where he crouched in damp brush where the sweat dampened dust rolled in little balls down his arms and face and where large leafed plants waved in his gun site, blocking the targets, shadowing them, confusing him.

As he shot again and again, sweat ran into his eyes. His buttocks throbbed with a new pain, his leg stiff to where he had to keep it straight behind him, even in a crouch. His injured right shoulder pained intensely with the recoil at each pull of the trigger. His mind shut down to private thoughts of survival and stayed on automatic. He shot again and again, changing the magazine automatically as it rung free on each eighth bullet. He found a target and tracked it, slowly. Squeeze the trigger. It's an amusement park. Move to another target. There they are. That tree. No, the next one. Right. That's a man there. The shadow. The target. See, it moved again. "Crack." The weapon banged against his shoulder like Nick Vergis picking a fight with him in the eighth grade. His nose burned from the powder and the dirt in the air. His ears rang like a locked on fire bell.

One figure kept moving closer through the trees. It wore a helmet. The other's wore pith hats or no hat at all. An officer maybe? Vincent kept on him, slowly, deliberately. "There, now!" "Crack." The helmet spun off into the dusty air. The man dropped like a concrete sack.

"They evera'ware. Evera'ware." Tucker was screaming again.

"Shut up. Shut up. Fuck you." He aimed at the mid-section of a man. He shot. The man's face burst red. Another man spun and dropped. Tucker had shot him. Another NVA soldier jumped from behind a tree, his arm pulled back, a grenade in it. He'd forgotten they might throw grenades.

"Shit! Shit!, Tucker!" The man's hand hit a tree branch. The grenade fell. He grabbed at it, kicked it, grabbed again, missed. He spun to run from his fatal error. The explosive burst threw the small body forward to smack face-first against a large scraggly barked tree trunk. The arms of the man grabbed at the trunk for a few seconds. His back and neck turned shiny. He slid slowly to the ground as though someone had pulled his blood's drain plug.

Vincent was crazed. Tucker was screaming, "Ah'm runnin' out. A'hm runnin' out." He was shooting the M-16 one bullet at a time.

The helo was back, low and close. Randy Hill's gattling gun ripped into the trees again. They'd been gone less than a minute.

"Oh motha' of mothers, the chopper will shoot *us*." Tucker yelled. His eyes were bugged out, pupils centered exactly.

The gattling gun ripped the greenery and the ground around them. There was a scream off to the right loud enough to be heard over the sound of the big engine. The scream continued long and eerie like a stomach shot coyote had once screamed on an Uncle's ranch in Southern Idaho. As quickly as it appeared, the helo was gone, the scene quiet as in dense winter snow. The firestorm of the gattling gun placed some kind of finality on the fighting. Both Vincent and Tucker stood up cautiously. Vincent was drawn by the quiet to whisper. "Tucker? They'll be back to get us."

"The helo …or the gooks?"

"The helo, godammit!" Vincent laughed from false relief. "We're not done yet."

The two men moved back toward the clearing. As they moved through the bushes a soldier broke from near them much as a rabbit darts from cover in a late autumn cornfield. Pure survival was now leading Vincent's every move. The M-1 jerked into shooting position as though it were on its own. It fired, twice. The back of the man's neck exploded, then the cloth of his uniform over his upper right shoulder ripped open. He spun around and around as though in a mini-tornado, then dropped, suddenly still, just a little dust in the air.

"He was runnin' Paul." Tucker spun and looked about. "They' is a runnin' away. They runnin' from us." Tucker hadn't fired at the man. Vincent grabbed at him. "Look." he screamed at the red-faced man. "Your fuckin' piece is empty." Tucker looked exhausted standing there with the last full magazine in his hand. "Load it." Vincent yelled.

Tucker snapped the magazine into place but he still looked crazed. "Whar's the radio, Chief?"

Vincent panicked. Where had he dropped it? "Thar'!" Tucker yelled. The radio was on Vincent's belt. His voice softened. "You had it."

"I forgot, I forgot." Vincent turned the radio on. DiNoble's frantic voice was on the air.

"How you hear me? Over?"

Vincent listened but couldn't hear the helo engine. He answered DiNoble. "Spot One by the clearing. You loud and clear. Where are you? Over." He gave no thought to transmission safety.

They came to the edge of the clearing. DiNoble's voice filled the air again. "Gattling gun do it? How's it look?"

"He's gone. Lake's gone." Tucker shrilled.

Lake wasn't anywhere to be seen. Where had he hidden?

The radio popped again. DiNoble sounded impatient. "How's it look, over?"

"They've taken Abie Lake. The NVA took him, over."

"We saw 'em runnin' with a man, on a slide …in blue dungarees. We held our fire. North." The pitch of DiNoble's voice changed. "We comin' in or no, Master Chief?"

"Don't know. They keep comin' back. What you think? Over?"

"Chief … We comin' in, or no. Tell me."

"Do it." Vincent hooked the radio on his belt, gave Abie away for the moment and grabbed Tucker's arm. "C'mon."

They ran once again to near the center of the clearing. The helo circled in, coming down fast, the blades clipped leaves from the tallest of the nearby trees. The usually cautious DiNoble was playing a little reckless. They could see Randy Hill's face in the side door, an M-16 in his hands, his head jerking back and forth scanning the trees around them. Soon, Vincent thought, we'll be back to the gray ship and to people we know.

He reached for a handrail as the brush and dust rose against them. The hot exhaust roared in his face and shook his clothes against his body. Tucker's 'Tonkin Gulf Yacht Club' ball cap flew off and away as he grabbed a hand rail. The flap-flap of the engine gave way to a roar. It was working.

But a million rounds of havoc ripped into the soft skin of the chopper. The machine dropped the last three feet and broke a strut. Three fingernails were ripped from Vincent's left hand. Randy Hill's face went white in front of Vincent. Hill fell from the helo and crumpled to the ground, "Jesus" a small hole centered above his left eye, another below his right eye. "Jesus." Vincent went down, Tucker fell on top of him and rolled off. DiNoble came out of the helo but tripped on a loose cargo belt. He flew out the door and landed on his face, his drawn forty-five went off in the dirt, grazed the side of his face and took most of his left ear off. The ship sat there rocking and bucking against the earth like a frightened and panicked horse.

"Hill's dead—HILL'S DEAD." Tucker was screaming but the words were mostly lost to the noise. "I'm shot. I'M SHOT." DiNoble screamed, rising to a vulnerable standing position. Tucker jerked him back to the ground. "RUN."

Pings and bangs, noises, thumps and grinding crunches came from the helo. DiNoble jumped back up again, grabbed Vincent by the shirt sleeve and pulled. "THE ROTOR—THE BLADES" He yelled. As he flicked his head to run, blood from his ear spattered on Vincent's face.

Crouching and running, Vincent followed DiNoble and Tucker around behind the Seasprite and away from the direction of the spraying bullets. They ran as fast as possible. As luck goes, when foot soldiers shoot hand held weapons at running targets, they tend to shoot high. Bullets were splitting into the leave of trees ahead of them.

As the three men dove low among those same trees, the ship was sprayed with another storm of flying steel bullets. The rotors jammed with a huge thwaaaangg noise and the sounds behind the running men stopped. It was dead silent for several seconds, then, the chatter of a light machine gun. The trees popped and flapped around them again.

Blood poured down from DiNoble's ear and colored the shoulder and back of his orange flight suit. Tucker suddenly yelled. "RUN! RUN!"

They ran together as Vincent and Tucker had run before, past where they had stood off the NVA. They sprinted, stumbled and leaped over fallen NVA bodies and broken tree parts. An explosion sounded behind them but no one stopped. The engine had flamed and blown. They ran, blindly dodging trees, falling, running ahead for their very lives. Vincent gasped for air. "So close." He thought. "So close to the end of this."

Up a slope, and up another they ran. They ran through a small gulch and up a hill following Tucker's big limping strides. Up another hill, to the top, they ran until they each realized the NVA had not bothered to follow them. They may even be back there laughing at the running men, laughing over their fright. The NVA had gotten their big prize, the helo, and, they'd killed Hill, the man who fired the gattling gun into them. And, they'd taken Abie Lake. Five strangers in a strange land. One dead, one in enemy hands. The NVA could hunt the remaining three men anytime.

"Mary Magdelana." Tucker whispered.

CHAPTER TWENTY NINE
Vil A-12 and the Bell

The three survivors gathered under a gnarled tree whose rutted bark glistened with thousands of silvery pupa. Dropping to one knee, Vincent's shoulder brushed roughly against the tree. Several of the empty and dried cavities fell weightlessly to the grass while those still heavy with larva clung stubbornly. Vincent poked a fingertip against one of the larva-laden pupa.

"Stay in there, worms. It's safer." He turned to Tucker and DiNoble.

"Abie and I go back ten years." He said without emotion. "He's my friend …they got him …"

DiNoble interrupted. "And I can't believe Hill is dead, *really*. Maybe he's just hit?" His voice flat, he was trying to examine his bloody ear in the reflection of his UCLA class ring. He would not touch the ear though as if denying it had been nearly amputated by the piteous accident. Despite the flat voice there was considerable emotion revealed by his statements. "I keep thinking; what if he isn't dead. What if we walked away too soon an' he's bleeding?"

"C'mon," Paul tried. "I was looking at him when it happened." I saw two …bullets …" He let his sentence hang incomplete. He didn't want to say 'two bullets in his head'.

Tucker, now sitting on his haunches and looking at the two senior men, vocalized his own thoughts. "That Abie?" He focused on the ground for an instant, then looked up and added: "He one of them black guys who don't say 'axe me' when they mean 'ask me'. I like that." For Tucker to appreciate anyone's use of correct vocabulary was incongruous enough to pull smiles from all three of the men. It was also enough to draw them together.

"Okay." Vincent started what had to be started. "Let's talk this out. We got a lot to think of." He turned to the lieutenant. "First off, where we stand in regard to the ship?"

Holding his left hand an inch or so from the dried blood covering his ear, the rattled Lieutenant seemed to fight for order within his thoughts, then spoke cautiously. "Until they hear otherwise I think Truaxe will likely, probably …assume we, me and Hill picked you guys up. They'll wait for a message sayin' we made it to a ship on Yankee Station."

"So it'll be hours a'fore anyone learns we ain't thar, right?"

"Right, when we don't show someplace? There'll be SAR all over this place …."

"How long till a SAR?" Vincent was speculation.

"Maybe seven hours, maybe more. Depends on who else is down, and where. If and when … " He re-emphasized the words strongly, "*IF, when*, a SAR comes in, we gotta' make radio contact with'em, locate a safe clearing …which ain't been the easiest thing so far … "

Tucker silenced DiNoble with the wave of an impatient hand as if signaling: 'enough pessimism, enough'. "What about Abie?" He asked into the air. Assured the Lieutenant had stopped talking, Tucker turned to Vincent and repeated his question. "What about Abie?"

Holding one hand up as if to stall any interruptions, Vincent tracked every development to the moment. "Piper, Hollander, Hill, maybe Lake, dead." He said in a lusterless tone. "Now soon, maybe you, Tuck, the Lieutenant here …maybe me. All for a failed mission." He kept the stall hand in the air. DiNoble and Tucker both started to speak. He shook the stall hand. "Hang loose a minute." He said. The two others obediently waited.

After several seconds Vincent started absently flicking empty pupa from the tree trunk with one fingertip. He spoke a few words between each flick. "I can't tell if its objective sense," flick-flick, "or plain ol' bein' beat tired that's driving me to consider," flick-flick. "to cut losses, ignore Lake and leave the area." Flick, flick. "But not going for Lake most likely means erasing him," flick. "if they haven't already." Remember, we were ready to jump on the chopper and leave him 'til it was shot down …"

"He gots a wife, Chief. An we wuz' caught up in savin' our asses with no time to think. We thinkin' now."

"I agree." His finger emptied a ten-inch rut of fifteen to twenty of the cotton like pupa. Ziiippp!

Could he look in a mirror and shave after telling Veronica he decided not to go for Abie? "Where, Paul? She'll ask me. Oh where oh where is my Abie?" Returning to one pupa removal at a time, he tried what might be an easy way out. "You're the lieutenant, Lieutenant." He said. "Make some decisions."

The statement sounded like a command and startled DiNoble.

"Wait up, now." He stood up, worked a kink out of his right knee, re-cupped his hand over his ear and looked at Vincent. "This isn't my call, Chief, really." The man looked back and forth from Vincent to Tucker, a little twig jiggling in the corner of his mouth. "I don't know jack shit in-country. I haven't even been to and E and E in-country escape school."

"You're the Lieutenant."

"I've lost a man …" His expression said 'don't do this to me'.

"I've lost Lake, and two CIA agents." Vincent rebutted.

"But you've been here all day. Hear me, Chief?"

"It sounds like you guys is voting. Though you shouldn't be," Tucker drawled slowly. "Lookin' fer Abie in these woods makes us like a color-blind hound with a nose cold. But, you been callin' the shots and we still 'live, Pappy. That's DeWitt's vote."

"Who?"

"Ohh … DeWitt? Inside joke, family shit. That's mah' vote"

STREAM →
N.
SCRUB + TREES
THICK TREES ON HILL
6
5
4
3
2
1.
BIKE
VIL A-12

At noon, the strong smell of burned metal announced in advance they were nearing the clearing and the smoking ribcage of the Seasprite. Tucker scanned the area through binoculars.

"NVA could be anywhar', Chief."

"True …keep looking."

The sun was hot and birds were moving about, chirping, fluttering, even around the wreckage of the copter.

"Fuckin' little shitbirds." Tucker scolded. "They're sing-song chirpin' makes it impossible to hear the V.C."

"Shitbirds?" DiNoble retorted. "My parents are bird people. These little tiny guys are called Munias. I've seen Red and Plain ones today. I been watchin' 'em. Like over there?" He pointed with the elbow of the hand cupped around his ear. "That's a Pekin Robin."

"From Peking?"

"No, *Pekin.* Not Peking." Three busy colorful birds about the size of an eastern U.S. Robin fluttered into a bush in front of Tucker.

"There," DiNoble said. "The brown-gray guy with the gold under-neck, orange yellow wings. Pretty?"

"Back home we'd shoot the fucker."

"Is nothing sacred, Tucker?"

"Abie is, today. Birds ain't."

When they thought it safe, they moved to the helo for the final story about Hill.

His stark white and unmoving body was still there, on its back, an almost serene expression on his boyish face. "Son-of-a-bitch" DiNoble uttered. "They just … " The man backed away, paled, then started to cry.

Tucker picked up two M-16 magazines which lay next to Hill's bug covered body and grabbed the Lieutenant by the arm. "You'all come over heah'. You got that 'jes' lost a quart of blood' look, L.T." He pulled the younger man off a few yards into the clearing.

"This's awful." DiNoble said, giving in to Tucker's pulls. "I can't handle this kind of stuff. Never could." He turned and walked further away on his own, sobbing quietly. Tucker returned to beside Vincent, who was completing the dog tag ceremony with Hill.

"That Lieutenant ain't gonna' be much hep' fer' us, Chief." Tucker said quietly.

"Yeah …just wait, Tuck."

DiNoble was walking back toward them, a hand now firmly pressed against the scabbing ear. "Listen, we gotta' get outta' here now. I'll fly back in here for the body later, really. But hear me, Chief?" (Hear me, Mom, Dad?)—"I'll get Hill to a G.R.U. for burial. You let me have a helo and I'll take people in to even find Lake. Really. " (Buy me a puppy and I'll take out the trash every day—clean my room, do my homework). As he talked, he discovered there was fresh blood on the hand covering his ear. Looking at his hand with disbelief, "God, lookit' this." He turned straight to Vincent and asked outright. "Can I wait? Not go for Lake until I have a chopper under me again?"

Vincent answered the man with a line usually used effectively by parents. "We'll see, Lieutenant. We'll see. Let's look around here first."

With that, Paul Vincent took charge.

They poked about outside of the clearing. The NVA had gathered all of their dead and wounded. "Took Abie ...an' took their own too." Tucker noted.

Vincent speculated as he looked about. "Must have wanted him for a reason, questions, hostage ... ?"

"You said he was too wounded to be of any value ...wasn't he?" DiNoble questioned.

"Lake doesn't know shit secrets. Still, they could'a killed him but didn't." Vincent seemed puzzled.

"Maybe 'cause he's a black'un?"

In a small grove of trees fifty yards north of the smoking helo, the three men faced one another as though stopping to chat outside a sporting goods store in a mall on a quiet Sunday in a town near their home. Tucker started it.

"Ah' gott'a question fer' you, Lieutenant."

"Huh?"

"Whar' the hell the ship when we got hit by that gook boat?"

"Why'd no one come after us?" Vincent followed.

"Is that what happened? A boat?"

"Rammed ...torpedo boat. We called Mayday ... "

"I wasn't on the bridge. " DiNoble snapped the sentence to the two men, and then seemed to begin apologizing. "We got called off station t' go south. Way south." He whined. "Shot out some radar sights down by Annam Gate. You guys temporarily became stick pins on a chart."

"Had they written us off?"

"No! No! It looked pretty safe to leave you guys in here. There was no intelligence to lead the navy to ever believe there was NVA in here ... 'cept the question about A12."

"No intelligence same as bad intelligence." Tucker said, disgust in his voice.

"From the number of troops I saw from the air, looks like the gooks knew you were comin'. Then too, I had to beat Clifford in the eye practically to get him to let me take this one more sweep in ...really."

"Why so?"

"The ship was called even further south. The regular SAR teams were busy around the DMZ. I had the only wings within reach of you, really.

"They jes' left us, didn't they?"

"Not really, but yes. Looked like just a long wait ...but now we know better. Soon as we get back? We fill 70.8 in and blow the shit out of this area—I hope, really."

"Well, before we blow anything up," Vincent said with authority, "let's look for Lake."

As exhausted as inner city school children in their first country hike, the three searched doggedly until they located a trail where several drag sleds were pulled on dirt paths. Without a word, they began following the clear tracks.

"We gonna' follow 'em to that vil?" DiNoble asked at one point.

"Not sure." Vincent said.

"We could use a hand if we do. Really!" DiNoble added.

"Only hand we gonna' get is on the end of our wrist." Tucker cracked.

Vincent kept checking his map. "We're here. That vil, A12? Its north and I think right up this trail we're on." He thumbnail marked the wrinkled map for DiNoble and Tucker and pointed ahead. "I think A12's where we're heading."

They soon came to a place where the trail split. All but one of the drag sleds went left, west. The lone one went north."

"What think? Abie in the group? Or alone?"

"Alone. Believe me." Tucker spoke right up.

"Sounds right." Vincent agreed. "Dead and wounded that way, POW to the command post at A12. Determining if A12's really a C.P. might be the only part of this mission we'll pull off."

DiNoble came to life a little. "I flew over the thing with Hill." Here, lookit' this." Taking a stick, he scratched out some shapes in the center of the path. "There's six little 'hootches', in'na "L" shape. These five, each about twelve maybe fifteen foot square. The building that makes the L foot? Maybe twice that size. If we come in from here, the south, the "L" building will be on our right, the rest leading away from us ...like so."

"What's here?" Vincent asked.

"Trees to the north and east. A big hill west. Left to right on the south end is like a man made hill, an old dike maybe ...but no water 'round it. There's a stream north of the village a few yards ...runs off toward the gulf."

They continued walking.

'Where oh where oh where is Abie, where oh where oh where is Abie. Where oh where oh where is Abie? Way down yonder in the paw-paw patch.' The senseless tune hyperventilated its way into Vincent's breathing pattern as the three men cautiously made their way along the now widening trail. Vincent led the way, DiNoble walked right behind him. Tucker, the M-16 balanced on his shoulder, a finger in its trigger, brought up the rear.

"Chief, do you really think Lake is still alive?" DiNoble asked as his breath puffed. He seemed more out of shape than the other two. Vincent didn't answer him.

DiNoble kept talking. "Should we really be trying this?" His voice fluttered some, like a tape player with a bad drive wheel.

"I don't know anything," Vincent sighed, "except we are about to go in and look. Just wait." He said impatiently.

"I mean, you saw the soldiers. Are they ...tough? Good?"

"We're still alive from luck." Vince said, honestly. "Dumb luck. Guy dropped his rifle. Another blew himself up. Poorly trained, frightened."

"Lahk' us." Tucker added as he walked past and took the lead.

"We had it out with hand guns." Vincent continued. "A lotta' men died, but not us. The gattling gun ran 'em off best. We're lucky to be alive and to answer your question? I think we're pushing it to look for Lake."

"Pushing what? Chief?"

"Luck, Lieutenant." He cracked impatiently. "Luck ...we're pushing ours. Drop it, will you?"

DiNoble stopped Vincent with a touch to his arm. Vincent often forgot the impact he, as a Master Chief made on young officers. He was reminded of it as he watched DiNoble's throat move up and down in a series of involuntary swallows. "Lookit, Chief. I don't know if…" Fear filled, he stopped talking and with a helpless, trapped look on his face stared at Vincent.

"Can you do it?" Vincent asked. "You gotta' tell me." Vincent worried. The bravado from the freshest troop was failing. Vincent turned to Tucker who was watching them from a few yards up the trail. Tucker didn't wait for a question.

"You're the boss, boss. Let's go in thar'."

"Let's stay with plan 'A'." Vincent said. "The NVA won't expect an attack on their stronghold by three idiots. That's how I see it."

DiNoble again cupped a hand over the damaged ear and fell in line without another word.

At 2 p.m., after a lot of quiet walking and no opposition, they heard a rooster crow and a tinny sounding radio playing ching-chang music into the air. With a finger-over-lips caution from Vincent, the three crawled up a fifteen-foot rise that DiNoble had correctly identified as part of an unused dike edge. At the top, the relative warmth of the late afternoon sun brought a smell of garlic, manure, kerosene smoke and garbage over the edge of the dike. They could hear voices. With a deep breath and rapid heartbeats they took their first look at village A12 through green and yellow *Guzmania Vella* leaves at the dike edge.

Five uniformed NVA and two black clad V.C. troops were squatted in the center of a twenty foot wide path that stretched the length of the village. The Vietnamese were eating and talking. Except for the soldiers' presence, DiNoble's briefing had been very close to correct. A large hootch was to the right, five more strung out away from them paralleling the path where the soldiers squatted and talked.

The six buildings were made from gray weathered planks hammered together vertically. The roofs were part thatch, part tarpaper. Some small windows had glass; larger openings were partly protected by bamboo slats made into crude, roll-up shades. The first three hootches had little porch areas on the southern sides covered with roughly made latticework. Jungle brush grew right to the backs of the hootches to Vincent's right. Chickens were pecking around outside all of the buildings. Two light brown dogs slept near one building causing Vincent's pulse to race. They watched the dogs carefully but the two animals seemed to have given up caring about intrusions long ago.

"We're lookin' north?"

"Right … shh. Look." Vincent pointed. A radio antenna, half hidden by vines peaked out of the roof of hootch number one.

"Right." DiNoble said. "With that, and the uniformed guys here, this *is* a C.P. of some type."

"Two rifles." Tucker whispered. "An' two AK's by those big cans thar'."

A soldier came out of hootch number one frightening the three men into ducking their heads. The soldier called to the two who were eating. The three sailors raised their heads in time to see the three soldiers walk into hootch number three.

"Thar's our boy." Tucker pointed. Just beyond where the soldiers were eating and just outside of hootch three was Lake, lying on the ground in a crude stretcher. He was partly hidden by a stack of several olive drab five-gallon cans and a neatly stacked pile of gallon sized glass jars all covered by thatched camouflage, weighted down by a rusted *Pepsi-Cola* sign. One of Lake's arms moved.

Tucker peered through binoculars. "Look. His leg's in a cast?"

"One of these people is likely a doctor of some sort." Vincent said. "We'll get Abie out." He seemed confident.

They lay for twenty minutes watching the village and forming a plan. There were eleven uniformed soldiers, three civilian men and two women in the village.

"They'll put a bullet into Abie at any sign of an attack."

"Probably."

The unmistakable hiss of a radio receiver erupted from hootch number one and filled the air with a commanding Vietnamese voice. The village sprang to life, alarming the three nervous men. Vincent cocked the forty-five.

"Wait, really!" DiNoble said. "They're covering up."

Any uniformed soldiers disappeared into the hootches. A woman led three goats from the brush and tethered them to a post near hootch number two. Laundry appeared on a clothes line. Two soldiers reappeared, wearing farmer's hats and cotton shirts over their uniforms. In a scurry, two men grabbed Lake and pulled him into hootch number three. Lake seemed to be consciously looking around.

A very quiet U.S. Air Force L-5 observation plane zoomed in very low over the village. Vincent pulled the other two back and under a willow tree to where only he had a view of the Vietnamese. Chickens scurried in the village, the goats jerked on their tethers. The dogs looked up but didn't get up. The slow but very maneuverable little plane with the tandem seating arrangement for pilot and observer circled and made three passes over the village. The women and civilian dressed soldiers waved at the plane. The observer waved back. Was this part of an early SAR looking for them, Vincent wondered, or was it just one more uncoordinated intelligence opportunity checking the village? If it were the latter, the plane crew had likely been fooled.

"Someone sure toll' them that plane was comin'."

"Shh."

In minutes the village was as before and as the three sailors re-positioned themselves behind the Vella leaves, the card game resumed. The village had fooled the plane without a touch of panic or fright.

A middle aged woman in flip-flop sandals, a faded gray dress, and carrying several rags and a dripping pan of water, went into hootch three where Lake had been taken. She came out of the hootch within a minute and went into hootch number one. She returned again carrying what appeared to be a very large cardboard box of U.S. supplied bandages, the *Johnson and Johnson—New Brunswick, NJ, 08903,* clearly visible. As she returned to Abie's hootch she said something to the card players. Her voice was very screechy. The men seemed to ignore her.

"Doctor?" DiNoble asked.

"I don't know …nurse? Shh."

At three p.m. the village held some kind of a general meeting. Everyone present went into hootch number one except for one man who continued to nap and the two card players who had moved the game with the afternoon sun and were now close to the stack of five gallon cans. There was no way of telling for sure how many people, if any, remained in the other hootches.

"I count twelve in hootch number one" Vincent whispered. "including one of the women. The gray dress lady-doctor-nurse is still with Lake, right?"

"Yes." DiNoble seemed more centered than before. "Just the three men outside. Everyone we've seen thus far seems accounted for."

"Come." Vincent motioned. While Vincent led his two men thirty-yards down a path, his mind moved again into automatic professional mode.

"Okay." Vincent said, retaining leadership. "I'd like to catch 'em while they're still in that meeting. So talk fast. Give me ideas." As the men talked, realistic points went into a pragmatic file in Vincent's mind. "We outnumbered, outgunned, got hardly no bullets left an' it's their neighborhood." Any ideas requiring luck, hope, or guesses, "wait for a plane to come back and radio 'em to attack, jes' barge in shootin', maybe the VC were ready to surrender themselves," were discarded by Vincent's 'no'. After three minutes of brainstorming, Vincent shushed the other two with a wave of his hand and set the plan.

"This is how I see it, but let's not rely on me bein' right. I'm a radioman, not a Marine. Tell me if you think you can handle your end of this idea. Alright?"

"I have a feeling anything we're trying is really more hope than anything." DiNoble said, still sounding negative and frightened.

Ignoring DiNoble, Tucker bent in to listen to Vincent. "Talk," He said to his chief. DiNoble sighed, held his hand near his ear and kept looking over his shoulder toward the village.

"In a real battle." Vincent began, "So I read, you gotta' have the three D's. *Disguise*, we have none. *Decoys,* we have none, and *Deception.* Maybe we have a little of the deception on our side. So we can't go at this like a real battle."

"Talk English, Chief."

"Stop that 'poor me, I'm a country dummy' shit, Tucker." Vincent snapped at the man. "I've had enough of it."

"Of what?"

"The homespun patronizing, don't talk too fast for me—shit."

Tucker's face reddened a little as though he were deciding if he was to be offended, or not. A big artificial grin broke through the redness. "Okay, …you da' boss."

Vincent continued. "Most are in hootch one. Three men outside. Lake, the woman and maybe a guard are in hootch three." He waited, the two men nodded. Vincent turned to Tucker. "Hear me, Tuck. I'll go in the bushes behind and to the right of the hootches and get in hootch three. There's likely a guard in there, maybe only the woman, maybe. Surprise is my best weapon, and maybe …use a club, knife her at the worst."

Tucker seemed distracted. "You listening, Tuck?"

"Yep … Talk."

"I'll take Abie out the back way, into the brush. Drag him around to here somewhere …" He looked and pointed down the path. " …to that big tree down there."

Tucker grabbed Paul's arm. "Wait, Chief. Let me do that part."

"What?"

"Drag Abie out."

"Why?"

"Why?" The man looked surprised. "Ah. One …ah'm bigger. An' gimmie that knife. I don' think you've ever carved anythin' 'cept maybe a turkey … I'll do that part."

"DiNoble?"

"Don' have'ta as't the L.T. I wanna' do it."

"I agree, Chief. He's bigger. Might be a guard in there, or two."

Vincent thought over the change in plans. "Okay, Tuck. You do hootch three and get Abie down to that tree. We'll look five minutes after you go in. After six minutes? DiNoble and I will head away down the trail we came up on."

"But"

"Wait! Tucker. Wait." Vincent held up both hands. "Lemmie tell it all." (As if, "I've got the big picture, damn you."). He turned to face DiNoble. "You wait at the end of the path, on the dike. You'll have the M-16 and the spare rounds. From there, you can see me, the three men and see Tuck if he comes out the *front* of number three. I'll be by hootch number one with two armed grenades and a forty-five. If Tucker comes out the front that means he's been discovered. If discovered, Gooks are gonna' scatter outta' hootch number one like cockroaches with a light switched on. Your *job* will be to *first* shoot the two card players and the napper. You shooting is how I'll know all's gone to hell with Tucker." Vincent turned to Tucker. "Give'm the M-16." Back to DiNoble. "Can you shoot this thing?"

"I think so."

"Fuck, *'think'*. Can you shoot it?" Vincent glared, patience gone. DiNoble's face locked up and his body tensed and froze. The man was a mess. His blown away ear looked pus infected and very bad. He seemed to have no resources for strength besides the pressured bravado Vincent was putting on him. Vincent noticed the man's clothes were soaked from sweat but for that matter, his own sweat was burning his own eyes.

"Di-Di." Vincent said with a forced calm voice. "Can you shoot the thing?"

Looking much like a challenged school boy, DiNoble glared back at Vincent. "Yes … I can shoot the fuckin' thing, really."

"OK," Vincent went on, uneasily. "If Tucker comes out the front, you shoot the M-16. If that happens, I'll put both grenades into hootch one, and get anyone left after they explode." He stopped talking. Looking at his own clothes, even his thigh fronts were dark with sweat.

"Can we do this? Tucker? Can you do your part?" Tucker seemed pale. "Want to change with me, we will." Vincent said.

Tucker perked up a bit. "I still gots two balls. Ah' kin' do it."

"DiNoble?"

"I don't like the 'balls' crack, Tucker." DiNoble said with a projective whine. Tucker looked away silently. DiNoble spoke to Vincent. "I can do this, Chief …really."

Vincent ignored the strife between the two. "Okay, remember, we have no idea how many are actually in there. Noise will bring real trouble. I have a hunch Tucker will be able to get out the back …and away …"

"We're working on a hunch?" DiNoble seemed about to panic.

"Yeah, a hunch. A hunch is things …info I didn't even know I had 'til now. A hunch is hope with some experience thrown in. Best we've got. "

"Fuck this, Chief."

"I know 'fuck this'. But Listen. Shooting is the last fucking thing we'll be doing in there. I mean that. The L-A-S-T thing we'll do. So, I use my hunch."

Everyone became still. Tucker handed the M-16 magazines to DiNoble who pushed them into his front waist. Using his ear holding hand, the frightened looking flyer began rubbing his palm up and down the barrel of the M-16. He was breathing shallow, sweat ran in the creases of his folded arms and on the hairy backs of his hands.

"Listen." Vincent's exasperation and fatigue showed on his face and in his words. "We agreed I'm in charge of this shit. A piece of me says just slip in there and kill Abie." He paused. No one seemed shocked by his statement. "I'm remembering what was done to the agents and … I don't want Abie or any of us to end up that way. If you think all you can accomplish in there, Tuck, is taking Abie out …can you do that? I'll understand. Hear me?" As Vincent spoke those words, Clifford's words shot out at him from the Truaxe Bridge the day of the slap. "And so I decided who does get killed".

"Ah' hear ya, Chief." Tucker's face was grave. "But if they wanted Abie dead, I think they'da' done it by now."

"Maybe, maybe … If you want to though, Tuck, I'll change positions with you again. You take the grenades."

"Shut up with that."

"Okay."

DiNoble addressed Tucker one-on-one. "Hey! Considering the consequences …and all …really …" His voice trailed away. "Maybe doin' Lake a favor is the idea right now, really." He stopped talking and looked away into the air. His fear was very obvious, too obvious to the others than he wanted it to be. He nursed the terrible fact that he was being tested and despite being a chopper jockey, a big guy with brains and an education, he was failing the male-bullshit side of life that had always beaten him.

Tucker looked DiNoble over carefully and pushed one finger into the man's shoulder. "Lieutenant, don't you shoot me with that thing if'n I come out the front. Ya' hear?"

DiNoble wiped sweat from his eyes with the back of his wet wrists. "I hear."

"Lieutenant? Listen a minute." Vincent needed more confidence from the man who would be the double lookout and initially the main trigger. "Remember, we don't *want* to shoot. But we *can* shoot. Tucker is carrying the *tough* load here. He'll likely be out the back of that hootch with Abie. If it goes to hell? Only *then* the load shifts to you and I. Do you want to shoot those three jerks in there? Or blow up hootch one? Tell me. This is real life. There wont be any 'take-two' on this."

"I'll do the M-16. Leaves you freer."

"Imagine one of those three killed Randy Hill. That might help you hold your end up. You can do this ..." Vincent sounded too much like a father telling a son he could make it to the far end of the pool if he really tries.

"I'll do it." DiNoble almost screamed.

Vincent took the lead again. "LISTEN." He said. "This is THEIR territory. Did we miss anything?"

"Onla' this. If'n all goes to hell and we get scattered? We kin' meet fifty yards south o' the helo clearin' at sun-up. That an idea?"

"Good idea. But this'll work." DiNoble offered. It was his first but vague vote of confidence but it was a vote.

"Okay. Here we go, and five minutes after Tucker is to be in hootch three, we rendezvous down by that big tree."

"Fuck!" Tucker bleated. "Mah fuckin' watch stopped." He stood shaking his right wrist then looking at, then listening to the small black time piece.

"No matter, Tuck. Just go. We have to time *you*. Just don't dilly dally."

As DiNoble and Vincent slipped back up the path, Tucker moved off to the right. They were committed. Vincent again recalled the old war motto, often proven: 'No plan ever survives the first contact with the enemy.' "Shit." He said aloud.

DiNoble took a position at the top of the ridge and had a clear view through the plants to the front of the hootches facing the wide dirt lane of the village. Vincent stood beside hootch number one, below a small opened window. By leaning to his right he could see DiNoble. The little transistor radio still played ching-chang music into the air. Tucker had been gone one minute. Chickens clucked here and there. Two minutes. Vincent's sweaty khaki's were chilled by a slight breeze. He wondered if Orientals could smell sweaty Occidentals. Three minutes. He watched a beetle crawl up a thin leafed plant. Another minute. As sweaty as he was on the outside, there was not a single ounce of moisture to be called upon in his mouth.

At the rear of hootch number three, Cecil Tucker, whose American name was Winston Dewitt but whose code name was 'Bell' whispered in perfect Vietnamese: "I'm coming in, I am a friend. Do not make any noise." This surprise action proved to the world that Cynthia Howser's perception of his comments at the pier were exactly correct; Tucker was Bell.

Inside the hootch he stood with his forty-five pointed at the head of an older NVA soldier named Trong Chuc. A middle aged Chinese woman named Meling stood silently and watched. Tucker spoke in Vietnamese without a trace of an accent.

"I am named Bell. This man here is not Bell. I am glad you tried to save my life, even though you got the wrong person. I am the man who has been on the radio to you. I am the man you were to sneak to Yulin Naval Base on Hainan island, or to Hong Kong. I've been to Hong Kong but got trapped into returning here." Tucker pulled a paper from his pocket and showed it to Trong. The old man squinted and tried to read it but the print was too small, his vision too bad.

Tucker put the paper back in his shirt pocket.

Trong Chuc spoke in English and was obviously very confused. "But, we thought …the American voice …on radio."

"That I might be a black man?" Tucker, alias Bell, actually Winston Dewitt, laughed quietly at the mistake. "No. I am white."

"Why you hold gun?"

"Because! Listen! Other Americans are out there, many." He lied. "I am taking this man out the back door here. I need to take him to safety. He is a good man. A nice man. I want to just leave. If I decide to come back for an escape I'll contact you later. But for now, help me escape with this man."

Trong Chuc had been a soldier since 1954 when he felt the only right thing to do was to become part of the Viet Minh movement. Since then, he had been wounded three times fighting the French and the U.S. He'd been blinded in one eye, his right knee was locked permanently and, because of poor food, terrible living conditions and marginal medical care, parasites had damaged his liver. Of limited usefulness because of his injuries, Trong knew he would remain a lowly ranked soldier unless he could somehow prove himself brave or valuable. Today, with the help of the round-faced Chinese nurse, Meling, he had been given the job of watching over the famous American who had been so helpful in giving them U.S. secrets for the past months, the man code named 'Bell'. To let the man go away would only confirm he had limited value in the eyes of his superiors. He could not begin to consider, in any favorable way, what Tucker was saying. Tucker was stupid, Trong thought to himself, to not see my position here.

"I only got about two more minutes an they attack all you guys. This man is a good man." Tucker tried again, to be convincing. "I have made a mistake thinking that all Americans are killers. I have watched this man. He and others are family men who hate the killing. I want to take them back to safety. I have been wrong. You must help me." As Tucker repeated parts of the plea in Vietnamese, Trong Chuc surprisingly snatched for the forty-five. But his one-eyed vision was no match for Tucker's youth and energy. Tucker smacked Trong in the head with the barrel of the forty-five and without slowing the motion also caught Meling's upper arm with the last few inches of the blow. Both Trong and Meling dropped to the dirt floor. Tucker then turned to Abie Lake who was lying awake but quiet on the floor of the smelly hootch. There were new bandages on his chest.

"Tuck, you fuck. What is this? Where? What? … "

"Jes' lay still, little buddy. You an' me is goin' out the back door heah'."

"You been talkin' gook. What is this?"

"I talk gook …that's what."

Trong Chuc's knife arched through the air and would have landed exactly between Tucker's shoulder blades had Abie not cried out. Tucker dropped, turned, caught Trong's wrist and jerked as hard as he could. The force of the jerk caused the crippled man to fly through the doorway out onto the village pathway, twenty feet from the card players. Discovery imminent, Tucker didn't hesitate. He lifted his forty-five and fired through the open doorway, putting a round into Trong's back. Meling, on hands and knees, crawled under a small table. Her flip-flops fell away as she pulled her legs up close to her chest, rocked over onto her right side, closed her eyes and lost bladder control.

Within a second of Tucker's forty-five bullet hitting Trong, DiNoble jerked the trigger of the M-16. Bullets immediately bounced in the dirt outside of the hootch. When Tucker saw the napper and the card players fall, he grabbed Abie's litter and pulled it out the *front* door.

With one second of Tucker's first bullet penetrating Trong's back, Vincent jumped up and flung the first grenade through the hootch window. It clanged against something metal and thumped to the floorboards. There were several yells of fear and outrage from inside. He jumped to the front of the hootch just as the doorway opened. He threw the second grenade as hard as he would throw a baseball. It smacked a small man hard on the side of the face and bounced on inside. The man dropped. At that instant, the first grenade exploded with a flash but only a little noise. A MISFIRE?

Screaming and yelling, two men flew out of the doorway. DiNoble was standing right there squinting, his mouth contorted. His M-16, moving slowly back and forth ripped splattering holes in the two men. The second grenade exploded, flinging a third man out through the doorway and almost into Vincent's face. Vincent shot into him without further thought. As the hootch burst into flames, heavy gray smoked filled the air and blew down around everyone.

"I've got 'em here," Vincent yelled to DiNoble, "Help Tucker." DiNoble turned back to the street side. A fourth man ran from hootch one, his clothes smoking. The open air fanned his smoking shirt, causing it to ignite and burn. Vincent shot at him but missed, nearly hitting DiNoble. The man turned and ran past DiNoble, right toward Tucker. DiNoble raised the M-16. Tucker raised his forty-five.

"NO!" Tucker shouted. DiNoble jerked the M-16 sideways. "NO!" Two rounds spun off into the trees. "NO!" Tucker shot the running man with one bullet from his forty-five. The man dropped onto his front and burned, his feet kicking up and down, stubbing into the hard packed dirt.

Tucker came into Vincent's view from the right, dragging the litter. Abie's head was flipping up and down as the litter bounced. His eyes were open, his mouth moving.

"I almost shot you ... I almost shot you ... " DiNoble's eyes were bulged out, his tongue stuck way out of his mouth. The wounded ear was bleeding freely again. He kept fanning the M-16, shooting little bursts at anything that moved. He had shot the napper and the card players, the dogs and the goats. Overall, the frightened DiNoble had done a good job but Vincent was afraid he still might shoot Tucker or even him.

"Di-Di ... COOL-IT!"

A man moved into the corner of Vincent's vision, darting from behind the burning hootch. He ran sidelong, watching Vincent. He darted behind hootch two. Vincent lost sight of him but ran to intercept him. He rounded hootch two and saw the man running in a weird half crouch, backwards, looking directly at Vincent's pistol. He'd been hit by grenade fragments. The front of his shirt was all bloodied, but he was holding a rifle. He tripped backward and fell down.

The forty-five pointed right at the man's face, Vincent ran to within ten feet of him. Their eyes touched. The Vietnamese eyes were deep blue. They danced back and forth from

Vincent's face to the end of the forty-five and back to Vincent's face so rapidly the blue color came in flashes. The face was pale and lean. His dry lips flared back and showed clean teeth. His skin was covered with discolored blotches. The man looked at Vincent's gun, then Vincent's face, then his own rifle that was griped by the barrel in his right hand.

Vincent's mind raced back to capture his long unused Vietnamese words, learned the hard way during the swift boat days. *"Toi chi? Muon chu'ns ta' tio? Thanh ban,"* Vincent said, hoping to say calmly to the man, "No, we want to be friends." But his language file had become confused. His Vietnamese of the Swift boat days mixed with the Chinese of the shore patrol days. Exaggerating the shape of his lips he had confused the man by mistakenly saying 'no, we'd like to be boyfriends'.

The soldier answered in very quiet Vietnamese; *"Toi muo'n so'ng."* Vincent couldn't patch together the softly spoken plea—'I want to live.' He couldn't tell if the words formed a question, an answer, or a prayer. The man's face showed only fear.

"Lam o'n." (Please) Vincent said, remembering the word correctly. The man's face remained the same. Vincent tried his muddy Vietnamese again and told the man to not move, that he would leave him there. *"Dung yen. Toi so' di yen cho anh."*

The man's hand moved slowly down the rifle toward the trigger. "NO! Godammit." Vincent's hands soaked with anxiety. He wanted to turn and run. He was repulsed by the thought he might have to kill the helpless looking man with the humanized blue eyes and soft voice. The thought 'in cold blood' rang through his mind. His body shook with aversion.

Vincent dropped his own gun to his thigh ...maybe he'd recognize it as a peaceable sign. "I'm not ...not a murderous man." He said. "We can spare one another." But no, the man's hand moved even closer toward the trigger of the rifle.

"Hay tin toi." Vincent pleaded for trust but realized the man couldn't possibly trust him. He had blown up the man's hootch, killed the small man's friends. The man had to fear him, hate him.

Vincent lifted the forty-five and leveled it at the blue eyes. The eyes tracked the gun's upward course. Vincent still couldn't distance himself from the human sense of the man. Did some woman love those eyes? Pulling the trigger would be sickening. *"Thoi ti."* Vincent tried but the man wasn't hearing the appeal to forget it all and go on with life. He was too caught up in looking at the barrel opening of Vincent's gun. Reality clicked in. He'd have to shoot the man.

Vincent tracked the man's eyes. "God damn you." He watched for the eyes to betray his move.

The eyes flicked. The man jerked the rifle.

Vincent's finger pulled, three times. The man's face exploded, then his shoulder, then his chest. Parts of the man blew backward and the blue-black forty-five kept jumping in Vincent's hand.

Vincent yelled and words formed. "Stop this ... Stop. Stop."

"Stop, Chief. STOP!" DiNoble pulled his arm.

"STOP." DiNoble yelled again. Then quietly, "The man's dead. Abie's over here." Vincent let the forty-five drop to the dirt. DiNoble picked it up and shoved it back in Vincent's holster.

Vincent tried walking away with DiNoble but his feet rooted to the spot. "Never told me this part." He said into the air.

"What, Chief?"

"Nothing'." He said, except there was something. There had been no mention in *The Bluejacket's Manual* they gave out in boot camp of fate or luck or instants of happenstance such as facing a man with blue eyes and blowing him into another world. Vincent wondered: Did someone know a million years ago that Paul Vincent would shoot this man's face off on this late afternoon at a village the Americans dubbed A12? Was it fate? Was there fate? Could the blue eyed man have known ten years ago, twenty, that some day he would be sitting in a hootch when a grenade would go off and burn him, cut him, force him to run outside to meet face to face with a man from Steubenville who didn't want to be there? Vincent marveled, would it make a difference in the man's afterlife to know he had been killed by a man who did not want to kill him?

DiNoble and Tucker were standing looking at him. He looked frightening as a leader but their confused faces re-reminded him of Admiral Halsey's words: "If you're in command, dammit, command." He looked quickly around. The crazy plan had survived contact with the enemy, thus far. They were alive. They had Abie. Abie was alive.

"Get, get." He chased DiNoble and Tucker ahead to drag Lake. He hung back at the edge of the village to insure they weren't followed.

The bodies of the napping man and the card players were lumped on the ground, their lives soaked into the dust. One of the dogs whined and gasped as it also bled from a bullet lodged somewhere in its body. He shot the dog through the head with the last bullet in the forty-five.

A motion, a flash of color in the corner of an eye. Who? Gray dress, the round-faced nurse. His shot into the dog had startled her from where she was kneeling in the dirt, Trong Chuc's lifeless head on her lap. No danger, Paul thought instinctively. She'd nursed Abie. She had taken Abie bandages and water. Woman help in war. She must have a name. *"Ten Co Lagi."* He asked, his rusty Vietnamese returning.

The woman didn't answer. Instead, she jerked back from Vincent's eyes and struggled to her feet favoring one leg as though it were lame. Her front was covered with Trong Chuc's blood and her own drying urine. She hunched her shoulders inward and upward, covered her chest with both arms, pulled her thighs together self-protectively. Her friend was suddenly and shockingly dead, all the others were dead. She unwillingly readied herself to die.

"Ten Co Lagi." He asked again for her name. Then tried his meager Chinese. *"Jiao? Jiao?"* She understood the Chinese.

"Meling." She said and her whole body jerked as though startled by her own voice.

"Hello, Meling. Go home now." He said it unthinkingly in English, unable to recall the words in Vietnamese or Chinese. "Go home."

"Go home." She repeated.

Vincent pushed a fresh magazine of shells into the handle of the forty-five. Meling heard that 'racking' noise pistols make but, because he was holding it pointed upwards she relaxed some. "No." He said to her. "No more." She didn't understand his English but she did understand when he put the pistol back into his holster. She nodded once, then again.

He turned away from her. With just her eyes she watched him walk about the village. "Bizarre." He said into the air and then, spinning to face her again startled the woman to rapt attention. "Humans?" He said directly to her. "We're intrigued by bizarre. You know that, Meling? Humans go to freak shows back home. They do that here?" Her arms and thighs relaxed just a touch. Something about the sound of his voice. "We slow down and look at auto accidents, almost find romance in murder and rape stories. Death fascinates us. A preview perhaps of something we'll all know?" He spun about and looked the village over again. He spoke into the air. "We even have a holiday to frighten ourselves with." He turned and faced her suddenly but spoke softly. "Trick or treat, Meling!" She stepped back one pace and watched him tentatively.

"You understand me at all?" He asked with hands on hips. Meling's face still expressed the intensity of her earlier fears, but was softening just a touch, subsiding somewhat to some gentleness coming from the strange talking man.

"You wouldn't like Halloween night, Lady." Paul chuckled. He thought of future Halloweens and how flat they would fall with fake blood, hunched-up cardboard cats and plastic monster faces.

Hurry, he thought. Get out. Get to the ship. Take Cynthia to America where you belong. Make new friends. Forget this murder. He turned back to face Meling's creased eyebrows. "The U.S. can't 'win' here. Y'know that, lady?" Meling's head shook a little from side to side but her face didn't change expressions. Vincent seemed to jump to a different thought.

"What do you know anyway, dumb fucking woman." He mumbled. "You're probably alive right now because I can't kill anyone else. Or because you helped Abie ...and you don't even know he and I are friends. Or you remind me of Mia. Or else you're alive simply because you've got a vagina. One of those reasons ...but the last one is probably the truest."

He kicked at a dead chicken. "We can't win here though, so relax." He said words to Meling as he addressed himself with thoughts. Go back home, Paul Vincent, back where your heart can beat monotonously again. Back where you're not afraid to let one nerve touch another. The culture here can't be disrupted in this way. Like everything else, it can't be forced ahead of its time. Some human cultural sense of timing must be honored here.

"Know what communism is, Meling?" She said nothing in response but the puzzled questioning look on her round face indicated she knew she was to answer something. "Didn't think so." He smirked. "Well you're testing it right now. Your communism? It promises so much but, thus far anyway, Lady ...its delivered war, a lot of misunderstanding, disregard for you ...and, probably soon again? Some more war." He pulled his ball cap off and wiped sweat from his face with its crumpled soft cloth. "We'll wait!" He called to Meling. "We'll all wait."

"Wait?" She mouthed, not understanding.

"This village name? Meling? *Jiao?*" He kept pointing all about the village and asking 'Jiao'.

"Jiao? Tho Bac."

"Tho Bac?"

"Tho Bac." She said pointing all around her.

"It *will* be over someday." He said to her. Then he thought: Sit back, P.V., and wait and watch. The Vietnamese will make their own futures in villages like *Tho Bac* and *Ap Bac* and others.

"Your kids …my kids? If I ever have any? They'll talk 'bout this war …maybe even village A12, Tho Bac. But, they'll more likely forget. Ol President Truman once said, 'the only part of the future we don't understand is the history we haven't read.' Ain't that the truth. In ten years, they'll be reading fuck-me books and travel guides and mystery stories …and this war will be lost to history, and all its mistakes repeated."

"War?" Meling mouthed almost without a sound.

"Yes …war." He turned away as if dismissing her, and stood wide legged. "I know this now." He pulled the forty-five again and waved it about. He talked crazily into the air, to Meling and to the dead around him. "I know with no doubt what-so-ever …" His voice rose in volume. "HEAR MEEEE!" He yelled psychotically and heard his words echo from the nearby valley. Meling backed away to the doorway of her hootch. She was unconsciously holding both of her hands to her face, sniffing the dried blood as she watched the frightening man address the air and the jungle.

"Mercy …merciful? Fuck those words. They'll never have meaning again." He staggered a few steps as though drunk, took in a deep breath, rose to his toes and yelled. "NO ONE WHO HAS LIVED THIS DAY …" One hand repeatedly pointed to the earth beside him. "THIS DAY RIGHT HERE" and borrowing from his Cynthia. "AND THIS MOMENT, AND THIS MOMENT … WILL EVER PLAY OUT OR CAUSE … ANOTHER DAY SUCH AS THIS. HEAR MEEEE!"

He strode kind of stiff legged to the slight rise at the top of the dike. He turned and again addressed the dead audience but this time quietly, reverently. "But I also know, my friends. No one else *has* lived this day, not exactly as *we* have." Tears from a new source with new chemistry ran from his eyes as the logic in his thoughts fell apart. You'd have to have wars so everyone involved then could know not to have a war. He turned and yelled into the trees: "UNTIL EVERYONE HAS LIVED A DAY LIKE TODAY." And then said quietly. "But that's stupid … 'cause only me, and that lady, and maybe Tucker and Abie and the frightened Di-Di will be left. Who will listen to us? No one. They'll pat our hands and say 'there-there. They'll go on having wars until they have their hands patted."

He shivered visibly as he turned to leave, but then felt a new compulsion. He spun back once again to face the dead.

"THANK YOU. ALL OF YOU." The words had feeling. Meling stepped forward and knelt again with Trong Chuc. She crossed herself surprising Paul.

"Does that make it better, Meling? If he died for God or because of God, is that better? The Lord loves and forgives a righteous death?" He heard his own bitter anger and stepped back from it. This woman is too innocent for that. "To give him a moment of grace and dignity, Meling? If that's the reason, I understand."

Then quietly, Vincent mumbled to all those around hootch number one. "You did your parts, I'll go back and say *no* to the war now." Then he thought to himself. "But, of course, who will listen?"

He looked toward the smoldering bodies in hootch number one. He asked the plant with the beetle still crawling on its leaf. "Why we do this? For freedom, you say?" He spun suddenly, startling Meling. He yelled into the trees. "I say to you. NEVER! Have I felt less free or seen less freedom."

He strode back to the dike edge and was stopped with a jolt. DiNoble and Tucker had been standing just out of his sight, looking at him and listening to him. On the stretcher, Abie Lake's eyes were open. He was also staring at him.

He checked the forty-five to be sure he'd put its last magazine into place. He cocked a round into the chamber and again erroneously ejected a bullet. "Shit," he said, picked the bullet from the ground, rubbed it clean on his shirt front, dropped it into his shirt pocket, jammed the heavy pistol back into the holster and barged ahead down the path.

"See?" He said. "And I thought Clifford was crazy? C'mon, let's look for the beach, you three."

The three dusty sweated traumatized men dragged the object of their wonderful effort down the trail toward *whatever* was coming.

CHAPTER THIRTY
Pink 113 and Doctor Pepper Time

"GOT ONE!" DiNoble screeched loud enough to be heard a mile away. Jumping to his feet, the small radio jammed against his good ear, his eyes squinted. He repeated, "Got one." Very good, Vincent thought, the shaky pilot kept his promise.

"Pink 1-1-3 this is Four Down. Over" He turned to Paul. "I was gonna' say 'four blind mice' ...but."

The answering signals were weak, interrupted with static and riddled with white noise. DiNoble lifted the radio and he and Vincent both bent in to listen.

"Say again, sta—call—Pink 1-3. You—and bare—. Over."

"This is DOWN FOUR, FOUR DOWN. Can you hear me? I'll give you a long count. Tune me in. One Two Three ..."

As DiNoble counted into the radio Vincent looked to Tucker and gave him a thumbs up sign. Tucker, sitting on a large log on the sandy dune of the beach was expressionless. Lake lay quietly nearby on the litter. An uncontrolled smile broke across Vincent's face as the unlikely hope of rescue seemed suddenly plausible. As DiNoble started a second long count into the radio, Vincent worried about the batteries lasting, and wished the pilot had a higher level of common sense abut those sorts of things.

Twenty seven year old U.S. Air Force Captain Miguel Sanchez had just completed seven low altitude runs over the Ben Hai area, spotting targets for the Marine Corps artillery. Usually these two-seater planes used both a pilot and an official spotter, but today there had been a shortage of men at Da Nang. Miguel had been doing both jobs and was irritable and drained. On the last run he heard the unmistakable 'thuck-thuck' sound of two bullets snapping through the canopy of his Cessna L-19. He wasn't hit personally, the plane seemed to fly all right, but it scared hell out of him and he took it as a sign to be through for the day. He pushed the throttle full forward on the small plane, skirted the trees and headed east toward the gulf, just slightly south of the DMZ.

Miguel Sanchez was a flyer. He'd wanted to fly since he was thirteen years old. The Air Force had given him that chance after he'd worked his way through Arizona State University and received a degree in mechanical engineering. However, looking for enemy troop positions was not flying to him, it was tortured pressure and concentrated hell. Flying was supposed to be as 19 year old poet John McGee said in *High Flight*; "*to slip the surly bonds of earth and dance the sky on laughter silvered wings* ... " Miguel Sanchez decided to climb high for a few minutes to relax, to "*push his eager craft through footless halls of space*" away from the anxiety and danger of the low runs. At seven thousand feet he leveled off "*where never lark or even eagle flew ...in the high untrespassed sanctity of space* ..." He relaxed. He calmed. After several minutes of towering about and feeling the plane under him he returned to the moment. He changed frequencies to contact his home base.

He immediately heard DiNoble's frantic voice. "Mayday, Mayday …down four. Do you hear me. Over?" As he listened to DiNoble counting over the circuit, Miguel pushed the rudder over and started a slow climbing circle, searching for the best reception. It was then he answered DiNoble directly.

"This is Pink 1-1-3. You are clearer. What can I do for you Down Four?" The Air Force pilot's soft-spoken calm was completely out of context with the situation on the ground.

"Get the map goin' Tell the man … "

"Down Four, this is Pink one one three—low fuel here. Start talking, over.

Vincent ripped open the stained and splitting map and spread it in front of the lieutenant. Something distracted DiNoble.

The sweating flyer pointed south.

"Look." He said. Somewhat over a mile away, coming around the end of a jut of land were the dim outlines of several foot soldiers. Tucker was also pointing, only to the north.

"Someone was movin' up thar'." Tucker stuck an arm out toward the northernmost point of land. There was movement there also, slightly closer than the movement to the south.

"Shit. Give the plane our coordinates but also tell him we're swimming straight out from here. Do it." He was very direct to DiNoble.

"Can't do that, Chief." Tucker said without affect.

Vincent was puzzled by Tucker's hesitance and said directly to him: "We've no bullets, no weapons, fool. Someone from the fleet can get to us on those coords before very long. We can't take on another fight." Deciding to ignore the worried looking Tucker, he took the radio from DiNoble and called the L-19.

"Pink 1-1-3, this Four Down. We headin' from zero eight mike charlie to two zero alfa charlie (08MC to 20AC). Where are you. Over?"

Miguel Sanchez scribbled the numbers on the small pad strapped to his right knee and answered the call. "This Pink 1-1-3. I'm seaward of Co Lieu, heading south. I copy the coords but makes no sense. Over"

Vincent's eyes scrambled over the map for the identifying logo. "We using COMSEVENTHFLEET map 11-319 of February 68. You got that one?"

"This 1-1-3. Negative. But is it 11-319 February? Over?"

"Affirmative 11-319 Feb. 08MC to 20AC. We doin' a Huck Finn. You understand what we doin' here? Over."

"Got that. I know you're going Huck Finn to get to 08MC to 20AC on a map I don't have. Need a time reference. Over." The radio signal was fading.

"Roger on that and we being crowded out down here." Vincent seemed confident again. He thought of times, then of the *Dr. Pepper* soft drink advertisements where everyone is encouraged to drink one at 'ten', 'two' and 'four'. He looked at the chart. If they got into the water and moved at about two miles per hour they should be close to the coords by three a.m.

"Pink 1-1-3—This is Down Four—Make our ETA between the last two *Doctor Pepper* times, plus twelve hours. You got that?"

"This' Pink 1-1-3—Roger, *Doctor Pepper* last two plus twelve. Got that one."

"This Down Four. Relay that data to Fireworks Zebra, or SAR …anyone …you are God right now. It's Disneyland here."

"Roger. Look for first sign of assistance at about *Johnny Carson* time. Got that?"

"Right. Carson time."

"This is God, signing out. I'm going to change frequency now and drop this info on Fireworks Zebra." Vincent slipped the radio into a fold in the bandages on Abie's chest. Lake stirred and opened his eyes. Abie said he could remember 'the water' and 'the woman' and Vincent wondered if the NVA had medicated him in some positive way beyond the leg cast and clean bandages. Within a forced smile, Vincent told his friend he had a broken leg and a cut on his chest, but should recover.

"Paul." Abie smiled back. "Don't shit an old shitter. I got no feelin' in my legs, I got no dick." Vincent immediately poked around Abie's legs with a twig. He got no responses to several jabs.

"See." Abie cried fighting tears. "Nothin'. And I'm only cold on top. I broke somethin' real valuable, didn't I?"

"Don't know, Ab. Wait for now. Could be something bruised bad." Vincent didn't want to deal with a panicked man in the water. "We'll get to sea, get picked up. Get you to a hospital."

"I'm afraid of water, Paul. You know that." Abie was frantic again.

"No, Abie. Veronica says you're not afraid of water, you're afraid of drownin'. So am I. And, I'm not plannin' on drowning. Hear me?"

"I can't swim."

"I got you, Abie. I got you. You'll be fine."

Abie pointed behind Vincent, his eyes wide and glazed. "LOOK!" There was a series of loud click sounds. Vincent spun around. Several black uniformed Viet Cong soldiers were standing in the soft sand fifty feet from them. The V.C. had weapons pointed directly at his small group.

"Mother fuck." Vincent's exasperated curse said it all. Fear for his life was followed closely by guilt and confusion over having failed. At that instant, Cecil Tucker broke into a flurry of fluent Vietnamese, jumping Vincent's confusion even further toward bewilderment. He had no idea what Tucker was saying but the cluster of V.C. lowered their weapons.

Still talking rapidly, Tucker reached into his shirt pocket and handed one of the V.C. a folded paper. There was more jabbering in Vietnamese as the paper was handed from man to man. Vincent took in information and watched. Abie lifted his head from the litter.

"Paul? He was talkin' gook back with that woman." Vincent had no idea what the hell Abie was talking about.

The one V.C. with lieutenant marks on his collar spoke in English. "You Bell?"

"Yes. Ah'am Bell."

"This man an' this man an' this man?" The lieutenant pointed with his AK-47 to Vincent, DiNoble and Lake.

"What the fuck is this?" Vincent asked Tucker.

"Shut up, Chief. Let me do this."

"What don't I know, Tucker?

DiNoble found his voice, "What the hell is this, really?" He shut up when one of the V.C. stuffed the end of a MAS rifle into his neck and pushed him to his knees in the sand. Poking more, the man prompted DiNoble's arms into the air. Vincent raised his.

Tucker spoke again in Vietnamese and Vincent got some sort of a picture. Eight V.C., their disheveled black cotton uniforms worn and soiled, crowded around the four Americans. Some were smiling and many had teeth missing. Two had open runny sores on their hands, arms and necks. While most seemed they were too quickly out of a cradle and into the world, they were listening attentively to Tucker's patter of speech.

Vincent shivered as fear mixed with the first chill of night air. His confusion gave way to some primitive understanding that Tucker seemed very at home with the Vietnamese and that they seemed to know him. He couldn't be a true enemy though, Vincent felt, he had watched him shoot the NVA early that day. Who was fooling whom, he wondered?

Talk to me, Tucker." He demanded.

"Shut up, Chief. Not one word and maybe I kin git' ya' outa' this alive. Hear me? You owe Abie if nothin else." Tucker was stern faced when he spoke to Vincent but shifted quickly to a smile as he addressed the V.C. lieutenant, whom he was now calling Cahn. There was more Vietnamese talking, some laughing. Tucker would point to Vincent and Abie and slow his speech, sound compassionate and caring. When he pointed to DiNoble, his words and affect became harsh. He made machine gun sounds with his throat and moved his hand through the air imitating a helicopter in flight. He pointed seaward and mimicked a ship and cannon blasting: 'pow, pow, crash, crash', he said over and over. He pantomimed men falling and screaming. He took a stick and flicked it at the sand at their feet. Telling the story of the bombardment of the NVA soldiers, he pointed to DiNoble again and imitated the gattling gun.

"Wait." Said DiNoble. "Really, that's not true, not fair … "

"Bien Cao." One of the Vietnamese said, and jabbered excitedly.

Tucker turned to Vincent. "This man knew the commander of those soldiers killed by the ship. A lieutenant, nama' Bien Cao."

"Gia Dinh, and Theu." The V.C. Lieutenant said.

"They knew all of those men, Paul. They trained together near here. I just told them how you tried to capture them. To save their lives. I also told them of Clifford's bombing them to hell." Tucker turned back to the V.C. but Vincent called to him.

"What about the farmers killed? What do they know about them?"

Tucker's face became grim. He turned to Vincent and talked to him as one would a foolish child. "Don't bring it up, stupid. They're not." He turned back to the V.C. and smiled again. He pointed toward Vincent and continued in Vietnamese. He pantomimed climbing a ladder, arguing with someone, actually jumping back and forth playing both parts. He pointed to Vincent again then swung his fist and fell backwards saying 'Captain, Captain.' The Vietnamese cheered and pointed to Vincent.

"What? What?" Vincent asked.

"I told 'em you hit the Cap'n for shelling the NVA's. Now shut up."

"Shut up." The Vietnamese Lieutenant echoed.

"Shut up?" Abie asked into the air causing the Vietnamese lieutenant to come closer and look him over. Tucker babbled more in Vietnamese as the lieutenant examined Abie's wounds and bandages. The Lieutenant did not ask how he'd gotten bandaged.

Moving in close, Tucker whispered to Vincent. "If I work this right, you and Abie will get out of here alive." As he moved away, Tucker added: "May cost us the Lieutenant ..."

"WHAT?" Color drained from DiNoble's ruddy complexion and his eyes darted back and forth in frantic driven jerks. "You cannot ..."

"Shut up." A soldier threatened him with a push from his rifle barrel.

The V.C. lieutenant forced Vincent and DiNoble to sit cross-legged in the damp sand. The position caused Vincent's left leg to cramp in pain but a look from Tucker told him to shut up and wait. Next to Vincent, DiNoble's face was white even through his three day beard growth. "What the fuck, Chief. I came in to save his ass, really, and now he's bad mouthing me."

"Shut up." Lieutenant Cahn said strongly to DiNoble.

"Shut up." Several of his troops echoed the words.

"Shut up." Lake said from where he lay.

Lieutenant Cahn and Tucker walked toward the water and talked for several minutes. The remainder of the disheveled group of soldiers stood around. Some lighted cigarettes, some talked among themselves and with hatred on their faces, would point to Tucker and the other Americans. Vincent realized that while Tucker had a lot of influence over the Vietnamese, he might not have a total hold.

There was sudden commotion off in the dusk and the V.C. grabbed their weapons. Tucker and Lieutenant Canh dropped to the sand but got up quickly, Canh laughing. Several NVA regulars came onto the brush-covered dune. At first the NVA wanted to shoot the Americans but Lieutenant Canh became quite assertive. As they spoke in hurried Vietnamese, the name 'Bell' came up again and again as did the words 'Master Chief'. Vincent listened to the strange language wondering if these men had come by way of the burned out A12.

Tucker had to re-tell his stories. As he talked, the NVA calmed and relaxed their weapons. Some became animated, as did a few of the V.C. who were helping Tucker with the story.

The western sky, which just a few minutes before had looked like a tie-dyed T-shirt, was now dimly blue black. The eastern sky was near totally black. Tucker, Lieutenant Canh and the leader of the NVA squad walked away into the darkness. Vincent could hardly make out their figures. A very light mist moved in and chilled the air further. Some of the V.C. and NVA drew parkas over their shoulders. Vincent shivered, as did DiNoble.

In six or eight minutes, Tucker and the two leaders returned to where Vincent sat with DiNoble next to Lake's litter. Tucker moved in close and belched. He smelled of sweat and garlic breath. "Whoee. I jes' had one of them plankton sandwiches they eat ...dry. But, no matter." He belched again then swallowed hard. "Ah toll' 'em we was goin' to float out to the ship on them logs you had us tie together. Ah didn't tell them 'bout no plane. They don' know we's the one's what left those dead guys back there marked 'for parts only'."

"They won't kill us?"

"Ah' cain't tell if they truly feel the same way I do 'bout you and Abie, or not, Chief."

"How is that?" Was Vincent's first question.

"Ah think you an okay person, Chief."

"Who the hell are you, Tucker? Why they know you?"

"Woah now, Chief. I'm not who the navy thinks ah' am. I came 'board Truaxe for two reasons. One, to find out why the agent on board wasn't doin ...his ..."

"Wait!" Vincent interrupted, and Tucker waited. "An agent on board? Who the hell?"

"Wait now, Chief. You'll figure it out soon 'nuff. You ain't no dummy. Anyhoo', I was to get him back to basics and then I was ... "

"Back to basics?"

"The man wasn't doin' his job of ... " He smiled broadly. "Of good ol' spy shit." He shrugged his shoulders and moved the index fingers of both hands in and out like triggers. "Spy stuff, Chief." He laughed out loud. "But I was also to mess up anything I could mess up, see what U.S. Navy stuff I could pass on to the NVA by radio."

"You had a radio?"

"No, you guys did, you idiot. Why you think I was always checkin' those radios out on the ship? I talked with the NVA a lot. Like the night before we went inna' first boat? They fren's o' mine, Chief. They couldn't locate the fust' CIA agents 'cause they got there too late. Could'a saved 'em a trip if'n I'da know'd for sure Clifford'a gunned them down like he did. They got the second set o' agents 'cause I ah' toll 'em whar' to look fer' 'em."

"You knew we'd find 'em dead like that?"

"Well, not 'zactly like that. That was awful. But yes, find 'em dead somewhere. You 'member me clickin' that microphone on and off, and bein' off freq?

"Yes."

Ten clicks, ten minutes, on 67.5 Megahertz. Truaxe never heard no Mayday signal 'cause I'd taken the antenna off."

"Fuck you, Tucker."

"Fuck me? Look around here. I got the guns. The V.C. are on my team. I jes' ate a sandwich an' you say fuck me? Fuck you, Chief. Maybe you ain't too crazy smart after all."

"But you've been killin' Vietnamese too. . "

"Whoops ..." Tucker's eyes flicked toward Cahn, then back. His voice was tense. "Now don't say that agin', Chief."

"They'll figure we did the village, Tucker. They'll know you been fighting on our side today."

"Listen, Chief. Those two gooks I shot with the M-16 didn't shoot us first 'cause they thought Lake was me, was Bell ...bein' dragged. I could'a talked to 'em. I'm not real sure why I shot 'em. But hell with that. 'Member our fust' night inn'a boat? When you said Cynthia Howser's name? With the letter from her?"

"Yes." Vaguely remembering, Vincent's heart balled up like a fist.

"Hell, that was one of mah' Hong Kong contact's name so you likely knew her unless there is more than one with her name. Ah' was to get to H.K. on Truaxe and contact her or Shaman, or Speckle, or Star, or Monique, or Au-yeung. See, Ah' know alla' names, and they're other names. Ah' had phone numbers memorized—how does 428-9330 sound to you? Familiar?"

Vincent said nothing.

"Thas' your sweetie's telephone. Hell, I thought you might be a contact man fer me when I saw Howser's name on the envelope Lake handed you. Tried my Bell code name on you twice't, on her onc't. But none o' ya' answered none."

"Wait now. Your girl was his contact?" DiNoble asked with a disbelieving whine.

Vincent ignored the Lieutenant and concentrated on Tucker. Again, someone he'd trusted had tricked him.

Tucker continued to brag. "Ah' wasn't able to make contact with anybody 'cause the code words didn't get to me or my man on the ship 'til the mornin' the ship got called back out."

"Code words?" Cynthia had talked of code words.

"Ah' was to get a new identity from your sweetie-pie's organization and get out of H.K. But I missed my Hong Kong contact man, Polov or Palof. You think all Chinese *people* look alike? All Chinese *streets* look more alike bet your ass. I wasn't too worried though, knew I could get the code words from contact people in Monique's bar."

"In the bar?" Vincent's mind backtracked. "Contact people? Clifford was there with two British officers and Stumpf. Was Merryweather there? That was before Balkin, or was it? Griffith was in the background. Who else? Tucker, Lake, Boswell. Was Abadar there? Yes, and someone else too."

"You worry over it, Chief. It'll come to you." Tucker seemed to be enjoying his position of power. "But remember, if you get's too softhearted over that Cynthia woman? Remember, if we had her cunt? We wouldn't be crawlin' 'round in the dirt and mud out heah' Ever think o' that?"

Vincent swallowed any response to the newly found foe.

By then, all faces were only shadows. Some of the V.C. scrambled around to gather brush for a fire. Tucker kept talking. As an Electrician Third Class, he had fallen from the fantail of the U.S.S. Chicago as it steamed in the Tonkin Gulf one night in 1962. "Gots' picked up by a fishing boat. Ate fish shit and worms for seven months in prison." After a year in prison he spent another few months in Haiphong in what he referred to as an 'education program.' He said he had met Ho Chi Minh and Pham Van Dong, the two major revolutionaries. "They know what's right for people, Chief. An' it ain't the U.S. way."

Convinced by the Vietnamese that Westerners were wrong in the war, he came back to the navy with forged identification to work against his own country. "Them Ruskies? They would catch a sailor, a guy with no relatives? Catch him between duty stations? I'd take over fer him. Easy."

Vincent felt more of the same numbness of discovery he felt when Cynthia told her side of this story. "Did they kill those replaced men?"

"Kill 'em? Maybe. Buy them off? More likely. Ah' don't really know, my Yankee fren'. Never asked. Onc't I took over for a dead man from a swift boat down near Tra Cu. Took his I.D., wandered into a hospital and acted a little crazy. No questions asked, I was sent to Tripler Hospital in Hawaii 'til ah' got better some. Then ah' went back to duty."

"Earlier when you said the NVA knew we were in here. You really meant that, didn't you?"

"Yeah, sorta', I guess. I tried ta' hint a hunnert' times that you didn't have the whole pich'a."

"But they rammed us, rammed you too, Tucker."

"Ah' know. Been talkin' to Canh heaah' 'bout that. There is dumb officers everywhere, Chief, not just in the U.S. of N. This here Lieutenant Canh told me they all felt sorry 'bout that and was lookin' fer me 'round heah. Earlier they thought Abie was me 'cause hesa' nigger and 'cause ah' talk kind'a southern nigger-like. Imagine that?"

Vincent could no longer see Tucker's expression in the dark but he *could* sense the smirking smile as Tucker talked on about his distaste for the war. He also described having been teased and pushed around by the sailors on the Chicago who picked on his under-socialized naiveté and his down-home accent. Tucker admitted he might have been simply getting even, in a childish sort of way for having been bullied by American sailors.

"Why tell me this."

"Why not? Maybe I jes' like tellin' it."

"You're a double agent, Tucker. They just don't know it yet."

"I'm not."

"You are. Look, why help Abie? Why did you fight your V.C. friends?"

"You fucked over ma' head some, Chiefee boy, thas' why. When Clifford killed the NVA, an' you hit him? I didn't think there was any regular navy people who thought like you think. I figured if you could change others could change and maybe the war would stop. My ship's contact man disagreed with me. He said you were …nasty, would be better off dead. In fact, Chief, I was to kill you inland, with Abie, except for one thing."

"What the hell was that?"

"I outrank the man on the ship. As ah' said before, I was sent to the ship 'cause that man wasn't doing his real job and I was to convince him his lack of work was being taken seriously …by authority. An agent. . . " Tucker laughed a phony laugh. " …who wasn't agenting."

"Pardon?"

"He was being won over, but not by you. He's a Russian, U.S. citizen type. He was to keep the Soviets up on U.S. navy stuff, but he slowed. He was won over by the good ol' U.S. of A. dream."

"Tucker, what …"

"That's another thing. Names not Tucker, it's … . "

"Wait." Vincent stopped him. "I don't want to know your name. Then have you figure you can't let us go 'cause we know it."

"No worry, Chiefee. Ah'm retirin' from all this." In the growing light of the V.C.'s fire, Tucker smiled what appeared to be a genuine smile. "Ah've had 'nuff." He stood up, grabbed Vincent by the wrist and pulled him to his feet. His left leg resisted being straightened out. Tucker did not pull DiNoble to his feet.

"Chief, you an' Abie get to go on a float ride."

"Wait." DiNoble tried to stand. Several rifles swung to point at his head. He dropped back to the sand.

"What is this, Tucker." Vincent asked.

"You are swimmin' out."

"Don't make us swim out alone." Vincent said, stalling.

"Yeah?" Tucker laughed. "Don't throw me inta' the briar patch? Bullshit, Pappy. Lake tol' me you swim like a duck."

"But Lake's hurt … Tucker"

"Actual …" Tucker interrupted. "I didn't hurt Lake. For the record? The name's Dewitt, Winston Dewitt, Electrician mate third class, USN, at your service. The navy has me down as drowned probably, back in sixty two. So don' call me Tucker." Winston Dewitt pointed toward Abie. "Seems like you and this Chief buddy o' yours gets to go back home, Abie. But, DiNoble here. He's too quick with a gattlin' gun trigger."

"Wait." DiNoble was on his feet. "I was ordered." The several rifles didn't slow him down. He actually shoved two of the barrels away.

"I was ordered?" Tucker mocked. "Thas' what the Germans said after they burnt the Jews. It's time we started speakin' up against those who order the wrong orders AND," he yelled, "AGAINST YOU WHO FOLLOW THE WRONG FUCKIN' orders. Vincent did, he slapped the S.O.B. you took the murdering order from. So fuck you, L.T."

"What is this?" DiNoble said and looked to Vincent who could only look back helplessly. He looked to Lieutenant Canh who returned the look with one of hatred.

"Tucker." DiNoble said finally, playing a chip for his life. "If it wasn't for me, you wouldn't have gotten out of that vil."

"Wrong, flyboy. I could've walked out of that vil." He laughed again. "But I really didn't want Vincent and Lake to die. I figure Vincent here to get back to Mrs., whoops whoops, almost said Mrs. double cups', sorry 'bout the crack but I figure you and her to start makin' noise against the war." He turned back to DiNoble. "As fer' you? You the real enemy. Planes and college and money and jokes. Nothin' serious, ever …your kind never give back to the world." He leaned into DiNoble's face close enough to cover him with the bad breath. "REALLY! Lou-fucking-tenant."

"You're psychotic." DiNoble said the word like everything would go away if it just had the correct title on it.

Tucker again put his face real close to DiNoble's. "So's your ol' man psychotic. Now get ready to shit yourself." He turned to Canh. Canh pulled out a pistol and before anyone could move or speak, the V.C. officer's pistol blew the side of DiNoble's head away.

"No, Tucker" Vincent yelled. "God-dammit you're doin' what you hate us doing. Goddamn you!" Lieutenant Canh pointed his Pistol at Vincent. Tucker shoved Vincent back.

"Ah ah, Chief. I ain't sayin' this is right. But this is the onliest' way you and Abie gets out of here. Hate me if you want, but fuck you."

There is no reasoning here, Vincent knew. There was only time to pack it in and save what he could. "Fact is, in Hong Kong?" Tucker began again. "Abie would have gone over the hill with me, right, Abie? Last day or so he got to really hating the navy, being mistreated as a black, the war, the Clifford's, the Griffith's."

"I don't believe that, Tucker."

"Believe it. Ask him. Well, better not. He's scared now. But that las' mornin'? Abie talked me into goin' back to the ship with him to drop off the packages, so we could go back to them honey pies? We *fell* inta' that recall accidental like. I was scared for sure, but then, there she was standing there in the greatest sweater since they invented them, Ms. 428-9330. Sent to rescue the hero of the battles, me. I figured she'd ...made her way to the ship to give me the passport and so on."

"Bull shit."

"Yeah, bullshit. An' you're not standin' next to a dead U.S. pilot on the beach while the V.C. light my cigarettes? Wake up and smell the gunpowder. Too bad you didn't know the code words."

"What code words?"

"With your woman? The crack I made about bells, and being an overworked travel agent. Remember?"

"I remember you makin' an ass of yourself. "

"Anyhoo, Chief. The lady didn't return my code. I was stuck then. I wondered what was wrong with her. I then figured either she was stupid, which she ain't, or a traitor to the cause because of you in her life, which I don't know ...or, she really had ...no friggin' idea I was her pickup man standing right there in front of her."

"Two out of three, I'd bet."

"But who cares what you bet? My ship contact also failed me that mornin' so I jes' says 'what the fuck' and came back out. The worse to happen is I'd get back in'na boat to here and git back to H.K. via the NVA underground. Which I did and which I'll do ...likely."

Suddenly Tucker was through talking. The Chief reached to DiNoble and removed one of his dog tags and put it on the chain with his own, Hill's and the others. As he did so, he was shaking from fear, from the murder, from the chills of the night, or all three.

"You get into that water now, you an' Lake. In about ten minutes, I have a feeling these guys are gonna' start tossing shots out after you. Seems they kinda' go through the evenin' crazies, kinda' like cats do? Best I can do. OK?"

"And they're the good guys in this war?"

"Chief, get it straight. In a war? There ain't no good guys. Now git. I never cared much for anyone with two first names, anyhoo ... Paul Vincent."

The water was actually warmer than the night air.

"I heard 'em talkin'. I heard everything." Lake was frightened as the water closed in around him on the log raft. "Tucker's a murderer, isn't he? He's murderin' us now isn't he?"

"Shhh, Abie." Vincent countered. "Shut up. We're okay now. We'll be free of 'em in just a few minutes."

"But he said he'd be shootin' at us."

"I doubt it. I'll get us out." He lost patience with Abie but stayed kind. "Shit, Abie. You've been 'born-again', not like religious born-again, but *really* born again, since we found you in that vil. We thought you were dead. I'm not losing you now. Veronica will kill me if I lose you twice. We'll be okay in that big ocean."

The V.C. had strapped Abie's litter to the top of the log float. Although he was high and almost dry, the injured man seemed to come in and out of understanding. Vincent wanted him to just relax, shut up, and float along.

With his high school friends in Steubenville, Paul Vincent had often swum from one set of locks on the Ohio river to the other, some six miles, just to have the Fourth of July boat racing crowds applaud them. He swam for the YMCA swim team through high school winters and had won a couple of medals for distance crawls. He once swam the 800 meter free-style in 10:02.

"Considering the alternatives, Abie. Going into the gulf for a couple hours seems reasonable."

"I don't swim."

His watch said it was three minutes before nine p.m. when they entered the water and started moving east. After just a few minutes he reached down and released his borrowed shoes and let them sink. After several more minutes he removed his trousers and tied them to the logs to be rid of the extra wet weight. Her panties were still in the back right pocket. He let his shirt float away.

He held onto the rear of the two-log float and pushed by kicking his legs slowly up and down. Now and then Abie would try to help by moving his hands in the water but his tries were ineffective. Abie talked and at times, made sense.

"Tell Veronica I'm sorry she wasn't the last woman I made love to. Will'ya tell 'er that?" At other times he would rave crazily, cursing Tucker, Clifford, the navy. He made Vincent laugh at one point when he yelled into the night over and over: 'murder is a frog'.

Vincent worried for his friend. His spinal cord was obviously injured. He pictured Abie in a wheel chair the rest of his life, Veronica fluttering around him. The thoughts caused him to push the raft with vigor and watch the night sky for signs of rescuing helos or ships. Despite the chancy position they were in, he felt very good they had gotten away from Vietnam soil alive even though, without DiNoble or Tucker as he planned earlier, he was captain, navigator, morale officer, engineer and main propulsion of the crude craft.

The moon popped through the clouds and several stars shown through. It was enough light to reflect off Abie's black wet face but not enough to reveal an expression.

"Where we, Pappy?" Abie asked.

"Movin' east. Just rest."

Until about six miles out he would be able to judge his position by the light of the large V.C. fire on the beach and by some lights from a village to the south. If it took three hours to reach a point where the lights were below the horizon, he would be very pleased with their progress. Anytime after that would be *Johnny Carson* time and he would expect to see searchlights from lead choppers in the darkened water. At worst, he figured, he would swim all the way to the final rendezvous position by five a.m. At the absolute worst, if the message didn't get relayed, they would be in well-traveled U.S. ship lanes by a few hours into daylight. He felt confident they would be found shortly after daybreak. He chose not to think about being found by a V.C. torpedo boat or by a Sampan filled with angry North Vietnamese civilians. He wondered how long they could *really* go without fresh water.

To get ready for an air search coming in, Vincent reached for the radio in Abie's bandages. "Fuck." It was gone. Tucker likely had lifted it. Vincent cursed him quietly but gained some strength from the curses. Abie asked openly—"Pappy, is this really the dawning of the age of Aquarius?" Paul decided not to answer.

The water became choppy about ten-thirty, jerky enough to make it difficult to swim smoothly. The waves seemed to reach up and slap him just as he timed for a breath. By eleven p.m., he was tiring. He lay his head on his arms on the logs and propelled very slowly by kicking.

"Paul?"

"What?"

"Time'sit?"

"Wait." The bright moon cast shadows and the hands on the watch were wet and reflective, impossible to read in the moonlight. "Perhaps midnight." He told Abie.

"Should be planes now." Abie seemed alert again, his comment correct. Midnight and they were still alone in the gulf.

"Somethin's been blown." Abie said.

"Patience, Abie. We still alive." He kicked and pushed for another thirty minutes and something caught his eye. Lifting himself partly on the logs, he recognized helo lights brushing back and forth on the surface of the sea several miles to the south. The lights were farther away than they had already paddled.

"That's our SAR Paul." Abie also saw the lights. "They miles off our track."

The scene to the south looked like seven or eight flashlights moving about and shining down from a near cloudless sky. Something was wrong with their plan.

"I might'a misjudged the set and drift of the tides, Ab."

"No, don' tell me that shit."

Could they really be miles north of their track in just three hours?

"I can't recall if I figured the tides, the drift. Or if DiNoble and I ..."

"What other mistakes you made?"

"Slow down, Abie" (Fuck you.) "We're in the water for the night. Slow down. Relax. Easy does it for now."

He was torn for a few minutes between continuing eastward for the ship lanes or heading south in case the SAR continued into morning.

He pushed and kicked for another hour. As his arms brushed his bearded face with each stroke, he recalled the YMCA coach Jim Davis insisting they keep their young thin bodies shaved when on the swim team. "Stops resistance" Davis would declare. 'Pedophile', Paul thought. But tonight, he wondered if the few days' growth hampered his speed in the salt water.

The lights to the south clicked off one by one. In an hour there were only two left.

"Paul." Abie sounded panicky.

"Yes?"

"This raft is sinkin', isn't it?"

He swam to the end where Abie's head was. Water was up around the man's chest and shoulders. The casted leg was floating, where before it had been above the water.

"Shit."

"It's water logging, Paul. Is it? Is it?"

Vincent felt defeated. The desperate trouble had simply shifted from the beach to the sea. He had pulled the man out of the village at the cost of other lives. He could not lose him now over misjudged water logging. His father had abandoned, tricked and betrayed *him*. He could not do the same to Abie.

"We gonna' … . make it … Ab." He puffed, breathless from struggling to right the logs.

"I don't swim. I'm …just a signalman. But I want to live. Find out who I can still yet be, Paul."

"We …we'll get to land. "

"We gotta', Paul. I know."

Vincent swung the sinking raft around and headed for shore. He kicked three times the pace he used coming out. After thirty minutes he knew the raft was sinking faster than his pace would take them ashore. He pulled ahead of the raft and hooked one foot to the tied trousers. Starting a crawl stroke he let his foot drag the raft behind. After several strokes he had it timed well. They were moving along a good speed. He went on swimmer's automatic as he had in the river as a teenager. He swam for over an hour without missing a stroke. He kept one thought and goal in his head. They'd be ashore soon. Back to the beach. But, that's back to Vietnam? Vietnam, filled with V.C. Back to angry farmers and children who tell V.C. soldiers where Americans are. Back to soldiers whose friends have been killed by a grenade in a village called A12 or Tho Bac. Back to Tucker's confused mind. Back to the farmers in the rice field, now dead. They'll know Vincent killed their brothers in the village and in the helo clearing. They'll let Meling take out her revenge over Trong's death and let other women pull Abie's dead legs from his broken body and beat Paul Vincent with the legs. They'll beat his neck and back with Abie's gangrenous legs because that's all they let the women do for revenge in the man's war. They'll beat his arms and shoulders until he hurts with throbbing bruises. They'll beat the cords of his neck, they'll pull his arms from the sockets and pull his leg from its hip socket by the ankle, and they'll call his name over and over. "Paul, Paul! Paul! Stop it, Paul."

Abie was calling him from behind. "STOP. STOP swimming." He was a motor, he couldn't stop swimming.

"STOP! PAUL!"

He stopped. His body fought against stopping. What did Abie want?

"Paul, s'no good." Abie was crying. "You're goin' crazy. You're hollering' an' talkin' crazy. Crazy stuff."

Vincent looked around him. His eyes burned, his body ached, his ankle was raw from rubbing the trouser loop. There were no signs of where he was. There was no landmass visible in the moonlight. He'd been in a swimming trance, almost like being asleep. He had turned randomly and lost time.

Determined to maintain, he judged the moon's position through the billowed clouds and headed again for where he thought the beach should be. Abie was crying aloud. He ignored the cries and started robot-like strokes again.

Don't think, stroke.

Remember the training as a swimmer. Coach Jim Davis at the YMCA would holler and say; "stroke, stroke, stroke, just stroke and you are there. You're working, not playing, damn you boy …damn you, stroke, stroke, stroke. Feel the greasy water slick off your back and slide past you. Hear me boy? Stroke, stroke, stroke. Each stroke …reach for the end of the pool, the bar at the end of the pool." Paul Vincent reached for the bar at the end of the pool. He again became a machine, his arms pulled, his legs churned, his mouth a channel to draw in and expel the air.

Abie kept yelling at him.

"Shut up, Abie." Stroke. "Shut the fuck up." Stroke. "I need to swim."

Should the moon have been in the west?

His heart began thumping very hard but he couldn't tell if it was from fatigue or fear. He shifted around, shoved the float ahead of him again and began to swim again, nudging the float with his hands, his head, his shoulders.

Pump, kick, stroke, push.

Pump, kick, stroke.

Pump, kick, stroke, push.

"Paul, gotta wait …water … " Abie was spitting water, nearly under, his neck strained upward. The cast had soaked through and became added dead weight. His legs were useless.

"Oh, God!" Vincent prayed. "Is there a God?" Could the logs not last a little longer? He shifted Abie on the float and got his head above water. He tore at the water soaked cast and it fell apart in his hands. "We gonna' do …it, Ab'." He gasped. He hooked his foot to the front log again and tried again. Minutes went by quickly. He began to tire. He searched for motivation. Revenge over Tucker? No. Screw Tucker. Veronica's smile when he brought Abie in? No, not enough. Cynthia could be enough. Cynthia. Her great breasts, her great sweet target breasts. First-class airline tickets. Yes, go to Cynthia. Go 'first-class.' Never mind she had lied. Never mind she had been tricked and wronged and had lied. Go for her breasts and her arms and her warm sweet smells mixed with Schiaparelli. Concentrate on the strokes of making love with her, push against the water, pull against the raft. Not fast enough, break through, run to her. A world famous runner goes to Cynthia. Over the Sierras, through Death Valley, south to the Rockies, pump-pump, run-run across the Great Plains, through Indiana and the low hills of Ohio, running east and now only ten miles from Steubenville, from High Street. Wait—It isn't Cynthia. Its Rachael. Rachael, waiting with young mocking blue eyes and blond hair and the ground suddenly ankle deep warm sticky syrup. That's Ben laughing in the background. No! It cannot be Rachael, she's gone. Rachael had been eighteen and vulnerable and unknowing. Cynthia had never been eighteen. She had sprung fully formed into life, a full grown wai-da of a woman of life and of the world.

"Paul … Jesus. I'm …sinking."

The logs had broken apart.

"NO!" Vincent yelled into the night but choked on inhaled water. He gagged as he pulled Abie to him. His panicked friend flailed his arms, smacking Vincent in the face, once, twice. Paul's vision flashed colored lights. He shoved Abie away and located the sinking log with the trousers tied to it. He pulled the knot free and tied the trouser legs together. He zipped it closed, buttoned the top button and swung them into the air. The daintiness of her white panties flew free of the pocket and onto the water in front of his face. He bit into them and swung the trousers again. Once, no. Once again, no. He tired. He floated for a few seconds, teeth and lips pursed to hold Cynthia's via the panties, he sucked the water through them. She was there then, as in the window at Monk's.

He tried again to float the trousers. They filled with air.

Resting, he took her panties, placed his head through the open waist and pushed through one leg opening, to hear them rip slightly. They fell into place right where he wanted them, around his neck like her arms.

He jerked Abie's face from the water. "The pants. Hold them. Let your legs float behind you …or sink, bastard. Just hold them in …front . . . of you."

Abie grabbed weakly at the trousers. They collapsed. "NO!" He let them slip away. Abie screamed sounds that did not form words. Vincent slapped his friend's face. Abie slapped back.

"Fill your lungs, Abie! " Vincent screamed and pushed away. He caught the sinking pants and pushed away from Lake's flailing arms. He filled the pants with air again and returned for Abie. He was under the surface. Paul caught Abie's collar and pulled, dead weight, then, suddenly, flailing and fighting. Vincent slapped him again, spit at him and cursed him. He jammed the pant's into Abie's hands and squeezed his fingers around them.

"Hold them. " He yelled.

Abie would not, or could not, hold them.

Clenching the buoyant trousers with the hand that had hit Ben Bristol was made impossible by pain. He shifted hands and grabbed Abie with the injured one. He held for two minutes and both men settled into the temporary safety. Vincent strained to think of something more to do. Nothing came.

"Pappy, we're goin' ta' die … ?"

Vincent coaxed and goaded him to relax and let his body sink a little and float. "You have to help me, Abie."

"I've no legs." He puffed and gasped. "I'm tryin', Pappy. Please!"

Vincent moved him onto his back and with the inflated pants in one hand held Abie in the classic rescue hold. Every four to six minutes he had to let go to refill the pants with air. His energy drained like a grounded battery. He pretended it could go on and on but after several fillings of air, knew his strength was being used too rapidly. For a while, he floated Abie on top of his own body while he tried floating on his back. Abie cried like a frightened boy cries.

Suddenly Abie panicked again and tried crawling atop Vincent. "Pappy, Pappy, oh … "

Vincent kicked away and lost Abie in the dark. He found him again floating motionless, face down. He jerked him around and blew into his mouth. His chest felt slick as he turned him over. His wounds had opened again, the bandages loose from the water and the fighting.

Vincent tried to plan. He had no idea where he was relative to anyplace. The watch Cynthia had given him was lost in the fighting. He grabbed Abie again and lay back to float. Abie calmed again.

OH GOD, NO. He'd lost him someplace. He'd fallen asleep or something. ABIE WAS UNDER THE WATER SOMEPLACE. He went under and reached crazily about. Nothing. He surfaced. Abie was floating right there, face down. The flotation pants were nowhere to be found. He blew life into the man's mouth again. He could smell Abie's blood. Minutes passed holding him.

"Paul ...not like this. Not like this, Pappy."

Paul held him in his arms. Their faces barely stayed above the water. Paul's breath was gone, his spirit gone, his body ached beyond pain he had ever known. His body had reached that part body builders speak of, the point of muscle failure, nothing left.

"Pappy, I ... "

"We need to sleep, Abie. Just let it go." Each time he closed down to die, his body received a flash of rest, enough to pump a moment's more life under Abie's body. The shots of strength would come and then he would drift off again into some easing sort of sleep. The dream? Cynthia. The dream and the sleep was the easiest part.

"I can't do more, Pappy. I can't do more."

"I can't keep us both going ... "

"I know, Pappy, I know."

Tears leaped into Paul's voice. "Abie, I gotta' let you go." He heard a deep sigh.

"I know, Pappy, I know." There was another sigh. "Tell Veronica ... "

"I will. I will."

"I love you, Pappy.

"I know, Abie. I know." Paul wrapped his arms around Abie's waist being careful not to squeeze his wounds more. He cuddled him in his arms as he rolled over onto his back to try to float again. The water seemed to rock them, gently. Paul felt he wanted to sleep then, forever. They floated several restful seconds then Abie's hand closed on Vincent's wrist and tightened like a power tool. He tried to ease it away but the grip tightened even more.

"I love you, Pappy. I do."

"I know, Abie. I do know."

The water folded over them both. The two men sank under. The grip tightened even more. Vincent felt pain there over his pain everywhere. They sank together, deep and darker. It was good and soothing and so untroubled to just drift down into the womb-like gulf. Seconds ticked to become a minute. Vincent reached slowly to Abie's hand and held it. With care, he pulled one of the fingers away from his wrist not wanting to disturb him as one doesn't want to disturb a child fallen asleep in the crook of your arm. The finger did not close again. In the dark silence of the deep water, Abie's last breath was suddenly all around their faces in the form of lighted glowing bubbles slipping upward past them.

The bubbles stopped.

One at a time, he removed his friend's remaining fingers. He pushed up into the water, vividly aware the body sliding past him was Abie. Braking surface his own body rolled over automatically. His lungs heaved and thumped against his chest. He gasped over and over. He ached. He breathed. He rested. Strength returned to wasted muscle.

"I saved him to kill him."

The need to sleep was gone with the loss of Abie. Vincent kicked his legs and moved his arms. Where was this strength when he needed it moments before? He tried to think but Abie's face was in his face, lying on the bottom of the gulf, bouncing gently among the sea grasses. Abie, Abie. So much so fast, so wrong, so very unfair. "Oh, Veronica, what will I say?"

In days maybe, Abie would float to the surface and wash slowly ashore. Maybe Vincent would be near him then. Maybe he'd wash alongside of Abie Lake on the beach in Vietnam. Dry, withered by water and salt and sun and sand, never to be found or never to be recognized. Would anyone ever know or care?

What will he say to Veronica?

The moon became clearly visible again. He turned and tried to move to the south where the lights had been earlier. It was a direction, a place to go. His heart pounded but he needed to hear it to know he was still alive.

Water filled his lungs painfully. He was following Abie down.

"Move." A voice said. "Move. For us, live, for us. I've been so wrong and now I can be so right. Don't take away you, just as I have finally found you." He heard Cynthia's caring and begging voice asking him to try. He heard David Selesky tell him they had 'a history now as friends' and he wanted Paul to survive. Survival as a friend had been with him in the boat when they were rammed, in the water swimming ashore, in the clearing in front of the NVA guns, in the brush when the soldier dropped his rifle and in his skill as he shot the M-1. Survival had been with him in the village and again, so far, this night. It was surrender that caused him to sink under but each time survival would push upward again. How long can I do this? How many more times would his heart pump and pump again? When would his mind fail to tell him that his nose was too filled with water to breathe? When would he be too tired to live the next second?

He tried pumping his arms and kicking again. It worked before, but not again. He became too tired, too thirsty to even think. His mouth filled with dry rags. The droning and thumping of his own heart wouldn't stop in his ears. The thumping dominated. His heart would burst soon. THUMP, THUMP, like the five inch shells.

ABIE IS BACK. GRIPPING HIM, PULLING HIM. HE'D SWUM IN CIRCLES. Fight him off. One hand, fight it. Two hands, fight them. Three hands, pulling on him. Keep fighting. "DO NOT STOP MOVING," he screamed to himself. He would die if he stopped. Abie stopped moving, Abie died. "DON'T STOP MOVING," He screamed.

"HEY! Buddy. We got you."

It was his mind, trying to trick him like Tucker tricked him. Signals in his brain screamed out to not be tricked.

"Lift him ... NOW!" His body was in the air.

"I've got you, Buddy. You're safe." Strong hands held his wrists.

"Dammit, RELAX MAN."

"We got you."

"Got me?"

"Got you, Buddy. Navy got you."

Got me? The words didn't come out.

Next he was swinging through the sky in a sling. The pounding and droning and roaring were fierce above him. A voice coaxed him to relax but when he tried to stop moving, his body would convulse and keep trying to swim. His throat closed in raspy thirsty spasms. He felt people touch him. Some hands pulled at his neck, pulled something free of his neck.

"NO!" And Cynthia was gone. All was gone.

The touches ached. He saw the orange balloon shape of a moving life jacket. Two faces came and went, a wet khaki collar with a Chief's anchor insignia. He was alive. A Chief had pulled him from the sea. Chiefs are to save people. Chiefs protect their men.

"I lost my men."

"I'm sorry, Buddy. That happens. I'm sure you tried your best. Hang in there a bit. You're home. Welcome home, Buddy."

CHAPTER THIRTY ONE
Kittyhawk

"I hurt, therefore I am. I hurt, therefore I am. I hurt, therefore I am." The crazy thought ran through his mind over and over while voices came in and out of his hearing like a FM station on a 3 AM Nevada Highway.

"I wonder which one he is?"

"Several dog tags on his chain ..."

The Chief Corpsman on the Sumner class destroyer, U.S.S. Maddox was in conversation with Doctor Timothy Brandenberg, the ship's physician. "But all tags are single except the one, 'Vincent, Paul R., USN, Type A, Protestant'."

"Probably him." Brandenberg said, hardly looking up from his patient. "But right now, this tissue damage is severe. Prune wrinkling. Mucosa areas burned. "Long time ina' water."

The corpsman put the jumble of dog tags aside and leaned down with the doctor. "Lacerations here, Doctor."

Gentle hands manipulated Vincent's arms and rotated his legs.

"Contusions a many." The doctor diagnosed aloud. "Cut on right buttock. It'll take a stitch or two. Infected also. Leg wound, infected, jagged." Doctor Brandenberg turned toward the corner of the small room and addressed a man dressed in dungarees and blue lab coat who was shaking a beaker.

"Got anything on that smear, Tandini?"

Second Class corpsman Angelo Tandini set the beaker down, bent over and adjusted a large black microscope. "Okay. Gram Negative from here. But ...enteric bacilli ...present. Normal gut flora ..."

"There's shit in his leg?" The doctor asked.

"You got it. Shit in the leg wound. Be a spear if we were around the Plain of Reeds. Probably a punji up here."

Brandenberg turned to his Chief Corpsman. "Wonder if he's allergic to isomerics?"

"Should I get it ready?"

"Yes, but we'll alert to reaction."

"No." Vincent screamed, but it came out a whisper.

"Hey. This guys hearing us." Doctor Brandenberg leaned into Vincent's face. "What? You allergic to penicillin?"

"Yes." He yelled again but again it came out in an unintelligible rasp.

"Vocal cords—salt probably. Don't talk now. Unless you have to."

"Okay."

The door to the sick bay opened and a very tall, thin and pale looking officer wearing a *Command at Sea* insignia entered the well lighted, mostly stainless steel sick bay. Keeping his head dipped and shoulders hunched buzzard-like to keep from bumping against the low ceiling, the Captain spoke in a quiet voice. "Helo's hovering aft, Doc. He ready to move?"

"Yes, sir. Good as we'll get him."

"Get him out there then."

"Aye aye, sir."

As he was carried on the stretcher Vincent felt pain everywhere. The gaunt face of the Maddox's tall Captain seemed to float along just above Vincent's, and the cooing caring voice brought a childhood comfort to him. His childhood mentor from Steubenville, Owen Edwards used to call him *lad.*

"Rest easy, lad. You're headin' home now, lad …just go easy."

On the fantail of Maddox the roar of the helo was unsettling enough to where he tried to get out of the stretcher.

"No, no, good buddy. Just wait a bit." Strong hands pulled firm straps over his chest and arms. "It'll be okay."

His chin was tucked under a warm white blanket and the stretcher snapped to a sky hook. The exhaust was too hot as he swung up and past its blast. WHERE IS DINOBLE AND HILL? He was swung inside the helicopter and bounced on the thin metal floor. WHERE IS ABIE? The engine roared even more. WHERE IS MY SHIP? He went into a half consciousness.

They flew for a long distance. Something was stuck into his arm, a bottle swung over his chest. A young man in a gray flight suit sat near him. Whenever Vincent opened his eyes the man would call 'doctor'. Was the ship's doctor flying with him? Was he that bad off?

As they landed he saw an aircraft carrier superstructure, a very blurred number '63' painted on its side. The number seemed familiar, why was it blurred? 'To fool the enemy', he thought. He was carried again and a thousand faces looked in at him. As they swung him through gray and green passageways he slept some more. Voices murmured all around him. He wanted it to be quieter. "Everyone be quiet." He rasped into the air.

"Sure, Buddy. We'll be quiet."

It became dark again, then lighter. Bottles were hanging over him but his vision was blurred as though he were looking through Vaseline. He could barely make out the ship's vents and pipes above his bed which were marked with large black arrows showing direction of whatever flowed within them. He hated that he couldn't see clearly. Someone asked him his name but he kept it to himself. His last secret would be his name.

He choked on things placed in his mouth. Hands caressed him again but he played dead. It might be the V.C. Other arms lifted him. His left leg was wrapped tightly and hooked to something that prevented him from moving it. He cursed but it would not budge. He quit trying to move the leg. He let the warm hands do for him. He slept secretly so they wouldn't know he was there.

Something soft was in his mouth, then gone. Too cool for her breast. Then something wet to sip. Cynthia was playfully giving him chilled wine. He heard her laugh. He gulped for fresh water. He strained to see but couldn't. Hands patted him again but withheld most of the liquid. It had to be the V.C.

Sometimes he awoke when they were tending his body but even awake it was black in the room. "Ouch!" What was wrong there? Did that thing in the jungle near the clearing cut *that* deep? What of the leg cut?

They bathed him. Needles woke him, needles let him sleep and dream. Someone tenderly fed him food and water. Meling? He couldn't see. It mattered greatly to him that he couldn't see but he didn't want to let them know that. What if he were in the village? The air smelled like alcohol. A clever way to cover village smells.

Then bottles and wires and vents hung above him. His eyes felt better, no more burning. He saw dim forms like oranges and apples being squeezed into juices to run into his mouth ...and grapes made into wines. Cynnie, Cynnie. God he wanted her to touch him again.

"Paul Vincent? Right?"

A man in light green was talking and smiling, inches from Vincent's eyes. He wanted to remain silent and just watch a familiar face. Kurt?

"Been awhile for you? Right?"

He had dark hair and a thin moustache. He smiled all of the time. He called his name correctly, Paul Vincent. Paul's throat ached and scratched as he tried to answer the kindly voice, but he had to force the words out. "Yes" How did the man know his name? Does Rachael know? Does Cynthia know? Does Abie know? Abie? Abie is dead. Abie will not know. Or, Abie will know everything.

"Abie is dead." He told the smiling face.

"Do you know that for sure?"

"I know nothing for sure except my name and rank and serial number."

"What is that?"

"A secret."

"Ok. Rest for now."

The doctor was there again. "This is corpsman Bryant behind me." He stepped aside and Vincent could barely make out a heavy-set red-headed man. The man waved and grinned. The blurred doctor moved into his vision again. "You'll be fine after some bed rest, Buddy. We've treated you for shock. You've recovered pretty much from that. You experienced a pretty good sprain in your lower back, lumbar sprain they call it. Classic 'bad back', ok? There's a deep infected cut we stitched on your ass, classic pain in the ass for awhile." The man laughed easily.

"Nothing is chronic or threatening. You've got an infected cut above your left ankle bone but its responding. Your left knee took some serious banging out there. Doctor Mantanis removed some fluids and probably will remove more in a few days. The leg's in a cast for strength but nothing's broken." He hesitated as Vincent watched the blur of a man pick up a cloudy note board from what had to be the foot of the bed. "Oh, yes. Your eyes were damaged from exposure. We had them bandaged for three days. They'll be ok soon. You seein' me good?"

"A little muddy." He forced the raspy words out. He looked at pipes and dials and tubes to check his vision.

"Sore throat and fuzzy vision for awhile, Chief. That's all."

Vincent nodded. He was alive. His throat hurt as he asked his first important question. "Where am I?"

"On Kittyhawk. In the Gulf."

The number '63', his memory was working again.

"DiNoble. Tucker. Lake. Randy Hill. The CIA people, I can't remember names." He spoke with some panic in his voice. "They're all gone now. I killed several people and I killed Lake too."

The soothing voice asked. "How do you know that?"

"He died under me. Sank …in the water …" Raspy words tumbled out of the pain filled throat. "Hill was shot by the NVA. Shot in the head in the clearing by the helo. With his eyes still open. So was DiNoble, shot. DiNoble was cold blooded murder. Killed by a Lieutenant, Canh, a V.C. officer." Then he remembered. "Tucker was one of them. TUCKER IS A V.C. SPY." He tried to rise up. The doctor stopped the effort.

"Ok, Chief. Rest now. Let's talk later."

"No, dammit. Tucker is a fuckin' spy and had DiNoble killed. He also set up the killing of Piper and Hollender."

"Who the hell is Piper and Hollender?"

"There on these dog tags, Doctor." Bryant's voice popped in from out of sight. The doctor scribbled some notes.

Vincent continued rambling. "I got their dog tags …listen to me. We gotta' tell someone. There's a spy on my ship. Also—somethin' was wrong with our SAR coordinates. I fucked 'em up or someone changed them. Someone *tried* to kill me an' Abie."

"Paranoia?" A voice said from the background.

"Shut up. I just think he's trying to tell us something." The doctor made a note to check on the dog tag names then turned back to Vincent. "Ok, OK. I'll get someone for you to talk to." He then signaled Bryant who primed a syringe.

"No, don't to that now. I've gotta' tell my ship … "

"I'll get right on it." Between Bryant's comforting words and the contents of the needle Paul Vincent went sound to sleep.

The men on Truaxe were also being washed by the events that took place ashore, and now aboard Kittyhawk.

Lieutenant Balkin, standing with Lieutenant Stumpf, the Captain and others, was reading the first message concerning the man picked out of the water.

"They're requesting dental records on Vincent, Hill, Lieutenant DiNoble … Tucker …anything forensic. The individual on Kittyhawk suffers deliriums, as indicated in their message. They're attempting I.D. Whomever it is recuperating has several dog tags on him, DiNoble, Hill, Piper, Vincent, Hollender. Not Lake's, nor Tucker's … The rescued person might even be one of the CIA."

"Send 'em what they ask for but tell 'em they'll have to furnish the transport chopper. Ours has obviously gotten into some shit in-country."

"Aye, aye, Sir.

Clifford was squinty eyed in thought as he dismissed Balkin and turned to the other officers. "That boat crew hadn't done anything right yet." He said into the air. "Tellin' the SAR people to search off Ha Tinh when they were up by Ben Thuy? Couldn't they read a map?"

It was difficult to tell the feeling behind Clifford's statements. He had personally taken the relayed message from Air Force Captain Miguel Sanchez just after 1800 on March fifth when Truaxe was in the middle of an NGFS mission. He had given the message to the other officers on watch and one of them had, at Clifford's direct order, personally relayed it on to the Search and Rescue coordination center at Nha Trang and to the COMSEVENTHFLEET flagship. For whatever reason though, the all night SAR effort had been a bust.

However, the morning after the overnight SAR, a mess cook was dumping garbage from the world-war-II veteran destroyer, Maddox, and had spotted a man in the water. Using a boat and swimmers, the Maddox had rescued the man but that took place some thirty-three miles north of the boat crew's SAR track. No one had connected the two until Kittyhawk reported the names on the dog tags.

"How the fuck he get that far north?" Clifford demanded as he paced back and forth on the bridge wing while Griffith leaned against a signal light. "Remember when we first got those SAR cords? The 08MC by 20AC? It was to be four men swimmin' out. The single man found I figured it was a pilot in the water. It wasn't enough men, plus, Vincent would not have miss-navigated that far off."

Griffith growled. "Never thought Vincent to be the navigator you felt he was …is … Sir"

"Well, I want to know who they pulled out. Hell, they didn't even say if it was a nigger they have." Clifford jammed his cigarette out against the ships paint work and stared at Griffith as if to dare him to call him on either the demeaning term, 'nigger', or that he put his smoke out on the good paint. Griffith said nothing but he did break eye contact. Clifford went on. "At least then we'd a' known it was that cut-buddy of Vincent's, that signalman."

"They'd of said if he was a negro, Captain. We must assume it was a white man. Could be any of them."

"I hate this waiting."

"The time will pass … Cap'n."

Clifford locked a stern look onto Griffith's face again. "This is my ship. These are my men. I've got one investigation pending. Do I need another? God dammit, man, can I have some empathy from you?"

Griffith wasn't surprised the Captain was thinking of the pending investigation as he assimilated the news of the four men. Clifford could be hurt by the testimony of most of the Truaxe men who had been in-country. Later, Griffith sat back, feet up in his stateroom and replayed the events of the night of March fifth.

Truaxe was off the coast of Da Nang about to make a high speed run to the beach to fire upon V.C. targets. Having been directed out of the spot boat's area, and as soon as the boat missed a radio check, Clifford had sent his helo north. That had been hours earlier.

They were awaiting word from DiNoble who was to hopefully make a rescue and proceed to a landing place of opportunity on Yankee Station. Clifford seemed nervous, but anyone would be nervous under the circumstances.

The ship was at general quarters and Clifford had the conn. Just a few seconds after Clifford ordered full speed into the firing run, Griffith saw him answer a call on the small radio that was assigned to the spot boat team. Clifford scribbled something on a small paper and pushed the radio back into the carrying pouch hooked to his belt.

"Griffith!" He had called. "Looks like they found our people."

"Yes, sir." As Griffith moved toward Clifford, Corrigan, Balkin, Stumpf and Lieutenant Lukarmo all converged onto the bridge wing and entered the conversation.

"Here," Clifford said, wiping sweat from his eyes with an open palm, "I've just got this fuckin' message from one of the Pink team spotter people. These coordinates came from a boat crew, probably ours, who are swimming out. He said they called themselves 'Down Four'. " Both Balkin and Griffith reached for the paper but Clifford stepped past them all and entered the pilot house. The officers followed.

Clifford ripped a piece of paper from the OOD clipboard, wrote some figures on it and handed that paper to Griffith.

"Plot these, and get 'em to SAR. No, wait!" He hesitated. "Get 'em to SAR and *then* plot 'em."

He pointed to the first set of numbers on the paper. "Four men are swimmin' out, and SAR is to look for them at this spot at twenty-three hundred." He pointed to a second set of numbers. "Then, they're aiming for this spot by three a.m. You people get a message out to the search people," he repeated.

Griffith took the paper but hesitated for a few seconds. Lukarmo leaned in and looked over his shoulder. Stumpf grabbed the paper, scanned the numbers and handed it to Corrigan. Corrigan took one glance but the paper was pulled from his grip by Balkin. Clifford stepped back toward the bridge wing but turned and looked at the five officers. Strong feelings prompted numerous expressions among the six men. Clifford stepped back in close and spoke up.

"I know what you all are thinking. And I don't like it."

"What ...?"

"I'm not thinking ..."

"Bullshit. Considering there's to be an investigation of those first two agents? You people are hoping the survivors are the ones who could do me the most harm."

"Cap'n, no." Griffith spoke up. "Counting the boat crew, the helo team and the two new CIA agents, there were seven men ashore. Its natural we're wondering whose left if there are only four left."

"Yeah? Natural? No thoughts about me?"

"Not from me, Cap'n."

"Nor I." Stumpf said almost silently.

Clifford turned and bolted out onto the bridge wing where he yelled at a lookout for not scanning ahead with binoculars.

Back in the pilot house the five remaining officers exchanged glances but not comments.

Balkin thought to himself. The pilot; DiNoble, and the gunner; Hill could probably hurt Clifford the most. They were the ones who actually found the two CIA bodies ashore, after the slap incident. They could testify that the agents had been blown away by the ship's firepower.

Lukarmo was also alert to the possibilities. If Vincent is a survivor, he'll likely bring the slap incident to the investigation. Clifford does not want that brought up.

Corrigan was also thinking. I'll bet the exec is hoping none of them make it back, and this investigation thing dies away. I know Griffith would rather be recommended for command by a Captain who had *not* been censored for poor performance, rather than by one who had.

Corrigan's eyes met Lieutenant Stumpf's blank stare. Stumpf spoke up as though he'd been in the center of everyone's thoughts. "There is only one advantage for the Captain." He said straight out. "DiNoble and Hill found the CIA bodies, they're trouble if they come back. Vincent wasn't court-martialed for the slap. Why not, they'll ask. If the four swimming out are anyone other than the two agents, and Lake and Tucker, Clifford will not fare well in an investigation."

Lukarmo spoke up. "He'll benefit most if its Lake, Tucker, an' rescued agents."

"Lowest rank? Easiest to intimidate?" Balkin asked.

"Of course."

"What you think, Commander?" Balkin asked Griffith.

"I agree." Griffith said quietly. "Captain has got to be hoping the survivors are Lake and Tucker. Lake intimidates easily …but Tucker. I don't know the man." To himself, Griffith became torn by feelings. With no love lost between them, he noted that Clifford was actually hurrying his own bad news by relaying the coordinates to the SAR team. He admired the man for not just dropping the message over the side after he'd received it. But, that would have been chancy, he thought. "I don't believe that any good ever comes of a commanding officer being censored in an investigation. We should all hope for the best for the Captain."

Ah-hah, Corrigan thought to himself. Griffith *is* worrying about his own fitness report.

Griffith took the small paper away from Corrigan, looked at his watch, made some notes on the paper and rechecked the coordinates against the Captain's figures on the bridge chart. Then, while Stumpf stayed on the bridge as OOD, Griffith went into CIC with Lukarmo, Corrigan and Balkin close on his heels.

Lukarmo spoke again as they followed Griffith in. "So, for the Captain's sake, we're hoping for Tucker and Lake …and we deal with it later if its any other way?"

"Right." Griffith said. "Or, overall better off if its Lake and Hill."

"Whatever, Sir."

Other events had been taking place on Truaxe between March third when the spot boat went in, and March fifth when Vincent was recovered. Mail was received.

Yankee Station ships rely on regular flights from Subic Bay to the Yankee Station aircraft carriers for the delivery of mail. After being sorted aboard the carriers, mail is delivered space available, by helo or launch, to the surrounding smaller ships. Truaxe had received mail on March fourth.

Dear Commander Griffith

I will not sign this letter, for obvious reasons. But, straight to the point. The three hundred dollar check as a donation to the Ben Bristol defense fund was well timed. Because of conversations I've had with one Barbara Griffith—I understand a lot of things now.

You have been covering for something aboard your ship having to do with an attempted mutiny by a Chief named Vincent. You are also covering something you must know about Vincent and the homosexual Doctor, Selesky, USN. Also, Barbara has given me other information that leads me to believe I can expect a similar monthly donation to the Ben Bristol defense funds. I can usually accept someone's religion, politics or sex things—but you've taken it too far. Barbara has told me everything.

Don't take this lightly.

After the injection from Bryant, Paul Vincent slept for ten hours. The sleep was filled with terror, sweats, confusion and five main themes. Hill's sudden death beside the helo, the unwanted shooting of the blue-eyed man near hootch number three, Tucker's two faces, DiNoble's surprise murder and the unwanted processing and re-processing in his mind of Abie's drowning. No sooner had the dreams finished but they would start again like a horrible movie shown on all four walls and inside your head. He couldn't escape the replays but could brace himself for each brutal detail. The scenes repeated again and again, preventing truly restful REM sleep.

In concert with the dreams, his mind reached for answers. Why had they been left in the water so long? Had he misread the coordinates to DiNoble by that much? Did the pilot copy them wrong? Could Tucker have used the stolen radio and changed them later?

Voices hummed in the background of his dreams and broke his slight concentration. The white overhead startled him from sleep as he parted his eyelids. He felt a headache but for the first time in days his eyes weren't burning. He had clear vision of the pipe markings on the overhead of the sick bay; 'Steam vent', 'Fresh water aft' 'Fire main' 'Vent 3-111-V'

Bryant and the doctor were suddenly over him, discussing him. The doctor turned and looked directly into his eyes.

"Chief, we've got to stop meeting in these strange places."

IT WAS DAVID SELESKY—AGAIN.

To understate, the same questions flew through him as had on the drug barge in Honk Kong. How? From where? Why?

It had been Selesky with him all the time. He now recognized the caring familiar voice, the thinning hair, the intent gray eyes, the friendly grin and the crisp green smock.

Why was this man sent to him for a third time? Vincent suddenly tensed with anger. He'd been aboard four days now, maybe five?

"I've told you there's a spy on my ship and I get you, Selesky."

"Tell me about the spy." Vincent almost replied to the question, but then backed away.

"Fuck you. That's a shrink question. You think I'm crazy, right?"

"Wrong. Tell me about the spy. Yesterday you said Tucker was a spy but there is no sign of him now. Like he too died in there."

"If he'd'a died. I'd'a brought his dog tag."

"You might have lost it, forgotten it … "

"I don't know for sure …anything. I just got off a merry-go-round." Questions filled his mind but he couldn't tell which were sound and which a part of a new fear that was building. Was this a set up? Were they using their prized shrink to draw evidence about how Lake died? He decided to stay silent until he learned more.

"Paul, listen to me. You've been through some deep shit, tell me …"

Deep shit. 'A world of shit'. He understands, maybe. "But you lie, Selesky …you lied on that barge." Jesus Christ! He thought to himself. He *did* lie. He lied about Patrick Balkin. Balkin was on Truaxe and could well be Tucker's contact man. He breathed deep and tried to center his thoughts. Was Balkin at Monique's that first night, behind the beads when Tucker and Abie were there? No. Wait! Think. He hadn't come aboard as of then. Or had he? Would it matter? He could have been at Monique's. After all, he'd been on the barge the following night.

His mind wouldn't track hindsight, hard as he tried. Selesky could also have been at Monique's.

Fear bolted through his body. The openly spoken anti-war Selesky had power of life and death over him as the M.D. He could not let Selesky know he suspected him or Balkin.

"Paul? You look miles away. What can I do for you right now? What do you need most of all?"

He stalled to think. "That's like asking me how old I'd be if I didn't know how old I am, isn't it?" Selesky backed away.

He looked behind Selesky. Bryant was leaning in and watching. Could he possibly trust that Bryant wasn't in with Selesky on some sort of deviousness? Luck jumped to Vincent's side: two others entered the four-bed ward. One was a doctor, the second an enlisted corpsman. Paul Vincent took a chance.

"Call those two over here. HEY!" He called out. "Come over here." The two stopped their motion and stared at him. They moved closer.

"What's going on?" The dark complexioned doctor asked.

"The chief here needs something." Selesky answered evenly. He turned to Vincent. "Chief, this' Doctor Mantanis, Nick. He's worked on your leg and on your butt."

"You get a Punji stake wound, Chief?" The doctor asked. Selesky continued talking, pointing to the second man, a corpsman with acne blazing across his face in humps, lumps and mini-white tips. "This is Auggie Ingres, Augustine." Selesky said. Vincent received a grinning smile from Ingres, which faded when not returned. The four men all looked at Vincent and waited. He couldn't tell by their expressions if they were patronizing a crazy man or if they were genuinely concerned.

"O.K. guys, get ready." He said, and took a few seconds to make eye contact with each man. He tried to settle his speech patterns and to not appear crazy. "I suspect *everyone* right now." He started, but hesitated. "I have a feeling you'll think I'll sound …ah …y'know … " he searched for the word.

"Paranoid?" The shy, dark, second generation Mediterranean looking Doctor Mantanis supplied the word.

"Paranoid. But just humor me. Ok?"

"I have no problem with this, Chief." Mantanis replied.

"Say what you have to say." Auggie added. "You among friends here."

"What time is it?" Three of the four men checked watches. "Fourteen ten."—"Two ten." "Yeah."

"Get set for a long story, gentlemen.

Vincent started with the slap of Clifford, a story Selesky had already heard in Hong Kong. When he got to the discovery of Selesky and Balkin in Hong Kong, he skipped over the homosexual side. Selesky interrupted him.

"The gay stuff is ok in present company. Not beyond we four though."

Vincent learned in those few words that some of the navy accepts that some small percent of the men around them are likely homosexual.

At six p.m. when Auggie Ingres slipped topside for sandwiches and coffee, Vincent had just covered the details of the dinner with Cynthia and Captain Clifford, and of Cynthia's confession to spying. By the time they were through the sandwiches and were trying coffee in paper cups, he had taken the fascinated listeners in-country and to village A12, Tho Bac. At eight p.m., Vincent was still filling in corners about DiNoble's death, and the ultimate loss of Abie Lake. 'Jesus.' was said several times by the listeners, as was 'No shit?', 'Good Christ' and 'Who will believe it all?'

Selesky had made several pages of notes on a yellow pad.

"And the reason you wanted Nick and Auggie here is because you figured Patrick might be the contact man?"

"You got it. I took a chance you couldn't all be in on it. Fact, when you said the gay stuff was ok in the present company, I got worried again that the four of you might be in a conspiracy." The others laughed but Vincent didn't.

"Well, none of us are against you, against the U.S, or against anything." Mantanis said.

"And only one of us is a faggot." Selesky grinned a sheepish broad smile.

"Then who is the agent?" Bryant asked and looked as though he loved the idea of a mystery. "Who is the likely contact man on Truaxe?"

"Perhaps by now, Patrick knows, Paul. You know why he was sent there in the first place?"

"He was to relieve as communications officer."

"No. Remember we told you we were N.I.S.? In Hong Kong?"

"True?"

"Partly true. Patrick is N.I.S. He'd been sent down from Yo'kuska to board Truaxe. If we hadn't been found by you, he would have gone aboard and you would never have connected him to me. As it was, he was sent aboard by CINCPACFLEET because … " Selesky stopped and looked about. " …have to keep this under hats, Nick, Auggie, Bryant. You also, Chief. OK?"

Everyone agreed the secret would stay secret.

"Your comm officer is Admiral Stumpf's son, right?

"Right."

"Well, he hasn't liked Clifford's version of the navy for months. He complained to big daddy—lack of training, injuries, fighting between the Captain and the Exec, arguing among the troops, fighting between nukes and black-shoe sailors, extremes of poor morale …so on."

"So Admiral Stumpf was taking a look, informally via Patrick?"

"Right." Selesky agreed. "No one expected to find *real* scandal like you're saying exists. At worse, they were anticipating quietly relieving Clifford as C.O."

He stopped talking, reached into a pocket, pulled out and unfolded a grayed paper. "I've been carrying this for two days, Chief. A letter I received from what has to be your wifey's brother, Ben the jerk—even though he hasn't signed it.

"Ex-wifey." Vincent corrected.

"Well, still a jerk." He adjusted the letter to his glasses and read it aloud.

"Dear Doctor Queer,"

He glanced up at the men and rolled his eyes.

"Smart people are putting three hundred dollars a month into the Ben Bristol Defense Fund, over a little problem here, care of the address on the envelope. Dumb people do not, and find other letters are mailed around. You aren't a dumb person. So far."

"Shit, David. I told Rachael you were gay. Stupid, stupid, I was."

"Yes. That was stupid."

"It has to be from Ben. Can he hurt you?"

"I've talked to a legal officer and he suggests either ignore him and take a chance, or, mail him at least one check to be cashed. Then, he suggests I actually go to civil authorities and follow through on a blackmail charge. Considering he's already in legal trouble …he'll probably run away."

Vincent apologized too much for having told Rachael of the homosexual issue.

"I have another piece of equally private news." Selesky reached to another pocket and out came a second letter, this one from Patrick Balkin. He scanned it for an instant and located the paragraph he wanted.

" …and it seems that CTG 70.8, not knowing I am aboard here, has found enough reason to start an investigation of their own over the deaths of two CIA agents in early Feb. Further, it seems that your friend, Chief Vincent, has been very busy here …"

He lowered the letter and looked at Vincent. "He goes on to tell about you slapping Clifford and of various crew member's reactions to that stunt."

"What were reactions, over time?" Vincent was keeping score should it actually end up in a court martial forum.

"Patrick seems to think it falls out at about fifty-fifty. Those actually on the bridge figure in your favor. Rest of the crew mostly think you were nuts."

Having expended much energy for a man in a weakened condition, Paul Vincent faded rapidly from that point. Again though, his sleep was filled with terror. He relived watching DiNoble's death, again and again. His dreams compared the headshot to DiNoble with the headshot to the blue-eyed Vietnamese, then the headshot to Randy Hill in flash, flash, flash sequences. Twisted into the same dream, the man Vincent had shot near the helo clearing was testifying against him at some sort of an international trial on cruelty. The inexperienced soldier stood before a board of skeleton judges, a black and white volleyball sticking out of his back where Paul's two bullets had blown through him. The man cried and complained about having to have a volley ball in his back forever, even though he was in what he referred to in broken English as 'innocent young soldier's heaven'.

He also dreamed of the CIA agent's mutilated bodies and Tucker almost crying over them, to later show no emotion at DiNoble's head being blown away. In his dreams, Tucker began to always have two heads and two faces, one caring and laughing *with* him, a second face cruel and laughing *at* him as he pushed the float into the gulf with an unusually large foot. In the dream, Tucker also fastened several twenty-five pound dog tags to a heavy chain around Vincent's neck.

The next Vincent knew, it was ten A.M., the following day.

He quickly penned a letter to Cynthia, telling all. He warned her of a man named Polof or Polot and also warned that her husband probably knew much more about the spies than he had ever told her. He used a British sounding woman's name as a return address, mailed the letter to her home address in Hong Kong and only hoped Cynthia would get it and not Kurt. He then made Bryant promise to hand it to the next pilot heading for Subic Bay or Japan.

Selesky showed up later and had something to say that Paul wasn't sure he followed.

"Way I see it, Paul, unbeknownst to you, Clifford has had you in some sort of a mentor position for a long time."

"Mentor?"

"Yes. You didn't know you were his hero 'cause you were busy looking for your own hero in him. That's what he drunkenly expressed at the dinner in H.K.

"Something like that," Paul agreed, "Cynthia brought it up as being like the worse kind of envy.

"You were his hero …hell, in a way, you're my hero, Paul. You seem to do it *all* correctly. You're not out to get anyone. Women love you, men respect you. Clifford was reacting to those same traits … "

"I have no idea of this shit, David."

"Paul, listen. After Clifford fired on the troops? Adrenaline is what took you to the bridge that day, pure adrenaline."

Selesky reached into his shirt pocket and pulled out a package of mints. "Gotta' quit smoking. Instead of rotting my lungs though, I'm rotting my teeth on these things." He offered one to Vincent. He took it. Selesky went on, carefully forming each word as though asking Vincent to pay close attention.

"Can I stop you?"

"No."

"Will I understand it?"

"Probably." Selesky pulled himself up and sat on one of the stainless steel cabinets near the bed. He rocked his legs back and forth. "Paul, love develops between men in the service, especially in combat but it can't be openly recognized or acknowledged. Tell me if I'm wrong now. A man in combat counts on another man. That second man does his job well, keeps the first man alive. The longer the reliance continues, the stronger the bond between the two men. The bond is not openly acknowledged. You guys don't run around out there saying; 'I love you, Pete for doing your job good', right?"

"Right."

"In combat ..." Selesky continued. "men care for one another in very serious life and death stuff situations." He stopped and unwrapped a second mint. Didn't offer one to Vincent. "Men in combat say to one another every day, in a lot of different ways—'I care enough about you to pay attention to my job so that you aren't killed. And, I expect the same caring from you.' And they get it and give it."

"But we get love at home to." Even as he said it, he passed the thought that he truly had not felt very much love from anyone in the USA for years.

"Men going back home feel they've been tricked by Uncle Sam into doing something that causes them to be hated by their own countrymen. At home, you'll get none of the acceptance you guys have for one another over here. It sets the closeness with the men in Vietnam in a very special place deep inside."

"And when I need acceptance, only remembering the acceptance of these men will make me feel ok?"

He let himself down from the cabinet and stood closer to the bed. "Just be ready. Try to understand, we're only now learning about these things, Paul. Maybe we can teach it if we learn it, and we can only learn it from guys like you."

"You gonna' write about this, Selesky?"

"I can't write well."

"Shit. Abie always said to write a book, you just take a dictionary and scratch out all the words you don't want to use. What's left is your book."

"No wonder he was special."

"Yeah."

Vincent nodded off again at two p.m. As before, his sleep took him back in-country. But this time he was simply an observer of the turmoil of others. He saw the pain, but didn't feel it. He was aware of trouble and problems and differences, but his new reaction was to accept that it is futile to try to solve the differences by fighting a war.

"I love you, Pappy.—I know, Abie." He could let it be without reservation, remorse or embarrassment. He had loved Abie and the only sad part was that he hadn't acknowledged it until the last moment of life.

Paul Vincent, like others, according to Selesky's caring study might someday cry surprising but uncontrolled tears when someone in their future does not say 'welcome home', or when someone puts them down for having fought in Vietnam, or, perhaps even, if they eventually *do* say, with a smile or a look of acceptance: 'welcome home' During those awkward moments they may well remember the friends of the past, those who did admire them, those who did trust them and need them. Needing those feeling they may well lock on to the names on a veteran's memorial, or a remembered unselfish understanding face of a friend now dead. Then quietly, within themselves, they will stand and grieve the loss of the love, and say 'fuck you' to anyone who pretends they know better, but do not.

"My God,'" Paul Vincent felt. "Please welcome me home from this."

CHAPTER THIRTY TWO
If It Goes Around, It Comes Around

When Paul Vincent returned from having walked to his first meal in the Chief's Mess on Kittyhawk, Bryant handed him several letters forwarded him from Truaxe. Vincent sat awkwardly on a tall stool, his left leg thumping from the walk on the rolling decks and the steep shipboard ladders. He tore Cynthia's very thick letter open. As he read, his left hand unconsciously massaged his left knee.

March 5th—Hong Kong B.C.
My Dearest Paul
My hands and thoughts shake as I write. The cable office would not send any cable to your ship using any controversial word or sentence to tell you Cecil Tucker is a Soviet sponsored spy. His contact name is 'Bell'. Don't you know, Paul, I realized he was the spy right after your ship left Hong Kong but even now I fear you'll believe I protected him, but no. I am fearful for your life and the lives of others, especially knowing you might go back into a boat with him. I beg, I pray —and not to suffer fools, all is all right.

Kurt has stayed away from me but I pursued him in order to find out more concerning Bell/Tucker. We were to furnish a new I.D. and remove a man named Bell from H.K.. It was too sparse a thought he was on your ship. Somehow Kurt tangled up contacting Bell. He blames our fight. Now he said if he would have contacted with Bell, he would have asked him to kill you. He doesn't trust me any longer so I am now staying clear of him. I can't tell Mia where I am for fear of jeopardizing her to Kurt.

Not knowing what else to do, I have approached your Eddie Monk at Shore Patrol. At this point I can't tell if I have somehow been taken crazy, or if the world around me has. Eddie Monk is sort of 'not to bother' with me. Kurt has intervened with his political influence and has immobilized my reputation. I fear for my life now, but I also fear for yours.

Bizarre as it sounds, perchance there is a second agent aboard ship. The only help I have is that Tucker/Bell knew him and that he had come and gone at Monique's. I did pick up that Tucker/Bell is his senior so it is probably not an officer—but can we be sure?

I have spoken with the U.S. Consulate here but I could tell, Kurt had been ahead of me. They patted my hand and sent me on my way. Same with the British Crown representatives of Hong Kong.

My fears are for your well-being. If I have been the cause of your injury or worse,

I have failed your innocent life and my mixed up one. God, I cannot breathe as I write those words. While no doubt finished as one of Kurt's followers, I still know their rules. If I haven't been satisfied you are alive and well by my best estimate of all things considered, by the 16th, Kurt and those responsible will rue the day they declared to keep you and I from being.

In my worse moments I picture both you and I being killed by 'them' and this letter being studied by some stuffy official. So, the attached pages include the details that will indict Kurt and others. You may choose to read the attached, or not. You will hate some of what you read, it addresses some of your unanswered questions of my past with them.

I have already told Eddie Monk all of this, but, true as he is to you, I still don't believe he believes me.

Write to me care of him. Please. And be safe.

Cyn

There was also a second letter to Vincent, a one page note from Eddie Monk.

March 5th Hong Kong

Dear Paul

I don't know what to believe here so I thought I'd go straight to you on this. Cynthia Howser is telling me something that she claims you know all about. A story of spies and agents and Monique's place, yet, Kurt Howser has visited, telling me to expect Cynthia, who he certifies is crazy as a loon and to expect will be raving about spy stories. He even brought her psychiatrist who states he's treated her for years and that she is very disturbed. Her psychiatric record is some forty pages thick and dated back six or more years. It looked authentic to me.

I've asked around the city. This Kurt Howser is untouchable, his reputation solid as far as the governor's office and beyond. So, because I know you've dated Cynthia I'm going along with her but there is nothing I can do until I hear from you. To be frank, she acts a little crazy. She's staying here in a cell, her choice. Says Kurt will 'kill' her. Kurt just shrugs his shoulders but offers any help we might want. I'm afraid to do anything with her until I hear from you.

Wherever you are, give 'em hell.

Eddie Monk

Vincent immediately wrote to Monk's office, filling him in on Tucker. Again, he asked Bryant to make sure some pilot had it in his hands, so it would not be delayed in the regular mail.

Bryant approached Lieutenant Carl Hanson who was flying a routine C.O.D. flight from Kittyhawk to Cubi Point Air Station near Subic Bay. He promised the excited and strange acting corpsman he would put the letter in international mail as soon as he touched down in

Subic. Hanson's light plane blew a tire when landing at Subic. It broke a strut and spun out on the runway. Although Hanson was not seriously injured, he spent the first day in traction in the sick bay at Cubi Point. He forgot about the letter for one full day and then, remembering the anxious begging voice of Bryant, handed it to a nurse to mail.

Nurse Elizabeth Hanover put the letter in her uniform pocket and remembered it during her lunch. She handed it to the second class corpsman who handled the hospital's internal sorting, filing and office delivery of mail. The corpsman dropped the letter in the outgoing mail box just after four p.m. on the eleventh of March. It lay there overnight.

On March 12th the letter was placed on a helicopter out of Subic and arrived at Clark AFB near Manila where it lay unsorted until 10 p.m. that evening. On March 13th, at mid-day the letter left Clark AFB for Hawaii on a KC-135 flight. The letter crossed the international dateline and arrived at Hickam AFB on Oahu in Hawaii on March 12th, the letter was trucked to the Fleet Post Office at Peal Harbor before it was actually discovered to be an international letter. It lay overnight.

The following morning the letter was shuttled to the downtown central Post Office in Honolulu and put into the international mail system.

The international agreement concerning postage was one of cross-acceptance. The U.S. would deliver mail coming in at whatever international rate of postage was on the letter, providing that particular country would do the same. Vincent's letter was delayed in Honolulu for the weekend and delayed another day being hand sorted through the 'cross-acceptance' desk run by Mrs. Amala Kalikotani. Amala, being a bit slow but having twenty years of service, made it a habit of checking each letter against the cross-acceptance list, so as to not jeopardize her job. Vincent's letter left the Honolulu international letter drop area on March 14th. If asked, a mail clerk was to inform anyone mailing a letter from Honolulu to Hong Kong to expect delivery within five working days.

"Mr. Balkin? There's a secret message in crypto. Eyes only for the C.O.."

"Very well."

Lieutenant Patrick Balkin had relieved Lieutenant Harry Stumpf as communications officer on Truaxe. One of his duties was to ensure the commanding officer had access to secret codes for extremely private or sensitive messages. He escorted Clifford to the small crypto room and set up the special machine for Clifford to read the 'eyes only' very private message.

"FOR COMMANDING OFFICER—EYES ONLY—COMMANDER SEVENTH FLEET SENDS PERSONALLY.

1. UNUSUAL LOSS OF AGENTS MARCH AND HINKLE, FEB 3 (CURRENTLY UNDER INVESTIGATION) NOW FURTHER INFLUENCED BY REAL POSSIBILITY ALSO OF DEATHS OF TWO MORE AGENTS, HOLLENDER AND PIPER, MAR 2-3. DEATHS APPEAR TIED TO INCORRECT PROCEDURES BY TRUAXE PERSONNEL. C.O. COOPERATION REQUIRED.

2. TRUAXE DIRECTED PROCEED HONG KONG UPON RECEIPT OF MESSAGE ORDERS TO "RESUME INTERRUPTED FEB R&R". ARRIVE H.K. 16 MAR.

3. C.O. KITTYHAWK WILL BE DIRECTED RETURN HONG KONG SAME REASON AND TO ACT AS CONVENING AUTHORITY INVESTIGATION DEATHS OF AGENTS.

4. C.O. IS HEREBY OFFICIALLY NOTIFIED NAVAL INVESTIGATIVE OFFICER IS CURRENTLY ABOARD TRUAXE AND WILL APPROACH C.O. FOR ASSISTANCE IF REQUIRED. END.

Lieutenant Lukarmo was talking with Commanders Corrigan, Valentino and Lieutenant Balkin, in CIC. "Shit, you'd think the Cap'n 'ud be happier for this surprise rest back in H.K."

Valentino was his usual objective self. "Nothing but a long face since the boat crew bought it, but, I can understand his grief."

"I think I can understand best," Corrigan chimed in with a smile. "Losing that boat crew and a brand new chopper after losing the first mission? I've been passed over enough to read 'passover fear' in the Cap'n's eyes." He smiled but the three officers didn't return it. It was far too early to be making even the slightest joke over the deaths of the crewmembers and all Corrigan's remark accomplished was to reaffirm he was his usual insensitive self. Valentino looked away from the man, Lukarmo got busy updating some charts and Balkin adjusted the volume on an air control circuit speaker.

"Just a minute, you guys." Corrigan chimed in. "Don't cold shoulder me over this. DiNoble and Hill were in my division. I always liked Vincent …though I leaned hard on him. He was sharp. He qualified as OOD faster than most officers I know of, and the way he went after the Captain was fearless …well …foolhardy maybe, but fearless. And he's smart and can control men. So I make a crack? I'm dealin' with this mess too."

Before any of the officers could respond to Corrigan's personal remarks, Arnold Griffith walked into CIC and addressed the group with his own agenda.

"Gentlemen." He nodded around. "Anyone here know of a naval officer, a doctor, named David Selesky?"

His question perked Balkin's ears but the other three looked blank.

"Comin' aboard here?" Valentino asked.

"No. Something else going on." Griffith kept face-shopping. He locked on Balkin who seemed unsettled. "You know him?"

"Me? No. Don't think so." Balkin was visibly nervous. "Why?" How would this executive officer know his well-protected homosexual lover's name?

"Nothing really. Have my reasons." Then he boldly stated: "You know him, don't you?"

Balkin feigned a laugh. "I said I don't think so." Then he tried to cover. "Name rang a bell but it's a big navy."

Griffith stared at the man for enough seconds to make both of them feel awkward. Then he added: "Friend asking if I knew him, that's all." Satisfied he wasn't going to gain any knowledge about Selesky, Griffith walked away leaving the already busted conversation even more stilted. Lukarmo tried to return it to unofficial 'shoot the breeze' but it wouldn't work. The men each went their own way.

On March 11th at eleven a.m. Winston DeWitt, alias Bell, alias Cecil Tucker, having ridden the ancient train and some trucks north from near Vil A-12, boarded the Soviet Lama class missile support ship, *General Ryabikov* as it swung at anchor in Haiphong harbor, North Vietnam. The 470 foot diesel powered vessel had arrived in Haiphong ten days earlier with a load of over one hundred SA-N-5 SAM missiles for the NVA and several Grail type SAM mobile launchers intended to be installed on trucks for use against U.S. aircraft in the central Vietnam region.

The *General Ryabikov* was moored at anchor alongside the Ugra class submarine support ship *Ivan Kolyshkin. Kolyshkin*, an enlarged version of the Don class submarine support ship had been especially sent to Haiphong since the Soviet Submarine *Pedrokli,* under command of Captain Betov Nikolayev had experienced serious nuclear reactor flaws. The December high-speed run from the eastern South China Sea to Hainan Island with U.S. destroyers and frigates harassing her had been too much for the aging submarine. The *Pedrokli* was moored alongside *Kolyshkin* but its crew had been evacuated and the ship completely sealed with a special foam designed to lock in the radiation of certain types of leaks. The crew of *Pedrokli* had been transferred to the *General Ryabikov* for transport back to mother Russia.

Captain Nikolayev and his first officer, Mr. Medkolonivich were standing on the forecastle of the *General Ryabikov* when Tucker walked aboard and tossed his duffel bags to the deck.

"Wha'el, wha'el. We do meet agin'." Tucker extended his hand to the two Soviet officers but only Nikolayev placed the face.

"Ah! One of the men in the boat in the Philippines. Mr. Bell, Yes?"

"Right on, Captain. Nice seein' ya'."

"I have wondered now and again if the American frigate found you and the other man, perhaps with their helicopter."

"We walked off that beach big as birds." Tucker's eyes skipped to the submarine alongside. Although the Russians had done their best to cover up the fact the ship was a total loss, Tucker could see tell-tale signs.

"My ol' taxi now a candidate for razor blades?"

"Pardon?" Nikolayev couldn't follow the American's humor.

"Dead boat?" Tucker pointed to the sub.

"Old and tired. Like me." Nikolayev said with a wry smile but totally without affect. "We going home, to Russia. Deserved rest. Are you going to Russia?"

"Naw. They be letting me off near Macau by the sixteenth. Ah've got one more job to do in Hong Kong before ah' take a long permanent vacation in France."

"What is it you are to do?" Nikolayev asked, curious as to what spies truly do. "If I might ask?"

"Well. Ya' kin ask. God knows ah' have no secrets from you, Cap'n. Some people who were to git me out of H.K. last month screwed up after taking good money for the job. I think someone has decided they are unreliable 'nuff to have their business closed."

"Are you a business closer?" It sounded like cheap revenge to the Captain.

"Ah've been known to close some, but usually U.S. businesses, in Vietnam. This my first real business in Hong Kong."

"Once they got you, they don't let go, do they?"

"Huh?" Nikolayev's comment went over Tucker's head.

"You have a long life, Mister Bell. You live and learn … " Nikolayev said looking into the air. He then turned and took hold of Tucker's shoulders and said directly into his eyes. " … Or you won't live *to* learn."

"Huh?"

Nikolayev turned away and motioned for his second officer to follow, leaving Tucker a puzzled look on his freckled face. It was nearing noon and the two officers had been ordered to meet for medication with Doctor Rothesmenn, the young Estonian physician.

During the sub chase, the *Pedrokli's* outdated steam control and passing system had blown three main valves within a matter of minutes. High levels of radiation were released into the sealed compartments of the old November submarine. Radiation monitoring meters had pegged at 60 REMs. The crew of Pedrokli had been exposed to enough radiation to require they all be transported to one of the 'widow-maker' hospitals in the eastern USSR. Doctor Rothesmenn anticipated fifty percent of them would likely die within 200 days, the remainder destined to suffer out their remaining days with radiation sickness; lowered white blood count, stomach pains, chronic diarrhea, dehydration, and slow but sure early death. Doctor Rothesmenn handed out pain killing capsules to any man who requested them. Her job, and she knew it, was to ensure the men suffered as little as necessary over the remaining months.

Rachael Vincent sat in one of the four chairs in David Selesky's old office in the clinic near the naval base in San Diego. Her elbows tight to her sides, she held the nearly ever-present ball of worn tissues on her lap, pulling nervously at it with the fingers of both hands. Barbara Griffith sat next to her looking equally apprehensive, a saucer balanced on her open left palm, the teacup, shaking slightly, held an inch above the saucer.

"Ben is in the waiting room but he doesn't know why we're here, Sarah." Rachael spoke without making eye contact.

Sarah Barkley, Selesky's one time intern, would have been amused at the turn of events if the two women in front of her didn't look so serious. Rachael had telephoned shortly after ten in the morning on the fourteenth of March and luckily, had caught Sarah between patients. Rachael, crying that she had no where to turn, insisted on coming in immediately.

Sarah felt a little apprehensive. The last she had heard, in January, Rachael Vincent had referred to her with a stream of swear words and a vow to never see her again. But, being a professional, she put her own personality aside and turned to her patient.

"Now that the three of us are here. What can we do, Rachael?"

Barbara Griffith answered for the two women. "There's something we have to tell."

"Yes." Rachael agreed. Sarah Barkley reached over and pressed the 'on' button of her reel-to-reel tape recorder. Neither of the women objected but they also didn't seem to notice.

"Paul Vincent has been protecting Doctor Selesky because Dr. Selesky is queer." Rachael began abruptly. Sarah Barkley relaxed immediately. As a friend and colleague, she had known of David and Patrick's homosexual relationship for nearly ten years. She had become part of the family of accepting and supportive heterosexual friends and professionals. Sarah braced herself for what she anticipated as a therapy session she had found herself part of before: helping someone deal with understanding the presence of a newly discovered homosexual friend, acquaintance or relative. She wondered if Rachael and Barbara were going to reveal that Paul Vincent himself was homosexual, or, closer to home, perhaps Ben Bristol, the brother, was also gay.

Sarah opened with a standard therapy question. "And how does Doctor Selesky's homosexuality effect you, Rachael?"

"Ben is blackmailing Doctor Selesky in some typical Ben way." Rachael said but Barbara interrupted. " …and I believe he is also blackmailing Rachael's husband … Paul …over the same thing. You know, pay me something or I tell the navy you protected a queer?" Rachael took the conversation back: " …and if Paul pays Ben money, that's money that won't be available for me." Sarah wasn't surprised Rachael's overall interest was self-invested.

"But that's not all." Barbara added quickly. "We also believe somehow, that Ben …" She looked at Rachael's face as though searching for permission to continue. Rachael's expression didn't change. "is somehow . . blackmailing my husband also … "

Sarah became confused. "Blackmailing Commander Griffith over Doctor Selesky being homosexual? Doesn't make sense."

"No!" Rachael said. Blackmailing him over the *other* …something." As she said 'other something' she nervously ripped the tissues she held into several more pieces. A scattering of the pieces dropped to the carpet.

"Other something?" Sarah questioned. "What is the 'other' something?" She flicked two wiggling fingers into the air in quote marks.

The two women closed up. Several times they glanced to one another then to the floor. Sarah reached into her professional skills. "It seems like this is a difficult subject to talk about. Would it be easier if only one of you were here to tell me, and the other waited outside?"

The two women looked at one another again but looked quickly back to the floor. Neither spoke. Sarah went in with more skills.

"Does this new issue have something to do with something other than the homosexuality?"

The two women spoke almost in unison. "Yes—Yes."

"Does it also concern both of your husbands?" "Yes—Yes." "And it's also blackmail-able? "Yes—Yes." "Can it hurt their careers?" "Yes—Yes." "Can either of them be hurt beyond just a career?" "Yes—Yes." "Can you two be hurt by this?" Neither woman spoke. Sarah felt apprehensive. She had opened something.

Thirty minutes later she was standing in the waiting room of the Commanding Officer of the San Diego Naval Station. She had Doctor Hans Gasser-Swieler, who had been David Selesky's relief, in tow. The base legal officer and the Chief of Staff for the Commander Cruiser Destroyer Force of the Pacific Fleet, a tenant on the naval station, were also present. They exchanged introductions and hand shakes as they waited for the Naval Station C.O. to call them into his inner office.

On March fourteenth, as Kittyhawk left station for Hong Kong to resume their R and R on the sixteenth, Paul Vincent showed Cynthia's letters to Selesky. After asking Vincent several questions and adding two more pages of notes to his already thick yellow pad, Selesky took everything he knew thus far to his own C.O., Captain Edward Gibbons, Commanding Officer of Kittyhawk.

Captain Gibbons, a man in his mid-forties, had been Commanding Officer of Kittyhawk since just before deploying from San Diego. Although he had some reservations about training levels on Truaxe from his observations of exercises while transiting the Pacific, he was not ready to accept that Clifford's ship was terminally flawed. Further, he was hesitant to accept any story about a spy on board, despite Selesky's insistence that Vincent, the source, was sane.

"Give us a break here, Doctor." The tall slightly overweight dark haired but crown-balding Captain addressed David Selesky. "This Vincent spends two days in hell in-country, closest friend lost, died in his arms yet, loss of two men he was to rescue. Chopper crashes around him. He's raving about having shot some V.C. regulars, struck his C.O., something that would be all over the navy by now, his leg's in a cast, wound on his ass, eyes blurred, punji stake wound—c'mon. Are all of you psychiatrists as gullible as this?"

"Captain Gibbons, please. Bear with me." He handed Gibbons some papers. "Here is additional information. Letter from an N.I.S. agent, Edward Monk, in Hong Kong. He's a personal friend of Vincent's and a man I know to be *very* professional." Selesky told him a few sentences about having observed Monk's behavior during the drug raid, but he did not disclose his position during the raid.

"And, here is a letter from Cynthia Howser to Vincent which names names." Selesky held back the letter he had received from Patrick. Although Patrick referred to the slap incident, he had also disclosed the existence of a confidential investigation, technically breaching investigator ethics. He waited and hoped the several pages of information from Cynthia, and the comments from Eddie Monk would be enough to sway Captain Gibbons.

Without comment the Captain read and browsed the several pages. Six to eight minutes passed. He finally stopped reading, fluffed the pages into a square on the corner of his desk and snapped a paper clip to them. He dropped them in the center of the green blotter on his desk, leaned back, put both hands behind his neck and looked straight at Selesky. "This' real hard for me to swallow, Doctor. This Cynthia woman goes on and on like a story out of a blue novel. This Monk guy, you say is a professional? He says the lady's a nut." He dropped his hands to his shirt front "However, I'm aware, doctor, for every on the one hand, there's a case for on the other hand. I need some time to think on this."

Selesky stepped forward and put two hands on the desk corner. "At least send a message to Truaxe confirming the slap on the C.O., Please!"

The Captain's hands went back to behind his neck. "Yeah. I send a message for all to see. 'Dear Captain Clifford, did your RMCM slap you last month and you then let him go ashore on liberty and then send him on an important mission'? Can't do that even to a blackshoe skipper I don't think too much of already."

Selesky stood upright, flicked his unbuttoned green smock aside and jammed his hands into his khaki trouser pockets. He squinted his eyes slightly and put his best clinical psychiatrist face on. "You *can* do it, Captain. The answer will be 'yes' or 'no'. If its 'yes' you can send a message to appropriate authorities, navy and otherwise, and, simply walk forward to flag officer's country and tell COMSEVENTHFLEET."

COMSEVENTHFLEET, Admiral Thomas Ferrent, was embarked aboard Kittyhawk. COMSEVENTHFLEET generally rode aboard one of the navy's cruisers in the gulf, or aboard a special flagship, but, at times, would embark on a carrier to stay close to the air war or, as this trip permitted, gain some time in Hong Kong. Although Admiral Ferrent had been staying abreast of what was happening aboard Truaxe concerning the dead CIA agents, that incident was only one very small circumstance concerning him and his large staff. Ferrent had the naval end of the war as his primary concern and Truaxe's troubles, until that morning, had been left to lesser officers. Gibbons resisted taking something that seemed like gossip to the admiral.

Captain Gibbons folded his hands in front of him on the edge of his desk. He turned his head sideways and scratched his chin on his right shoulder. "And if the answer is 'no'?"

"It won't be. I'm sure." His voice hesitated, Selesky *seemed* unsure.

"Doctor." Gibbons came up with a slight smile. "I think you've been over here too long. Are you absolutely sure this man is not hallucinating with help from this Cynthia woman? Absolutely, without a doubt?"

"Nothing is absolute, Captain. . but. . "

The Captain stood up behind his desk and motioned to the door with one hand. "Enough. I'll think on it. Plus, I also think maybe you *have* been here too long."

"I've only been here four weeks."

Gibbons smiled. "That could still be too long, Doctor." He dropped back into his chair and picked up a yellow folder. Selesky had been dismissed.

The frustrated psychiatrist stepped out of the Captain's office and back to the ward where he filled Vincent in. Both men experienced that helpless emptiness felt by any subordinate when their authority says 'no'.

"Maybe I should go straight to Ferrent?" Selesky mused.

"No, No. Don't anger a Captain by goin' over his head …just yet."

They tried to decide on a next step, some means to alert Truaxe to the spy potential. Selesky looked into sending a private telegram to Patrick Balkin under the system known as 'class echo' whereby personal 'Western Union' type messages can be transmitted over naval circuits under emergency conditions.

"No way." Vincent cautioned him, speaking as a radioman. "The system is too controlled and structured. It's for obvious emergencies. Besides, being a commercial message it has to go unclassified, and anyone can read it along the way, including, the radioman who tears it off of the machine on Truaxe."

"You're the communicator, Chief …" Selesky was cleaning his glasses on his shirt tail.

Vincent sat in his shorts on the edge of the sick bay bed. A weight was tied to his left ankle and he swung the leg up and back exercising the fluid drained knee joint. He continued to educate Selesky. "But you can't send words such as 'spy', or 'conspiracy' and you can't say anything that compromises a ship's movements …or …lists names of an individual stationed aboard a ship …nothin' like that." He puffed slightly against the exertion of the leg exercises. "The message goes through a civilian clearing house in a foreign country, for Christ's sake …"

"Bullshit system you radiomen have then." Selesky seemed frustrated.

"Its not *my* system, David. Lighten up."

"Frustrated, Paul."

"I know, I know."

The mid-March sunshine kept the large loft on Hankow Street much warmer than did December sun despite that the dirt on the windows blocked more than half the available rays. It was so warm, David Chen, who Cynthia told Paul was called Au-yeung removed his worn corduroy jacket. He looked about for a clean place to lay it, discovered the dust was thick everywhere, and put it back on. Rasha, who Cynthia said was called *Speckle*, was actually dressed summery in mini skirt and loose fitting blouse, her extreme pony-tail waving behind her whenever she moved. She had placed a white handkerchief on the very front of one of the dusty wooden folding chairs and was sitting on it.

Monique, who Cynthia said used the name *Star*, seemed opposite, she pulled her sweater around her shoulders and complained it was cold. Polav, the Russian middle man held his overcoat over his right arm, leaned against the banister next to the stairwell and lit a cigar. The group of troubled agents were waiting for Shaman who had called the emergency meeting.

"That god-dam Annie." Monique spoke, her French accent a little more spicy than usual. "I knew zat' whan she came to zee' group tha' she be mush' t'double. Za' beetch'."

"That was years ago, Star." Au-yeung protested. "She's been very good. And do we know for sure she has caused any trouble? I don't feel good about hating her."

Rasha spoke up in her clipped sentences. "That Paul? He told me the night I slept with him …he loved her enough to not want to have sex with anyone else." She flicked her head back and forth with two jerks, her pony tail flipped behind her like a snapped rope.

"But," Monique's voice continued angry, but slightly less French. "He still fooked' you though. Or you lie?"

Rasha looked down and away, her face flushed slightly. "Well, yes. But in a way, I did it to him, in the night. You know …it happened."

"You sucker for the big dick, Speckle." Au-yeung laughed toward Rasha. No one else laughed.

"David, that wasn't kind."

"Don't call me David, use other name."

Monique exploded in French. "*J'ai mal au coeur—ca empire* (I feel sick and this is all getting worse)" Then shifted to English. "Fuck all 'zis false intrigue, 'zis phony nomes, za' code words. All to keep Shaman's fantasy."

"Cool down, Star." Au-yeung got very nervous when Monique exploded."

"Cool down yourself, old man. Look where it has gotten us."

"It has worked so far." Au-yeung countered. "We should listen to Kurt … I mean, Shaman … " Frustrated with his own error, Au-yeung's face became red. He turned away into heavy coughing, his face turning even deeper red, tears at the corners of his eyes. He jerked a grayed handkerchief from his sport coat pocket and jammed its balled shape against his open mouth. Everyone became silent.

"Heavens." Kurt's voice surprised everyone as he poked his head above the stairwell and projected the one word into the room. He then paced quickly to the center of the large loft, crossed his arms and stood there as though purposefully mimicking Yul Brynner's famous stance in *The King and I*. "I can hear your bloody cough the other side of Kowloon, Au-yeung." He remained in the center of the room but shifted to hands on hips. He surveyed everyone. "Ah-hah, all are here who count."

"There is no Annie." Au-yeung noted.

Kurt ignored the remark and nodded to the Russian. " Hello, Palov."

"Polav." The Russian corrected the slight error in his name. "Everyone gets it wrong."

"Polav." Kurt corrected his pronunciation. "Good you are here." He greeted each member. "Star, Speckle, Au-yeung." There was an obvious hesitancy. He kept the floor but didn't speak for a few seconds. He looked almost tearful.

"KURT." Monique used his actual name in a loud purposefully pronounced tone. "We've decided to not use the phony names."

"I didn't agree, Star." Ay-yeung countered but started coughing and again turned away.

"Well, I decided. I can't use them. Is stupid any more with Annie …well, Cynthia on loose someplace. The names are gone. Paul Vincent and others probably know everything. . I …think we've. . "

"Enough." Kurt spoke directly to Monique. "Enough. We don't know anything about Vincent except his ship has left and as far as Cyn … Annie. I have her covered." His air of bravado continued. "She's been all over town but my reputation has countered her at every turn. She is seen now as a blundering mixed up woman, suffering a psychotic break …" He turned to Chen. ". . nervous breakdown, Au-yeung." Au-yeung nodded acknowledgement, now recovered from his coughing spell. Monique seemed beaten back by Kurt's assertive style.

Polav spoke. "Shaman …this is your organization, I acknowledge. However, I believe I must pull away. You may feel everything is controlled. However … I am not so sure."

"Wait, Polav." Kurt's open palms faced Polav. "Please. Do not move too fast. We must discuss this through. I can give you every reason to continue your trust in us. All is fine. We have to keep a little low until we decide how far Cyn …dammit. " He snapped his fingers over his own breach of the name rule, but continued. " …how far Annie is able to go. I have certain plans to discuss with my people today. I need three quarters of an hour."

Polav took a long pull on the fat cigar. He purposely blew smoke over Kurt's head. He shifted his overcoat to the arm where he held the cigar and pulled a handkerchief from his hip pocket. He wiped at his nose and looked directly at Kurt. "I hope you are to discuss …

Annie ...should be eliminated from this group ...before I can return my faith." Polav spoke what others may have been thinking. "She too dangerous to have like a cannon loose on a storm ship."

Kurt snapped at Polav, "LEAVE US ALONE." then immediately changed his approach. He moved toward the Russian with his hands outstretched. "Wait, Polav, my friend. Wait. I am upset. Please understand." Polav stood expressionless. Kurt continued. "Please leave us alone for a few minutes ..." Kurt looked to each of the others and back to Polav. He tried a smile. "While I tell of a plan which, if it wasn't for certain privacy we need, you could hear. Go to the coffee shop at the corner hotel and one of us will telephone the bar for Heinrich, shortly. Please understand."

Polav shrugged his shoulders, shifted his heavy overcoat back to the other arm and reached for the handrail of the stairs. "I will wait. But, Bell will be back soon, I am told, perhaps is already here. He will be anxious to speak with whoever it was messed up his pickup." He paused at the top of the stairs and looked down to assure his footing. "Understand, Shaman. I *must* have Bell moved on. You had several chances to contact him last time, and failed. Your carelessness put him in jeopardy. How the man has faired thus far?" He left the question in the air and became directive toward Shaman. "We *must* have professionalism—better cooperation."

"Yes, you must." Kurt was patronizing the man. He playfully shooed Polav down the stairs before he turned back to his small band.

Monique spoke right up. *"J'en ai ras le bol de Cynthia."*

"English—English, Star." Au-yeung begged,

"*Oui.* I am fed up with Cynthia. I say we zacrifice her to keep ze' Bell job, and the future Russian money and confidence."

"Agree." Au-yeung spoke up quickly.

"Agree also." Rasha turned her back to Kurt as though afraid to look directly at him while supporting the other's strong conviction.

"Sacrifice? Jesus." Kurt said and turned away and looked down. "Jesus." He repeated, spinning to face Monique. "By the light, we are talking of Annie."

"We are talking of CYNTHIA." Monique sizzled the name out. "The woman who has had you wrapped around her fingers for years. The child-girl with the woman body ...who has fooled you. Fooled all of us. She hates us. That is clear to me that she hates us, hates you ..."

"Hate? Us? Me?"

"For turning away her lover. You fool, Kurt, to have thought that wouldn't explode some day? Some day he leave his wife ...and she leave you. He raptures her, fool."

Kurt glared at her but Monique held fast. She stood from her chair as if ready to do battle. Chen and Rasha moved in and the four stood as points on a compass. Kurt felt weak and powerless.

"But, its Cynthia." He said quietly. "How can you ...how can I ... ?" He dropped his eyes to the floor, nearly in tears.

Monique changed tones just slightly. "Kurt, we know this is difficult." Her words were filled with genuine sounding sympathy. "You haf' a long history with her. I am sorry I call you a fool. We have all been fools over lovers. You shouldn't be immune. Look at Rasha, who once took beatings just to be loved by her Swede giant. Nor David here, who has been made a fool by countless young little girls without pussy hair." She waited until she saw the response she shopped for in Kurt. He raised his eyes toward her. She opened her arms and stepped toward him. He moved to her. She hugged him closely and patted his shoulder. The man began to cry openly against her hair.

"My Cynthia. . " He sobbed. "I've fouled it all up—everything."

David Chen moved close also and patted Kurt's shoulder. Rasha moved in but she did not pat the man's shoulder. She took a long narrow stiletto from under her mini-skirt. With a gasp for strength she rammed the pointed dagger into Kurt's lower right back and jerked it upwards, hard, just as Monique pushed him, hard. As his body flew backward, Rasha held the dagger tightly, letting it rip its way up and around his right side. The tip of the knife had sliced the right kidney hilum, punctured the hepatic vein, half severed the abdominal aorta and sliced the renal artery completely through. His body cavity rushed with blood. As Kurt fell, his thrashing arm struck Rasha, his hand tightened on her pony-tail. She was jerked to the floor by her hair. As the two fell, Au-yeung fell with them and grabbed the knife from Rasha's hand. With the movement of an artist flicking a brush against an easel, he slashed Kurt's throat just above the vocal fold, once, twice and a third stroke. His larynx fell away. The last slash severed the base of his tongue so completely it spurted out of his mouth and fell to the floor. An artery gushed blood in surges onto the boards of the loft. Kurt's eyes bulged. His arms flailed for four to five seconds. All movement stopped quickly as blood no longer reached his brain. He lay quiet, a circle of wet appeared at the crotch of his light gray trousers. Chen rolled away from Kurt's body and broke into an uncontrolled coughing fit. Rasha jerked her hair from Kurt's fist and stood up. Blood covered her front. She tried holding back tears but failed. She sobbed openly and ran to a corner of the room where she continued a muffled cry, alone

The plan the three had secretly made the day before was now nearly completed.

"*Au revoir*, Kurt." Monique said softly. She then turned to David Chen. "Call the Russian." She commanded. "He must see we mean business."

CHAPTER THIRTY THREE
A Long Way Since 'One If by Land'

Thank you again, Ella, for the ride, Dear." Martha smiled as she carefully pushed the passenger door closed with a flat opened hand. She stepped flat footed back a step, then, with just a slight grunt, hoisted her large frame up onto the curb in front of her house.

"You are surely welcome, Martha. Peter Paul fixed the car and said he'll fix it anytime for me."

"Now who is Peter Paul, exactly, Ella?" Martha asked as she habitually pulled the flowered polyester dress away from its plastered position across her large hips.

Ella adjusted her rear view mirror as she does every twenty seconds or so, and spoke without looking at Martha. "He's that nice young man, who lives in the house back of next door? I told you about him."

"Yes, he's such a nice quiet man, always waves to me."

"That's him. Peter Paul." Still looking in the rear view mirror, Ella flicked a blotch of dried makeup from the right corner of her mouth. "Bye now, Martha. Call later."

"I will."

Peter Paul Jammison, who friends at work jokingly called 'PP', had lived in the small sixty year old house in the two hundred block of University Avenue for seven years. No one ever said much about Peter Paul other than that he seemed like such a nice young man who never played loud music, never got drunk, never left his trash can out an extra day, and never went on a vacation. The neighbors knew Peter Paul to be quiet, to never go bowling or drinking, to never date, nor belong to a club. In his neighborhood of mostly older and retired homeowners, predictability drew respect.

Peter Paul had worked as an electrician's helper for Matranac Shipbuilding Corporation in San Diego for over seventeen years and it was understood he sent his mother a check each month which kept her well taken care of in a board and care home someplace in Georgia. But, what the neighbors didn't know, was that PP was also a specialty agent for the KGB.

As a low rated, class 17, low profile covert artist who received an annual retainer of less than four thousand dollars in carefully laundered cash, Peter Paul had a specialty skill. His special skill wasn't called upon very often but when needed, the KGB required quick action from him.

On March thirteenth, Peter Paul ripped open the flowered envelope that fell through his mail slot. With a pleased expression on his unshaven face, he carried the hand printed single page to the one bedroom and withdrew a worn leather satchel from a crowded closet floor. Sitting on his unmade bed, PP opened the satchel and withdrew a worn six inch by eight inch red colored booklet marked 'candles'. From a small drawer, he withdrew two standard elementary school compasses and set them to the distances indicated on the flowered letter paper, and began working back and forth between the 'candle' book and the letter. After a few calculations he began to write single blocked letters on a small notebook paper.

X B-E-N X B-R-I-S-T-O-L X 1-4-1-8 X I-L-L-I-N-O-I-S—S-T X B-E-N-S X B-A-R X C-O-L-O-N-I-A-L—X

He then looked up the word 'COLONIAL' in a separate small booklet marked 'select'. Peter Paul stared at the 'select' booklet and the paper for several seconds and then, balancing them back and forth from hand to hand, he burned both the paper and the incoming letter. He watched the few ashes break up as they disappeared down the stained slow flushing toilet bowl. He replaced the satchel in the closet and took a blue map book from a cluttered shelf behind his bed. He picked up a dented green fishing tackle box, put a soiled Dodgers ball cap on his head and left his house by the back door. He waved to Ella who was shaking a small rug over the banister of her back porch, and walked to the narrow alley behind the house where he climbed into his neglected 1958 Ford. He drove to 1418 Illinois Street and found that a neatly lettered sign temporarily stopped his plans.

"This establishment has been closed by order of the
San Diego County Marshall's Office
Do not enter
Contact county office, 107 C street, office 166—refer to case 603-68.

Moving around San Diego in his car, the resourceful Peter Paul took less than three hours and slightly more than four hundred dollars to locate Ben's home address. He found him to be living with his wife, Bunny, two children, and a sister, Rachael, in a naval housing residence at 3654 McCandless Street just east of the thirty-second street naval station, about one half block from the Chief Petty Officer's club, on the side of the street near the school used primarily for retarded children.

Peter Paul drove his car to a chain linked but open gated parking lot outside of the naval station and boldly selected a dust covered abandoned looking 1958 black *Chevrolet* convertible that appeared to have been sitting for some time, the owner likely a sailor who had gone to sea. Taking a large ring of keys from the fishing tackle box, it took Peter Paul only six minutes to enter and start the car. He let it idle for several minutes while the gray smoke of inactivity burned through the carburetor and smoothed out to a quiet three-quarter cam rumble. He used a book taken from the trunk to knock the heavy rain spattered dust from its windows. Cleaning his hands on his trousers and on the seat of the car, he felt lucky to find over a half a tank of gasoline in the Chevy.

He drove that car to within three blocks of his University Avenue house and parked it. The following day, he called in sick at Matranac and used the black Chevy to trail Ben Bristol.

At around noon on March fourteenth, Peter Paul watched Ben Bristol drive his two children to a *Jack In The Box* restaurant on National Avenue near where San Diego merged with National City. They returned home by one p.m. Peter Paul parked a half block away, opened a western novel, crawled inside the pages and watched the house out of one eye.

The two children played in the front of the small duplex but Ben remained inside and out of sight. At three p.m., two women arrived at the house and parked a 1962 Ford sedan at the curb. Both were blondes, possibly bleached, in pedal pushers, light nylon jackets, with rollers in their hair under colorful scarves. The children clustered immediately around the two women and Peter Paul decided they were Ben's wife, Bunny and sister, Rachael.

At six p.m. Ben left the house on McCandless in the tan Ford sedan and drove three miles to the *Beef and Barter* restaurant on the east side of Highland Avenue near Eighteenth Street in National City. He met a rather attractive brunette woman for dinner. Peter Paul dusted himself off well and waited in the bar. He drank soda water.

At nine p.m. Ben and the woman left the restaurant in the woman's car. Ben drove to a small motel on Broadway in the city of Chula Vista, seven minutes south of the National City restaurant. Traffic was light, but heavy enough for Peter Paul to remain inconspicuous as he followed the couple. Parking away from the glare of the street lights, in the shadows of a curbside tree, he waited outside of the motel for over five hours.

At two twenty-five a.m. Ben left the motel by taxi. The brunette must have stayed in the room, her car was still there when PP pulled away to follow Bristol. Ben Bristol's taxi returned to where he had parked his 1962 Ford sedan behind the now darkened restaurant on a deserted Highland Avenue. Peter Paul stopped his car at the curb in front of the restaurant, unnoticed. He waited and watched Ben argue with the cab driver, probably over the fare.

"Fuck you." He could hear Bristol's voice. He sounded drunk.

"Fuck you too, ass-hole. Its still, four bucks, fifty." The cab driver had no patience for a belligerent late night customer.

When the cab eventually pulled away from Bristol, its headlights gave Peter Paul a clear look at the entire near empty parking area. There were two unwashed darkened cars parked nose-in at the rear of the lot next to three overfilled green dumpsters. One car had a Baja California license plate hanging by only one screw. When the taxi lights scanned the dumpsters, a white cat jumped from one and ran, tail down, ears back, to under the Baja car.

The closed restaurant was to PP's left. A high wall made up the rear and right sides of the parking lot. The darkened windows of a few apartments were above and several feet beyond the right wall which was the south end of the lot. Bristol's car sat by itself, nosed into space number five of twelve spaces marked clearly on the south wall. A loan company and used furniture store across the street from the parking area were dark. A corner traffic light cast intermittent red, green and yellow lights onto some surfaces in the parking area, but not bright enough to see much by. There was one dim street light about fifty yards to the south which threw enough light into the parking area to move around by. Peter Paul couldn't see any automobile traffic on Highland Avenue in either direction.

A slightly built man dressed in white with a long soiled apron suddenly came from behind the back of the restaurant and, startling Peter Paul with a crashing noise, threw two large bags into the first open dumpster. Without looking around at all, the man smacked his hands together in a flicking motion and walked back out of sight behind the restaurant.

With headlights off, Peter Paul drove into the restaurant parking lot and blocked Ben's car. From the fishing box, he picked a pair of blue rubber gloves, the type used for cleaning toilets, and pulled them into place. It was two fifty-six a.m.

Ben Bristol was the type to try a bluff but was also quick to back off if a bluff failed. He shoved the Ford's door opened and yelled toward Peter Paul. "Hey!" He snarled. "Move the car, Buddy." The car didn't move. In fact, Peter Paul got out of the car and walked toward Ben.

Panicked, Ben made sure his windows were rolled up and the doors locked. He started the engine, half planning on ramming backward into the Chevy, if necessary. He waited in the seat, his heart beating rapidly.

Peter Paul stepped to Ben's window and pulled a large caliber silenced automatic from his front waistband. He tapped on the glass with the tip of the barrel and pointed it directly at Ben's face.

"Shut off the motor. I just want money." He spoke just loud enough to be heard through the closed glass and over the noise of the two engines. "I'm not going to hurt you …unless you don't give me no money."

Ben didn't hesitate to quickly reach forward and kill the car's engine.

"Money!" Peter Paul repeated. "And move slowly." Bristol reached into his right pants pocket where he kept his bills rolled together within a stained brassy looking money clip. He held it up for Peter Paul to see.

"Hand it out to me."

Heartbeat flying, Ben delayed for a few seconds but Peter Paul ceremoniously cocked the automatic and put the end of the barrel against Ben's window, pointed straight at his face. Ben rolled the window down two inches and lifted the clip of bills toward the waiting fingers of Peter Paul's left hand. When the window was opened less than two inches, Peter Paul let the barrel of the gun slide up the glass and poke inside just an inch or so. Ben leaned forward to be out of the direct aim of the barrel.

With just thumb and forefinger of his left gloved hand, Peter Paul reached in the small opening above the glass and pinched the money clip. The instant the money clip was his, he jerked the direction of the barrel toward Ben's head and squeezed the trigger. There was a fairly loud explosion in the still night air and the recoil of the automatic banged its barrel tip upward against the top of the window frame, and down, to chip away a large chunk of glass.

The impact of the large bullet exploded through Bristol's left ear with enough force to totally short circuit his brain stem. Ben fell forward in the Ford's seat as though someone had unplugged him from an energy source. Peter Paul panicked for an instant for fear Ben would rest against the car's horn. But no, he bounced off the steering wheel and fell to his right into a slumped final position.

Peter Paul looked quickly about as he freed the bills from the money clip and dropped the clip to the pavement. The man in the white apron and another still smaller man appeared in the dim light near the dumpsters.

"Git! Back in there." Peter Paul yelled. The two men disappeared. He scurried to his car and drove quickly out of the darkened parking lot. He stayed in the right hand lane and headed north on Highland Avenue with his window rolled down, listening for police sirens. He turned left on Division Street. Once on the residential street he pulled over to the curb, shut out the car's lights and waited a few moments.

When he was sure no one was following, he stayed with Division Street west toward the naval station, passed the navy commissary store and returned to where he had stolen the Chevy. He parked it in the same space he had taken it from earlier. Keeping the blue gloves on, he wiped everywhere he might have touched to be sure there were no clear fingerprints remaining. In his own car, he returned to San Diego proper via Pacific Coast Highway and up Washington Street to his University Avenue house. It was four a.m., Ella was sleeping.

In his bedroom, Peter Paul selected a second small booklet from his closeted satchel. This booklet was marked 'book'. Within ten minutes he had encrypted a letter on flowered stationery and addressed it to his contact on the U.S.S. Truaxe, care of the fleet post office, San Francisco.

The following evening, March fifteenth, Peter Paul smiled to himself as he sifted through the *Evening Tribune* and located the small article that covered the robbery and murder of one Benjamin Bristol of San Diego. An elderly woman who had been unable to sleep said she had watched the robbery from the window of her apartment house. Emanual Rodriguez and Jose Escaban who had been working in the restaurant nearby said they had not heard the single gunshot. The police were looking for a white man of average height and build who drove a dark colored convertible with a Naval Base sticker clearly visible on its front left bumper.

Peter Paul then flipped to the automobile section of the paper to check the prices of newer cars. The five thousand dollars that would be arriving within thirty days was a nice surprise to begin spring with. He could get rid of the Ford that he always felt left an oil slick taste in his mouth after driving it.

When he went to his mailbox later that day, there was another flowered envelope. He took it into the bedroom, very pleased with the increased tempo of his part time job.

At five a.m. on March 15th, David Selesky hurried to the Kittyhawk sick bay and shook Paul Vincent awake. "C'mon, drop your cock, grab your socks. Captain Gibbons, and guess who else, wants to talk?"

"Who else?" Vincent came quickly awake. "I'll bite, who else?"

"Admiral Ferrent."

"Great." He said as he flipped the covers aside and rose quickly from the bed. "Ouch!" He slowed his movements, touched his left knee. "Still doesn't bend right."

With Selesky lifting him by one arm Vincent got to his feet and reached for his uniform. Wearing it had become a symbol that he was returning to a sense of normal. The seas were calm, he noticed, the ship was riding smooth. It would be easier for him to get around than when the ship was tossing. Balancing easily, he dressed in khaki trousers, long sleeved khaki shirt and tie. Selesky seemed nervous and impatient as Vincent clipped new Master Chief double-star-anchor collar devices into place.

With a knock, Selesky and Vincent were invited into the Kittyhawk's *Flag Officer Quarters* where Admiral Ferrent and others waited. The large but crowded dark paneled office smelled like new carpeting and pipe smoke. Through two open ports, Vincent could hear the swish noise of the ship's port quarter pushing against the seas outside and below the quarters. Vincent was introduced to Admiral Ferrent, Captain Gibbons, Commander Eric Fenno the Kittyhawk executive officer, Captain Ronald Westhaven the COMSEVENTHFLEET intelligence officer, Fred 'something', the Kittyhawk communications officer, their legal officer whose name Vincent missed completely, and the Admiral's writer, Rob Langley, a Chief Yoeman Vincent had been introduced to earlier in the Chief's Quarters. Langley nodded and stood near the paneled doorway, pen and pad in hand. Doctor Mantanis was also present and seemed as joyous at being part of the intrigue as he had when Vincent first told the story.

Admiral Ferrent, a slender and dark haired man with a thin moustache, high cheek bones and alert eyes was seated behind his desk, smoking a pipe. He was the only person seated but Selesky motioned Vincent into a chair in the center of the room in front of Ferrent's polished desk. The remainder of the men balanced on the gently rolling deck by habitually shifting their weight from one foot to the next, or by touching or leaning inconspicuously, when necessary for balance, against a bulkhead.

Captain Westhaven, Admiral Ferrent's intelligence officer, handed Vincent a saucer and a full cup of black coffee. He spoke directly to Vincent.

"This conversation has been classified, at this moment, Chief, as Top Secret—need to know. Understood?"

"Yes, Sir."

Captain Westhaven nodded and stepped to beside the Admiral's desk. Captain Gibbons took over. "I tried to sleep on it overnight but I guess I got to the end of my rope about the same time as Doctor Selocky did."

"Selesky." Vincent corrected him involuntarily.

"Right." Gibbons acknowledged. "Doctor Selesky came knocking on my door at two a.m., Chief. His arguments paralleled mine. Right Doc?" The Captain nodded toward Selesky.

"Yes, Sir. I don't know what I was going to say when I knocked on your door but I knew I had to try one more time." Selesky was beaming. Gibbons took the speaker's role back.

"Master Chief, I've never thought a man to be crazy one day and then see him as totally sane the next." Gibbons leaned against the bulkhead near Admiral Ferrent's desk next to a round faced black clock with white numerals and hands. It was 5:22 a.m. Gibbons had just lit a cigarette and was shaking the match to cool. "But that's what I'm doing." He turned and dropped the match into a brass ashtray on the corner of Ferrent's desk.

"I understand, Sir." Vincent felt very good he was going to be listened to. The Admiral's pipe smoke clouded with Gibbons' cigarette smoke in a round stream of first morning sunlight that suddenly shown through one of the ports in the topside office. For a moment, the sun-in-smoke blocked Ferrent's facial expression. Vincent spoke anyway. "Thank you for being part of this, Admiral."

Admiral Ferrent leaned forward, waved an open hand back and forth to clear the smoke cloud. He nodded to Vincent but didn't speak. At the moment, Ferrent seemed like a quiet rather passive man as he drew on the white Merchem pipe, but Vincent knew he couldn't possibly be very passive and be the Commander of the Seventh Fleet. Gibbons talked again, taking everyone's attention.

"What if there is truth to Vincent's stories?" Captain Gibbons said into the air. "That's what my dream kept asking. If there's a spy on a U.S. ship, Admiral Ferrent should be made party to that. If not true, no one is hurt. A crazy Master Chief would still just be a crazy Master Chief, but, we don't see crazy Master Chief's." He nodded to Selesky. "Doctor, go on with the story as we've worked it out, please."

Selesky stepped one pace forward and took the stage. "There are a lot of 'ifs' in this, Chief Vincent. If Tucker is a spy, and if he has a consort on Truaxe, Tucker would not have bothered to have his consort alter Vincent's coordinates. If Tucker wanted Vincent dead he would have killed him as he killed DiNoble. So someone *else* wanted you or the boat and helo crew, dead. So, altered coordinates have nothing to do with Tucker or spies. They've more to do with someone's fear of you, of the boat crew or the helo crew. Possibly fear of you guys living to testify over the careless killing of the first two CIA agents, or, Clifford's shooting of the surrendering NVA troops. The common denominator there can only be … " He hesitated as if for effect. " … Captain Clifford."

Selesky stepped back a pace. Captain Gibbons took over again, turning to Admiral Ferrent. He stuck four fingers into the air. "The Pink Team pilot identified four men down. Assuming within those four could be Vincent, DiNoble, Hill and Lake, *or*, the second two CIA agents, one person who would benefit from those four survivors being out of the picture would be Captain Clifford, but only if someone were to make a case out of what Vincent says is true—that Clifford fired irresponsibly on the surrendering NVA …or, that poor training support by the C.O. caused the poor marksmanship overshoot and the CIA agent deaths. Either way, Clifford is under the gun."

Vincent spoke up. "My agreement with Clifford was that I would *not* say anything once he and I had talked in his room that night, agreed it was all a series of errors." Vincent said hesitantly.

"Were you coerced?"

"Coerced? Hard to tell, Captain. We were both in a no-win. It was the first time I had stood toe to toe with my C.O. Perhaps because my personal desires won out, I may not have realized I was coerced."

"Tell them of the no-win and the desires, Chief." Selesky encouraged,

"The Captain's desires seemed to be to keep a clean record, make admiral …which he openly spoke of … "

"And yours, Chief?" Gibbons asked.

"My desire, if you will sir, was to make port in Hong Kong and see someone there. And, by the way, Captain. I believe Captain Clifford trusted me, accepted my word that I would drop all of my concerns over the CIA deaths, the farmers, the NVA."

"So, you traded favors without really realizing it?"

"Oh, I think they were realized." Selesky answered for Vincent.

"Agree, now when I look back at it." Vincent agreed.

"So," Gibbons ventured. "Consider every possible angle, including the rather hard to believe raving stories of the Howser woman …who else might benefit from you being dead, or, from any member of the boat team or helo crew being dead …beside Clifford?"

Everyone went silent for several awkward seconds. Mantanis stepped to the coffee pot and topped off his small cup. He signaled a replenishment to others and both Gibbons and the Admiral accepted.

Five minutes of detailed discussion over Cynthia's letter resulted in a general feeling that if she hadn't been tricking Paul Vincent in a very sophisticated way, then Kurt Howser could surely want to see Vincent dead. But, the officers felt, there was no conceivable way Kurt could have controlled Tucker, or for that matter, controlled anyone on Truaxe, considering the distance.

"So, we're back to suspecting Captain Clifford." Gibbons said.

"Wait now." Vincent offered to the elite group. "Captain Clifford is a lot of things but I don't see him as … " He searched for words.

"As a spy, Chief?" Gibbons asked.

"Right, Sir. I see Captain Clifford, if I may say so right up front, as, well, pretty disturbed."

"Disturbed?"

"Yes, Sir." He liked using a conservative term he's heard Selesky use, rather than calling Clifford 'nuts'. "Disturbed in a true sense, but I'm not qualified in any way to say for sure."

Selesky interrupted. "He may be more qualified on this subject than he thinks, Admiral. Go ahead, Chief, go over the behaviors you've described to me."

"Well, Clifford often goes from subject to subject without finishing any of them. He is friendly one second and hateful the next. He trusts no one, accuses me of being after him, insists his father hates him, feels Lieutenant Stumpf makes reports on him to Admiral Stumpf …like he's …rather. ." He searched for a descriptive term. " …what I often think I am."

"Paranoid?" Selesky gave him the word he wanted.

"Describe paranoia for us, Doctor Selesky, if you will …layman stuff." Admiral Ferrent directed.

"Paranoid, sir? Suspects without basis, that others are exploiting or deceiving him. Reluctance to confide in others for fear it will be used against him. Unwarranted expectations of being tricked or harmed, taking unneeded precautions, scanning, hyper-vigilance …fear. Bears grudges. Doubts the loyalty or trust of friends or officers. Secretiveness. Reads hidden meaning or threats in benign remarks of others. Quick to take offense, …enough?"

"Enough. Thank you. Sounds like most of the people I know." The Admiral guffawed then let everyone take his turn following the relief of laughter.

Vincent waited, then continued. "He's all Doctor Selesky says …but, he's *not* stupid. He's super tuned-in to anything that might hurt his image. In changing coordinates, something stupid as that, something that can be traced—is too big a chance for Clifford … "

"But not if it would have worked …if *you* were dead. If you were dead, Chief, no one in the world would have thought of a coordinate change." Commander Fenno was probably correct there.

"Desperate men do desperate stupid things." Selesky commented.

"But wait." Admiral Ferrent spoke up. All eyes turned to his. "I see it a little different. It *is* stupid if Clifford changed coordinates to kill the Master Chief. Even with Vincent testifying against him, Clifford would likely have survived an investigation of NVA killing. This is wartime, you know."

"What are you saying, Admiral?" Gibbons questioned.

"I believe there is some missing link in this, Ed—and the link *must* be that Clifford had more to cover than just a potential investigation. Clifford and this Tucker could well be the co-agents. Based on Vincent saying Tucker told him the agent aboard Truaxe wasn't agenting, Clifford may have wanted to rid himself of Tucker's threat. He could have assumed Tucker was also swimming back out …so, he alters the coordinates, *not* to necessarily get rid of Vincent …but to get rid of his nemesis."

"That's my vote." Ferrent's intelligence officer backed him up.

"I can agree to that also, with very little imagination." Captain Gibbons added.

"And me too." Even Doctor Mantanis the orthopedic surgeon added his vote on the intelligence matter. Captain Westhaven nodded to Mantanis but smothered a smile.

The group fell silent for several seconds. Everyone exchanged glances with everyone else. Gibbons spoke again, to Vincent. "You aren't buying this, are you, Chief?"

"I'm sorry, Gentlemen." Vincent chose his words carefully, nervous not to offend the group who totally outranked him. "I still see Clifford, although crazy, as too US of N to be an actual spy." He then shrugged a 'but what do I know, shrug'.

Admiral Ferrent leaned forward at his desk and bumped his pipe against the heavy brass ashtray. The ash spilled out in a tight ball. He turned specifically to face Paul Vincent. "Master Chief, listen to me, from my seat. And this is very privileged information. This causes us, the navy, to *officially* wonder if Clifford is simply a screwed up officer trying crazily to protect a faltering career, or, if he is in fact …was in fact …when he acted, the second half of an espionage team. We must investigate either behavior, but be very wary of the potential of the latter. "

The seriousness of the comment coming from the Commander, Seventh Fleet overwhelmed Vincent. It must have shone on his face.

"We appreciate this is very difficult for you, Chief." Admiral Ferrent seemed almost fatherly. "You may be too close to it all. God knows we've been sitting here high and dry while you've been in the melting pot, so to speak. Just be patient with us, Chief." Vincent saw the man as a true gentleman.

"So, where do we begin? What do you want from me?" Vincent asked.

Selesky pulled out a well worn, rolled yellow pad. It flopped open on Ferrent's desk corner. He flicked back through several pages. Not looking at Vincent, he addressed him. "Can you remember the name Tucker gave you? His correct name?"

Vincent searched his memory but came up blank.

"Chief, I've written it here …first time you said it. But you were rambling so I didn't put much strength in it then. I'm just checking to see if you can repeat it."

"Prompt my memory."

Selesky turned to Ferrent. "May I, Sir?"

The Admiral shrugged—'whatever'.

"Twice governor of New York?" Selesky threw the words at Vincent and poised himself, awaiting a reply.

Vincent squinted his eyes. "Means nothing to me."

"Windy city, 1962?" Selesky tried again. Vincent's eyes opened wide. He snapped his fingers. "Chicago. Tucker fell off the Chicago … Dewitt . . Dewitt something."

"You got it, Paul." Selesky turned the yellow pad toward Gibbons and Ferrent, his finger indicating a penciled notation. Gibbons read aloud.

"Winston Dewitt, EM3, the Chicago, 1962."

Gibbons turned quickly to his communication officer. "Fred, I want a priority message to the bureau. Let's find out if a Winston Dewitt fell off Chicago and so on. Wake someone up back there. I want an answer ASAP. Then, let's get a tracer from Pink Team on those coordinates and see how they arrived and how they looked when relayed from Truaxe, how they ended up at SAR, so on. Also, ask the bureau what they have on what's-his-name … Cecil Tucker."

"Right." Vincent said. "Tucker said he took over once for a man from a swift boat in the delta off Tra Cu. Said he acted crazy and was sent to that army hospital in Hawaii where they just sorta' believed him. Even got a new I.D. card there."

The communications officer jerked a wall phone from its holder and spun the rotary dial. As he spoke quietly into the phone, Admiral Ferrent leaned toward David Selesky. "What the hell was the 'twice governor of New York' question, Doctor?" He asked.

"I don't remember *much* from U.S. History but a brain cell let that info go when I looked at the name 'Dewitt' here in the pad. Dewitt Clinton was twice governor of New York. So sue me?" The Admiral laughed. Captain's Gibbons and Westhaven laughed in turn. Vincent waited until the laughter rotated down to his rank level. He and the Chief Yoeman let in the last appreciative chuckle.

Paul Vincent again stared at the sick bay pipes and wiring overhead. He couldn't accept that Clifford was actually the spy contact. His stereotyped picture of a spy was either the *James Bond*, 007 type, or a shadowy covert personality way out of suspicion. He could not see an open bumbler like Clifford going so far as to intentionally frustrate the efforts of his own country. But then, he remembered. He would never have believed Cynthia Howser capable of spying for profit, nor had Tucker's hillbilly style even slightly garnered suspicions. He also would never have guessed the mild mannered Kurt Howser was anything more than some harmless intellectual whose life centered on the gathering of money and comfort. Further yet, for heaven's sake, David Chen was still the farthermost from a spy model. For that matter, Patrick Balkin not only didn't appear homosexual, he hadn't seemed to be Naval Investigative material either. To take it a step more, David Selesky had not seemed homosexual on first meeting nor did he seem like a liberal to the point of openly being against the Vietnam war. Nor had Barbara Griffith looked like an officer's wife who would sleep around with a low-life like Ben Bristol. With more thought he decided that only Monique and Rasha might fit his image of intrigue and spying. Their accents, being prostitutes and secretive filled the image.

By the time Vincent was overtaken by fatigue to the point of falling asleep, he decided he had not been a very good judge of character for most of his life. Look at his marriage to Rachael and how he kept looking for her brothers to begin to shine. He then felt that deciding people's true character was probably best left to Admiral Ferrent and Captain Gibbons' experienced staffs.

"Good Christ." His thoughts jerked him wide awake. "Abie's death was murder, murder in a true sense. If Clifford had changed the coordinates, no matter his reasons, he was guilty of premeditated murder." He lay back in the bunk. His head began to ache, his ulcer flared discomfort. He was so tense, the Ben Bristol hand competed with the healing knee for pain attention. He was unable to fall asleep.

He looked at the new watch that Selesky had bought for him from the Kittyhawk exchange store. The temporary *Timex* indicated it was noon, March 15th. Kittyhawk would arrive in Hong Kong in eighteen hours. He wanted to sleep. He needed his strength to go ashore to find Cynthia.

After Paul Vincent and some of the others left, Admiral Ferrent continued in discussion with the small group of officers.

"As COMSEVENTHFLEET, I am senior military commander involved. I would not like to try to resolve all of this over communication circuits, not at this time. I can't trust we can get a message to that Lieutenant Balkin on Truaxe without Captain Clifford getting wind of it. "

The Admiral leaned back in his chair and started stuffing tobacco from a leather pouch into the bowl of the white pipe. "Clifford is wearing two hats right now and we must be alert for him to act from either position when he reaches Hong Kong. Hat number one is a C.O., scared for his career. He knows we know of that hat because of the first investigation ref the first agents. Hat two is as a frightened agent. I'm hoping he doesn't think that's been uncovered. I'm planning to stall until we make Hong Kong and then, simply arrest Clifford, let their executive officer, this Griffith guy, take command. Get Clifford out on the next plane and let the national security people take over. "

"Might I suggest something, Admiral?" Fenno leaned in.

"Please."

"I recommend we send a message to all higher-ups, a phony message, making Truaxe an addressee on it. Tell'um Chief Vincent has died, or is totally psychotic."

"What's your point?"

"Remove Vincent as threat to Clifford. See my point? If Clifford is an agent, his value to whomever he works for, probably the Kremlin, is as C.O. of a nuclear ship. If we take away any threat of loss of that position … "

"He's less likely to do something stupid, like run, when he hits Hong Kong?"

"Yes, Sir."

"Good idea, Eric." The Admiral joked.. "This is why the navy pays you the medium big bucks isn't it?"

Eric Fenno just smiled. The message was drafted and sent.

After a quick telephone call to Admiral Forrest Brentwood, Commander of the Eleventh Naval District in San Diego, the San Diego Naval Station Commanding Officer, Captain James Steele learned for sure, that under a 1957 law, a psychotherapist can break patient privilege over what has been said in a therapy session only if it is revealed that someone's life is in danger.

"Yes, Admiral, that information does fit the *threat to life* category." Pause. "Yes, Sir." Pause. "Yes, Sir." Pause. "Right now, Sir."

Captain Steele drafted a message to COMSEVENTHFLEET and to Truaxe for action, informing them of the information given by Rachael and Barbara to Sarah Barkley. Because of its importance, the message was also addressed to the State Department, The Nuclear Regulatory Committee, Federal Bureau of Investigation, Bureau of Naval Personnel, Chief of Naval Operations, Commander in Chief of the U.S. Pacific Fleet, Commander Naval Forces Vietnam and other lesser but interested commands.

When a naval message is destined to a ship at sea, it is routed through a system of teletype circuits. The actual destination of the message is controlled by a six to nine digit tape-punched routing indicator that is read by computer or, in most cases in 1968 where the system has not been modernized, is read by sight by the radiomen on watch at each relay station.

The message concerning Truaxe was punched into half inch wide waxed yellow paper teletype tape at the naval station San Diego and entered the 82B1 automated communication system at one a.m. Hong Kong time. It was sent as an 'immediate' message, indicating action was to be taken on its contents 'immediately' and that it was to be handled at each relay point 'immediately', not permitted to be delayed by messages of lesser precedence.

The message left the naval station by landline and switched automatically to the Naval Communication Relay Station (NAVCOMMSTA) San Diego located on the waterfront at the corner of Harbor Drive and Broadway. As soon as the 'immediate' sensor was activated, a landline circuit opened to the NAVCOMMSTA San Francisco, located in Stockton California near state route 99. The San Diego watch supervisor noted the message had only been 'in house' about thirty seconds since it arrived from the Naval Station communications center.

Stockton had not yet been switched to the 82B1 system. Instead of automatically activating an on-going circuit, the message spilled out in tape form to be hand read.

"Hey ...got a hot one for Hawaii." The message tape was then hand carried 'cross-office' and placed into a transmitting switch, 'click', to be sent via radio to the NAVCOMMSTA in Hawaii located in the center of the island of Oahu near the small town of Waihiawa.

"That hot one go yet?" Asked the watch supervisor, Radioman first class Pete Peterson.

"Yep, that's its tail right there ...now."

Radiomen at Waihiawa manage the major east-west military message relay center. Some forty radiomen and communication yeoman receive, interpret, route, carry cross-office and introduce, thousands of teletype tapes a day in and out of the hundreds of linked circuits that cross the pacific. The digits of the routing indicators typed at the beginning of each yellow tape direct which link the tapes are to be placed into. The message going to COMSEVENTHFLEET, Commander Naval Forces Vietnam, and to Truaxe had a common routing indicator, heading west.

"Hey, hot one, fer' San Miguiel."

"Backed up here. Two ahead of you."

The radioman on watch slipped his *immediate* message tape in the third slot down on the "awaiting action" tape holder grid, and informed his supervisor ... "Wilbur, high precedence? Backed up three to San Migoo'."

"Okay. I'll watch."

Within eight minutes, the message arrived for onward relay at NAVCOMMSTA Philippines located at the San Miguiel naval communications station, in the mountains a few miles from Subic Bay.

NAVCOMMSTA San Miguiel was in the middle of switching over from manual to the 82B1 system. Each day as new circuits were switched, it was difficult to keep up to the *exact* status of any tributary station at any one given time. Eight by ten inch hand written cardboard signs were used temporarily to inform the watchstanders of the latest status.

This particular message spilled out in tape form onto the floor of the teletype relay center at 4:40 a.m. Hong Kong time and was picked up by nineteen year old radioman third class Richard Glass who was in his sixteenth month of COMMSTA duty. Glass carried the message to the 'duplicate router' where a copy was made of the tape to go into the COMSEVENTHFLEET special circuit, a second copy to go onto the fleet broadcast where Truaxe radiomen would be alert for messages addressed to them, and a third copy to be relayed on to Commander Naval Forces Vietnam.

"Hayden, you keepin' those circuit changes well marked?"

"Yeah, Chief. With grease pencil signs for now. I'll have printed signs made when the mess is over."

Naval Forces Vietnam (NAVFORV) had been one of the first stations switched to an automatic key and their copy of the message went right out. COMSEVENTHFLEET and the fleet broadcast had been switched that day. Only low priority stations remained on the manual system; stations such as the American Red Cross representative Subic Bay, (AMCROSS SUBIC) and AMCROSS Sangley Point, Industrial Management office (Indman) Subic Bay, Naval Weather Station Sangley Point, U.S. Consulate Office Manila, and other administrative stations.

In the changeover, the actual machine, number twenty three, that was once the manual fleet broadcast transmit device had been changed to become the AMCROSS SUBIC circuit, simply because it was a well maintained machine and shouldn't go to waste. The previous COMSEVENTHFLEET transmit device, number thirty seven, had been moved to become U.S. Consulate Office, Manila. It had a grease pencil sign taped to it as Radioman Hayden promised. Busy in conversation with Radioman Harold Long about the weekend they had just spent with two new-found lovelies in Baguio City, Radioman Glass was operating on braggart automatic.

"Boy, that lady could peel a grape with that thing." He scanned the routing indicators on the tape meant for Truaxe.

"That'd be okay if you're grape size, I guess." Harold Long quipped. "Now for me. My name actually indicates to the ladies what to expect." He guffawed.

Radioman Glass put a bold penciled 'X' over the Truaxe routing indicator, to mean it had been transmitted to that station.

"It wasn't grapes she wanted put in there." Glass jibbed. Caught in the sparring conversation with Radioman Long, Radioman Glass habitually put the tape into machine twenty-three. It went to the American Red Cross office Subic Bay.

"I'm seein' mine again tonight." Long yelled over the clackity noise of the busy station. "What 'bout you, Glass?" A second black 'X' and the tape for COMSEVENTHFLEET dumped out on the floor of the office of the U.S. Consulate, Manila. Both offices were closed until 0900 the following day.

"Naw, not me, I'm staying in the barracks and getting some sleep. I'm so pooped I can hardly see."

CHAPTER THIRTY FOUR
Get Your Programs Here

Cynthia Howser no longer had the advantage of overlooking the harbor from her home on Victoria Peak. Believing Eddie Monk felt she was too crazy to take seriously, she started fearing Kurt might be able to hurt her even in Monk's protective jail cell. On the thirteenth she slipped away and was living anonymously in the now run down *Fandian Ho* hotel on the Aberdeen side of the island. Each day at noon she would call Monk and ask her standard questions: Was there a letter for her from Paul? Did he know anything of the ship's movements, or of Paul's welfare. Thus far, Monk had no valuable answers.

At three p.m. on the fifteenth, three hours after Cynthia's call, Monk's office received a routine message report announcing the arrival of Truaxe and Kittyhawk first thing the morning of the sixteenth.

"Rats." He thought aloud. Then: "Oh, well. I'll tell her when she calls tomorrow. Chances are, if she goes to her home above the tram, she'll see them come in anyway."

On the sixteenth, Cynthia changed her pattern. Instead of waiting until noon, she telephoned Monk shortly before eight a.m. Eddie had already left to have a semi-business breakfast with two Hong Kong policemen. He then planned to walk to the British Pier to meet Truaxe, greet Vincent for the sake of their friendship and to sort the myriad of stories and try to have more information for Cynthia's anticipated noon telephone call. The timing was off.

"Shore Patrol, Officer Esplanade."

"Officer Monk, please."

"Not here, Lady. I help you?"

"I'm Cynthia Howser. Is there a letter there for me?"

"A what?" Tex-Mex had to put her on hold twice to answer other calls, and was also making neglected log entries as he talked to her.

"A letter. It was to come to me via Officer Monk."

"Hav'ta ask him that later, lady." Tex-Mex waved two S.P.'s into the back room for a meeting. " ...and he's out."

"Where'd he go?"

"Lady ... I don't know." He tossed a pencil into the air over his shoulder. "He's my boss. Doesn't check in and out with me. Can you call later?"

It was the sixteenth of March, the date she had carefully picked to hear from Paul and to decide if he was alive or dead. Cradling the black phone, Cynthia turned to the small hotel room window and gazed without seeing past Lantau Island toward Macau a few miles to the west. Large clear tears rolled down her cheeks. She watched a bent over old man swish-sloshing another man in a tiny square fronted boat. The scene drew her. People moving about the waterways seemed to have purpose, peace, somewhere to be going, someone to be with and someone to be returning to.

With a noiseless sigh she put the few things she had collected during her days on the run into a paper bag. Habitually she looked into the mirror above the worn oak dresser and searched for the light in her eyes, the light Paul always said he saw and cherished. She couldn't see it through the tears. She brushed at her hair but the usual light feelings which accompanied prettying herself were replaced by a heavy, complete and terrible thought: The reason she wanted to be beautiful, the man she wanted to be beautiful for, was likely gone from life.

"My stupidity about Tucker. I'll never see him again." Sobs of sorrow for Paul and pity for herself burst forth uncontrolled. She pressed the plastic prongs of the hairbrush into the flesh at the side of her neck, trying to feel *something* besides the deadening heartache. Suspecting that the powerful sadness she was experiencing would be with her forever, she wanted to alter that power in some way and make use of it for her new main purpose of life.

"Reprisal." She mouthed the word and it felt so gratifying she voiced more such words. "Retribution, retaliation, revenge, reprisal toward Kurt, Bell, Monique. Revenge with Rasha, Polav, David Chen, Beebe, anyone connected to the deceptions of those wasted years." Her breathing became shallow and difficult as she planned the redress.

She left the small hotel in her car at 8:30 a.m. neither seeing nor hearing anything of the world around her. Within thirty minutes, her heart beating strongly and deliberately, she drove to the top of the lookout where she and Paul had first kissed. Adjusting to being alone and still planning her revenge, she gazed out over the city and the harbor, at first without seeing. She opened her purse and the vial of 'shocking' which so represented time spent with him on that overlook. She saturated her already tear socked handkerchief with the perfume and draped it over a low tree branch. The aroma filled the air and for a brief second brought his arms around her.

Suddenly, there it was. The gray ship with the white side number '55'.

"He *is* still alive."

Driving the car, her thoughts darted with optimism; "Yes, Yes! He lives ...he's looking for me," to pessimism; "no, he'll be gone. They'll say he is dead." She pushed the eager Mercedes toward the navy pier.

Turning into the large concrete area she had waved goodbye from just days earlier, she saw the bow of Truaxe moored at the end of the British naval pier, sixty yards away. Several people were gathered around the pier's gate, many more walking to and from the ship.

She drove the car as close as the Chinese policeman would permit. Leaving the motor running, the door open, she ran through the chain link gate, past others and down the pier. The skirt of her light dress was continually lifted by the wind off the harbor. Running awkwardly she kept it pressed against her sides with both hands. People she passed, mostly salesmen and merchants looked at her strangely as she ran. Ahead of her, near the fantail of the ship was a large crowd of people milling around. One group of about ten khaki clad uniformed U.S. sailors were single filing up the narrow gangway.

Crazed, she stopped near the bow and talked to the first crewmen she saw with *Truaxe* on the shoulder above his rating stripe.

"Chief Vincent. Is he aboard? Is he OK?" The beautiful but teary eyed woman with the wind blown hair startled Enginemen Bill Higgins and Tony Medich as they connected the ship's fresh water lines to the pier. The two men looked at one another."Ma'am, Chief Vincent and some others were lost in-country. Right Tony?"

"Sure were, lady." The tall man in sweaty working blues pulled his white-hat from his head in unconscious reverence. "Right now I believe that's where it stands, Ma'am. "

Bill Higgins turned and yelled to a third man who stood on the foc'sle of Truaxe. "Andy …ain't the latest on the Master Chief that he and them others is MIA?"

"That's it. Higgy."

"MIA? Cynthia asked.

"Missing, ma'am. Ain't good."

Pushing her way through the crowd of salesmen and line handlers she made it half way up the narrow gangway before Vernon Putney, a first class petty officer acting as the Junior O.O.D., stopped her.

"Ma'am. Who are you representing?"

She asked her question.

Vernon Putney was a first class storekeeper who had only been aboard a few days, having transferred over from U.S.S. Halsey on request to remain in the Western Pacific where he could get more time near his Filipino wife's family, in Manila. He knew of the loss of the men in-country, of course, but he hadn't known any of them personally.

"Ma'am, I can't say anything officially, but last known …most of 'em are de …de … deceased. If you want to wait … " He turned from her and walked up the gangway.

Cynthia couldn't remember the teary eyed walk back to the car, nor could she remember driving again to Victoria Peak, but within thirty minutes, just before ten AM, her heart beating strongly and deliberately, she stopped her car on Amber Lane a quarter mile from her house.

The garage doors were closed. She couldn't tell if Kurt was at home. She slipped in a side door with a key that was always hidden beneath a certain mossy stone. She stood silently in the living room and listened. The quiet house smelled closed and damp. No sign or smell of an early morning shower or of morning meals having been prepared. Considerable mail lay below the drop slot inside the front door.

Staying away from Mia's end of the house she made her way quietly to her old bedroom. She had to pass Kurt's room. The door was closed. She pressed her ear to its smooth painted wood and listened, scarcely breathing. Without a sound she turned the knob gently and pushed it open. The door's bottom edge hissed slightly against the carpet. The room smelled like sandalwood and cedar and was very warm. A small space heater was glowing in the center of the room. There were no signs of Kurt.

She closed the door quietly and made her way toward her own bedroom. She repeated the same ritual before entering. Her room was cooler and smelled of lotions and potpourri. She reached down and pulled off her flat shoes and stood in stockings on the familiar carpet. Next to her bed, in the same drawer where she kept the measurement compact was the nine-millimeter automatic. She lifted it. It felt colder and heavier than ever before. Holding it to her side she pushed some papers aside and located two spare magazines of bullets. Following a developing thought and plan, she dumped her small purse contents on the bed and looked for and found a large blue shoulder bag from a shelf in Kurt's closet.

She raked inside of it with one hand. As remembered, there were several hundred American dollars in the bag and most of all a passport folder. She quickly scraped the few things from the bed into the larger bag. Returning to the bed she made sure the gun and magazines were out of sight in the contents of the shoulder bag.

Her heart pounding, her breathing erratic, she dropped all of her clothes to the carpet except the white bra and garter belt and started selecting more practical outer things to wear. Standing nearly naked she suddenly felt vulnerable. She heard a 'click' behind her.

Mia stood in the doorway, a surprised look on her face.

"Tian Tian." (Sweet one.) The little Chinese woman let out a cry of relief and delight and hurried to Cynthia's arms. They hugged unashamed and Mia cried. "I look all of Xianggang, (Hong Kong) tomorrow Zhonghua' (All of China)". Cynthia felt even more sad and lonely. Mia jabbered.

"Mister Kurt he tell me alla' time what he do and when he come home. He say nothing 'bout Missy Cyn when I ast' him. I know he mad, I think you fight."

Mia helped Cynthia dress in fresh stockings, blue jeans and a long sleeved yellow sweater, all the while talking rapidly and repeating herself. "He alla' time ast' me if you call I say no and he no believe Mia but I say no. But he no believe Mia."

"You did good, Mia. I'm sorry I didn't call. I was afraid to let you know for fear Kurt would …"

"He stay home ebery night, watch redivusion, 'til two nights. Now he go, stay go."

"Gone two days?"

"Yes, two day."

Cynthia became afraid then. He could walk into the house at any moment.

"Also, Missy Cyn. No ring-ring dianhua-phone. Otha' ladies not dianhua' anymore. Otha ladies and Dabid Chen? He dianhua' alla' time afore, ring-ring. E'bery day, two, 'tree times dianhua', ast' for you. Rashta the hair lady, and Moni' lady and Dabid Chen, they hab' dinna' two times here on v-ranna', eben' when too cold. But now not dianhua since Mister Kurt not come back home."

"Kurt is surely with them then, Mia." Cynthia tried to calm her old friend. "He'll pop up."

"No, no! He no with them." Mia said excitedly. "I dianhua Moni' lady hotel. She say no and tell me again …she say 'not dianhua' 'gain, godammit'." The little Asian face boiled over into tears.

Cynthia held her close and spoke into the top of the little ladies head. "I'm going to look for Kurt today, Mia. I'll phone you."

Mia stopped wringing her hands only long enough to help Cynthia into a pale blue lightweight jacket. Handing Cynthia the shoulder bag, Mia felt the extra weight. The old woman's wrinkled face drained of color.

"Gun. Why gun?" Her words were almost shrieks. "No! No! Cyn. No gun." Crazily she tried pulling Cynthia's purse from her hands.

"Mia! No!." Cynthia pulled back and jerked free of the old woman's uncontrolled grabs. "No, Mia. Stop!" She slipped the purse strap over her right shoulder and reached for Mia's shoulders. Cynthia shook her friend, hard. Mia backed away a step and stopped fighting, both hands pressed against her mouth.

"It's O.K., Mia." Cynthia prepared to lie. "I'm taking it to sell it. Kurt and I are going to break up, it seems. I need some money because he's stopped my access to the bank accounts."

Mia believed the woman who had never lied to her before, ever. "I have Meigu'o—Meiyua'n, 'Merican. I have, you have." She turned and ran from the bedroom. Cynthia knew it would be useless to protest.

From habit Cynthia stopped at the mirror near the bedroom door. She ignored her red eyes but examined her figure. She tucked the yellow sweater into her tight jeans and watched it mold around her upper body.

"Wait!" She said aloud and stepped back into the room, pulling the jacket off and jerking the yellow sweater over her head. She stood a few seconds in bra and jeans. Mia came running flat-footed back into the room. She had several U.S. bills clutched in her right hand. She looked surprised at Cynthia's state of undress.

"Bu' yao nei ge? (Don't want that one?) You want 'notha brouse or sweatta', Cyn?" Mia let the handful of bills flutter to the bedspread and stepped to Cynthia.

"Wait." Cynthia said again. She reached behind her back and flipped her bra free.

"Tai xiao?" (Too small?) Mia fluttered around her mistress. Cynthia reached into a dresser drawer and fumbled through her lingerie. She pulled another bra from a pile of folded things. "I like this one, Mia."

"Is Wai-da." Mia said looking puzzled. "Mister Paul in Hong Kong?"

"Yes, Mia." Cynthia lied again as she pulled the straps onto her shoulders and stood while Mia smoothed the material and snapped the hooks into place at her back. She could not bring herself to tell Mia what all had taken place, that she was wearing it simply for a sensation of closeness with Paul and that she was going off to do something desperate. When she slipped the yellow sweater back on, the results were startling.

"There, Mia." She said, looking into the mirror. "He'll like me in this." She turned to her old friend. "I'll find him now in Hong Kong." She locked her jaw to clamp back tears as she lied again.

"You find him." Mia said, pressing the U.S. money into Cyntha's hand. Cynthia couldn't argue with Mia over the money. Instead she took the three hundred dollars and hugged the anxious-to-please old lady.

"I'm afraid something very wrong, Missy, Cyn."

"No, no, Mia. I'll dianhua' later. Tell you all."

"Don't stay 'way, Missy Cyn. I worry worry. Prease'! Don't go and stay go."

As soon as she walked away from Mia, Cynthia slipped one magazine into the automatic, cocked a round into its ready chamber and released the thumb-flip safety. She left the house by the same door she had entered but this time kept her hand in her shoulder slung purse and around the handle of the gun. She watched for signs of Kurt or the others.

At ten twenty a.m., carrying the light jacket, she hurried down the graveled path at the side of the curved blacktop roadway. Four Europeans and three Chinese workmen were constructing a room addition on the house next to where she had parked. The men hooted at her exciting figure as she bounced the last few steps to the car. Not looking at them, she tossed her purse and jacket to the far seat and turned to face the group of workmen. With a defiant look she extended her right middle finger and, exhilarated by going so far out of her subdued character, she jammed her left hand into the crook of her right arm, thrust the international sign toward the men. "Fuck you all," she said through new tears, and she yelled a line she remembered from an American movie. "You wouldn't make a pimple on Paul Vincent's great tight ass."

The men, understanding no English, but knowing full well the meaning of the finger, responded with a series of hoots, leg slaps and nudges.

Fumbling some with the keys, she soon roared away in the red Mercedes. The tears on her face dried quickly from the wind of the open window.

A few minutes after ten a.m., Cecil Tucker/Bell/Winston Dewitt crawled up the last rungs of the rusted metal ladder and stepped onto the concrete pier near Cherry Street just south of the Tai-Kok-Tsui ferry landing in the bay called the Yaumatei Typhoon Shelter. The wrinkled and stooped old Portuguese oarsman climbed the ladder behind him and stood puffing for breath, one grimy hand held palm up. It had been a long damp trip overnight and they both seemed glad to be out of the uncomfortable small red and yellow boat.

Two nights earlier the Russian ship had sneaked him by boat into Tai O city on the western edge of Lantau Island. Looking and hopefully acting like one of the local Portuguese fishermen, Tucker boldly took a taxi the fifteen miles to the eastern end of the island at Mui Wo city where passports and visa's were not important. Without either, he decided it was safer for him to continue his Portuguese impersonation and sneak into Kowloon proper in one of the small boats that seem to come and go as they pleased.

Three hours earlier had Tucker looked to the east and into the window of the small hotel in Aberdeen, he might have seen Cynthia's tear filled face looking directly at him as the boat passed Lantau island on its way sneaking in from Macau.

Without a word the old man poked at Tucker's arm with a half balled fist. Tucker reached into his pocket and produced a single worn and faded U.S. one hundred dollar bill and stuck it in the dirty upturned palm. The oarsman looked the bill over for an instant then stuffed it in a bagged out sweater pocket. He turned from Tucker and gave a jerk to the thin line that trailed down to the front of the boat they had just climbed from. Still without speaking, the oarsman walked away and even when Tucker said 'goodbye' and 'thanks' in rough Portuguese, the old man made no notice. The boat jerked slightly and bumped along the pier's pilings, obediently following the old man.

Tucker shrugged his shoulders, dropped his two duffel bags of personal things he had recovered from storage in Haiphong and pulled a hand drawn map from under his jacket.

Looking about for landmarks, he decided he was about thirty blocks north of the tailor loft on Hankow road, the loft where he was to meet Polav, at noon. Unknown to Tucker, he was heading to the same loft where Rasha, Monique and David Chen had murdered Kurt Howser.

He folded the map, tucked it under his jacket and scratched at his beard covered face. Since the Russian ship had virtually no fresh water to spare, Tucker hadn't shaved nor showered for days He itched all over, especially arm pits and crotch. He seriously wondered if there was someplace he could bathe and clean-up before meeting with Polav.

Hoisting the two heavy duffel bags one to each shoulder he moved toward Ferry Street and looked for a taxi. It was ten a.m. He was beginning to feel warmed by the sun.

Most officers were present for breakfast in the wardroom of Truaxe as they fell in behind Kittyhawk to enter Hong Kong. There were two general feelings in the air: 'Oh boy! Hong Kong again', and, 'something doesn't seem right'.

Captain Clifford looked under-shaved and very nervous as he stood near the door of the wardroom pantry, his cup and saucer of black coffee balanced in his left hand. Griffith sat at his usual seat to his right. Dressed in the single-breasted khaki jacket and tie, Clifford's face showed a lot of theater as he watched the other officers coming and going. Even Commander Valentino seemed not his usual calm Henry Fonda self. He was thumbing nervously through a huge pile of maintenance request forms but also seemed to be monitoring the Captain. Lieutenant Stumpf spilled orange juice on his shirt front and said once to the man next to him that he was anxious to get some mail, some important word coming from his father. Mr. Lukarmo, his voice muffled by a mouthful of Danish, hollered at someone over the telephone: "But it's sea detail in a few minutes to get this ship into port. I want lights out in CIC and those circuits posted clearly, each freq like in the dammed book."

Commander Deiter complained to the supply officer that his men had goofed off so much the last time in Hong Kong he was worried that some reactor maintenance hadn't been completed correctly. Corrigan was borderline mean to everyone around him and was picking on a steward because his eggs were underdone. Even Lieutenant Beauford, the personnel officer was complaining into the air that he didn't quite know how to make the proper diary entry concerning the MIA status of Vincent, Lake, DiNoble, Hill and Tucker.

One of the younger officers, Ensign Wrobel, came into the room like an overconfident Walter Cronkite and didn't notice the tension. He spoke directly to Captain Clifford. "Good to be back to good ol' Hong Kong, for a rest, Captain?" His question struck some button in Clifford and the man realized it the moment the words were in the air.

"Rest?—Rest, shit." Clifford's loud comment stopped all conversation. Every head turned his way, cups and forks held in mid-move. The young officer stumbled backward into Lieutenant Lukarmo. Lukarmo dropped his Danish, grabbed for it but bumped the table, hard. Coffee from three cups and juice from three glasses sloshed over onto the mess table. Several men reached to clean up the mess. Clifford seemed not to notice, his attention full on the Ensign.

"Rest? There ain't no rest for *me* here. Know what I've got comin' in?" He changed his attention from the Ensign to the room in general. "A god-dammed board of investigation.

That's what I've got comin' in. A *secret* investigation at that." Commander Valentino rose from his chair, concerned. Not only was the man speaking too loud even for the vent noises of the smoky room, his comment violated a direct order from COMSEVENTHFLEET. The Captain was so out of line the expressions on the officer's faces revealed they were grasping for a correct response. Some of them eased toward the door to eliminate their discomforts.

"Wait!" Clifford yelled. "Just wait." He waved his arm and sloshed coffee down his front and onto the deck. "No one leave here right now. We're having a meeting."

Griffith approached the Captain. "Sir, we have sea detail in five minutes. Maybe the meeting could ..."

"I know what we have, Mr. Griffith." He snapped, backing Griffith away. "But what I have is a god-by-jesus-dammed naval investigative fuckin' officer ridin' on my ship—some secret spy asshole on my ship. Might even be you, Arnie ... " His eyes were flared wide open, his mouth held at an odd angle. He spun and pointed a finger toward Lieutenant Stumpf who jerked to his feet defensively.

"But it's probably you, Stumpf, spyin' for your prejudiced father." He quickly added. "Who I respect, mind you, but warily."

Stumpf whipped his chin with a white napkin and stepped back from the table. He looked ready to flee. Commander Valentino moved in next to the Captain.

"Captain. This is not the place nor the time." He squeezed his hand *very* hard around the biceps of Clifford's right arm. Clifford tried to jerk away but Valentino persisted. For some reason, likely because of the no-nonsense grip from Valentino, Clifford stopped struggling. His expression relaxed and his face paled considerably. He picked a napkin from the nearby table and started wiping at the spilled coffee on his shirtfront.

A self-assured looking Valentino maintained his grip on Clifford's arm and turned to face the room-full of officers. He said matter-of-factly; "Gentlemen, man your special sea detail stations, let's get this ship into Hong Kong." Though the message was clear, no one would move without completing the picture of exactly what was happening to the commander of the ship

By turning to Commander Griffith and using a formal term, Valentino set the stage. "Executive officer? I believe you are in command, Sir." Without hesitation, he continued addressing Griffith but speaking loudly so as to be heard clearly over the vent noises. "With your permission, Sir, I'll go to the bridge and conn the ship into port. I would appreciate it, however, Commander, if you would assist Commander Deiter with Captain Clifford." Valentino also nodded toward two young husky ensigns and face motioned that they go along to help, if necessary.

Griffith seemed stunned but was adjusting to the events quickly. His next comment locked in the stage set by Valentino. "Very well, Commander Valentino. You take the conn. I will escort Captain Clifford."

The wardroom emptied.

Clifford fell quiet. Deiter took Clifford's right arm, Griffith took his left. They escorted the man out of the forward doorway of the wardroom and toward Clifford's office and stateroom. Patrick Balkin moved in beside Commander Valentino.

"Commander, please note this." He held up an opened identification billfold. "I am Commander Patrick Balkin, N.I.S. I am under CINCPACFLEET's personal and secret orders. I don't know how the Captain's discovered my presence …but it has upset him, considerably."

"Twisted him right out of the center of the navy's bell curve, for now." Valentino said calmly.

He extended his hand. "Welcome aboard, again, Commander. Let me know what I can do to be of assistance. As it seems right now, I'm assuming Commander Griffith has taken command. Any objections?"

"None."

Ten minutes later, Valentino went to the bridge to bring the ship into port. After several minutes, Griffith appeared topside and approached Valentino on the starboard bridge wing.

"Dom? 'Member awhile back I mentioned some stuff going on with Barbara?"

"Not really, but yes?"

"Look. We should be moored by 0850. I've got to get to a phone as soon as we anchor."

"Not goin' ta' anchor, Commander." Valentino said. He stepped away from Griffith and looked aft to check the status of mooring lines that were being pulled from stowage. "Just got a flashing light message from Kittyhawk. We're goin' to moor at the Brit pier."

"Oh." Griffith's face filled with responsive expressions. "First class treatment. Pays to take British officers to dinner."

"Maybe."

"I can get to the overseas phone at the S.P. office on the pier."

"Do what you have to do, Arnie."

Griffith shifted subjects. "Dom? The Captain seemed calm when I left him five minutes ago. He's staying in his quarters with Deiter and some others. I'm going below. I'll skip my sea detail station as long as you are okay here with the conn. I have to do something else before I go ashore."

"Of course, Arnie." Valentino smiled at the man's obvious discomfort, but he also recognized that disturbed as Clifford appeared to be, Griffith was assuming command of a troubled ship.

Truaxe moored promptly at 0850. As always, it was very busy on the quarterdeck for the first few hours. The lines and gangway had to be tied with the correct amount of slack to permit the ship to rise and fall with the tides, but not so much as to be banged against the pier by the winds or waves. Several crewmembers came and went over the gangway to make line adjustments while the officer of the deck maintained ship's security at the gangway. Deck hands, sweaty and dirty from handling the mooring lines carried large awkward-to-manage aluminum rat guards from the ship to fasten to the mooring lines. Telephone circuit wires were weaved from the ship to the dock's connectors and, as usual, there was some difficulty because of the lack of standardized jacks and plugs. Ship fitters and hull technicians busily connected hoses to replenish fresh water and to top off aviation fuel tanks even though they had no helo. As soon as fresh water was available, deck hands commenced washing the salt spray from the ship's superstructure. Water ran everywhere topside and splashed down from one deck to the next, slopping at times on fresh uniforms worn by the men lining up for the quarterdeck OOD watch or on those expecting to go ashore early.

The OOD, his Junior OOD and a team of messengers, while dodging splashes of the falling water, started their watch and began to manage the barrage of salesmen and representatives who want aboard to see the stores officer, the tour guides who wish to leave pamphlets, and church representatives and other do-gooders who want to invite the crew to services throughout the city. Further, Hong Kong police officers and Eddie Monk's S.P. office were there with a list of rules and to identify places off limits to servicemen. The ship's shore patrol waited on the quarterdeck for instructions, mail was received and off loaded and all the while, as is usual in a port like Hong Kong, V.I.P's and officials, military and otherwise were arriving to make protocol visits. Though in the good hands of Lieutenant Hicks, the quarterdeck area seemed like a general madhouse.

It was 0855 a.m. Though Lieutenant Hicks, First Class Petty Officer Vernon Putney and three seaman messengers were managing the initial barrage of visitors, they were not ready for the surprise arrival of the Commander of the Seventh Fleet and a twelve-man inspection party. Hicks became somewhat rattled by the very assertive and well organized group.

Captain Westhaven, COMSEVENTHFLEET's intelligence officer was very firm as he presented Lieutenant Hicks with the proper clearances and identification for the inspection team.

"Do *not* announce us formally, Lieutenant. Simply have us escorted to the wardroom and to Captain Clifford's quarters."

Seventh Fleet's communication officer was escorted immediately to the radio room to, if possible, sort out voice circuit tapes and logs and verify the figures of Vincent's coordinate message as it came in to Truaxe. His Senior Chief quartermaster was to be escorted to the bridge to take possession of applicable charts and maps and to see if Vincent's coordinates were ever actually charted. One of his airframes officers was to gather the onboard helicopter logs and see what might be gained from those records. One of his top intelligence officers was to collect all CIC voice circuit logs and tapes, tracking charts, gunfire support charts and ammunition logs. Clifford was being professionally ganged up on.

As Lieutenant Hicks logged the names of the inspection team, he was surprised to see Master Chief Vincent's name on the list. Looking about, he saw Vincent standing in the center of the boarding party. As he tried to get Vincent's attention, his JOOD, Petty Officer Putney interrupted him with some story about a woman wanting to know something. He dismissed Putney,—"take *care* of it yourself"—but was again distracted before he could catch Vincent's eye. He was also surprised to see Lieutenant Patrick Balkin greeting the inspection team, introducing himself as a Naval Commander, not as a Lieutenant, and as a Naval Intelligence Officer.

At 0902, Commander Griffith walked aft to go ashore to make his telephone call. Noticing the extra commotion of the inspection party, but not wanting to be distracted from his personal mission, he ducked behind the after gun mount and stayed out of sight. As soon as the bulk of the boarding party had been escorted forward, Griffith, briefcase in hand, walked quickly down the gangway.

"Can't wait for ship's phones, Lieutenant Hicks," he said with a salute, "going down the pier to make an important call. Back soon." He turned toward the end of the long concrete pier to his left. Captain Gibbons, half way forward on the topside starboard passageway noticed Griffith leaving the ship.

"Who's that officer?" Gibbons asked the yeoman escort.

"That's Commander Griffith, Sir. He's our exec."

Gibbons turned to Lieutenant Baker, his aide. "That's the man who will be taking command shortly. Ask that Lieutenant on the quarterdeck where the exec is going ...and tell him I wish to see the man as soon as possible."

"Aye, aye, Sir."

At the end of the pier, at 0910, Griffith passed through the gate and walked quickly for the S.P. building. He didn't recognize that the red Mercedes coupe that maneuvered past him with other traffic was the one Paul Vincent had been in the morning of the emergency recall. Nor did the distracted Cynthia Howser recognize Griffith in the assembly of people around the gangway and on the pier.

The same moment Admiral Ferrent's aid assisted Lieutenant Hicks in logging the names of the inspection party, Petty Officer Putney noticed Cynthia pushing her way up the gangway through the waiting police officers, salesmen and clergy.

"Ma'am. Who are you representing?"

She told her story.

"Ma'am, I can't say anything officially, but last known ...most of 'em are de-de-ceased. If you want to wait?" He said, holding up two palms in a 'stand still' sign, and across the quarterdeck to Lieutenant Hicks.

"That woman, Lieutenant ...?" Putney interrupted Hicks.

Hicks didn't look up from the log. "Dammit Putney, handle the visitors will you. I'm over my head here."

"But, she wants to know if . . ."

"Take *care* of it ... " He was very firm.

"Yes, Sir." He took the few steps back to where Cynthia stood half-way up the gangway but he was cut off by a crowd of sailors with rat guards. He gave Cynthia a shoulder shrug and an arms akimbo helpless look that meant; "having trouble finding out for sure". But she took his body language to say; "I'm sorry, deceased, that's how it is, sorry".

At 0915 she spun and ran away down the gangway. "Ma'am, I can't say anything else ...but when we're not ...so. . . .busy ..." He let his voice trail off. It had been lost to three toots of a nearby tugboat whistle anyhow.

Putney thought he saw the lady crying but wasn't sure. He was looking for one of his messengers to send after her but was immediately distracted by a pushy vendor who tried sneaking past him with three worn wicker suitcases filled with smelly shell-craft that had that made-at-home-with-loving-hands look.

Cynthia Howser had missed being on the quarterdeck when Paul Vincent was there, by less than four minutes.

At 0930 on the sixteenth, Marion Dumbrowski, the State Department communication clerk at the Consulate office, Manila, whose job it was to distribute incoming messages to the correct consulate offices, got around to unrolling the teletype paper from under the printers in the security room. Assuming the messages on the floor were routine and administrative in nature, as they usually were, Marion wasn't in any particular hurry. Standard operating procedures were set up that if a high precedent message arrived at night for the consulate, the NAVCOMMSTA personnel would telephone Marion, or one of the other three clerks at home. They would then drive to the consulate message room and take whatever action was required by the message, which usually meant awaking the appropriate consulate officer. No one had been called the night before so Marion was in no real hurry to begin her daily task of cutting the messages into the correct length for the duplicating machine, making the right number of copies, and delivering them throughout the building.

By ten thirty a.m. she had worked her way to near the end of the string of over twenty-five messages. She wasn't real surprised when she found the misrouted message. It had happened before.

She picked up the telephone and called the error desk at NAVCOMMSTA San Miguiel.

"NAVCOMMSTA service desk, This' Petty Officer Barns, this is a-non-secure line—may I help you, sir."

"I'm a 'ma'am', Barney? Marion D from the consulate?"

"Hi Babes."

"You dropped us one that's not ours."

"What number?"

"Near the end."

"Hot one?"

"Didn't notice—But its to COMSEVENTHFLEET and some ship."

"Shit," Barns said and ran for the consulate circuit file tapes. He spun the reels of three quarter inch paper tape out onto the floor, watching for certain patterns indicating the start and end of each message. He stopped the spinning reel after each ending pattern so he could examine the addressees on the following message. Message after message was correctly addressed to the consulate. After 19 messages and over three minutes of searching, he found what he was looking for.

"Christ, tell Chief Doak, we dropped a SEVENTHFLEET immediate message." He looked at his watch. "Shit, seven-eight hours ago."

Barns tore the copy of the tape from the reel and, leaving the consulate tape splayed out on the floor temporarily, ran to the new 82B1 outgoing line for COMSEVENTHFLEET. He placed the message in the transmit sensor head and snapped the keyer lid over it. At the instant it passed through the transmit head it was printing on COMSEVENTHFLEET's incoming teletype machine aboard the flagship Kittyhawk. Impatiently, Barnes stood next to the transmit device and waited as the message passed through the keyer head at 100 words per minute. As soon as enough tape had passed through, he led the end of the tape several machines away and introduced it into the fleet broadcast machine transmit head in order to get it on the air to Truaxe.

"Shit, shit. A non-delivery, to of all people—Admiral Ferrent." Senior Chief Doak began to sweat in the air-conditioned communication center as he showed the message to the Communication Watch Officer.

"Jesus, Chief ...you read this thing?"

"Yeah ...we dropped a hot one."

On the same morning, the sixteenth in Hong Kong, the fifteenth in San Diego, Nick Bristol, Ben's younger brother stood with his arm around Bunny Bristol. Bunny's eyes were red, her face pale. She stood stoop shouldered in the crowded living room of her sister-in-law's house on McCandless Street. There were several other people in the room including Barbara Griffith, Rachael Vincent and three FBI agents. The group had been waiting in the small house for ten hours. One of the agents spoke.

"It's three eighteen p.m. That's what? Nine eighteen a.m. Hong Kong?"

"Yeah, the sixteenth ...nine eighteen a.m. tomorrow."

"I'm tired. Wish he'd call."

"Me too."

Usually, waiting for long periods was routine duty for the three FBI agents, but weariness and tension showed on the faces of the others, especially Rachael and Barbara.

Rachael lit a cigarette, all three agents insisted she put it out.

"That'll kill you. Don't you read the papers?" Rachael silently obeyed.

The living room telephone rang once and moved the agents to action.

Tony Vargas, a tall and serious looking FBI investigator pushed the recorder button at the instant of the first ring. Two other agents, the short stocky black man, Ralph Bunch who was the telephone taping expert and Roy DanHauser, the slightly built mustached FBI psychologist, picked up a single headset and leaned in to share its ear pieces. All three men nodded to Rachael.

Rachael, her shoulders pulled in pointing forward, hands shaking, her face pale, reached reluctantly for the telephone. Hesitating once more, she said. "What if its not Paul?"

"Answer it, lady." Vargas ordered.

"Hello?"

All any of them heard was the garbled word 'Hong Kong' and a request to accept charges. Tony Vargas nodded, 'yes'.

It was not Paul Vincent on the noisy line.

Rachael became speechless, the telephone in one hand, the end of her blond pony-tail twisting in the fingers of the other. Looking frightened, she covered the mouthpiece and with a helpless and panic look, spoke to Vargas: "What'll I do, it's Mister Griffith?" Bunny Bristol immediately burst into tears and was led out of the room by her brother-in-law, Nick.

Griffith spoke over the miles. "Mrs. Vincent? I've got to get a message to Barbara."

Rachael's mouth opened but that's as far as she went. Griffith spoke again.

"This is Arnold," Then he started over again, very assertively. "This is *Commander* Griffith. I *must* get a message to my wife, right now. Where is she?" Tony Vargas motioned to Barbara Griffith—'take the phone'. From the nearby bedroom they could hear Bunny crying and talking loudly to her brother. "But it's him. I'm afraid. What'll I do? What'll I do?"

Roy Danhauser motioned to Ralph Bunch to shut Bunny up. Danhauser then took Barbara Griffith by the elbow of her left arm.

"Talk to him." He whispered hoarsely.

Rachael blurted: "She's right here," and held the phone toward a dazed looking Barbara Griffith. With Danhauser pushing her slightly, Barbara walked the few steps to Rachael but instead of taking the telephone, stood fingering the side hems of her light blue dress, her face colorless. Agent Danhauser whispered to her:

"Help us and you help yourself stay out of prison."

She made a frustrated finishing school 'umph' sound, pulled a snap-on earring from her right ear and took the phone from Rachael. Rachael began sobbing, took two steps toward the corner of the small living room and dropped to the floor looking dazed and red-faced. Sitting on the carpet, she pulled her legs up to her chest, wrapped her arms around them and buried her face into her knees. Roy Danhauser looked from Rachael to Tony Vargis and rolled his eyes. From the adjacent bedroom they all heard Bunny yell something which including referring to Ralph Bunch as a 'nigger'.

Barbara, hand's shaking as she held the telephone to her face closed her eyes.

"Yes, Arnie?" She managed to sound cheerful but tears leaked through the tightened eyes.

"Good. I found you. You alright?"

"Yes ...but ..."

"Good." Griffith's voice sounded excited and far away. "Listen, I've tried calling you at our place but they say the phone's been disconnected. What the hell's going on." Arnold Griffith swore so seldom, Barbara knew he was very upset. Griffith went on. "I have to warn you, Barbara, stay away from that Bristol fella ...he's going to ... "

"NO!" Barbara screamed, "Arnie, don't talk!"

She threw the phone down and bolted toward the door of the navy house but tripped over Rachael's feet and went down. Ralph Bunch, having heard her scream bounded into the room. He grabbed Barbara's arm in time to prevent her from falling all the way to the floor. Roy Danhauser snatched the swinging telephone to his face and grabbed Rachael Vincent's arm, hard.

"Griffith?" He said into the phone.

"Yes? Who is this?" Barbara Griffith started a scream but Bunch closed his hand over her mouth. Not in time.

"What was that?" Griffith snapped. "What's happening there? Who is this?"

"This is Ben Bristol." Danhauser lied, then commenced mimicking Ben's character. "What you sayin' to Barbara that caused her to cry?"

But Griffith became suspicious. He spoke slowly, "If you're ...really Bristol. . " Then his words sped up. "Tell me ...how much money did I send in my last check?"

Danhauser stalled and shrugged his shoulders. Spinning one hand in a 'help me' signal, Danhauser stalled. "Why should I tell you how much you sent me? How do I know you're really Griffith?"

"I sent it to the Bristol Foundation. That's how you know who I am."

Tony Vargas flipped his headset from his ears, grabbed both Rachael and Barbara very tightly by the upper arm and whispered. "How much was the last check to Bristol?"

Barbara jerked her mouth away from the hand of Ralph Bunch and lied. "SEVENTY FIVE DOLLARS. CUBA—CUBA," She screamed, intending Griffith to hear.

"No!". Rachael called out. "NO!" She called out. "Three hundred dollars."

Griffith had heard it all. By the time Danhauser tried to continue his facade, the line was dead. Danhauser turned to Barbara. Vargas threw his headset down on a chair. Bunch pulled Barbara around to face him.

"That was a very *very* big mistake, Mrs. Griffith, *especially* …during a time of war." He pulled a pair of handcuffs from his inside pocket, pulled Barbara Griffith's hands to behind her back and snapped the cuffs into place.

"Well, you guys," Danhauser said with a smirk. "Emerson said only shallow men believe in luck. That make us shallow?"

Vargas said, "Mirandize all of 'em."

"The dumb brother, too?"

"He's not dumb." Rachael said seemingly unaware of the seriousness of the moment. "He just looks dumb and acts it sometimes … "

"Well, he surely isn't the dumbest one here, that's for sure." Vargas said.

Bunch began a monotone: "You have a right to remain silent …you have the right … "

Tony Vargas pulled Rachael to her feet and placed handcuffs on her wrists and repeated the same phrases. Rachael Vincent spoke into the air. "Oh, Paul …oh, Paul. I'm so sorry …help me, forgive me …"

"What are you sayin', Lady? Is he involved in this?"

"I ain't sayin' anything …anything."

CHAPTER THIRTY FIVE
The Fan is Hit

At 9:32 a.m., after his telephone call to San Diego, Arnold Griffith, heart beating rapidly, walked quickly up the gangway returning to Truaxe. Once under the canvas awning, he returned Lieutenant Hicks' sharp salute.

"I'll only be aboard a few minutes, Mister Hicks. Personal problem I have to square away ashore."

"You aware what's goin' on aboard here, Commander?" Hicks asked.

"No."

"Investigation. And guess what? That Balkin? An N.I.S. investigator. Don't know what he's been investigatin' but Master Chief Vincent was in the Admiral's party ..." Hicks saw Griffith's face turn white. He hesitated.

"Vincent is aboard? With what Admiral?"

"Yes, With Admiral Ferrent, COMSEVENTHFLEET ... "

Griffith's eyes widened but just for a mini-second.

" ...and you're supposed to go right to him ..."

"Very well, Lieutenant. I'll do that." He turned and walked away from the quarterdeck at a very casual pace just as Eddie Monk walked up the gangway and presented his N.I.S. identification to Lieutenant Hicks.

"Looking for Master Chief Vincent, please."

Out of earshot of Lieutenant Hicks and Monk, Griffith's face, already a little warm from his brisk walk in the March sunshine seemed to flood with perspiration as the back of his khaki shirt also wet quickly through. His thoughts sprinted. Stopped in the passageway adjacent to the ship's engine room he became lost enough in deep thought to ignore the morning greetings of several crewmembers who passed by.

After many seconds he jerked to life. Looking both ways in the dimly lighted passageway he punched in the combination lock numbers and swung the hatch to the engine room open, entered and shut it behind him. It was immediately cool and quiet in the well air-conditioned upper level of the immaculately white nuclear spaces.

He was greeted by a watch-stander. "Morning Commander."

"Good morning, Amhurst. Got to get something from my locker."

Just inside the main hatch were several white metal lockers similar to those seen in sport facility dressing rooms. Originally intended as general storage, they'd been adopted for personal use by the senior engineering officers and enlisted men. Most kept their personal copies of classified engineering manuals stored there along with specialty tools, test equipment, spare uniforms, cameras, cigarettes and the like. As the most senior 'nuke' officer, Griffith had taken over a locker on his first day aboard, two years earlier.

He set his briefcase down on the gray rubber mats on the aluminum deck, selected a key from his pocket and opened a locker marked 'X.O. only'. Keeping his back to Amhurst, he removed a small gray metal case from one of two drawers inside the locker. The case had several wires spiraling out from it, connected somewhere in the rear half of the locker drawer. Opening the case and continually looking over his shoulder to see if Amhurst was still preoccupied, he manipulated several dials on an elaborate looking electronic device fastened inside the gray box.

Holding the device in one hand, allowing the wires on the device to uncoil and follow him down, Griffith then dropped to one knee and opened his briefcase. He removed an orange paper from the briefcase and held it close to his chest. Looking from the paper to the electronic device, he moved several mini switches to the 'up' position, several others to a 'down'. He then removed a twelve-by twelve-by-two-inch plastic box from the briefcase and sat it and the electronic box side by side on the middle shelf of the locker. He gently worked the device's wires back into the rear half of the drawer. He then took two pre-prepared wires with a P-60 type phonograph plugs on each end from his briefcase and connected the plastic box to the electronic box by inserting the plugs into jacks.

"Don't touch anything here, Amhurst," he said and went immediately down the ladder to the reactor core panel deck, just ten feet below where he had been standing. Next to core panel number three, he located an electrical junction box marked L-201-E and removed its cover. With the tip of a screwdriver he moved the position of a very small switch that was taped inside the electrical box. It made a slight 'click' noise. He glanced up at Amhurst to assure the man was still busy with his clip-board duties.

Griffith then went to the master core control panel and with a small especially designed hand made tool taken from the briefcase, turned the dial faces on indicators numbers 7, 9 and 11 to read "Free" instead of "Bound". He then pulled three faceplates from the briefcase identical to the ones he just changed and placed them exactly over the changed ones. The new faceplates indicated the dials were in their correct 'bound' positions.

He returned up the ladder and placed two short wooden dowels into holes he had drilled in the locker frame over a year ago. He ripped two pieces of red heavy aviation tape from a roll and taped the locker door tightly to the dowels. The doors were held firmly in a slightly open position. He turned and interrupted Amhurst.

"Look, Amhurst. How long are you on watch?"

"Till noon, Commander."

"Good." He said and looked at his watch. "I'm taking some very critical ambient temp readings in this space ...some new data required by the status of forces agreement with Hong Kong. I . . I want you to leave this locker door just as it is. Pass that word on to your relief. Do *not* open it further, do *not* close it for any reason."

Amhurst, a man who lifted weights and worked-out continually and who had that extremely husky well muscled upper body look, seemed puzzled. Griffith took his 'tough toes Arnie' stance and accompanied it with his 'I'm the executive officer, just shut up and listen', facial expression. "Do you understand, Amhurst?"

Amhurst snapped to attention. Despite his huge arms and muscled neck, he looked fearful of Griffith. "Yes, Sir. I was only ..."

"Only nothing." Griffith snapped. "I'll be back now and again to record the monitor, and it had best be ...best be ..."

"Just as it is now, Sir."

"Right."

At 10:18, Griffith left the engine room and hurried topside. He passed Lieutenant Hicks on the quarterdeck and lied. "That's Admiral Ferrent alright, Mister Hicks. I'm now off like an errand boy for the Admiral."

"Very well, Sir." Hicks laughed and returned Griffith's very proper salute as the executive officer hurried down the ship's gangway, briefcase in hand.

Walking fast, Griffith caught a taxi near the S.P. building and headed toward Harbor View Street in the Central District. It was an eight-minute ride. Letting his taxi go he ducked into a pharmacy to locate a telephone. Pulling out his phrase book he spoke hesitatingly to a small man in a white coat.

"*Duoshao gongyong dianhua?*" His question came out: "*how much* is a public telephone?"

The man looked confused. "Seventy cents Hong Kong." He answered. Griffith went back to his phrase book.

He tried to ask: "Where is one". "*Wo xihuan zhei ge?* " He actually said "I'd like one."

"Over there." The man pointed to a corner of the pharmacy area, then chuckled: "Throw that book away, your Chinese is terrible."

Griffith dialed three different numbers from a list in his briefcase before he located David Chen. After a brief conversation, he left the pharmacy and stepped quickly a few doors east to a men's ready-to-wear store and bought a white sport shirt and an inexpensive blue blazer. He put his khaki uniform coat, shirt, tie and hat into a large paper bag and walked briskly to the Star Ferry building. It was 10:55 a.m.

After leaving Mia, Cynthia cried uncontrollably and drove without direction for nearly twenty minutes. There had been a bad accident just next to the YWCA at MacDonnel Road and she found herself trapped in slow moving traffic. She banged helplessly several times on the steering wheel. A woman on her right, whose print skirt hung out below the driver's door looked at her curiously. Suddenly self-conscious, Cynthia stared straight ahead and tried to calm herself and think clearly. During the next ten minutes the car moved only a few feet but Cynthia found herself more able to concentrate. A flat feeling overcame her, a flatness pressed against the only sense of identity that remained inside of her. That of hatred, determination, revenge.

She further shaped her plan.

With the large purse strapped on her shoulder, pistol inside, she left the red Mercedes at the curb on Cotton Tree Drive and walked down Garden Road, through Chatter Garden to Connaught Road Central and through the familiar car park to the Star Ferry building, a distance of about one mile. The last few minutes she hurried, wanting to catch the 11:30 ferry. But no, rounding the corner of the ferry building she saw a long line was already formed for the next trip. Buying a ticket she fell into line but was back at the white colored posts, indicating she would not catch the next ferry and it would be thirty minutes before she would leave for Kowloon.

Accepting the delay she stood in the line in the warm sun. The Chinese chatter of her fellow travelers and the strong fishy smell of the harbor were familiar and relaxing to her ear. She was glad to feel calmer as she looked about. From where she stood she could see the fantail end of Truaxe moored to Navy pier a half mile away. A large U.S. aircraft carrier was anchored in the bay, several boats trailing white tails coming and going from gangways and ladders. Relax, she told herself. Relax. The wait for the ferry would be a good time to further strengthen her plan.

Taking a deep breath she leaned one shoulder blade against a thin light pole and folded her arms beneath her breasts. Something pulled her attention to the rear upper deck of the departing ferry, about a hundred feet away. A familiar form stood there looking off toward where Truaxe was moored. It was David Chen. He was talking to a tall man whose back was to her. The man turned and almost made eye contact. Dressed in blue blazer and khaki trousers was Arnold Griffith.

Her heart vaulted. Her senses activated like a computer in search mode. Where? When? Who? Think back. Look for it. Feel it. Smell it. Reach for it. Taste it? Yes, taste, that's close. The Dinner. Hear it? Yes! Hear it. Details of Captain Clifford's dinner night were struggling to become vivid in her mind. Choppy pieces of conversations with the Truaxe officers in the lobby snapped in and out of memory.

"You cause me to miss home. . " No, that was that Mr. Merryweather.

"The world went to hell in the dining room a few . . " No, Mr. Stumpf talking about Clifford.

"You're a real bell-ringer. Perhaps we'll meet again."

"YES!" she said aloud. "Griffith said that. The contact words. He is Bell's man on Truaxe." She rose to her feet, her eyes locked on the ferry as it moved away. "Chen knows him so Kurt must know him. They're going to see Kurt."

She was speaking aloud. An older Chinese couple stared at her. Cynthia looked away, nervous again. Now anxious to hurry, her ride was still twenty minutes away. She could only hope the two men who were ahead of her were heading for the tailor loft.

At 11:45 the crowd on the Hong Kong side became restless, not used to delays. They could all see the ferry was stopped half-way from Kowloon. People began looking at their watches, pushing a little, jockeying for position at the anticipated gangway location. Some went to the window marked *Shoukuantai'*.

One nervous looking little fat man asked into the air: *"Da'o Kowloon zenme zou?"* He received no answer for his stuckmates.

A police boat moved quickly toward the ferry that appeared to be drifting freely in the center of the bay, and tied to its stern. Some men went aboard. A second police boat and a fire fighting boat sped in from the east.

Five minutes passed. It looked like the ferry had headway again. The fire fighting boat slowed. Cynthia nervously checked her watch. It was 11:50. The police boat left the ferry's side as everything seemed to return to normal.

Cynthia fought against the crowd and held her ground. The ferry arrived and word spread as it loaded the next group of passengers: There had been a small fire in its engine room. Nothing serious. Cynthia was now inside the *green* posts. She would be on the *next* ferry, at noon.

After another fifteen minutes, she was on her way to Kowloon but the delay had seemed endless to her. Before the ferry actually landed, she pushed to the head of the line and jumped ashore. The attendant yelled at her in English.

"You dumb get hurt, woman'."

Walking briskly toward Hankow street in jeans, tight sweater and opened light jacket with her shoulders slightly back and her small heels clicking, she attracted the attention Paul often teased her about but yet seemed to feed on. Two U.S. sailors tried to pick her up. One murmured in stereotyped sailor talk.

"Baby, anymore 'round here like you?"

The other stopped, turned and stared. "Now *THAT*, is a sweater girl."

Regretting now having worn the wai-da and further realizing how no one could understand the reach for love behind wearing it, she crossed her arms self-consciously over her breasts and continued walking fast, tears drying from the wind. She wanted the look those sailors had given her, she thought, but not from *them*. She wanted it only from her Paul where it was safe and was part of their loving one another. Convinced by circumstances of the day that she could never have that *safe* love again, her eyes, nose and mouth simultaneously burst forth in completely uncontrolled sobs.

Turning the corner onto Hankow Street she hesitated and pressed herself against a store doorway directly across the narrow crowded street from a busy restaurant, four storefronts from the familiar tailor shop. She thought she recognized Polav the Russian enter the tailor shop but she wasn't sure. She did see shadowy figures reflected in the front window of the loft over the shop.

Tina, Cynthia's seamstress and wife of the man who owned the shop came out of the street level door and stood for a minute with hands on hips. She had on a gray mini, a baggy black jacket and white pumps. Pulling the jacket sleeves up, Tina looked up and down the street as though looking specifically for someone, but did not see Cynthia. She went back inside, closed the entrance door and pulled the shade over the glass. A thin hand reached into view and suspended a *closed* sign on the door shade.

Cynthia reached into her shoulder bag with both hands, made sure there was truly a bullet in the chamber of the automatic, put the safety on and positioned it under her thumb. With no idea of exactly what she was to do, she walked boldly across the street and banged on the door of the shop. Once. Twice.

Tina opened the door. "*Ni hao*, Annie," she said but did not step back.

"Excuse me." Cynthia said sharply and pushed her way passed Tina. "Where is the American named Griffith?" She demanded.

Tina said nothing but she lowered her eyes. The place was very quiet and smelled of an odor she knew but could not immediately place. "Where are Griffith and Chen?" She asked again.

"I hear my name?" Griffith spoke as he and Chen stepped from behind the loft stairway. Both were smiling. "I've hoped we'd meet again, Annie." Griffith approached her with an outstretched hand.

Cynthia tightened her grip on the automatic but kept it in the purse. "Don't refer to me as 'Annie'. You're Bell's contact on Truaxe, aren't you?"

"Whoa! Whoa!" Griffith said putting two hands in front of his chest as though pleading. "Me and Bell? Is that so bad?" He and Chen both moved toward Cynthia, the glassy smiles remained on their faces. The six or seven vacant faced Chinese workmen in the shop were watching everyone closely. Tina moved in beside Cynthia and a wide smile took over her face.

"You look good, Cynthia." The comment didn't seem appropriate. Cynthia ignored the little woman.

Chen actually leaned in to peck her cheek. Griffith re-extended a hand but she ignored it again.

"You seem very upset, Ms. Howser." Griffith patronized.

"What is it, Dear?" Chen asked.

"Where is Kurt? Where is Polav, and …and …where is Paul Vincent?"

Griffith put a thumb and forefinger to his chin. "Oh …that's it." He put a hand on her shoulder. "No wonder you seem upset."

"Paul has been lost in Vietnam." She said. "Bell had something to do with it."

"No! No!" Chen said quickly. " Paul Vincent is on the American ship."

"He is not." She snapped back. "I was there this morning. I was told by four different people he's dead or MIA" Her voice cracked followed by residual tears.

Griffith took over. Keeping his hand on her shoulder he spoke very softly. "My dear, Cynthia. Paul Vincent is on the Kittyhawk, anchored in the bay. He is alive, and well. Believe me."

They could tell by her eyes they had distracted her from her desperation. Griffith continued. "He was hurt in Vietnam, yes. But has recouped well, we understand. In fact, was to come over to Truaxe today."

"But … "

"Is true, Annie." Chen chimed in.

"Is true." Tina agreed.

"How would you know, David … Tina?"

"C'mon … Annie." Griffith re-used her code name. "You picked it right, I was Bell's man on Truaxe. I've brought these folks up to date."

"But where is Kurt …the others?"

Griffith stayed in close. Alert, he assumed Cynthia's hand was on a gun. "Kurt and the others are to meet us at his home, your home. Soon now." He jerked the purse from her hand and the gun fell away to the floor. All of the workmen ducked for cover. Tina fell on the gun then stood up with it. A dirty tatter ran down the leg of her hose.

"Easy now …wait." Griffith took the automatic from Tina. "Wait, now." He turned to Cynthia. "Please understand. We are on your side, Annie."

"Don't call me that."

"Okay. Whatever you ask." He was very patronizing. "But hear me." He pushed the snap and caught the magazine that dropped from the small automatic. He ejected the round from the chamber and watched it bounce across the wooden floor. "You came in here very upset." He continued, "And, I don't blame you. None of us blame you. By your questions we can see the American navy has lied to you, likely on purpose. When you asked just now where Paul Vincent was? I knew the navy was keeping that from you ...weren't they?"

She thought of her daily calls to Monk and his repeated report that he had heard nothing of Vincent.

"Yes, maybe." Confused again, she wondered; had the man on the quarterdeck lied?

Griffith picked Cynthia's purse from the floor and opened it. He picked through its contents for a second or two and handed it back to her.

"Here, my dear. Please believe us." He then handed her the automatic, picked up the fallen bullet, slipped it back into the magazine and handed that to her also.

"We are all still a team here." He said.

"When someone hands you back your loaded gun, Annie, we can't be all bad." The sweet David Chen smiled so nicely, the dear man she'd known over the years seemed determined to comfort her. Tina also put an arm around her and hugged her sincerely. Stepping back she looked at Cynthia from head to foot.

"You been crying so sad." She took a tissue and dabbed at Cynthia's eyes. "No more tears. You have on sweater I make?" She seemed pleased. "Woo-woo!" She kidded and hugged her again. Cynthia had known this lady for eight years, had known Chen for nine. She did not like Griffith but she was beginning to feel better.

Griffith stepped back, still smiling. Chen and Tina filled Cynthia in with a story. They hadn't seen much of Kurt, they lied, but they were to meet at his house later in the day. Kurt's idea. No, Polav hadn't been in the shop that day. They hadn't seen Monique nor Rasha.

Griffith and Chen invited Cynthia to accompany them back to Hong Kong island where Chen's car was parked near the ferry landing. They could hurry and take her to the fleet landing where she could ask again of Paul's whereabouts, or possibly even catch a boat out to Kittyhawk where, Griffith explained, Paul could likely still be in the sick bay.

Commander Griffith picked up his uniform bag as they gathered to leave. Cynthia waved to Tina's husband, Lom Quon, as she always had done in the past when she'd leave. He seemed nervous and awkward as he waved back, as though anxious to see them all leave the shop.

At 1:20 p.m., on the ferry, Griffith and Chen continued to be charming as they crossed the bay.

"You two go on." She said as she stepped onto the wooden landing on the Hong Kong side. "I'll catch a taxi to the fleet landing." She started stepping ahead.

"Wait! Cynthia." Griffith grabbed her arm as they neared Chen's beige 1966 Opel sedan.

"What?"

"Get in the car," he ordered.

"NO!"

"Get in car, Annie." Chen's voice was mean. It broke into a cough. She was not afraid of Chen but Griffith was very strong. He shoved her into the front seat of the car and looked around to see if anyone was watching them abduct the attractive woman. He pushed in beside her on the front seat passenger side of the right hand drive Opel and immediately jerked her purse from her hands. In just seconds he re-loaded and cocked the automatic. He tossed her purse to the back floor of the car after snatching the American money from it. Breathing heavily, Chen pushed in on the driver's side.

"Drive, Chen." Griffith ordered, counting the money.

"But? Why? What can I do?" Cynthia was completely confused again.

"Chen here has quite an eye for a figure like yours, even from a distance. He saw you on the ferry landing, behind us. We didn't know how long you might have been following us. We had some business to take care of at the loft. People to meet. I started a fire on the ferry to delay you …but they musta' put it out."

"Why, why?" She repeated.

"Could not take chance, Annie." Chen added. "We know Kurt have everyone believe you crazy …but we not know what you might do."

"Besides" Griffith made clear, "we need money, more than you have with you, and there's money at your house. Now you show us where. Saves Chenny and I having to take the place apart."

"Is Paul Vincent really alive?" It was a foolish question.

"Who cares." Griffith tossed aside.

"There's no money at our house. I just took it all. I was just there."

"Shut up, Annie. There is money and you know where it is." Chen said as he moved into the traffic on Connaught Road Central. "You *will* show us."

Griffith locked a strong grip on the back of Cynthia's neck and kept it there as they drove.

Cynthia hoped Chen would take Cotton Drive and get caught in the same traffic she had been in, but no. He cleverly rushed up Ice House Street, creatively took some back streets and headed up Victoria Peak on Arbuthnot Road through the newly opened Botanical Gardens.

As she unconsciously ran her fingertips over the tiny cracks of the worn leather seat, Cynthia Howser accepted she had been artfully tricked. She felt flawed to have been so needy as to fall for their lies and tricks. This all means Paul is surely dead, she thought, yes. Accept it as truth. Kurt was surely involved in his death in some way. She had likely lost the chance for the revenge she had promised herself. She wondered; would she live through this day?

Earlier, at exactly 9:33 a.m., after having his business breakfast, Monk boarded Truaxe just behind Commander Griffith. He showed his N.I.S. and shore patrol I.D. to Lieutenant Hicks and asked for Master Chief Vincent. Hicks telephoned the wardroom where the COMSEVENTHFLEET intelligence officer was manning the inspection team's telephone. Hicks announced Monk's arrival to visit Vincent.

"Mr. Balkin is coming aft to escort Mr. Monk to the wardroom, have him wait, please."

"Very well, Sir."

Not aware Captain Clifford had lost his composure earlier and had been confined to his stateroom by Commander Valentino and the exec, the Admiral's party including Captain Gibbons and the inspection team of twelve plus Paul Vincent and David Selesky, crowded into the wardroom.

Vincent watched as Selesky and Balkin greeted one another. They shook hands as old friends might and Vincent witnessed what he saw as extreme restraint as the two men protected their relationship from discovery. Admiral Ferrent took a seat across from Captain Gibbons, leaving the chair at the head of the table open for Clifford.

Patrick Balkin returned to the wardroom and introduced Eddie Monk all around, which included a bear hug between he and Paul Vincent and a warm handshake for David Selesky. Lieutenant Stumpf, accompanied by the Admiral's communication officer, Fred something, also entered the room looking nervous and anxious to announce some news.

"Yes, Lieutenant? Captain Westhaven asked of the COMMO.

"Sir, just took this flashing light message from Kittyhawk." He pointed to a standard message form held on a clipboard. "From Bureau of Personnel. Winston DeWitt, it appears, was the name of a man who was reported overboard from U.S.S. Chicago earlier in the war ... they describe him here. According to Lieutenant Stumpf, it sounds like it could be Tucker."

"Good." Ferrent almost shouted. "Chief Vincent makes more sense as each hour passes."

"Also, Sir." Fred referred to a second message. "Tripler Army hospital treated a Cecil Tucker for anxiety and stress in March, 1967 and returned him to duty. But, instead of him goin' back to his original PBR squadron on the Long Tau River? The navy moved him over to an ATC squadron near the Plain of Reeds. However, Admiral ... " The man fumbled with the messages on the clip board and pulled one from the bottom of the pile. " ...according to a second communication from the Bureau, the real Cecil Tucker is a dark complexioned white male, second class bos'n mate, brown hair and eyes, six foot three, 185 pounds." He looked up from the clipboard as Mr. Stumpf took over the conversation.

"Our Cecil Tucker's a fish belly white red head, Admiral." Stumpf said. "The man's an imposter for sure."

"The real Cecil Tucker is likely rotting in a lagoon somewhere for over a year." Someone offered from the back of the room.

Commander Deiter and the two Truaxe escort officers, Ensign Sycycky and Ensign Gable accompanied Clifford into the wardroom. When Clifford entered, all men stood to face him. Vincent noticed Selesky touch Balkin's elbow as they juggled for standing room by the table. When the Captain saw Admiral Ferrent, he became animated.

"An Admiral, on our ship." He leaned forward and actually pulled Ferrent's hand away from his side and shook it, surprising the Admiral. Clifford then turned to Deiter. "Have we made arrangements for lunch?" He yelled toward the wardroom pantry. "STEWARD! Come out here." He turned to Admiral Ferrent. "Will you and your entire staff be embarked on Truaxe, Admiral?" Not waiting for a response he spun again to Deiter and this time whispered. "Which Admiral is this?" Captain Robert Clifford was well into a psychotic episode.

Despite Clifford obviously breaking down, Admiral Ferrent continued his own mission. He pulled his pipe from a trouser pocket and fumbled with it. "Captain Clifford," He said to the quieting room, "I am holding an investigative mast right this moment … "

"Mast? For whom?" Clifford managed.

Ferrent continued. "I wish to announce to you …that as a result of a preliminary investigation by N.I.S. investigator Balkin and others, that at this very moment members of my staff are searching your ship for information and evidence." He motioned to Clifford to take a seat at the head of the table. Clifford became quiet and appeared to calm. He sat down and began to scratch at his earlobe. Ferrent continued, "Until further notice, you are relieved of command of Truaxe. Commander Arnold Griffith will relieve you as commanding officer … "

"Relieved of my command by that do-gooder?" Clifford rose slowly from his chair. His head was turning from side to side, his eyes wide. "Deiter?" The man looked like a lost child. "What is this? Admiral? … Sir?"

"Sit down, Captain." Ferrent said firmly and then nodded to his intelligence officer. "Captain Westhaven, read the charges please."

Clifford sat at rigid attention although he hadn't been directed to do so. He became white faced and stiff-jawed as Westhaven read charges.

" …inability, as Commanding Officer, to establish and maintain good order and discipline …falsifying readiness and training status, resulting in unqualified gunfire support effort …and gunfire which caused the deaths of … CIA agents …failure to report the nature of the CIA agent's deaths …failure to initiate a board of investigation into the deaths … attempt to cover up information …suspicion of conspiracy to obtain information for an enemy government … "

"WHAT! ?"

" …suspicion of conspiracy to reveal to enemy agents the location of CIA agents Piper and Hollender, ultimately resulting in their discover by enemy forces and resulting in their deaths …"

"What! ?"

" …suspicion of conspiracy to reveal the location of a rescue boat and crew to the enemy through the use of USN radios …resulting in the boat being located, rammed and sunk by NVA forces … "

"NO!!!, NO!!!"

" …suspicion …altering search and rescue coordinates of Master Chief Paul R. Vincent and his crew resulting in SAR efforts being located some thirty miles off location, resulting in the death of Lake, A. B. Signalman second class, USN … "

As Robert Clifford rose to his feet the color drained from his face. He immediately sank to the deck but Commander Deiter and Ensign Sycycky held him nearly straight up by the armpits. Doctor Selesky moved to Clifford's side, produced a pocketed stethoscope and pressed it to the man's chest.

"Fainted, Admiral. Put him on one of these tables."

Monk took advantage of the first relatively free moment to address Vincent. Eddie could tell by his friend's colorless appearance he'd been through something rough.

"You look like hell." He whispered pulling his chair closer. "Hear anything from Cynthia?"

"No. Not a thing. I thought you had her safely in a cell."

"She's been calling in daily, but hasn't called in yet today. I've got her home number, tried it over and over but all I get is the maid who claims she knows nothing."

Vincent continued to whisper. "Glad you're here. Some of my end of the story you'll hear now. But … " He leaned even closer to Monk and invited Selesky to also hear. "Do not bring up Cynthia Howser, unless asked to do so … OK? I want to get out of here and find her."

Monk looked puzzled and Selesky looked solemn faced as both men nodded agreement to Vincent's request.

Twenty minutes later Clifford was again seated in his usual wardroom chair, facing Admiral Ferrent and the staff of questioning officers. Because the ships' corpsman, Senior Chief Bellefontaine had access to any medical paraphernalia he might need, he'd been called in to watch over the Captain. This freed Selesky. Bellefontaine smiled toward Paul, "How's that hand, Chief?"

Vincent nodded and wiggled a few fingers toward the man.

Meanwhile, Clifford was pulling hard at a button on his right shirt pocket. He seemed unaware he had passed out or that the Chief corpsman had awakened him with smelling salts.

"I'm not the best officer, I know." His gaze swept from face to face. "My father tells me so. Tells me I walk to the drip of a different faucet?" He locked on to Admiral Ferrent's gaze. "I never thought that was funny either, Admiral … But, Admiral … I am not a conspirator." The captain's words seemed futile and trite, the same words used by anyone in his position. "I am an American." Clifford boasted. "This is my country … " He seemed impassioned by the need to convince.

"Who am I supposed to have been in conspiracy with?"

"You know well, Captain." Westhaven checked his notes. "Cecil Tucker, the engine man. But this will all come out later."

"Tucker?" Clifford looked bewildered. "Don't even know the man." Clifford stuck out his chin and rubbed his throat as if trying to ease tension there.

"He was in my boat crew." Vincent spoke up. Clifford's head snapped to the direction of Vincent's voice.

"Vincent! You're here? You're in on this?" He turned to the admiral. "Now I understand. This man …this man is responsible for *everything* going wrong. Not me. This man did it all. Ask him."

Ferrent ignored the accusatory outburst.

"Tucker was in my boat crew, you've spoken to him. The country man."

Clifford tried to concentrate. "Yes, the hillbilly guy that came in by helo?"

"That's him."

"He's a clod-hoppin' hillbilly idiot." Clifford said strongly. "How can he be a …what'd you say? A conspirator?"

Although Ferrent felt Clifford was too disturbed to make any real progress in an investigation, he tried some preliminary probes and asked some opening questions about training levels, the flawed training readiness report Clifford had sent in January, the injuries of the crew resulting thus far from poor training. Clifford defended, but not well.

Interrupting the questioning, the COMSEVENTHFLEET communication officer entered the wardroom with Mr. Stumpf, who has resumed duties as Truaxe communication officer. Stumpf stepped aside while his counterpart had a brief whispering session with Ferrent, Gibbons and Captain Westhaven. Stumpf then handed some papers to Westhaven. The intelligence officer looked them over for more than a minute, and then confronted Clifford.

"The SAR coordinates sent in by Master Chief Vincent here?" He nodded toward Vincent, "*Were* changed on board this ship, Captain Clifford." Westhaven seemed very angry.

Vincent felt his own heartbeat increase. "Jesus," he thought, "they're right …" Which was followed by one more thought: "Or are they?"

Clifford seemed genuinely surprised. "NO!" He said. If he was acting, he was doing a very good job. "How could anyone do that?"

"We got from two directions, comparison with what Pink team sent, to what ended up at the SAR station …and … " Westhaven held up one hand in order to keep Clifford from talking. "Incoming voice monitor tape on the circuit you manned, coming from Pink team?"

"Yes."

" …compared to the tape monitor of the outgoing circuit to SAR …" Westhaven waved the papers in front of Clifford. "You changed those coordinates, Captain."

"Did not." Clifford screamed back. "Did not. I know those coordinates, even now, I did NOT CHANGE THEM," he screamed. He then turned to Paul Vincent. "Chief, Eight MC to twenty AC—Right? Right?"

Vincent was amazed at what he assumed was a dramatic bluff by Clifford. All old coordinates sound alike. Vincent couldn't remember the actual numbers. However, Captain Westhaven tapped Vincent's shoulder and drew his attention to one of the pages on the table-top. Clifford had stated the incoming coordinates correctly.

"How do you remember those coordinates so exactly?" Ferrent asked. "Why those?"

"Why not." Clifford seemed surprised by the question. "I remembered them. I remember a lot of things, numbers especially. Those numbers and letters were easy. " He became very animated. "In fact, in my stateroom I've got the piece of paper I copied those coordinates on. It's in my scrapbook. Have a steward bring the scrapbook. Top right above my bunk." Admiral Ferrent nodded to one of his officers to follow through.

"Those coords?" Clifford said to Gibbons. "08-MC and 20-AC? Those are easy for me to remember. I keep tract of curious happenstance. 08 and 20 is the 8th month and 20th day, August 20th, my birthday. That's partially why I kept the figures for my scrapbook. Luck you know. But the rest is the other initials. The M.C. is for Melinda Clifford, my wife. The A.C.? Arthur Clifford, my son's initials. I kept it 'cause it fits things I collect. My lucky charms … "

"Why would you keep an incoming message of such importance? How did you relay it?" Westhaven pounded at Clifford.

"I, I , well, I just kept it. I recopied the coords on a piece of paper and gave them to … " Clifford's hands dropped to his sides, his eyes widened. "Gave it to the OOD. No. To Corrigan likely, or Lukarmo. Probably it was Corrigan changed them. He's told me he hates Vincent. But wait. No." Clifford jumped to his feet and pointed straight at Paul Vincent's face.

"GRIFFITH CHANGED THEM. IT HAD TO BE HIM." He leaned forward, reached at an angle over the table and grabbed Admiral Ferrent's right wrist. "Griffith is your man, Admiral, not me." He sat down again, very self pleased.

Ferrent lifted Clifford's hand from his wrist and rose from the table. "Gentleman, this has gone far enough for now." He looked from face to face. "I don't think we can gain anything more from this man at this time." The others began to rise and gather notebooks, folders and the like. Ferrent continued. "Where's that Commander Griffith anyway? Didn't we tell the OOD to have him report here?"

"Yes, Sir."

"Send someone to locate him, will you?"

"Yes, Sir."

Paul Vincent spoke up, a very serious and questioning look on his face. "Admiral? Commander Griffith once insisted I understand something."

"Yes?"

"He said …quote—to protect ourselves, we often must protect our commanding officer'."

"So?"

"So there may be something to Griffith's changing the coord's. Just a moment, Admiral." The admiral seemed surprised.

"Please." Vincent said. He rose from his chair and stepped to his right until he could look straight at Clifford, who was looking at him.

"Captain? I hear what you said. You jumped at the idea of Commander Griffith as the spy."

"Yes. He has to be. But they won't listen to me."

"Why do you say it was Griffith, Captain?"

Clifford looked from Vincent to Admiral Ferrent. "May I, Sir?" He seemed completely calmed. His mood had swung as Vincent had seen so many times before. Clifford looked capable and military.

"Talk." Ferrent said.

"Two reasons … Admiral. One:" He dropped back into his chair, leaned forward and rested on one elbow, pointing with that hand into the air. "I gave the correct coordinates to Commander Griffith on the bridge and directed him to relay them to SAR."

"So?"

"If they were changed leaving this ship, his voice was the one that changed them. So he's the spy."

"A weak attempt at self protection, Cap'n." Ferrent replied and stirred as if to return to his original idea of adjourning.

"Wait, Sir. Please." Vincent said. Ferrent sat back and waited.

Vincent leaned two fists on the end of the wardroom table and stared at Clifford as though trying to make his Captain's brain react in a certain direction. "There's more though, isn't there, Captain?"

Clifford leaned back in his chair and stared back at Vincent. He spoke. "I know it, Chief. But I can't bring it here right now. Give me a clue?"

Every eye moved to Vincent.

"The social security number. Tucker's SSN." Vincent said to Clifford.

Clifford jumped to life and banged one fist on the tabletop. He turned to Ferrent. "RIGHT! Dammit that's it and that's what I thought of earlier when you said 'Tucker'."

"What are you talking about?" Westhaven tried to understand.

"Tucker came aboard here, but EPDOPAC kept tossing his name out of their computer. Said he didn't match up as someone they had ordered to this command. That happens now and then, so I didn't think much of it." Clifford looked back to Vincent. "Chief's right though. Griffith kept stalling EPDOPAC with letters, saying Tucker's SSN had been inverted, things like that. He'd send letters too, not messages. Letters delayed it all. See? I remember dates and numbers. Look at the ship's letter file, around February 12th. Griffith was covering for that man bein' aboard Truaxe."

Two staff officers left the wardroom, one to find the steward mates to recover Clifford's scrapbook, the other to check the letters to EPDOPAC concerning Tucker's SSN.

"Also." Vincent jumped in. "Griffith and Tucker were always talking, privately, secret-like. Arguing, but yet Tucker said they weren't." He related the steward mates' story about hearing the yelling between Tucker and Griffith, later denied by Tucker. "Further, Admiral," Vincent added. "Tucker told me his discussions with Griffith were over not getting paid. Tucker even borrowed money from me in Hong Kong …to prove he was broke. But he wasn't. He had enough money to loan a hundred to Lake."

"So the money arrangement story was a cover up for arguments going on, agent to agent?" Ferrent thought aloud.

"Right." Clifford was on his feet again. "And Griffith or Tucker could have been those men on the fantail that night after we left Hong Kong, messing with the Spot Boat radios. Right Vincent?"

"Speculation." Westhaven said.

"Circumstantial yes." Clifford responded. "But, it's not me that's a spy, Admiral." Clifford was actually smiling. "Further, against my actual better wishes, Griffith insisted Tucker accompany the first *and* the second spot boat ashore, as boat's engine man. I am not your spy." His smile shifted suddenly to tears, possibly, of relief. Clifford turned to face Paul Vincent.

"Chief?"

"Yes, Sir."

"You believed in me, didn't you?"

"I guess I did, Sir."

"Why do you?" Clifford asked. Vincent hesitated. Admiral Ferrent answered for him and appeared to be smiling.

"The chief here, yesterday? He said you were too USN to be an agent. He trusted you." Ferrent's smile became very real. Clifford turned back to Vincent.

"For whatever reasons, Chief." Clifford managed a very nervous grin that locked into place and quivered. "You helped me out of a fire here,." Clifford snatched a pencil from the tabletop and launched it across the room. He yelled out crazily: "Of all people, TOUGH TOES ARNIE IS A FUCKIN' SPY. Tell my father THAT!"

At that instant the officer who had been dispatched by Ferrent to find Griffith and bring him to the wardroom returned to announce that Griffith had lied to the OOD and left the ship. "Something about being on an errand for you, Admiral."

"Shit." Ferrent said openly.

The steward returned with Captain Clifford's scrapbook that held the scrap of paper he had copied the coordinates on.

"08-MC, 20-AC." Ferrent read.

The ship's Chief Yeoman, Senior Chief McCullough appeared with the February 12th letter to EPDOPAC. "We got somethin' going on here." Ferrent agreed.

A ship's radioman, accompanied by the COMSEVENTHFLEET communication officer came into the wardroom with a secret, 'immediate' precedence message addressed to COMSEVENTHFLEET and to Truaxe. Both men looked very nervous.

"This message was delayed six to ten hours, Admiral, at NAVCOMMSTA PHIL. We'll learn more about why, later."

"Read it, please, Mr. Stumpf."

FROM: CO NAVSTA SDIEGO
TO COMSEVENTHFLEET
U.S.S. TRAUXE.
INFO U.S. DEPT OF STATE, CIA FBI, BUPERS, CNO, CINCPACFLT, COMELEVEN COMTWELVE, COMNAVFORVIETNAM, COMCRUDESPAC, CINCPAC, NIS YOKO.

-

SECRET NOFORN

1. TAKE IMMEDIATELY INTO CUSTODY COMMANDER ARNOLD GRIFFITH, USN, SER 0101123. CURRENT EXECUTIVE OFFICER TRUAXE. CONSIDERED ARMED AND DANGEROUS.

2. PSYCHOTHERAPY SESSION WITH NAVAL CONTRACT THERAPIST SARAH BARKLEY REVEALS RACHAEL BRISTOL VINCENT, (DEPN ID#75761) WIFE OF MASTER CHIEF RADIOMAN PAUL R. VINCENT OF TRAUXE AND BARBARA GRIFFITH,(DEPN ID#56662) WIFE OF COMMANDER ARNOLD GRIFFITH, SWEAR TO THE FOLLOWING.

A. ARNOLD GRIFFITH IS KGB AGENT WHO LATELY HAD BECOME PRO-US AND, UNTIL RECENTLY, HAD DECIDED TO DEFECT TO U.S.

B. HOWEVER, DUE EXTRAMARITAL AFFAIR BETWEEN MRS GRIFFITH AND RACHAEL BRISTOL VINCENT'S BROTHER, ONE BENJAMIN BRISTOL, GRIFFITH'S IDENTITY AS AGENT WAS REVEALED TO BRISTOL. BRISTOL HAS BLACKMAILED GRIFFITH FOR MONEY ON AT LEAST TWO OCCASIONS.

C. MRS GRIFFITH REVEALS THAT BECAUSE TRUE IDENTITY COMPROMISED, GRIFFITH'S FINAL KGB DUTY IS TO CAUSE NUCLEAR ACCIDENT/INCIDENT ON TRUAXE.
D. RECENT ASSASSINATION DEATH OF BEN BRISTOL AND ARREST OF KNOWN KGB AGENT PETER PAUL JAMMISON REVEALS GRIFFITH MIGHT HAVE REVERTED TO FORMER STRONG KGB SUPPORTIVE ROLE. MAY HAVE TAKEN STEPS TO SABOTAGE TRUAXE NUCLEAR REACTOR.
ADVISE STATUS ASAP.
END

Admiral Ferrent and his staff jerked into action. On warning from Clifford and Vincent, Ferrent's staff became suspicious of Griffith's briefcase. Lieutenant Hicks couldn't remember if Griffith had it with him when he left the ship.

Paul Vincent turned to Selesky. "Christ. Ben Bristol is dead. Assassinated, yet. I've wished him dead, now he is.

"So?"

"A forgotten boomerang that's come back to smack me. That's all."

"Easy with the magic thinking now, Paul." Selesky said. "And no need to rescue Rachael. Look up the word 'divorce'."

"Rescue? Whoa! Maybe. Who does she have left?"

"She'll manage that, Paul. Appropriate phone call to her later, Yes. Run off to rescue her? Not on your fucking life."

"But Christ, David. Right now I'm squirming here under orders. All I really want is to be ashore and find Cynthia. Isn't *that* a rescue?"

"This is a therapy conversation for another time. But right now? I'm going with you to find her. OK?"

"Yes. You, me ...and Monk."

"And, we've got to hurry." Monk said. "I've got another barge raid tonight at 9 PM. ..."

" ...and I've the medical duty aboard Kittyhawk tonight about the same." Selesky added. "I'll telephone and try to get a standby. . but ..."

Within twenty minutes, at 1:20 p.m., Griffith's office was torn apart and his safe opened by Truaxe's Senior Chief Hull Technician and bomb expert, Joseph Algeria. Nothing was found to indicate where Griffith might have fled.

Eddie Monk made telephone calls to local authorities alerting them to Griffith's appearance, that he could be armed and dangerous, and, requesting he be picked up immediately.

"We found the bomb, Admiral." Captain Westhaven burst into the wardroom. "We are recommending immediate evacuation of the ship by all personnel not actually required.

"What is the nature of the bomb, Ron?" Ferrent addressed Westhaven.

"Sophisticated. Exceptionally sophisticated device. Not seen by the ship's man before. Electronic keyer, located in a locker above the reactor. He's had over a year to install it. And he'd been with the reactor for two years prior to that."

"How complicated is this?"

"We believe the bomb itself is actually part of the reactor. There are several wires leading from the obvious timing device to a second device, which might be the explosive itself, which also has more wires leading into a steel bulkhead behind some cabinets. Those wires are intermingled with and tagged to imitate the ship's regular wiring. It's a very tangled array of confusion leading down toward the reactor space. It appears he has explosives planted somewhere in a vulnerable spot of the reactor itself."

"Are we in deep shit here?"

"We're in deep shit, Admiral. We better get this ship to open sea."

CHAPTER THIRTY SIX
SNAFU Now Thorny Miss

With the real chance for a nuclear disaster facing Admiral Ferrent, his command abilities were severely tested. Getting more volunteers than needed, he ordered Truaxe taken to sea under its own power in order to protect the areas of Hong Kong, potentially save lives and save the United States an international scandal. His own Captain Westhaven volunteered to represent him and to command Truaxe. Commander Deiter insisted on acting as executive officer to be available to add his expertise as nuclear engineering officer.

"What time you getting underway, Captain?" Ferrent asked through the clenched pipe teeth.

"Three p.m. Got a skeleton crew, thirty-three. All good men, no grandstanders, just loyal U.S. of N.

"All of you, Westy," Ferrent said, "you included, are good people. Thank you for going. Guys like that Griffith? They just don't understand the difference between them and us. Truaxe, our ship, *any* ship is as much the United States as is any few acres of any land back home. We'll defend it, protect it and even coddle it. He's missing that."

"Why do they hate us so?"

"I think, but I'm not sure. It's that freedom offers so much to consider ...it's overwhelming to them. They want predictability no matter the autonomy it costs them. Something such as that."

"Well, I wish I could have some predictability right now, Admiral."

"Well, let's go for some. Take Truaxe into South China Sea as discussed." Ferrent said. "Get between Hainan Island and Luzon. No significant land masses."

"And the sea will grant each man new hope?" Westhaven quoted history.

"Yes. We'll all hope Columbus was right." Ferrent supported.

"Amen."

"I'll order Henry Fitch and the carrier *America* from Yankee Station." Ferrent continued describing the plans. "They can helo evac you guys once the nuclear people at the Regulatory Association and N.E.C. advise how best to manage the affair."

"Take us ten hours to get there, top speed. Then circle on station?"

"What'd the Master Chief's boat crewman say? 'Circle like a fundamentalist Viking'."

"Yeah. But we'll cover you leaving here and once you are there. The whole affair has officially been designated by the president as 'top secret, restricted data, no foreign nations, except England'. We've got a code name too, *Thorny Miss*.

After watching Truaxe leave the fragrant harbor, Admiral Ferrent moved his investigation and advisory team to Kittyhawk and to the room it had all started in days earlier with the interview of Paul Vincent. This team consisted of Captain Gibbons, C.O. Kittyhawk, Lieutenant Commander Valentino, operations officer, Truaxe, Commander Patrick Balkin, N.I.S., Commander Selesky, psychiatrist, Lieutenant Stumpf, communication coordinator, Eddie Monk, N.I.S. and acting as Hong Kong police liaison, and Master Chief Vincent, a center post.

Admiral Ferrent also had Captain Clifford transferred to a stateroom on board Kittyhawk where Clifford was to remain restricted to quarters under guard, pending further investigation.

At three p.m., Commander Dominic Valentino spoke to Admiral Ferrent and the investigation team. "Now it's clearer why Griffith seldom left the ship, even refused to visit his wife the night before we sailed from San Diego. If he was defecting, he was likely afraid his own people would find him ashore."

Patrick Balkin spoke up. "This is supported from another direction. According to Vincent, Tucker was actually sent aboard Truaxe to motivate an agent who wasn't 'agenting' very well."

"I recall another point," Paul Vincent added. "That evening, right after the slap incident, I spoke to Abie Lake by telephone from my quarters. Now follow this, gentlemen. Lake told me that *Tucker* had told *him*, that Griffith mentioned the killing by overshoot of the first two CIA agents.

"So?"

"So, ..." Vincent added, "that isn't something an executive officer shares routinely with a second class engine man. See, the signs were all around us that Griffith wasn't what he appeared to be."

"And we missed them all." Dieter said. "He's surely tricked us."

"Don't sound so defeated, Commander." Monk joined. "Someone, I think it was De La Fontaine, said —'It is doubly pleasing to trick the trickster'."

"What?" Dieter asked, confused.

"He quotes things that fit." Vincent plugged cheerily, "and, he's an eternal optimist to boot. Both traits have aggravated the hell out of me for years now."

"We need a future teller now, not just an optimist." Dieter concluded.

There was a knock at the paneled room door. Paul checked his wrist, it was 2:20 p.m. He was churning inside over his need to find Cynthia, yet each time he tried to ease away to start searching, someone had a question that only he had answers for.

In answer to the knock, Captain Clifford came into the room looking pale, upset and very out of sorts. The two Ensigns were right behind him, looking helpless. Clifford stood just inside the doorway, his hat in one hand, a wrinkled white paper in the other. He had reading glasses on, something he'd never worn before in front of the crew. His khaki uniform was rumpled and his zippered fly open. A fresh cigarette was clenched between pursed lips, the smoke causing him to blink continually. Everyone seemed surprised to see him.

Admiral Ferrent spoke politely through his pipe. "Yes, Captain?"

Clifford seemed breathless as he spoke. "Admiral Ferrent, Captain Gibbons. —Sirs." He stuffed his hat under his left arm and began shifting the white paper from one hand to the next. He nodded toward the accompanying Ensigns. "Don't blame these men, Admiral. I've bullied them to let me out of those quarters."

"What do you want, Captain" Ferrent asked.

"I really did mess up ship's training … I deserved bein' investigated. I've served …over a year with a Russian agent and never caught on …"

"Wait." Ferrent interrupted him. "I have no need for you to grovel here, Captain. And we are very busy right now."

"Who the fuck is groveling?" Clifford's words were angrily spoken. Ferrent showed no affect other than a quick glance about the area near Clifford, as though seeing if any potential weapons might be at hand.

"Here it comes." Selesky whispered to Vincent.

Clifford went on, turning his gaze from Ferrent to Vincent. "You … I became afraid of you …" He looked back to Ferrent. "I think Vincent tried to goad me into wrecking my own career. Oh, yes, while I did *not* change the coordinates? I *knew* Griffith had." That statement caused Ferrent to look around to the faces of everyone in the silent group.

"Jesus." Gibbons whispered.

"Fooled *me* ." Selesky whispered.

Clifford began a ritual familiar to Vincent; picking at his ear, the cigarette shaking between his lips, an inability to maintain eye contact.

"When I became aware Griffith had altered the coords, I assumed he'd done it just to get the Chief out of my hair, make me easier to live with." He forced a laugh, blowing ashes into the air, a large group falling onto his shirtfront. "I actually admired Griffith's dedication to me then." He dabbed at the ashes on his shirt. "I had no idea Griffith had his own motives. I've been a class alpha fool. That's what I've been turnin' over and over in my room."

Ferrent seemed ready to let the man further hang himself.

Selesky asked a question. "How'd you feel after you knew Vincent might die in there?"

"Shit. For a few hours I *hoped* he would die in there. He couldn't testify against me then. No one could get to me … "

"I asked what you *felt*, Captain, not what you *thought*."

Clifford seemed taken back. "Felt? Don't know …let's see." He looked toward the overhead and back to Selesky. "I was afraid, but also, but, I no longer liked myself. Fear, and I hated myself …more fear when Vincent ended up alive."

"More fear?"

"Fear he was coming to get me." Clifford paused and puffed a cloud of smoke from his cigarette.

"I've always been afraid of *something*. Afraid of responsibility, of my father's pushing me …but I also wanted to be like Vincent here. I knew after shelling the NVA's my career would come to an end. I will never be selected now. I cannot face my father." He turned to face Ferrent. "You've got what I've wanted …but I've not really wanted it. I just knew I'd never be accepted until I was an admiral."

"Accepted where?" Selesky asked quietly.

"Anyplace ... " Clifford answered quickly. "Home, wife, kids, the clubs, the selection boards, the quarterdecks of every ship in the navy. The list of photo's on the living room wall ...but I'm too tall, or something ...they know I'm lazy. They know I want command but if I had it, they'd see I did it better ... I'm better at command ...look how I did those fuckin' NVA's in. Wham, Wham ... 28 dead assholes. Vincent and that nigger? Friends they were." He snapped his face toward Vincent. "Can't truly be friends with a nigger, y'know, or with those fuckin' gooks, with the flips'. I know this stuff and they know I know it and if I was COMSEVENTHFLEET I'd fired 'em all out of this man's navy ...and," he turned to Ferrent, "things you should be doin' but you're like Admiral Stumpf. Weak. Weak excuse for an admiral ... Excuse my bluntness, Sir." Clifford dropped into a chair. "Fuck you, fuck you all." He said. He looked as whipped as he had that night after the dinner in Hong Kong. "Take me home ...country road."

Ferrent shifted in his chair. He appeared touched by it all. "Captain, go back to your quarters, please. We'll talk about this later." The two ensigns gathered Clifford by his armpits and led him out of the very quiet room. The silence took over the group of men for several minutes, then Admiral Ferrent spoke up.

"Perhaps some dim feeling of kinship I'm feeling. The man's tried hard, he simply failed. We all try hard, some fail now and then. Some of the failures are deserved. Some not. He surely brought his to us today."

"What makes a man think he has to do something he doesn't want to do?" Balkin asked into the air.

"He told us, Patrick." Selesky said. "Vulnerable to the father."

Gibbons dismissed it. "Another crazy Captain." He said. "Ever since the *Bounty* and *Caine Mutiny*, the one in hundreds who goes crazy gets all the press. The hundreds of others out there bustin' their asses get little or nothin'."

"If we were ashore, I'd sure have a drink on this one." Ferrent disclosed.

Vincent leaned over and spoke softly to Selesky, Balkin and Monk.

"Clifford is crazy. Griffith, or *someone*, has set a bomb on the ship. Look, its 2:40. I can't sit around here like this, I've got to try and find Cynthia."

Selesky turned to Ferrent. "Admiral, I recommend, under the circumstances, Chief Vincent be excused from all this, for a much needed rest."

"Of course, of course, Doctor. I think we can all use a break from the tension. Master Chief, you came closer to being killed by a conspiracy than we all thought at first. You get some rest, lad."

But the tension was only transferred. While Patrick Balkin had to stay aboard Kittyhawk to draft an update report to CINCPACFLEET, Paul Vincent, Eddie Monk, David Selesky and Tex-Mex stood in Monk's office and poured over Cynthia's lengthy letter about Kurt's organization.

Monk reported he hadn't seen Cynthia for three days, and they didn't know she had spoken with Tex-Mex that morning until her name came up in the conversation. Tex-Mex banged his fist on the counter top very hard and cursed. "Son-of-a-bitch, I was busy as shit. Coulda' talked her in here if I'da' only knew."

He turned to Vincent with a pleading 'I'm sorry look' but Paul didn't comfort him, being caught up in his own version of 'ah, what might have been'.

Vincent spoke to the group. "This is the day she said she would get revenge if she hadn't heard from me." He turned to Monk. "I just assumed she would be with you, Eddie, waiting at the pier."

"We've all fucked this up." Monk consoled. "If I'da' believed in her, I'd still have her here … "

"Ok, Ok, you guys. Let's quit beating ourselves and one another up." Selesky said patiently and turned to a map of the city. "She's gotta' be someplace."

At that instant Lieutenant Han of the Hong Kong Police walked into Monk's office to assist. After being introduced all around and briefed by Monk, Han turned to Vincent.

"Chiep? 'Member I changed gun with Officer Tie after shooting on baa'ge that night?"

"Yes. To keep Tie out of the investigation?"

"Yes. Well, wrong gun. Your gun do away with that man."

"What?" Vincent went white faced. "I've killed someone and didn't even know about it?"

"See … " Selesky jumped in to steady him. "Truly …what you don't know often doesn't hurt you. Those men in-country were not the first you've killed." He shook Paul lightly by one shoulder. "Let go. Let it go. We've work to do."

Ignoring Vincent who was distracted by the news from Han, the more objective others poured over the letters and the map. By 3:20 p.m. they decided most things centered on a loft in Kowloon but they couldn't figure the exact location. They pushed Paul into action. He called Cynthia's house but there was no answer.

"We hab to make a pran." Lieutenant Han said. "Come with me."

With six of Han's best plain clothed officers, some of who had met Selesky and Vincent during the raid on the drug barge, the group swept into Monique's hotel at precisely 3:30. They cornered Dartmouth behind the registration desk. The man frightened right up.

Vincent sounded menacing as he held the alarmed man's shirtfront. "The Kowloon address, Dartmouth."

Dartmouth's thick British accent sounded whiny. "Ah' know no ah'dress. Ah' know nothing of Kowloon. Ah' hoven't even been thea'h for five yea'ahs'."

Tex-Mex took the man into a back room while Vincent and the others searched through the registration area and searched Monique's private office for any sort of clue to a Kowloon address. Nothing.

Lieutenant Han became nervous and spoke privately with Monk.

Monk approached Vincent. "Look, I think I'm losing Han's cooperation. We've no search warrants. So far, we've got an absent crazy lady with an unbelievable story, an AWOL navy Commander who *might* be KGB, a bunch of flashing lights in a box that *might* be a bomb, a missing British husband with a reputation of walking on water, a hillbilly spy who hitches rides on U.S. ships, a hotel full of hookers who are really agents, and a message from someone's wife saying her hubby is a Russian agent about to blow up a ship." He hesitated but kept the floor. Looking directly into Vincent's eyes he rubbed his hand through his thick hair and stepped back a pace. "Sure, Paul. And I've a tunnel from Hong Kong to Kowloon to sell to you."

"Say what you mean, Eddie."

"We need a meeting of the minds of everyone involved. British, U.S.N., Hong Kong police, CIA We need a starting place."

"We've already had too many meetings. We've lost today with meetings. I've got a lady out there …"

Tex-Mex interrupted by appearing with Dartmouth who was bent over clutching his stomach. His shirt front was covered with vomit.

"There ain't no Kowloon address in this guy, Eddie, or I'd have it by now."

"Shit!" Vincent said and moved immediately for a telephone. "I can't think straight, or I'd'a thought of this before." He dialed 428-9330, again. This time he reached Mia.

"Mia? Mr. Paul. I'm looking for Cynthia." He took a chance.

The squeaky little voice filled his ears. "No Cyn here, Mister Paul. Cyn no here for days then come today. Now go Kowloon side I theenk. She hab chong in handbag. I bery 'fraid."

"Chong? What's chong?"

"Gun." Han piped up.

"Yes." Mia said. "Gun, she hab gun, she hab burrets."

"Mia. Steady now. Where in Kowloon? No one knows address. Do you?"

"She hab' gun. She hab' Bullets. She wear Wai-da. Yerrow sweatta'. Say she see you. You no see her?" The line went silent except for its buzzing noise.

"Mia—NO, I no see her." He was very impatient with her. He felt stupid speaking in broken English. "Where Kowloon office? Where loft?"

"Mister Paul? Address on Hankow Road, bery fine tailor shop. Lom Quon own tailor shop. His wife make Wai-da's for Cyn … Tina, name."

Vincent handed the telephone to Lieutenant Han. "You try, please."

Speaking in Chinese, Han exchanged several sentences with Mia then the line went silent.

"What?" Vincent asked.

"Someone at door there. I asked her see if Cynthia."

Soon Mia returned to the phone and hurried Han to Kowloon.

"Let's go." Han said to the group. "I know where prace is …your girlfriend in yellow sweata' brue' jacket and American …pants." He said. He spoke in Chinese and ordered two of his men to remain at Monique's with orders to take her and Rasha Din for questioning.

It was three-fifty p.m.

Breaking the speed limit in two police cars they arrived at the Star ferry landing in six minutes. Lieutenant Han used his car radio to contact the Kowloon Police as the double-decked ferry traveled the short run to Kowloon. The Kowloon Police station was just across the street from the Star House restaurant next to the ferry landing. The group was met by six additional uniformed police officers and an additional squad car. It was exactly four thirty five p.m. and the sky was just slightly gray with clouds.

In five minutes they approached the row of buildings that housed the tailor shop. Three men were sent to the rear of the building by way of the curio shop next door.

"We could find anything here, right?" Tex-Mex asked.

"Or nothing." Vincent answered.

"Or we'll find this Kurt Howser. Maybe more of the group of Cynthia's so called agents or whatever the hell this is about." Monk added. "Shit, if this is our day, we'll find your Commander Griffith here. They're all linked via Tucker, right?"

Han ordered Vincent and David Selesky to stand fast. "You stay outside, saila's." He meant it.

Han, Monk, Tex-Mex, and nine police officers entered the building. Within sixty seconds Monk leaned out of an upstairs window and waved to Vincent. "Come up the stairs, both of you, quickly."

Inside the tailor shop police officers held five Chinese men and one woman against a shelf lined wall. Three of the men were in undershirts and baggy cotton pants, one in a suit and tie and the last in grimy looking coveralls. The woman was dressed in a trendy western style mini, white pumps and baggy jacket. There was also a European man dressed only in shirt, shoes, tie and striped boxer shorts. Like the others, he held his hands in the air, most likely an unfortunate customer caught while being measured for a suit. He looked very worried.

It was warm in the shop and a sweet scented incense saturated the air. Three inoperable large fans hung overhead, their wooden blades covered with thick dust. A young boy of about eight years of age was seated at one of three old treadle sewing machines. He held a paper cup with a straw in it and, straw end in mouth but without a marked expression, seemed to be just watching the grownups play some new game.

Two officers were questioning one of the undershirted Chinese men. The man seemed petrified as he tried without success to manage a smile of innocence and surprise. He kept his hands clutched together and held just below his chin. His face glowed from sweat. Paul noticed the man had a huge vaccination mark high on his right shoulder. When his smile would flash, his upper teeth were spotted with gray rot.

Vincent and Selesky hip-wiggled their way through the narrow shop and past the men. Their presence in U.S. Navy uniforms caused the tailors to look even more alarmed.

Vincent led the way and climbed the narrow steep stairs into the even warmer loft.

He saw nothing out of the ordinary and assumed they had simply been too late or too early to find anyone. He found himself breathing in slowly, trying to detect signs of Cynthia's perfume. He smelled only the incense from below and the dust that hung in the rays of the late afternoon sun glaring through the dirty windows.

"Over here, Paul." It was Monk. He was bent over in front of one of a half dozen three foot high wooden doors built into the one windowless wall of the loft, just in front of where the angle of the slanted roof would not permit a man to stand to full height. The low slung doors all stood open. The small spaces, used for storage, revealed several long forgotten wooden boxes, stacks of paper bags still tied together and eight to ten rolls of tailor cloth material. Everything was so covered with dust to all be the same dull gray in color, except for four large gray plastic bags, bags normally used on the adjacent piers for storing incoming raw cotton bails. They were not dust covered.

Monk pointed. At first Vincent couldn't tell what he was seeing. He squinted. He made out shadowy gray semi-transparent plastic and through the plastic, a woman's shoe, and an ankle, then a bare leg. Cynthia?

Sheer panic stuck his very soul. He leaned into the small compartment and grabbed at the plastic wrapped body. Two policemen pulled him away.

"Wait. Cynthia?" He said jerking his arms free.

"Wait, Paul." Monk snapped and then, grabbing his arm at the elbow, softened his tone. "They'll bring them out, step back. This is their show. There are four plastic bags in there, each with a body in it." He watched Vincent turn white. "I know. Just wait a minute."

Vincent began to sweat. Selesky moved in next to him and put a hand on his right shoulder. "Hang in there, now, more than ever. I'm hangin' with you."

The Chinese officers pulled the bags from the compartment one at a time. One of the bags split and filled the room with the odor of feces. Han spoke firmly in Chinese. One of his men ran to the top of the stairs and yelled below in Chinese. A second officer bent over the bags and with a piece of wooden crate, pushed the plastic against whatever was inside. You could make out distinct parts of human shapes.

Two officers appeared with the one undershirted tailor who had been singled out below. He was cuffed with his hands behind his back. They spoke to him in Chinese and pushed him reluctantly toward the bags. The man cringed and began to whine, and then to cry. Han smacked the man open handed in the face and yelled at him. The man started bowing repeatedly toward Han and talking a steady stream in strong dialect.

"This man, name Lom Quon, put them in the bags, it looks like. " Monk said to Vincent.

Hah crouched over the bags and took out a small penknife. When it was obvious he was going to cut them open, several men pulled out handkerchiefs and held them against their noses. Vincent followed suit. Han slit the first bag.

The small body inside was almost hidden from view by masses of dark and shining hair. Hair like only Rasha Din had. Vincent felt actual relief.

"Not Cyn," He breathed toward Monk

"Right."

Han cut away the entire bag. Rasha was dressed in a blood covered short blue skirt and light blouse. Her throat had been severed. Her bowels had emptied. Everyone held handkerchief's tightly to their noses, expressions strained as they tried to ignore the powerful odors.

Also holding his nose, Vincent felt no recognizable emotion looking at the dead woman. He was more dazed or fascinated than anything; similar to when he and Tucker had discovered the two agents tied to the tree in-country. But, he rationalized; he didn't know this person, actually. Since learning from Cynthia that Rasha had been an agent, all human feelings about her had left him. He felt only a dull sadness, mostly for himself.

"Rasha Dim, or Din, alias 'Shampoo'." Vincent said to Monk and Selesky. "She worked at Monique's."

"What she do dere?" Han asked from across the room.

He thought for several seconds. What did Rasha do? Who was Rasha? He felt cold and angered toward her. "She's a hooker and …" He tried to identify her. "and a . . non-political, rather money hungry seducer of unwary intelligence sources." He laughed at his feigned clinical description. Han turned away without comment.

A nervous looking and slightly overweight and balding Chinese man in a dark suit entered the loft. He was carrying a worn and cracked dark brown medical bag. He looked oddly at Vincent and Selesky, seemingly puzzled by their uniforms. He greeted Han in Chinese and nodded to several others in the room. Appearing not distracted by the odor he took something from his bag and leaned over Rasha. He poked at her neck, chest and lower body eight to ten times with two sharp instruments. He stood and spoke to Han in Chinese. Monk interpreted for Vincent and educated him to the scene.

"This man's the coroner. Egbert Ling. Good man. He's answering Han's question. Rigor mortise begins to set at the jaw line, Paul, and goes down to the feet. After about twelve hours, it begins to leave the body, starting at the feet and working back to the jaw. By twenty-eight to thirty-two hours, the body is relaxed again. By poking, Ling can tell how long the person's been dead … " Selesky took over and commented.

"He'll wait a few minutes and poke again and see if the rigor is just beginning to set, or is reversing. We'll have a good idea of how long they've been here because the temp has been pretty constant."

Monk agreed.

The officers pulled a second bag into view and slit it open. There was a woman in this bag also. Vincent's muscles flexed involuntarily.

"Monique." He said to Monk, a little too loud.

Han rose from his stooped position and looked to Vincent. "Monique DuBois," he said. "night lady, hotel lady. I liked her."

"Me too, once." Vincent said.

Monique flopped out of the bag leaking like a dead battery. She had clearly been knifed to death in the chest and stomach. Her eyes were open as was her mouth. Han closed her eyes with the butt of his penknife. One of them popped open again. He cursed in Chinese. The coroner leaned over and pushed them shut with one thumb. The eyes stayed closed. The man commented in Chinese as he poked at Monique's body with the sharp instruments.

"There's a bullet hole in her hair." Monk interpreted. The coroner and Han quickly returned to Rasha's body. They poked around in her hair. The coroner spoke again in Chinese.

"Bullet in her head also." Monk said.

There was a large older man in the third bag and for an instant Vincent anticipated it might be David Chen. But, the man was too heavy for Chen, and was not Asian.

"Know him?" Monk asked. Han looked to Vincent, waiting for his answer.

"No idea." But noticing the heavy woolen clothing and the out-of-date necktie, he remembered. "Cynthia wrote about a Russian, Tucker said something about a Soviet contact man … Potal …Poval? Something."

"Look in his pockets." Monk suggested to Han.

A fly buzzed in Paul's face. Then another. Monk touched his arm and pointed to Rasha's body. Flies were working over her wounds like building inspectors. This caused unfamiliar nausea to swarm in over Paul. He turned away and tried to ignore all thoughts and feelings. The flies soon discovered Shampoo and the old man.

Vincent wished he hadn't suggested they take time to check the older man's pockets. It delayed the opening of the last bag. Hands shaking, he braced himself as he tried to discern the figure in the remaining bag. It could only be Cynthia, Kurt or David Chen. Whoever was *not* in the bag most likely had done the killing. He looked to Han's handcuffed prisoner. What could that man tell him about Cynthia?

Vincent felt lightheaded for several seconds and was reminded by Selesky that this was his first full day on his feet. Selesky found him a shaky wooden folding chair. He sat and tried to be patient.

When Han rolled the old man over, everyone could see a distinct bullet hole above his right eye, in a bushy brow. His throat had *not* been cut. His pockets revealed a red handled Swiss Army Knife, some change, three unwritten postal cards, and, in the suit coat pocket, a small paper-back novel in Russian.

"Russian." Han said.

"Why kill the KGB man?" Vincent asked.

"If this gang failed to get Tucker out, as you say, Paul … " Monk offered.

" … Get rid of the man?"

"Right, get rid of him before he informs the KGB of the failures?"

"Fuckin' people, Eddie." Vincent said, sounding even more worried. "And Cynthia is one of their enemies."

"Yes." Han said and turned to the fourth bag. Vincent began to sweat clearly. Han cut the bag open. White fleshy arms flopped out into the room with two thuds. Long white arms, Freckles, red hair.

"Jesus Christ." Vincent uttered with restraint. "It's Cecil Tucker." Lightheaded again he turned to Monk as if for an explanation but Monk was stopped by it all.

"It's Tucker … Dewitt … No doubt. He's Bell also." Vincent added.

"Could you be wrong?"

"Only if he has a twin." He walked next to the bodies and pointed to Tucker with one foot. "It's Winston DeWitt Tucker … USN asshole." The flies zoomed in on Tucker's half-opened eyes and mouth. "Check. He'll have a punji wound on his shin."

Han was writing what Vincent was saying. The coroner poked at Tucker's body. He found the punji scar. He spoke to Han.

"They've been dead four hours or so, Monk interpreted. "This Tucker guy? Dead longer than the others …by maybe two hour."

"Where is Cynthia?" Vincent asked.

"Where is Kurt Howser?" Monk answered with a question.

"And where is this Dabid Chen." Han asked.

"Where is Griffith?" Selesky said, adding to the conundrum.

By the time they left the scene in Kowloon it was after seven p.m. and dark in the city. Lom Quon, Han's prisoner, claimed to not know anything of Cynthia. When Vincent wanted to push the questioning with the obviously whipped and frightened little man, Han had backed him away. Han said he couldn't get the man to admit anything except he had been forced to hide the bodies in the plastic bags by a man with a mask on who threatened his family, a story Han didn't believe. Lom Quon said he was to get rid of the bodies after dark or the man with the mask would burn down the building and kill him and his wife and son. Han would work more on the interrogation later. Vincent noticed Han's men also arrested the mini skirted wife, the Taiwanese woman named Tina who had been in the tailor shop with the others. An older tailor took the crying and kicking child home from the shop. Paul deduced correctly that she was Tina, the seamstress and author of the wai-da labels.

Once back to Monk's office at the pier, the Hong Kong police with close cooperation from the U.S. Consulate, the FBI and CIA operatives, officially took over the case.

Vincent's head ached, his leg hurt and the Ben Bristol hand thumped anew. They had not uncovered a single clue to Cynthia's whereabouts.

Monk begged off. He had his own scheduled work to do and said he could spend more time helping Vincent in the morning. Selesky made several calls to *Kittyhawk* to try to get someone to take his duty, but no. He had to return to the ship.

"Paul, look. I don't like you crawling around this city on your own, this tired, this upset. Come back with me."

"David, trust me. I know this town. I've lived here before. I'll not get in trouble, not in my beat-up condition. I'll stay here at Monk's," he lied, "and be fresh to meet with you tomorrow." Selesky tried ordering him but Vincent knew their relationship was no longer one of officer and enlisted man.

"No." He said not too politely. "I can't go back to USN right now."

Selesky's growing respect for Vincent's ordeal helped him understand and accept.

As soon as Selesky left, Paul borrowed a heavy black S.P. Humber sedan and drove straight atop the tram area and parked at the same turnout where he and Cynthia had first kissed. For an instant, he was sure he smelled her perfume as he stared out over the lighted city toward Kowloon. Somewhere in those lights he thought to himself, is Cynthia. Somewhere also, is Kurt Howser, David Chen, and now among the key players, the new enemy, Arnold Griffith.

Where might they be? According to Cynthia's written pages to him and Monk, Kurt was the main enemy at least until Griffith came into view. Could the three of them have been masterminding this all along? All of it? The soft spoken and gentle David Chen had such a long and close history with Kurt, Paul decided Chen must be Kurt's helper, or at least in on it. He was struck that he had always paid so little attention to Chen, he could not come up with a single lead as to where the old man might be, who his friends are, or where he spends time. One woman reported once socially 'David is like being in a restaurant after a full meal. There is nothing there for you.'

He tried to bring Arnold Griffith into the killing scene in some way but he couldn't put the educated and proper Griffith into the middle of shooting and knifing. But, didn't the message from San Diego say something about an assassin killing Ben? Is Griffith that cold beneath his narcissism?

Wait now, Paul thought. Griffith had best be running from the city soon. He was one of the few people aware of the potential of a nuclear disaster and possible fallout. Paul figured him to be at least trying to get out of the area before Hong Kong was filled with gamma radiation from the blown reactor.

"Where, Cynthia? Where—are you?" He said into the air.

On instinct he drove to her house only one mile away. He wanted to talk more with Mia about where Cynthia had been during the time he was gone, what exactly had she said earlier in the day?

He parked the black Humber in the gravel a few feet from where Cynthia had parked her Mercedes that same day. Was Schaparelli in the air? No, there was only enough ambient light from the city to keep him from stumbling as he walked quietly toward the front of the familiar place. He stopped forty feet from the entrance and stood for several minutes behind a large bush and waited while he further developed night eyes.

There were two drape-covered but lighted windows that he could see. One from Mia's bedroom behind the kitchen to his left, the other from near Kurt's study at the right front corner of the spread one story house. Could Kurt be there? Would he be armed? Dangerous?

He had a shocking thought. Cynthia could be there, with Kurt.

He tried to think. She'd fooled him once, for years. Was he still in the part of a fool?

The light went out in the study area. Within a few seconds he saw dim light flood out from the windows at the rear right side of the house. Someone had moved from Kurt's study to the back of the house where the bedrooms were side by side.

He heard a loud 'click' noise near the front entrance but the area was hidden in shadows. He heard a scrape of feet on concrete. Someone was walking toward him from the house. Paul eased more fully behind the bush. The form moved closer and closer to him, walking slowly and unsteadily. Whoever it was coughed.

It was David Chen.

Vincent stepped from behind the bush and readied himself to attack if the old man tried to resist. Chen stopped, shuddered with fright and pulled his thin arms up to cover his face.

"David." Vincent said. "Don't move and don't talk. I have a gun." He lied.

"Paul Vincent?" Chen was very distressed. He dropped his arms and moved his head as if trying to focus in the dim lights. "What are you …" He broke into a cough.

"What are *you* doing here?" Vincent asked.

"I was visiting … " He hesitated.

"Visiting who? Is Kurt in there?"

"Kurt?" Vincent couldn't read Chen's expression in the shadowy light.

"Cynthia in there?"

Chen didn't answer. He grabbed Chen's right wrist and twisted the old man's arm to behind his back in a classic arm lock. "Walk, back to the house. Ring the bell."

"Wait. What is happening? I have to get something from my Opel, up road." Chen resisted but was easily overpowered. "Why you so cross at me?" Vincent hesitated for a few seconds. Chen wasn't *acting* like an enemy. He relaxed his grip. Chen pulled his arm to his front and moved it slowly back and forth as if to restart circulation.

"Why are you so …crazy, Paul?"

"I was at the loft just now. Do you know about the loft?"

"Loft? I don't go to loft anymore." Was Chen this uninformed? "What are you talking about, Paul. Let's go inside …we can talk." Chen turned toward the house, breathing heavily, his feet scraping and shuffling.

Vincent walked ahead of him, his thoughts racing. Who is in the house? It had to be Kurt.

"No one in house, Paul." Chen offered. "Only crazy house lady … Mia."

"Ring the bell." Paul ordered.

David Chen pushed the softly lighted bell switch. It chimed dimly beyond the door. Only then did Vincent make a decision—to not trust Chen. He pushed his long time old friend to one side and threatened him with a hissing whisper. "Not one word or you get the first bullet."

The front door swung inward. Vincent braced himself for Kurt. A light shadow revealed an automatic pistol in a right hand.

It was Arnold Griffith.

Vincent brought his left fist fully in a circle to land along side Griffith's head. The handgun flew out of Griffith's grip and into the house. Both men went down just inside the doorway but Vincent was immediately on top bringing downward blows with both fists locked together. Griffith covered up and bucked against him but one final blow of his right fist detonated against Griffith's head, silencing him but also exploding renewed pain to the Ben Bristol injury.

Griffith was out, unmoving, face flushed. Vincent was immediately on his feet. He flicked the switches near the door, flooding the living room and the outside area with light. He ran out through the open door, caught Chen only a few feet up the driveway, dragged him back and threw him into the house where he crashed against a library table and fell to the carpet.

Mia was suddenly there wrapped in a rumpled green terry cloth robe, her arms tied behind her back with scarves, her mouth and nose covered with what appeared to be rolled bandages. With purpose, Mia threw herself onto the living room floor from the hallway entrance. She rolled over and let out a sound of pain as one hand closed around the handle of the small automatic. Frantic, she tried to maneuver to gripe the pistol but it slipped away.

"MIA!" Vincent called from the doorway. She jerked her head but looked wide-eyed and fearful until she recognized him. She made muffled sounds through the *Ace* bandage. Vincent jerked the gag from Mia's mouth. Chen, on the floor, was coughing and gasping for breath. Mia started talking rapidly in Chinese. "*Qu', Wo' de Cyn hua'i le.*"

"Speak English, Mia." Paul commanded.

Motioning toward Griffith with jerks of her head, she said in clear English—"They come when I talk telephone with police man, Mr. Han. My Cyn is hurt. That man, that man …he hurt …my Cynnie."

"Hurt"? Vincent grabbed Griffith and spun him around on the floor. His head flopped lazily, still unconscious. He turned and grabbed Chen by the shirtfront and lifted him to his feet. "Talk to me." While gasping for air, Chen weakly brought a knee up into Vincent's groin, too slow. Vincent blocked the blow with one leg and countered with an upward fist to Chen's neck. There was an audible 'snap' sound and Chen crumpled straight down onto the carpet. Vincent, his face grimaced stood shaking his right fist slowly up and down in front of him.

Griffith stirred.

"Cyn in oddur' room …she be …hurt with gun." The old woman's face puckered, she screamed *"DAIFU DAIFU."* She kept yelling in mixed Chinese and English and Vincent couldn't understand her. Something about a doctor and danger and the back of the house, but there was more. He grabbed her shoulders, shook her and yelled.

"Is anyone else back there, Mia?"

"CYN DEAD! Bedroom …trouble."

He yelled to Mia. "Is Kurt back there?" He tried to find out the level of danger as his racing mind would not permit any phrase in that had 'Cyn' and 'Dead' in it.

Mia became sober faced. "Mr. Kurt dead. They say they kill him, dead." Vincent couldn't believe her.

Vincent stepped to Griffith and kicked him a hard blow to the stomach and then to the left side of his head to keep him from leaving. Griffith stayed unconscious. Not knowing what or who would be there, Vincent then picked up the automatic and ran boldly into the darkened rear of the house, throwing each door open that he passed.

He found her on Kurt's bedroom floor. She was not moving. Her yellow sweater had been pulled up to under her armpits; her jeans were tangled at her ankles. Her panties were torn and soiled looking. There was what looked like a puncture wound in her throat and one white wai-da cup was deeply blood soaked. There was a dinner plate sized bloodstain on the white carpet. He pressed his ear against her breast to listen and felt warm blood on his cheek.

She was breathing.

He returned to Mia and untied her. "Telephone, ambulance. Police. You hear me? Understand me?"

"*Daifu, Dianhua. Yiyuan.* . Porice." She yelled back.

Following Mia to the living room, and not wanting Griffith to escape, Vincent leaned over and punched the prone man in the head again and again kicked the unmoving man in the stomach. He turned to Chen who was also very still. He ran back to Cynthia, afraid of moving her.

He actually prayed "Oh God! Oh God! Please!" as he heard Mia on the telephone, yelling in Chinese.

He returned to the living room and grabbed Griffith's feet. With pure adrenaline effort he lifted and dragged him back to where Cynthia lay. He put two of Kurt's belts from a closet around Griffith's ankles, flipped the man on his stomach and belted his wrists behind his back. He then put a third belt around Griffith's neck like a dog leash and led it back to tie to the ankle belts. He repeated a similar security move with Chen although the old man was limp as a rag.

Mia came into the bedroom and began screaming in Chinese.

"ENGLISH, MIA!"

"Police coming snappy time." She looked at Griffith and Chen and pointed wildly. "They get Cyn at Kowloon side, bring her here in Dabid Chen car, today." She puffed for breath. "Just when I talk on telephone …with Porice Lieutenant Han. They put gun my face. Then they hide Dabid Chen car someprace. They tie me in this room with her then they fight with words. I hear but have rag on my eyes. I no see but hear. Tall man," She nodded toward Griffith, "He bery angry to Cyn, he curse her, 'bout money. No hab money. I tell them I hab money but tall man put rag on my mouth. I hear slap and Cyn cry out. He then tell David Chen to stop touching with Cyn, I theenk he try sex with her. Chen call her 'big tits', *women ya* sex, sex but Chinese words, bad words. Dabid and big man word fight. I hear *chong* after big man tell Dabid Chen to gib' him a pirrow from bed. *Chong* go 'bump-bump', not bang-bang. He musta' put *chong* in pirrow. Then Cyn not talk more."

Mia's face rumpled further into tears. "I thenk they shoot Mia next, but they didn't. He tell Dabid go to car …purses something. Next I know I shake hands from tie-tie and hear fight by you."

Mia struggled to stop crying and shifted subjects as she locked on to Vincent's eyes. "Mister Kurt is dead, Dabid Chen say. Say Moni-lady kill him."

"Monique killed Kurt?" He was even further puzzled. "But Monique was in a bag? Today, dead, Mia."

Mia shut Vincent out then and dropped to beside Cynthia. "*Ni nar bu' shufu, tang nu-er Cyn? Qu' yiyuan. Deng yi deng, Daifu—wu fen zhong.*" She cried hurting and desperate tears.

"What? What are you saying, Mia?" Vincent demanded.

Mia held Cynthia and re-sobbed the words in broken English. "What wrong my sweet daughter Cyn? Go to hospital wait, wait, just for a moment—doctor in five minutes." Vincent found himself crying with her. Crouched on the floor next to them, his hand felt something different. Half under the bed was the pillow that had been used as the silencer.

The ambulance arrived before the police but no one spoke English. Vincent was torn. Go with Cynthia and chance losing Griffith and Chen?

About that time, Griffith became conscious and vomited on himself and on the carpet. After vomiting, he lay quietly without struggling against the belts. He stared at Vincent and at one point moved his face into what Vincent saw as a smirk. Vincent stomped him in the face with the heel of his right shoe. Griffith went unconscious again.

The ambulance crew seemed very professional and went right to work on Cynthia. One of the crew examined David Chen and spoke to Mia. Mia pulled her hands to her cheeks and turned to Paul.

"Dabid Chen dead, Mister Paul." Her face expressed a further intense look of abhorrence and confusion. "You know dead now too?"

Vincent said nothing, but chased the crew away from Chen and, with his poor Chinese, begged them to hurry with Cynthia. Mia begged also, interpreting for Paul when necessary. Within three minutes of the ambulance arriving, Cynthia was on her way to St. Mercy hospital at the bottom of the hill.

The police arrived in the form of Lieutenant Han with two of the officers from the loft. Vincent quickly brought him up to date. Han instructed his men to take Griffith into very careful custody and to call the coroner over Chen.

A U.S. consulate car pulled into the curved drive and Gregory Winsthrop, a consulate officer who Han seemed to know real well stepped out of the black Dodge and introduced himself as the state department representative for *Thorny Miss.* Han sent him to his two officers to search for evidence and investigate the scene. Vincent told them of the pillow.

Paul and Mia ran for the black Humber but Han interceded.

"No. I take you with siren. St. Mercy hospital?"

On the ride to the hospital Mia apologized over and over for having lied to Paul about Cynthia being in Europe in February. She said she hated doing it. Paul accepted the apology with a hug for the frightened old woman who had been through such a horrible day. With the hug, Mia moved against him as a frightened ten year old might.

They wouldn't let Paul or Mia close to Cynthia's room. They watched hopefully but helplessly as Chinese doctors and nurses came and went. He tried to read their faces but they all had that hollow professional look that hides any clue to progress or prognosis. Mia, a catholic, went into the small hospital multi-faith chapel to pray. Paul stood at the doorway of the draped and carpeted chapel and watched. Maybe, he thought, I'll learn how to pray and help Mia.

Within a few minutes three of Mia's close friends appeared and the four of them started a ritual with their Rosaries. Paul released his worry for Mia to the three friends. He paced. He waited. He could not stop tension shudders of helplessness. He wept but not in a shuddering head down manner, just that tears ran freely from his eyes.

'People cry when they experience feelings they don't have coping skills for.' Selesky had said. But he'd said the same thing about anger. 'People show anger the most when they experience things they haven't learned to cope with. Sometimes they cry."

Two hours passed. Paul's tears changed to blunted anger. Selesky was right *again.* He did not have coping skills for his helpless feelings and for the potential death of Cynthia.

By one a.m., probably through Lieutenant Han's efforts, the word of Cynthia's gunshot wounds spread to Kittyhawk. The navy was showing up in support. David Selesky arrived in civilian clothes. Admiral Ferrent, also in civilian clothes was there briefly with Lieutenant Stumpf and Commander Valentino, who were in uniform. The uniformed Captain Gibbons in the company of two uniformed British naval officers also stood several yards down the marble floored hallway and nodded to Vincent. They left him alone with Selesky who said Patrick Balkin had been called in to help interrogate Griffith, who, to continue the odyssey, had been admitted to the police wing in the basement of the same hospital.

At four thirty a.m. a doctor named Lu spoke to Paul in very good English. He described Cynthia's wounds as being caused by three small caliber bullets, but all Paul actually heard was that there would be a wait of several hours. No he couldn't sit with her, she was in surgery. She had been shot in the heart. No, there was nothing he could do at the moment. No, he couldn't predict with accuracy if she would recover. Yes, they had plenty of her type of blood and that was not the problem.

Fighting for sanity, Paul asked his friend. "What can I do, David?"

"Hope, cross fingers. Have faith. Some people pray. This is open-heart repair, Paul. A terrible intrusion on a person. But, my frightened friend …surgeons really know their way around in there these days."

Eddie Monk strode up to the pair. "Admiral Ferrent sent me to find out how we can help? Said do anything he or the navy or I can manage."

"Take me to Griffith?"

"Sounds fair."

In the elevator, Canadian Ian Tyson's smooth cowboy voice sang softly through masked speakers. *"I wish I'd done things different, ah but wishin' don't make it so."*

CHAPTER THIRTY SEVEN
Right and Wrong Defined

This Griffith? If he's truly one of the big boys." Admiral Ferrent said, lighting his pipe. "We caught him too easily. Where was the KGB? If they organized to get this Bell person out of Hong Kong, how come Griffith seemed to be on his own?"

"This man is, or *was*, an important, expensive nuke trained top agent." Balkin agreed. "The complexity of the timing devices. The clever way he's hidden both his and Barbara's identity all these years ..."

"That puzzles me, also." Selesky acknowledged. "His wife having an affair with Ben Bristol ...telling Vincent's wife her husband is an agent. That's out of character for a matched pair of spies."

"That's what I'm thinking also, Doctor." Ferrent continued. "Her having the affair is bad enough ...but his reacting so badly to it? Wow! And compromising himself further with the telephone call to warn his wife. Answering Bristol's blackmail letter ...puling whatever strings to get Bristol murdered. And, did he *really* change Vincent's coordinates?"

"All of that is out of character," Selesky interrupted, "but the antagonism everyone says he felt toward Vincent is also out of line. Seemed irritated by Vincent's mere presence ..."

Ferrent re-interrupted and completed the sentence. "to the point of making stupid errors. Showing up at Howsers with the Howser woman. I don't understand it. What was he after? Money? Seems incongruous. All these years of planning and to be short of cash?"

Selesky added. "Whatever it was, it was important to him ....very much so. Was it *her*, Cynthia Howser he was after, and sex, as with the old man?"

"Well, Admiral," Balkin offered, "We get a crack at him now and I want Vincent present to keep him off guard. We're banking that whatever is behind Griffith's hatred for Vincent might have enough fuel to cause him to make mistakes under questioning. Help defuse the bomb aboard Truaxe."

With fingers crossed, Ferrent and the state department representative approved Balkin's basic plan for questioning Griffith. They approved Vincent as part of the interrogation team. Lieutenant Han would represent the police, Balkin, the navy's investigating team and Monk, with the rules stretched but because of his hard-working reputation would represent the British government's of Hong Kong's interest. David Selesky, to be introduced as an intelligence officer was included as Paul's moral support and to observe Griffith from an unsuspected psychiatric point of view. They'd use the name "Seltzer" to keep Griffith from name recognition.

Outside of the cool basement hospital room which was guarded by two serious looking Hong Kong police officers, the police doctor, Angela Sen, with just a slight accent, briefed the interrogation team.

"X-rays reveal Mr. Griffith have at least two broken ribs, slight concussion, several bruises to his chest, stomach and back. Because of beating, he complaining of chest pains, blindness in one eye …and some being dizzy. They tell us he dangerous man. So we move him to special prisoner room here at St. Mercy."

The group entered the large tiled white room to find Griffith in the nearest of two beds, the second bed being empty and stripped to the springs. The room smelled of fresh paint. Three large banks of fluorescent fixtures dominated the ceiling; the resultant lighting was very bright, almost to the point of distraction.

"Once was an operating theater," Dr. Sen revealed, "bright lights."

Griffith stirred when the group entered but he couldn't move far.

"Restrained by body belt and locked wrist cuffs." Doctor Sen pointed out.

Lying on the bed but not making eye contact, Griffith was in a green hospital gown and had a white bandage over his left eye. His bottom lip was puffed and split, slightly to the left of center. He kept licking at the lip, which was covered with a clear greasy ointment.

Dr. Sen motioned the group to the far corner of the room. Pointing to the patch, she explained there was a deep laceration above his left eye that penetrated what she described as the orbicularis muscle and the front tip of the levator muscle, causing his upper lid to relax and block his vision.

"He'll be a droopy eye the rest of his life?" Monk seemed pleased.

"Yes, likely." Sen whispered. "There some hemorrhaging to the vitreous body of that eye, also, and a cut through the suspensory ligament of the lens."

"Meaning? Can it be fixed?" Vincent asked the serious looking woman.

"I don't know if a surgeon could repair that kind of damage. He likely have trouble with that eye for the rest of his life."

"Ol' one eye." Monk said real loud.

Griffith stirred and peered at them with the one good eye. He seemed to be trying to catch what he could of their conversation.

Balkin whispered. "He denies knowing anything about the bomb. Even bringing Petty Officer Amhurst to him earlier didn't budge the denial."

"Once he breaks with anything, we'll get it all I believe." Monk said. "I'd like to know a lot of things: Is Kurt Howser really dead? If not, where is he? Who actually did the murders in the loft? Is the dead Russian a KGB man? "

"Fook murder in loft," Han interjected. "I get from Lom Quon who did murders. We need only one information from dis' guy. Make bomb safe." He patted Vincent on the arm. "Use whatevah' you hab' to use, guys."

They all turned to Griffith's bed.

Griffith moaned but received no sympathy from the group that surrounded him. Doctor Sen left the room and pulled the large door behind her. There was an echo quality to the room with the door closed. Griffith smelled of perspiration and fatigue.

Up close, he looked terribly damaged. In addition to the split lip and the eye patch, his face was overall bruised from the beating. He looked pale from recurrent nausea and vomiting caused by the concussion.

"I want a lawyer." Griffith tried to sound demanding but looked vulnerable and helpless.

"A lawyer? This isn't California." Balkin seemed joyful to pick at Griffith. "You've been arrested in a foreign country, it's the Hong Kong police, not the highway patrol."

"I am a naval commander, Lieutenant Balkin, I expect respect for a superior officer.

"Fuck you," Balkin surprised Griffith, "You are under arrest for the attempted murder of Mrs. Howser, and, you gave away any incoming respect the instant you set that timer. Are you getting the picture?"

Griffith became quiet but kept his one eye sweeping from one face to the next.

Seltzer (Selesky) left the room and returned carrying two folding chairs. A pudgy Chinese woman orderly followed him into the room with two more. Balkin and Seltzer sat on Griffith's left, Han on his right. Monk positioned his chair backward at the foot of the bed, straddled the brown plastic seat and leaned his arms on the metal chair back. A toothpick wiggled in his mouth. Paul Vincent stood between Monk and Seltzer and leaned against the curved chrome bar that shaped the foot of the bed. He pushed his chief's hat to the back of his head.

Han chased the orderly out of the room, "Qu-Qu", lit a smelly local cigarette and blew smoke over Griffith's face. "You in chaage', Chiep Bincent. It's your lady he hurt."

Griffith's one visible eye jerked from Han to Vincent's face. His brow furrowed.

Having cleared it with Han, and taking a chance the others would understand, Vincent reached deliberately into his pants pocket and withdrew Cynthia's small automatic, the one he had taken from Griffith. He cocked the weapon and a live round flipped into the air. Monk flicked one hand in double-quick time, caught the small bullet and tossed it to land on Griffith's chest. Han, who knew Vincent less than anyone, suddenly became nervous over the gun in the hands of the angry man with the lover near death. He fought to stay outwardly calm and trust Monk's judgment.

"One." Vincent said to Griffith. "The combination to the device on the ship."

"I know nothing of a device." Griffith peered at Vincent with his one visible eye.

There was a scraping of chair legs on the tile floor. Han threw his cigarette to the floor and slapped his foot over it like he was crushing a bug. Han, taking a further chance motioned to the men to leave the room with him. "We leave Chiep heah'. This is man who hurt Chiep's lady fren'. I 'spect we get more we leave them 'lone, Gentlemen."

All the men rose to leave.

"You can't do this." Griffith feigned a very nervous laugh and tried to call Han's bluff.

Han turned back to face Griffith and put on his best Charlie Chan face. "Listen carepully to me. No one know you still 'live when we pick you up, Mister Grippith. 'Cept' the' police oppicers who live Hong Kong which will be dangerous when ship blow up. They not say anythin' 'bout you dead. You 'stand me?"

"This is against the law." Griffith said.

"I am the law. I don't feel anything against me, 'cept you."

"You can't deal this way."

"I deal in crime …you are crime."

"This is against the law." Griffith repeated, looking at Han.

Han shrugged his shoulders. "Putting bomb 'gainst law."

Griffith seemed to fold in. "Give me pen and paper," He said with resignation, "and, please, take off these restraints. I'm not going anywhere."

Han produced a key and unsnapped the wrist cuffs from the steel bed-side-bars. Within minutes, by pulling the paper close to his good eye, Griffith drew a rather detailed sketch of the device in the locker onboard Truaxe.

"These positions of the toggles make it inactive. After these toggles are in these positions," He drew a star next to the drawing on the page, "only then can you remove the plugs and take the first bomb, the gray box, to safety."

"First bomb?" Balkin asked.

Griffith actually smiled but cut it short when the split lip reopened and flooded with fresh blood. He reached and rubbed the lip with one finger, visually inspected the fingertip, licked it, and turned back to Balkin.. "Let's get to it." He said. "I know by now you've taken that ship to sea. We're in no danger here. Neither is anyone else in this city."

"Not true." Balkin lied. "We'll diffuse the bomb here."

Vincent touched the pistol through the thin blanket and against Griffith's crotch. "Remember, no one knows how many wounds or what kinds of wounds you had when you arrived here, or, for that matter, if you even ever arrived here."

"That woman doctor does." Griffith fought the bluff.

Han, who had still not left the room as he threatened to do leaned over Griffith. "That woman doctor? She my daughter in-law best fren'. They go medical school Unibersity Calipornia, L.A. They like U.S.A." He rocked back on his heels slightly. "Any questions?"

"We have time here." Griffith said, appearing less cocky. "Listen, I know you'll not trust my figures but my briefcase is hidden in Howser's house." His eye flicked to Vincent's face. "Under the woman's bed. In it … " His eyes swept from face to face, and returned to Vincent's. "under the bitches bed …is a orange colored paper that'll verify these switch positions."

"So?" Han asked.

"So …call the ship and tell them these positions. The first bomb will deactivate." The man seemed very cool and was talking like someone who had the upper hand. He actually asked Seltzer to crank the head of the bed up, which David did.

"How much time do we have on the bomb?" Balkin asked.

"I'll keep that info to myself for now." Griffith countered. "However, to show my good faith …you better hurry to disconnect the first bomb. Once disconnected … I'll trade you for the second bomb's location and secret …"

"Fuck you." Monk said and reached between the bars at the foot of the bed and grabbed Griffith's ankles. "What say you release that waist strap and I jerk this guy down here and crush his balls on these bars?"

"AND …" Griffith actually hollered. " …you must open the *yellow* snap switch on the brief case *before* the white switch."

"Bomb inside satchel?" Han seemed to catch every detail.

"Yes."

Monk got a strong grip on Griffith's ankles. "Unlock the waist strap."

"Wait." Han cautioned. Calling for the policemen who were waiting outside the door, Han reconnected Griffith's wrist restraints and motioned to the group of Americans. "Policemen stay here, you come me."

"Wait!" Griffith called out. "Leave me that paper pad and a pen, and leave me arm room to write. I mean it."

"Do what he ask." Han spoke to his men in English.

They left the hospital room and hurried to a police van next to the hospital emergency entrance.

Han dialed 428-9330 and spoke to the two Chinese officers and the U.S. consulate officer, Gregory Winthrop. Within five minutes the briefcase had been safely opened on Cynthia's bed and Gregory Winthrop was speaking to the police van by telephone.

"Look for orange card." Han said and switched to a speaker-phone.

Winthrop described the contents of the briefcase to Balkin and the others. "There are several notebooks with addresses, look like code names for people ...and recent dates with coded entries." The group in the van could hear Winthrop rustling papers in the briefcase. "I have two obvious code books. One marked 'candle'—'nother marked 'select'. Mean anything?"

"No."

"Wait, here's an orange card. Bunch of symbols."

"Those are switch positions. Tell me them." Monk seemed excited but focused.

Winthrop read from the card. Han and the others compared his description to Griffith's rough sketch.

"If he's not lying, at least it *looks like* the first bomb can be deactivated." Monk said.

Balkin and Monk took over Han's communication van for several minutes. They reached Kittyhawk on 2716 kilocycles, the standard harbor frequency, and passed the switch positions to COMSEVENTHFLEET's communications officer to be relayed by long-range circuit to the detonation experts on Truaxe.

"We'll know soon." Balkin whispered.

Winthrop continued to describe the contents of the briefcase. "There are three pills in a small bottle, possibly poison. Here, see if this means anything, Commander Balkin. I'm reading from a hand printed notebook. Quote: Kurt Howser is called 'Shaman', S-H-A-M-A-N, Cynthia Howser is 'Annie', Rasha Din is 'Speckle', Monique DuBois, D-U-B-O-I-S, is 'Star', and David Chen is known as 'Au-yeung'. Do I have to spell that?"

"No!"

"A man named Polav P-O-L-A-V, is a Russian contact who will use code words quote: ring a bell—bell ringer—bell tone—unquote, to be followed by some question about quote: traveling someplace—travel agent—unquote."

"Old news." Vincent said, jerking a clenched fist into the air. "I learned all that code shit from Bell. But before the Captain's dinner? Griffith said Cynthia was a 'bell ringer'."

Vincent's eyes focused upward in concentration. "Also, on the pier before we left Hong Kong? Tucker said something ...to her—'rang a bell'—something—and, said he'd 'been in and out of more ports than a travel agent' ...something like that. I thought ...at the time, he seemed so intimidated by her, he was just rambling.

"So," Balkin said, "Griffith was involved enough to have had true identification on everyone. That info alone will get him fifty years in Leavenworth." He turned to the speaker-phone. "Keep talking, Winthrop."

As the group stood around the speaker in the crowded van, now filled with Han's smelly cigarette smoke, Winthrop went on. "I'm now reading from a hand written letter that has been decoded in its margin, in longhand. Christ, get this: He had advance information that Cecil Tucker, code name 'Bell', would be dropped by submarine near Subic Bay. Come aboard U.S. ship, Truaxe, ... Jesus, this is hot stuff ...around late January, 1968. He would be an engine man second class, as a cover. He would approach Griffith who was to turn over some reactor information that Griffith apparently had been withholding from his contacts. Griffith was also to later get Tucker to Polav via the Howser organization. . and get Tucker out of the country ...that was back in Feb."

The local CIA and U.S. State Department representatives had a lengthy conversation with the Hong Kong police, the British government, and the Navy. It was agreed Captain Gibbons, to have rank to make final negotiations with Griffith, would join the original team of Han, Balkin, Seltzer, Monk and Vincent.

While waiting for Gibbons to arrive, Vincent pumped the attending physicians for anything encouraging concerning Cynthia. He got very little. When Gibbons arrived, Vincent took a deep breath and followed the critical team into Griffith's brightly lighted room.

"Let's talk about the offer, Griffith." Gibbons opened.

"The first bomb came apart as I said, I suppose?" Griffith asked.

"True."

"Now, where is Truaxe?"

"None of your business."

Griffith sipped from a cup of tea, holding his left hand pressed slightly against the eye patch. "I'll ignore your rudeness, Captain Gibbons, luckily for you. But I need to know speed and hours on that reactor ... " He reached and pulled at Gibbons wrist and looked at the man's wristwatch, " ...since noon yesterday." With one fingertip, he again blotted a drop of blood away from the split lip.

Gibbons looked to Balkin. Balkin shrugged.

"Forty knots, ten hours to the safety area." Gibbons said.

Griffith suddenly seemed worried. "Slow to fifteen knots, do not back the port engine, do not scram the reactor."

"What if we ignore you?"

"Hurry ...do it." .

Balkin stepped quickly to the doorway and leaned out of it. He spoke to the waiting CIA representative who took off on the run to pass the message to Kittyhawk and on to Truaxe.

"Don't fuck this up, Griffith." Balkin said when he returned.

Griffith smiled and turned to Seltzer. "Ask everyone to leave the room except you, if you please." He pointed to Seltzer again, then turned to Balkin. "Give me a match or a lighter, I know you smoke." Balkin handed him a Kittyhawk *Zippo* lighter. The room was cleared.

As soon as the door closed, Griffith held one finger to his lips in a 'shh' signal and motioned to David to come closer. He whispered quite softly, "I know who you are. You're that MD Shrink of Vincent's. Didn't fool me with that *intelligence officer* Seltzer crap." He then held a hand printed paper for Selesky to see.

"DO NOT READ THIS ALOUD. THIS ROOM IS PROBABLY BUGGED.
MY WIFE HAS VINCENT'S LETTER TO HIS WIFE, TELLING THAT YOU ARE HOMOSEXUAL. I ALSO KNOW YOUR LOVER IS THE LT. BALKIN. UNLESS I GET COOPERATION FROM YOU CONCERNING MY NEXT MOVE AGAINST THE POWERS THAT BE, THE PROOF I HAVE WILL SHOW UP IN THE MAIL AT THE BUREAU LEVEL.
NOD IF YOU UNDERSTAND THAT I MEAN BUSINESS.

Selesky nodded. Griffith took Balkin's lighter and burned the paper, letting the ashes drop to the floor on the left side of the bed. He kept rubbing at the bandaged eye.

"Is your eye bothering you?' Selesky asked.

"No." He answered with a snap. "Now, send Vincent in, same circumstances."

Griffith repeated the same introductory warning to Vincent and showed him a second note.

I HAVE TWO THINGS THAT I BELIEVE WILL GUARANTEE YOUR COOPERATION WITH ME.
1. YOU PROTECTED SELESKY'S HOMOSEXUALITY FROM THE NAVY, A VIOLATION OF NAVY REGS. I HAVE PROOF—YOUR LETTERS WRITTEN TO YOUR EX-WIFE.
2. SINCE 1963 OR SO, YOU GAVE VALUABLE MILITARY INFORMATION TO THE HOWSERS, MUCH OF WHICH I HAVE DOCUMENTED IN WRITING FROM THE HOWSERS. YES, FROM BOTH OF THEM. ALSO FROM MONIQUE, WHO KEPT VERY GOOD RECORDS.
UNLESS I GET COOPERATION FROM YOU CONCERNING MY NEXT MOVE AGAINST THE POWERS THAT BE, THE PROOF I HAVE WILL SHOW UP IN THE MAIL AT THE BUREAU LEVEL
NOD IF YOU UNDERSTAND THAT I MEAN BUSINESS.

"Bullshit! What do I care what you try to do to me."

"Shhh." Griffith hissed. "Don't test me too far. There's a ship out there that'll go ka-boom. Now send Balkin in, same circumstances."

Griffith showed Patrick Balkin a similar note. Balkin made no response of any kind to the man. Griffith just grunted, burned the final pre-written note and let its ashes float to the floor beside the bed.

He asked for everyone to return to the room.

"Gentlemen, I want several first class OPEN tickets on several flights out of Hong Kong. I want my passport validated with diplomatic visas for several countries. I want absolute trust that I will not be followed. Further, Captain Gibbons, I want three copies of a letter of transactional immunity … "

"Immunity?" Gibbons seemed indignant.

"Right. Transactional immunity, to be exact. It can be granted by an admiral. I believe Admiral Ferrent will be glad to do it, to get his blessed Truaxe back."

"This is an espionage case, Griffith." Gibbons snapped back. "Admiral Ferrent will have to take this through the wickets at the department of justice before it would be valid."

"Well, *mein capitain* …Get on it! Hurry hurry." Griffith was especially cocky. "Ask the President, for all I care. AND, I want one copy of the letter to carry with me, one given to the Hong Kong French consulate and one to the Hong Kong office of the International Red Cross."

"That will take days …hours anyway." Balkin seemed overwhelmed.

"Get on it, hurry hurry."

Gibbons motioned to Balkin. Patrick walked to the door again but this time it closed behind him.

"Once I'm safely landed, I repeat, *landed* at the country of my choice, and sure I have not been followed, I'll make sure you learn the correct way to defuse the secondary explosive device, and … " He stalled for a reaction but no one spoke. "Very well then, if this isn't funny to you all … I will also instruct you how to defuse the final backup device."

"Is there really a third device?" Gibbons asked, holding his hat in his hands and wiping his brow with a white handkerchief.

"Of course."

"But Tucker inferred you wanted to be friendly to the U.S." Selesky was doing 'nice guy.'

"Isn't this friendly?" He grinned at Selesky. "Just because my plans to become a U.S. citizen have been temporarily fouled …and I emphasize—*temporarily*, just because the country I wanted to become a *real* citizen of is becoming more and more immoral, like Vincent, decadent, like Ben Bristol, perverse, like the crew chasing these Hong Kong whores. . " He looked off into space and rambled. " …a country spends more money on cat food than baby food. Vandalism rampant. Writing on freeway walls, drugs in colleges, a whole generation of moral agnostics showing up. Gangs govern neighborhoods, government waste which we see every day out here, now they talk of this acid rain, fraud in religion …unfit air worse than in East Germany." He tossed his hands into the air and seemed to refocus. "Need I go on? No? Someday I'll be a U.S. citizen."

"But people who know all of this will watch for you if you get out of this." Selesky said.

"THAT, kind sir, is why I want immunity. I know its not possible now, but I once thought it would be quite nice to have my own U.S. command, especially one of Admiral Rickover's submarines ... I could have had my cake ...play captain, and be protected by KGB also. They hunger for any intelligence I could play out to them. Life would have been wonderful. Remember, I was seventeen when I was recruited by the KGB. At first it seemed like an honor. All for mother Russia, that stuff. Then I saw true freedom was possible, not exactly how the U.S. is today ...but somewhere in there was something good. I wanted to be a U.S. Navy Commanding Officer, own an R.V, have a family, my children free to pick their own professions. I married Barbara. She knew I was an agent. She loved it, but she wasn't real smart about anything. You know? Every time that woman would pull up to a gas pump? the gas cap was on the wrong side"

"Then," he continued, "the KGB changed. From good guys to trouble. They hounded me, threatened my wife. She feared them. Then, when I got to Truaxe? I saw how stupid Clifford is, yet he was the C.O. I doubt the guy could sell insurance as a civilian. I hated that. I wanted to prove to the U.S., to Barbara ...that I too could be a commanding officer. So, I did all I could to protect Clifford so any fitness report he wrote on me, would be of value ...not from some laughable fool. I was ready to turncoat to the CIA but only if they would let me continue as a naval officer. I would have approached the CIA after this trip, but ...but ... "

"But Tucker fouled it up for you?"

"NO!" He yelled. "That clod wasn't experienced enough to hamper me, much. Oh, he gave me some trouble but I arranged for the torpedo boat to get him, and Vincent, and Lake."

"Why Lake?" Selesky asked.

"You know? I actually thought the black one was KGB. Someone they'd slipped in on me. He was so buddy-buddy with Tucker ...who I knew was KGB. Too bad they missed ...and missed Vincent here, also."

"If it wasn't Tucker who fouled it all up for you. Who was it?" Selesky asked calmly.

"It was my wife."

"She didn't want to defect?"

"Barbara was impatient." He looked directly at Vincent. "You see. She was just like you." Griffith's one visible eye opened very wide. He spoke slow and deliberate. "Because of her weaknesses, sexual ...glandular weaknesses, the so called need for love?" His voice sped up. "She got messed up. Forgot our goals, values. But now? Once again, Barbara is screaming to me to help her, protect her, fix the world for her."

"Is that what she's done in the past?" Selesky was speaking in his best therapy voice.

"I am the man, she is the woman." His voice took on the tones of a preacher. "Men take care of women. That's only right." Selesky's eyes flicked to Vincent's and rolled slightly. "If the U.S. has their way, my Barbara will spend the next fifty years in prison. I can't let that happen."

"So to keep up your image, you'll give up your triumph over Truaxe if we give Barbara Griffith back to you?"

"That's it, Doctor Selesky. You've guessed it."

"But it seems she'll need to be rescued or protected forever." Selesky argued.

"No. This time she'll have learned." Griffith held one hand against the eye patch and pointed with one finger of the other hand directly at Vincent. "You see? Sex ruined her life. Love didn't ruin it. I love her and I didn't ruin her life. That Bristol relative of yours? Ruined her life. Sex ruined your life too, Vincent. Because of the Howser woman dangling her pretty self in your face, you left your wife when your duty was to protect your wife." He crossed both hands on his chest and more or less proclaimed: "Men are to protect women."

"You hated Vincent for letting his wife down?"

"God surely knows I was doing my best to protect my Barbara, but she was not only too impatient, but too filled with longing, loneliness …for men. Can you imagine her sleeping with Ben Bristol?"

"That had to hurt very much." Selesky said.

"Only to remind me of how I let her down. But now Bristol is dead, and I'll soon have my Barbara back."

"And you've gotten even with Vincent by killing Cynthia?" Selesky's question caused the hair to stand on Vincent's back.

Griffith's face jerked back to Selesky. "No, never. I hate what he is, true. He acts entitled and he isn't …isn't anything. Just a radioman. Not even college."

"Why'd you try to kill Cynthia Howser?"

Griffith kept his eyes covered with both hands. "Don't know if I did try that. Now that Vincent here hurt my eye, broke my ribs … I hope maybe she does die." Monk moved in close to prevent Vincent from attacking Griffith. Griffith was still talking.

" …the money maybe. I needed money to get away. Until I was totally free, I couldn't go to the KGB, *nor* to the U.S. I got a few hundred from the whores' purse, but needed more. Au-yeung said there was plenty money at the Howser's house, or I wouldn't have even bothered to go there. He was lying. When we got back to the house? He wouldn't help look for money. He just wanted sex from her. But the ol' man couldn't get it up."

Selesky squeezed Vincent's hand to caution him. Vincent stepped back, more tense than ever.

"He tried sex with Cynthia?" Selesky asked Griffith.

"He tried *something*. Kept fondling her, tried undressing her. That maid was noisy and had to be gagged and tied up. Stupid distractions. I got bored. There was no money. At least none of those women seemed to know where any was."

"So you shot her?"

"No. He's dead now. That guy Chen? He shot her, not me."

"Why lie?" Selesky said evenly. "The maid said you shot her."

"What does she know? She was blindfolded."

Griffith dropped his hands to his chest and turned to face Gibbons as if dismissing Selesky. Several distinct deep breathing patterns could be heard in the room.

Griffith broke the silence. "Well, Captain Gibbons. Do I get my plane tickets? Or does the USN try to explain the loss of a brand new nuclear powered destroyer." He grinned a stage smile. The lip split again. The smile stopped. "Yes, the entire story. A Truaxe idiot for a captain. A nuclear trained agent as executive officer. Successful embarrassing conspiracy resulting in CIA agent deaths …twice over." He laughed evilly and ignored his lip. "Make a complete fool out of the U.S. of N and of the United States itself. It'll finish the nuclear programs, raise international hell over safety. No U.S. nuclear powered ship will be permitted in any foreign port. The liberals will be marching. Peace-niks'll be speeding around in their little boats …raving about danger to the environment. You'll be like Chamberlain dealing with Hitler. You'll pick between war and shame and get both. Congressmen and newsmen will be out at night like marauding roaches, licking and sucking for information. They'll be investigating why the CIA and FBI didn't discover me years earlier. Once I make complete disclosure and I do mean complete—to the *New York Times,* the *London Times*, and others. Mind you, other agents already have the paperwork ready to drop in the mail slots."

"So we let you go and we keep Truaxe?"

"And save face, the U.S. face …that's what I'm saying."

"How can we trust you?"

Griffith's face became serious and concerned looking. "I want my wife back safe and sound. Running from the KGB these past two years has cost me Barbara. She wasn't strong enough. I drove her to Bristol. She'll be happy to be with me once she knows I was responsible for her getting out of trouble. That's why you can trust me."

Gibbons clicked his tongue against his teeth. "We have no choice."

No one spoke. Everyone left the hospital room leaving a nervous Griffith under the guard of two policemen and a second CIA man.

Gibbons, with Admiral Ferrent was on the Kittyhawk single-side-band encrypted voice circuit to the pentagon within ten minutes. They were told to wait thirty minutes before answering Griffith. The president was consulted.

At the curb in front of St. Mercy hospital, Griffith would have looked like any middle class businessman in the sport coat and slacks Balkin had purchased for him, but the black eye patch, split lip and bruises altered his appearance and attracted the stares of the curious passing by.

Vincent stood next to Monk, both men extremely tense. Monk quipped; "Whomever said 'evil never wins' and 'crime doesn't pay' hadn't met this ass-hole."

A sober faced Captain Gibbons handed Griffith an official looking envelope and handed matching envelopes to Mr. Charles Yen, representative of the International Red Cross and to Miss Andrea Delvaulx, an officer from the French consulate.

"The immunity, signed and valid," he said stiffly.

Griffith started inspecting the paperwork but Gibbons distracted him by pushing several envelopes containing flight tickets into his hands. "Here, take these also. You wanted them. I wanted nothing to do with this."

Vincent also spoke. "If I had five minutes with you. I'd get the bomb's released and anything else we …'

" …but, you're just an ass, Vincent." Griffith snarled.

"Still, if I had my way …"

"But you don't." Griffith barked.

At Gibbons unspoken but clear visual plea, Vincent stepped back and let Griffith alone. He watched the man sort through the airline tickets. The hated position that Ben Bristol had filled in Vincent for years was now taken over by Griffith.

"Christ, do I always have to have someone to hate, David?"

"Maybe so, maybe no." Selesky whispered helplessly. "This man is pretty easy to put that emotion onto."

The beat-up looking Commander Griffith finished sorting through the pile of envelopes and very carefully stuffed them in the left inside pocket of the navy blue sport coat. He cockily pulled on Gibbon's arm and looked at the man's watch. It was almost noon.

"Gentlemen, the latest arrival of these flights is, considering I may go east, I may go west, is ...noon tomorrow, local time. I suggest Truaxe jog in place ... "

"Will they be safe?" Gibbons asked quietly.

"Yes. Of course they'll be safe. You'll hear from me by then, most likely through a call to a U.S. embassy. I suggest you alert them all over the world." He was relishing his power position. "The information I give them will be very technical in nature. Of course, as planned, I will only call an embassy after I have spoken with Barbara at the Ambassador Hotel in Havana, *and*," he repeated the word to stress his position, "*and* she ensures me she can get away from your man."

Balkin, still representing U.S. interests replied to Griffith. "Our man has orders to stay very close to her until Truaxe tells us the bombs are harmless. Then, and only then can you have your Barbara ..."

Griffith skillfully kept the Navy in a no-win situation. "No, No, gentlemen, that is when you'll find out *IF* I actually *want* my Barbara ... The key word is 'if', the bomb's defuse." Griffith reflected as close to a smirk as anyone with an eye patch and a painful split lip could. "See, I've really got you."

Balkin said nothing.

"So I leave now. And I know you will follow me, or try to. But I mean it. First sign I am covered by someone tracking me, I become mute. As far as idle threats to me? threaten away." He turned to Vincent.

"As far as *you* threatening me. You're a primal coward who runs from it when the going gets rough in a marriage. You couldn't even stand it when Clifford shot those stupid NVA's. I know you couldn't have pulled the trigger on me in that hospital room." He pushed one finger into Vincent's chest and his face became red, his voice harsh and threatening.

"I owe you for this eye, Vincent. You've ruined my face, how I look, and I won't forget it, *ever*." He stepped back a pace and lightened up his tune. "But, I believe we are even." Vincent knew what Griffith was going to say even before the words spat from his split lip. "I hope the bitch is dead."

Monk caught Vincent's hand in mid-flight as Griffith jumped backward so quickly he nearly stepped in front of a taxi pulling to the curb.

Vincent shook Monk's grip free. He looked at Griffith with hatred on his face, but still honoring Gibbons' request to let the man go, Vincent's words seemed calm.

" For now, you've got the best of us." Griffith seemed taken back. Even Selesky seemed surprised at Vincent's compliance. Then Vincent added: "My day will come, out of the blue, to you."

Griffith climbed into a taxi and quickly rolled the window down. "By the by, gentlemen." Everyone turned to hear his parting shot. "The Shaman guy ... Howser? Au-Yeung and the women killed him a few days ago. They're a bunch of omnivores. They knifed him up, had that Chink guy dump his body at sea. Thought you'd want to know." He raised both hands and opened all fingers into the air. "It wasn't me."

The taxi pulled away.

The President himself considered Griffith's escape to be a small price to pay for nuclear continuity. But, as Captain Gibbons, Lieutenant Han and the others watched Griffith pull away they knew that because of the terrain, the crowds and even limited help for Griffith from the Hong Kong KGB, tracking Griffith without being noticed was going to be very difficult. Gibbon's hands were tied officially from the White House ... 'do not track the man.' But Lt. Han went immediately to his van and set his only plan into motion.

From that moment, Vincent was pushed to the background of the investigation scene and went back into the hospital to see if there was any change in Cynthia.

CHAPTER THIRTY EIGHT
The Wounds and the Rage

"You may come in with me, Mr. Vincent. But be very calming." It was Doctor Sen, doing a favor at Han's request. She took hold of one of Paul's hands and spoke directly and clearly.

"Miss Cynthia have three bullets. One enter throat, right of epiglottis and miss vocal fold. Hit only flesh. Missed spinalis, very lucky. If that only bullet, she be up now." Paul didn't grasp the anatomical terms but he nodded, awaiting the final prognosis.

"One bullet enter left lung at the top, but from up heading down." She poised her index finger pointing downward and plunged it up and down several times. "Left lung very damaged. May never be good. Understand?"

"Yes."

"Second bullet also from top downward, enter heart and do damage but only partly puncture important places. Much blood loss, replaced now. Very lucky. Heart surgery was maybe good."

"Will she live?"

"We all watch, we all hope. We all love her here. She one of our sisters in hospital."

"You've done all you can?"

"Of course! Doctor Smyth and Doctor Lou and I do surgery. She healthy. We pray now." Doctor Sen stepped away and motioned for Paul to enter the room.

Cynthia lay on her back in the single bed observation room. Paul's flowers, and others, including some from Frenchie were sitting outside, not permitted to disrupt the fragile atmosphere. A Chinese R.N. at Cynthia's side came immediately to him.

"You are Paul." She acknowledged with a whisper. Her nametag read 'Nina Fong—Pulmonary Team'.

"Yes."

Fong was wearing a uniform identical to the one Cynthia had worn in years past. She pointed toward Cynthia's bed. "She one of our sisters." The woman had been crying. "We do our bery best."

"Thank you."

Sister Fong stepped aside and let him get close to her bed. He breathed deep and tried to not be intimidated by the scene. A bottle that Dr. Sen explained was an anti-biotic and something else ran to her left arm, a huge bluish bruise surrounded the connecting needle. Her face was colorless, her hair dull and lifeless. Her neck was wrapped in thick white bandages. The transparent cannula tube ran into her nostrils. Her breath made slight gurgling sounds. Beneath the hospital gown he could see her entire upper body was also wrapped in bandages.

His heart ached at the recurring visual of her chest having been penetrated first by Griffith's bullets, then by the surgeon's scalpel and by the cruel looking device that split her sternum and held it open during surgery. He hated Griffith with a renewed and boiling passion.

"Jesus, Jesus." He muttered. Dr. Sen patted his arm and left with the sister. Paul took a chair at Cynthia's right. Through misted eyes he watched her breath for nearly thirty minutes, using each second to relive all the moments he could recall from their lives together. My God, he thought . . 'how I love her' . . .'how I wasted both of our lives.'

She opened her eyes. At first they seemed glazed and unfocused. She saw the man she had previously thought was dead but the vision simply melded into the recurring images that had wracked her since she had been shot.

But suddenly the dream was different.

'It IS Paul'. He was moving, smiling, talking. There were tears in his eyes. She heard his voice, felt a touch. It was his fingers on her cheek. Her body shook with sobs of exhilaration and sobs of anguish over the stupidity of a revenge that had cost her so dearly.

She tried a smile.

He leaned close. "You are safe now. I love you."

Her mouth moved but her lips were dry and stuck to one another. He reached into a water glass and wet her lips with water from his fingers.

" Tucker . . .was to kill you." She sobbed causing her body to tense with pain. "Oh, Paul. I was told you were dead."

Her eyes closed for one moment, then another, then another. Paul held her right hand and waited. After twenty minutes: "Come close." She whispered. He leaned. His ear touched her mouth.

"His passport is in the back seat." He could barely hear her and thought she might be delirious, her mind hampered by medications and by the pain.

"It's over now. It's all over." He said, but he felt defeated by his fear of her injuries. He was not sure he could comfort her. He wanted to retaliate, now, with Griffith. He truly regretted not killing the man when he had a chance in the hospital room or at the curb. He felt a deep sense of disadvantage that Griffith was free and that Cynthia was so terribly exposed.

"Tell me." She whispered. "Am I OK?"

"Everything came out fine in surgery." He wanted so badly to protect her. "There is no one left to hurt either of us."

"Kurt is dead, isn't he?"

"Yes." He said softly. "That's what I understand."

"Good." She said. That surprised him. She closed her eyes. Her breathing changed to deeper, more purposeful moves. He held her hand ever so softly and watched her sleep. On impulse he removed his navy ring from his finger and placed it on hers. It was too big but he liked seeing it there. Turning it, the gold band part became a wedding band.

By two thirty p.m. her breathing had changed to where she gasped at times. Her face began to glow from perspiration. Dr. Sen said it was okay to wipe her brow when he wanted to.

At four p.m. her eyes flicked open and she seemed startled. "PAUL!"

"I'm here."

"Griffith …he tried …to kill me. He'll use John Henry Handler."

"But you'll be ok now." John Henry Handler meant nothing to him.

"No. You must get Griffith."

"We have him." He lied. He wanted her to rest, sleep, get well. He couldn't control his tears but immediately behind the tears was a locked in rage of helplessness.

"His plan to get away. Clever … John Henry Handler."

She slept again but fitfully. She blurted words unclearly. "Handler—Chen's—the car—the purse."

At six thirty she awoke, again startled.

"Paul!"

"I'm here."

"The passport is in Chen's car …the back floor. My purse." She seemed determined now.

"Yes, Dear. It's ok now."

She squeezed his hand very hard. Her nails dug into his skin. "Listen to me." Her voice was raspy, demanding and didn't seem like Cynthia. He motioned through the two-way window for Dr. Sen to come in.

"Paul. Listen to me." Tears ran from the outside corners of both of her eyes. Dr. Sen took Cynthia's pulse.

"Tell me. Do you hurt?" He asked.

"Chen's car. My purse."

"I'll get it. Where is his car?" She worried about her purse. A practiced, habitual worry, he thought.

She closed her eyes and for a few seconds he thought she had passed out again. She then breathed deeply and spoke without opening her eyes. "North of my house, left turn, at vacant lot, take side road under willow tree. Don't you see?"

"What do you want me to see?"

She spoke again but he couldn't make out her words. He only heard: 'Griffith—passport—and Hong Kong'.

"Cynthia. You don't have to talk now. Can this wait?"

"No." She squeezed his Ben Bristol hand very hard. He suppressed the response and leaned even closer. Her breath was hot against his face. Her eyes opened. "Please. Get him. Griffith is going … John Handler …" Her eyes closed but she squeezed his hand again. ". . to use Tucker's passport to slip out of Hong Kong. My purse for weeks waiting for Bell." Her hand released his.

It was clear. "Shit!" He said aloud.

"Yes!" She whispered, excitedly.

Griffith's flippant attitude over getting away now made sense. It was all a facade. He wasn't planning on using the U.S. furnished tickets at all. He knew U.S. agents would cover them. He had his own way out which made all of his promises meaningless.

Cynthia's eyes had opened. She sensed his change in manner.

"Paul? You don't really have him, do you?" She tried to rise up from the bed but her arms collapsed under the effort. She panted for breath.

"No. We don't." He stood and tried to help her get comfortable. Her pillow was wet from perspiration. He held her head up and gently turned the pillow over and lowered her head into it. His tears flowed even more, torn between nursing her and with the thoughts of Griffith.

"Griffith's set a bomb on the ship. He's promised to defuse the bomb if we let him get away."

"No. He told David Chen that was his … " Her eyes closed.

"It was his 'what', Cynthia. Try to tell me."

She spoke but he couldn't hear her. Her eyes closed. Her breathing stopped. Paul yelled for Dr. Sen who came in immediately having seen changes on the monitors in the outer room. Paul was pushed out of the way, roughly.

Her eyes opened wide again, but they seemed blank "Paul?"

The light that he'd always seen in her eyes was gone. She seemed to know it too.

"Yes." He said. Dr. Sen and her group of nurses stepped back from the bed.

"Griffith." Her voice was very weak. "Ace in hole. He'll wait until dark. He'll sneak to Chen's Opel and get to my purse. I heard him and Chen discuss it as I lay on the floor. "

"Discuss what?"

"He sent Chenny to the car to get my purse …right after I was shot. I heard his plan talked … " She closed her eyes. "You were by me on the floor in the bedroom, with Mia." As he listened, she became very excited but only for an instant before her skin color faded very quickly and her eyes closed again.

He again held her hand and watched her face. If he would have arrived at Amber Lane five minutes earlier he might have stopped it all. Or, he might have also been shot.

She awoke with a jerk against his hand. "Get him, please, get him. For me."

"It doesn't matter, Cyn. He'll get away and call us to defuse the bomb. He wants his wife back. He's crazy about some need to rescue her."

"NO NO!" She tried to scream but her voice made only a gurgling sound. Her face flushed very red and then immediately white. Dr. Sen moved in. Paul was pushed away again. Cynthia was raving but Dr. Sen put a needle to her arm.

"Wait!" Cynthia cried out. Dr. Sen turned to Paul.

"Talk to her."

He knew that instant; his Cyn was not going to live.

She seemed to know also.

He moved in close and put his ear to her mouth. "I love you," she said.

"I love you." He pressed his lips to her cheek. She pulled his right hand up to near her cheek and held it there.

"I'm still your wai-da?"

"The greatest wai-da in all of the universe." He felt love for her very strongly. "You know." He whispered and smiled into her eyes. "If we could back up life like it was a tape?" He spoke softly and directly. "If I got the letter asking me to go with you?"

"Oh, yes." Her hand moved his hand back and forth against her cheek.

"I would have gone with you, in a second."

"I know that now. I love you, Paul."

"I know, Cyn. I know."

He stayed near, his face touching hers. She closed her eyes but held his hand tightly. "Stay close." She whispered.

"Yes."

She breathed several deep breaths, and spoke again, surprising him. "Griffith? . . he hates his wife. He told me …and Chenny. He wants to blow up the ship …and embarrass the U.S."

"I believe you."

"Go, now. Get him, Paul. He's just pretending he wants her back. Go to Chenny's car. My purse. Before dark."

"I will, but … I want …for just a few more minutes." He said

"A few more minutes." She repeated.

"We have this moment, and this one," he said, acknowledging once and for all that her moments mattered.

"Yes!" she said and she closed her eyes again and pulled at his hand. He leaned in close to her mouth and looked at every turn and line of her lips, of her eyes, of her brow. He needed to remember her loveliness. Instead of being allowed to witness the years pass over her face, he knew it was down to only moments, or seconds. He kissed her lips with just a touch of his. She returned the kiss ever so softly. She whispered, "Next time … I'd bring my letter to you myself."

Cynthia Howser died.. Her last conscious knowledge was that her face was touching his.

Paul sat back in the chair and felt unbelievably alone. More alone than he thought could be experienced. He wondered if she truly returned to wherever it was she was before she was born and if he could join her there someday to continue their moments.

David Selesky was at his side, his hand touched Paul's shoulder.

"This is new, *this* pain." Paul Vincent was staring blankly into the room, no tears, his jaw set, his eyes cold and locked.

"What are you saying, Paul? What do you need from me?"

"This is the deepest pain I have ever known."

"Whatever I can do …to help this moment, Paul. Say the word."

"I know where Griffith is. He's lied to us all. The ship's going to explode."

"Jesus."

"Let's go get him."

It was only thirty minutes or so before dark. Selesky and Patrick Balkin accompanied him in Monk's S.P. Humber. Paul drove in silence but the two men jabbered awkwardly.

"Fucker, imagine him trying to blackmail us over faggotry."

"Yeah, If the fuckin' navy wasn't so homophobic there couldn't be this type of blackmail."

"F.T.N."

"Yeah, Fuck The Navy."

Within ten minutes they passed Cynthia's house and saw Gregory Winthrop's black Dodge and four police cars parked there. The police cars had blue lights flashing. A crowd of fifty or so curious were crowded along the sides of the narrow roadway.

"It's getting dark soon." Selesky reminded.

"We'll be able to see another half hour at most." Paul guessed.

"Police are going over that house to the last degree."

"Don't stop."

They drove two hundred feet north of Cynthia's house and turned left as she had directed. They checked two side roads before they found Chen's beige 1966 Opel Rekord sedan sitting under a large willow tree. They parked the Humber fifty yards further down the small road and started to walk back. Selesky stopped Paul by taking his arm.

"Gotta talk."

"What?"

"First. I didn't think the car would be here. I thought you were in some daze, or Cynthia's story was a fantasy … I don't know."

Vincent read his friend's face. "You're scared, David? I understand if you are."

"Afraid? Yeah. Guess I am. But not of Griffith showing up at that car."

"Of what?" Balkin asked.

"Of Paul here. Going off the deep end …"

" …killin' Griffith? You afraid that's all I want here?"

"Listen to me." Selesky said, trying to lock Paul's gaze in. "I don't have to remind you. Look what you've been through. I'm just afraid … "

"Of what?"

"The narcissistic wound …" Selesky spouted some psychiatric jargon, "the wound to yourself of her death . . is followed by the narcissistic rage, Paul. I'm afraid your rage will sprout out any second and take charge."

"Wounded? Yes, I'm wounded over her death. Rage? I'll manage my rage, David. My first priority here is to get the *ship* freed up. I promise. Can you trust that?"

"I want to. But Griffith has all the chips."

"All but one." Paul said.

"See. That's what I hate. You have this mysterious bullshit look on your face that you have the answers."

"I think I do have *one* of them, dammit. Back at the hospital, you said you'd do anything. It's okay if you back down, but this is important to me. Leave me alone if you want to. But I'm going back to that car before he comes and gets what he's after."

"*If* he comes." Balkin said.

"Yeah, if." David echoed. "And if he comes, Paul. What is this master plan?" Selesky was very challenging, out of character.

"You see how pissed he was about his face, his eye? Go for his vanity. I think if we threaten to harm his face more? He'll cave in. I'm willing to try it …"

"We can be court-martialed for withholding knowing about this car . . ." Balkin reminded them.

"Fuck you." Paul exploded. "We found out at the last minute . . .saw him come here . . .we were visiting Cynthia's house . . .it'll be easy."

"Let's go." Selesky said to Balkin as he turned to Paul. "But listen. One promise?"

"What?"

"The Rage is close to the surface. Hear that 'fuck-you' a few seconds ago? Will you agree we're more objective than you right now."

"No."

'Humor me. If we say stop. We stop. Agree?"

"Agreed."

Anxiously they walked toward the Opel. It was locked and had that leaky fuel or bad carburetor smell some cars have. Cynthia's shoulder-bag purse was visible on the floor of the back seat.

"We back off. Wait. At my move, we rush from three directions. Agreed?"

"Agreed. As long as we can see." Selesky reminded.

"Your signal." Balkin agreed.

The three men fanned out and hid in the thick bushes on the vacant land. For Vincent, the intervals between heartbeats marked the passing seconds as once again he found himself waiting on the periphery of potential violence, while watching a bug crawl slowly up a thin leafed liverwort plant.

His mind hung heavily on those last moments with Cynthia. He suppressed his rage with thoughts of how to honor his memories of her and of 'her moments'.

'Verdi', he thought, 'would write an opera to her. Bach, a refrain. The good Russians would make an icon to her. Shakespeare would surely pen a play to top all stories of love, including Romeo and Juliet.'

It was now too dark to see the bug.

At that instant a taxi pulled into the lot, circled the Opel and moved back toward the main roadway where it stopped. Griffith got out of the passenger's side. He had changed clothes to a conservative dark suit and dress hat. In the headlights Paul could see the patch was gone from his left eye. Vincent thought to himself. "Unless the Cabbie is a cop or there's an invisible soundless helo overhead . . .which there isn't, he's shaken the CIA"

"Please wait right over there, Cabbie." Paul cringed at the sound of Griffith's voice. The hair on his arms stiffened.

Griffith walked to the Opel and tried the doors. He looked around on the ground. After several seconds he located a piece of tree branch and smashed it against the rear right door window. The branch broke. Griffith mumbled.

He searched the ground again and soon broke into a trot over to where the taxi driver had turned the car's lights off. With the lights removed from the scene, Paul was getting some night vision.

The driver got out of the taxi and opened the trunk. Paul could barely make out what they were doing. Soon Griffith hurried back to the Opel. He had a tire rod in his hand.

Without so much as looking around he smashed the side window and unsnapped the door lock. When he opened the door and leaned in, Paul was on him in six long adrenaline-driven strides.

"Get him!" He yelled as he crashed into the car's back seat and pounded Griffith on the back of the neck. Griffith's mouth smashed against a door handle, splitting both lips and breaking off three top teeth. Driven by a visual of Cynthia's pale face, Paul snatched at the back of the man's collar and jerked him up.

"Wait." Balkin cried. "Don't kill him."

The taxi spun tires in gravel and left the scene. Paul looked. It may have been KGB assistance for Griffith.

Paul pulled Griffith out onto the ground and dragged him to the front of the Opel.

"Turn on the car lights, David."

Balkin opened Cynthia's purse and located a British passport. "Here it is. John Henry Handler."

"Cynthia was right all the time. She knew. This was to be Tucker's passport out of Hong Kong." In the flood of car lights, Paul twisted Griffith to a sitting position against the car's bumper. Griffith's mouth and lips were bleeding. A piece of broken tooth stuck to his upper lip. The lid of the left injured eye was somehow stuck open and looked wild and red. The other eye opened. The man jerked to fight Paul but was shoved backward hard against the car's bumper. A torn edge of the license plate cut deep into the flesh behind Griffith's right ear. He screamed in surprise and pain. He stopped struggling and put a hand to the gash. Paul let him.

The lid of the bad eye dropped closed but the good eye tracked Paul's every move. Griffith's tongue dragged through the new opening where the broken teeth were snapped off, his words came out unclear. "My mouph. My fath." He panicked.

"SURPRISE!" Paul said and sounded delighted. He then whispered from deep in his throat: "Got you, mother fucker."

His voice pulled chills of fear from deep within whoever Arnold Griffith really was. The man whined painfully.

Paul took Griffith by both ears, dug in his nails and twisted. The flesh behind the right ear tore more where it had been cut by the license plate. The man screamed and jerked away, crazed. Paul slapped him along side the right side of his head and he fell quiet.

"Don't kill him." Balkin said. "Revenge is not good now."

Paul turned to face Patrick. "Revenge? Listen." Vincent's voice was even, but he was winded. "This." He shook Griffith by the collar. " . . is the fucking *real* enemy. Look up the word. He's a Soviet agent, he killed Cynthia …*hear me?* I don't want revenge … I want simple human fucking *justice* …and," He turned and faced Griffith again and pulled him to his feet by the shirt front. " I also want my goddammed ship back."

Griffith only moaned.

"Talk, Paul." It was David's trusting voice.

"Men on Truaxe are waiting for him to call in. Nuclear energy, right or wrong, he has no right to put that reactor to the bottom of an ocean. Christ only knows what that'll bring about."

"You can't beat it out of him, Paul. He's a human being." Selesky was almost pleading.

"I'm *counting* on that. If he is a human being, then he has a basic fear, like all of us. Even Clifford said everyone has one human weakness."

"His is vanity?"

"THE vanity. I can make him talk …mess up his good looks." He looked at both men's faces. "Just don't stop me now. We can't let Griffith win this way."

"Just don't ruin your life over this ass, Paul."

"Ruin it? He killed Cynthia. How can he ruin my life now? It is he and I and you two."

"Paul, you're not back in a Vietnam war now." Balkin said. Paul wasn't sure if Balkin was sincerely afraid, or was doing a realistic slide of good cop bad cop.

Paul snapped back. "The war is right here, right here." He let go of Griffith's shirtfront and the man folded slowly to the ground. Paul looked to Selesky, then to Balkin. He knelt beside Griffith again and looked at him and tried to think priorities. He thought back to Kurt intercepting the 1962 letter. How that one act had taken them all to this day, was fantastic. His rage that Selesky had named so correctly, originally directed to Kurt for setting it all up, transferred easily to Griffith. He felt Kurt and Griffith exuded the same kind of blind, self invested disregard for consequences.

"This man is …is . Can you imagine if we …if that ship blows a nuclear cloud over the south China Sea? He cannot win this one. Help me get him to where those police can hook us to a radio to Kittyhawk."

Paul and Patrick lifted Griffith between them and carried and dragged him the two hundred yards or so toward Cynthia's home. The crowd of onlookers at the house moved out of the way of the three uniformed men and the injured civilian.

Gregory Winthrop stepped from several uniformed police, took one look and seemed shocked. "What! What! What?"

"Take us inside. This is Griffith."

Stammering, "But, but we let him go … I thought," he led the three into Kurt Howser's bedroom. The Chinese officers stayed outside of the room. Paul put Griffith in a wing back chair identical to the one in Cynthia's room, the one he had held her so closely in the night before Truaxe was recalled.

Winthrop started to telephone for an ambulance but Paul's threat stopped him. "I'm his fucking ambulance." Winthrop backed off and became a spectator.

Selesky thrashed about the room's small bar and came up with a bottle of soda water. He poured it over Griffith's head and face. Griffith snapped awake, arms swinging. Paul knelt in front of the chair, grabbed Griffith's wrists and twisted them, surprised at the strength control he had over the bigger man. Griffith stopped struggling and just looked at Paul's face. He seemed very frightened. Paul put a knee into Griffith's stomach and took hold of his ears as he had under the willow tree, one in each hand.

"Start talking right now." He said, and dug his nails into the flesh.

Griffith cursed him.

"I mean it." Paul yelled, his breath blowing into Griffith's face. "I'll rip your fucking ear off …away."

"Paul, this isn't right." Balkin said taking hold of one of Paul's arms.

"Isn't *right?*" Paul spoke unevenly, out of breath. "The major fuckin' human weakness always come up when we are pressed to decide what is *actually* …and *truly* right or wrong, fucker."

"I know when something isn't right, Paul. Stop this." Balkin insisted.

Paul dropped Griffith's shirt front and faced Balkin *and* Selesky. "Who in the fuck are you or me to decide now what is right or not? Right and wrong doesn't even get measured except by humans. We goin' to let this ass-hole define either of them by letting him blow the ship? Back off now, and, and we'll see right versus wrong."

He turned to Griffith and took his ears in his hands again.

"Listen fucker. I'm measuring your big wrong against my little one that is about to come as I rip your fucking ear off.

Perhaps taking strength from Balkin's stance, it looked like Griffith laughed a mocking smirk.

Paul spit in Griffith's face and jerked on the right ear. The rage of Cynthia's death was in his grip. With sort of a sucking noise, the cut ear actually tore away. Paul was surprised but so involved he didn't show it. He kept pulling. Griffith started a long howling sound. From the temporal area downward through the flesh as deep as the cerumen glands, a fist sized piece of pulp and hair hung down the right side of Griffith's temple and jaw. Griffith screamed an unholy sound into the room. Paul rubbed the fleshy side of the injured ear and jammed his hand into Griffith's face, covering him with his own blood. Without warning, Paul struck Griffith's nose with the side of an open hand, causing blood to gush. He stepped back from Griffith and looked at Balkin.

"Right?" He yelled into the air. "Or wrong?"

The near crazed spy grabbed at his ear and his nose and rocked back and forth in the chair. All expression was lost in the bloodied mess.

Patrick Balkin vomited in the corner of the room. Winthrop cranked a rear window open.

Selesky pulled at Paul's arm. "Paul, you're crazy now."

Paul remembered their agreement. "Are you telling me to stop?"

Selesky hesitated. "No. Will it be worth it? This is craziness …for me. "

"Fuck *you.* Think of Abie Lake. He was murdered by Griffith. Think of the blackmail notes in the hospital room. Think of Cynthia now back to wherever she was before she was born. Think of ME, goddamn you."

"You're killing him." Winthrop stepped next to Paul. Paul let go of Griffith and confronted Winthrop with a yelling voice, more for Griffith than for Winthrop.

"You're fucking wrong. I will *never* kill him. I'll only ruin his face and looks and rack him with pain like he's racked me. He *killed* Cynthia, and *killed* Lake—people I loved. He caused the death of—DiNoble—Randy Hill—Piper, Hollender, others …" He dropped the sound of his voice to a low murmur. " …he drove Cap'n Clifford over the edge." He shoved Winthrop's chest and yelled again. " Back off!"

Winthrop stepped away, Griffith's blood staining the front of his white shirt. Intimidated by Paul's rage, he reached under his suit coat and drew a revolver from his back waistband. Paul saw him but ignored the move. He turned back to Griffith's chair.

"Take his arms, David." Paul commanded his passive friend then told Balkin to find a mirror for Griffith to see himself in. Selesky tried grabbing both arms but Griffith fought him. Balkin stepped in, a small mirror under one arm pit. He took one arm, Selesky the other, pulled them behind the chair and held the mirror very close to Griffith's eyes. Griffith let out a loud uncontrolled moan. "My mouf', my p-face." He shook his head violently and blood flicked freely onto his jacket and white shirt.

Someone chattered in Chinese near the doorway. Lieutenant Han came into the room and looked at Griffith and Paul and at Winthrop's drawn revolver. He reached for his own gun under his armpit.

"Not necessary, Han." Selesky said boldly. "We have new information. Unless we get words from this asshole, the ship's gonna' blow. All that crap he said in the hospital about his wife? Was just crap. Cynthia Howser overheard his true plans."

Han's hand came out without a gun and he stepped behind Griffith's winged back chair, pushing Selesky and Balkin aside. "This man now tell everything, right Commander?"

Griffith tried pulling away but Han held his head in a tight arm lock. Paul wasn't sure what it was, but he read something cooperative and realistic in Han's face. He took a chance and spoke directly into Griffith's face.

"Now, tell Balkin how to defuse the second and third bombs."

"NO!"

"I remember the gutted bodies of the CIA agents." Paul continued. "I saw their faces pulled away from itself. It's *your* turn." He nodded toward Han who reached over the taller man's shoulders and rammed a finger deep into each of Griffith's nostrils. "I'll pull des' off the face."

"Helb me… helb me." Griffith's one eye pleaded to Greg Winthrop who stood there with a revolver in his hand.

Winthrop wimpled back. "You're the Commaner'. *Order* them to stop." Thank heaven, Vincent thought. Winthrop had come off the fence.

The crazed man they worked on knew if he were ever to return to the Russia he had betrayed, he would at least have to carry out the destruction of Truaxe. It was his only chance out of there. He knew he had to hold out. He glared into the room as though not seeing. "Lem'me goooo!" He yelled and again tried to break from Han's grip.

Excited, Han yelled at Paul in Chinese but Paul ignored the man and yelled at Griffith. "You murdered Cynthia. I have no mercy for you …you hear me? I have NO mercy in me. Last chance. Tell Balkin … NOW!"

"Nooooo!" Griffith moaned. "Please, no!"

There was no stopping Han at this time. He put all the strength he could into the bent fingers that were lodged in Griffith's nostrils. He jerked upward with a smooth magician-like motion. The flesh lifted away from the rubbery mass of the nasal cavity deeply into the membrane below. Griffith twisted one arm free of Selesky's grip and swung upward, his backhand struck Paul in the mouth. Han jerked the nose again. Griffith let out a frightening long and eerie scream of pain and disbelief. The bulk of his nose was pulled clear of his face and hung from a skin flap between his eyes. Blood flowed profusely into his mouth.

Paul's upper lip swelled immediately.

Han threw Griffith's head forward as one might toss a rotted melon.

Selesky was there with a pillow case and jammed it into Griffith's bloodied face.

"You killed him, Han. You killed the man." Winthrop said evenly.

Han looked over his shoulder and yelled in Chinese. "Yisheng—Yisheng." One of his men broke from near the doorway and ran

"Sent for doctor." Han said. .

"I'm a doctor." Selesky said. He won't die from this." Han stepped away.

"He'll just be very, very ugly." Paul said, flicking at Griffith's blood on his shirt sleeves.

Selesky and Paul pulled Griffith to Kurt's bed and flopped him on his back. He immediately began to choke on his own blood. Selesky jammed a pillow under his neck, came up with more towels from the nearby bath and covered the wounded nose and ear. Griffith kept choking and fighting for breath. Selesky located a box of Cynthia's body powder and poured it over the fleshy face and ear. It clotted the blood.

Though Han had stepped back and seemed awed by his own deed, Paul wouldn't stop. He pulled out the small automatic, cocked it and pressed it between Griffith's eyes.

"No." Griffith was conscious but dazed. He actually seemed calmed by the trauma. Selesky pulled Vincent aside.

"Listen, his wounds?"

"Yes?"

"A kind of natural anesthesia get pumped into the system, like maybe endorphins. The person feels a psychotic unexplained calm. That's where Griffith is right now."

"And?"

"You've got to get him out of that state or he'll not be frightened."

"Shit." Paul moaned, but turned back to Griffith. He pressed the gun right between Griffith's eyes and pushed it tight. "On 'three' you'll have talked, or I'll have blown your brains away. One … "

Griffith rolled his one good eye to lock on Paul's

"Two … "

Griffith said nothing.

"Three." Paul pulled the trigger. It clicked on empty.

"Hah." He shouted like a delighted prank player. He then flicked the magazine free of the gun's handle and, inches from Griffith's good eye, carefully placed three bullets from his pocket into the magazine. As Paul slowly slid the magazine back into the gun handle, Griffith followed the movements with his one good eye. 'Click, whip slick, click.' Paul cocked it again and placed the barrel back between Griffith's eyes. Han left the room. Balkin turned his face away. Winthrop started to speak. His mouth came open but it froze, mute.

"Listen, these men will let me have my way with you … You killed Cynthia."

"Hurp me …and the ship …blowb." Griffith tried to talk.

"Hurt you? Ship blow? I haven't even *begun* to hurt you. I'm just making you ugly forever, before we let you go with Tucker's passport. See, we knew all about it." He pulled the passport from his pocket and shoved it against Griffith's face. "See, John Henry Handler is it? You think you KILLED Cynthia? Wrong motherfucker. She got you. She sent me after you at the Opel. Dumb ass-ass. She got you best, BASTARD."

"Wait!" Griffith seemed stopped by that remark. "She 'libe?" He couldn't form 'v' sounds.

"Yes, asshole." Paul lied but loved the feeling. "You failed everywhere. And we don't even *care* about the ship. None of us do. We hate the war, asshole. Sinking that nuke truck is the best thing you ever did. It'll stop all this nuke bullshit. Right, David?"

"Far as I'm concerned, it's just so much steel at the bottom of the South China fuckin' Sea." Balkin said, having returned with new energy.

Selesky borrowed an unprofessional line from boot-camp days. "Fuckin-a-ditty-bag." There were tears in his eyes.

"You betta' tell sallah'." Han added from the doorway. Winthrop, who was also red-eyed, stood frozen, revolver in hand. Han pulled the gun away from the white faced man.

Griffith's one good eye gazed crazily at Paul's face. He spoke but no one could understand the words.

"You trying to tell us how to defuse the bomb?" Selesky asked.

"No."

Vincent new he must actually cause what he had loathed when he saw it done to Piper and Hollander. He understood the powerful force that could overtake humans, and make a life valueless. Whatever had driven the men to mutilate Piper and Hollender, was now unbridled within him. My God, he thought, how deeply the hatred is for the Americans in Vietnam.

"This is called hatred, Griffith." He said evenly. "Watch it, no, feel it, happen." He pulled the gun away from Griffith's head and spoke evenly. "I'm thinking now of Cynthia and of the two CIA men with their bodies cut to pieces. I'm going to shoot off both of your balls, Griffith, then pull off your other ear." The man's entire body began to flinch involuntarily. It was all Selesky and Balkin could do to hold him on the bed.

"Then ...never mind." Paul said. The automatic exploded into the mattress between Griffith's legs. He missed the testicles, but the piece ripped from the scrotal sack was close enough.

Within minutes the telephone to the police station transmitter room was patched by radio to Kittyhawk's radio central where it was further patched into a tactical data support circuit to Truaxe. On board Truaxe, the circuit was connected to the ship's P.A. system in the engine room.

Griffith spoke. "The secon' bobb is ..." The nerve centers in Griffith's face were erratic and distorted by pain and disbelief. His body shook involuntarily. He could hardly form words.

Balkin relayed into the telephone. "The second bomb is. . "

"Phobbo line ell' two zebo un.. . .' Griffith struggled to talk and breath. Blood mixed with saliva ran freely from his mouth. Selesky made a pretense of tending his wounds.

"Follow line L-two zero one." Balkin translated into the telephone.

"'Rectric rine ... "

"Electric line ... "

On Truaxe the team of men, lead by Commander Deiter followed the instructions that came slowly over the quiet clear P.A. system.

"Follow electric line L-201-E, through the mass of wires to a two by three inch junction box. It looks like a small standard electric switch box. It'll be behind reactor core panel three—that's panel 'three.' On the front right bottom of the box is a small letter K as in 'Kilo' pounded into the box cover. Remove the two screws. He says there is a basic on-off switch in there with the toggle broken off. Take a screwdriver and push it upward. That kills the circuit."

Deiter himself removed the cover and positioned the screwdriver.

Paul Vincent pulled Griffith into a sitting position on the side of the blood-covered bed. He stood in front of him and placed his thumbs beside the bridge of Griffith's nose, buried slightly into the corners of each of his eyes. The energy came from the visual image of Cynthia with her chest held open by the retractor, surgeons hands manipulating her heart, searching, removing pieces of the bullet inflicted by Griffith, sewing up her body's parts. He relived her last breath then addressed Griffith.

"If they throw that switch ...and anything happens ...beside killing that bomb circuit ... I'm thumbing out this bad eye and shoving it down your bastard throat. Then, with the other eye, you can look at your helpless ugliness forever, each day. IS THAT FUCKING CLEAR?"

Griffith slouched limp but said nothing. Paul pushed slightly into the eye socket. Griffith knew he would do it. There was no bravado left in the double turncoat agent. "WAIT!" He yelled. Wait ..."

"Wait." Balkin yelled into the telephone.

" ...bepore they trow thwitch, first ... " Griffith was in uncontrolled tears. Selesky moved to the front of the man and knelt. "Tell us about it, Commander."

Within the next three minutes, Deiter and one of his Chiefs were turning the dial faces on control panels 7, 9 and 11 to read 'free' vice 'bound.' Commander Deiter agreed over the circuit that those moves made sense to him. They threw the switch in the junction box marked 'K'. Griffith then directed them to a panel in the seawater control valve area. They located the explosives.

Balkin could hear cheers over the phone circuit.

An ambulance arrived for Griffith.

Vincent, Selesky, Balkin, Han, Winthrop and the two Chinese officers were called by Han into Cynthia's back bedroom. The circle of her blood on the carpet was now dark brown. Selesky dropped a pillow over the spot.

"Listen." Han said with conviction. "Never anything this important before to any of us. But listen. That officer? He arrived on doorstep here, badly torn apart. He say by KGB. He was screaming his willingness to stop the sabotage of Truaxe. You understan'? This be most important secret you ever will have …to tell no one but we men. No matta' twenty years away? No talk."

They all knew they could never tell the truth.

EPILOGUE
Reprisal complete

A message was sent to the president of the United States. A second message was sent to the CIA operatives who had sneaked Barbara Griffith into Cuba: "Return her". She was tried for espionage and is serving an undetermined sentence in a federal prison, but not with her husband.

The U.S. Navy formally thanked Rachael Bristol Vincent for convincing Barbara to see Doctor Sarah Barkley and reveal it all. She even got her name in the *San Diego Union* and in the *San Diego Evening Tribune.*

Dr. Sarah Barkley married a retired Navy Master Chief and had three sons. She recently retired from private practice in La Jolla California, one of the most respected marriage and family therapists in the country.

Bunny Bristol and her two children returned to her parents in Weirton West Virginia. Nick Bristol went to work for a National City department store as a truck driver's helper. Mia went to work for Mr. and Mrs. Eddie Monk and, oddly enough, after Kurt and Cynthia's wills were probated, found herself to be the owner of the house she had lovingly served Cynthia in. She sold the home to the Monks and stayed in their employ.

Months after the incident, Mia was able to sort through Cynthia's things. One day Paul received a letter from Mia, written by Eddie Monk with simple good wishes and a little red label taped to a piece of paper. It was one of the smaller wai-da tags. Paul slipped it into his billfold.

David Selesky and Patrick Balkin both retired from the navy by 1977. They bought a home together in upstate New York and became very active in gay rights. As a complete puzzlement to the human condition, the together-appearing Selesky became addicted to prescription drugs and was indicted in 1983 for writing bogus prescriptions for controlled medications. In 1985 he lost his medical license, guilty of grooming several psychologically vulnerable patients for sex, not unlike how a pedophile 'grooms' a naive child.

Patrick Balkin, fearing for his own struggling reputation as an entertainment promoter left Selesky in 1985 and moved to Long Island. To add to the puzzle, both he and Selesky were among the earlier victims of AIDS. They died in 1987 within weeks of one another.

Dressed in black complete with full facial veil, Vera 'Veronica' Lake accepted Abie Lake's posthumous medals but would not talk with Paul Vincent during or after the ceremony. Her mother told Paul that Vera just couldn't understand how he could leave his friend to die. The mother patted his hand and walked away with Veronica.

Captain Clifford spent almost two years in Mental Hospitals after Truaxe was saved. Following unofficial but widely practiced navy custom, Clifford was acknowledged for his years of *good* service and not punished for his few months of not-so-good service. He was discreetly promoted to flag rank and retired in 1973. Benefiting from psychotherapy, he finally neutralized the impact of his father on his personality. 'Our New Admiral', as the family calls him, can be seen most early mornings making his way across the golf course at NAS North Island or on the public city course in Coronado California. He doesn't say anything much about his career nor do the few cronies who play regularly with him ask. Bless them all.

'Our Admiral' wrote a moving article for the Naval Institute Magazine on the potential hazards of living vicariously through an adult child's achievements. Harry Stumpf quit the navy and currently lives in Hawaii where he publishes music videos.

Captain Betov Nekolayev died in his Mother Russia in 1970 from the influences of radiation poisoning from the submarine, Pedrokli. He was given the award of 'Hero of the Sovetskikh Sotsialisticheskikh Republik'. His son, Betov II, a MIG pilot officer in the Soviet Air Force was seen with friends, throwing the medal into the Volga River in March, 1971, just a day or two before he defected to Israel, with a brand new MIG fighter.

Commander Merideth Deiter, after publishing a revealing paper on the genesis of troublesome rivalry between nuclear trained and general service trained sailors, took over as commanding officer of Truaxe. Commander Dominic Valentino became his executive officer.

After 1968, if you looked up 'handsome' in a dictionary, contrary to Abie's earlier remark, you would no longer find 'see Arnold Griffith'. In a federal prison, Griffith's face became a ringed mass of scars and disfigured folds, his right ear a crude plastic mold, his nose permanently shrunken and misshapen. The no longer vain, no longer handsome Arnold Griffith was traded in 1976 for one of the west's agents who had been held for years in a prison on the Kamchatka Peninsula. It was later learned that Griffith, whose parents were Russian Jews, Hadra and Leoniev Gorniyak, eventually migrated to Israel under still another name.

Mysteriously, in 1979, Griffith was found murdered in his rented house in the small village of El Bira just west of the old city of Jericho in what is now the West Bank Territory. The Israeli intelligence community reported to the U.S. that Griffith had been shot once in the throat, once in a lung, and once into his heart. A baseball cap was found on his chest. It was blue and gold and had a patch above its visor:

—Tonkin Gulf Yacht Club—

1968

Paul Vincent was transferred to serve as senior instructor at the navy evasion and escape school at Warner Springs near San Diego. It is understood he retired honorably from the navy in 1975 and shortly thereafter went on an endless-summer type of world-wide trip, grabbing rides catch-as-catch-can on military flights as retirees can do. No one has taken the time to trace records to see if reprisal took him to the West Bank.

In 1978, determined to find answers to the *right* and wrong questions, he entered the *United States International University in San Diego* to study psychology and human behavior. We'll hear from him again.

Oh yes, his Ben Bristol hand never did quite heal all the way.

Reprisal is an engaging journey of unexpected emotions. Two stories, each of which could stand alone, intertwine the worlds of men and women because of a war, and of those men and women despite the war. *Reprisal* presents relationships in intimate detail - love, sex and the accompanying conflicted choices. Vince Huntington's wonderful details will cause you to move off to a private place to read.

Maureen Shanahan. National Fashion Director, SAKS 5th Ave, N.Y. and San Diego

Reprisal is a great story, a fine read. I first read it a few years ago 'in progress' and encouraged Vince Huntington to finish the work. I loved it then. You'll love it now. He writes so well the reader can openly relate to each individual in the story.

Fritz Klein, MD. Author: *Life, Sex, and the Pursuit of Happiness*, Haworth Press, 2005.

Reprisal defined. In warfare, a reprisal is a limited and deliberate violation of the laws of war to punish an enemy for breaking the laws of war. A legally executed reprisal is not an atrocity. To be legally justified, a reprisal can only be directed against the party carrying out the original violation . . . as a last resort and with 'formal notice'. (Wikipedia).

Though internationally argumentative, a reprisal is not technically an act of war because it is solely in response to conduct (often personal) that violated International law. (Author's Phantom Editor).

Made in the USA